To Richard

All our love on your 11th Birthday

Gran & Grandy

Kiss

CW01648496

THE GIANT BOOK OF
# HORROR

# THE GIANT BOOK OF
# **HORROR**

Edited by Stephen Jones

·PARRAGON·

This edition published and distributed by Parragon Book Service Ltd 1996,
produced by Magpie Books, an imprint of Robinson Publishing, London

Parragon Book Service Ltd
Unit 13–17, Avonbridge Trading Estate
Atlantic Road, Avonmouth
Bristol BS11 9QD

Previously published as
*The Mammoth Book of Terror* and
*The Anthology of Horror Stories*
by Robinson Publishing



ISBN 0 75251 846 1

A copy of the British Library Cataloguing in Publication Data
is available from the British Library.

Printed and bound by Firmin-Didot (France),
Group Herissey. No d'impression : 35235.

# CONTENTS

# ACKNOWLEDGEMENTS

"The Last Illusion" copyright (c) 1985 by Clive Barker. Originally published in *Clive Barker's Books of Blood Volume 6: The Life of Death*. Reprinted by permission of Sphere Books and Pocket Books, a division of Simon & Schuster Inc.

"Bunny Didn't Tell Us" copyright (c) 1985 by David J. Schow. Originally published in *Night Cry*, Winter 1985. Reprinted by permission of the author.

"Murgunstrumm" copyright (c) 1932 by The Clayton Magazines, Inc. Originally published in *Strange Tales*, January 1933. Reprinted by permission of the author.

"The Late Shift" copyright (c) 1980 by Dennis Etchison. Originally published in *Dark Forces*. reprinted by permission of the author. Portions of lyrics from "Light My Fire", words by the Doors, (c) 1967, Doors Music Co., used by permission of the authors and publisher.

"The Horse Lord" copyright (c) 1977 by The Mercury Press, Inc. Copyright (c) 1983 by Lisa Tuttle. Originally published in *The Magazine of Fantasy and Science Fiction*, June 1977. Reprinted by permission of the author.

"The Jumpity-Jim" copyright (c) 1974 by Ronald Chetwynd-Hayes. Originally published in *The Elemental*. Reprinted by permission of the author.

"Out of Copyright" copyright (c) 1980 by Ramsey Campbell. Originally published in *Hot Air*. Reprinted by permission of the author.

"The River of Night's Dreaming" copyright (c) 1981 by Stuart David Schiff. Originally published in *Whispers III*. Reprinted by permission of the author.

"Amber Print" copyright (c) 1968 by Basil Copper. Originally published in *Dr. Caligari's Black Book*. Reprinted by permission of the author.

"The House of the Temple" copyright (c) 1981 by Brian Lumley.

# Clive Barker

## The Last Illusion

CLIVE BARKER made his impressive debut as a horror writer in 1984 with six volumes of short stories, published under the collective title *Clive Barker's Books of Blood*. These were followed by such acclaimed novels as *The Damnation Game*, *Weaveworld*, *Cabal* and *The Great and Secret Show* and the movies *Hellraiser* and *Nightbreed*.

The following story introduces readers to Barker's down-at-heel occult private eye, Harry D'Amour. One of the author's forthcoming film projects will be based around Harry's exploits, and the character also turns up in the short story "Lost Souls" as well as *The Great and Secret Show* and its sequels. So prepare to enter a world of supernatural terror that reads like Raymond Chandler meets H.P. Lovecraft, but with that extra twist of imagination that makes it undeniably Barker's own . . .

WHAT HAPPENED THEN—when the magician, having mesmerised the caged tiger, pulled the tasselled cord that released a dozen swords upon its head—was the subject of heated argument both in the bar of the theatre and later, when Swann's performance was over, on the sidewalk of 51st Street. Some claimed to have glimpsed the bottom of the cage opening in the split second that all other eyes were on the descending blades, and seen the tiger swiftly spirited away as the woman in the red dress took its place behind the lacquered bars. Others were just as adamant that the animal had never been in the cage to begin with, its presence merely a projection which had been extinguished as a mechanism propelled the woman from beneath the stage; this, of course, at such a speed that it deceived the eye of all but those swift and suspicious enough to catch it. And the swords? The nature of the trick which had transformed them in the mere seconds of their gleaming descent from steel to rose-petals was yet further fuel for debate. The explanations ranged from the prosaic to the elaborate, but few of the throng that left the theatre lacked some theory. Nor did the arguments finish there, on the sidewalk. They raged on, no doubt, in the apartments and restaurants of New York.

The pleasure to be had from Swann's illusions was, it seemed, twofold. First: the spectacle of the trick itself—in the breathless moment when disbelief was, if not suspended, at least taken on tip-toe. And second, when the moment was over and logic restored, in the debate as to how the trick had been achieved.

"How do you do it, Mr Swann?" Barbara Bernstein was eager to know.

"It's magic," Swann replied. He had invited her back-stage to examine the tiger's cage for any sign of fakery in its construction; she had found none. She had examined the swords: they were lethal. And the petals, fragrant. Still she insisted:

"Yes, but *really* . . ." she leaned close to him. "You can tell me," she said, "I promise I won't breathe a word to a soul."

He returned her a slow smile in place of a reply.

"Oh, I know . . ." she said, "you're going to tell me that you've signed some kind of oath."

"That's right," Swann said.

"—And you're forbidden to give away any trade secrets."

"The intention is to give you pleasure," he told her. "Have I failed in that?"

"Oh no," she replied, without a moment's hesitation. "Everybody's talking about the show. You're the toast of New York."

"No," he protested.

"Truly," she said, "I know people who would give their eye-teeth to get into this theatre. And to have a guided tour backstage . . . well, I'll be the envy of everybody."

"I'm pleased," he said, and touched her face. She had clearly been anticipating such a move on his part. It would be something else for her to boast of: her seduction by the man critics had dubbed the Magus of Manhattan.

"I'd like to make love to you," he whispered to her.

"Here?" she said.

"No," he told her. "Not within ear-shot of the tigers."

She laughed. She preferred her lovers twenty years Swann's junior—he looked, someone had observed, like a man in mourning for his profile, but his touch promised wit no boy could offer. She liked the tang of dissolution she sensed beneath his gentlemanly façade. Swann was a dangerous man. If she turned him down she might never find another.

"We could go to a hotel," she suggested.

"A hotel," he said, "is a good idea."

A look of doubt had crossed her face.

"What about your wife . . .?" she said. "We might be seen."

He took her hand. "Shall we be invisible, then?"

"I'm serious."

"So am I," he insisted. "Take it from me; seeing is not believing. I should know. It's the cornerstone of my profession." She did not look much reassured. "If anyone recognises us," he told her, "I'll simply tell them their eyes are playing tricks."

She smiled at this, and he kissed her. She returned the kiss with unquestionable fervour.

"Miraculous," he said, when their mouths parted. "Shall we go before the tigers gossip?"

He led her across the stage. The cleaners had not yet got about their business, and there, lying on the boards, was a litter of rose-buds. Some had been trampled, a few had not. Swann took his hand from hers, and walked across to where the flowers lay.

She watched him stoop to pluck a rose from the ground, enchanted by the gesture, but before he could stand upright again something in the air above him caught her eye. She looked up and her gaze met a slice of silver that was even now plunging towards him. She made to warn him, but the sword was quicker than her tongue. At the last possible moment he seemed to sense the danger he was in and looked round, the bud in his hand, as the point met his back. The sword's momentum carried it through his body to the hilt. Blood fled from his chest, and splashed the floor. He made no sound, but fell forward, forcing two-thirds of the sword's length out of his body again as he hit the stage.

She would have screamed, but that her attention was claimed by a sound from the clutter of magical apparatus arrayed in the wings behind her, a muttered growl which was indisputably the voice of the tiger. She froze. There were probably instructions on how best to stare down rogue tigers, but as a Manhattanite born and bred they were techniques she wasn't acquainted with.

"Swann?" she said, hoping this yet might be some baroque illusion staged purely for her benefit. "Swann. Please get up."

But the magician only lay where he had fallen, the pool spreading from beneath him.

"If this is a joke—" she said testily, "—I'm not amused." When he didn't rise to her remark she tried a sweeter tactic. "Swann, my sweet, I'd like to go now, if you don't mind."

The growl came again. She didn't want to turn and seek out its source, but equally she didn't want to be sprung upon from behind.

Cautiously she looked round. The wings were in darkness. The clutter of properties kept her from working out the precise location of the beast. She could hear it still, however: its tread, its growl. Step by step, she retreated towards the apron of the stage. The closed curtains sealed her off from the auditorium, but she hoped she might scramble under them before the tiger reached her.

As she backed against the heavy fabric, one of the shadows in the wings forsook its ambiguity, and the animal appeared. It was not beautiful, as she had thought it when behind bars. It was vast and lethal and hungry. She went down on her haunches and reached for the hem of the curtain. The fabric was heavily weighted, and she had more difficulty lifting it than she'd expected, but she had managed to slide halfway under the drape when, head and hands pressed to the boards, she sensed the thump of the tiger's advance. An instant later she felt the splash of its breath on her bare back, and screamed as it hooked its talons into her body and hauled her from the sight of safety towards its steaming jaws.

Even then, she refused to give up her life. She kicked at it, and tore out its fur in handfuls, and delivered a hail of punches to its snout. But her resistance was negligible in the face of such authority; her assault, for all its ferocity, did not slow the beast a jot. It ripped open her body with one casual clout. Mercifully, with that first wound her senses gave up all claim to verisimilitude, and took instead to preposterous invention. It seemed to her that she heard applause from somewhere, and the roar of an approving audience, and that in place of the blood that was surely springing from her body there came fountains of sparkling light. The agony her nerve-endings were suffering didn't touch her at all. Even when the animal had divided her into three or four parts her head lay on its side at the edge of the stage and watched as her torso was mauled and her limbs devoured.

And all the while, when she wondered how all this could be possible—that her eyes could live to witness this last supper—the only reply she could think of was Swann's:

"*It's magic,*" he'd said.

Indeed, she was thinking that very thing, that this must *be* magic, when the tiger ambled across to her head, and swallowed it down in one bite.

Amongst a certain set Harry D'Amour liked to believe he had some small reputation—a coterie which did not, alas, include his ex-wife, his creditors or those anonymous critics who regularly posted dog's excrement through his office letterbox. But the woman who was on the phone now, her voice so full of grief she might have been crying for half a year, and was about to begin again, *she* knew him for the paragon he was.

"—I need your help, Mr D'Amour; very badly."

"I'm busy on several cases at the moment," he told her. "Maybe you could come to the office?"

"I can't leave the house," the woman informed him. "I'll explain everything. Please come."

He was sorely tempted. But there *were* several outstanding cases, one of which, if not solved soon, might end in fratricide. He suggested she try elsewhere.

"I can't go to just anybody," the woman insisted.

"Why me?"

"I read about you. About what happened in Brooklyn."

Making mention of his most conspicuous failure was not the surest method of securing his services, Harry thought, but it certainly got his attention. What had happened in Wyckoff Street had begun innocently enough, with a husband who'd employed him to spy on his adulterous wife, and had ended on the top storey of the Lomax house with the world he thought he'd known turning inside out. When the body-count was done, and the surviving priests dispatched, he was left with a fear of stairs, and more questions than he'd ever answer this side of the family plot. He took no pleasure in being reminded of those terrors.

"I don't like to talk about Brooklyn," he said.

"Forgive me," the woman replied, "but I need somebody who has experience with . . . with the occult." She stopped speaking for a moment. He could still hear her breath down the line: soft, but erratic.

"I need you," she said. He had already decided, in that pause when only her fear had been audible, what reply he would make.

"I'll come."

"I'm grateful to you," she said. "The house is on East 61st Street—" He scribbled down the details. Her last words were, "Please hurry." Then she put down the phone.

He made some calls, in the vain hope of placating two of his more excitable clients, then pulled on his jacket, locked the office, and started downstairs. The landing and the lobby smelt pungent. As he reached the front door he caught Chaplin, the janitor, emerging from the basement.

"This place stinks," he told the man.

"It's disinfectant."

"It's cat's piss," Harry said. "Get something done about it, will you? I've got a reputation to protect."

He left the man laughing.

The brownstone on East 61st Street was in pristine condition. He stood on the scrubbed step, sweaty and sour-breathed, and felt like a slob. The expression on the face that met him when the door opened did nothing to dissuade him of that opinion.

"Yes?" it wanted to know.

"I'm Harry D'Amour," he said. "I got a call."

The man nodded. "You'd better come in," he said, without enthusiasm.

It was cooler in than out; and sweeter. The place reeked of perfume. Harry followed the disapproving face down the hallway and into a large room, on the other side of which—across an oriental carpet that had everything woven into its pattern but the price—sat a widow. She didn't suit black; nor tears. She stood up and offered her hand.

"Mr D'Amour?"

"Yes."

"Valentin will get you something to drink if you'd like."

"Please. Milk, if you have it." His belly had been jittering for the last hour; since her talk of Wyckoff Street, in fact.

Valentin retired from the room, not taking his beady eyes

off Harry until the last possible moment.

"Somebody died," said Harry, once the man had gone.

"That's right," the widow said, sitting down again. At her invitation he sat opposite her, amongst enough cushions to furnish a harem. "My husband."

"I'm sorry."

"There's no time to be sorry," she said, her every look and gesture betraying her words. He was glad of her grief; the tearstains and the fatigue blemished a beauty which, had he seen it unimpaired, might have rendered him dumb with admiration.

"They say that my husband's death was an accident," she was saying. "I know it wasn't."

"May I ask . . . your name?"

"I'm sorry. My name is Swann, Mr D'Amour. Dorothea Swann. You may have heard of my husband?"

"The magician?"

"*Illusionist*," she said.

"I read about it. Tragic."

"Did you ever see his performance?"

Harry shook his head. "I can't afford Broadway, Mrs Swann."

"We were only over for three months, while his show ran. We were going back in September . . ."

"Back?"

"To Hamburg," she said. "I don't like this city. It's too hot. And too cruel."

"Don't blame New York," he said. "It can't help itself."

"Maybe," she replied, nodding. "Perhaps what happened to Swann would have happened anyway, wherever we'd been. People keep telling me: it was an accident. That's all. Just an accident."

"But you don't believe it?"

Valentin had appeared with a glass of milk. He set it down on the table in front of Harry. As he made to leave, she said: "Valentin. The letter?"

He looked at her strangely, almost as though she'd said something obscene.

"*The letter*," she repeated.

He exited.

"You were saying—"

She frowned. "What?"

"About it being an accident."

"Oh yes. I lived with Swann seven and a half years, and I got to understand him as well as anybody ever could. I learned to sense when he wanted me around, and when he didn't. When he didn't, I'd take myself off somewhere and let him have his privacy. Genius needs privacy. And he *was* a genius, you know. The greatest illusionist since Houdini."

"Is that so?"

"I'd think sometimes—it was a kind of miracle that he let me into his life . . ."

Harry wanted to say Swann would have been mad not to have done so, but the comment was inappropriate. She didn't want blandishments; didn't need them. Didn't need anything, perhaps, but her husband alive again.

"Now I think I didn't know him at all," she went on, "didn't *understand* him. I think maybe it was another trick. Another part of his magic."

"I called him a magician a while back," Harry said. "You corrected me."

"So I did," she said, conceding his point with an apologetic look. "Forgive me. That was Swann talking. He *hated* to be called a magician. He said that was a word that had to be kept for miracle-workers."

"And he was no miracle-worker?"

"He used to call himself the Great Pretender," she said. The thought made her smile.

Valentin had re-appeared, his lugubrious features rife with suspicion. He carried an envelope, which he clearly had no desire to give up. Dorothea had to cross the carpet and take it from his hands.

"Is this wise?" he said.

"Yes," she told him.

He turned on his heel and made a smart withdrawal.

"He's grief stricken," she said. "Forgive him his behaviour. He was with Swann from the beginning of his career. I think he loved my husband as much as I did."

She ran her finger down into the envelope and pulled the letter out. The paper was pale yellow, and gossamer-thin.

"A few hours after he died, this letter was delivered here by hand," she said. "It was addressed to him. I opened it. I think you ought to read it."

She passed it to him. The hand it was written in was solid and unaffected.

*Dorothea,* he had written, *if you are reading this, then I am dead.*

*You know how little store I set by dreams and premonitions and such; but for the last few days strange thoughts have just crept into my head, and I have the suspicion that death is very close to me. If so, so. There's no help for it. Don't waste time trying to puzzle out the whys and wherefores; they're old news now. Just know that I love you, and that I have always loved you in my way. I'm sorry for whatever unhappiness I've caused, or am causing now, but it was out of my hands.*

*I have some instructions regarding the disposal of my body. Please adhere to them* to the letter. *Don't let anybody try to persuade you out of doing as I ask.*

*I want you to have my body watched* night and day *until I'm cremated. Don't try and take my remains back to Europe. Have me cremated here,* as soon as possible, *then throw the ashes in the East River.*

*My sweet darling, I'm* afraid. *Not of bad dreams, or of what might happen to me in this life, but of what my enemies may try to do once I'm dead. You know how critics can be: they wait until you can't fight them back, then they start the character assassinations. It's too long a business to try and explain all of this, so I must simply trust you to do as I say.*

*Again, I love you, and I hope you never have to read this letter,*

*Your adoring,*

*Swann.*"

"Some farewell note," Harry commented when he'd read it through twice. He folded it up and passed it back to the widow.

"I'd like you to stay with him," she said. "Corpse-sit, if you will. Just until all the legal formalities are dealt with and I can make arrangements for his cremation. It shouldn't take them long. I've got a lawyer working on it now."

"Again: why me?"

She avoided his gaze. "As he says in the letter, he was never superstitious. But I am. I believe in omens. And there was an odd atmosphere about the place in the days before he died. As if we were watched."

"You think he was murdered?"

She mused on this, then said: "I don't believe it was an accident."

"These enemies he talks about . . ."

"He was a great man. Much envied."

"Professional jealousy? Is that a motive for murder?"

"Anything can be a motive, can't it?" she said. "People get killed for the colour of their eyes, don't they?"

Harry was impressed. It had taken him twenty years to learn how arbitrary things were. She spoke it as conventional wisdom.

"Where is your husband?" he asked her.

"Upstairs," she said. "I had the body brought back here, where I could look after him. I can't pretend I understand what's going on, but I'm not going to risk ignoring his instructions."

Harry nodded.

"Swann was my life," she added softly, apropos of nothing; and everything.

She took him upstairs. The perfume that had met him at the door intensified. The master bedroom had been turned into a Chapel of Rest, knee-deep in sprays and wreaths of every shape and variety; their mingled scents verged on the hallucinogenic. In the midst of this abundance, the casket—an elaborate affair in black and silver—was mounted on trestles. The upper half of the lid stood open, the plush overlay folded back. At Dorothea's invitation he waded through the tributes to view the deceased. He liked Swann's face; it had humour, and a certain guile; it was even handsome in its weary way. More: it had inspired the love of Dorothea; a face could have few better recommendations. Harry stood waist high in flowers and, absurd as it was, felt a twinge of envy for the love this man must have enjoyed.

"Will you help me, Mr D'Amour?"

What could he say but: "Yes, of course I'll help." That, and: "Call me Harry."

He would be missed at Wing's Pavilion tonight. He had occupied the best table there every Friday night for the past six and a half years, eating at one sitting enough to compensate for what his diet lacked in excellence and variety the other six days of the week. This feast—the best Chinese cuisine to be had south of Canal Street—came *gratis*, thanks to services he had once rendered the owner. Tonight the table would go empty.

Not that his stomach suffered. He had only been sitting with Swann an hour or so when Valentin came up and said:

"How do you like your steak?"

"Just shy of burned," Harry replied.

Valentin was none too pleased by the response. "I hate to overcook good steak," he said.

"And I hate the sight of blood," Harry said, "even if it isn't my own."

The chef clearly despaired of his guest's palate, and turned to go.

"Valentin?"

The man looked round.

"Is that your Christian name?" Harry asked.

"Christian names are for Christians," came the reply.

Harry nodded. "You don't like my being here, am I right?"

Valentin made no reply. His eyes had drifted past Harry to the open coffin.

"I'm not going to be here for long," Harry said, "but while I am, can't we be friends?"

Valentin's gaze found him once more.

"I don't have any friends," he said without enmity or self-pity. "Not now."

"OK. I'm sorry."

"What's to be sorry for?" Valentin wanted to know. "Swann's dead. It's all over, bar the shouting."

The doleful face stoically refused tears. A stone would weep sooner, Harry guessed. But there was grief there, and all the more acute for being dumb.

"One question."

"Only one?"

"Why didn't you want me to read his letter?"

Valentin raised his eyebrows slightly; they were fine enough to have been pencilled on. "He wasn't insane," he said. "I didn't want you thinking he was a crazy man, because of what he wrote. What you read you keep to yourself. Swann was a legend. I don't want his memory besmirched."

"You should write a book," Harry said. "Tell the whole story once and for all. You were with him a long time, I hear."

"Oh yes," said Valentin. "Long enough to know better than to tell the truth."

So saying he made an exit, leaving the flowers to wilt, and Harry with more puzzles on his hands than he'd begun with.

Twenty minutes later, Valentin brought up a tray of food: a large salad, bread, wine, and the steak. It was one degree short of charcoal.

"Just the way I like it," Harry said, and set to guzzling.

He didn't see Dorothea Swann, though God knows he thought about her often enough. Every time he heard a whisper on the stairs, or footsteps along the carpetted landing, he hoped her face would appear at the door, an invitation on her lips. Not perhaps the most appropriate of thoughts, given the proximity of her husband's corpse, but what would the illusionist care now? He was dead and gone. If he had any generosity of spirit he wouldn't want to see his widow drown in her grief.

Harry drank the half-carafe of wine Valentin had brought, and when—three-quarters of an hour later—the man reappeared with coffee and Calvados, he told him to leave the bottle.

Nightfall was near. The traffic was noisy on Lexington and Third. Out of boredom he took to watching the street from the window. Two lovers feuded loudly on the sidewalk, and only stopped when a brunette with a hare-lip and a pekinese stood watching them shamelessly. There were preparations for a party in the brownstone opposite: he watched a table lovingly laid, and candles lit. After a time the spying began to depress him, so he called Valentin and asked if there was a portable television he could have access to. No sooner said than provided, and for the next two hours he sat with the small black and white monitor on the floor amongst the orchids and the lilies, watching whatever mindless entertainment it offered, the silver luminescence flickering on the blooms like excitable moonlight.

A quarter after midnight, with the party across the street in full swing, Valentin came up. "You want a night-cap?" he asked.

"Sure."

"Milk; or something stronger?"

"Something stronger."

He produced a bottle of fine cognac, and two glasses. Together they toasted the dead man.

"Mr Swann."

"Mr Swann."

"If you need anything more tonight," Valentin said, "I'm in the room directly above. Mrs Swann is downstairs, so if you hear somebody moving about don't worry. She doesn't sleep well these nights."

"Who does?" Harry replied.

Valentin left him to his vigil. Harry heard the man's tread on the stairs and then the creaking of floorboards on the level above. He returned his attention to the television, but he'd lost the thread of the movie he'd been watching. It was a long stretch 'til dawn; meanwhile New York would be having itself a fine Friday night: dancing, fighting, fooling around.

The picture on the television set began to flicker. He stood up, and started to walk across to the set, but he never got there. Two steps from the chair where he'd been sitting the picture folded up and went out altogether, plunging the room into total darkness. Harry briefly had time to register that no light was finding its way through the windows from the street. Then the insanity began.

Something moved in the blackness: vague forms rose and fell. It took him a moment to recognise them. The flowers! Invisible hands were tearing the wreaths and tributes apart, and tossing the blossoms up into the air. He followed their descent, but they didn't hit the ground. It seemed the floorboards had lost all faith in themselves, and disappeared, so the blossoms just kept falling—*down, down*—through the floor of the room below, and through the basement floor, away to God alone knew what destination. Fear gripped Harry, like some old dope-pusher promising a terrible high. Even those few boards that remained beneath his feet were becoming insubstantial. In seconds he would go the way of the blossoms.

He reeled around to locate the chair he'd got up from—some fixed point in this vertiginous nightmare. The chair was still there; he could just discern its form in the gloom. With torn blossoms raining down upon him he reached for it, but even as his hand took hold of the arm, the floor beneath the chair gave up the ghost, and now, by a ghastly light that was thrown up from the pit that yawned beneath his feet, Harry saw it tumble away into Hell, turning over and over 'til it was pin-prick small.

Then it was gone; and the flowers were gone, and the walls and the windows and every damn thing was gone but *him*.

Not quite everything. Swann's casket remained, its lid still standing open, its overlay neatly turned back like the sheet on a child's bed. The trestle had gone, as had the floor beneath the trestle. But the casket floated in the dark air for all the world like some morbid illusion, while from the depths a rumbling sound accompanied the trick like the roll of a snare-drum.

Harry felt the last solidity failing beneath him; felt the pit call. Even as his feet left the ground, that ground faded to nothing, and for a terrifying moment he hung over the Gulfs, his hands seeking the lip of the casket. His right hand caught hold of one of the handles, and closed thankfully around it. His arm was almost jerked from its socket as it took his body-weight, but he flung his other arm up and found the casket-edge. Using it as purchase, he hauled himself up like a half-drowned sailor. It was a strange life-boat, but then this was a strange sea. Infinitely deep, infinitely terrible.

Even as he laboured to secure himself a better hand-hold, the casket shook, and Harry looked up to discover that the dead man was sitting upright. Swann's eyes opened wide. He turned them on Harry; they were far from benign. The next moment the dead illusionist was scrambling to his feet—the floating casket rocking ever more violently with each movement. Once vertical, Swann proceeded to dislodge his guest by grinding his heel in Harry's knuckles. Harry looked up at Swann, begging for him to stop.

The Great Pretender was a sight to see. His eyes were starting from his sockets; his shirt was torn open to display the exit-wound in his chest. It was bleeding afresh. A rain of cold blood fell upon Harry's upturned face. And still the heel ground at his hands. Harry felt his grip slipping. Swann, sensing his approaching triumph, began to smile.

"Fall, boy!" he said. "Fall!"

Harry could take no more. In a frenzied effort to save himself he let go of the handle in his right hand, and reached up to snatch at Swann's trouser-leg. His fingers found the hem, and he pulled. The smile vanished from the illusionist's face as he felt his balance go. He reached behind him to take hold of the casket lid for support, but the gesture only tipped the casket further over. The plush cushion tumbled past Harry's head; blossoms followed.

Swann howled in his fury and delivered a vicious kick to Harry's hand. It was an error. The casket tipped over entirely and pitched the man out. Harry had time to glimpse Swann's appalled face as the illusionist fell past him. Then he too lost his grip and tumbled after him.

The dark air whined past his ears. Beneath him, the Gulfs spread their empty arms. And then, behind the rushing in his head, another sound: a human voice.

"Is he dead?" it inquired.

"No," another voice replied, "no, I don't think so. What's his name, Dorothea?"

"D'Amour."

"Mr D'Amour? Mr D'Amour?"

Harry's descent slowed somewhat. Beneath him, the Gulfs roared their rage.

The voice came again, cultivated but unmelodious. "Mr D'Amour."

"Harry," said Dorothea.

At that word, from that voice, he stopped falling; felt himself borne up. He opened his eyes. He was lying on a solid floor, his head inches from the blank television screen. The flowers were all in place around the room, Swann in his casket, and God—if the rumours were to be believed—in his Heaven.

"I'm alive," he said.

He had quite an audience for his resurrection. Dorothea of course, and two strangers. One, the owner of the voice he'd first heard, stood close to the door. His features were unremarkable, except for his brows and lashes, which were pale to the point of invisibility. His female companion stood nearby. She shared with him this distressing banality, stripped bare of any feature that offered a clue to their natures.

"Help him up, angel," the man said, and the woman bent to comply. She was stronger than she looked, readily hauling Harry to his feet. He had vomited in his strange sleep. He felt dirty and ridiculous.

"What the hell happened?" he asked, as the woman escorted him to the chair. He sat down.

"He tried to poison you," the man said.

"Who did?"

"Valentin, of course."

"Valentin?"

"He's gone," Dorothea said. "Just disappeared." She was shaking. "I heard you call out, and came in here to find you on the floor. I thought you were going to choke."

"It's all right," said the man, "everything is in order now."

"Yes," said Dorothea, clearly reassured by his bland smile. "This is the lawyer I was telling you about, Harry. Mr Butterfield."

Harry wiped his mouth. "Pleased to meet you," he said.

"Why don't we all go downstairs?" Butterfield said. "And I can pay Mr D'Amour what he's due."

"It's all right," Harry said, "I never take my fee until the job's done."

"But it is done," Butterfield said. "Your services are no longer required here."

Harry threw a glance at Dorothea. She was plucking a withered anthurium from an otherwise healthy spray.

"I was contracted to stay with the body—"

"The arrangements for the disposal of Swann's body have been made," Butterfield returned. His courtesy was only just intact. "Isn't that right, Dorothea?"

"It's the middle of the night," Harry protested. "You won't get a cremation until tomorrow morning at the earliest."

"Thank you for your help," Dorothea said. "But I'm sure everything will be fine now that Mr Butterfield has arrived. Just fine."

Butterfield turned to his companion.

"Why don't you go out and find a cab for Mr D'Amour?" he said. Then, looking at Harry: "We don't want you walking the streets, do we?"

All the way downstairs, and in the hallway as Butterfield paid him off, Harry was willing Dorothea to contradict the lawyer and tell him she wanted Harry to stay. But she didn't even offer him a word of farewell as he was ushered out of the house. The two hundred dollars he'd been given were, of course, more than adequate recompense for the few hours of idleness he'd spent there, but he would happily have burned all the bills for one sign that Dorothea gave a damn that they were parting. Quite clearly she did not. On past experience it would take his bruised ego a full twenty-four hours to recover from such indifference.

He got out of the cab on 3rd around 83rd Street, and walked through to a bar on Lexington where he knew he could put half a bottle of bourbon between himself and the dreams he'd had.

It was well after one. The street was deserted, except for him, and for the echo his footsteps had recently acquired. He turned the corner into Lexington, and waited. A few beats later, Valentin rounded the same corner. Harry took hold of him by his tie.

"Not a bad noose," he said, hauling the man off his heels.

Valentin made no attempt to free himself. "Thank God you're alive," he said.

"No thanks to you," Harry said. "What did you put in the drink?"

"Nothing," Valentin insisted. "Why should I?"

"So how come I found myself on the floor? How come the bad dreams?"

"Butterfield," Valentin said. "Whatever you dreamt, he brought with him, believe me. I panicked as soon as I heard him in the house, I admit it. I know I should have warned you, but I knew if I didn't get out quickly I wouldn't get out at all."

"Are you telling me he would have killed you?"

"Not personally; but yes." Harry looked incredulous. "We go way back, him and me."

"He's welcome to you," Harry said, letting go of the tie. "I'm too damn tired to take any more of this shit." He turned from Valentin and began to walk away.

"Wait—" said the other man, "—I know I wasn't too sweet with you back at the house, but you've got to understand, things are going to get bad. For both of us."

"I thought you said it was all over bar the shouting?"

"I thought it was. I thought we had it all sewn up. Then Butterfield arrived and I realised how naïve I was being. They're not going to let Swann rest in peace. Not now, not ever. We have to save him, D'Amour."

Harry stopped walking and studied the man's face. To pass him in the street, he mused, you wouldn't have taken him for a lunatic.

"Did Butterfield go upstairs?" Valentin enquired.

"Yes he did. Why"

"Do you remember if he approached the casket?"

Harry shook his head.

"Good," said Valentin. "Then the defences are holding, which gives us a little time. Swann was a fine tactician, you know. But he could be careless. That was how they caught him. Sheer carelessness. He knew they were coming for him. I told him outright, I said we should cancel the remaining performances and go home. At least he had some sanctuary there."

"You think he was murdered?"

"Jesus Christ," said Valentin, almost despairing of Harry, "of course he was murdered."

"So he's past saving, right? The man's dead."

"Dead; yes. Past saving? no."

"Do you talk gibberish to everyone?"

Valentin put his hand on Harry's shoulder, "Oh no," he said, with unfeigned sincerity. "I don't trust anyone the way I trust you."

"This is very sudden," said Harry. "May I ask why?"

"Because you're in this up to your neck, the way I am," Valentin replied.

"No I'm not," said Harry, but Valentin ignored the denial, and went on with his talk. "At the moment we don't know how many of them there are, of course. They might simply have sent Butterfield, but I think that's unlikely."

"Who's Butterfield with? The Mafia?"

"We should be so lucky," said Valentin. He reached in his pocket and pulled out a piece of paper. "This is the woman Swann was with," he said, "the night at the theatre. It's possible she knows something of their strength."

"There was a witness?"

"She didn't come forward, but yes, there was. I was his procurer you see. I helped arrange his several adulteries, so that none ever embarrassed him. See if you can get to her—" He stopped abruptly. Somewhere close by, music was being played. It sounded like a drunken jazz band extemporising on bagpipes; a wheezing, rambling cacophony. Valentin's face instantly became a portrait of distress. "God help us . . ." he said softly, and began to back away from Harry.

"What's the problem?"

"Do you know how to pray?" Valentin asked him as he retreated down 83rd Street. The volume of the music was rising with every interval.

"I haven't prayed in twenty years," Harry replied.

"Then *learn*," came the response, and Valentin turned to run.

As he did so a ripple of darkness moved down the street from the north, dimming the lustre of bar-signs and street-lamps as it came. Neon announcements suddenly guttered and died; there were protests out of upstairs windows as the lights failed and, as if encouraged by the curses, the music took on a fresh and yet more hectic rhythm. Above his head Harry heard a wailing sound, and looked up to see a ragged silhouette against the clouds which trailed tendrils like a man o' war as it descended upon the street, leaving the stench of rotting fish in its wake. Its target was clearly Valentin. He shouted above the wail and the music and the panic from the black-out, but no sooner had he yelled than he heard Valentin shout out from the darkness; a pleading cry that was rudely cut short.

He stood in the murk, his feet unwilling to carry him a step nearer the place from which the plea had come. The smell still stung his nostrils; nosing it, his nausea returned. And then, so did the lights; a wave of power igniting the lamps and the bar-signs as it washed back down the street. It reached Harry, and moved on to the spot where he had last seen Valentin. It was deserted; indeed the sidewalk was empty all the way down the next intersection.

The drivelling jazz has stopped.

Eyes peeled for man, beast, or the remnants of either, Harry wandered down the sidewalk. Twenty yards from where he had been standing the concrete was wet. Not with blood, he was pleased to see; the fluid was the colour of bile,and stank to high Heaven. Amongst the splashes were several slivers of what might have been human tissue. Evidently Valentin had fought, and succeeded in opening a wound in his attacker. There were more traces of the blood further down the sidewalk, as if the injured thing had crawled some way before taking flight again. With Valentin, presumably. In the face of such strength Harry knew his meagre powers would have availed him not at all, but he felt guilty nevertheless. He'd heard the cry—seen the assailant swoop—and yet fear had sealed his soles to the ground.

He'd last felt fear the equal of this in Wyckoff Street, when Mimi Lomax's demon-lover had finally thrown off any pretence to humanity. The room had filled with the stink of ether and human dirt, and the demon had stood there in its appalling nakedness and shown him scenes that had turned his bowels to water. They were with him now, those scenes. They would be with him forever.

He looked down at the scrap of paper Valentin had given him: the name and address had been rapidly scrawled, but they were just decipherable.

A wise man, Harry reminded himself, would screw this note up and throw it down into the gutter. But if the events in Wyckoff Street had taught him anything, it was that once touched by such malignancy as he had seen and dreamt in the last few hours, there could be no casual disposal of it. He had to follow it to its source, however repugnant that thought was, and make with it whatever bargains the strength of his hand allowed.

There was no good time to do business like this: the present would have to suffice. He walked back to Lexington and caught a cab to the address on the paper. He got no response from the bell marked Bernstein, but roused the doorman, and engaged in a frustrating debate with him through the glass door. The man was angry to have been raised at such an hour; Miss Bernstein was not in her apartment, he insisted, and remained untouched even when Harry intimated that there might be some life-or-death urgency in the matter. It was only when he produced his wallet that the fellow displayed the least flicker of concern. Finally, he let Harry in.

"She's not up there," he said, pocketing the bills. "She's not been in for days."

Harry took the elevator: his shins were aching, and his back too. He wanted sleep; bourbon, then sleep. There was no reply at the apartment as the doorman had predicted, but he kept knocking, and calling her.

"Miss Bernstein? Are you there?"

There was no sign of life from within; not at least, until he said:

"I want to talk about Swann."

He heard an intake of breath, close to the door.

"Is somebody there?" he asked. "Please answer. There's nothing to be afraid of."

After several seconds a slurred and melancholy voice murmured: "Swann's dead."

At least *she* wasn't, Harry thought. Whatever forces had snatched Valentin away, they had not yet reached this corner of Manhattan. "May I talk to you?" he requested.

"No," she replied. Her voice was a candle flame on the verge of extinction.

"Just a few questions, Barbara."

"I'm in the tiger's belly," the slow reply came, "and it doesn't want me to let you in."

Perhaps they *had* got here before him.

"Can't you reach the door?" he coaxed her. "It's not so far . . ."

"But it's eaten me," she said.

"*Try*, Barbara. The tiger won't mind. *Reach.*"

There was silence from the other side of the door, then a shuffling sound. Was she doing as he had requested? It seemed so. He heard her fingers fumbling with the catch.

"That's it," he encouraged her. "Can you turn it? Try to turn it."

At the last instant he thought: suppose she's telling the truth, and there *is* a tiger in there with her? It was too late for retreat, the door was opening. There was no animal in the hallway. Just a woman, and the smell of dirt. She had clearly neither washed nor changed her clothes since fleeing from the theatre. The evening gown she wore was soiled and torn, her skin was grey with grime. He stepped into the apartment. She moved down the hallway away from him, desperate to avoid his touch.

"It's all right," he said, "there's no tiger here."

Her wide eyes were almost empty; what presence roved there was lost to sanity.

"Oh there is," she said, "I'm in the tiger. I'm in it forever."

As he had neither the time nor the skill required to dissuade her from this madness, he decided it was wiser to go with it.

"How did you get there?" he asked her. "Into the tiger? Was it when you were with Swann?"

She nodded.

"You remember that, do you?"

"Oh yes."

"What do you remember?"

"There was a sword; it fell. He was picking up—" She stopped and frowned.

"Picking up what?"

She seemed suddenly more distracted than ever. "How can you hear me," she wondered, "when I'm in the tiger? Are you in the tiger too?

"Maybe I am," he said, not wanting to analyse the metaphor too closely.

"We're here forever, you know," she informed him. "We'll never be let out."

"Who told you that?"

She didn't reply, but cocked her head a little.

"Can you hear?" she said.

"Hear?"

She took another step back down the hallway. Harry listened, but he could hear nothing. The growing agitation on Barbara's face was sufficient to send him back to the front door and open it, however. The elevator was in operation. He could hear its soft hum across the landing. Worse: the lights in the hallway and on the stairs were deteriorating; the bulbs losing power with every foot the elevator ascended.

He turned back into the apartment and went to take hold of Barbara's wrist. She made no protest. Her eyes were fixed on the doorway through which she seemed to know her judgement would come.

"We'll take the stairs," he told her, and led her out on to the landing. The lights were within an ace of failing. He glanced up at the floor numbers being ticked off above the elevator doors. Was this the top floor they were on, or one shy of it? He couldn't remember, and there was no time to think before the lights went out entirely.

He stumbled across the unfamiliar territory of the landing with the girl in tow, hoping to God he'd find the stairs before the elevator reached this floor. Barbara wanted to loiter, but he bullied her to pick up her pace. As his foot found the top stair the elevator finished its ascent.

The doors hissed open, and a cold fluorescence washed the landing. He couldn't see its source, nor did he wish to, but its effect was to reveal to the naked eye every stain and blemish, every sign of decay and creeping rot that the paintwork sought to camouflage. The show stole Harry's attention for a moment only, then he took a firmer hold of the woman's hand and they began their descent. Barbara was not interested in escape however, but in events on the landing. Thus occupied she tripped and fell heavily against Harry. The two would have toppled but that he caught hold of the banister. Angered, he turned to her. They were out of sight of the landing, but the light crept down the stairs and washed over Barbara's face. Beneath its uncharitable scrutiny Harry saw decay busy in her. Saw rot in her teeth, and the death in her skin and hair and nails. No doubt he would have appeared much the same to her, were she to have looked, but she was still staring back over her shoulder and up the stairs. The light-source was on the move. Voices accompanied it.

"The door's open," a woman said.

"What are you waiting for?" a voice replied. It was Butterfield.

Harry held both breath and wrist as the light-source moved again, towards the door presumably, and then was partially eclipsed as it disappeared into the apartment.

"We have to be quick," he told Barbara. She went with him down three or four steps and then, without warning, her hand leapt for his face, nails opening his cheek. He let go of her hand to protect himself, and in that instant she was away—back up the stairs.

He cursed and stumbled in pursuit of her, but her former sluggishness had lifted; she was startlingly nimble. By the dregs of light from the landing he watched her reach the top of the stairs and disappear from sight.

"Here I am," she called out as she went.

He stood immobile on the stairway, unable to decide whether to go or stay, and so unable to move at all. Ever since Wyckoff Street he'd hated stairs. Momentarily the light from above flared up, throwing the shadows of the banisters across him; then it died again. He put his hand to his face. She had raised weals, but there was little blood. What could he hope from her if he went to her aid? Only more of the same. She was a lost cause.

Even as he despaired of her he heard a sound from round the corner at the head of the stairs; a soft sound that might have been either a footstep or a sigh. Had she escaped their influence after all? Or perhaps not even reached the apartment door, but thought better of it and about-turned? Even as he was weighing up the odds he heard her say:

"Help me . . ." The voice was a ghost of a ghost; but it was indisputably her, and she was in terror.

He reached for his .38, and started up the stairs again. Even before he had turned the corner he felt the nape of his neck itch as his hackles rose.

She was there. But so was the tiger. It stood on the landing, mere feet from Harry, its body humming with latent power. Its eyes were molten; its open maw impossibly large. And there, already in its vast throat, was Barbara. He met her eyes out of the tiger's mouth, and saw a flicker of comprehension in them that was worse than any madness. Then the beast threw its head back and forth to settle its prey in its gut. She had been swallowed whole, apparently. There was no blood on the landing, nor about the tiger's muzzle; only the appalling sight of the girl's face disappearing down the tunnel of the animal's throat.

She loosed a final cry from the belly of the thing, and as it rose it seemed to Harry that the beast attempted a grin. Its face crinkled up grotesquely, the eyes narrowing like those of a laughing Buddha, the lips peeling back to expose a sickle of brilliant teeth. Behind this display the cry was finally hushed. In that instant the tiger leapt.

Harry fired into its devouring bulk and as the shot met its flesh the leer and the maw and the whole striped mass of it unwove in a single beat. Suddenly it was gone, and there was only a drizzle of pastel confetti spiralling down around him. The shot had aroused interest. There were raised voices in one or two of the apartments, and the light that had accompanied Butterfield from the elevator was brightening through the open door of the Bernstein residence. He was almost tempted to stay and see the light-bringer, but discretion bettered his curiosity, and he turned and made his descent, taking the stairs two and three at a time. The confetti tumbled after him, as if it had a life of its own. Barbara's life, perhaps; transformed into paper pieces and tossed away.

He reached the lobby breathless. The doorman was standing there, staring up the stairs vacantly.

"Somebody get shot?" he enquired.

"No," said Harry, "eaten."

As he headed for the door he heard the elevator start to hum as it descended. Perhaps merely a tenant, coming down for a pre-dawn stroll. Perhaps not.

He left the doorman as he had found him, sullen and confused, and made his escape into the street, putting two block lengths between him and the apartment building before he stopped running. They did not bother to come after him. He was beneath their concern, most likely.

So what was he to do now? Valentin was dead, Barbara Bernstein too. He was none the wiser now than he'd been at the outset, except that he'd learned again the lesson he'd been taught in Wyckoff Street: that when dealing with the Gulfs it was wiser never to believe your eyes. The moment you trusted your senses, the moment you believed a tiger to *be* a tiger, you were half theirs.

Not a complicated lesson, but it seemed he had forgotten it, like a fool, and it had taken two deaths to teach it him afresh. Maybe it would be simpler to have the rule tattooed on the back of his hand, so that he couldn't check the time without being reminded: *Never believe your eyes*.

The principle was still fresh in his mind as he walked back towards his apartment and a man stepped out of the doorway and said:

"Harry."

It *looked* like Valentin; a wounded Valentin, a Valentin who'd been dismembered and sewn together again by a committee of blind surgeons, but the same man in essence. But then the tiger had looked like a tiger, hadn't it?

"It's me," he said.

"Oh no," Harry said. "Not this time."

"What are you talking about? *It's Valentin.*"

"So prove it."

The other man looked puzzled. "This is no time for games," he said, "we're in desperate straits."

Harry took his .38 from his pocket and pointed at Valentin's chest. "Prove it or I shoot you," he said.

"Are you out of your mind?"

"I saw you torn apart."

"Not quite," said Valentin. His left arm was swathed in makeshift bandaging from fingertip to mid-bicep. "It was touch and go . . ." he said, ". . . but everything has its Achilles' heel. It's just a question of finding the right spot."

Harry peered at the man. He wanted to believe that this was indeed Valentin, but it was too incredible to believe that the frail form in front of him could have survived the monstrosity he'd seen on 83rd Street. No; this was another illusion. Like the tiger: paper and malice.

The man broke Harry's train of thought. "Your steak . . ." he said.

"My steak?"

"You like it almost burned," Valentin said. "I protested, remember?"

Harry remembered. "Go on," he said.

"And you said you hated the sight of blood. Even if it wasn't your own."

"Yes," said Harry. His doubts were lifting. "That's right."

"You asked me to prove I'm Valentin. That's the best I can do." Harry was almost persuaded. "In God's name," Valentin said, "do we have to debate this standing on the street?"

"You'd better come in."

The apartment was small, but tonight it felt more stifling than ever. Valentin sat himself down with a good view of the door. He refused spirits or first-aid. Harry helped himself to bourbon. He was on his third shot when Valentin finally said:

"We have to go back to the house, Harry."

"*What?*"

"We have to claim Swann's body before Butterfield."

"I did my best already. It's not my business any more."

"So you leave Swann to the Pit?" Valentin said.

"*She* doesn't care, why should I?"

"You mean Dorothea? She doesn't know what Swann was involved with. That's why she's so trusting. She has suspicions maybe, but, insofar as it is possible to be guiltless in all of this, she is." He paused to adjust the position of his injured arm. "She was a prostitute, you know. I don't suppose she told you that. Swann once said to me he married her because only prostitutes know the value of love."

Harry let this apparent paradox go.

"Why did she stay with him?" he asked. "He wasn't exactly faithful, was he?"

"She loved him," Valentin replied. "It's not unheard of."

"And you?"

"Oh I loved him too, in spite of his stupidities. That's why we have to help him. If Butterfield and his associates get their hands on Swann's mortal remains, there'll be all Hell to pay."

"I know. I got a glimpse at the Bernstein place."

"What did you see?"

"Something and nothing," said Harry. "A tiger, I thought; only it wasn't."

"The old paraphernalia," Valentin commented.

"And there was something else with Butterfield. Something that shed light: I didn't see what."

"The Castrato," Valentin muttered to himself, clearly discomfited. "We'll have to be careful."

He stood up, the movement causing him to wince. "I think we should be on our way, Harry."

"Are you paying me for this?" Harry inquired, "or am I doing it all for love?"

"You're doing it because of what happened at Wyckoff Street," came the softly-spoken reply. "Because you lost poor Mimi Lomax to the Gulfs, and you don't want to lose Swann. That is, if you've not already done so."

They caught a cab on Madison Avenue and headed back uptown to 61st Street, keeping their silence as they rode. Harry had half a hundred questions to ask of Valentin. Who was Butterfield for one, and what was Swann's crime that he be pursued to death and beyond? So many puzzles. But Valentin looked sick and unfit for plying with questions. Besides, Harry sensed that the more he knew the less enthusiastic he would be about the journey they were now taking.

"We have perhaps one advantage—" Valentin said as they approached 61st Street. "They can't be expecting this frontal attack. Butterfield presumes I'm dead, and probably thinks you're hiding your head in mortal terror."

"I'm working on it."

"You're not in danger," Valentin replied, "at least not the way Swann is. If they were to take you apart limb by limb it would be nothing beside the torments they have waiting for the magician."

"Illusionist," Harry corrected him, but Valentin shook his head.

"Magician he was; magician he will always be."

The driver interrupted before Harry could quote Dorothea on the subject.

"What number you people want?" he said.

"Just drop us here on the right," Valentin instructed him. "And wait for us, understand?"

"Sure."

Valentin turned to Harry. "Give the man fifty dollars."

"*Fifty*?"

"Do you want him to wait or not?"

Harry counted four tens and ten singles into the driver's hand.

"You'd better keep the engine running," he said.

"Anything to oblige," the driver grinned.

Harry joined Valentin on the sidewalk and they walked the twenty-five yards to the house. The street was still noisy, despite the hour: the party that Harry had seen in preparation half a night ago was at its height. There was no sign of life at the Swann residence however.

Perhaps they *don't* expect us, Harry thought. Certainly this head-on assault was about the most foolhardy tactic imaginable, and as such might catch the enemy off-guard. But were such forces ever off-guard? Was there ever a minute in their maggoty lives when their eyelids drooped and sleep tamed them for a space? No. In Harry's experience it was only the good who needed sleep; iniquity and its practitioners were awake every eager moment, planning fresh felonies.

"How do we get in?" he asked as they stood outside the house.

"I have the key," Valentin replied, and went to the door.

There was no retreat now. The key was turned, the door was open, and they were stepping out of the comparative safety of the street. The house was as dark within as it had appeared from without. There was no sound of human presence on any of the floors. Was it possible that the defences Swann had laid around his corpse had indeed rebuffed Butterfield, and that he and his cohorts had retreated? Valentin quashed such misplaced optimism almost immediately, taking hold of Harry's arm and leaning close to whisper:

"*They're here.*"

This was not the time to ask Valentin how he knew, but Harry made a mental note to enquire when, or rather *if*, they got out of the house with their tongues still in their heads.

Valentin was already on the stairs. Harry, his eyes still accustoming themselves to the vestigial light that crept in from the street, crossed the hallway after him. The other man moved confidently in the gloom, and Harry was glad of it. Without Valentin plucking at his sleeve, and guiding him around the half-landing he might well have crippled himself.

Despite what Valentin had said, there was no more sound or sight of occupancy up here than there had been below, but as they advanced towards the master bedroom where Swann lay, a rotten tooth in Harry's lower jaw that had lately been quiescent began to throb afresh, and his bowels ached to break wind. The anticipation was crucifying. He felt a barely suppressible urge to yell out, and to oblige the enemy to show its hand, if indeed it had hands to show.

Valentin had reached the door. He turned his head in Harry's direction, and even in the murk it was apparent that fear was taking its toll on him too. His skin glistened; he stank of fresh sweat.

He pointed towards the door. Harry nodded. He was as ready as he was ever going to be. Valentin reached for the door handle. The sound of the lock-mechanism seemed deafeningly loud, but it brought no response from anywhere in the house. The door swung open, and the heady scent of flowers met them. They had begun to decay in the forced heat of the house; there was a rankness beneath the perfume. More welcome than the scent was the light. The curtains in the room had not been entirely drawn, and the streetlamps described the interior: the flowers massed like clouds around the casket; the chair where Harry had sat, the Calvados bottle beside it; the mirror above the fireplace showing the room its secret self.

Valentin was already moving across to the casket, and Harry heard him sigh as he set eyes on his old master.

He wasted little time, but immediately set to lifting the lower half of the casket lid. It defeated his single arm however and Harry went to his assistance, eager to get the job done and be away. Touching the solid wood of the casket brought his nightmare back with breath-snatching force: the Pit opening beneath him, the illusionist rising from his bed like a sleeper unwillingly woken. There was no such spectacle now, however. Indeed a little life in the corpse might have made the job easier. Swann was a big man, and his limp body was uncooperative to a fault. The simple act of lifting him from his casket took all their breath and attention. He came at last, though reluctantly, his long limbs flopping about.

"Now . . ." said Valentin ". . . downstairs."

As they moved to the door something in the street ignited, or so it seemed, for the interior suddenly brightened. The light was not kind to their burden. It revealed the crudity of the cosmetics applied to Swann's face, and the burgeoning putresence beneath. Harry had an instant only to appreciate these felicities, and then the light brightened again, and he realised that it wasn't *out*side, but *in*.

He looked up at Valentin, and almost despaired. The luminescence was even less charitable to servant than to master; it seemed to strip the flesh from Valentin's face. Harry caught only a glimpse of what it revealed beneath—events stole his attention an instant later—but he saw enough to know that had Valentin not been his accomplice in this venture he might well have run from him.

"*Get him out of here*!" Valentin yelled.

He let go of Swann's legs, leaving Harry to steer Swann single-handed. The corpse proved recalcitrant however. Harry had only made two cursing steps towards the exit when things took a turn for the cataclysmic.

He heard Valentin unloose an oath, and looked up to see that the mirror had given up all pretence to reflection, and that something was moving up from its liquid depths, bringing the light with it.

"What is it?" Harry breathed.

"The Castrato," came the reply. "Will you *go*?"

There was no time to obey Valentin's panicked instruction however, before the hidden thing broke the plane of the mirror and invaded the room. Harry had been wrong. It did not carry the light with it as it came: it *was* the light. Or rather, some holocaust blazed in its bowels, the glare of which escaped through the creature's body by whatever route it could. It had once been human; a mountain of a man with the belly and the breasts of a neolithic Venus. But the fire in its body had twisted it out of true, breaking out through its palms and its navel, burning its mouth and nostrils into one ragged hole. It had, as its name implied, been unsexed; from that hole too, light spilled. By it, the decay of the flowers speeded into seconds. The blossoms withered and died. The room was filled in moments with the stench of rotting vegetable matter.

Harry heard Valentin call his name, once, and again. Only then did he remember the body in his arms. He dragged his eyes from the hovering Castrato, and carried Swann another yard. The door was at his back, and open. He dragged his burden out into the landing as the Castrato kicked over the casket. He heard the din, and then shouts from Valentin. There followed another terrible commotion, and the high-pitched voice of the Castrato, talking through that hole in its face.

"Die and be happy," it said, and a hail of furniture was flung against the wall with such force chairs embedded themselves in the plaster. Valentin had escaped the assault however, or so it seemed, for an instant later Harry heard the Castrato shriek. It was an appalling sound: pitiful and revolting. He would have stopped his ears, but that he had his hands full.

He had almost reached the top of the stairs. Dragging Swann a few steps further he laid the body down. The Castrato's light was not dimmed, despite its complaints; it still flickered on the bedroom wall like a midsummer thunderstorm. For the third time tonight—once on 83rd Street, and again on the stairs of the Bernstein place—Harry hesitated. If he went back to help Valentin perhaps there would be worse sights to see than ever Wyckoff Street had offered. But there could be no retreat this time. Without Valentin he was lost. He raced back down the landing and flung open the door. The air was thick; the lamps rocking. In the middle of the room hung the Castrato, still defying gravity. It had hold of Valentin by his hair. Its other hand was poised, first and middle fingers spread like twin horns, about to stab out its captive's eyes.

Harry pulled his .38 from his pocket, aimed, and fired. He had always been a bad shot when given more than a moment to take aim, but *in extremis*, when instinct governed rational thought, he was not half bad. This was such an occasion. The bullet found the Castrato's neck, and opened another wound. More in surprise than pain perhaps it let Valentin go. There was a leakage of light from the hole in its neck, and it put its hand to the place.

Valentin was quickly on his feet.

"Again," he called to Harry. "*Fire again*!"

Harry obeyed the instruction. His second bullet pierced the creature's chest, his third its belly. This last wound seemed particularly traumatic; the distended flesh, ripe for bursting, broke—and the trickle of light that spilled from the wound rapidly became a flood as the abdomen split.

Again the Castrato howled, this time in panic, and lost all control of its flight. It reeled like a pricked balloon towards the ceiling, its fat hands desperately attempting to stem the mutiny in its substance. But it had reached critical mass; there was no making good the damage done. Lumps of its flesh began to break from it. Valentin, either too stunned or too fascinated, stood staring up at the disintegration while rains of cooked meat fell around him. Harry took hold of him and hauled him back towards the door.

The Castrato was finally earning its name, unloosing a desolate ear-piercing note. Harry didn't wait to watch its demise, but slammed the bedroom door as the voice reached an awesome pitch, and the windows smashed.

Valentin was grinning.

"Do you know what we did?" he said.

"Never mind. Let's just get the fuck out of here."

The sight of Swann's corpse at the top of the stairs seemed to chasten Valentin. Harry instructed him to assist, and he did so as efficiently as his dazed condition allowed. Together they began to escort the illusionist down the stairs. As they reached the front door there was a final shriek from above, as the Castrato came apart at the seams. Then silence.

The commotion had not gone unnoticed. Revellers had appeared from the house opposite, a crowd of late-night pedestrians had assembled on the sidewalk. "Some party," one of them said as the trio emerged.

Harry had half expected the cab to have deserted them, but he had reckoned without the driver's curiosity. The man was out of his vehicle and staring up at the first floor window.

"Does he need a hospital?" he asked as they bundled Swann into the back of the cab.

"No," Harry returned. "He's about as good as he's going to get."

"Will you *drive*?" said Valentin.

"Sure. Just tell me where to."

"Anywhere," came the weary reply. "Just get out of here."

"Hold it a minute," the driver said, "I don't want any trouble."

"Then you'd better *move*," said Valentin. The driver met his passenger's gaze. Whatever he saw there, his next words were:

"I'm driving," and they took off along East 61st like the proverbial bat out of Hell.

"We did it, Harry," Valentin said when they'd been travelling for a few minutes. "We got him back."

"And that *thing*? Tell me about it."

"The Castrato? What's to tell? Butterfield must have left it as a watch-dog, until he could bring in a technician to de-code Swann's defence mechanisms. We were lucky. It was in need of milking. That makes them unstable."

"How do you know so much about all of this?"

"It's a long story," said Valentin. "And not for a cab ride."

"So what now? We can't drive round in circles all night."

Valentin looked across at the body that sat between them, prey to every whim of the cab's suspension and road-menders' craft. Gently, he put Swann's hands on his lap.

"You're right of course," he said. "We have to make arrangements for the cremation, as swiftly as possible."

The cab bounced across a pot-hole. Valentin's face tightened.

"Are you in pain?" Harry asked him.

"I've been in worse."

"We could go back to my apartment, and rest there."

Valentin shook his head. "Not very clever," he said, "it's the first place they'll look."

"My offices, then—"

"The second place."

"Well, Jesus, this cab's going to run out of gas eventually."

At this point the driver intervened.

"Say, did you people mention cremation?"

"Maybe," Valentin replied.

"Only my brother-in-law's got a funeral business out in Queens."

"Is that so?" said Harry.

"Very reasonable rates. I can recommend him. No shit."

"Could you contact him *now*?" Valentin said.

"It's two in the morning."

"We're in a hurry."

The driver reached up and adjusted his mirror; he was looking at Swann.

"You don't mind me asking, do you?" he said. "But is that a body you got back there?"

"It is," said Harry. "And he's getting impatient."

The driver made a whooping sound. "Shit!" he said. "I've had a woman drop twins in that seat; I've had whores do business; I even had an alligator back there one time. But this beats them all!" He pondered for a moment, then said: "You kill him, did you?"

"No," said Harry.

"Guess we'd be heading for the East River if you had, eh?"

"That's right. We just want a decent cremation. And *quickly.*"

"That's understandable."

"What's your name?" Harry asked him.

"Winston Jowitt. But everybody calls me Byron. I'm a poet, see? Leastways, I am at weekends."

"Byron."

"See, any other driver would be freaked out right? Finding two guys with a body in the back seat. But the way I see it, it's all material."

"For the poems."

"Right," said Byron. "The Muse is a fickle mistress. You have to take it where you find it, you know? Speaking of which, you gentlemen got any idea where you want to go?"

"Make it your offices," Valentin told Harry. "And he can call his brother-in-law."

"Good," said Harry. Then, to Byron:

"Head west along 45th Street to 8th."

"You got it," said Byron, and the cab's speed doubled in the space of twenty yards. "Say," he said, "you fellows fancy a poem?"

"Now?" said Harry.

"I like to improvise," Byron replied. "Pick a subject. Any subject."

Valentin hugged his wounded arm close. Quietly, he said: "How about the end of the world?"

"Good subject," the poet replied, "just give me a minute or two."

"So soon?" said Valentin.

They took a circuitous route to the offices, while Byron Jowitt tried a selection of rhymes for Apocalypse. The sleepwalkers were out on 45th Street, in search of one high or another; some sat in the doorways, one lay sprawled across the sidewalk. None of them gave the cab or its occupants more than the briefest perusal. Harry unlocked the front door and he and Byron carried Swann up to the third floor.

The office was home from home: cramped and chaotic. They put Swann in the swivel chair behind the furred coffee cups and the alimony demands heaped on the desk. He looked easily the healthiest of the quartet. Byron was sweating like a bull after the climb; Harry felt—and surely looked—as though he hadn't slept in sixty days; Valentin sat slumped in the client's chair, so drained of vitality he might have been at death's door.

"You look terrible," Harry told him.

"No matter," he said. "It'll all be done soon."

Harry turned to Byron. "How about calling this brother-in-law of yours?"

While Byron set to doing so, Harry returned his attention to Valentin.

"I've got a first-aid box somewhere about," he said. "Shall I bandage up that arm?"

"Thank you, but no. Like you, I hate the sight of blood. Especially my own."

Byron was on the phone, chastising his brother-in-law for his ingratitude. "What's your beef? I got you a client! I *know* the time, for Christ's sake, but business is business . . ."

"Tell him we'll pay double his normal rate," Valentin said.

"You hear that, Mel? *Twice* your usual fee. So get over here, will you?" He gave the address to his brother-in-law, and put down the receiver. "He's coming over," he announced.

"Now?" said Harry.

"Now," Byron glanced at his watch. "My belly thinks my throat's cut. How about we eat? You got an all night place near here?"

"There's one a block down from here."

"You want food?" Byron asked Valentin.

"I don't think so," he said. He was looking worse by the moment.

"OK," Byron said to Harry, "just you and me then. You got ten I could borrow?"

Harry gave him a bill, the keys to the street door and an order for doughnuts and coffee, and Byron went on his way. Only when he'd gone did Harry wish he'd convinced the poet to stave off his hunger pangs a while. The office was distressingly quiet without him: Swann in residence behind the desk, Valentin succumbing to sleep in the other chair. The hush brought to mind another such silence, during that last, awesome night at the Lomax house when Mimi's demon-lover, wounded by Father Hesse, had slipped away into the walls for a while, and left them waiting and waiting, knowing it would come back but not certain of when or how. Six hours they'd sat—Mimi occasionally breaking the silence with laughter or gibberish—and the first Harry had known of its return was the smell of cooking excrement, and Mimi's cry of "Sodomite!" as Hesse surrendered to an act his faith had too long forbidden him. There had been no more silence then, not for a long space: only Hesse's cries, and Harry's pleas for forgetfulness. They had all gone unanswered.

It seemed he could hear the demon's voice now; its demands, its invitations. But no; it was only Valentin. The man was tossing his head back and forth in sleep, his face knotted up. Suddenly he started from his chair, one word on his lips:

"*Swann!*"

His eyes opened, and as they alighted on the illusionist's body, which was propped in the chair opposite, tears came uncontrollably, wracking him.

"He's dead," he said, as though in his dream he had forgotten that bitter fact. "I failed him, D'Amour. That's why he's dead. Because of my negligence."

"You're doing your best for him now," Harry said, though he knew the words were poor compensation. "Nobody could ask for a better friend."

"I was never his friend," Valentin said, staring at the corpse with brimming eyes. "I always hoped he'd one day trust me entirely. But he never did."

"Why not?"

"He couldn't afford to trust anybody. Not in his situation." He wiped his cheeks with the back of his hand.

"Maybe," Harry said, "it's about time you told me what all this is about."

"If you want to hear."

"I want to hear."

"Very well," said Valentin. "Thirty-two years ago, Swann made a bargain with the Gulfs. He agreed to be an ambassador for them if they, in return, gave him magic."

"*Magic*?"

"The ability to perform miracles. To transform matter. To bewitch souls. Even to drive out God."

"That's a miracle?"

"It's more difficult than you think," Valentin replied.

"So Swann *was* a genuine magician?"

"Indeed he was."

"Then why didn't he use his powers?"

"He did," Valentin replied. "He used them every night, at every performance."

Harry was baffled. "I don't follow."

"Nothing the Prince of Lies offers to humankind is of the least value," Valentin said, "or it wouldn't be offered. Swann didn't know that when he first made his Covenant. But he soon learned. Miracles are useless. Magic is a distraction from the real concerns. It's rhetoric. Melodrama."

"So what exactly are the real concerns?"

"You should know better than I," Valentin replied. "Fellowship, maybe? Curiosity? Certainly it matters not in the least if water can be made into wine, or Lazarus to live another year."

Harry saw the wisdom of this, but not how it had brought the magician to Broadway. As it was, he didn't need to ask. Valentin had taken up the story afresh. His tears had cleared with the telling; some trace of animation had crept back into his features.

"It didn't take Swann long to realise he'd sold his soul for a mess of pottage," he explained. "And when he did he was inconsolable. At least he was for a while. Then he began to contrive a revenge."

"How?"

"By taking Hell's name in vain. By using the magic which it boasted of as a trivial entertainment, degrading the power of the Gulfs by passing off their wonder-working as mere illusion. It was, you see, an act of heroic perversity. Every time a trick of Swann's was explained away as sleight-of-hand, the Gulfs squirmed."

"Why didn't they kill him?" Harry said.

"Oh they tried. Many times. But he had allies. Agents in their camp who warned him of their plots against him. He escaped their retribution for years that way."

"Until now?"

"Until now," Valentin sighed. "He was careless, and so was I. Now he's dead, and the Gulfs are itching for him."

"I see."

"But we were not entirely unprepared for this eventuality. He had made his apologies to Heaven; and I dare to hope he's been forgiven his trespasses. Pray that he has. There's more than *his* salvation at stake tonight."

"Yours too?"

"All of us who loved him are tainted," Valentin replied, "but if we can destroy his physical remains before the Gulfs claim them we may yet avoid the consequences of his Covenant."

"Why did you wait so long? Why didn't you just cremate him the day he died?"

"Their lawyers are not fools. The Covenant specifically prescribes a period of lying-in-state. If we had attempted to ignore that clause his soul would have been forfeited automatically."

"So when is this period up?"

"Three hours ago, at midnight," Valentin replied. "That's why they're so desperate, you see. And so dangerous."

Another poem came to Byron Jowitt as he ambled back up 8th Avenue, working his way through a tuna salad sandwich. His Muse was not to be rushed. Poems could take as long as five minutes to be finalised; longer if they involved a double rhyme. He didn't hurry on his journey back to the offices therefore, but wandered in a dreamy sort of mood, turning the lines every which way to make them fit. That way he hoped to arrive back with another finished poem. Two in one night was damn good going.

He had not perfected the final couplet however, by the time he reached the door. Operating on automatic pilot he fumbled in his pocket for the keys D'Amour had loaned him, and let himself in. He was about to close the door again when a woman stepped through the gap, smiling at him. She was a beauty, and Byron, being a poet, was a fool for beauty.

"Please," she said to him, "I need your help."

"What can I do for you?" said Byron through a mouthful of food.

"Do you know a man by the name of D'Amour? Harry D'Amour?"

"Indeed I do. I'm going up to his place right now."

"Perhaps you could show me the way?" the woman asked him, as Byron closed the door.

"Be my pleasure," he replied, and led her across the lobby to the bottom of the stairs.

"You know, you're very sweet," she told him; and Byron melted.

Valentin stood at the window.

"Something wrong?" Harry asked.

"Just a feeling," Valentin commented." I have a suspicion maybe the Devil's in Manhattan."

"So what's new?"

"That maybe he's coming for us." As if on cue there was a knock at the door. Harry jumped. "It's all right," Valentin said, "he never knocks."

Harry went to the door, feeling like a fool.

"Is that you, Byron?" he asked before unlocking it.

"Please," said a voice he thought he'd never hear again. "Help me . . ."

He opened the door. It was Dorothea, of course. She was colourless as water, and as unpredictable. Even before Harry had invited her across the office threshold a dozen expressions, or hints of such, had crossed her face: anguish, suspicion, terror. And now, as her eyes alighted upon the body of her beloved Swann, relief and gratitude.

"You *do* have him," she said, stepping into the office.

Harry closed the door. There was a chill from up the stairs.

"Thank God. Thank God." She took Harry's face in her hands and kissed him lightly on the lips. Only then did she notice Valentin.

She dropped her hands.

"What's *he* doing here?" she asked.

"He's with me. With us."

She looked doubtful. "No," she said.

"We can trust him."

"I said *no*! Get him out, Harry." There was a cold fury in her; she shook with it. "*Get him out*!"

Valentin stared at her, glassy-eyed. "The lady doth protest too much," he murmured.

Dorothea put her fingers to her lips as if to stifle any further outburst. "I'm sorry," she said, turning back to Harry, "but you must be told what this man is capable of—"

"Without him your husband would still be at the house, Mrs Swann," Harry pointed out. "*He's* the one you should be grateful to, not me."

At this, Dorothea's expression softened, through bafflement to a new gentility.

"Oh?" she said. Now she looked back at Valentin. "I'm sorry. When you ran from the house I assumed some complicity . . ."

"With whom?" Valentin inquired.

She made a tiny shake of her head; then said, "Your arm. Are you hurt?"

"A minor injury," he returned.

"I've already tried to get it rebandaged," Harry said. "But the bastard's too stubborn."

"Stubborn I am," Valentin replied, without inflection.

"But we'll be finished here soon—" said Harry.

Valentin broke in. "Don't tell her anything," he snapped.

"I'm just going to explain about the brother-in-law—" Harry said.

"The brother-in-law?" Dorothea said, sitting down. The sigh of her legs crossing was the most enchanting sound

Harry had heard in twenty-four hours. "Oh please tell me about the brother-in-law . . ."

Before Harry could open his mouth to speak, Valentin said: "It's not her, Harry."

The words, spoken without a trace of drama, took a few seconds to make sense. Even when they did, their lunacy was self-evident. Here she was in the flesh, perfect in every detail.

"What are you talking about?" Harry said.

"How much more plainly can I say it?" Valentin replied. "*It's not her.* It's a trick. An illusion. They know where we are, and they sent *this* up to spy out our defences."

Harry would have laughed, but that these accusations were bringing tears to Dorothea's eyes.

"Stop it," he told Valentin.

"No, Harry. You *think* for a moment. All the traps they've laid, all the beasts they've mustered. You suppose she could have escaped that?" He moved away from the window towards Dorothea. "Where's Butterfield?" he spat. "Down the hall, waiting for your signal?"

"Shut up," said Harry.

"He's scared to come up here himself, isn't he?" Valentin went on. "Scared of Swann, scared of us, probably, after what we did to his gelding."

Dorothea looked at Harry. "Make him stop," she said.

Harry halted Valentin's advance with a hand on his bony chest.

"You heard the lady," he said.

"That's no lady," Valentin replied, his eyes blazing. "I don't know what it is, but it's no lady."

Dorothea stood up. "I came here because I hoped I'd be safe," she said.

"You *are* safe," Harry said.

"Not with him around, I'm not," she replied, looking back at Valentin. "I think I'd be wiser going."

Harry touched her arm.

"No," he told her.

"Mr D'Amour," she said sweetly, "you've already earned your fee ten times over. Now I think it's time *I* took responsibility for my husband."

Harry scanned that mercurial face. There wasn't a trace of deception in it.

"I have a car downstairs," she said. "I wonder . . . could you carry him downstairs for me?"

Harry heard a noise like a cornered dog behind him and turned to see Valentin standing beside Swann's corpse. He had picked up the heavy-duty cigarette lighter from the desk, and was flicking it. Sparks came, but no flame.

"What the hell are you doing?" Harry demanded.

Valentin didn't look at the speaker, but at Dorothea.

"She knows," he said.

He had got the knack of the lighter; the flame flared up.

Dorothea made a small, desperate sound.

"Please don't," she said.

"We'll all burn with him if necessary," Valentin said.

"He's insane," Dorothea's tears had suddenly gone.

"She's right," Harry told Valentin, "you're acting like a madman."

"And you're a fool to fall for a few tears!" came the reply. "Can't you see that if she takes him we've lost everything we've fought for?"

"Don't listen," she murmured. "You know me, Harry. You trust me."

"What's under that face of yours?" Valentin said. "What are you? A Coprolite? Homunculus?"

The names meant nothing to Harry. All he knew was the proximity of the woman at his side; her hand laid upon his arm.

"And what about you?" she said to Valentin. Then, more softly, "why don't you show us your wound?"

She forsook the shelter of Harry's side, and crossed to the desk. The lighter flame guttered at her approach.

"Go on . . ." she said, her voice no louder than a breath. ". . . I *dare* you."

She glanced round at Harry. "Ask him, D'Amour," she said. "Ask him to show you what he's got hidden under the bandages."

"What's she talking about?" Harry asked. The glimmer of trepidation in Valentin's eyes was enough to convince Harry there was merit in Dorothea's request. "Explain," he said.

Valentin didn't get the chance however. Distracted by Harry's demand he was easy prey when Dorothea reached across the desk and knocked the lighter from his hand. He bent to retrieve it, but she seized on the *ad hoc* bundle of bandaging and pulled. It tore, and fell away.

She stepped back. "See?" she said.

Valentin stood revealed. The creature on 83rd Street had torn the sham of humanity from his arm; the limb beneath was a mass of blue-black scales. Each digit of the blistered hand ended in a nail that opened and closed like a parrot's beak. He made no attempt to conceal the truth. Shame eclipsed every other response.

"I warned you," she said, "I warned you he wasn't to be trusted."

Valentin stared at Harry. "I have no excuses," he said. "I only ask you to believe that I want what's best for Swann."

"How can you?" Dorothea said. "You're a demon."

"More than that," Valentin replied, "I'm Swann's Tempter. His familiar; his creature. But I belong to him more than I ever belonged to the Gulfs. And I will defy them—" he looked at Dorothea, "—and their agents."

She turned to Harry. "You have a gun," she said. "Shoot the filth. You mustn't suffer a thing like that to live."

Harry looked at the pustulent arm; at the clacking fingernails: what further repugnance was there in wait behind the flesh façade?

"Shoot it," the woman said.

He took his gun from his pocket. Valentin seemed to have shrunk in the moments since the revelation of his true nature. Now he leaned against the wall, his face slimy with despair.

"Kill me then," he said to Harry, "kill me if I revolt you so much. But Harry, I *beg* you, don't give Swann to her. Promise me that. Wait for the driver to come back, and dispose of the body by whatever means you can. Just don't give it to her!"

"Don't listen," Dorothea said. "He doesn't care about Swann the way I do."

Harry raised the gun. Even looking straight at death, Valentin did not flinch.

"You've failed, Judas," she said to Valentin. "The magician's mine."

"What magician?" said Harry.

"Why Swann, of course!" she replied lightly. "How many magicians have you got up here?"

Harry dropped his bead on Valentin.

"He's an illusionist," he said, "you told me that at the very beginning. Never call him a magician, you said."

"Don't be pedantic," she replied, trying to laugh off her *faux pas*.

He levelled the gun at her. She threw back her head suddenly, her face contracting, and unloosed a sound of which, had Harry not heard it from a human throat, he would not have believed the larynx capable. It rang down the corridor and the stairs, in search of some waiting ear.

"Butterfield is here," said Valentin flatly.

Harry nodded. In the same moment she came towards him, her features grotesquely contorted. She was strong and quick; a blur of venom that took him off-guard. He heard Valentin tell him to kill her, before she transformed. It took him a moment to grasp the significance of this, by which time she had her teeth at his throat. One of her hands was a cold vice around his wrist; he sensed strength in her sufficient to powder his bones. His fingers were already numbed by her grip; he had no time to do more than depress the trigger. The gun went off. Her breath on his throat seemed to gush from her. Then she loosed her hold on him, and staggered back. The shot had blown open her abdomen.

He shook to see what he had done. The creature, for all its shriek, still resembled a woman he might have loved.

"Good," said Valentin as the blood hit the office floor in gouts. "Now it must show itself."

Hearing him, she shook her head. "This is all there is to show," she said.

Harry threw the gun down. "My God," he said softly, "it's her . . ."

Dorothea grimaced. The blood continued to come. "Some *part* of her," she replied.

"Have you always been with them then?" Valentin asked.

"Of course not."

"Why then?"

"Nowhere to go . . ." she said, her voice fading by the syllable. "Nothing to believe in. All lies. Everything: *lies*."

"So you sided with Butterfield?"

"Better Hell," she said, "than a false Heaven."

"Who taught you that?" Harry murmured.

"Who do you think?" she replied, turning her gaze on him. Though her strength was going out of her with the blood, her eyes still blazed. "You're finished, D'Amour," she said. "You, and the demon, and Swann. There's nobody left to help you now."

Despite the contempt in her words he couldn't stand and watch her bleed to death. Ignoring Valentin's imperative that he keep clear, he went across to her. As he stepped within range she lashed out at him with astonishing force. The blow blinded him a moment; he fell against the tall filing cabinet, which toppled sideways. He and it hit the ground together. *It* spilled papers; he, curses. He was vaguely aware that the woman was moving past him to escape, but he was too busy keeping his head from spinning to prevent her. When equilibrium returned she had gone, leaving her bloody handprints on wall and door.

Chaplin, the janitor, was protective of his territory. The basement of the building was a private domain in which he sorted through office trash, and fed his beloved furnace, and read aloud his favourite passages from the Good Book; all without fear of interruption. His bowels—which were far from healthy—allowed him little slumber. A couple of hours a night, no more, which he supplemented with dozing through the day. It was not so bad. He had the seclusion of the basement to retire to whenever life upstairs became too demanding; and the forced heat would sometimes bring strange waking dreams.

Was this such a dream: this insipid fellow in his fine suit? If not, how had he gained access to the basement, when the door was locked and bolted? He asked no questions of the intruder. Something about the way the man stared at him baffled his tongue. "Chaplin," the fellow said, his thin lips barely moving, "I'd like you to open the furnace."

In other circumstances he might well have picked up his shovel and clouted the stranger across the head. The furnace was his baby. He knew, as no-one else knew, its quirks and occasional petulance; he loved, as no-one else loved, the roar it gave when it was content; he did not take kindly to the proprietorial tone the man used. But he'd lost the will to resist. He picked up a rag and opened the peeling door, offering its hot heart to this man as Lot had offered his daughters to the stranger in Sodom.

Butterfield smiled at the smell of heat from the furnace. From three floors above he heard the woman crying out for help; and then, a few moments later, a shot. She had failed. He had thought she would. But her life was forfeit anyway. There was no loss in sending her into the breach, in the slim chance that she might have coaxed the body from its keepers. It would have saved the inconvenience of a full-scale attack, but no matter. To have Swann's soul was worth any effort. He had defiled the good name of the Prince of Lies. For that he would suffer as no other miscreant magician ever had. Beside Swann's punishment, Faust's would be an inconvenience, and Napoleon's a pleasure-cruise.

As the echoes of the shot died above, he took the black lacquer box from his jacket pocket. The janitor's eyes were turned heavenward. He too had heard the shot.

"It was nothing," Butterfield told him. "Stoke the fire."

Chaplin obeyed. The heat in the cramped basement rapidly grew. The janitor began to sweat; his visitor did not. He stood mere feet from the open furnace door and gazed into the brightness with impassive features. At last, he seemed satisfied.

"Enough," he said, and opened the lacquer box. Chaplin thought he glimpsed movement in the box, as though it were full to the lid with maggots, but before he had a chance to look more closely both the box and contents were pitched into the flames.

"Close the door," Butterfield said. Chaplin obeyed. "You may watch over them awhile, if it pleases you. They need the heat. It makes them mighty."

He left the janitor to keep his vigil beside the furnace, and went back up to the hallway. He had left the street door open, and a pusher had come in out of the cold to do business with a client. They bartered in the shadows, until the pusher caught sight of the lawyer.

"Don't mind me," Butterfield said, and started up the stairs. He found the widow Swann on the first landing. She was not quite dead, but he quickly finished the job D'Amour had started.

"We're in trouble," said Valentin. "I hear noises downstairs. Is there any other way out of here?"

Harry sat on the floor, leaning against the toppled cabinet, and tried not to think of Dorothea's face as the bullet found her, or of the creature he was now reduced to needing.

"There's a fire escape," he said, "it runs down to the back of the building."

"Show me," said Valentin, attempting to haul him to his feet.

"Keep your hands off me!"

Valentin withdrew, bruised by the rebuff. "I'm sorry," he said. "Maybe I shouldn't hope for your acceptance. But I do."

Harry said nothing, just got to his feet amongst the litter of reports and photographs. He'd had a dirty life: spying on adulteries for vengeful spouses; dredging gutters for lost children; keeping company with scum because it rose to the top, and the rest just drowned. Could Valentin's soul be much grimier?

"The fire escape's down the hall," he said.

"We can still get Swann out," Valentin said. "Still give him a decent cremation—" The demon's obsession with his master's dignity was chastening, in its way. "But you have to help me, Harry."

"I'll help you," he said, avoiding sight of the creature. "Just don't expect love and affection."

If it were possible to hear a smile, that's what he heard.

"They want this over and done with before dawn," the demon said.

"It can't be far from that now."

"An hour, maybe," Valentin replied. "But it's enough. Either way, it's enough."

The sound of the furnace soothed Chaplin; its rumbles and rattlings were as familiar as the complaint of his own intestines. But there was another sound growing behind the door, the like of which he'd never heard before. His mind made foolish pictures to go with it. Of pigs laughing; of glass and barbed wire being ground between the teeth; of hoofed feet dancing on the door. As the noises grew so did his trepidation, but when he went to the basement door to summon help it was locked; the key had gone. And now, as if matters weren't bad enough, the light went out.

He began to fumble for a prayer—

"Holy Mary, Mother of God, pray for us sinners now and at the hour—"

But he stopped when a voice addressed him, quite clearly.

"Michelmas," it said.

It was unmistakably his mother. And there could be no doubt of its source, either. It came from the furnace.

"*Michelmas,*" she demanded, "are you going to let me cook in here?"

It wasn't possible, of course, that she was there in the flesh: she'd been dead thirteen long years. But some phantom, perhaps? He believed in phantoms. Indeed he'd seen them on occasion, coming and going from the cinemas on 42nd Street, arm in arm.

"Open up, Michelmas," his mother told him, in that special voice she used when she had some treat for him.

Like a good child, he approached the door. He had never felt such heat off the furnace as he felt now; he could smell the hairs on his arms wither.

"*Open the door*," Mother said again. There was no denying her. Despite the searing air, he reached to comply.

"That fucking janitor," said Harry, giving the sealed fire escape door a vengeful kick. "This door's supposed to be left unlocked at all times." He pulled at the chains that were wrapped around the handles. "We'll have to take the stairs."

There was a noise from back down the corridor; a roar in the heating system which made the antiquated radiators rattle. At that moment, down in the basement, Michelmas Chaplin was obeying his mother, and opening the furnace door. A scream climbed from below as his face was blasted off. Then, the sound of the basement door being smashed open.

Harry looked at Valentin, his repugnance momentarily forgotten.

"We shan't be taking the stairs," the demon said.

Bellowings and chatterings and screechings were already on the rise. Whatever had found birth in the basement, it was precocious.

"We have to find something to break down the door," Valentin said, "*anything*."

Harry tried to think his way through the adjacent offices, his mind's eye peeled for some tool that would make an impression on either the fire door or the substantial chains which kept it closed. But there was nothing useful: only typewriters and filing cabinets.

"*Think*, man," said Valentin.

He ransacked his memory. Some heavy-duty instrument was required. A crowbar; a hammer. An axe! There was an agent called Shapiro on the floor below, who exclusively represented porno performers, one of whom had attempted to blow his balls off the month before. She'd failed, but he'd boasted one day on the stairs that he had now purchased the biggest axe he could find, and would happily take the head of any client who attempted an attack upon his person.

The commotion from below was simmering down. The hush was, in its way, more distressing than the din that had preceded it.

"We haven't got much time," the demon said.

Harry left him at the chained door. "Can you get Swann?" he said, as he ran.

"I'll do my best."

By the time Harry reached the top of the stairs the last chatterings were dying away; as he began down the flight they ceased altogether. There was no way now to judge how close the enemy were. On the next floor? Round the next corner? He tried not to think of them, but his feverish imagination populated every dirty shadow.

He reached the bottom of the flight without incident, however, and slunk along the darkened second-floor corridor to Shapiro's office. Half way to his destination, he heard a low hiss behind him. He looked over his shoulder, his body itching to run. One of the radiators, heated beyond its limits, had sprung a leak. Steam was escaping from its pipes, and hissing as it went. He let his heart climb down out of his mouth, and then hurried on to the door of Shapiro's office, praying that the man hadn't simply been shooting the breeze with his talk of axes. If so, they were done for. The office was locked, of course, but he elbowed the frosted glass out, and reached through to let himself in, fumbling for the light switch. The walls were plastered with photographs of sex-goddesses. They scarcely claimed Harry's attention; his panic fed upon itself with every heartbeat he spent here. Clumsily he scoured the office, turning furniture over in his impatience. But there was no sign of Shapiro's axe.

Now, another noise from below. It crept up the staircase and along the corridor in search of him—an unearthly cacophony like the one he'd heard on 83rd Street. It set his teeth on edge; the nerve of his rotting molar began to throb afresh. What did the music signal? Their advance?

In desperation he crossed to Shapiro's desk to see if the man had any other item that might be pressed into service, and there tucked out of sight between desk and wall, he found the axe. He pulled it from hiding. As Shapiro had boasted, it was hefty, its weight the first reassurance Harry had felt in too long. He returned to the corridor. The steam from the fractured pipe had thickened. Through its veils it was apparent that the concert had taken on new fervour. The doleful wailing rose and fell, punctuated by some flaccid percussion.

He braved the cloud of steam and hurried to the stairs. As he put his foot on the bottom step the music seemed to catch him by the back of the neck, and whisper: "*Listen*" in his ear. He had no desire to listen; the music was vile. But somehow—while he was distracted by finding the axe—it had wormed its way into his skull. It drained his limbs of strength. In moments the axe began to seem an impossible burden.

"*Come on down,*" the music coaxed him, "*come on down and join the band.*"

Though he tried to form the simple word "No", the music was gaining influence upon him with every note played. He began to hear melodies in the caterwauling; long circuitous themes that made his blood sluggish and his thoughts idiot. He knew there was no pleasure to be had at the music's source—that it tempted him only to pain and desolation—yet he could not shake its delirium off. His feet began to move to the call of the pipers. He forgot Valentin, Swann and all ambition for escape, and instead began to descend the stairs. The melody became more intricate. He could hear voices now, singing some charmless accompaniment in a language he didn't comprehend. From somewhere above, he heard his name called, but he ignored the summons. The music clutched him close, and now—as he descended the next flight of stairs—the musicians came into view.

They were brighter than he had anticipated, and more various. More baroque in their configurations (the manes, the multiple heads); more particular in their decoration (the suit of flayed faces; the rouged anus); and, his drugged eyes now stung to see, more atrocious in their choice of instruments. Such instruments! Byron was there, his bones sucked clean and drilled with stops, his bladder and lungs teased through slashes in his body as reservoirs for the piper's breath. He was draped, inverted, across the musician's lap, and even now was played upon—the sacs ballooning, the tongueless head giving out a wheezing note. Dorothea was slumped beside him, no less transformed, the strings of her gut made taut between her splinted legs like an obscene lyre; her breasts drummed upon. There were other instruments too, men who had come off the street and fallen prey to the band. Even Chaplin was there, much of his flesh burned away, his rib-cage played upon indifferently well.

"I didn't take you for a music lover," Butterfield said, drawing upon a cigarette, and smiling in welcome. "Put down your axe and join us."

The word *axe* reminded Harry of the weight in his hands, though he couldn't find his way through the bars of music to remember what it signified.

"Don't be afraid," Butterfield said, "you're an innocent in this. We hold no grudge against you."

"Dorothea . . ." he said.

"She was an innocent too," said the lawyer, "until we showed her some sights."

Harry looked at the woman's body; at the terrible changes that they had wrought upon her. Seeing them, a tremor began in him, and something came between him and the music; the imminence of tears blotted it out.

"Put down the axe," Butterfield told him.

But the sound of the concert could not compete with the grief that was mounting in him. Butterfield seemed to see the change in his eyes; the disgust and anger growing there. He dropped his half-smoked cigarette and signalled for the music-making to stop.

"Must it be death, then?" Butterfield said, but the enquiry was scarcely voiced before Harry started down the last few stairs towards him. He raised the axe and swung it at the lawyer but the blow was misplaced. The blade ploughed the plaster of the wall, missing its target by a foot.

At this eruption of violence the musicians threw down their instruments and began across the lobby, trailing their coats and tails in blood and grease. Harry caught their advance from the corner of his eye. Behind the horde, still rooted in the shadows, was another form, larger than the largest of the mustered demons, from which there now came a thump that might have been that of a vast jack-hammer. He tried to make sense of sound or sight, but could do neither. There was no time for curiosity; the demons were almost upon him.

Butterfield glanced round to encourage their advance, and Harry—catching the moment—swung the axe a second time. The blow caught Butterfield's shoulder; the arm was instantly severed. The lawyer shrieked; blood sprayed the wall. There was no time for a third blow, however. The demons were reaching for him, smiles lethal.

He turned on the stairs, and began up them, taking the steps two, three and four at a time. Butterfield was still shrieking below; from the flight above he heard Valentin calling his name. He had neither time nor breath to answer.

They were on his heels, their ascent a din of grunts and shouts and beating wings. And behind it all, the jack-hammer thumped its way to the bottom of the flight, its noise more intimidating by far than the chatterings of the berserkers at his back. It was in his belly, that thump; in his bowels. Like death's heartbeat, steady and irrevocable.

On the second landing he heard a whirring sound behind him, and half turned to see a human-headed moth the size of a vulture climbing the air towards him. He met it with the axe blade, and hacked it down. There was a cry of excitement from below as the body flapped down the stairs, its wings working like paddles. Harry sped up the remaining flight to where Valentin was standing, listening. It wasn't the chatter he was attending to, nor the cries of the lawyer; it was the jack-hammer.

"They brought the Raparee," he said.

"I wounded Butterfield—"

"I heard. But that won't stop them."

"We can still try the door."

"I think we're too late, my friend."

"*No*!" said Harry, pushing past Valentin. The demon had given up trying to drag Swann's body to the door, and had laid the magician out in the middle of the corridor, his hands crossed on his chest. In some last mysterious act of reverence he had set folded paper bowls at Swann's head and feet, and laid a tiny origami flower at his lips. Harry lingered only long enough to re-acquaint himself with the sweetness of Swann's expression, and then ran to the door and proceeded to hack at the chains. It would be a long job. The assault did more damage to the axe than to the steel links. He didn't dare give up, however. This was their only escape route now, other than flinging themselves to their deaths from one of the windows. That he would do, he decided, if the worst came to the worst. Jump and die, rather than be their plaything.

His arms soon became numb with the repeated blows. It was a lost cause; the chain was unimpaired. His despair was further fuelled by a cry from Valentin—a high, weeping call that he could not leave unanswered. He left the fire door and returned past the body of Swann to the head of the stairs.

The demons had Valentin. They swarmed on him like wasps on a sugar stick, tearing him apart. For the briefest of moments he struggled free of their rage, and Harry saw the mask of humanity in rags and the truth glistening bloodily beneath. He was as vile as those besetting him, but Harry went to his aid anyway, as much to wound the demons as to save their prey.

The wielded axe did damage this way and that, sending Valentin's tormentors reeling back down the stairs, limbs lopped, faces opened. They did not all bleed. One sliced belly spilled eggs in thousands, one wounded head gave birth to tiny eels, which fled to the ceiling and hung there by their lips. In the mêlée he lost sight of Valentin. Forgot about him, indeed, until he heard the jack-hammer again, and remembered the broken look on Valentin's face when he'd named the thing. He'd called it the *Raparee*, or something like.

And now, as his memory shaped the word, it came into sight. It shared no trait with its fellows; it had neither wings nor mane nor vanity. It seemed scarcely even to be flesh, but *forged*, an engine that needed only malice to keep its wheels turning.

At its appearance, the rest retreated, leaving Harry at the top of the stairs in a litter of spawn. Its progress was slow, its half dozen limbs moving in oiled and elaborate configurations to pierce the walls of the staircase and so haul itself up. It brought to mind a man on crutches, throwing the sticks ahead of him and levering his weight after, but there was nothing invalid in the thunder of its body; no pain in the white eye that burned in his sickle-head.

Harry thought he had known despair, but he had not. Only now did he taste its ash in his throat. There was only the window left for him. That, and the welcoming ground. He backed away from the top of the stairs, forsaking the axe.

Valentin was in the corridor. He was not dead, as Harry had presumed, but kneeling beside the corpse of Swann, his own body drooling from a hundred wounds. Now he bent close to the magician. Offering his apologies to his dead master, no doubt. But no. There was more to it than that. He had the cigarette lighter in his hand, and was lighting a taper. Then, murmuring some prayer to himself as he went, he lowered the taper to the mouth of the magician. The origami flower caught and flared up. Its flame was oddly bright, and spread with supernatural efficiency across Swann's face and down his body. Valentin hauled himself to his feet, the firelight burnishing his scales. He found enough strength to incline his head to the body as its cremation began, and then his wounds overcame him. He fell backwards, and lay still. Harry watched as the flames mounted. Clearly the body had been sprinkled with gasoline or something similar, for the fire raged up in moments, gold and green.

Suddenly, something took hold of his leg. He looked down to see that a demon, with flesh like ripe raspberries, still had an appetite for him. Its tongue was coiled around Harry's shin; its claws reached for his groin. The assault made him forget the cremation or the Raparee. He bent to tear at the tongue with his bare hands, but its slickness confounded his attempts. He staggered back as the demon climbed his body, its limbs embracing him.

The struggle took them to the ground, and they rolled away from the stairs, along the other arm of the corridor. The struggle was far from uneven; Harry's repugnance was at least the match of the demon's ardour. His torso pressed to the ground, he suddenly remembered the Raparee. Its advance reverberated in every board and wall.

Now it came into sight at the top of the stairs, and turned its slow head towards Swann's funeral pyre. Even from this distance Harry could see that Valentin's last-ditch attempts to destroy his master's body had failed. The fire had scarcely begun to devour the magician. They would have him still.

Eyes on the Raparee, Harry neglected his more intimate enemy, and it thrust a piece of flesh into his mouth. His throat filled up with pungent fluid; he felt himself choking. Opening his mouth he bit down hard upon the organ, severing it. The demon did not cry out, but released sprays of scalding excrement from pores along its back, and disengaged itself. Harry spat its muscle out as the demon crawled away. Then he looked back towards the fire.

All other concerns were forgotten in the face of what he saw.

*Swann had stood up.*

He was burning from head to foot. His hair, his clothes, his skin. There was no part of him that was not alight. But he was standing, nevertheless, and raising his hands to his audience in welcome.

The Raparee had ceased its advance. It stood a yard or two from Swann, its limbs absolutely still, as if it were mesmerised by this astonishing trick.

Harry saw another figure emerge from the head of the stairs. It was Butterfield. His stump was roughly tied off; a demon supported his lop-sided body.

"Put out the fire," demanded the lawyer of the Raparee. "It's not so difficult."

The creature did not move.

"*Go on*," said Butterfield. "It's just a trick of his. He's dead, damn you. It's just conjuring."

"No," said Harry.

Butterfield looked his way. The lawyer had always been insipid. Now he was so pale his existence was surely in question.

"What do you know?" he said.

"It's not conjuring," said Harry. "It's *magic*."

Swann seemed to hear the word. His eyelids fluttered open, and he slowly reached into his jacket and with a flourish produced a handkerchief. It too was on fire. It too was unconsumed. As he shook it out tiny bright birds leapt from its folds on humming wings. The Raparee was entranced by this sleight-of-hand. Its gaze followed the illusory birds as they rose and were dispersed, and in that moment the magician stepped forward and embraced the engine.

It caught Swann's fire immediately, the flames spreading over its flailing limbs. Though it fought to work itself free of the magician's hold, Swann was not to be denied. He clasped it closer than a long-lost brother, and would not leave it be until the creature began to wither in the heat. Once the decay began it seemed the Raparee was devoured in seconds, but it was difficult to be certain. The moment—as in the best performances—was held suspended. Did it last a minute? Two minutes? Five? Harry would never know. Nor did he care to analyse. Disbelief was for cowards; and doubt a fashion that crippled the spine. He was content to watch—not knowing if Swann lived or died, if birds, fire, corridor or if he himself—Harry D'Amour—were real or illusory.

Finally, the Raparee was gone. Harry got to his feet. Swann was also standing, but his farewell performance was clearly over.

The defeat of the Raparee had bested the courage of the horde. They had fled, leaving Butterfield alone at the top of the stairs.

"This won't be forgotten, or forgiven," he said to Harry. "There's no rest for you. Ever. I am your enemy."

"I hope so," said Harry.

He looked back towards Swann, leaving Butterfield to his retreat. The magician had laid himself down again. His eyes were closed, his hands replaced on his chest. It was as if he had never moved. But now the fire was showing its true teeth. Swann's flesh began to bubble, his clothes to peel off in smuts and smoke. It took a long while to do the job, but eventually the fire reduced the man to ash.

By that time it was after dawn, but today was Sunday, and Harry knew there would be no visitors to interrupt his labours. He would have time to gather up the remains; to pound the boneshards and put them with the ashes in a carrier bag. Then he would go out and find himself a bridge or a dock, and put Swann into the river.

There was precious little of the magician left once the fire had done its work; and nothing that vaguely resembled a man.

Things came and went away; that was a kind of magic. And in between?; pursuits and conjurings; horrors, guises. The occasional joy.

That there was room for joy; ah! that was magic too.

# David J. Schow

## Bunny Didn't Tell Us

DAVID J. SCHOW is perhaps best known as the man who coined the term "splatter punk", although his own fiction shows a depth and subtlety that puts it well above most of the work currently being churned out under that movement's aegis. Winner of the *Twilight Zone Magazine*'s readers poll for his short story, "Coming Soon to a Theatre Near You", a string of appearances in Karl Edward Wagner's *The Year's Best Horror Stories* inevitably led to the 1987 World Fantasy Award for his tale "Red Light".

He has written several pseudonymous novelizations, and is also the co-author of *The Outer Limits: The Official Companion*. His novels include *The Kill Riff* and *The Shaft*, he edited *Silver Scream*, and two collections, *Seeing Red* and *Lost Angels*, appeared last year. He also scripted *The Texas Chainsaw Massacre 3* and is currently working on a new screenplay entitled *Deadly Metal*.

"Bunny Didn't Tell Us" is a blackly humorous slice of grue that in style owes more than a passing debt to the classic EC Comics of the '50s.

THE GRAVE ROBBERS worked as quickly and silently as they were able. It began to rain lightly.

It sounded more like the opening to a bad grade-school joke, but the fact was that most of the embalming crew on the night shift at Forest Lawn consisted of tae-kwon-do freaks. They spent more of the wee hours showing off new moves than tending the latest batch of customers, and were so self-involved they represented no threat at all. Ditto the hired security. They hated blundering about the vast cemetery in the rain. Professionalism was one matter, superstition another.

Riff favored working in the rain no matter what the scam. Water washed away both guards and their willingness to pry, as well as providing a safe background of white noise for nocturnal endeavors with noise potential.

He and Klondike were knee-deep in the hole. Riff gathered a clump of turf in one hand and squinted at it as he crumbled it apart. Rain funneled in a steady stream from the vee of his hat. "Recently tamped," was all he said, wiping his hand on his grimy topcoat. All around them the rainfall hissed into the thick, manicured landscaping.

Mechanically, Riff jabbed his folding army spade into the dirt, stomped on the edge, and chucked the bladeful of earth over his shoulder to the right. Klondike faced him in the hole, duplicating the moves one half-beat later. Both had learned how to turn out a foxhole in Korea, and in no time they were four feet down, then five.

Klondike's spade was the first to thump against something solid and hollow. "Bingo," the larger man muttered.

Riff hesitated, then tossed back another gout of dirt anyway. Klondike smelled like a wet bearskin, and his permanent facial shadow of black beard stubble served to camouflage his face in the darkness. Riff did not necessarily enjoy working with someone as coarse as Klondike, but all his life he had made a virtue of never questioning orders.

"Wait," he said, and the big man froze like a pointer. Riff tapped the surface beneath their feet with his spade. "Sounds funny."

They knelt and swept away clots of dirt with their gloved hands.

"Time," said Riff.

Klondike peeled back the cuff of his glove and read his luminous watch face. "0345 hours," he said. The fingertips of his gloves were stylishly sawn off, and Klondike promptly used the moment of dead time to pick his nose. "Ain't got us much time," he whispered. "Funk-hole's turning to mud."

"I know that," Riff said, hunkering down in the bottom of their excavation and resisting the urge to add *you imbecile*. He plucked a surgical penlight from a coat pocket and cupped his palm around the beam, leaning close. "Look at this."

The dime-sized dot of light revealed a silver dent—left by Riff's spade—in a smooth surface of brilliant, fire-engine red enamel. Klondike ran his fingers over it, and stared dumbly at his hand while the tiny scar in the otherwise flawless surface refilled with water.

"Bloody hell!" snapped Riff. "Bunny didn't tell us that the guy was buried in his goddamn *car*!"

Suddenly the drumming of rain on the exposed metal surface seemed to become incriminatingly loud.

Riff's ties to Bunny Beaudine ran back to the middle 1970s, and a half-witted punchline Bunny had formulated about finding employment for needy military vets. A decade before, Bunny had been just another seedy Sunset Boulevard pimp, chauffeuring his anemic, scabby stable of trotters around in a creaking, third-hand Cadillac whose paint job was eighty percent primer. Then Bunny discovered cocaine, and his future turned to tinsel. Coke required bodyguards, and Bunny learned to be Bad.

Riff suspected that Bunny got a kick out of two things: hiring white dudes to accomplish his dirty work, and vigorously dipping into his inventory for personal gratification, both the ladies and the face Drāno. His usual checklist of dumb jobs included low-power dope deliveries, playing cabbie for the girls—Bunny now captained a fleet of Mercedes from the cabin of his own Corsair limo—and the odd bit of mop-up. It was a living.

Bunny's strongarm boys packed Magnums and broke bones with the frequency Riff broke wind after a plate of lasagna. Once he'd taken that first job for Bunny (a cash pass deliberately miscounted, as a test for Riff's honesty), Riff understood that there was no shaking hands, no clean leavetakings. Since he had no other prospects—1976 was a lousy job year for vets—it was just as well.

Until this current assignment came along. Riff remembered how it had gone down in Bunny's Brentwood "office."

Bunny had been laughing, flashing his ten-thousand-dollar teeth. "Poor old Desmond," he cackled. "Pour soul."

Riff had gotten a phone call and had shown up precisely on the half hour. "What became of Desmond?" Desmond was one of Bunny's competitors. They cursed each other in private and slapped each other's shoulders, trading power handshakes, whenever anyone else was watching.

Two of Bunny's boys bellowed deep basso laughter from across the room.

"Why, poor old Desmond somehow got his ass blowed off," said Bunny. "Terrible thing. You can't even live in the city anymore. . . ."

The watchdogs stopped guffawing at a wave of Bunny's hand. His pinkie ring glittered and his broad-planed African face went dead serious. Riff stood, arms folded, waiting for the show to end so business could become relevant.

"What it is," Bunny said to Riff, "is this. You remember Desmond, Riff, my man?"

"I saw him a few times."

"You remember all those rings and slave bracelets and shit he used to wear all over his hands?"

"Yeah," said Riff. "Mandarin fingernails, too."

"Thems was for tooting. But you recall, right?" Bunny was nodding up and down. So far so good. "One of them rings was a cut-down from that diamond they called the Orb in the papers—stolen from that bitch in Manhattan last year."

"The one married to the toilet-paper tycoon." Riff knew the ring. It was cut-down, alright, but was still of vulgar size, and worth at least a hundred grand.

"You got it. Well, here's a little piece of trivia that nobody knows. Poor old Desmond was buried wearing that ring."

Riff was already beginning to get the picture. As with all pimps up from gutter level, Desmond had insisted on burial as lavish as his lifestyle, and in a boneyard as obscene as the diamond he'd hired stolen. Riff looked back at the bodyguards. "Why didn't you just have your goons steal the ring after they blew the back of his head off?" he said, smiling.

Bunny kept his happy face on. "Why, there ain't nobody in the world would finger me; that was a accident, man," he said, his voice singsong and full of bogus innocence. "Besides, we take the ring *then*, that means Desmond's boys be hunting it, and I don't want to end this life in the trunk of some Mexican's Chevy being drug out of the ocean by the police." He pronounced it *po*-lice. He shrugged. "But now—now, as far as Desmond's people are concerned, that rock is a permanent resident of Forest Lawn, by the freeway. Ain't nobody gonna miss it now."

The goons chuckled on cue. Riff drew Klondike as an accomplice mostly because the hulking halfwit was the wrong color to make it in the world as a bodyguard for Bunny, but the bonus Bunny pushed in Riff's direction erased any objections. The only hitch was that no amount of cash could get Riff clear of Bunny now.

That was how Riff's adventure in the rain had begun.

"Shit!" Klondike beefed. "Asshole pimp six feet under in his muthafuggin' pimpmobile!"

"Watch your language," said Riff. "And keep your voice down!" Slick mud was beginning to join them in the hole in force. He scooped out the bilge with his hands.

"What kinda car is it?"

*Who cares*, though Riff. Dumb question; dumb goon. "Just dig, before we drown." He wanted to find out if they were near a car window they could break, to cut excavation time. They'd been putzing around on the roof for nearly half an hour. Riff realized they were on top when he found the insulated rectangle of the sunroof. The car was gigantic—maybe a full-stretch limousine. He traced the outline of the sunroof with a finger while Klondike continued to bail sludge in an awkward squat.

"Crowbar!" Riff said over his shoulder. Soon the horizon would turn pink-gray with predawn light, and he mentally damned daylight savings time again.

Klondike poked his head out of the hole, did a quick three-sixty, and returned with the crowbar. His own private mud-slide was right behind him. Things were getting gooey.

"All clear topside," he said.

Not sure which side the sunroof opened from, Riff had a moment of indecision, and that was when he heard the grinding noise. It was a low whirring basso against the lighter sound of the pattering rain.

The sunroof was opening. Yellow cabin light sprayed upward from the widening hatchway.

Things happened too fast for Riff to keep track.

He fell backward onto his rump in surprise, thinking, *It's one of Bunny's goddamn tricks, goddamn Bunny, its—*

It seemed a funny thing to hear a big lug like Klondike screaming. His voice spiked Riff's ears, cracking high with terror.

"Riff! It's got my leg and I can't *Riff help HELP ME!*"

And in the sickly glow of the limousine's interior lights, Riff saw what had hold of Klondike's leg.

The suit sleeve was crushed black velvet; the cuffs, ruffled lace. The kind of overblown getup a showoff like Desmond would demand to be buried in. The ebony claw dragging Klondike backwards was threaded with luminescent white mold. The brown jelly of rot glistened in the light, and the dagger fingernails that were Desmond's coke-snorting tools, now jagged and cracked, gathered, seating themselves in Klondike's left calf.

Klondike hollered.

Riff was backed into the humid mound of turned earth. He might have yelled, but his throat seemed stuffed up with grave dirt, and his tongue hugged the roof of his mouth in fear.

There was nothing for Klondike to grab as an anchor, and the relentless tow of the slime-clotted hand pulled him, wriggling, to block the light from within the buried car. Another arm slid through the crack of space and snaked around Klondike's waist in a hideous bear-hug, from below. Dense black mud was dripping down into the car as Klondike thrashed to no gain against the dead, locked embrace.

Riff could still see, too well.

The pressure increased. Gray knuckle bones popped through wet splits in the decayed meat, and Klondike screamed one last time.

The sound of his back breaking apart was the splintering of dry bamboo, the crunching of ice between the teeth. It cut off the screaming. Then Klondike, all of him, began to fold into the hole in a way Riff had never seen a human body bend before.

Riff's own body thawed enough to move, and one hand grasped the spade. He took a single step closer.

Klondike's body hung upward in a ludicrous bow-shape, feet and arms in the night air. Something else in his body suddenly gave way with a sharp, breaking carrot noise, and he sagged a few inches further down into the sunroof.

Riff, trembling, raised the spade, blade-down. Klondike was dead as a side of beef. Riff was not watching him so much as the moldering hands that pulled him down. There, on the middle finger of one, was the diamond.

When he lifted the spade to strike, the oily, dark mud greasing the roof of the car skimmed his feet from beneath him, and he sprawled headlong on top of what was left of Klondike.

Now Riff screamed, because the groping claw had locked around the lapel of his topcoat three inches from his nose, pulling him inexorably downward along with its inert partner. Klondike's stale, animal odor stung Riff's nostrils for a fast instant before being washed away by the eye-steaming stench of putrefaction. Riff's guts boiled and heaved. He was sinking into the impossibly small sunroof.

He flailed; got his heel against the lip of the hole. Like a hungry spider, the graveyard hand was making for his

Adam's apple, and he fought to slow it down. When his fingers sank into the oleaginous dead flesh he killed the onrushing spasm of revulsion by jerking backward hard enough to dislocate his shoulder.

He had a grip on the ring when he did it.

The thick, drenched tweed of the coat separated with a heavy purr drowned out by the rain. Riff plunged backward and wedged into the rapidly dissolving dirt mound, shuddering uncontrollably, teeth clacking, completely apeshit with panic.

In the sickly yellow glow, he saw that the maggoty flesh of the ring finger had stripped away like a rotten banana peel, exposing a still-clutching skeleton finger. The sound it made against the red enamel was like a fork tine raked against a porcelain sink.

Brown gunk was leaking from between his own fingers, and he opened his fist to reveal a diamond almost as big as a golf ball, nestled in clumps of buttery skin that was warm only because it had been inside Riff's closed hand.

Riff's body would not move; he was frozen from the bowels down, his back married to the pit wall. If he looked away, all he would see were dancing, round-edged rectangles of yellow light.

Klondike's chin was still perched on the edge of the sunroof. The now-ringless hand in lace and black velvet circled his body and tugged. Klondike's upper row of teeth caught on the rubber insulation strip. Another tug, and his forehead bonked against the hatch. Then the rest of him slid into the hole all at once and he was gone.

Riff was whimpering now, still cemented to the spot, transfixed by the waiting yellow hole. He could just see the upper curve of one of the phony electric braziers on either end of the front windows. Yellow squares overlapped in his pupils; in his mind he saw a million times over the rotting hand emerging again, grasping, pulling up a shoulder, revealing a head and torso. . . .

"Here!" he yelled, his bones finally grinding into motion. "Here, goddamnit! Keep it! Bunny wanted it, not me!

*Take it back!*" He flung the diamond without aiming. It bounced on the roof with a thunk, and wandered toward the sunroof like a crystal beebee in a Brobdingnagian puzzle maze.

It decided at last to drop in, and vanished noiselessly.

Riff's treacherous body now insisted that he run, that he set an Olympic record for running in the rain.

The sunroof began to whirr slowly shut, paring away the light. Riff's heartbeat punched away at his throat. The last of the ooze in his hand was rinsed away.

Then he piled out of the hole and hauled his poor white ass toward the freeway at maximum speed. In forty-five minutes the rain changed to a five-alarm downpour, and Riff stood in his own private puddle, facing the singularly unamused gaze of Bunny.

"Turn him out," said Bunny flatly, and two of his boys winnowed Riff down to his waterlogged skivvies.

"I told you I don't have the ring," said Riff, still shivering. "But you're not going to believe that any more than you'll believe that Klondike—"

"Pulled a doublecross, bashed you with a shovel, tied you up with your own coat, and took the diamond?" finished Bunny. His eyes bugged, watery and yellow with sickle-cell. "Shit. Any one 'o them things, maybe—but Klondike didn't have enough battery power to invent all four. You're jerking me around, Riff my friend. Maybe you didn't even make it out to the grave, huh?"

Riff swallowed. Bunny was getting ready to do something nasty.

"I'm not lying," he said carefully. "Klondike is still at the gravesite."

Anticipating Bunny's next accusation, one of the hulks flanking the doorway to the office stepped forward. "I know what you're thinking, boss," he said in a voice as deep and growly as a diesel truck engine. "That boy Desmond is as dead as one of them barbecued chickens in the market. Me and Tango was a hundred percent sure." He back-stepped to his place at the door, and Riff thought of a cuckoo clock.

"You took a hundred percent of my green," said Bunny. "You *better* be goddamn sure." He said *gah-dam*.

"Can I have my pants back?" said Riff. Regrettably, it drew Bunny's pique away from his bulldogs and refocused it on himself.

"Give him his duds," said Bunny. "He's going out there with us." He rose to his buggywhip-skinny six-two and wired an expensive pair of rose-tinted shades around his face. "And if you're snowjobbin' me, boy—"

"I know." Riff nodded as he fought his way back into his sodden clothing. "I'll have a hard time peddling Veteran's Day poppies wearing a cast up to my eyebrows."

"You got it."

They made the drive in funeral silence, and nobody cared about the dawn and the dirty floormop hue it turned the horizon. LA's surface streets were flooding by now, and the homeowners in the Hollywood Hills would be cursing the mudslides, and it was obvious that visitor business at Forest Lawn would be just . . . Well, thought Riff—they were assured of no disturbances, anyway.

The gorilla named Tango broke out three umbrellas in basic black, and nobody moved to share one with Riff, who led them down to Plot #60 from an access road charmingly called Magnolia View Terrace. It proved a lot easier than sneaking up from the freeway. The heavily saturated turf around Desmond's final resting place made their shoes squish. Bunny's Gucci loafers were goners, Riff thought with not a little satisfaction.

Forest Lawn was discreet concerning such peccadilloes as vandalism. No matter what happened to Desmond's grave, the news would never make the *Times*, and the wad of bills Tango had slapped into the gatekeeper's palm guaranteed privacy for proper mourning.

One of those characteristic Astroturf tarps had been pegged over the hole. Desmond's garish monument stone spired toward outer space like a granite ICBM.

"So what?" Bunny said loudly as a jolt of thunder shook the ground.

"They covered it up!" said Riff.

All three men turned to look at him. "I can see that, null and void," Bunny snapped. "Get on with it!" The pimp stood with his hands deep in the pockets of his black overcoat, Tango's buddy holding an umbrella over him like a dutiful Egyptian slave. Riff never could dredge up the guy's name—the two were as interchangeable as knife-maniac movies—so he pointed at Tango. "Help him," Bunny said, and Tango eyed the tarp doubtfully before stepping sidewise down into the pit. Bunny thought he could hear a noise through the downpour, a kind of electric fly-buzzing. Maybe construction equipment was working somewhere nearby.

Riff held up the corner of the tarp for Tango. There was a very dim yellow glow emanating from beneath it, and water had pooled in its middle, causing it to sag.

As Tango ducked under the tarp, Riff planted his foot dead bang into the bigger man's ass, driving him inside. The tarp flopped wetly back into place. Tango's partner saw it happen, and automatically broke his police revolver from its armpit holster, bringing it to bear on the bridge of Riff's nose.

But by then, Tango had started screaming.

He shot up against the tarp from beneath, hurling water all over the trio just as Bunny shouted, "Blow him away!" meaning Riff, and took a miscalculated backward step that dumped him onto his butt in the mud.

Riff grabbed the big Magnum barrel just as it went off in his face. There was a gentle backward tug as the slug whizzed cleanly through the sleeve of his overcoat. The *pistolero*'s second shot headed off into the stratosphere as the slimed incline of the pit came apart like warm gelatin under his heels. He slid indecorously down into Riff's embrace. As he flailed for balance Riff wrested away the gun and gave him a no-nonsense bash in the face with it that flattened his nose to pulpsteak and rolled his eyeballs up into dreamtown.

It had taken maybe two seconds, total. Riff quickly climbed to the rim of the grave. He knew how, by now. The gunman's semiconscious body oozed slowly downward until his legs were beneath the tarp edge. Then he was pulled the rest of the way inside.

Topside, Bunny was still on his back, trying to scramble his own petite shooting iron past the silver buttons on his double-breasted overcoat. He looked up, glaring hotly, and saw a dripping, mud-caked bog monster pointing an equally mud-caked revolver in his direction. His hands stopped moving and his eyes became very white.

From behind Riff, there came a sound like a green tree branch being twisted in half, followed by nothing except the patter of the new rain. One of the tent pegs popped loose and the tarp sagged into the hole.

Bunny's face was a livid crimson-black with rage. The knowledge he had been outdrawn, however, did not stop him from trying to preserve his image by saying, "I'll kill your ass for this, you know," in his quiet, bad-pimp's hiss.

"What it is, Bunny," said Riff, gesturing with the gun, "is you need to climb down into his hole."

"*Tango!*" Bunny screeched, trying to crawl backward.

Riff frowned and shot Bunny once, in the left leg just below the kneecap. Blood mingled with the mud and gore, spoiling his nine-hundred-dollar suit. "This isn't a *movie*, Bunny; just get in the hole."

Hiding his pain behind clenched teeth, Bunny began to drag himself toward the pit. When he backed down into it, on top of the tarp, his hands going wrist-deep in the muck, he looked up at Riff and in his best snake-charming voice said, "Why?" mostly to buy a couple of seconds more. It was extra seconds that always counted in rescue time.

"Because I gotta change my life, Bunny," he said, looming over him with the gun.

*Buy more seconds.* "I'll let you," said Bunny, gasping now. "Anything you want, man. Partners. We'll—"

Riff was about to tell Bunny not to bullshit a bullshitter when the ruglike tarp heaved mightily up, splitting in the middle. The first thing that came out was yellow light. The second thing that came out was a black velvet-clad arm that captured Bunny's wounded leg in its trash-compacter grip very nicely. Bunny slid three more feet with a loud cry of pain.

One thing about those limos, Riff thought as he turned away and walked back up the slope. He'd noticed it during the ride out in Bunny's own chariot. They sure had a lot of room inside.

Behind him, Bunny's pocket pistol went off four, five times and then stopped. No slugs came Riff's way.

Riff pawed around under the limousine's bumper for the magnetic case containing the spare keys, and when he got behind the wheel he involuntarily glanced at the car's sunroof. The two cars were probably a lot alike.

He did not stick around to hear the tiny whirring noise coming from Plot #60. Nor did he ever see the ridiculously fat diamond left at the edge of the grave, as payment. A Forest Lawn worker, finding it later in the day and assuming it to be a cheap crystal because of its large size, took it to his Pasadena apartment and hung it in the kitchen window, where it threw the setting sun's rainbow colors against his breakfast nook for the next fifteen years.

# Hugh B. Cave

# Murgunstrumm

HUGH B. CAVE is one of the great masters of macabre fiction. Born in Chester, England, in 1910, he emigrated to America with his family when he was five. While editing trade journals he sold his first story, "Corpse on the Grating", to the pulp magazines in 1930. Quickly establishing himself as an inventive and hugely prolific writer, he became a regular contributor to *Weird Tales*, *Strange Tales*, *Ghost Stories*, *Black Book Detective Magazine*, *Thrilling Mysteries*, *Spicy Mystery Stories* and the legendary "shudder-pulps" *Horror Stories* and *Terror Tales*.

Cave left the field for almost three decades, before returning in late 1977 with a hefty collection of his best horror stories, *Murgunstrumm and Others*. Since then he has produced a dazzling array of new novels, including *Legion of the Dead*, *The Nebulon Horror*, *The Evil*, *Shades of Evil*, *Disciples of Dread*, *The Lower Deep*, *Lucifer's Eye* and *Forbidden Passage*. As if that wasn't enough, he has also written two young-adult novels, *The Voyage* and *Conquering Kilmarnie*, and has recently finished a blockbuster mainstream novel covering the last four decades of events in Haiti and Jamaica, where he spent 23 years of his life.

The short novel that follows perhaps best exemplifies the no-holds-barred gothic horror thillers of the '30s. Prepare to be transported back to the days of the Depression where your genial host, Murgunstrumm, welcomes you to the Gray Toad Inn for an evening of entertainment you'll never live to forget!

## 1. 3 A.M.

THE NIGHT HOURS ARE TERRIFYING in that part of the country, away from traveled roads and the voices of sane men. They bring the moan of lost winds, the furtive whisper of swaying trees, the agony wail of frequent storms. They bring madness to men already mad, and fear and gibbering and horrible screams of torment. And sometimes peals of wild hideous laughter a thousand times worse.

And with the dread of darkness, that night, came other fears more acute and more terrifying, to clutch viciously at the man who sought to escape. Macabre horrors of the past, breeding anew in the slough of his memory. Visions of the future, huge and black before him. Grim dread of detection!

The square clock at the end of the long corridor, radium-dialed for the guard's benefit, told him silently that the hour was 3 A.M. The hour when darkness deepens before groping dawn; when man is so close to that other-world of mystery that a mere closing of his eyes, a mere clutching of the subconscious, brings contact with nameless shapeless entities of abhorrent magnitude. The hour when the night watch in this grim gray structure, and the solitary guard on the outer walls, would be least alert. *His* hour, for which he had waited seven months of eternity!

His eyes were wide, staring, fearful. He crept like a cat along the corridor, listening for every separate sound. Somewhere in the tiers above him a man was screeching violently, thumping on a locked door with frenzied fists. That would be Kennery, whom they had dragged in only a week ago. They had warned him to be still at night, poor devil. In the morning he would learn the awful loneliness and silence of solitary confinement. God! And men like that had to go on living, had to wait for death, slowly!

He prowled forward again, trembling, hugging the wall with thin fingers. Three more corridors now and he would be in the yard. He clutched the key feverishly, looking down at it with hungry eyes. The yard, then the last great gate to freedom, and then. . . .

His groping hands touched a closed door. He stopped abruptly. Over his head hung the number 23. The V. D. ward. And he shuddered. Someone was mumbling, laughing, inside—Halsey, the poor diseased idiot who had been here eighteen endless years. He would be on hands and knees, crawling over the floor, searching for beetles. He would seek and seek; and then, triumphant at last, he would sit for hours on his cot, holding a terrified insect cupped in his huge hands while he laughed gleefully at its frantic struggles.

Sickness surged over the fugitive's crouching body. He slunk on again quickly. God, he was glad when that mad caterwauling was smothered by a bend in the corridor! It clung in his brain as he tiptoed to the end of the passage. He fingered the key savagely. Eagerness glared in his eyes.

That key was his. His own! His own cunning had won it. During the past month he had obtained an impression of every separate lock between him and escape. Furtively, secretly, he had taken chewing-gum forms of every infernal slot. And no one knew. No one but Martin LeGeurn, Ruth's brother, who had come once each week, on visiting day, and carried the impressions back to the city, and had a master key made. A master key! Not successful at first. But he himself, with a steel nail file, had scraped and scraped at the thing until it fitted. And now, tonight. . . .

He descended the staircase warily, feeling his way every step. It was 3:10 now. The emergency ward would be open, with its stink of ether and its ghastly white tables on wheels. He could hide there until the guard passed. Every move according to schedule!

The door was open. He crept toward it, reached it, and stopped to peer anxiously behind him. Then he darted over the threshold and clung silently to the wall, and waited.

Hours passed. Frantic hours of doubt and uncertainty. Strange shapes came out of nowhere, out of his distorted mind, to leer and point at him. God! Would those memories never die? Would the horrors of that hour of madness, seven months gone, torment him forever, night after night, bringing back visions of those hideous creatures of living death and the awful limping thing of the inn? Was it not enough that they had already made a soul-twisted wreck of him and sent him to his black house of dread? Would they—

Footsteps! They were audible now, approaching down the corridor outside. They came closer, closer. They scuffed past with an ominous *shf-shf-shf*, whispering their way. With them came the muffled clink of keys, dangling from a great ring at the guard's belt. And the sounds died away.

The fugitive straightened up and stepped forward jerkily. And then he was running wildly down the passage in the opposite direction. A massive door loomed before him. He flung himself upon it, thrusting his own key into the lock. The door swung open. Cold, sweet air rushed into his face. Outside lay the yard, bleak, empty, and the towering walls that barred the world beyond.

His terror was gone now. His movements were mechanical and precise. Silently he locked the barrier behind him and slunk sideways along the wall of the building. If he made the slightest sound, the slightest false move, those glaring, accusing, penetrating searchlights would clank on and sweep the enclosure from one end to the other. The great siren would scream a lurid warning for miles and miles around, howling fiendishly that Paul Hill had escaped.

But if he went cautiously, noiselessly, he would be only a part of the darkness. There was no moon. The night was like pitch. The guard on the wall would not see.

A step at a time he moved along the stone, hesitating before each venture. Now a hundred feet lay between him and the gate. Now fifty; and the guard had not heard. Now twenty. . . .

His breath caught in his throat as he darted across the final ten feet. Flat against the last barrier of all, he fumbled with the huge lock. His fingers turned the key with maddening slowness, to muffle any fatal thud. Then, putting his shoulder to the mass, he pushed. The big gate inched outward.

Without a sound he squeezed through the narrow aperture. His teeth were clenched; his lips tasted of blood. But he was out, outside! No one had seen him! Feverishly he pushed the great block of iron back into place. On hands and knees he crawled along the base of the wall, crawled and crawled, until the guard's turret was only a grim gray blur against the black sky. Then, rising abruptly to his feet, he stumbled into the well of darkness beyond.

"Thank God!" he whispered hoarsely. And then he was hacking, slashing his way through tangled black underbrush, with huge trees massed all about him and the inky sky blotted out overhead.

## 2. Armand LeGeurn

NO ONE, that night, saw the disheveled gray-clad figure that stumbled blindly from the woods and slunk silently, furtively down the state road. No one saw the unholy lust for freedom in his eyes, or the thin whiteness of his compressed lips.

He was violently afraid. He turned continually to glance behind him. But his fists were clenched viciously. If that hideous siren sounded now, when he was so close to ultimate freedom, they would never take him back there alive. Never! Once before, during his seven hellish months of confinement, the siren had screamed. That was the time Jenson—foolish, idiotic Jenson, mad as a hatter—had scaled the walls. The bloodhounds had uncovered his hiding place in the heart of the woods, and he had been dragged back, whimpering, broken.

But not this time! This time the escaped fugitive was no madman. Horror, not madness, had thrust him into that den of cackling idiots and screeching imbeciles. Stark horror, born of an experience beyond the minds of men. Horror of another world, a world of death and undead demons. And to-night, at four o'clock, Martin LeGeurn would be waiting at the crossroads, with a car. Martin would not be late.

Paul Hill began to run. On and on he ran. Once he turned abruptly and plunged into the edge of the woods as a passing bus roared up behind him. Then, as the bus bellowed past, he leaped to the shoulder of the road again, racing frantically.

A sob of relief soughed through his lips as he rounded the last sharp bend and saw, far ahead, a pair of stationary headlights glaring dimly toward him. He stumbled, caught himself. His legs were dead and heavy and aching sullenly, but he lurched on. And then he was gripping the side of the car with white nerveless hands, and Martin LeGeurn was dragging him into the seat.

There was no delay now. Everything had been arranged! The motor roared sharply. The roadster jerked forward and gathered momentum. The clock on the dash said five minutes past four. By five o'clock they would be in the city. The city, and Ruth, and—and then he would be free to finish it in his own way. Free to fight!

He fumbled with the leather bag under his feet.

"Why didn't Ruth come to see me?"

"Listen!" Martin LeGeurn said sibilantly.

Paul stiffened. He heard it. The sound was a moaning mutter, trembling on the still air, somehow audible above the drone of the motor. It rose higher, clearer, vibrating like a living voice. Paul's fingers dug cruelly into the leather seat cushion. The color seeped out of his face.

He knew that sound. It was a lurid screaming now, filling the night with shrill significance. The night watch had discovered his absence. He had blundered somewhere. Some door left open; some twist of unforeseen fate—and now, up there in the tower, a black-faced fiend was whirling the handle of the great siren faster and faster, gloating over its hellish voice. The same awful wail had seared the countryside when Jenson had fled into the woods, four months ago.

A terrible shudder shook Paul's body. He cringed against his companion. Courage left him. Incoherent mumblings came from his mouth.

"They know," Martin said jerkily. "In ten minutes the

road will be patrolled. Every car will be stopped. Get into your clothes. Quick!"

Paul stiffened. Suddenly he sat erect, fists clenched savagely.

"They'll never take me back! I'll kill them! Do you hear? I'll kill them all!"

Then he was tearing at the leather bag between his knees. He got it open, dragged out the light brown suit and tan shirt, the necktie and shoes. Feverishly, as the car rushed on at reckless speed with Martin LeGeurn hunched over the wheel, he ripped off his asylum garb and struggled into the other. Deliberately he stuffed the gray clothes into the bag, and snapped the lock.

"Get off this road. Take the first right."

Martin glanced at him quickly, frowning.

"It's madness. If we hurry, they may not—"

"We can't make it. The state police will—"

"But if we turn off—"

"I know the way, I tell you! Let me drive!"

Martin's foot jammed on the brake. Even before the car had trembled to a stop, Paul snapped his door open and leaped out. And he was no longer a ghastly spectre in gaunt gray as he stumbled in the glare of the headlights. He was a lean, powerful young man, decently dressed, resolute and determined and fighting viciously to overcome his own natural terror. He slid behind the wheel without a word. The car shot forward again under more expert hands. Roaring over the crest of the hill, it swerved suddenly to the right and lumbered into a narrow sub-highway of dirt and gravel.

And the siren screeched behind it. The whole of creation was vibrant with that infernal moan. It would throb and throb all through the night, flinging its message over an unbelievable radius. It would never stop!

But Paul paid no attention to it. He said curtly: "Heave that bag out. They'll never find it in here." And later, when Martin had obeyed, he said abruptly, scowling: "Why didn't Ruth come to see me?"

"She—she just couldn't, Paul."

"Why?"

"You wouldn't understand."

"She's waiting for me now. Is she?"

"I"—Martin stared straight at the windshield, biting his lips—"I don't know, Paul."

"She never tried to help me," Paul said bitterly. "Good God, she knew why I was in there! She could have gone to Kermeff and Allenby and made them listen."

"They left the city," Martin mumbled.

"That's a lie."

"She—"

"I know," Paul said heavily. "She went to them and they wouldn't listen. They're not supposed to listen. Doctor Anton Kermeff and Doctor Franklin Allenby,"—the words were bitter as acid—"that's who they are. Too big to believe the truth. Their job was to put me away and sign a statement that I was mad. That's all they cared."

"I don't think Ruth went to see them, Paul."

Paul's hands tightened on the wheel. The stiffening of his body was visible, so visible that Martin said abruptly, as the car lurched dangerously to the side of the road and jerked back again:

"You—you don't understand, Paul. Please! Wait until you've talked to Father."

"Father?" And the voice was tinged with sudden suspicion. "Why not Ruth?"

"You'll know everything soon, Paul. Please."

Paul was silent. He did not look at his companion again. A vague dread caught at him. Something was wrong. He knew it. He could feel it, like a lurking shape leering and grinning beside him. Like those other lurking undead demons of seven months ago. But Martin LeGeurn could not tell him. Martin was his friend. Someone else would have to blurt out the truth.

The big roadster droned on through the night.

It was daylight when they reached the city. Murky, sodden daylight, choked with drizzling rain. Street lights still smirked above drooling sidewalks. The elevated trestle loomed overhead, a gleaming, sweating mastodon of steel. Silence, which had held sway for the past hour over black country roads, gave way to a rumble of sound.

"Better let me take the wheel," Martin LeGeurn said dully. And when Paul had swung the car to the curb: "We're safe now. They won't look for you here. Not yet."

Not yet! Paul's laugh was mockery. Before the day was over, the news of his escape would be in every headline, glaring over town. Newsboys would be shrilling it. News flashes on the radio would blurt it to millions of listeners. "Special Journal Dispatch! At an early hour this morning, Paul Hill, twenty-three-year-old inmate of the State Insane Asylum, escaped. . . ."

The car moved on again through slanting rain. The windshield wiper clicked monotonously, muttering endless words to the beat of Paul's brain. "Police of this state and neighboring states are conducting an unceasing search for the escaped madman who eluded the dragnet last night. . . ."

"You want to go straight to the house?" Martin LeGeurn said suddenly.

"Of course. Why shouldn't I?"

"I'm not going in with you."

"Why?"

"I've got something to do. Got to go to Morrisdale, and get there before night. But Father's waiting for you. You can talk to him."

He drove on. The streets were deserted, here in the lower downtown sector. The roadster picked its way through intricate short cuts and sideways, and emerged presently on the South Side, to purr softly along glistening boulevards.

"You're going to Morrisdale?" Paul frowned.

"Yes."

"What for?"

"For—Ruth," Martin said grimly. "It's your own idea, Paul. Your method of escape. Just what I couldn't think of myself, though I sat up night after night, half mad."

"What do you mean?"

"I'll tell you—when it's over," Martin muttered. He was

staring through the crescent of gleaming glass before him. His lips were tight, bloodless. "We're almost there," he said abruptly.

They were entering the residential sector of the South Side. The car groped its way more slowly. Paul stared on both sides, remembering the houses, the great church on the corner, the rows of stores: things he had forgotten during the past months. And presently Martin swung the wheel. The roadster skidded into a tree-lined road. Lovely homes with immaculate driveways and wide lawns loomed gray in the drizzle. The car slowed to an awkward stop. Martin turned abruptly, thrusting out his hand.

"Good-by, Paul. Don't worry."

"But—"

"I've got to go. Got to reach Morrisdale on time to-night. Talk to Father, Paul. And trust me."

Paul gripped the outstretched hand. Then he was out of the car, hurrying up the drive. And the car was roaring down the road again, into the murk, like a great greyhound.

Paul's fingers pressed the bell. He waited, nervously. The door opened. Old Armand LeGeurn, Ruth's father, stood there on the sill, arms outthrust.

After that, things blurred. The door closed, and Paul was pacing down the thick carpet with LeGeurn's arm around him. Then he was in the luxurious library, slumped in a huge chair, folding and unfolding his hands, while Old LeGeurn talked slowly, softly.

"She couldn't come to see you, Paul. They've sent her away. The same two physicians, Kermeff and Allenby. Less than a week after they sent you. Mad, they said. They're big men, Paul. Too big. She never returned here after leaving the hospital at Marssen. They took her straight from there to Morrisdale."

"Morrisdale," Paul muttered feebly. Suddenly he was on his feet, eyes wide and body tense. "That's where Martin's gone!"

"He's been often, Paul. That's how you got your letters. He mailed them from here. She didn't want you to know."

"But there *must* be some way of getting her out."

"No, Paul. Not yet. We've tried. Tried everything—money, influence, threats. Kermeff and Allenby are bigger than that, boy. They put their names to the paper. No power on earth can convince them they're wrong. No power on this earth—yet."

"Then she's got to stay?" Paul pleaded. "She's got to. . . ." He relaxed again with a heavy shudder. "It's not right, Mr LeGeurn! It's horrible! Why, those places are—are. . . ."

"I know what they are, boy. We're doing all we can. But we must wait. She still remembers those other things: Murgunstrumm and the awful creatures of the inn. They rush upon her. They affect her—queerly. You understand, boy. You know what it means. Until she's forgotten all that, we can only wait. No physician in the country would disagree with Kermeff and Allenby. Not with such evidence. In time she'll forget."

"She'll never forget, in there!" Paul cried harshly. "At night, in the dark, the whole thing comes back. It's awful. Night after night it haunted me. I could hear that horrible laughter, and the screams. And those inhuman shapes would come out of nowhere, grinning and pointing and leering. She'll never forget. If we don't get her away. . . ."

"Escape, son?"

"Yes! Escape!"

"It won't do. She couldn't face it. She's not strong enough to be hunted down as you'll be."

Paul stood up savagely, pushing his fingers through his hair. He stared mutely at the man before him. Then his nerves gave way. He buried his face in his hands, sobbing.

"You'll stay here to-night, Paul?" he heard Armand LeGeurn asking.

Paul shook his head heavily. No, he couldn't stay here. The first place they'd look for him would be here in Ruth's home. As soon as they discovered that he had wriggled through their unholy dragnet, they'd come here and question, and search, and watch.

"I want to think," he said wearily. "It's all so tangled. I want to be alone."

"I know, son." Armand LeGeurn rose quietly and offered his hand. "Let me know where you are, always. If you need money or help, come here for it. We believe in you."

Paul nodded. He didn't need money. There was a wallet in the pocket of the coat Martin had given him. He could go and get a room somewhere, and think the thing out alone. More than anything else he wanted to be by himself.

"I'll go to the North End," he said, "and—"

But Armand LeGeurn was pacing to the door. When he returned, he carried a small suit-case in his hand.

"Take this," he advised. "It won't do for you to go prowling about the stores, getting what you need. Everything is here. And—be careful, Paul."

Paul took the suit-case silently. Abruptly he thrust out his hand. Then he hurried down the hall and went out the front door.

## 3. "To Rehobeth"

PAUL FOUND lodgings in a third-rate rooming house, deep in the twisted cobblestoned streets of the North End slums. There, late in the afternoon, he sat on the slovenly bed and stared fixedly at the single window. The suit-case, open but not unpacked, lay between his feet; and on top, grinning up at him like a black beetle nestling in the clean white folds of the shirt beneath it, lay a loaded revolver. Armand LeGeurn, acting evidently on the spur of the minute, had dropped it there just before clicking the bag shut.

It was raining. A drooling porous mist fogged the window pane. The room was a chill, dark, secluded retreat high above the muttering side street below. A radio, somewhere in the bowels of the house, mumbled dance music and crooning voices.

Paul sat motionless. He was not afraid of realities any more. It was not fear of tangible things that kept the color out of his face and made him sit rigid. The police would never look here for him, at least not until they had combed the rest of the city first. He was in no immediate danger. He had money, clothes, and friends if he needed them.

But the torment had returned—torment a hundred times more vicious than fear of capture. Macabre shadows stalked the room. Nameless voices laughed horribly. Fingers pointed at him. Red, red lips, set fiendishly in chalk-colored dead-alive faces, curled back over protruding teeth to grin malignantly. A significant malicious name hissed back and forth, back and forth, never ceasing. *Murgunstrumm! Murgunstrumm!*

Ruth was in the asylum at Morrisdale. Martin LeGeurn had gone there. Something was wrong. Martin had seemed preoccupied, mysterious. He hadn't wanted to talk. Now he was gone. Only Armand LeGeurn was left, and Armand had tried every method possible; had tried to convince Kermeff and Allenby that she was not mad.

Paul's fists clenched. He mouthed the two names over and over, twisting them bitterly. Kermeff and Allenby. It was their fault! He jerked to his feet, clutching at the wooden bed-post with both hands, cursing loudly, violently.

Then he sat down again, staring at the black revolver which leered up at him. A truck rumbled over the cobblestones, far below. Someone was turning the dials of the radio, bringing in snatches of deep-throated music and jangling voices. Paul reached down slowly and took the revolver in his hands. He fingered it silently, turning it over and over. Then he sat very still, looking at it.

Ten minutes later, without a word, he stood up and put the revolver in his pocket. He bent over the suit-case. Very quietly he walked to the door. His lips were thin and tight, and his eyes glaring.

He paced noiselessly down the narrow stairs to the lower hall. The street door opened and closed. He hurried out into the rain, along the sidewalk.

Suit-case in hand, he groped his way through the maze of gleaming streets, avoiding the lighted thoroughfares as much as possible, yet bearing ever toward the uptown sector. He glanced neither to right nor left, but strode along without hesitating, carried forward recklessly by the hate in his heart and the sudden resolution which had come to him. Not until he reached the outskirts of the slums did he consider his own peril again. Then he stopped, stepped quickly into a black doorway, and stared furtively about him.

He was mad, walking through the streets like this. What if the police down here had been given his description? What if they were even now looking for him? Probably they had and they were. If he stepped on a bus or boarded a street car, or even hailed a cab, he would be playing squarely into their hands. He couldn't reach the LeGeurn home that way. And he couldn't go on walking, like a blind fool, waiting for some stranger to peer suddenly into his face and scream an alarm.

He studied the street in both directions. A hundred yards distant, on the corner, a red-and-white electric sign, blinking in the drizzle, designated a drugstore. Warily Paul crept out of the doorway and moved along the sidewalk. He was afraid again now, and nervous. He kept his face hidden when hurrying men and women brushed past him. Reaching the drugstore, he slipped inside without attracting attention and looked quickly for a telephone booth. An instant later, with a little gasp of relief, he swung the booth door behind him and groped in his pockets for a coin.

The nickel jangled noisily. With stiff fingers Paul dialed the LeGeurn number and waited fretfully until the resultant hum clicked off.

A masculine voice, Armand LeGeurn's, answered almost inaudibly.

"Mr LeGeurn," Paul said slowly, fumbling for the right thing to say. "I want to—"

His words had a surprising effect. LeGeurn, instead of waiting for him to finish, interrupted with a hearty laugh and sputtered quickly:

"Hello, Frank, hello! By the Lord, man, it's a downright joy to hear that voice of yours. I'm all tied up here. Police watching the house, and the phone wires tapped in the bargain. Damned inconvenient, I'm telling you! What's up? What d'you want?"

Paul's reply choked on his lips. He stiffened, and his fingers tightened on the receiver. Phone wires tapped! Police at the house! Then abruptly he understood Armand LeGeurn's ruse. Regaining his composure, he answered with assumed astonishment:

"Police? Why, what's wrong?"

"What's wrong! Don't you read the papers?"

"You don't mean," Paul said, frowning, "it's about that chap who got away from the nut house? Good Lord, what's that got to do with you?"

"Plenty. Tell you later, when you're sober."

"I'm sober now. That is, almost."

"What's on your mind then?"

"Nothing much." Then Paul added quickly: "That is, nothing but the fact that I'm getting thoroughly soaked and I'm stranded in the slums without a sou in my pocket, old man. I was going to demand your car to escort me home, if your pugilistic chauffeur isn't asleep or something. But if you're tied up. . . ."

"The car, eh? Where'd you say you were?"

"Down in the heart of the most miserable, sloppy, filthy section of this confounded city, my boy." Paul flung back desperately. "And not enjoying it a bit."

"Really? Well, you can have the car. Welcome to it. Where'll I send it?"

Paul named the streets hurriedly. As an afterthought he said as carelessly as he could: "Tell Jeremy to pull up at the dinky little drugstore just around the corner of Haviland. Yeah, I'll be in there getting my feet dry. And say—thanks, mister. Thanks a lot. I appreciate it."

The telephone clicked ominously. Releasing it, Paul leaned against the side of the booth, limp, frightened, with cold sweat trickling down his face. It was another moment before he could steel himself to open the door and step out. Then, with a forced slouch, he picked up his bag, pushed the door wide, and strode across the tile floor.

He couldn't wait in the store. That would be dangerous. The police might see fit to check the call and send someone to investigate. But he could wait outside, in some convenient doorway a short distance up the street. And then, when he saw the car coming, he could walk casually toward it without being seen.

Outside, with the rain beating in his face, he sought a suitable niche and found one. Huddled there, he wondered if his plan was plausible. It wasn't. The element of risk was too great. If the police came to the drugstore, seeking him, they would be suspicious when they found him gone. They too would wait for the car. Then, if he stepped out. . . .

But the car, coming from the suburbs, would have to pass along the avenue before turning into Haviland Street. That was it! Paul knew the machine by sight—a long low black roadster, inconspicuous among others, but easily discerned by one who knew it intimately. And it would have to cross the avenue intersection, have to pass the lights.

Very quickly Paul slipped out of the doorway and hurried into the rain.

He had to wait long when he reached the square. While he waited, leaning against the wall of a building, with his coat collar pulled high above his neck and face, he watched the lights blink from red to green and green to red, endlessly. Slow lights they were, and the corner was a dangerous one, choked with traffic and scurrying pedestrians. The cars that snaked past, scintillating and gleaming, were like huge moving gems as they groped their way with sluggish caution.

The whole square was bright with illumination. Brilliant store windows threw out walls of color. Sparkling electric signs twinkled overhead. Street-lamps glared accusingly, sullenly, striving to penetrate the rain. It was maddening to stand there, waiting and waiting. . . .

Once a policeman, in rustling rubber coat, swung past with mechanical steps. Paul stiffened and watched him. But pedestrians were waiting at the same time for the traffic lights to become red and yellow; and the policeman paid no attention. He passed on idly, and Paul relaxed with a shudder.

Five minutes passed, and ten. And then the car came. The lights were against it. It slowed cautiously as it approached; and as it stopped, Paul darted forward across the gleaming avenue. Skirting two intervening machines, he leaped to the running-board and clawed the door open. And then he was in the seat beside the lean, wiry form of Matt Jeremy, and muttering harshly:

"I prayed for that light, Jeremy, prayed it would be red when you came. If you hadn't stopped. . . ."

Jeremy glanced at him quickly, bewildered.

"What's wrong, sir? I was going to the drugstore, like you told Mr LeGeurn. I thought you wanted—"

The light changed. Paul clutched the man's arm and said abruptly, thickly:

"Turn right. Get out of here quickly!"

Jeremy grunted. The car jerked forward, hesitated an instant to nose its way through cross traffic, and swung sharply off the avenue. Gaining speed, it droned on through the rain, leaving the clamor and congestion of the main thoroughfare behind.

"You'll have to get home the best way you can," Paul said evenly, a little later. "I've got to have the machine."

"That's what Mr LeGeurn said, sir," Jeremy nodded.

"He'll understand. That's why I phoned."

"Yes, sir. He understands all right. He said for me to go with you."

"What?"

"I'm to stick with you, sir. That's what he said. If you want me."

Paul drew a deep breath and stared squarely into the man's grinning face.

"Want you! Jeremy, I—"

"I might come in handy, maybe," Jeremy shrugged. "Trouble's my middle name, sir. Where to?"

"To Rehobeth," Paul said grimly. "To Rehobeth and the Gray Toad Inn. And the rest is up to God, if there is a God in that unholy place."

## 4. "They Don't Come Out, Sir."

FOR YEARS, old Henry Gates had squeezed a meager existence out of the ancient Rehobeth Hotel. For years he had scuffed quietly about the village, minding his own affairs and seldom intruding, but wise in his knowledge of what went on about him. For years he had lived in silent dread of what might some day happen.

To-night he stood silently on his veranda, gazing down into the deepening dusk of the valley below. The air was cold and sweet with the smell of rain-soaked earth. Darkness was creeping in on all sides, hovering deep and restless above the village.

Across the way a light blinked, announcing that Tom Horrigan's boy was working in the stables. Other lights, feeble and futile, winked on either side. Beyond them the woods were still and dark, and the leaden sky hung low with threatening rain.

"A night of evil," Gates mumbled, sucking his pipe. "There'll be doin's to-night. There'll be laughin' and screamin' on the Marssen Road."

The light across the way went out suddenly. A boy appeared, framed in the stable doorway. The door creaked on rusty wheels, jarring shut. The boy turned, glanced toward the hotel, waved his hand.

"Hi there, Mr Gates! A fair black night it'll be, hey? I was walkin' to town."

"Ye've changed your mind, I'm thinkin'," Gates retorted.

"That I have. I'll be goin' home and to bed, and lockin' my windows this night."

The boy hurried away. Other lights blinked out. Henry Gates gazed into the valley again, muttering to himself.

"There'll be screamin' and laughin' in the old inn to-night."

He turned and hobbled inside. The door closed; the bolt thudded noisily. The village of Rehobeth was dormant, slumbering, huddled and afraid, waiting for daylight to arouse it.

An hour later the black roadster purred softly out of the darkness. The car was a dusty gaunt shape now, after three hours travel over sixty-odd miles of paved highways and black, deserted country roads. Matt Jeremy hung wearily over the wheel. Paul Hill, slumped beside him, stretched arms and legs with a grumble of complaint, and opened the door.

Shadows filled the valley below. Here the road, after climbing steadily for five miles, rested in the uncouth little hamlet before venturing the last mile or so over the ridge into the next state. And Rehobeth had not changed since that day, more than seven months past, when Paul Hill had stood in this same spot—stood here with Ruth LeGeurn and laughed, because they were marooned with a broken-down car and had to spend the night in the ancient hotel beside them.

No, Rehobeth had not altered. It was still the same lonely isolated village, looking down upon a world all its own—a shadowed gray world, blanketed with bleak snow during the long winter months, swathed in murky sunlight through the summer. Only sixty miles from the big city, only twenty-odd miles from civilization, but in reality a million miles from anywhere, sordid, aloof, forgotten.

"Well, what do you think?" Paul said with a shrug. "Like the place?"

"Not much, sir," Jeremy confessed. "Still, I reckon it's a pretty good hide-away, and it ain't so far you can't keep track of things."

"I'm not hiding, Jeremy."

"No? Then what are we doin' here, sir? I thought"—Jeremy released the wheel and slid out—"I thought we were just goin' to lay low and wait."

Paul climbed the hotel steps slowly. The door was locked. Evidently it was bolted on the inside, and the inmates of the place had gone to bed.

"Old Gates," Paul smiled, "must be upstairs. They don't expect visitors at this hour."

He hammered loudly. "Gates!" he called out. "Henry Gates!"

A long interval passed, and presently a *scuff-scuff* of footsteps was audible inside. But the door did not open immediately. A face was suddenly framed in the window at the right, and a groping glare of lamplight illuminated the veranda. Then the face and the light vanished, and the bolt rattled. The door opened cautiously.

"Ye're lookin' for me, sir?"

"You're Gates?" Paul said, knowing that he was.

"Yes, sir. I am that."

"Good. We're staying here a day or two, Gates. You've two good rooms vacant?"

"Ye're stayin' here, sir? Here?"

"Yes. Why not? Full up, are you?"

"No, no, sir. I've got rooms. Sure I've got 'em. Only the likes of you, with an automobile like that un, don't generally—"

Paul forced a laugh. He knew what Gates was thinking.

"That's all right," he shrugged. "Quite all right. We want to do a bit of looking around. Might even decide to set up a hunting camp around here somewhere. Just show us the rooms and never mind about the car."

Old Gates was willing enough, once his fears were allayed. He held the door wide. Paul and Jeremy passed inside casually and gazed about them.

There was nothing inspiring. Bare, cracked walls leered down as if resenting the intrusion. A musty lounge, long unused, leaned on scarred legs. A squat table, bearing the flickering oil lamp which Gates had first held, stood in the middle of the floor. Beyond, a flight of stairs angled up into darkness.

"D'ye mind tellin' me your names, sir?" Gates said hesitantly. "I'll show ye to your rooms, and then I'll be makin' out the register."

"Mr James Potter will do," Paul nodded. "James Potter and chauffeur. And by the way, Gates, have you a typewriter?"

"Typewriter, sir?" Gates hobbled behind the desk and took down a key. "Afraid not, sir. I used to have, but you see business ain't what it used to be." He wheezed up the stairs with Paul and Jeremy following him. "Rehobeth be such an out-of-the-way place, sir, and nobody comes this way very often lately, and. . . ."

The rooms were at the end of the upper corridor, adjoining each other and connected by an open door. Paul inspected them quietly and smiled, and pressed a bill into the old man's hand. And presently, alone in Paul's chamber with the hall door shut, the two newcomers stared at each other and nodded grimly. That much was over with.

"Didn't recognize me," Paul said evenly.

"Recognize you, sir?" Jeremy frowned.

"This is the place, Jeremy, where Miss Ruth and I stopped that night. You don't know the details. You were in Florida with Mr LeGeurn."

"Oh. I see, sir. And you thought he might—"

"Remember me? Yes. But seven months is a long time. The madhouse can change a man in less time than that. Open the bag, Jeremy, will you?"

Jeremy did so, putting his knee to the leather and jerking the straps loose. Lifting the suit-case to the bed, Paul fumbled a moment with the contents, then stepped to the old-fashioned desk and sat down with paper and fountain pen in hand.

And he wrote two letters, one to Doctor Anton Kermeff, the other to Doctor Franklin Allenby, addressing both to the State Hospital in the city he had just left. The letter to Kermeff read:

*My dear Kermeff:*

*You will, I am sure, consider this note most carefully and act upon it as soon as possible. Mr Paul Hill, the young man whom you and Allenby declared insane some seven months ago, and who escaped only very recently from confinement, is now at the Rehobeth Hotel in a state of most complete and mystifying coma. Fortunately I am on my vacation and was passing through Rehobeth at the time of his attack, and I am now attending him.*

*The case, I assure you, is worth your gravest attention. It is the most unusual condition I have ever had the fortune to stumble upon. Of course, I am remaining here incognito. The name is James Potter. I suggest that you come at once, saying nothing to arouse undue attention to yourselves or to me. Later, of course, the patient must be returned to confinement; but meanwhile I believe I have something worthy of your esteemed consideration.*

*A copy of this letter I am also sending to Allenby, since you are both equally interested in the case.*

*Yours in haste,*
*Hendrick Von Heller, M.D.*

The letter to Allenby was an exact duplicate. Paul sat very still, staring at what he had created. He was gambling, of course. Only one thing he was sure of: that Von Heller, the very noted specialist, was actually somewhere in this part of the state, on vacation. Von Heller had discussed that with the doctors at the asylum, on one of his regular visits.

As for the rest, Von Heller was known, by reputation at least, to both Kermeff and Allenby. But would the handwriting of the letters prove fatal? That was the risk. It might; it might not. Possibly Kermeff and Allenby had never seen, or never particularly noticed, Von Heller's script. Perhaps—and it was very likely, considering the man's importance and prestige—he had employed a secretary. At any rate, the element of chance was there. A typewriter would have lessened it, and could easily have been purchased on the way here. But old Gates had none, and it was too late now.

"We'll have to face it," Paul shrugged. "We can't be sure."

"If it means a scrap, sir. . . ."

"It might, Jeremy. Part of it might. But we'll need minds, as well. *Wills.*"

"Well now—"

"Never mind," Paul said. "It's getting late. Come."

He shoved the door open. Henry Gates had lighted the oil burners in the corridor, filling the upper part of the inn with a furtive, uneasy, yellowish glare. Probably those burners had not been ignited in months past. Perhaps not for seven months. And the lower lobby, illuminated only by the oil lamp on the desk, was deep with moving shadows, gaunt and repelling.

Gates was writing in the register when Paul and Jeremy descended. He looked up and grunted, obviously startled. Holding his pen at an awkward angle, he said hurriedly:

"Just puttin' your names down, sir, I was. Be ye goin' out?"

"For a short drive," Paul nodded.

"M-m-m. It be a dark night, sir. Not a star in the sky when I looked out the window just now. And no moon at all to speak of. These be lonely roads about here."

Paul smiled bitterly. Lord, what mockery! Gates, huddled here, mumbling to him—to *him*—about the loneliness of the surrounding roads! As if he didn't know! As if he hadn't learned every conceivable horror there was to learn, seven months ago!

"You've a mail box here?" he questioned curtly.

"I'll take it, sir," Gates replied, eyeing the white oblongs in Paul's hand. "Two of 'em, hey? Ain't often the postman gets anythin' here, sir. He'll be comin' by in the mornin', on his route."

"They'll get to the city before night?"

"Well, sir, the postman takes 'em to Marssen in his tin lizzie."

"That's quite all right, then. Come, Jeremy."

"Be ye goin' anywheres in particular, sir?" Gates blinked, raising his eyebrows.

"I thought we might turn down the old road that cuts in a mile or so below here. Looked rather interesting when we came through. Leads to Marssen, doesn't it?"

"It does that."

"Hm-m. I think I've been over it before. Vaguely familiar, somehow. If I'm right, there ought to be an old inn about two miles down. The Gray Goose, or the Gray Gull, or—"

"Ye mean the Gray Toad?"

"That's it, I guess. Closed up, is it?"

"No, sir," Gates' voice was a whisper as he came out from behind his barlike desk and scuffed forward ominously. "It ain't closed, sir. And if I was you—"

"Who runs the place, I wonder? Do you know?"

"I know, sir. Yus, I know. It's a queer cripple as runs it, sir. A queer foreigner what never goes nowhere nor comes into the village, nor ever does anythin' but limp around inside his own dwellin'. Murgunstrumm is his name, sir. Murgunstrumm."

"Strange name," Paul mused, keeping his voice level with an effort. "And what's so wrong about the place, Gates?"

"I dunno, sir. Only I've heard noises which ain't the kind I like to hear. I've seen automobiles stop there, sir—fine automobiles, too—and ladies and gentlemen go inside, all dressed up in fine clothes. But I ain't never seen 'em again. They don't come out, sir. And I know one thing, as I'm certain of."

"Yes?"

"About seven months ago it happened, sir. I'm sittin' here behind my desk one night along about evenin', and a young couple comes walkin' down the road from the woods. A pretty girl she was, if ever there was one; and the young man was about your height and looks, only not—excusin' me, sir—so kind of pale-lookin' and thin. They said as how their car was broke down about a mile up the road, and could they use my telephone to call a garage feller in Marssen. And then—"

Gates peered furtively about him and came a step nearer. He was rubbing his hands together with an unpleasant sucking sound, as if he feared the consequences of saying too much.

"They had supper here, sir, the two of them, and then they went out for a walk. Said they might walk down the valley, seein' as how it was such a fine night. But they didn't get there, sir. No, sir, they didn't ever get there."

"They got lost?" Jeremy said curtly.

"I'm not knowin'. All I know is, I'm sittin' here about one o'clock in the mornin', havin' a bite to eat with the garage man after he'd got their automobile fixed up and waitin' for them to come back for it—and we sudden hear footsteps stumblin' up the steps. There's a shout, and we run out. And it's the young man, sir, walkin' like one in a dream and white as a ghost. And he's carryin' the girl in his arms, like she's dead; only she ain't dead, sir, because she's moanin' and mumblin' like she's gone clean mad. . . ."

Gates' voice choked off to a faltering hiss, leaving only a feeble echo to chase fretfully around the room. Jeremy was staring at him with wide eyes. Paul stood very stiff, white and silent.

"And what happened then?" Jeremy whispered.

"Well, the young man fell down on the floor here like a dead one for sure, and he never moved a muscle when me and the garage feller bent over him. The girl, she lay here twitchin' and sobbin' and talkin' a lot of words which didn't make sense. Then the garage man and me, we got both of 'em into the young man's car, and the garage feller he drove 'em as quick as he could to Marssen, to the hospital there. They called up the city for some real good doctors, and"—Gates shuddered violently and peered around him again—"and both the young man and his lady friend was put away in the insane-house," he finished fearfully.

There was silence for an instant. An unnatural, ugly silence, broken only by the sound of men breathing and the *pft-pft-pft* of the oil lamp on the desk. Then Paul laughed softly, queerly.

"The insane-house, eh?" he shrugged. "A good story, Gates. Not bad at all. And they're still there?"

"It's the God's honest truth, sir. I swear it is. And the young people are still locked up, they are. I'm tellin' ye, sir, I think of it even now on dark nights, sir, and I fair get the horrors from it!"

"Thanks. I guess we'll be moving along, Gates. We'll have a look at your ghastly inn."

"But nobody goes along that road no more, sir. Not after nightfall!"

"All right, old man," Paul shrugged, knowing that his voice faltered slightly and his assumed indifference lacked the sincerity he strove to stuff into it. "Don't sit up and worry about us. We won't come back the way the others did. I'd have a hard job carrying you, eh, Jeremy?"

Jeremy's laugh, too, was vaguely harsh. But he turned and followed to the door. And an instant later, leaving Gates stiff-legged and staring in the middle of the unclean floor, with the sputtering oil lamp casting spider-shadows on the wall behind him, Paul and Jeremy stepped over the threshold. The door creaked shut behind them. They descended the wooden steps slowly.

## 5. Murgunstrumm

THE LONELY untraveled road between Rehobeth and the buried little town of Marssen, twelve miles distant, was particularly black and abandoned that night. Leaving the main dirt highway a mile or so below the last of Rehobeth's straggling houses, it plunged immediately into sullen unbroken woods, where all sounds died to nothingness and the light was a dim, uneven, flickering gloom.

The mud-crusted black roadster, with Jeremy at the wheel, careened recklessly down the main road, boring its way with twin beams of bright light. At the intersection, it slowed to a crawl, and Jeremy swung the wheel. Then, more slowly, the car proceeded down the Marssen road; and presently it was moving at snail-speed, groping along a snake track of deep ruts and loose, damp sand.

"It ain't," Jeremy said laconically, "what you'd want to call a pleasure drive, sir. Fair gives me the creeps, it does, after the old guy's talk."

Paul nodded. He said nothing. He was thinking again, and remembering, in spite of himself. What Gates had narrated back at the hotel was true, and the old man's words had awakened memories which were better a thousand times dead.

Paul's face was strained, colorless now. His hands were clenched defensively. He stared straight ahead of him through the dirty windshield, watching every sudden twist of the way, every looming shadow. Once he touched the revolver in his pocket and felt suddenly relieved. But he remembered again, and knew that the weapon would mean nothing. And presently, after ten minutes of slow, cautious progress, he said quietly:

"Stop the car here, Jeremy."

"Here, sir?"

"We'll walk the rest. It isn't far. They mustn't see us."

Jeremy grunted. The roadster turned to the side of the road, scraped noisily against the thick bushes, and came to a jerky stop.

"Will I lock it, sir?"

"Yes. And keep the key in your hand. We may need it quickly."

Jeremy glanced at him quizzically. Then, with a shrug, he turned the ignition key, removed it, and slid out of his seat. In a moment Paul was beside him, gripping his arm.

"Sure you want to come, Jeremy?"

"Why not, sir? I'm pretty handy with my fists, ain't I?"

"That won't help, Jeremy. Nothing will help, if we're seen."

"Well then, we won't be seen. You're shiverin', sir!"

"Am I?" Paul's laugh was harsh, toneless. "That's bad. I shouldn't be. Not after what happened before. Shivering won't help, either. Come on."

They passed down the narrow road, leaving the roadster half hidden, black and silent, behind them. Paul, thinking again, peered furtively on either side, fighting back his fear of the darkness. Shadows leaped at him from matted walls of gloom. Faint whispers sucked down from above as the night breeze whimpered and muttered through rustling leaves. The horrors of the madhouse came back, vivid and close. Supernatural voices laughed hideously and screamed, and everywhere ahead, in the gloom, a limping shape seemed to be waiting and leering and pointing triumphantly.

Jeremy, more or less indifferent to intangible terror, plodded along with a set frown on his square features. Shadows and whispers did not trouble him. He did not know. And Paul, pressing close to him, found relief in the man's presence, and courage in his stolidness.

So they walked on and on, until presently out of the darkness ahead of them, on the right, a gray mass took form with maddening slowness. Paul stood quite still, drawing his companion close.

"That's the place," he said almost inaudibly.

"There's a light, sir," Jeremy observed.

Yes, there was a light. But it was a feeble thing, a mere oblong slit of illumination, visible faintly through a cracked shutter. And the house itself, upstairs and down, was sinister with darkness. Like an enormous humpbacked toad it squatted just off the road, isolated in its own desolate clearing, hemmed in on three sides by unbroken walls of gloom and silence.

Not a lovely place, the Gray Toad Inn. Not any more. At one time, Paul reflected, it had been a roadhouse of gay repute, situated pleasantly on an out-of-the-way road between semi-dead villages, with desirable seclusion a strong point in its favor. Here, night after night, had come revelers from the nearby city and even nearer towns, to laugh and drink and fill the big house with youthful clamor.

But not any more. All that had changed. The inn had grown cold and lonely. The road itself had fallen more and more into disuse and obscurity. That very isolation which had made the place a popular resort had now buried it in abject solitude and left it dark and dismal, hoary with interred memories, sinking into slow rot.

Yet a light glowed now in the lower level, winking out into the darkness. A wan yellow light, filtered through a cracked blind, clutching outward like a thin bony finger, as if pleading for old times to return. And Paul and Jeremy, staring at it, crept slowly, noiselessly, through the deep grass of the overgrown clearing toward it.

And there was something else, which the inn had never known in its days of laughter and gaiety—something which even Jeremy, who lacked imagination and feared no foe but of flesh and form, noticed furtively.

"There's somethin'," he whispered, reaching out to grasp Paul's coat, "there's somethin' awful queer here, sir. The air. . . ."

Paul stiffened. Fifty yards before him, the humpbacked structure bulged sullenly against the crawling sky above.

Deep grass rustled against his legs. He stared suddenly into Jeremy's set face.

"What do you mean?" he said thickly. But to himself, in his mind, he muttered triumphantly: "He's noticed it too! He's noticed it too! Ruth wouldn't believe me when we came here before, but it's true, it's true!"

"The air has a funny smell, sir," Jeremy said slowly. "Like—like earth, or dirt. Like a mushroom cellar or somethin'. I must be crazy, sir, but it seems to hang all around here, heavy-like."

Crazy? Paul choked out a jangling laugh, full of triumph. No, not crazy. Not yet. Jeremy was right. This place—this ancient abode of infernal silence and monstrous horror—was alive within itself. It breathed and felt. It was no part of the woods around it.

But Jeremy wouldn't understand. The explanation was far too intricate and vague and impossible for him. Yet it was true. The atmosphere surrounding this structure before them, the air that clung tenaciously to the entire clearing, was a living entity, a dull leaden *thing*, visible to eyes that dared seek it out. It was a part of the inn itself, having no connection, no acquaintance, with the air about it. It reeked up out of the very earth, and from the decaying walls of the building, and from the bodies of the dead-alive creatures who inhabited the place.

But to Jeremy it was simply a creepy sensation, vaguely inexplicable and unpleasant. And so Paul moved on, more and more slowly, cautioning his companion to complete silence.

Thus they reached the side of the inn itself, and Paul crouched there in utter darkness, with the great structure hunched over him, mastodonic and gaunt, enveloped in its pall of dull, moving, viscous exhalation.

For an instant Paul clung there, unable to put down his deepening dread. All the ancient horrors rushed upon him viciously, striving to shatter the walls of his mind and send him back, back down the road, reeling and laughing and screaming in madness, as they had done on that other night seven months ago. And then, slowly, he stood erect until he could peer through the cracked shutter. And hung there, rigid and flat-pressed against the window-ledge, staring.

Only a vague semicircle of illumination was visible inside through the filthy window glass. There at a small square table against the farther wall, unaware of Paul's presence, sat a long figure. The oil lamp on the table, peculiarly shaded with an agate cup-shaped globe, cast a restless, unreal glow into the man's face.

An ugly face it was, in the full horrible significance of the word. A sunken savage gargoyle, frog-like in shape, with narrow close-set eyes blinking continually beneath beetled brows that crawled together, like thick hairy fingers, in the center. The broad nose, twisted hookwise, seemed stuck on, like a squatting toad with bunched legs. And the mouth was wide, thick, sensuous, half leering as if it could assume no other expression.

The man made no movement. Apparently in a state of semi-stupor, he leaned on the table in the near gloom. Beyond him the feeble light played up and down the cream-colored wall and over the worn green carpet, revealing shadowed shapes of other tables and other chairs and objects without definite form.

Paul stared, utterly fascinated and terrified, clutching the window-sill with white hands, standing stiff and unalive in the darkness. He might have clung there indefinitely, remembering every separate fear of his last visit here, had not Jeremy's guarded voice hissed suddenly behind him:

"Somethin's comin', sir! A car!"

Paul turned. A faint purring sound came to his ears from somewhere down the road. He stepped forward violently and seized Jeremy's arm.

"Down!" he cried sharply. "Get down, man!" And then he was flat in the deep grass, heaving, breathing heavily, with Jeremy prone beside him, so close that their bodies fused together.

"What is it, sir?" Jeremy whispered.

"Be still!"

In the road, the purring became an audible drone, as of a motor. Nearer and nearer it came, and then, just once, a muted horn shrilled out, sending a muffled blast through the night. Twin headlights took form and grew into glaring, accusing orbs.

At that moment the door of the inn opened creaking back softly. A lantern swung in the aperture, dangling from an uplifted hand; and the man with the toad face scuffed slowly over the threshold, muttering to himself and blinking his eyes. Bent, twisted grotesquely, he limped down the stone flagging a dozen paces and stood still, holding the lantern high.

The headlights of the oncoming car became brilliant bowls of fire, cutting slantwise through the unearthly mist of the grounds. They slowed and stopped, and the drone of the engine became suddenly still. The lights were extinguished. The car door clicked and swung open. A voice—a girl's voice, vaguely timid and afraid and fantastically out of place in such sordid surroundings—said:

"This—this is the place you are bringing me?"

And the voice that answered her was somehow packed with subtlety, gloating and possessive in spite of its quiet smoothness.

"Certainly, my dear. You will enjoy yourself."

Two shapes materialized. Shadows in the gloom, nothing more, they moved down the path to where the lantern swayed before them. Then the outer rays of the light encompassed them, and Paul stared mutely with every ounce of color ebbed from his face.

A man and a girl. Man-and-a-girl. It surged over and over in his brain. God! After seven months, the horror was still going on, still happening! The man—the man was like all the others, tall, straight, smiling, attired in immaculate evening clothes. The girl was young and lovely and radiant in a trailing white gown and flame-colored velvet wrap. But she was not happy; she was not a willing guest. She was afraid and helpless, and her oval face was pathetically pale in the lantern glow—pale as alabaster; the face of one who was very close to death, and knew it, and had no resistance left in body or soul to fight against it.

She walked mechanically, staring straight ahead of her.

And then the glare of the lantern swept full over her, revealing a mark—but no one would have seen it who did not look closely. Jeremy did not notice it, certainly. Only Paul discerned it—Paul, who was praying that the mark would not be there.

A mere patch of whiteness, where the girl had tried in vain to cover, with powder, a pair of ghastly crimson incisions, fiendishly significant. And the marks themselves were faintly visible as she came closer in the accusing halo of the uplifted lantern.

She stopped very abruptly then, and peered at the hideous face behind the upraised arm. She trembled and shrank away from it, and a subdued frightened whisper came involuntarily from her lips. Her companion put his arm about her and laughed, glanced indifferently at the man with the lantern, and laughed again, mockingly.

"It's only Murgunstrumm, my dear. He wouldn't harm a fly. He wouldn't know how, really. Come."

The girl paced on, walking like one already dead, like one who had been so long in the clutch of fear that nothing more mattered. The lantern cast a long gaunt shadow on the walk as she stepped in front of it. One long shadow—only one. The man in evening clothes, pacing just behind his lovely comrade, left nothing. Nothing but empty glaring whiteness. . . .

They went inside; and Murgunstrumm, scuffing over the sill behind them, reached out an abnormally long arm to swing the heavy door shut. The last thing Paul saw, as the lantern light died behind the closing barrier, was the unholy grin which transfigured that toadlike face. Then—then something possessed him.

He was on his feet blindly, fists clenched until the palms of his hands stabbed with pain.

"Great God, don't let them do it! Don't—"

He stumbled forward, thrashing through the deep grass, retching with the sudden turmoil which roared within him. Frantically he staggered toward the door of the inn; mad, unreasoning, knowing only that he could not stand still and let the horror continue.

He would have rushed to the door, then, and hammered upon it, screaming to the heavens above him; would have slashed his way into the house and fought—fought with hands and teeth and feet in a mad attempt to drag the girl from that foul embrace; would have continued until they overwhelmed him, killed him. All to no purpose!

But luck saved him. His blundering foot twisted beneath him as it cracked against an immovable something in the grass. Agony welled up through his leg, letting him down. He pitched violently forward and plunged headlong.

And the madness left him as he lay there, gasping. Ahead of him he heard the door of the inn creak open. A probing shaft of lantern light swept the clearing, and Murgunstrumm stood there on the threshold, peering out. Then the innkeeper muttered something inaudible, and the door closed again. The light vanished. The clearing was very dark and still.

What a fool he was! In the fury of a moment's insanity he had come within an inch of condemning Ruth forever to the asylum. He had come within an instant of awful death, when life was the most necessary possession in the world.

The girl in the flame-colored wrap was beyond his power to save. Beyond any power, except of a merciful God. The mark of the vampire was already imprinted in her throat. She was a slave of the demon who had stolen her soul. Nothing could help her now.

Paul's hands dug savagely into his face. A snarl came from his throat as he lay there in the deep grass. And then another sound, behind him, took his attention as something wriggled close. Jeremy's voice said in a thick whisper:

"You—you're all right, sir?"

"Yes, I'm all right."

"You ain't hurt, sir?"

"No. Not—hurt."

"Will we try to break into the place? That girl, she looked as if they might mean to do some damage—"

"No. It's too late."

Paul reached out and gripped the big man's arm. He lay still for a moment then, waiting for strength to return.

Then, with a warning whisper, he began to crawl backward through the grass. Not once did he take his gaze from that closed barrier. Inch by inch he retreated until at last the deep grass gave way to underbrush and crackling bushes, and sheltering black trees loomed over him. Rising, he stood in the darkness until Jeremy joined him. Then together they crept silently back to the road.

"Listen," Jeremy cautioned him suddenly.

They stood quite still. A burst of laughter—feminine laughter, wild and shrill and vaguely mad—pursued them. Paul shuddered, took a step forward. Then, with an effort, he turned and hurried on again. He said nothing until the roadhouse, with its pall of evanescent vapor, was buried again in the gloom behind them. Then he muttered grimly:

"Did you see, clearly, the man in evening clothes?"

Jeremy's big body twitched as if something had jostled him. He turned a white, frightened face.

"That feller, sir," he whispered huskily, "there was somethin' creepy about him. When he stepped in front of the lantern back there—"

"You saw it too?"

"I don't know what it was, sir, but he didn't seem natural."

"I know," Paul said.

"Who is he, sir?"

"I don't know. I only know what he is."

"And the cripple, sir. He's the same Murgunstrumm feller the hotel man was tellin' us about?"

"The cripple," Paul replied, and his voice was low and vibrant and full of hate, "is Murgunstrumm."

They paced on in silence after that. Reaching the car, they got in quickly. Jeremy stuck the key in the slot and turned it. The motor coughed, purred softly. The black roadster jerked backward, swung fretfully about, reversed again, and straightened with a lunge.

"Back to the hotel, sir?" Jeremy said sharply.

Paul answered, almost inaudibly: "Yes. Back to the hotel."

## 6. Kermeff and Allenby

AT SEVEN O'CLOCK the following evening a large gray touring car, smeared and panting from sixty miles of fast travel, crunched to a stop before the Rehobeth Hotel. Twilight had already swooped down on the little community. A murky gloom welled up from the valley below. Lights blinked in the shadows, and the village lay silent and peaceful in the lassitude of coming night.

The car door clicked open. A gray-coated figure slid from the chauffeur's seat and moved quietly to the rear, glancing queerly, frowningly at the hotel. Mechanically he pulled open the rear door.

The two men who descended after him were, it was evident, somehow ill at ease and vaguely apprehensive. For an instant they clung close to the car, scowling unpleasantly and impatiently. They exchanged glances and comments. Then, with a word to the driver, they advanced to the steps.

Old Gates, aroused by the sound of the machine's arrival, met them in the doorway. Squinting at them, he asked hesitantly:

"Be ye lookin' for someone, sirs?"

"For Mr James Potter," the larger of the two said distinctly. "He expects us. We should like to go directly to his rooms, if you please."

"To be sure, sir," Gates grimaced. "I'll take ye right up now, I will. Come this way, sir."

"Er—it will perhaps be better if we go up alone. Will you direct us?"

Gates blinked, and stared more intently then, as if distrustful. But he turned with a shrug and said, rather stiffly:

"Of course, sir. Walk right through the lobby here and up the stairs, and turn right and go straight down the hall to the last door."

"Thank you."

Kermeff and Allenby ascended the stairs slowly, with Kermeff in the lead. They were strange companions, these two. Of different nationalities, they differed also in face and form, and obviously in temperament. Kermeff, the larger, was a bull-shouldered, aggressive man with huge hands that gripped the railing viciously. He possessed a sensitive mouth and keen eyes that declared him fiery, alert, possibly headstrong, and as stubborn as stone.

Allenby, trailing behind him, was smaller, wiry in stature, stern and deliberate of movement. Sullen, aloof, he climbed without a word and without a backward glance.

Together they strode along the upper landing to the door of James Potter's room. Kermeff knocked sharply. The door opened, framing Matt Jeremy on the threshold.

"Mr Potter?" Kermeff said gutturally.

"Yes, sir," Jeremy nodded. "Come right in."

Kermeff stepped over the sill. Allenby, hesitating an instant, peered up and down the corridor, shrugged and followed him closely. Very quietly, unobtrusively, Jeremy closed the door as he had been told to do.

A single lamp, not too efficient, burned on the desk in the corner. Beside it Paul Hill leaned silently against the wall, waiting. Kermeff and Allenby, pacing into the room, saw him each at the same moment.

The big man stiffened as if a wire had been drawn taut within him. He flung up his head and stared. He wet his lips and sucked a long noisy breath into them. Allenby took a sudden step forward, stopped abruptly and stood quite still.

"You!" Kermeff rasped violently. "Where is Doctor Von Heller?"

"Sit down, gentlemen," Paul said evenly.

"Where is Von Heller?"

"Von Heller is not here."

"What? What are you saying? Are you . . .?"

"I wrote the letters myself, gentlemen," Paul shrugged, "to bring you here."

Kermeff realized the truth. He had been trapped. He had gulped the bait completely. His one desire now was to spit it out again, to leave before the madman before him became violent. Kermeff swung about with a lurid growl.

But the exit was barred, and the physician stiffened again. The door was closed; Jeremy leaned against it. Kermeff stood on braced legs, swaying. He gathered himself. With a great oath he flung himself forward.

He stopped almost in the same movement. Jeremy's hand, sliding out of a bulging pocket, gripped a leveled revolver. Kermeff glared at it with animal hate. Turning again, very slowly and deliberately, he faced Paul.

"Sit down," Paul ordered.

"You are mad!"

"Sit down, I said."

Kermeff sank into a chair. He was trembling not with fear, but with rage. He sat like a coiled spring, ready to leap erect. He glared sullenly at his colleague, as if expecting Allenby to work the impossible.

Instead, Allenby glanced furtively from the rigid revolver to Paul's set face, and sat down also. Not until then did Paul move away from the wall. He, too, drew a revolver from his pocket.

"It is your car outside, I suppose?" he said quietly, addressing Kermeff. "Yes?"

"Yes."

"Come with me, then. At once, please."

Kermeff stood up, watching every move with smoldering eyes that threatened to blaze any moment into flame. He said harshly, gutturally:

"Why did you summon us here?"

"You will see, in time."

"It is an outrage! I demand—"

"Demanding will do you no good," Paul said crisply. "You are here and you will stay here. There will be no argument."

"I will have you arrested for forgery!"

"You are going downstairs with me and instruct your driver to return to town. You will tell him, very simply, that you have no further need for him. And you will make no false move, Kermeff. I didn't bring you here for pleasure or for any petty hate. If you attempt in any way to trick me, I will kill you."

Kermeff faltered. For an instant it seemed that he would give way to his violent anger and rush forward blindly, despite the twin revolvers that covered him. Then, trembling from head to foot, he turned to the door.

Jeremy held the door open as the physician strode into the hall. Paul followed silently, close enough behind to keep his protruding coat pocket, with his revolver buried in it, on a direct unwavering line with the man's back.

And Kermeff tried no tricks. Obviously he realized the grim severity of his position. He walked deliberately down the corridor, descended the stairs, and strode across the lobby. Gates, glancing at him from behind the desk, mumbled an inaudible greeting. Kermeff, without replying, went directly to the door and stepped out on the veranda, with Paul only inches behind him.

The chauffeur stood there, leaning indifferently against the rail. Kermeff looked squarely at him and said distinctly:

"We are staying here, Peter. You may go back to the city. We shall not need you."

"You won't want me, sir?"

"When we do, I will send for you."

The chauffeur touched his hand to his cap and turned to the steps. Kermeff, swinging on his heel, re-entered the hotel. He climbed the stairs with methodical precision. He said nothing. With Paul still behind him, very close and silent, he returned to the room he had just left.

And there, with the door closed again, Paul said evenly:

"That is all, gentlemen. I must ask you to remain here quietly until it is dark. Then. . ." He shrugged his shoulders.

Allenby, peering at him sharply, said in a thick voice:

"Then what?"

"I don't know. Perhaps we shall go mad."

Paul sat down, toying with the revolver. Kermeff and Allenby glared at him, then glanced significantly at each other. Jeremy, stolid and silent, remained standing at the door.

This occured at seven-thirty. At nine, Paul glanced at his watch, stirred impatiently in his chair, and stood up.

Crossing quickly to the window, he drew the shade and peered out. It was very dark outside. The village was a thing of brooding silence and blackness. The sky held no twinkling points of light, no visible moon. There was no need to wait longer.

He stepped to the bed and drew back the covers, exposing the white sheets beneath. Methodically he pulled the top sheet free and tore it into inch-wide strips and ripped the strips into sections. Jeremy was watching queerly. Kermeff and Allenby stared and said nothing. Perhaps they thought he was mad.

And perhaps he was! Certainly it was a mad thing he was doing—a crazy, fantastic idea which had crept into his mind while he sat there in the chair, thinking of what the night might hold. And now, as he pulled his suit-case from the corner and rummaged through it in search of the needle and thread which Armand LeGeurn had stowed there, a thin smile played on his lips. Without a doubt they would think him mad in another moment.

He found what he sought. Crossing quietly to the door, he put his revolver into Jeremy's hand and said simply: "Be careful." To do what he intended, he would have to bend over within reach of Kermeff's thick arms and then within reach of Allenby's. It would not do to leave the gun unguarded in his pocket, for a groping hand to seize.

He turned and gathered up the strips of white cloth. To Kermeff he said evenly:

"Put your hands behind you."

"What are you going to do?"

"Nothing to hurt you. Perhaps something that may save you from harm later. Put them behind you."

With a shrug, as if to imply that insane men must be humored, the big man complied.

Paul bent over him. Across the front of the man's vest he stretched a twelve-inch strip of cloth and sewed it quickly into place. A second strip, somewhat shorter, he sewed across the first, forming a large gleaming cross. The stitching was crude and clumsy, but it would hold. Unless clutching fingers or teeth tore the sheeting loose, the thing would remain in place.

Kermeff, meanwhile, was watching with hostile eyes. When the operation was finished he relaxed and held his coat open, studying the cross as if he could not quite believe. Then he scowled unpleasantly and peered again into Paul's face.

"In God's name, what is this for?"

"For your protection," Paul said grimly. "And you are right. Protection in God's name."

Kermeff laughed—a strained unnatural laugh that was more animal than human. But Paul was already at work upon Allenby, and presently he was attaching a third cross to his own body, in such a position that a single outward fling of his coat would reveal it to anyone who stood before him. Finally, pacing to the door, he took the two revolvers from Jeremy's hand and said quietly:

"Do the same to yourself, Jeremy. I'll stand guard. As soon as you've finished, we'll be leaving."

## 7. The Innkeeper

THE GRAY TOAD INN was half a mile ahead. Paul, huddled over the wheel of the roadster, glanced quickly into the face of the man beside him and wondered if Anton Kermeff were afraid. But there was no trace of fear in the big man's features. They were fixed and tense; the thick brows were knitted together in a set frown, the eyes focused straight ahead, unblinking. If anything, Kermeff was violently angry.

But he was also helpless. He was unarmed, and the door-pocket under his right hand contained nothing which might serve as a weapon. Paul has seen to that before leaving the hotel. And Paul's own hand, resting carelessly on the rim of the wheel, hovered only a few inches above the revolver in his coat pocket. If Kermeff made a single treacherous move, that hand could sweep down in a scant second and lash up again.

Moreover, the roadster's convertible top was down; and Matt Jeremy, in the spacious rumble-seat beside the huddled form of Franklin Allenby, commanded a view of the front. If Kermeff moved, Jeremy had orders to strike first. As for Allenby, the very presence of the powerful Jeremy beside him seemed to have driven all thought of resistance from his mind.

The car purred on, eating its way with twin shafts of light drilling the uncanny darkness. The Gray Toad Inn was just ahead.

This time Paul did not stop the car. Approaching on foot, under cover, would avail nothing to-night. The car was part of the plan. Paul clung to the wheel and drove steadily along the unused road, until at last the massive grotesquery of the inn materialized in the gloom on the right.

As before, a light glowed on the lower floor, struggling feebly to grope through the atmosphere of abomination that hung over the entire building. The car slowed to a groping pace, approaching almost noiselessly. Kermeff was staring. Paul looked at him, smiled thinly, and said in a low voice:

"The Gray Toad, Kermeff. You've heard of it before?"

The physician said nothing. He sat very stiff, his hands clenching and unclenching nervously. Obviously he was beginning to realize the peril of his position, the danger of being hauled blindly through the night, on a strange mission, by a madman who presumably sought revenge.

Ahead, the light winked suddenly as if an obstruction inside the grim walls had stepped momentarily in front of it. Then it glowed again. The door of the inn swung back.

Instinctively Paul's foot touched the brake. The car stopped with a tremor. With sudden dread Paul waited for whatever would emerge.

At first he saw nothing. He was looking for the wrong thing. He expected a human shape—the hunched body of Murgunstrumm or perhaps one of the immaculate evening-attired inhabitants. But it was no human form that slunk over the threshold into the night. It was an indistinct creature of low-slung belly and short legs. It crept forth, hugging the ground, and broke into a loping run straight for the road.

A long thin howl rose on the still air. The howl of a wolf.

Paul shuddered, still staring. Wolves, here in Murgunstrumm's house, meant only one thing! They were not flesh and blood, but—

Kermeff cried aloud. The loping thing ahead had reached the road and stopped quite still. Crouching, it swung about to face the car, as if seeing the machine for the first time. The twin lights fell full upon it as it bellied forward, revealing a sleek black body and glittering eyes of fire.

There was an instant of emptiness, of stiffening inaction, while the thing's eyes glared balefully. Then, all at once, it rushed forward with amazing speed, hurtling through the intervening space so quickly that it seemed to lose form as it came.

And it had no form! Even as it swept the last few yards it became a shapeless blur and vanished utterly; and in its place, swooping up before the headlight, came a flapping winged thing which drove straight at Paul's face.

Just once it struck. An unearthly stench invaded Paul's nostrils. The smell of the grave enveloped him, choking him. Then the creature was high above, hanging like a painted shape against the sky, with wings swaying slowly. And Kermeff was laughing in a peculiarly cracked shrill voice:

"It's a bat! It's only a bat!"

Paul's foot hit the accelerator sharply. The car jerked forward, careening down the road. But even as it groaned to a stop again before the driveway of the inn, Paul looked up again apprehensively, muttering to himself. And the bat still hovered near, seeming to eye the occupants of the car with a malicious hungry glare of hate.

"Come," Paul said sharply, climbing out. "Hurry!"

He strode toward the door. Somehow the thought that Kermeff and Allenby might choose this moment to chance an attack, or to attempt escape, seemed insignificant. The other peril was so much greater and closer that he could consider nothing else.

He was a fool—that was it! No sane man would be deliberately walking into the horrors of this diabolical place after once having had the luck to escape. Yet he was doing precisely that. He was risking something more than life, more than the lives of his three companions—for Ruth.

Still he advanced, not daring to hesitate or look above him. He knew, without looking, that the same significant shape hovered there—the thing which had once been a wolf and now was a bat, and in reality was neither. And it was there for a reason. Pangs of hunger had driven it out into the night, to prowl the countryside or perhaps to pay a visit to one of the nearby villages. And here—here at hand was a means of satiating that hunger, in the shape of four unwary visitors to the abode of evil. Four humans of flesh and blood. Flesh which meant nothing; blood which meant everything!

But it was too late to turn back. The door creaked open in Paul's face. A glare of light blinded him. A lantern swung before him, and behind it gleamed a pair of penetrating, searching eyes. Paul gazed fearfully into the eyes, into the contorted frowning mask of features in which they were set at incredible depth. With an effort he smothered his increasing fear and said in an uneven voice:

"You—you're still open, my good man?"

The repulsive face shook sideways. The thick lips parted soundlessly, mouthing an unspoken negative.

"Oh, come," Paul insisted, forcing something like a careless laugh. "We're hungry. We've come a long way and have even farther to go. Can't you stretch it a bit and scrape up something for us to eat and drink?"

Again Murgunstrumm shook his head without answering. The lantern swayed directly in front of Paul's face, vivid and repelling.

"We'll make it worth your while," Paul argued desperately. "We'll pay you—"

He did not finish. That same nauseating stench assailed him abruptly and a distorted black thing flopped past his head to careen against the lantern and lurch sideways into Murgunstrumm's face. Paul recoiled with an involuntary cry. But the thing had no evil intentions; it merely circled Murgunstrumm's shoulders erratically, uttering queer whispering sounds. And then all at once it darted away.

"We'll pay you double," Paul said again, recovering himself and stepping forward crisply. "We'll—" He stopped. Murgunstrumm was no longer scowling. The twisted face was fixed in a hungry grin. The sunken eyes were riveted, like the eyes of a starved animal, squarely in Paul's face. Murgunstrumm lifted the lantern higher and said thickly:

"You come in."

Paul stepped forward, knowing only that he felt suddenly weak and very afraid. Mechanically he crossed the sill. Kermeff followed him, and Allenby, and Jeremy entered last. Then the door swung shut and Murgunstrumm was leaning against it, the lantern dangling in his hand. His lips were spread in a huge idiotic grin. His eyes were twin sloes of fire, fixed and unmoving.

It was a queer room. The only two sources of light, the lantern and the slender-necked oil lamp on the table, were feeble and flickering, filling the entire chamber with a faltering, dancing yellow glow and uncouth crawling shadows. A bare floor, evidently once a polished dance surface, but now merely a layer of blackened boards, extended away into unlimited gloom. The walls were mere suggestions of shapes in the semidark, visible only when the fitful lamps were generous enough to spurt into restive brilliance.

There were tables—three, four of them. Round squat tables of dark color, holding candle stumps with black dejected wicks set in green glass holders, which threw out tiny jeweled facets of light.

And it was the light—lamplight and lanternlight—which put the room in motion and lent it that restless, quivering sensation of being furtively alive. First the lamp flare, sputtering and winking, fighting against stray drafts which came out of cracked walls and loose windows. And then, more particularly, the glare of the lantern in Murgunstrumm's hanging fist, jerking slowly into the center of the room as the cripple limped forward.

"Sit down, sirs," Murgunstrumm leered. "We be all alone here to-night."

He scuffed past, seeming to sink into the floor each time

his twisted right foot came in contact. His guests stared at him, fascinated utterly, as he hobbled to the farther wall. There, grinning at them indifferently, he raised the lantern face high and clawed up its globe with crooked fingers, and peered fixedly at the burning wick as if it were a thing of evil significance.

And his face was full in the realm of it—a gargoyle of malicious expectation. A contorted mass of shapeless features, assembled by some unholy chance or perhaps developed by some unholy habit. And then the lips protruded, the cheeks bloated for an instant. The thick tongue licked out, directing a gust of air into the lantern. The flame expired.

After that, Paul and his companions retreated to an out-of-the-way table, as near the door as possible, and sat very close together, in silence.

Murgunstrumm vanished, to reappear a moment later with a cloth, ghastly white in the contrasting gloom, slung over his stiffened arm. Grinning, he bent over the table, lifted the lamp, and spread the cloth in place. Lowering the lamp again, he said gutturally:

"Ye'll be wantin' food, huh?"

"Anything," Paul said, cringing from the hovering face. "Anything will do."

"Uh-uh. I'll find somethin', I will."

"And—er—"

"Yus?"

"Can't we have a bit more light here? It's—it's ghastly."

The innkeeper hesitated. It seemed to Paul for an instant that the man's lips tightened almost imperceptibly and the dull sheen of his eyes brightened as if some nerve, buried in that venomous head, had been short-circuited. Then with a shrug the fellow nodded and said:

"Yus, sir. We don't generally have much light here. I'll touch up the candles, I will."

He groped to the other tables and bent over them, one after another, scratching matches and holding his deformed, cupped hands over the cold candle wicks. And presently four tiny flames burned in the thick gloom, like tiny moving eyes, animal eyes glowing through fog.

"Who"—it was Anton Kermeff speaking for the first time—"who is that man?"

"Murgunstrumm," Paul said dully.

"He is horrible. Horrible!"

"He is more than that," Paul replied bitterly.

"I refuse to remain here. I shall go—"

"No." Paul bent over the table, gazing straight into the physician's face. "You will not leave so easily, Kermeff."

"You have no right!"

"I have nothing to do with it."

Kermeff's mouth tightened in the midst of a guttural exclamation. He said very sharply: "What?"

"You would never leave here alive. Wait, and watch."

Kermeff's face whitened. Allenby, sitting just opposite him, looked sharply, furtively, at Paul and trembled visibly. He licked his lips. He said falteringly, in a whisper:

"Why did we come here?"

"To wait—and watch."

"But it is madness! That man—"

"That man is all you imagine," Paul said, "and more. You will see, before the night is over."

His voice choked off. He was aware of no sound behind him, no scuff of feet or suck of breath; only of a ghastly sensation that something, someone, was very close and gloating over him. He could feel eyes, boring through and through, with the awful penetrating power of acid.

Abruptly he swung in his chair. He found himself staring straight into Murgunstrumm's prognathous countenance, and the man's mouth was lengthened in a mocking grin. Not of humor, but of mocking hate. And the eyes were boring, unblinking, unmoving.

An instant passed while Paul returned the glare. Then Allenby cracked under the strain. Half rising, he said in a sharp, childishly shrill voice:

"What do you want? Don't glare like that, man!"

The grinning lips opened. Murgunstrumm laughed. It seemed no laugh at all; it was soundless, merely a trembling of the man's breath.

"I bring wine now, or later? Huh?"

Allenby relaxed, white, trembling. Paul turned, released from the binding clutch of that unholy stare, and looked mechanically, mutely, at his companions. Kermeff nodded slowly. Jeremy, with fists clenched on the table, said raspingly:

"Tell him to bring some wine, sir. We need it."

Murgunstrumm, without a word, limped back into the gloom. His boots scraped ominously, accenting every second beat as his crooked leg thumped under him. There was no other sound.

And the silence persisted for many maddening minutes. The massive structure seemed to have stopped breathing. Paul's voice, when he spoke at last, was a sibilant hiss, whispering into the shadows and back again like a thing of separate being.

"Your watch, Kermeff. What time is it?"

"Eleven," Kermeff said lifelessly.

"Seven hours," Paul muttered. "Seven hours until daylight. They will soon be returning."

"They?"

"The others. The inhabitants. The awful—"

Paul's voice died. He twitched convulsively, as if a hand had been clapped across his mouth. But it was no hand; it was a sound—a sound that jangled down from far above, from the blackness beyond the cracked ceiling, seemingly from the very depths of the night; a mocking, muffled laugh that hung endlessly in the still air, like the vibrating twang of a loose violin string. Then silence, dead, stifling. And then, very suddenly, a thin scream of utter terror.

There was nothing else. The sound lived and died and was not reborn. Silence, as of the grave, possessed the room. Then, violently, Kermeff flung back his chair and lurched to his feet.

"What was that?"

No one answered him. Jeremy was without motion, gripping the table with huge hands. Allenby sat like a man dead, stark white, eyes horribly wide and ivory-hued. The lamp's flame gutted the dark. Paul said mechanically:

"Sit down."

"What was it?"

"I was wrong," Paul mumbled. "The inhabitants have not all left. One—at least one—is here still."

"That scream! It was a girl! A girl!"

"A girl," Paul said in a monotone. "A girl in a flame-colored wrap. But we can do nothing. It is too late. It was too late last night, when she came here. It is always too late, here."

"What do you mean?"

"Sit down, Kermeff."

Kermeff floundered into his chair and hunched there, quivering. Muttering aloud, he clawed at his throat and loosened his shirt collar. His hands slid down jerkily, fumbling with the buttons of his coat.

But Paul's hand, darting forward with incredible swiftness, closed over the man's wrists, holding them rigid.

"No, Kermeff."

"What?"

"Keep your coat buttoned, if you love life. Have you forgotten what we did at the hotel?"

Kermeff faced him without understanding. His hands unclenched and fell away.

"It is hot in here," he choked. "Too hot. I was going to—"

But another voice, soft and persuasive, interrupted him. Something scraped against the back of his chair. A long, deformed arm reached over his shoulder to place a tray with four glasses—thick greenish glasses, filled with brilliant carmine liquid—on the white cloth before him. And the voice, Murgunstrumm's voice, announced quietly:

"It be good wine. Very good wine. The meat'll be near ready, sirs."

Something snapped in Kermeff's brain. Perhaps it was the shock of that naked arm, gliding so unexpected before his face. Perhaps it was the sight of the red liquid, thick and sweet smelling and deep with color. Whatever it was, he swung about savagely and seized the cripple's arm in both hands.

"That scream!" he shouted luridly. "You heard it! What was it?"

"Scream?"

"You heard it! Don't deny it!"

The innkeeper's mouth writhed slowly into a smile, a significant, guarded smile. And his lips were wet and crimson—crimson with a liquid which had only recently passed through them.

"It was the night, sir," he said, bending forward a little. "Only the night, outside. These be lonely roads. No one comes or goes."

"You are lying! That sound came from upstairs!"

But Murgunstrumm released his arm from the clutching fingers and slid backward. He was grinning hideously. Without a word he retreated into the shadows of the doorway and vanished.

And Kermeff, turning again in his chair, sat quite without motion for more than a minute. He gazed at the glasses of red wine before him. Then, as if remembering something, he lifted both his hands, palms up, stared fixedly at them, and mumbled slowly, almost inaudibly:

"His arm—his arm was cold and flabby—cold like dead tissue. . . ."

## 8. The Winged Thing

MURGUNSTRUMM did not return. The four guests sat alone at their table, waiting. The room, with its pin points of groping, wavering, uncertain candle-light, was otherwise empty and very still. Paul, bending forward quietly, abnormally calm and self-contained now that the moment of action had arrived, said in a low voice:

"It is time to do what we came here to do."

Kermeff studied him intently, as if remembering all at once that they had come here for a reason. Allenby remained motionless, remembering other things more close at hand and more Tartarean. Matt Jeremy's fists knotted, eager to take something in their powerful grip and crush it.

"What do you mean?" Kermeff said warily.

"We must overpower him."

"But—"

"If I once get that filthy neck in my fingers," Jeremy flared, "I'll break it!"

"There are four of us," Paul said evenly. "We can handle him. Then, before the others return, we can explore this house from top to bottom."

"It won't take four, sir," Jeremy growled. "I'm just itchin' to show that dirty toad what two good human hands can do to him."

"Human hands?" It was Allenby interrupting in a cracked mumble. "Do you mean . . .?"

"I mean he ain't human, that's what! But when he comes back here, I'll—" Jeremy gulped a mouthful of red wine and laughed ominously in his throat—"I'll strangle him until he thinks he is!"

"Not when he first returns," Paul commanded sharply. "He suspects us already. He'll be on guard."

"Well, then—"

"Let him bring food. Then I'll ask him for—"

A sudden hissing sound came from Allenby's tight lips. Paul turned quickly. The door of the inner room had opened, and Murgunstrumm stood there, watching wolfishly, listening. He glared a moment, then vanished again. And presently, carrying a tray in his malformed hands, he limped into view again.

He said nothing as he lowered the tray to the table and slid the dishes onto the white cloth. Methodically he reached out with his long arms and placed four cracked plates in their proper positions. Knives and forks and spoons, black and lustreless, as if removed from some dark drawer for the first time in years, clinked dully as he pushed them before each of his guests. Then he stood back, his fists flat and bony on the cloth.

"It ain't often we have visitors here no more," he said curtly, looking from one face to another with intent eyes. "But the meat's fresh. Good and fresh. And I'll be askin' you to hurry with it. Near midnight it is, and I'm wantin' to be closin' up for the night."

Kermeff lifted his knife and touched the stuff on his plate. It was steak of some sort, red and rare in brown gravy. The vegetables piled about it were thick and sodden and obviously very old.

Paul said abruptly: "You're expecting visitors?"

"Huh?"

"You're expecting someone to come here?"

The innkeeper glared. His eyes seemed to draw together and become a single penetrating shaft of ochre-hued luminosity.

"No one comes here, I told you."

"Oh, I see. Well, we'll hurry and let you go to bed. Fetch some bread, will you?"

Murgunstrumm swept the table with his eyes. Mumbling, he limped away; and as he reached the doorway leading to the other room he turned and looked sharply back. Then he disappeared, and Paul said viciously, crowding over his plate:

"This time, Jeremy. As soon as he returns. If we fail—"

"Listen!"

There was a sound outside. The sound of a motor. It seeped into the room with a dull vibrant hum, growing louder. Out there in the road a car was approaching. Paul's hands clenched. If it were coming here—

He heard something else then. The shrill blast of a horn, just once. And then, from the inner room, Murgunstrumm came limping, one-two, one-two, one-two, with quick steps. He seized the lantern from its hook on the wall. He lit it and proceeded to the door, without a glance at the table.

Jeremy clutched the cloth spasmodically, ready to rise.

"No!" Paul cried in a whisper. "No! Not now!"

The door creaked open. Murgunstrumm scraped over the threshold. A breath of cold sweet air swept into the room, rustling the table cloth. The four men at the table sat quite still, silent, waiting.

There were voices outside, and the drone of the car's engine was suddenly still. Then footsteps crunched on the gravel walk and clicked on the stone flagging as they neared the door. An accusing, resentful voice, low yet audible, said thickly:

"That other car, Murgunstrumm? You have visitors?"

The innkeeper's reply was a whisper. Then, in a shrill feminine voice, lifted in mock horror, so typical of character that Paul could almost see the dainty eyebrows go up in assumed consternation:

"Goodness, what an odd hangout! I shan't stay here long. Why, I'd be thoroughly frightened to death."

Laughter—and then the door opened wider, revealing two figures very close together, and behind them the restive halo of Murgunstrumm's bobbing lantern.

The man was in evening clothes, straight, smiling, surveying the room with slightly narrowed eyes. Certainly he seemed out of place here, where every separate thing reeked of age and decay. Yet something about him was not so incongruous. His eyes glittered queerly, with a phosphorescent force that suggested ancient lust and wisdom. And his lips were thick, too thick, curled back in a sinister scowl as he peered suddenly at the four men at the table, and nodded. Then, whispering something to his companion, he moved toward the flickering candle-points in the misty gloom.

The woman was younger, perhaps twenty, perhaps less. A mere girl, Paul decided, watching her covertly. The sort of girl who would go anywhere in the spirit of reckless adventure, who ridiculed conventions and sought everlasting excitement, fearing nothing and conquering all doubts with ready laughter.

And she was lovely. Her gown was of deep restless black, trailing the crude floor as she moved into the shadows. Her white wrap—ermine, it must be—was a blob of dazzling brilliance in the well of semidarkness which leaped out to engulf her.

To a remote table near the wall they went together, and their conversation was merely a murmur, containing no audible words. They leaned there close to each other, their hands meeting between them. And Murgunstrumm, flat against the closed door with the lantern fuming in his dangling hand, followed their movements with eyes of abhorrent anticipation—sloe eyes that seemed to be no part of the man himself but separate twin orbs of malice.

Then it was that Jeremy, bending close over the table, said almost inaudibly:

"Shall I go for him, sir? Them others won't interfere."

"No," Paul said quickly. "Wait."

Jeremy subsided, muttering. His hands knotted and unclenched significantly. Then he stiffened, for Murgunstrumm was groping over the floor toward them, swinging the lantern. Stopping just behind Paul's chair, the proprietor blinked sullenly into each man's face, and said harshly, nervously:

"Ye'll have to go."

"But we've only just been served. We haven't had time to—"

"Ye'll have to go. Now."

"Look here," Paul said impatiently. "We're not bothering your guests. We're. . . ."

He stopped. Gazing at Murgunstrumm, he saw something in the far part of the room that caused the words to die on his lips and made him recoil involuntarily. His hands gripped the table. Murgunstrumm, seeing the sudden intentness of his gaze, turned slowly and peered in the same direction.

There in the near darkness a door had opened noiselessly. It hung open now, and the threshold was filled with a silent, erect human figure. Even as the four men at the table watched it fearfully, the figure moved out of the aperture and advanced with slow, mechanical steps.

The man was in black and white, the contrasting black and white of evening attire. But there was nothing immaculate about him. His hair was rumpled, crawling crudely about his flat forehead. His chalk-colored face was a mask, fixed and expressionless. He walked with the exaggerated stride of a man seeped, saturated with liquor. His eyes were wide open, gleaming. His lips were wet and red.

And there was something else, visible in ghastly detail as the lantern light fell upon it. A stain marred the crumpled whiteness of his stiff shirt-front—a fresh glistening stain of bright scarlet, which was blood.

He stood quite still, staring. For an instant there was no other movement in the room. Then, mumbling throaty words, Murgunstrumm placed the lantern on the table and cautiously advanced to meet him.

And then Paul and the others heard words—guarded, strangely vague words that for all their lack of meaning were nevertheless hideously suggestive, significant and, to Paul, who alone understood them, the ultimate of horror.

"You have finished?" Murgunstrumm demanded eagerly.

The other nodded heavily, searching the cripple's face with his eyes.

"I am finished. It is your turn now."

Trembling violently, Murgunstrumm reached out an unsteady hand to claw the man's arm.

"Now?" he cried hungrily, sucking his lips. "I can go now?"

"In a moment. First I would talk to you. These strangers here. . . ."

But Paul heard no more. The table quivered under his hands and lurched suddenly into him, hurling him backward. A harsh, growling cry came from the other side of it; and then, all at once, someone was racing to the door. It was Allenby, utterly unnerved by what he had just seen, and seeking desperately to escape.

And he was quick, amazingly quick. The door clattered back on its hinges before any other inmate of the room moved. Arms outflung, Allenby clawed his way through the aperture, shouting incoherently. And then Paul was on his feet, lurching forward.

"Stay here!" he cried to Jeremy, who would have followed him. "Hold Kermeff!"

The threshold was empty when he reached it. He stopped, bewildered by the vast darkness before him. Vaguely he saw that Murgunstrumm and the creature in black and white, standing in the middle of the room, were quite motionless, watching every move. Then he stumbled over the sill, into the gloom of the path.

Nothing moved. The clearing was a silent black expanse of shadow, flat and empty under its pall of decayed atmosphere. The air was cold, pungent, sweeping into Paul's face as he swayed there. High above, feeble stars were visible.

Blindly Paul ran down the driveway, staring on either side. He stopped again, muttering. There was no movement anywhere, no sign of the man who had fled. Nothing but night and cold darkness. And a low-hanging winding-sheet of shallow vapor, swirling lazily between earth and heaven.

But Allenby had to be found. If he escaped and got back to the Rehobeth Hotel, he would use Henry Gates' phone to summon help. He would call the police at Marssen. He would lead a searching party here. And then everything that mattered would be over. The madhouse again. And Ruth would never be released from the asylum at Morrisdale.

Savagely Paul slashed on through the deep grass, moving farther and farther from the open door of the inn. Allenby had not reached the road; that was certain. He was hiding, waiting for an opportunity to creep away unobserved.

Paul's lips whitened. He glanced toward the car. The car—that was it. The key was still in the lock. Allenby knew it was. Paul stood stock still, watching. Then, smiling grimly, he deliberately turned his back and moved in the opposite direction.

Without hesitating, he blundered on, as if searching the reeds for a prone figure which might be lying there. A long moment dragged by, and another. There was no sound.

And then it came. A scurrying of feet on the gravel walk, as a crouching figure darted from the shadows under the very wall of the house. An instant of scraping, scuttling desperation, as the man flung himself across that narrow stretch of intervening space. Then a sharp thud, as the car door was flung back.

Paul whirled. Like a hound he leaped forward, racing toward the road. The motor roared violently, just ahead of him. The car door was still open. Allenby was hunched over the wheel, struggling with the unfamiliar instruments.

And he was fiendishly quick, even then. Too quick. The

car jerked forward, bounding over the uneven surface. Like a great black beast it swept past the man who ran toward it, even as he reached the edge of the road. Then, with a triumphant roar, it was clear.

Clear! Paul stumbled to a stop. A dry moan came from his lips as his prey screamed beyond reach. He stood helpless—for a fraction of an instant.

Then, out of his pocket, his revolver leaped into his fist. He spun about. Twin spurts of flame burned toward the fleeing shape which was already careening from side to side in wild sweeps. There was an explosion, sharp and bellowing. The car lurched drunkenly, whirled sideways. Brakes screeched. Like a blundering mastodon the machine shot into the deep grass as the bursting tire threw it out of Allenby's feeble control.

And Paul was running again. He was beside the groaning shape before the driver could get out from behind the wheel. The revolver dug viciously into Allenby's ribs.

"Get out!"

Allenby hesitated, then obeyed, trembling.

"I—I won't go back there!"

The gun pressed deeper. Allenby stared suddenly into Paul's face. What he saw there made him shudder. He stood quite still. Then, pushing the revolver away nervously, he mumbled.

"You—you are not as mad as I thought."

"You should have known that before you tried to get away."

"Perhaps I should have."

"You're going back with me."

Allenby's voice trembled. "I have no alternative?"

"None."

With a shrug of defeat, the physician walked very quietly, very slowly, back toward the house.

The Gray Toad Inn had not changed. At one table Kermeff sat stiff and silent, under Jeremy's cold scrutiny. In the corner, among the shadows, sat the girl of the ermine wrap with her escort, only vaguely interested in what had happened.

Murgunstrumm still stood in the center of the floor, staring. The creature who had come, only a few moments before, from the bowels of the house, now sat alone at a nearby table. He glanced up as the door closed behind Paul and the physician. Then he looked down again, indifferently. And then, eagerly, Murgunstrumm approached him.

"Can I go now?" the cripple demanded.

"Yes. Get out."

Murgunstrumm rubbed thick hands together in anticipation. Breathing harshly, noisily, he wheeled about and limped quickly back to the table where his four guests were once again sitting quietly. His mouth was moving as he swept the lantern away and turned again.

He had forgotten, now, the presence of his undesirable guests. He did not look at them. His eyes, stark with want, were visioning something else—something he had waited for for hours. And he was trembling, as if in the grip of fever, as he started toward the door where the strange gentleman had first appeared.

But he did not reach it. Before he had covered half the intervening distance he stopped very abruptly and wheeled with a snarl of impatience, glaring at one of the covered windows. He stood rigid, listening.

Whatever he heard, it was a sound so inaudible and slight that only his own ears, attuned to it by long habit, caught its vibrations. The men at the table, turning jerkily to peer in the same direction, at the same window, saw nothing, heard nothing. But Murgunstrumm was scraping hurriedly toward the aperture, swinging his lantern resentfully.

He twisted the shade noisily. As it careened up, exposing the bleak oblong of unclean glass, the lantern light fell squarely upon the opening, revealing a fluttering shape outside. More than that the watching men did not discover, for the innkeeper's hands clawed at the window latch and heaved the barrier up quickly.

It was a winged thing that swooped through the opening into the room. The same hairy obscene creature that had whispered to Murgunstrumm, more than an hour ago, to admit the four unsuspecting guests! Rushing through the aperture now, it flopped erratically about the lantern, then darted to the ceiling and momentarily hung there, as if eyeing the occupants of the inn with satisfaction. Murgunstrumm closed the window hurriedly and drew the shade again. And the bat—for bat it was—dropped suddenly, plummet-like, to the table where sat the man who had recently come from the inner rooms.

It happened very quickly. At one moment, as Paul and his companions gazed in sudden dread, the winged thing was fluttering blindly about the ghastly white face of the man who sat there. Next moment there was no winged thing. It had vanished utterly, disintegrated into nothingness; and there at the table, instead of a solitary red-lipped man in evening clothes, sat two men. Two men strangely alike, similarly dressed, with the same colorless masks of faces.

They spoke in whispers for a moment, then turned, both of them, to glance at the four men near them. And one—the one who had appeared from the mysterious internals of the inn—said casually:

"We have visitors to-night, eh, Costillan?"

The answer was a triumphant gloating voice, obviously meant to be overheard.

"Ay, and why not? They were coming here as I was leaving. Our fool of an innkeeper would have refused them admission."

"So? But he was afraid. He is always afraid that he will one day be discovered. We must cure that, Costillan. Even now he has told your guests to leave."

The man called Costillan—he who had an instant before been something more than a man—turned sharply in his chair. Paul, staring at him mutely, saw a face suddenly distorted with passion. And the man's voice, flung suddenly into the silence, was vibrant with anger.

"Murgunstrumm!"

Hesitantly, furtively, the cripple limped toward him.

"What—what is it, sir?"

"You would have allowed our guests to depart, my pretty?"

"I—I was—"

"Afraid they would learn things, eh?" The man's fingers closed savagely over Murgunstrumm's wrist. He made no attempt to guard his voice. Obviously he held only contempt for the men who were listening. "Have we not promised you protection?"

"Yes, but—"

"But you would have let them leave! Did I not order you to keep them here? Did I not whisper to you that I might return—hungry?"

Murgunstrumm licked his lips, cringing. And suddenly, with a snarl, the creature flung him back.

"Go down to your foul den and stay there!"

At that Murgunstrumm scuttled away.

No sound came from Paul's lips. He sat without stirring, fascinated and afraid. And then a hand closed over his arm, and Jeremy's voice said thickly, harshly:

"I'm goin' to get out of here. This place ain't human!"

Paul clutched at the fingers and held them. Escape was impossible; he knew that. It meant death, now. But he had only two hands: he could not also hold Kermeff and the physician's terrified companion. Lurching to his feet, Kermeff snarled viciously:

"If we stay here another instant, those fiends will—"

"You cannot leave," Paul countered dully.

"We shall see!" And Kermeff kicked back his chair violently as he reeled away from the table. Allenby, rising after him, clung very close.

A revolver lay in Paul's pocket. His hand slid down and closed over it, then relaxed. Jeremy, frowning into his face, muttered thickly. The two physicians stumbled toward the door.

Sensing what was coming, Paul sat quite still and peered at the nearby table. The two men in evening attire had stopped talking. They were watching with hungry, triumphant eyes. They followed every movement as Kermeff and Allenby groped to the door. And then, silent as shadows, they rose from the table.

The two fleeing men saw them each at the same instant.

Both stood suddenly still. Kermeff's face lost every trace of color, even in the yellow hue of the lamp. Allenby cried aloud and trembled violently. The two creatures advanced with slow, deliberate steps, gliding steps, from such an angle that retreat to the door was cut off.

And then, abruptly, Paul saw something else, something infinitely more horrible.

The remaining two inhabitants of this place of evil—the man and woman who had entered together but a short time ago—were rising silently from their table near the wall. The man's face, swathed in the glow of the candlelight beneath it, was a thing of triumph, smiling hideously. The girl—the girl in the white ermine wrap—stood facing him like one in the grip of deep sleep. No expression marred her features; no light glowed in her eyes.

The candle flame flickered on the table between them. The man spoke. Spoke softly, persuasively, as one speaks to a mindless hypnotic. And then, taking her arm, he led her very quietly toward the door through which Murgunstrumm had vanished.

And, as on that other occasion when he had lain in the deep grass of the clearing outside, Paul's mind broke with sudden madness.

"No, no!" he shrieked. "Don't go with him!"

He rushed forward blindly, tumbling a chair out of his path. At the other end of the room, the creature turned to look at him, and laughed softly. And then the man and the girl were gone. The door swung silently shut. A lock clicked. Even as Paul's hands seized the knob, a vibrant laugh echoed through the heavy panels. And the door was fast.

Savagely Paul turned.

"Jeremy! Jeremy, help me! We can't let her go—"

The cry choked on his lips. Across the room, Jeremy was standing transfixed, staring. Kermeff and Allenby huddled together, rigid with fear. And the two macabre demons in evening clothes were advancing with arms outthrust.

## 9. A Strange Procession

THEY WERE no longer men. Like twin vultures they slunk forward, an unholy metamorphosis already taking place in their appearance. A misty bluish haze enveloped them, originating it seemed from the very pores of their obscene bodies, growing thicker and deeper until it was in itself a thing of motion, writhing about them like heavy opaque fog moved by an unseen breeze. More and more pungent it grew, until only a single feature of those original loathsome forms was visible—until only *eyes* glowed through it.

Kermeff and Allenby retreated before those eyes in stark terror. They were stabbing pits of swirling green flame, deep beyond human knowledge of depth, ghastly wide, hungry. They came on relentlessly, two separate awful pairs of them, glittering through dimly human shapes of sluggish, evil-smelling vapor.

As they came, those twin shapes of abomination, uncouth hands extended before them. Misty, distorted fingers curled forth to grope toward the two cringing victims. Allenby and Kermeff fell away from them like men already dead: Kermeff stiff, mechanical, frozen to a fear-wracked carcass of robotlike motion; Allenby mumbling, ghastly gray with terror.

Back, step by step, the two physicians retreated, until at last the wall pressed into their bodies, ending their flight. And still the twin forms of malevolence came on, vibrant with evil.

Not until then did reason return to the remaining two men in the room. Jeremy flung himself forward so violently that his careening hips sent the table skidding sideways with a clink of jumping china. Paul, rushing past him, flung out a rasping command.

"The cross! The cross under your coats!"

Perhaps it was the stark torment of the words, perhaps the very sound of his voice, as shrill as cutting steel. Something, at any rate, penetrated the fear that held Kermeff and Allenby helpless. Something drove into Kermeff's brain and gave him life, movement, power of thought. The physician's big hands clawed up and ripped down again. And there, gleaming white and livid on his chest hung the cross-shaped strips of cloth which Paul had sewn there.

Its effect was instantaneous. The advancing shapes of repugnance became suddenly quite still, then recoiled as if the cross were a thing of flame searing into them. Kermeff shouted luridly, madly. He stumbled a step forward, ripping his coat still farther apart. The shapes retreated with uncanny quickness, avoiding him.

But the eyes were pools of absolute hate. They drilled deep into Kermeff's soul, stopping him. He could not face them. And as he stood there, flat-pressed against the wall, the uncouth fiends before him began once again to assume their former shape. The bluish haze thinned. Outlines of black, blurred with the white of shirt-fronts, glowed through the swirling vapor. When Paul looked again the shapes were men: and the men stood close together, eyeing Kermeff and Allenby—and the cross—with desperate diabolical eyes.

Suddenly one of them, the one called Costillan, moved away. Swiftly he walked across the floor—was it walking or floating or some unearthly condition halfway between?—and vanished through the doorway which led to the mysterious rear rooms. The other, retreating slowly to the outside door, flattened there with both arms outflung, batlike, and waited, glaring with bottomless green orbs at the four men who confronted him.

And then Paul moved. Shrill words leaped to his lips: "That girl—we've got to get to her before—"

But the cry was drowned in another voice, Jeremy's. Stumbling erect, Jeremy said hoarsely:

"Come on. I'm gettin' out of here."

"Look out! You can't—"

But Jeremy was already across the intervening space, confronting the creature who barred the barrier.

"Get out of the way!" he bellowed. "I've had enough of this."

There was no answer. The vulture simply stood there, smiling a little in anticipation. And suddenly, viciously, a revolver leaped into Jeremy's fist.

"Get out of the way!"

The creature laughed. His boring eyes fixed themselves in Jeremy's face. They deepened in color, became luminous, virulent, flaming again. And Jeremy, staggering from the force of them, reeled backward.

"I'll kill you!" he screeched. "I'll—"

He lost control. Panic-stricken, he flung up the revolver and pulled the trigger again and again. The room trembled with the roar of the reports. And then the gun hung limp in Jeremy's fingers. He stood quite still, licking his lips, staring. Amazed, he stepped backward into the table, upsetting a glass of red liquid over the white cloth.

For the man in evening clothes, despite the bullets which had burned through him, still stood motionless against the closed door, and still laughed with that leering, abhorrent expression of triumph.

There was silence after that for many minutes, broken finally by the familiar *shf-shf-shf* of limping feet. Into the room, glaring from one still form to another, came Murgunstrumm, and behind him the companion of the undead fiend at the door.

Costillan pointed with a long thin arm at Kermeff, and at the white cross which hung on the physician's breast.

"Remove it," he said simply.

Murgunstrumm's lips curled. His huge hands lifted, as if only too eager to make contact with the cross and the human flesh beneath it. Slowly, malignantly, he advanced upon Kermeff's still form, arms outstretched, mouth twisted back over protruding teeth. And the mouth was fresh with blood—blood which had not come from the cripple's own lips.

But Paul was before him, and a revolver lay in Paul's fingers. The muzzle of the gun pointed squarely into the innkeeper's face.

"Stand back," Paul ordered curtly.

Murgunstrumm hesitated. He took another step forward.

"Back! Do you want to die?"

Fear showed in the cripple's features. He came no closer. And a thin breath of relief sobbed from Paul's lips as he realized the truth. He had not known, had not been sure, whether Murgunstrumm was a member of the ghoulish clan that inhabited this place, or was a mere servant, a mere confederate.

"Jeremy," Paul's voice was level again with resolution.

"What—what do you want, sir?"

"Lock every window and door in this room except the one behind me."

"But, sir—"

"Do as I say! We've got to find that girl before any harm comes to her—if it's not already too late. When you've locked the exits, take—You have a pencil?"

Jeremy groped in his pockets, frowning. Fumbling with what he drew out, he said falteringly:

"I've a square of chalk, sir. It's only cue chalk, from the master's billiard room."

"Good. When you've locked the doors and windows, make a cross on each one as clear and sharp as you can. Quickly!"

Jeremy stared, then moved away. The other occupants of the room watched him furtively. Only one moved—Costillan. And Costillan, snarling with sudden vehemence, stepped furtively to the door and flattened there.

One by one Jeremy secured the windows and marked them with a greenish cross, including the locked door in the farther shadows, through which the girl in the white wrap had vanished. When he turned at last to the final barrier, which led to the gravel walk outside, his way was blocked by the threatening shape which clung there, glowering at him, waiting for him to come within reach.

"One side," Jeremy blurted. "One side or I'll—"

"Not that way!" Paul cried sharply. "The cross on your chest, man. Show it."

Jeremy faltered, then laughed grimly. Deliberately he unbuttoned his jacket and advanced. The creature's eyes widened, glowing most strangely. Unflinching, Jeremy strode straight toward them.

Just once, as if fighting back an unconquerable dread, Costillan lifted his arms to strike. Then, cringing, he slunk sideways. And at the same moment, seeing the barrier unguarded, Kermeff lurched forward.

"I'm getting out of here!"

"You're staying, Kermeff."

The physician jerked around, glaring. Paul's revolver shifted very slightly away from Murgunstrumm's tense body to include Kermeff in its range of control. Kermeff's forehead contracted with hate.

"I tell you I won't stay!"

But he made no attempt to reach the door, and Paul said evenly to Jeremy:

"Lock it."

Jeremy locked it and made the sign of the cross. And then Paul's finger curled tighter on the trigger of the gun. The muzzle was still on a line with Murgunstrumm's cowering carcass. Paul said roughly:

"Allenby!"

"Yes?"

"You are remaining here, to make sure nothing attempts to enter from outside. Do you understand? And if the girl in the white wrap comes back through that door"—Paul pointed quickly to the locked barrier which had baffled him only an instant before—"or if that fiend comes back alone, lock the door on this side and keep the key!"

"I can't stay here alone!"

"Nothing will harm you, man. Keep your coat open, or strip it off. They can't come near the cross. Sit at the table and don't move. We're going."

"You're going? Where?" Allenby croaked.

"To find that girl, you fool! And you"—Paul glared into Murgunstrumm's bloated face—"are going to lead us."

A bestial growl issued from the innkeeper's lips. He fell back, rumbling. But the revolver followed him and menaced him with dire meaning, and he thought better of his refusal. Silently he scuffed backward toward the inner door.

"For your life, Allenby," Paul snapped, "don't lose your head and try to escape." He took the chalk from Jeremy's hand and dropped it on the table. "As soon as we've passed through this door, mark it with the sign of the cross, then stay here on pain of death. You're safe here, and with the door sanctified, and locked on the outside, these—these blood-hungry ghouls cannot escape. Do you hear?"

"I'll stay," Allenby muttered. "For the love of Heaven, come back soon. And—and give me a gun!"

"A gun is no good to you."

"But if I've got to stay here alone, I—"

Paul glared at the man suspiciously. But there was no sign of treachery in Allenby's white face. No sign that he perhaps wanted the revolver for another reason, to use on the men who had brought him here. And a gun might really prove valuable. It would give the man courage, at any rate.

But Paul took no chances. "Put your revolver on the table, Jeremy," he said curtly. "If you touch it before we're out of this room, Allenby, I'll shoot you. Do you understand?"

"I—I only want it for protection, I tell you!"

Jeremy slid the weapon within reach of the man's hand. Allenby stood stiff, staring at it. And then Paul's revolver pressed again into the thick flabbiness of Murgunstrumm's shrunken body, forcing the cripple over the threshold.

"Take the lantern, Jeremy."

The door closed then, shutting out the last view of the chamber—the last view of two thwarted demons in evening clothes, standing motionless, staring; and Allenby, close to the table, reaching for the revolver and flinging back his coat at the same time, to expose the stern white mark of protection on his chest.

The lantern sputtered eerily in Jeremy's hand. He turned, locked the door carefully, removed the key. Murgunstrumm watched silently.

"Now." Paul's weapon dug viciously into the cripple's abdomen. "Where is she? Quickly!"

"I—I ain't sure where they went. Maybe—"

"You know!"

"I tell you they might've gone anywhere. I ain't never sure."

"Then you'll show us every last room and corner of this devilish house until we find her. Cellar and all."

"Cellar?" The repeated word was a quick, passionate whisper. "No, no, there be no cellar here!"

"And if you try any tricks, I'll kill you."

It was a strange procession filing silently through the musty rooms and corridors of the ancient structure. Murgunstrumm, a contorted, malformed monkey swathed in dancing lantern light, led the way with limping steps, scraping resentfully over the bare floors. Very close behind him strode Paul, leveled revolver ready to cut short any move the man might make to escape or turn on his captors. Jeremy came next, huge and silent; and last of all, Kermeff, in whom all thought of rebellion had seemingly been replaced by deepening dread and his acute realization that here were things beyond the minds of men.

Room after room they hurried through—empty, dead rooms, with all windows locked and curtained, and every shutter closed. In one, obviously the kitchen, an oil stove was still warm and a large platter of fresh meat lay on the unclean table.

Room after room. Empty, all of them, of life and laughter. In some stood beds, stripped to bare springs; bare tables; chairs coated with dust. Like cells of a sunken dungeon the chambers extended deeper and deeper into the bowels of the house. From one to another the strange procession moved, eating its anxious way with the clutching glare of the lantern.

"There is nothing here," Kermeff said at last, scowling impatiently. "We are fools to go farther."

"There is something, somewhere."

Murgunstrumm, leering crookedly, said:

"They might've gone outdoors. I ain't never sure where."

"We have not yet explored upstairs."

"Huh?"

"Or down."

"Down? No, no! There be no downstairs! I told you—"

"We'll see. Here; here's something." Paul stopped as the advancing lantern rays touched a flight of black stairs winding up into complete darkness. "Lead on, Murgunstrumm. No tricks."

Murgunstrumm scuffed to the bottom of the steps and moved up with maddening slowness, gripping the rail. And suddenly, then, the man behind him hesitated. A single word, "Listen!" whispered softly through Paul's lips.

"What is it?" Kermeff said thickly.

"I heard—"

"No, no!" Murgunstrumm's cry was vibrant with fear. "There be no one up here!"

"Be still!"

The cracked voice subsided gutturally. Another sound was audible above it. A strange nameless sound, vaguely akin to the noise of sucking lips or the hiss of gusty air through a narrow tube. A grotesque sound, half human, half bestial.

"An animal," Kermeff declared in a low voice. "An animal of some sort, feeding—"

But Paul's shrill voice interrupted.

"Up, Murgunstrumm! Up quickly!"

"There be nothin', I tell you!"

"Be quiet!"

The cripple advanced again, moving reluctantly, as if some inner bonds held him back. His face was convulsed. He climbed morosely, slowly hesitatingly before each step. And his move, when it came, was utterly unexpected.

He whirled abruptly, confronting his captors. Luridly he cried out, so that his voice carried into every corner of the landing above:

"I tell you there be no one! I tell you—"

Paul's hand clapped savagely over his mouth, crushing the outcry into a gurgling hiss. Jeremy and Kermeff stood taut, dismayed. Then Paul's gun rammed into the cripple's back, prodding him on. No mistaking the meaning of that grim muzzle. One more sound would bring a bullet.

Groping again, Murgunstrumm at last reached the end of the climb, where the railing twisted sharply back on itself and the upper landing lay straight and level and empty before him. The sucking sounds had ceased. The corridor lay in absolute uncanny silence, nerve-wracking and repelling.

"That noise," Paul said curtly, "came from one of these rooms. We've got to locate it."

"What—what was it?"

There was no answer. The reply in Paul's mind could not be uttered aloud. Kermeff did not know, and the truth would make a gibbering idiot of him. Kermeff, for all his medical knowledge, was an ignorant blind fool in matters macabre.

And another array of gloomy rooms extended before them, waiting to be examined. With Murgunstrumm probing the way, the four men stole forward and visited each chamber, one after another. There was nothing. These rooms were like those below, abandoned, sinister with memories of long-dead laughter, dust-choked, broodingly still.

"Something," Kermeff gasped suddenly, "is watching us. I can feel it!"

The others glanced at him, and Jeremy forced a dry laugh. Half the corridor lay behind them; the remaining doors stretched ahead beyond the restless circle of light. Paul muttered fretfully and pushed the innkeeper before him over the next threshold. His companions blundered close behind. The lantern light flooded the chamber, disclosing a blackened window and yellowish time-scarred walls. A four-poster bed stood against the wall, covered with mattress and crumpled blanket.

And Paul, too, as he bent over the bed examining the peculiar brownish stains there, felt eyes upon him. He whirled about bitterly, facing the doorway—and stood as if a hand of ice had suddenly gripped his throat, forcing a frosty breath from his open mouth.

A man stood there, garbed meticulously in black evening clothes, smiling vindictively. He was the same creature who earlier in the evening had escorted the girl in the white ermine wrap into the inn. The same, but somehow different; for the man's eyes were glowing now with that hellish green light, and his lips were full, thick and very red.

He said nothing. His gaze passed from Paul's colorless face to Murgunstrumm's, and the cripple answered it with a triumphant step forward. Kermeff shrank back until the bed post crushed into his back and held him rigid. Jeremy crouched, waiting. The creature stirred slightly and advanced.

But Paul did not wait. He dared not. In one move he wrenched his coat open, baring the white sign beneath, and staggered forward. The intruder hesitated. The green eyes contracted desperately to slits of fire. The face writhed into a mask of hate. Violently the man spun back, recoiling with arms upflung. And the doorway, all at once, was empty.

For an instant Paul was limp, overcome. Then he was across the threshold, lurching into the hall in time to see a shape—a tawny, four-legged shape, wolfish in contour—race down the corridor and bound into darkness, to land soundlessly upon the stairs and vanish into lower gloom.

There was nothing else. Nothing but Kermeff, dragging at his arm and saying violently:

"He'll overpower Allenby downstairs!"

"Allenby's safe," Paul said dully, mechanically. "He has the cross."

He remembered the revolver in his hand and raised it quickly, swinging back to face Murgunstrumm. But the cripple was helpless, held in Jeremy's big hands, in the doorway.

And so they continued their investigation, and at the end of the long passageway, in the final room of all, found what Paul in the bottom of his heart had expected. There, on the white sheets of an enameled bed, lay the lady of the ermine wrap, arms outflung, head lolling over the side, lifeless hair trailing the floor.

Murgunstrumm, seeing her there, rushed forward to stand above her, glaring down, working his lips, muttering incoherent words. He would have dropped to his knees beside her, clawing at her fiendishly, had not Jeremy flung him back.

For she was dead. Kermeff, bending above her, announced that without hesitation. Her gown had been torn at the breast, exposing soft flesh as delicately white as fine-grained gypsum. An ethereal smile of bewilderment marred her lips. And upon her throat, vivid in the ochre glare of the lantern, were two blots of blood, two cruel incisions in the jugular vein.

Paul stepped back mutely, turning away. He waited at the door until Kermeff, examining the marks, stood up at last and came to him.

"I don't understand," the physician was saying stiffly. "Such marks—I have never encountered them before."

"The marks of the vampire," Paul muttered.

"What?"

"You wouldn't understand, Kermeff." And then Paul seized the man's arm abruptly, jerking him around. "Listen to me, Kermeff. I didn't force you to come to this horrible place for revenge. I only wanted to prove to you that I'm not mad. But we've got to destroy these fiends. It doesn't matter why we came here. We've got to make sure no one else ever comes. Do you understand?"

Kermeff hesitated, biting his lips nervously. Then he stiffened.

"Whatever you say," he said thickly, "I will do."

Paul swung about then, and called quickly to Jeremy. And Jeremy, looking up from the limp figure on the bed, had to drag Murgunstrumm with him in order to make the innkeeper move away. A fantastic hunger gleamed in Murgunstrumm's sunken eyes. His hands twitched convulsively. He peered back and continued to peer back until Jeremy shoved him roughly over the threshold and kicked the door shut.

"Lead the way, Murgunstrumm," Paul snapped. "We have not yet seen the cellars."

The cripple's lips twisted open.

"No, no! There be no cellars. I have told you—"

"Lead the way!"

## **10.** A Girl's Voice

THE CELLARS of the Gray Toad Inn were sunken pits of gloom and silence, deep below the last level of rotted timbers and plastered walls. From the obscurity of the lower corridor a flight of wooden steps plunged sharply into nothingness; and Murgunstrumm, groping down them, was forced to bend almost double lest a low-hanging beam crush his great malformed head.

No amount of prodding or whispered threats could induce the captured innkeeper to hurry. He probed each step with his clublike feet before descending. And there was that in his eyes, in the whole convulsed mask of his features, which spoke of virulent dread. The revolver in Paul's hand did not for an instant relax its vigil.

Like a trapped beast, lips moving soundlessly and huge hands twisting at his sides, the cripple reached the bottom and crouched, there against the damp wall, while his captors crowded about him, peering into surrounding darkness.

"Well," Paul said curtly, "what are you waiting for?"

A mutter was Murgunstrumm's only response. Sluggishly he felt his way; and the lantern light, hovering over him, revealed erratic lines of footprints, old and new, in the thick dust of the stone floor. Footprints, all of them, which harmonized with the shape and size of the cripple's own feet. He alone had visited these pits, or else the other visitors had left no marks! And the signs in the dust led deeper and deeper into a labyrinth of impossible gloom, luring the intruders onward.

And here, presently, as in the central square of some medieval, subterranean city, the floor was crossed and recrossed with many lines of footprints, and chambers gaped on all sides, chambers small and square, with irregular walls of stone and high ceilings of beams and plaster.

Broken chairs, tables, choked every corner, for these rooms had been used, in the years when the house above had been a place of merrymaking and laughter, as storage vaults. Now they were vaults of decay and impregnable gloom. Spiderwebs dangled in every dark corner; and the spiders themselves, brown and bloated and asleep, were the only living inhabitants.

And with each successive chamber Murgunstrumm's features contracted more noticeably to a mask of animal fear. Not fear of the revolver, but the dread of a caged beast that something dear to him—food, perhaps, or some object upon which he loved to feast his eyes—would be taken from him. As he approached a certain doorway, at last, he drew back, muttering.

"There be nothing more. I have told you there be nothing here."

Only the pressure of the revolver forced him on, and he seemed to shrivel into himself with apprehension as he clawed through the aperture and the lantern light revealed the chamber's contents.

There was a reason for his reluctance. The room was large enough to have been at one time two separate enclosures, made into a whole by the removal of the partition. And it was a display gallery of horrible possessions. The three men who entered behind Murgunstrumm, keeping close together, stood as if transfixed, while utter awe and abhorrence welled over them.

It was a vault, choked with things white and gleaming. Things moldy with the death that clung to them. And there was no sound, no intruding breeze to rustle the huge shapeless heap. It was death and mockery flung together in horror. And the men who looked upon it were for an interminable moment stricken mute with the fiendishness of it.

Then at last Kermeff stepped forward and cried involuntarily:

"Horrible! It is too horrible!"

Jeremy, turning in a slow circle, began to mumble to himself, as if clutching eagerly at something sane, something ordinary, to kill the throbbing of his heart.

"Bones! God, sir, it looks like a slaughterhouse!"

The lantern in Paul's hand was trembling violently, casting jiggling shadows over the array, throwing laughter and hate and passion into gaping faces which would never again, in reality, assume any expression other than the sunken empty glare of death. And Murgunstrumm was in the center of the floor, huddled into himself like a thing without shape. And Kermeff was pacing slowly about, inspecting the stack of disjointed things around him, poking at them professionally and scowling to himself.

"Women, all of them," he announced gutturally. "Young women. Impossible to estimate the number—"

"Let's get out of here!" Jeremy snarled.

Kermeff turned, nodded. And so, jerking Murgunstrumm's shoulder, Paul forced the cripple once again to lead the way. And the inspection continued.

Other chambers revealed nothing. The horror was not repeated. As the procession moved from doorway to doorway, Jeremy said bitterly, touching Paul's arm:

"Why don't you ask him what those things are, sir? He knows."

"I know, too," Paul said heavily.

Jeremy stared at him. The big man fell back, then, as Murgunstrumm, taking advantage of their lack of attention, attempted to scuff past a certain doorway without entering. Fresh footprints led into that particular aperture. And Kermeff was alert. Ignoring the cripple, Kermeff strode into the chamber alone, and suddenly cried aloud in a cracked voice.

There, upon a table, lay a thing infinitely more horrible than any heap of decayed human bones. Murgunstrumm, forced into the room by Paul, strove with a sharp cry to fall back from it, until he was caught up in Jeremy's arms and hurled forward again. And the three intruders stood mute, staring.

A sheet of canvas, ancient and very dirty, partly covered what lay there. A long, bone-handled knife was stuck upright beside it, in the table.

The operation, if such a fiendish process could be so termed, was half completed. Kermeff, faltering to the table, lifted the blanket halfway and let it drop again with a convulsive twitch. Jeremy looked only once. Then, twisting with insane rage, he seized Murgunstrumm's throat in his big hands.

"You did this!" he thundered. "You came down here when that rat came up and told you—told you he was finished. You came down here and—"

"Jeremy." Paul's voice was mechanical, lifeless. "Do you recognize her?"

Jeremy stiffened and looked again. And then a glint of mingled rage and horror and pity came into his eyes. He released the cripple abruptly and stood quite still.

"It's—it's the girl who came in here last night, sir!" he whispered hoarsely. "When you and I was outside alone, in the grass, watchin'—"

"God in Heaven!" Kermeff cried suddenly, reached up with both hands.

Paul had had enough. He swung about to grope to the door, and froze like a paralytic in his tracks.

There in the doorway a revolver was leveled at him in the hands of a leering creature in evening clothes. The revolver was Allenby's; and the man behind it, Costillan, was standing very still, very straight, with parted lips and penetrating eyes that were hypnotic.

Paul acted blindly, desperately, without thinking. Flinging up his own gun, he fired. An answering burst of flame roared in his face. Something razor-sharp and hot lashed into his shoulder, tearing the flesh. He stumbled back, falling across the table where lay that mutilated body. The gun slipped from his fingers; and the creature in the doorway was still there, still smiling, unharmed.

It was Jeremy who leaped for the fallen gun, and Murgunstrumm who fell upon it with the agility of a snake. The man in evening clothes, advancing very slowly, pointed his own weapon squarely at Jeremy's threatening face and said distinctly:

"Back, or you will taste death."

Then Murgunstrumm was up, to his knees, to his feet, clutching the retrieved gun in quivering fingers. Like an ape he stood there, peering first into the stark white faces of Paul's companions, then into the drilling eyes of his master. And Paul, at the same instant, staggered erect and stood swaying, clutching at his shoulder where blood was beginning to seep through the coat.

At sight of the blood, the creature's eyes widened hungrily. He glided forward, lips wide. Then he stopped, as if realizing what he had forgotten. To Murgunstrumm he said harshly:

"Remove that—that abomination! Tear down the cross and rip it to shreds!"

And Murgunstrumm did so. Protected by the menacing revolver in Costillan's hand, and the gun in his own fist, he tore the white cross from Paul's chest and ripped it apart. To Kermeff and Jeremy he did the same. And when he had finished, when the rags lay limp at his feet, the creature in black and white said, smiling:

"Upstairs it will be more pleasant. Come, my friends. This is Murgunstrumm's abbatoir, unfit for the business of fastidious men. Come."

Outside, two more of the macabre demons were waiting. They came close as the three victims filed out of the chamber. One of them was the man who had fled from the upper room where lay that other half-naked body with twin punctures in its crushed throat. The other was the companion of the smiling Costillan—the second of the two who had been left in the central room under Allenby's guard.

In grim silence the three horribles led their victims out of the pits, with Murgunstrumm limping triumphantly behind.

Cold dread clawed at Paul's soul during that short journey out of one world of horror into another; dread combined with a hopelessness that left him weak, shuddering. Somehow, now, the resistance had been drawn out of him. Further agony of mind and spirit could drag no more response from flesh and muscle.

He had been so close to success! He had learned every secret of this grim house of hell, and had shown Kermeff the same.

But the truth would avail nothing now. Paul, climbing the stairs slowly, mutely, glanced at Kermeff and moaned inwardly. Kermeff was convinced. Kermeff would have freed Ruth, signed a statement that the girl, after escaping from this house of evil seven months ago, had been not mad but horrified and delirious. But now Kermeff himself would never leave; there would be no statement. Ruth would remain indefinitely in the asylum.

A sound rose above the scrape of footsteps—a sudden hammering on some distant door, and the muffled vibration of a man's voice demanding entrance. The creatures beside Paul glanced at each other quickly. One said, in a low voice:

"It is Maronaine, returning from the city."

"With good fortune, probably. Trust Maronaine."

"Murgunstrumm, go and open the door to him. Wait. One of these fools has the key."

"This one has it," the cripple growled, prodding Jeremy.

"Then take it."

Jeremy stood stiff as the innkeeper's hands groped in his pockets. For an instant it seemed that he would clutch that thick neck in his grip and twist it, despite the danger that threatened. But he held himself rigid. Murgunstrumm, key in hand, stepped back and turned quickly into the dark, swinging the lantern as he limped away.

The revolver pressed again into Paul's back. His captor said quietly, in a voice soft with subtlety:

"And we go in the same direction, my friend, to pay a visit to your friend Allenby."

Allenby! What had happened to him? How had the vampires escaped from the prison chamber where he had been left to guard them? Pacing through the gloom, Paul found the problem almost a relief from the dread of what was coming. In some way the monsters had overcome Allenby. Somehow they had forced him to open one of the doors, or the windows. . . .

"Did you hear that, my friend?"

Paul stopped and peered into the colorless features of his persecutor. Kermeff and Jeremy were standing quite still.

"Hear what?"

"Listen."

It came again, the sound that had at first been so soft and muffled that Paul had not heard it. A girl's voice, pleading, uttering broken words. And as he heard it, a slow, terrible fear crept into Paul's face. The muscles of his body tightened to the breaking point. That voice, it was—

The gun touched him. Mechanically he moved forward again. Darkness hung all about him. Once, turning covertly, he saw that the gloom was so opaque that the moving shapes behind him were invisible. Only the sound of men breathing, and the scrape of feet; only the sight of three pairs of greenish eyes, like glowing balls of phosphorus. There was nothing else.

But resistance was madness. The demons behind him were ghouls born of darkness, vampires of the night, with the eyes of cats.

And so, presently, with deepening dread, he stumbled through the last black room and arrived at the threshold of the central chamber. And there, as his eyes became accustomed again to the glare of the lantern which stood on the table, he saw Allenby lying lifeless on the floor, just beyond the sill. The door closed behind him and he was forced forward; and suddenly the room seemed choked with moving forms. Kermeff and Jeremy were close beside him. The three macabre demons hovered near. Allenby lay there, silent and prone. Murgunstrumm—

Murgunstrumm was standing, bat-like, against the opposite barrier which led to the night outside, glaring, peering invidiously at two people who were visible at a nearby table. These were the guests whom the innkeeper had just admitted. Man and woman. The man, like all the others, was standing now beside the table with arms folded on his chest, lips curled in a hungry smile. The girl stared in mute horror straight into Paul's frozen face.

The girl was Ruth LeGeurn.

## 11. Compelling Eyes. . . .

"YOU SEE, your friend possessed a weakling's mind."

The man with the gun kicked Allenby's dead body dispassionately, grinning.

"He had no courage. He was bound with fear and unable to combat the force of two pairs of eyes upon him. He became—hypnotized, shall we say? And obedient, very obedient. Soon you will understand how it was done."

Paul hardly heard the words. He still stared at the girl, and she at him. For seven mad months he had longed for that face, moaned for it at night, screamed for it. Now his prayers were answered, and he would have given his very soul, his life, to have them recalled. Yet she was lovely, even in such surroundings, lovely despite the ghastly whiteness of her skin and the awful fear in her wide eyes.

And her companion, gloating over her, was telling triumphantly how he had obtained her.

"There were three of them," he leered, "in a machine, moving slowly along the road just below here. I met them and I was hungry, for nothing had come to me this night. There in the road I became human for their benefit, and held up my hand as befitting one who wishes to ask directions. They stopped. And then—then it was over very quickly, eh, my lovely bride? The boy, he lies beside the road even now. When he awakes, he will wonder and be very sad. Oh, so sad! The older man hangs over the door of the car, dead or alive I know not. And here—here is what I have brought home with me!"

"And look at her, Maronaine!"

"Look at her? Have I not looked?"

"Fool!" It was another of the vampires who spoke. "Look closely, and then examine this one!"

Eyes, frowning, penetrating eyes which seemed bottomless, examined Paul's features intently and turned to inspect the girl.

"What mean you, Francisco?"

"These are the two who came here before, so long ago, and escaped. Look at them, together!"

"Ah!" The exclamation was vibrant with understanding.

"These are the two, Maronaine."

A white hand gripped Paul's shoulder savagely. The face that came close to his was no longer leering with patient anticipation of satisfaction to come, but choked with hate and bestial fury.

"You will learn what it means to escape this house. You have come back to find out, eh? You and she, both. No others have ever departed from here, or ever will."

"They should be shown together, Francisco. No?"

"Together? Ah, because they are lovers and should be alone, eh?" The laugh was satanic.

"Up there"—an angry arm flung toward the ceiling—"where it is very quiet. You, Maronaine, and you, Costillan, it is your privilege. Francisco and I will amuse ourselves here with these other guests of ours."

A grunt of agreement muttered from Maronaine's lips. His fingers clasped the girl's arm, lifting her from the chair where she cringed in terror. Ugly hands dragged her forward.

"Paul—Paul! Oh, help!"

But Paul himself was helpless, caught in a savage grip from which there was no escape. His captor swung him toward the door. Struggling vainly, he was hauled over the threshold into the darkness beyond, and the girl was dragged after him.

The door rasped shut. The last Paul saw, as it closed, was a blurred vision of Jeremy and Kermeff flattened desperately against the wall, staring at the two remaining vampires; and Murgunstrumm, crouching against the opposite barrier, cutting off any possibility of retreat.

Then a voice growled curtly:

"Go back to your feast, Murgunstrumm. We have no use for you here. Go!"

And as the two victims were prodded up the twisting stairs to the upper reaches of the inn, the door below them opened and closed again. And Murgunstrumm scurried along the lower corridor, mumbling to himself, clawing his way fretfully toward the stairway that led down into the buried pits.

It was a cruel room into which they were thrust. Situated on the upper landing, directly across the hall from where that pitiful feminine figure lay on the musty bed, it was no larger than a dungeon cell, and illuminated only by a stump of candle which lay in a pool of its own gray wax on the window sill.

Here, forced into separate chairs by their captors, Paul and Ruth stared at each other—Ruth sobbing, with horror-filled eyes wide open; Paul sitting with unnatural stiffness, waiting.

Powerful hands groped over Paul's shoulder and held him motionless, as if knowing that he would soon be straining in torment. At the same time, the door clicked shut. The candlelight wavered and became smooth again. The second vampire advanced slowly toward Ruth.

A scream started from the girl's lips as she saw that face. The eyes were green again. The features were voluptuous, bloated beyond belief.

"We will show them what it means to escape this house. Her blood will be warm, Costillan. Warm and sweet. I will share it with you."

The girl struggled up, staring horribly, throwing out her hands to ward off the arms she expected to crush her. But those arms did not move. It was the eyes that changed, even as she cringed back half erect against the wall. The eyes followed her, boring, drilling, eating into her soul. She stood quite still. Then, moaning softly, she took a step forward, and another, faltering, and slumped again into the chair.

The creature bent over her triumphantly. Fingers caressed her hair, her cheeks, her mouth—the fingers of a slave buyer, appraising a prospective purchase. Very slowly, gently, they thrust the girl's limp head back, exposing the white, tender, lovely throat. And then the creature's lips came lower. His eyes were points of vivid fire. His mouth parted, his tongue curled over a protruding lower lip. Teeth gleamed.

Paul's voice pierced the room with a roar of animal fury. Violently he wrenched himself forward, only to be dragged back again by the amazingly powerful hands on his shoulders. But the demon beside Ruth straightened quickly, angrily, and glared.

"Can you not keep that fool still? Am I to be disturbed

with his discordant voice while—"

"Listen, Maronaine."

The room was deathly still. Suddenly the man called Costillan strode to the door and whipped it open. Standing there, he was motionless, alert. And there was no sound anywhere, no sound audible to human ears.

But those ears were not human. Costillan said curtly:

"Someone is outside the house, prowling. Come!"

"But these two here . . .?"

"The door, Maronaine, locks on the outside. They will be here when we return, and all the sweeter for having thought of us."

The chamber was suddenly empty of those macabre forms, and the door closed. A key turned in the slot outside. And then Paul was out of his chair with a bound. Out of it, and clawing frantically at the barrier.

A mocking laugh from the end of the corridor was the only answer.

No amount of straining would break that lock. An eternity passed while Paul struggled there. Time and again he flung himself against the panels. But one shoulder was already a limp, bleeding thing from that bullet wound, and the other could not work alone. And presently came the voice of Ruth LeGeurn behind him, very faint and far away.

"They said . . . someone outside, Paul. If it is Martin and Von Heller. . . ."

"Who?"

"I escaped from Morrisdale last night, Paul. Martin told me how to do it. He met me outside the walls. We drove straight to the city, to find you. You were gone."

Paul was leaning against the door, gasping. Wildly he stared about the room, seeking something to use as a bludgeon.

"Martin went to the hospital, to plead with Kermeff and Allenby for both of us, Paul. Your letters were there. He knew the handwriting. We traced you to Rehobeth to-night and—and we were on our way here when that horrible man in the road—"

"But Von Heller!" Paul raved. "Where does he come into it?"

"He was at the Rehobeth Hotel. He—he read the account of your escape and said he knew you would return there."

"He'll be no help now," Paul said bitterly, fighting again at the door. "I can't open this."

Ruth was suddenly beside him, tugging at him.

"If we can find some kind of protection from them, Paul, even for a little while, to hold them off until Martin and Von Heller find a way to help us! Von Heller will know a way!"

Protection! Paul stared about him with smoldering eyes. What protection could there be? The vampires had torn away his cross. There was nothing left.

Suddenly he swept past Ruth and fell on his knees beside the bed. The bed had blankets, sheets, covers! White sheets! Feverishly he tore at them, ripping them to shreds. When he turned again his eyes were aglow with fanatical light. He thrust a gleaming thing into Ruth's hands—a crudely fashioned cross, formed of two strips knotted in the center.

"Back to your chair!" he cried. "Quickly!"

Footsteps were audible in the corridor, outside the door. And muffled voices:

"You were hearing sounds which did not exist, Costillan."

"I tell you I heard—"

"Hold the cross before you," Paul ordered tersely, dragging his own chair close beside Ruth's. "Sit very still. For your life don't drop it from fear of anything you may see. Have courage, beloved."

The door was opening. Whether it was Costillan or Maronaine who entered first it was impossible to say. Those ghastly colorless faces, undead and abhorrent, contained no differentiating points strong enough to be so suddenly discernible in flickering candlelight. But whichever it was, the creature advanced quickly, hungrily, straight toward Ruth. And, close enough to see the white bars which she thrust out abruptly, he recoiled with sibilant hiss, to lurch into his companion behind him.

"The cross! They have found the cross! Ah!"

Nightmare came then. The door was shut. The candle glow revealed two crouching creeping figures; two gaunt, haggard, vicious faces; two pairs of glittering eyes. Like savage beasts fascinated by a feared and hated object, yet afraid to make contact, the vampires advanced with rigid arms outthrust, fingers curled.

"Back!" Paul cried. "Back!"

He was on his feet with the cross clutched before him. Ruth, trembling against him, did as he did. The two horribles retreated abruptly, snarling.

And then the transformation came. The twin bodies lost their definite outline and became blurred. Bluish vapor emanated from them, misty and swirling, becoming thicker and thicker with the passing seconds. And presently nothing remained but lurking shapes of phosphorescence, punctured by four glaring unblinking eyes of awful green.

Eyes!

Paul realized with a shudder what they were striving to do. He fought against them.

"Don't look at them," he muttered. "Don't!"

But he had to look at them. Despite the horror in his heart, his own gaze returned to those advancing bottomless pits of vivid green as if they possessed the power of lodestone. He found himself peering into them, and knew that Ruth too was staring.

Ages went by, then, while he fought against the subtle numbness that crept into his brain. He knew then what Allenby had gone through before merciful death. Another will was fighting his, crushing and smothering him. Other thoughts than his own were finding a way into his mind, no matter how he struggled to shut them out. And a voice—his own voice, coming from his own lips—was saying heavily, dully:

"Nothing will harm us. These are our friends. There is no need to hold the cross any longer. Throw down the cross. . . ."

Somehow, in desperation, he realized what he was doing, what he was saying. He lurched to his feet, shouting hoarsely:

"No, no, don't let them do it! Ruth, they are fiends, vampires! They are the undead, living on blood!"

His careening body struck the window ledge, crushing the last remnant of candle that clung there. The room was all at once in darkness, and the two mad shapes of bluish light were a thousand times more real and horrible and close. Completely unnerved, Paul flung out his hand and clawed at the window shade. It rattled up with the report of an explosion. His fingers clutched at the glass. He saw that the darkness outside had become a sodden gray murk.

Then he laughed madly, harshly, because he knew that escape was impossible. Death was the only way out of this chamber of torment. The window was high above the ground, overlooking the stone flagging of the walk. And the eyes were coming nearer. And Ruth was screeching luridly as two shapeless hands hovered over her throat.

Somewhere in the bowels of the house, under the floor, a revolver roared twice in quick succession. A voice—Jeremy's voice—bellowed in triumph. A long shrill scream vibrated high above everything else. There was a splintering crash as of a door breaking from its hinges—and footsteps on the stairs, running.

Paul hurled himself upon the bluish monstrosity which hung over Ruth's limp body. Wildly, desperately, he leaped forward, thrusting the cross straight into those boring eyes.

Something foul and fetid assailed his nostrils as he tripped and fell to the floor. He rolled over frantically, groping for the bits of white rag which had been torn from his hands on the bedpost as he fell. He knew that Ruth was flat against the wall, holding out both arms to embrace the earth-born fiend which advanced toward her. Her hands were empty. She had let the cross fall. She was no longer a woman, but a human without a will, utterly hypnotized by the eyes.

Paul's fingers found the bit of white rag. Instinctively he twisted backward over the floor, avoiding the uncouth hands that sought his throat. Then he was on his feet, leaping to Ruth's side. Even as that ghoulish mouth lowered to fasten on the girl's throat, the cross intervened. The mouth recoiled with a snarl of awful rage.

"Back!" Paul screamed. "Look, it is daylight!"

The snarling shape stiffened abruptly, as if unseen fingers had snatched at it.

"Daylight!" The word was a thin frightened whisper, lashing through the room and echoing sibilantly. The green eyes filled with apprehension. Suddenly, where the distorted shapes of swirling mist had stood, appeared men—the same men, Costillan and Maronaine, with faces of utter hate. The candlelight was not needed to reveal them now. The room was dim and cold with a thin gray glare from the window.

"Daylight," Costillan muttered, staring fixedly at the aperture. "We have only a moment, Maronaine. Come quickly."

His companion was standing with clenched hands, confronting the two prisoners.

"You have not won," he was saying harshly. "You will never escape. To the ends of hell we will follow you for what you have done this night."

"Come, Maronaine. Quickly!"

"Yours will be the most horrible of all deaths. I warn you—"

A mighty crash shook the door, and another. With sharp cries the two undead creatures whirled about. Triumphantly, Paul knew the thoughts in their malignant minds. They were demons of the night, these fiends. Their hours of existence endured only from sunset to sunrise. If they were not back in their graves. . . .

And now they were trapped, as the barrier clattered inward, torn and splintered from its hinges. A battering ram of human flesh—Jeremy—hurtled over the threshold. Other figures crowded in the doorway.

And suddenly the two vampires were gone. Even as the men in the corridor rushed forward, the twin shapes of black and white vanished. And only Paul saw the method of it. Only Paul saw the black-winged things that swirled with lightning speed through the aperture, into the gloom of the corridor beyond.

## 12. The Vault

STRONG HANDS held Paul up then. Jeremy and Martin LeGeurn stood beside him, supporting him. Kermeff was on his knees beside the limp unconscious form on the floor. And a stranger, a huge man with bearded face and great thick shoulders, was standing like a mastodon in the center of the room, glaring about him—Von Heller, the mightiest brain in medical circles; the man who understood what other men merely feared.

"Where are they?" he roared, whirling upon Paul. "Stand up, man. You're not hurt. Where did they go?"

"It was daylight," Paul whispered weakly. "They—"

"Daylight?" Von Heller swung savagely to face the window. "My God, what a fool I—Where are the cellars? Hurry. Take me to the cellars."

To Paul it was a blurred dream. He knew that strong hands gripped him and led him rapidly to the door. He heard Von Heller's booming voice commanding Kermeff to remain with the girl. Then moving shapes were all about him. Jeremy was close on one side. Martin LeGeurn was supporting him on the other, talking to him in a low voice of encouragement. Von Heller was striding furiously down the corridor.

The darkness here was as opaque as before, as thick and deep as the gloom of sunken dungeons. But there was no sound in the house; no sound anywhere, except Paul's own voice, muttering jerkily:

"Thank God, Martin, you came in time. If those demons had hurt Ruth or killed Jeremy and Kermeff. . . ."

The answer was a guttural laugh from Jeremy. And in the dark Paul saw on Jeremy's breast a gleaming green cross, glittering with its own fire. He stared mutely at it, then turned and looked back toward the room they had just left, as if visualizing the same on Kermeff's kneeling body. And he knew, then, why his companions were still alive; why they were not now lying lifeless and bloodless on the floor of the downstairs chamber.

One of them—Jeremy, probably—had rushed to Allenby's dead body and seized the square of chalk in the pocket of the corpse. And the pantomime of the upper room had been reenacted in the lower room, the same way, until Martin LeGeurn and Von Heller had battered down the outside door.

The revolver shots—Martin had fired them, more than likely. Martin did not know that bullets were useless.

"Thank God," Paul muttered again. And then he was descending the stairs to the lower floor, and descending more stairs, black and creaking, to the pits.

"Which way?" Von Heller demanded harshly. "We must find the coffins."

"Coffins?" It was Jeremy frowning. "There ain't no coffins down here, sir. We looked in every single room. Besides"—vicously—"them two fiends upstairs won't never need coffins any more. When you leaped on 'em sir, and made that cross mark over their filthy hearts with the chalk, they just folded up. Shriveled away to dust, they did. Lord, what a stench! I'll never forget—"

"Never mind that. Where is the burial vault?"

"But there ain't any burial vault. We were just—"

Jeremy's words ended abruptly. He stood still, one hand gripping the lower end of the railing, the other uplifted.

"Listen to that!"

There was a sound, emanating from somewhere deep in the gloom of the cellar—a sucking, grinding sound, utterly revolting, mingled with the mumbling and gurgling of a man's voice.

"An animal, eating," Von Heller said in a whisper.

"It ain't an animal, sir."

"My God! Murgunstrumm. Well, he'll be able to show us where the coffins are."

Von Heller groped forward, eyes burning with terrible eagerness. He was a man no longer, but a hound on a hot scent which meant to him more than life and death. Crouching, he advanced noiselessly through the pits, staring straight ahead, ignoring the chambers on all sides of him as he went deeper and deeper into the maze. And the others followed right at his heels in a group.

And the sight that met the eyes of the intruders, when they reached at last the threshold of the slaughter room, soured the blood in their veins and made them rigid. The lantern flared there, on the floor against the wall. The sodden canvas sheet had been torn from its former position and lay now in an ugly gray heap on the floor.

Murgunstrumm crouched there, unaware of the eyes that watched him.

Von Heller was upon him before he knew it. With awful rage the physician hurled him back from the table. Like a madman Von Heller stood over him, hurling frightful words upon the cripple's malformed head.

And the result was electrifying. Murgunstrumm's face whipped up. His sunken eyes, now completely mad with mingled fear and venom, glared into Von Heller's writhing countenance and into the masks of the men in the doorway. Then, with a great suck of breath, Murgunstrumm stiffened.

The jangling words which spewed from his lips were not English. They were guttural, thick Serbian. And even as they echoed and re-echoed through the chamber, through the entire cellar, the cripple sprang forward.

There was no stopping him. His move was too sudden and savage. Hurling Von Heller aside, he lunged to the table, grabbed the huge knife, then was at the threshold, tearing and slashing his way clear. And with a last violent scream he vanished into the outer dark.

A moment passed. No man moved. Then Von Heller seized the lantern and rushed forward.

"After him!"

"What did he say?"

"He thinks his masters betrayed him. Thinks they sent us here. He will destroy them, and I want them alive for research. After him, I say!"

Footprints led the way—footprints in the dust, twisting along the wall where other prints were not intermingled. With the lantern swaying crazily in his outflung hand, Von Heller ran forward. Straight to the smallest of the cell-like chambers the trail led him; and when the others reached his side he was standing in the center of the stone vault, glaring hungrily at a tall, rectangular opening in the wall.

Seeing it, Paul gasped. Jeremy said hoarsely:

"We looked in here before. There wasn't no—"

"You were blind!"

And Von Helfer was striding forward again, through the aperture. It was a narrow doorway; the barrier hung open, fashioned of stone, on concealed hinges. Little wonder that in the gloom Paul and Jeremy and Kermeff had not discovered it before. Every chamber had been alike then.

But not now. Now they were pacing onward through a blind tunnel. The stone walls were no longer stone, but thick boards on both sides and above and below, to hold out the earth behind them. This was not the cellar of the inn, but a cunningly contrived extension, leading into subterranean gloom.

Strange realizations came into Paul's mind. The Gray Toad had not always been an inn of death. At one time it had prospered with gaiety and life. Then the decay had come. Murgunstrumm had come here to live. And these creatures of the night had discovered the place and come here, too, and made Murgunstrumm their slave, promising him the remains of their grim feasts. They had brought their grave earth here. . . .

For twenty yards the passage continued, penetrating deeper and deeper at a sharp incline. And then it came to an end, and the lantern light revealed a buried chamber where every sound, every shred of light, was withheld by walls of unbroken earth. A tomb, sunk deep beneath the surface of the clearing above.

And the lantern disclosed other things. Long wooden boxes lay side by side in the center of the vault. Seven of them. Seven gaunt ancient coffins.

They were open, all but one. The lids were flung back. The corpses had been hauled out savagely, madly, and hurled upon the floor. They lay there now like sodden heaps of flesh in a slaughterhouse, covered with strips and shreds of evening clothes. Great pools of blood welled beneath them. The lantern glare revealed sunken shriveled faces, hideous in decay, already beginning to disintegrate. Gaunt bones protruded from rotting flesh.

And Murgunstrumm was there. He was no longer human, but a grave robber, a resurrection man with hideous intentions, as he crouched over the lid of the last oblong box, tearing it loose. Even as the men watched him, stricken motionless by the fiendishness of it, he leaped catlike upon the enclosed body and dragged it into the open. The man was Maronaine. And there, with inarticulate cries of hate, Murgunstrumm fell upon it, driving his knife again and again into the creature's heart, laughing horribly. Then he stumbled erect, and a discordant cackle jangled from his thick lips.

"Betrayed me! Betrayed me, did yer! Turned on old Murgunstrumm, which served yer for 'most twenty-eight years! Yer won't never betray no one else! I'll tear every limb of yer rotten bodies—"

He looked up then, and saw that he was not alone. His rasping voice stopped abruptly. He lurched back with uncanny quickness. His hands jerked up like claws. His convulsed face glared, masklike, between curled fingers. A screech of madness burned through his lips. For an instant he crouched there, twisting back into the wall. Then, with a cry tearing upward through his throat, he hurled himself forward.

In his madness he saw only Von Heller. Von Heller was the central object of his hate. Von Heller was the first to step forward to meet him.

It was horror, then. It was a shambles, executed in the gloom of a sunken burial vault with only the sputtering, dancing glow of the lantern to reveal it. Four men fought to overpower a mad beast gone amuck. Four lunging desperate shapes blundered about in the treacherous semidark, clawing, slashing, striking at the horribly swift creature in their midst.

For Murgunstrumm was human no longer. Madness made a bestial mask of his features. His thick, flailing arms possessed the strength of twenty men. His heaving, leaping body was a thing of unbound fury. His eyes were wells of gleaming white, pupil-less. His drooling mouth, curled back over protruding teeth, whined and whimpered and screamed sounds which had no human significance.

He had flung the knife away in that first vicious rush. Always, as he battled, his attention was centered on Von Heller. The others did not matter. They were only objects of interference to be hurled aside. And hurl them aside he did, at last, with the sheer savagery of his attack.

For a split second, alone in the center of the chamber, he crouched with arms and head outthrust, fingers writhing. He glared straight into Von Heller's face, as the physician flattened against the wall. And then, oblivious of the revolver which came into Von Heller's hand, the cripple leaped.

Von Heller's revolver belched flame directly in his path, again and again.

In mid-air, Murgunstrumm stiffened. His twisted foot struck the edge of the open coffin before him. He tripped, lunged forward. His writhing body sprawled in a shapeless mass.

A long rattling moan welled through his parted lips. He struggled again to his knees and swayed there, shrieking. His hands flailed empty air, clawed at nothingness. And then, with a great shudder, he collapsed.

His broken body crashed across the coffin lid. His head snapped down, burying itself in Maronaine's upturned features. And then he lay quite still, staring with wide dead eyes at the ceiling.

It was Von Heller who spoke first, after many minutes of complete silence. With a last glance at the scene, the physician turned very quietly and motioned to the doorway.

"Come."

Thus, with the lantern finding the way, the four men left the cellar of horror and returned to the upstairs room where Kermeff and Ruth LeGeurn awaited them. Kermeff, standing quickly erect, said in a husky voice:

"You found them?"

"It is over," Von Heller shrugged. "Quite over. As soon as Miss LeGeurn is better, we shall leave here and return—"

"To Morrisdale?" Paul cried, seizing the man's arm.

"To Miss LeGeurn's home, where Doctor Kermeff will sign the necessary papers. Kermeff made a very natural mistake, my boy. But he will rectify it."

"I was ignorant," Kermeff muttered. "I did not know."

"There was only one way to know, to learn the truth. Paul has shown you. Now we shall leave and. . . ."

But Paul was not listening. He was sitting on the edge of the bed, holding the girl's hands. The room was sweet and clean with daylight, and he was whispering words which he wished no one but Ruth to hear.

And later, as the big car droned through sun-streaked country roads toward the distant city, Ruth LeGeurn lay in the back seat, with her head in Paul's arms, and listened to the same whispered words over again. And she smiled, for the first time in months.

# Dennis Etchison

# The Late Shift

AFTER WINNING $250 in his teens for an essay entitled "What America Means to Me", British and World Fantasy Award winner Dennis Etchison has gone on to become one of the genre's most accomplished short story writers. His first professional sale was a science fiction story in 1961, since when he has contributed fiction to a wide variety of magazines and anthologies.

Etchison's own collections include *The Dark Country*, *Red Dreams* and *The Blood Kiss*, he has written two novels under his own name—*Darkside* and *The Fog*—and novelized *Halloween II* and *III* and *Videodrome* under the pseudonym "Jack Martin". He is also the editor of the anthologies *Cutting Edge*, *Lord John Ten* and three volumes of *Masters of Darkness*, and has written the scripts for several movies and television series.

"The Late Shift" is perhaps one of his most representative stories, set in a jaundiced, paranoid Southern California milieu; it was made into a short film in 1984 entitled *Killing Time*.

THEY WERE DRIVING BACK from a midnight screening of *The Texas Chainsaw Massacre* ("Who will survive and what will be left of them?") when one of them decided they should make the Stop 'N Start Market on the way home. Macklin couldn't be sure later who said it first, and it didn't really matter, for there was the all-night logo, its bright colors cutting through the fog before they had reached 26th Street, and as soon as he saw it Macklin moved over close to the curb and began coasting toward the only sign of life anywhere in town at a quarter to two in the morning.

They passed through the electric eye at the door, rubbing their faces in the sudden cold light. Macklin peeled off toward the news rack, feeling like a newborn before the LeBoyer Method. He reached into a row of well-thumbed magazines, but they were all chopper, custom car, detective and stroke books, as far as he could see.

"Please, please, sorry, thank you," the night clerk was saying.

"No, no," said a woman's voice, "can't you hear? I want that box, *that* one."

"Please, please," said the night man again.

Macklin glanced up.

A couple of guys were waiting in line behind her, next to the styrofoam ice chests. One of them cleared his throat and moved his feet.

The woman was trying to give back a small, oblong carton, but the clerk didn't seem to understand. He picked up the box, turned to the shelf, back to her again.

Then Macklin saw what it was: a package of one dozen prophylactics from behind the counter, back where they kept the cough syrup and airplane glue and film. That was all she wanted—a pack of Polaroid SX-70 Land Film.

Macklin wandered to the back of the store.

"How's it coming, Whitey?"

"I got the Beer Nuts," said Whitey, "and the Jiffy Pop, but I can't find any Olde English 800." He rummaged through the refrigerated case.

"Then get Schlitz Malt Liquor," said Macklin. "That ought to do the job." He jerked his head at the counter.

"Hey, did you catch that action up there?"

"What's that?"

Two more guys hurried in, heading for the wine display. "Never mind. Look, why don't you just take this stuff up there and get a place in line? I'll find us some Schlitz or something. Go on, they won't sell it to us after two o'clock."

He finally found a six-pack hidden behind some bottles, then picked up a quart of milk and a half-dozen eggs. When he got to the counter, the woman had already given up and gone home. The next man in line asked for cigarettes and beef jerky. Somehow the clerk managed to ring it up; the electronic register and UPC Code lines helped him a lot.

"Did you get a load of that one?" said Whitey. "Well, I'll be gonged. Old Juano's sure hit the skids, huh? The pits. They should have stood him in an aquarium."

"Who?"

"Juano. It *is* him right? Take another look." Whitey pretended to study the ceiling.

Macklin stared at the clerk. Slicked-back hair, dyed and greasy and parted in the middle, a phony Hitler moustache, thrift shop clothes that didn't fit. And his skin didn't look right somehow, like he was wearing makeup over a face that hadn't seen the light of day in ages. But Whitey was right. It was Juano. He had waited on Macklin too many times at that little Mexican restaurant over in East L.A., Mama Something's. Yes, that was it, Mama Carnita's on Whittier Boulevard. Macklin and his friends, including Whitey, had eaten there maybe fifty or a hundred times, back when they were taking classes at Cal State. It was Juano for sure.

Whitey set his things on the counter. "How's it going, man?" he said.

"Thank you," said Juano.

Macklin laid out the rest and reached for his money. The milk made a lumpy sound when he let go of it. He gave the carton a shake. "Forget this," he said. "It's gone sour." Then, "Haven't seen you around, old buddy. Juano, wasn't it?"

"Sorry. Sorry," said Juano. He sounded dazed, like a sleepwalker.

Whitey wouldn't give up. "Hey, they still make that good *menudo* over there?" He dug in his jeans for change. "God, I could eat about a gallon of it right now, I bet."

They were both waiting. The seconds ticked by. A radio in the store was playing an old '60s song. *Light My Fire*, Macklin thought. The Doors. "You remember me, don't you? Jim Macklin." He held out his hand. "And my trusted Indian companion, Whitey? He used to come in there with me on Tuesdays and Thursdays."

The clerk dragged his feet to the register, then turned back, turned again. His eyes were half-closed. "Sorry," he said. "Sorry. Please."

Macklin tossed down the bills, and Whitey counted his coins and slapped them onto the counter top. "Thanks," said Whitey, his upper lip curling back. He hooked a thumb in the direction of the door. "Come on. This place gives me the creeps."

As he left, Macklin caught a whiff of Juano or whoever he was. The scent was sickeningly sweet, like a gilded lily. His hair? Macklin felt a cold draft blow through his chest, and shuddered; the air conditioning, he thought.

At the door, Whitey spun around and glared.

"So what," said Macklin. "Let's go."

"What time does Tube City here close?"

"Never. Forget it." He touched his friend's arm.

"The hell I will," said Whitey. "I'm coming back when they change fucking shifts. About six o'clock, right? I'm going to be standing right there in the parking lot when he walks out. That son of a bitch still owes me twenty bucks."

"Please," muttered the man behind the counter, his eyes fixed on nothing. "Please. Sorry. Thank you."

The call came around ten. At first he thought it was a gag; he propped his eyelids up and peeked around the apartment, half-expecting to find Whitey still there, curled up asleep among the loaded ashtrays and pinched beer cans. But it was no joke.

"Okay, okay, I'll be right there," he grumbled, not yet comprehending, and hung up the phone.

St. John's Hospital on 14th. In the lobby, families milled about, dressed as if on their way to church, watching the elevators and waiting obediently for the clock to signal the start of visiting hours. Business hours, thought Macklin. He got the room number from the desk and went on up.

A police officer stood stiffly in the hall, taking notes on an accident report form. Macklin got the story from him and from an irritatingly healthy-looking doctor—the official story—and found himself, against his will, believing in it. In some of it.

His friend had been in an accident, sometime after dawn. His friend's car, the old VW, had gone over an embankment, not far from the Arroyo Seco. His friend had been found near the wreckage, covered with blood and reeking of alcohol. His friend had been drunk.

"Let's see here now. Any living relatives?" asked the officer. "All we could get out of him was your name. He was in a pretty bad state of shock, they tell me."

"No relatives," said Macklin. "Maybe back on the reservation. I don't know. I'm not even sure where the—"

A long, angry rumble of thunder sounded outside the windows. A steely light reflected off the clouds and filtered into the corridor. It mixed with the fluorescents in the ceiling, rendering the hospital interior a hard-edged, silvery gray. The faces of the policeman and the passing nurses took on a shaded, unnatural cast.

It made no sense. Whitey couldn't have been that drunk when he left Macklin's apartment. Of course he did not actually remember his friend leaving. But Whitey was going to the Stop 'N Start if he was going anywhere, not halfway across the county to—where? Arroyo Seco? It was crazy.

"Did you say there was liquor in the car?"

"Afraid so. We found an empty fifth of Jack Daniels wedged between the seats."

But Macklin knew he didn't keep anything hard at his place, and neither did Whitey, he was sure. Where was he supposed to have gotten it, with every liquor counter in the state shut down for the night?

And then it hit him. Whitey never, but never drank sour mash whiskey. In fact, Whitey never drank anything stronger than beer, anytime, anyplace. Because he couldn't. It was supposed to have something to do with his liver, as it did with other Amerinds. He just didn't have the right enzymes.

Macklin waited for the uniforms and coats to move away, then ducked inside.

"Whitey," he said slowly.

For there he was, set up against firm pillows, the upper torso and most of the hand bandaged. The arms were bare, except for an ID bracelet and an odd pattern of zigzag lines from wrist to shoulder. The lines seemed to have been painted by an unsteady hand, using a pale gray dye of some kind.

"Call me by my name," said Whitey groggily. "It's White Feather."

He was probably shot full of painkillers. But at least he was okay. Wasn't he? "So what's with the war paint, old buddy?"

"I saw the Death Angel last night."

Macklin faltered. "I—I hear you're getting out of here real soon," he tried. "You know, you almost had me worried there. But I reckon you're just not ready for the bone orchard yet."

"Did you hear what I said?"

"What? Uh, yeah. Yes." What had they shot him up with? Macklin cleared his throat and met his friend's eyes, which were focused beyond him. "What was it, a dream?"

"A dream," said Whitey. The eyes were glazed, burned out.

What happened? Whitey, he thought. Whitey. "You put that war paint on yourself?" he said gently.

"It's pHisoHex," said Whitey, "mixed with lead pencil. I put it on, the nurse washes it off, I put it on again."

"I see." He didn't, but went on. "So tell me what happened, partner. I couldn't get much out of the doctor."

The mouth smiled humorlessly, the lips cracking back from the teeth. "It was Juano," said Whitey. He started to laugh bitterly. He touched his ribs and stopped himself.

Macklin nodded, trying to get the drift. "Did you tell that to the cop out there?"

"Sure. Cops always believe a drunken Indian. Didn't you know that?"

"Look. I'll take care of Juano. Don't worry."

Whitey laughed suddenly in a high voice that Macklin had never heard before. "*He-he-he!* What are you going to do, kill him?"

"I don't know," he said, trying to think in spite of the clattering in the hall.

"They make a living from death, you know," said Whitey.

Just then a nurse swept into the room, pulling a cart behind her.

"How did you get in here?" she demanded.

"I'm just having a conversation with my friend here."

"Well, you'll have to leave. He's scheduled for surgery this afternoon."

"Do you know about the Trial of the Dead?" asked Whitey.

"Shh, now," said the nurse. "You can talk to your friend as long as you want to, later."

"I want to know," said Whitey, as she prepared a syringe.

"What is it we want to know, now?" she said, preoccupied. "What dead? Where?"

"Where?" repeated Whitey. "Why, here, of course. The dead are here. Aren't they." It was a statement. "Tell me something. What do you do with them?"

"Now what nonsense . . .?" The nurse swabbed his arm, clucking at the ritual lines on the skin.

"I'm asking you a question," said Whitey.

"Look, I'll be outside," said Macklin, "okay?"

"This is for you, too," said Whitey. "I want you to hear. Now if you'll just tell us, Miss Nurse. What do you do with the people who die in here?"

"Would you please—"

"I can't hear you." Whitey drew his arm away from her.

She sighed. "We take them downstairs. Really, this is most . . ."

But Whitey kept looking at her, nailing her with those expressionless eyes.

"Oh, the remains are tagged and kept in cold storage," she said, humoring him. "Until arrangements can be made with the family for services. There now, can we—?"

"But what happens? Between the time they become 'remains' and the services? How long is that? A couple of days? Three?"

She lost patience and plunged the needle into the arm.

"Listen," said Macklin, "I'll be around if you need me. And hey, buddy," he added, "we're going to have everything all set up for you when this is over. You'll see. A party, I swear. I can go and get them to send up a TV right now, at least."

"Like a bicycle for a fish," said Whitey.

Macklin attempted a laugh. "You take it easy, now."

And then he heard it again, that high, strange voice. "*He-he-he! tamunka sni kun.*"

Macklin needed suddenly to be out of there.

"Jim?"

"What?"

"I was wrong about something last night."

"Yeah?"

"Sure was. That place wasn't Tube City. This is. *He-he-he!*"

That's funny, thought Macklin, like an open grave. He walked out. The last thing he saw was the nurse bending over Whitey, drawing her syringe of blood like an old-fashioned phlebotomist.

All he could find out that afternoon was that the operation wasn't critical, and that there would be additional X-rays, tests and a period of "observation," though when pressed for details the hospital remained predictably vague no matter how he put the questions.

Instead of killing time, he made for the Stop 'N Start.

He stood around until the store was more or less empty,

then approached the counter. The manager, whom Macklin knew slightly, was working the register himself.

Raphael stonewalled Macklin at the first mention of Juano; his beady eyes receded into glacial ignorance. No, the night man was named Dom or Don; he mumbled so that Macklin couldn't be sure. No, Don (or Dom) had been working here for six, seven months; no, no, no.

Until Macklin came up with the magic word: police.

After a few minutes of bobbing and weaving, it started to come out. Raphe sounded almost scared, yet relieved to be able to talk about it to someone, even to Macklin.

"They bring me these guys, my friend," whispered Raphe. "I don't got nothing to do with it, believe me.

"The way it seems to me, it's company policy for all the stores, not just me. Sometimes they call and say to lay off my regular boy, you know, on the graveyard shift. 'Specially when there's been a lot of holdups. Hell, that's right by me. I don't want Dom shot up. He's my best man!

"See, I put the hours down on Dom's pay so it comes out right with the taxes, but he has to kick it back. It don't even go on his check. Then the district office, they got to pay the outfit that supplies these guys, only they don't give 'em the regular wage. I don't know if they're wetbacks or what. I hear they only get maybe $1.25 an hour, or at least the outfit that brings 'em in does, so the office is making money. You know how many stores, how many shifts that adds up to?

"Myself, I'm damn glad they only use 'em after dark, late, when things can get hairy for an all-night man. It's the way they look. But you already seen one, this Juano-Whatever. So you know. Right? You know something else, my friend? They *all* look messed up."

Macklin noticed goose bumps forming on Raphe's arms.

"*But I don't personally know nothing about it.*"

They, thought Macklin, poised outside the Stop 'N Start. Sure enough, like clockwork They had brought Juano to work at midnight. Right on schedule. With raw, burning eyes he had watched Them do something to Juano's shirt front and then point him at the door and let go. What did

They do, wind him up? But They would be back. Macklin was sure of that. They, whoever They were. The Paranoid They.

Well, he was sure as hell going to find out who They were now.

He popped another Dexamyl and swallowed dry until it stayed down.

Threats didn't work any better than questions with Juano himself. Macklin had had to learn that the hard way. The guy was so sublimely creepy it was all he could do to swivel back and forth between register and counter, slithering a hyaline hand over the change machine in the face of the most outraged customers, like Macklin, giving out with only the same pathetic, wheezing *please, please, sorry, thank you*, like a stretched cassette tape on its last loop.

Which had sent Macklin back to the car with exactly no options, nothing to do that might jar the nightmare loose except to pound the steering wheel and curse and dream redder and redder dreams of revenge. He had burned rubber between the parking lot and Sweeney Todd's Pub, turning over two pints of John Courage and a shot of Irish whiskey before he could think clearly enough to waste another dime calling the hospital, or even to look at his watch.

At six o'clock They would be back for Juano. And then. He would. Find out.

Two or three hours in the all-night movie theatre downtown, merging with the shadows on the tattered screen. The popcorn girl wiping stains off her uniform. The ticket girl staring through him, and again when he left. Something about her. He tried to think. Something about the people who work night owl shifts anywhere. He remembered faces down the years. It didn't matter what they looked like. The nightwalkers, insomniacs, addicts, those without money for a cheap hotel, they would always come back to the only game in town. They had no choice. It didn't matter that the ticket girl was messed up. It didn't matter that Juano was messed up. Why should it?

A blue van glided into the lot.

The Stop 'N Start sign dimmed, paling against the coming morning. The van braked. A man in rumpled clothes climbed out. There was a second figure in the front seat. The driver unlocked the back doors, silencing the birds that were gathering in the trees. Then he entered the store.

Macklin watched. Juano was led out. The a.m. relief man stood by, shaking his head.

Macklin hesitated. He wanted Juano, but what could he do now? What the hell had he been waiting for, exactly? There was still something else, something else. . . . It was like the glimpse of a shape under a sheet in a busy corridor. You didn't know what it was at first, but it was there; you knew what it might be, but you couldn't be sure, not until you got close and stayed next to it long enough to be able to read its true form.

The driver helped Juano into the van. He locked the door, started the engine and drove away.

Macklin, his lights out, followed.

He stayed with the van as it snaked a path across the city, nearer and nearer the foothills. The sides were unmarked, but he figured it must operate like one of those minibus porta-maid services he had seen leaving Malibu and Bel-Air late in the afternoon, or like the loads of kids trucked in to push magazine subscriptions and phony charities in the neighborhoods near where he lived.

The sky was still black, beginning to turn to slate close to the horizon. Once they passed a garbage collector already on his rounds. Macklin kept his distance.

They led him finally to a street that dead-ended at a construction site. Macklin idled by the corner, then saw the van turn back.

He let them pass, cruised to the end and made a slow turn.

Then he saw the van returning.

He pretended to park. He looked up.

They had stopped the van crosswise in front of him, blocking his passage.

The man in rumpled clothes jumped out and opened Macklin's door.

Macklin started to get out but was pushed back.

"You think you're a big enough man to be trailing people around?"

Macklin tried to penetrate the beam of the flashlight. "I saw my old friend Juano get into your truck," he began. "Didn't get a chance to talk to him. Thought I might as well follow him home and see what he's been up to."

The other man got out of the front seat of the van. He was younger, delicate-boned. He stood on one side, listening.

"I saw him get in," said Macklin, "back at the Stop 'N Start on Pico?" He groped under the seat for the tire iron. "I was driving by and—"

"Get out."

"What?"

"We saw you. Out of the car."

He shrugged and swung his legs around, lifting the iron behind him as he stood.

The younger man motioned with his head and the driver yanked Macklin forward by the shirt, kicking the door closed on Macklin's arm at the same time. He let out a yell as the tire iron clanged to the pavement.

"Another accident?" suggested the younger man.

"Too messy, after the one yesterday. Come on, pal, you're going to get to see your friend."

Macklin hunched over in pain. One of them jerked his bad arm up and he screamed. Over it all he felt a needle jab him high, in the armpit, and then he was falling.

The van was bumping along on the freeway when he came out of it. With his good hand he pawed his face, trying to clear his vision. His other arm didn't hurt, but it wouldn't move when he wanted it to.

He was sprawled on his back. He felt a wheel humming under him, below the tirewell. And there were the others. They were sitting up. One was Juano.

He was aware of a stink, sickeningly sweet, but with an overlay he remembered from his high school lab days but couldn't quite place. It sliced into his nostrils.

He didn't recognize the others. Pasty faces. Heads thrown forward, arms distended strangely with the wrists jutting out from the coat sleeves.

"Give me a hand," he said, not really expecting it.

He strained to sit up. He could make out the backs of two heads in the cab, on the other side of the grid.

He dropped his voice to a whisper. "Hey. Can you guys understand me?"

"Let us rest," someone said weakly.

He rose too quickly and his equilibrium failed. He had been shot up with something strong enough to knock him out, but it was probably the Dexamyl that had kept his mind from leaving his body completely. The van yawed, descending an off ramp, and he began to drift. He heard voices. They slipped in and out of his consciousness like fish in darkness, moving between his ears in blurred levels he could not always identify.

"There's still room at the cross." That was the younger, small-boned man, he was almost sure.

"Oh, I've been interested in Jesus for a long time, but I never could get a handle on him. . . ."

"Well, beware the wrath to come. You really should, you know."

He put his head back and became one with a dark dream. There was something he wanted to remember. He did not want to remember it. He turned his mind to doggerel, to the old song. *The time to hesitate is through*, he thought. *No time to wallow in the mire. Try now we can only lose/And our love become a funeral pyre.* The van bumped to a halt. His head bounced off steel.

The door opened. He watched it. It seemed to take forever.

Through slitted eyes: a man in a uniform that barely fit, hobbling his way to the back of the van, supported by the two of them. A line of gasoline pumps and a sign that read WE NEVER CLOSE—NEVER UNDERSOLD. The letters breathed. Before they let go of him, the one with rumpled clothes unbuttoned the attendant's shirt and stabbed a hypodermic into the chest, close to the heart and next to a strap that ran under the arms. The needle darted and flashed dully in the wan morning light.

"This one needs a booster," said the driver, or maybe it was the other one. Their voices ran together. "Just make sure you don't give him the same stuff you gave old Juano's sweetheart there. I want them to walk in on their own hind legs." "You think I want to carry 'em?" "We've done it before, brother. Yesterday, for instance." At that Macklin let his eyelids down the rest of the way, and then he was drifting again.

The wheels drummed under him.

"How much longer?" "Soon now. Soon."

These voices weak, like a folding and unfolding of paper.

Brakes grabbed. The doors opened again. A thin light played over Macklin's lids, forcing them up.

He had another moment of clarity; they were becoming more frequent now. He blinked and felt pain. This time the van was parked between low hills. Two men in Western costumes passed by, one of them leading a horse. The driver stopped a group of figures in togas. He seemed to be asking for directions.

Behind them, a castle lay in ruins. Part of a castle. And over to the side Macklin identified a church steeple, the corner of a turn-of-the-century street, a mock-up of a rocket launching pad and an old brick schoolhouse. Under the flat sky they receded into intersections of angles and vistas which teetered almost imperceptibly, ready to topple.

The driver and the other one set a stretcher on the tailgate. On the litter was a long, crumpled shape, sheeted and encased in a plastic bag. They sloughed it inside and started to secure the doors.

"You got the pacemaker back, I hope." "Stunt director said it's in the body bag." "It better be. Or it's our ass in a sling. Your ass. How'd he get so racked up, anyway?" "Ran him over a cliff in a sports car. Or no, maybe this one was the head-on they staged for, you know, that new cop series. That's what they want now, realism. Good thing he's a cremation—ain't no way Kelly or Dee's gonna get this one pretty again by tomorrow." "That's why, man. That's why they picked him. Ashes don't need makeup."

The van started up.

"Going home," someone said weakly.

"Yes . . ."

Macklin was awake now. Crouching by the bag, he scanned the faces, Juano's and the others'. The eyes were staring, fixed on a point as untouchable as the thinnest of plasma membranes, and quite unreadable.

He crawled over next to the one from the self-service gas station. The shirt hung open like folds of skin. He saw the silver box strapped to the flabby chest, directly over the heart. Pacemaker? he thought wildly.

He knelt and put his ear to the box.

He heard a humming, like an electric wristwatch.

What for? To keep the blood pumping just enough so the tissues don't rigor mortis and decay? For God's sake, for how much longer?

He remembered Whitey and the nurse. "*What happens? Between the time they become 'remains' and the services? How long is that? A couple of days? Three?*"

A wave of nausea broke inside him. When he gazed at them again the faces were wavering, because his eyes were filled with tears.

"Where are we?" he asked.

"I wish you could be here," said the gas station attendant.

"And where is that?"

"We have all been here before," said another voice.

"Going home," said another.

Yes, he thought, understanding. Soon you will have your rest; soon you will no longer be objects, commodities. You will be honored and grieved for and your personhood given back, and then you will at last rest in peace. It is not for nothing that you have labored so long and so patiently. You will see, all of you. Soon.

He wanted to tell them, but he couldn't. He hoped they already knew.

The van lurched and slowed. The hand brake ratcheted.

He lay down and closed his eyes.

He heard the door creak back.

"Let's go."

The driver began to herd the bodies out. There was the sound of heavy, dragging feet, and from outside the smell of fresh-cut grass and roses.

"What about this one?" said the driver, kicking Macklin's shoe.

"Oh, he'll do his 48-hours' service, don't worry. It's called utilizing your resources."

"Tell me about it. When do we get the Indian?"

"Soon as St. John's certificates him. He's overdue. The crash was sloppy."

"This one won't be. But first Dee'll want him to talk, what he knows and who he told. Two doggers in two days is too much. Then we'll probably run him back to his car and do it. And phone it in, so St. John's gets him. Even if it's DOA. Clean as hammered shit. Grab the other end."

He felt the body bag sliding against his leg. Grunting, they hauled it out and hefted it toward—where?

He opened his eyes. He hesitated only a second, to take a deep breath.

Then he was out of the van and running.

Gravel kicked up under his feet. He heard curses and metal slamming. He just kept his head down and his legs pumping. Once he twisted around and saw a man scurrying after him. The driver paused by the mortuary building and shouted. But Macklin kept moving.

He stayed on the path as long as he dared. It led him past mossy trees and bird-stained statues. Then he jumped and cut across a carpet of matted leaves and into a glade. He passed a gate that spelled DRY LAWN CEMETERY in old iron, kept running until he spotted a break in the fence where it sloped by the edge of the grounds. He tore through huge, dusty ivy and skidded down, down. And then he was on a sidewalk.

Cars revved at a wide intersection, impatient to get to work. He heard coughing and footsteps, but it was only a bus stop at the middle of the block. The air brakes of a commuter special hissed and squealed. A clutch of grim people rose from the bench and filed aboard like sleepwalkers.

He ran for it, but the doors flapped shut and the bus roared on.

More people at the corner, stepping blindly between each other. He hurried and merged with them.

Dry cleaners, laundromat, hamburger stand, parking lot, gas station, all closed. But there was a telephone at the gas station.

He ran against the light. He sealed the booth behind him and nearly collapsed against the glass.

He rattled money into the phone, dialed Operator and called for the police.

The air was close in the booth. He smelled hair tonic. Sweat swelled out of his pores and glazed his skin. Somewhere a radio was playing.

A sergeant punched onto the line. Macklin yelled for them to come and get him. Where was he? He looked around frantically, but there were no street signs. Only a newspaper rack chained to a post. NONE OF THE DEAD HAS BEEN IDENTIFIED, read the headline.

His throat tightened, his voice racing. "None of the dead has been identified," he said, practically babbling.

Silence.

So he went ahead, pouring it out about a van and a hospital and a man in rumpled clothes who shot guys up with some kind of super-adrenaline and electric pacemakers and nightclerks and crash tests. He struggled to get it all out before it was too late. A part of him heard what he was saying and wondered if he had lost his mind.

"Who will bury them?" he cried. "What kind of monsters—"

The line clicked off.

He hung onto the phone. His eyes were swimming with sweat. He was aware of his heart and counted the beats, while the moisture from his breath condensed on the glass.

He dropped another coin into the box.

"Good morning, St. John's, may I help you?"

He couldn't remember the room number. He described the man, the accident, the date. Sixth floor, yes, that was right. He kept talking until she got it.

There was a pause. Hold.

He waited.

"Sir?"

He didn't say anything. It was as if he had no words left.

"I'm terribly sorry . . ."

He felt the blood drain from him. His fingers were cold and numb.

". . . But I'm afraid the surgery wasn't successful. The party did not recover. If you wish I'll connect you with—"

"The party's name was White Feather," he said mechanically. The receiver fell and dangled, swinging like the pendulum of a clock.

He braced his legs against the sides of the booth. After what seemed like a very long time he found himself reaching reflexly for his cigarettes. He took one from the crushed pack, straightened it and hung it on his lips.

On the other side of the frosted glass, featureless shapes lumbered by on the boulevard. He watched them for a while.

He picked up a book of matches from the floor, lit two together and held them close to the glass. The flame burned a clear spot through the moisture.

*Try to set the night on fire*, he thought stupidly, repeating the words until they and any others he could think of lost meaning.

The fire started to burn his fingers. He hardly felt it. He wondered if there was anything else that would burn, anything and everything. He squeezed his eyelids together. When he opened them, he was looking down at his own clothing.

He peered out through the clear spot in the glass.

Outside, the outline fuzzy and distorted but quite unmistakable, was a blue van. It was waiting at the curb.

# Lisa Tuttle

# The Horse Lord

LISA TUTTLE was born in Houston, Texas, but since 1980 she has lived in Britain. A full-time writer and editor, she sold her first story in 1971, since when her books have included the novels *Windhaven* (with George R.R. Martin), *Familiar Spirit*, *Gabriel*, and the superb collection *A Nest of Nightmares*. She is also the author of *Encyclopedia of Feminism* and *Heroines: Women Inspired By Women*, and she recently edited the acclaimed anthology of new horror stories by women, *Skin of the Soul*.

The following story combines those two staples of horror fiction—children and possession—in a genuinely disturbing tale of ancient evil. *My Pretty Pony* it isn't . . .

THE DOUBLE BARN DOORS were secured by a length of stout, rust-encrusted chain, fastened with an old padlock.

Marilyn hefted the lock with one hand and tugged at the chain, which did not give. She looked up at the splintering grey wood of the doors and wondered how the children had got in.

Dusting red powder from her hands, Marilyn strolled around the side of the old barn. Dead leaves and dying grasses crunched beneath her sneakered feet, and she hunched her shoulders against the chill in the wind.

"There's plenty of room for horses," Kelly had said the night before at dinner. "There's a perfect barn. You can't say it would be impractical to keep a horse here." Kelly was Derek's daughter, eleven years old and mad about horses.

This barn had been used as a stable, Marilyn thought, and could be again. Why not get Kelly a horse? And why not one for herself as well? As a girl, Marilyn had ridden in Central Park. She stared down the length of the barn: for some reason, the door to each stall had been tightly boarded shut.

Marilyn realised she was shivering then, and she finished her circuit of the barn at a trot and jogged all the way back to the house.

The house was large and solid, built of grey stone 170 years before. It seemed a mistake, a misplaced object in this cold, empty land. Who would choose to settle here, who would try to eke out a living from the ungiving, stony soil?

The old house and the eerily empty countryside formed a setting very much like one Marilyn, who wrote suspense novels, had once created for a story. She liked the reality much less than her heroine had liked the fiction.

The big kitchen was warm and felt comforting after the outside air. Marilyn leaned against the sink to catch her breath and let herself relax. But she felt tense. The house seemed unnaturally quiet with all the children away at school. Marilyn smiled wryly at herself. A week before, the children had been driving her crazy with their constant noise and demands, and now that they were safely away at school for nine hours everyday she felt uncomfortable.

From one extreme to the other, thought Marilyn. The story of my life.

Only a year ago she and Derek, still newly married, were making comfortable plans to have a child—perhaps two—"someday".

Then Joan—Derek's ex-wife—had decided she'd had her fill of mothering, and almost before Marilyn had time to think about it, she'd found herself with a half-grown daughter.

And following quickly on that event—while Marilyn and Kelly were still wary of each other—Derek's widowed sister had died, leaving her four children in Derek's care.

Five children! Perhaps they wouldn't have seemed like such a herd if they had come in typical fashion, one at a time with a proper interval between.

It was the children, too, who had made living in New York City seem impossible. This house had been in Derek's family since it was built, but no one had lived in it for years. It had been used from time to time as a vacation home, but the land had nothing to recommend it to vacationers: no lakes or mountains, and the weather was usually unpleasant. It was inhospitable country, a neglected corner of New York state.

It should have been a perfect place for writing—their friends all said so. An old house, walls soaked in history, set in a brooding, rocky landscape, beneath an unlittered sky, far from the distractions and noise of the city. But Derek could write anywhere—he carried his own atmosphere with him, a part of his ingrained discipline and Marilyn needed the bars, restaurants, museums, shops and libraries of a large city to fill in the hours when words could not be commanded.

The silence was suddenly too much to bear. Derek wasn't typing—he might be wanting conversation. Marilyn walked down the long dark hallway—thinking to herself that this house needed more light fixtures, as well as pictures on the walls and rugs on the cold wooden floors.

Derek was sitting behind the big parson's table that was

his desk, cleaning one of his sixty-seven pipes. The worn but richly patterned rug on the floor, the glow of lamplight and the books which lined the walls made this room, the library and Derek's office, seem warmer and more comfortable than the rest of the house.

"Talk?" said Marilyn, standing with her hand on the doorknob.

"Sure, come on in. I was just stuck on how to get the chief slave into bed with the mistress of the plantation without making her yet another clichéd nymphomaniac."

"Have him comfort her in time of need," Marilyn said. She closed the door on the dark hallway. "He just happens to be on hand when she gets a letter informing her of her dear brother's death. In grief, and as an affirmation of life, she and the slave tumble into bed together."

"Pretty good," Derek said. "You got a problem I can help you with?"

"Not a literary one," she said, crossing the room to his side. Derek put an arm around her. "I was just wondering if we couldn't get a horse for Kelly. I was out to look at the barn. It's all boarded and locked up, but I'm sure we could get in and fix it up. And I don't think it could cost that much to keep a horse or two."

"Or two," he echoed. He cocked his head and gave her a sly look. "You sure you want to start using a barn with a rather grim history?"

"What do you mean?"

"Didn't I ever tell you the story of how my, hmmm, great-uncle, I guess he must have been—my great-uncle Martin, how he died?"

Marilyn shook her head, her expression suspicious.

"It's a pretty gruesome story."

"Derek . . ."

"It's true, I promise you. Well . . . remember my first slave novel?"

"How could I forget? It paid for our honeymoon."

"Remember the part where the evil boss-man who tortures his slaves and horses alike is finally killed by a crazed stallion?"

Marilyn grimaced. "Yeah. A bit much, I thought. Horses aren't carnivorous."

"I got the idea for that scene from my great-uncle Martin's death. His horses—and he kept a whole stable—went crazy, apparently. I don't know if they actually *ate* him, but he was pretty chewed up when someone found his body." Derek shifted in his chair. "Martin wasn't known to be a cruel man. He didn't abuse his horses; he loved them. He didn't love Indians, though, and the story was that the stables were built on ground sacred to the Indians, who put a curse on Martin or his horses in retaliation."

Marilyn shook her head. "Some story. When did all this happen?"

"Around 1880."

"And the barn has been boarded up ever since?"

"I guess so. I remember the few times Anna and I came out here as kids we could never find a way to get inside. We made up stories about the ghosts of the mad horses still being inside the barn. But because they were ghosts, they couldn't be held by normal walls, and roamed around at night. I can remember nights when we'd huddle together, certain we heard their ghostly neighing . . ." His eyes looked faraway. Remembering how much he had loved his sister, Marilyn felt guilty about her reluctance to take in Anna's children. After all, they were all Derek had left of his sister.

"So this place *is* haunted," she said, trying to joke. Her voice came out uneasy, however.

"Not the house," said Derek quickly. "Old Uncle Martin died in the barn."

"What about your ancestors who lived here before that? Didn't the Indian curse touch them?"

"Well . . ."

"Derek," she said warningly.

"OK. Straight dope. The first family, the first bunch of Hoskins who settled here were done in by Indians. The parents and the two bond-servants were slaughtered, and the children were stolen. The house was burned to the ground. That wasn't this house, obviously."

"But it stands on the same ground."

"Not exactly. That house stood on the other side of the barn—though I doubt the present barn stood then—Anna and I used to play around the foundations. I found a knife there once, and she found a little tin box which held ashes and a pewter ring."

"But you never found any ghosts."

Derek looked up at her. "Do ghosts hang around once their house is burned?"

"Maybe."

"No, we never did. Those Hoskins were too far back in time to bother with, maybe. We never saw any Indian ghosts, either."

"Did you ever see the ghost horses?"

"See them?" He looked thoughtful. "I don't remember. We might have. Funny what you can forget about childhood. No matter how important it seems to you as a child . . ."

"We become different people when we grow up." Marilyn said.

Derek gazed into space a moment, then roused himself to gesture at the wall of books behind him. "If you're interested in the family history, that little set in dark green leather was written by one of my uncles and published by a vanity press. He traces the Hoskins back to Shakespeare's time, if I recall. The longest I ever spent out here until now was one rainy summer when I was about twelve . . . it seemed like forever . . . and I read most of the books in the house, including those."

"I'd like to read them."

"Go ahead." He watched her cross the room and wheel the library ladder into position. "Why, are you thinking of writing a novel about my family?"

"No. I'm just curious to discover what perversity made your ancestor decide to build a house *here*, of all godforsaken places on the continent."

Marilyn thought of Jane Eyre as she settled into the window seat, the heavy green curtains falling back into place to shield her from the room. She glanced out at the chilly grey land and picked up the first volume.

James Hoskins won a parcel of land in upstate New York in a card game. Marilyn imagined his disappointment when he set eyes on his prize, but he was a stubborn man and frequently unlucky at cards. This land might not be much, but it was his own. He brought his family and household goods to a roughly built wooden house. A more permanent house, larger and built of native rock, would be built in time.

But James Hoskins would never see it built. In a letter to relatives in Philadelphia, Hoskins related:

"The land I have won is of great value, at least to a poor, wandering remnant of Indians. Two braves came to the house yesterday, and my dear wife was nearly in tears at their tales of powerful magic and vengeful spirits inhabiting this land.

"Go, they said, for this is a great spirit, as old as the rocks, and your God cannot protect you. This land is not good for people of any race. A spirit (whose name may not be pronounced) set his mark upon this land when the earth was still new. This land is cursed—and more of the same, on and on until I lost patience with them and told them to be off before I made powerful magic with my old Betsy.

"Tho' my wife trembled, my little daughter proved fiercer than her Ma, swearing she would chop up that pagan spirit and have it for her supper—which made me roar with laughter, and the Indians to shake their heads as they hurried away."

Marilyn wondered what had happened to that fierce little girl. Had the Indians stolen her, admiring her spirit?

She read on about the deaths of the unbelieving Hoskins. Not only had the Indians set fire to the hasty wooden house; they had first butchered the inhabitants.

"They were disemboweled and torn apart, ripped by knives in the most hungry, savage, inhuman manner, and all for the sin of living on land sacred to a nameless spirit."

Marilyn thought of the knife Derek had said he'd found as a child.

Something slapped the window. Marilyn's head jerked up and she stared out the window. It had begun to rain and a rising wind slung small fists of rain at the glass.

She stared out at the landscape, shrouded now by the driving rain, and wondered why this desolate rocky land should be thought of as sacred. Her mind moved vaguelv to thought of books on anthropology which might help, perhaps works on Indians of the region which might tell her more. The library in Janeville wouldn't have much—she had been there, and it wasn't much more than a small room full of historical novels and geology texts—but the librarian might be able to get books from other libraries around the state, perhaps one of the university libraries . . .

She glanced at her watch, realising that school had let out long before; the children might be waiting at the bus stop now, in this terrible weather. She pushed aside the heavy green curtains.

"Derek—"

But the room was empty. He had already gone for the children, she thought with relief. He certainly did better at this job of being a parent than she did.

Of course, Kelly was his child; he'd had years to adjust to fatherhood. She wondered if he would buy a horse for Kelly and hoped that he wouldn't.

Perhaps it was silly to be worried about ancient Indian curses and to fear that a long-ago event would be repeated, but Marilyn didn't want horses in a barn where horses had once gone mad. There were no Indians here now, and no horses. Perhaps they would be safe.

Marilyn glanced down at the books still piled beside her, thinking of looking up the section about the horses. But she recoiled uneasily from the thought. Derek had already told her the story; she could check the facts later, when she was not alone in the house.

She got up. She would go and busy herself in the kitchen, and have hot chocolate and cinnamon toast waiting for the children.

The scream still rang in her ears and vibrated through her

body. Marilyn lay still, breathing shallowly, and stared at the ceiling. What had she been dreaming?

It came again, muffled by distance, but as chilling as a blade of ice. It wasn't a dream; someone, not so very far away, was screaming.

Marilyn visualised the house on a map, trying to tell herself it had been nothing, the cry of some bird. No one could be out there, miles from everything, screaming; it didn't make sense. And Derek was still sleeping, undisturbed. She thought about waking him, then repressed the thought as unworthy and sat up. She'd better check on the children, just in case it was one of them crying out of a nightmare. She did not go to the window; there would be nothing to see, she told herself.

Marilyn found Kelly out of bed, her arms wrapped around herself as she stared out the window.

"What's the matter?"

Kelly didn't shift her gaze. "I heard a horse," she said softly. "I heard it neighing. It woke me up."

"A horse?"

"It must be wild. If I can catch it and tame it, can I keep it?" Now she looked around, her eyes bright in the moonlight.

"I don't think . . ."

"Please?"

"Kelly, you were probably just dreaming."

"I heard it. It woke me up. I heard it again. I'm not imagining things," she said tightly.

"Then it was probably a horse belonging to one of the farmers around here."

"I don't think it belongs to anyone."

Marilyn was suddenly aware of how tired she was. Her body ached. She didn't want to argue with Kelly. Perhaps there had been a horse—a neigh could sound like a scream, she thought.

"Go back to bed, Kelly. You have to go to school in the morning. You can't do anything about the horse now."

"I'm going to look for it, though," Kelly said, getting back into bed. "I'm going to find it."

"Later."

As long as she was up, Marilyn thought as she stepped out into the hall, she should check on the other children, to be sure they were all sleeping.

To her surprise, they were all awake. They turned sleepy, bewildered eyes on her when she came in and murmured broken fragments of their dreams as she kissed them each in turn.

Derek woke as she climbed in beside him. "Where were you?" he asked. He twitched. "Christ, your feet are like ice!"

"Kelly was awake. She thought she heard a horse neighing."

"I told you," Derek said with sleepy smugness. "That's our ghost horse, back again."

The sky was heavy with the threat of snow; the day was cold and too still. Marilyn stood up from her typewriter in disgust and went downstairs. The house was silent except for the distant chatter of Derek's typewriter.

"Where are the kids?" she asked from the doorway.

Derek gave her a distracted look, his hands still poised over the keys. "I think they all went out to clean up the barn."

"But the barn is closed—it's locked."

"Mmmm."

Marilyn sighed and left him. She felt weighted by the chores of supervision. If only the children could go to school every day, where they would be safe and out of her jurisdiction. She thought of how easily they could be hurt or die, their small bodies broken. So many dangers, she thought, getting her coral-coloured coat out of the front closet. How did people cope with the tremendous responsibility of other lives under their protection? It was an impossible task.

The children had mobilised into a small but diligent army, marching in and out of the barn with their arms full of hay, boards or tools. Marilyn looked for Kelly, who was standing just inside the big double doors and directing operations.

"The doors were chained shut," she said, confused. "How did you—"

"I cut it apart," Kelly said. "There was a hacksaw in the tool shed." She gave Marilyn a sidelong glance. "Daddy said we could take any tools from there that we needed."

Marilyn looked at her with uneasy respect, then glanced away to where the other children were working grimly with hands and hammers at the boards nailed across all the stall doors. The darkness of the barn was relieved by a storm lantern hanging from a hook.

"Somebody really locked this place up good," Kelly said. "Do you know why?"

Marilyn hesitated, then decided. "I suppose it was boarded up so tightly because of the way one of your early relatives died here."

Kelly's face tensed with interest. "Died? How? Was he murdered?"

"Not exactly. His horses killed him. They . . . turned on him one night, nobody ever knew why."

Kelly's eyes were knowing. "He must have been an awful man, then. Terribly cruel. Because horses will put up with almost anything. He must have done something so—"

"No. He wasn't supposed to have been a cruel man."

"Maybe not to *people.*"

"Some people thought his death was due to an Indian curse. The land here was supposed to be sacred; they thought this was the spirit's way of taking revenge."

Kelly laughed. "That's some excuse. Look, I got to get to work, OK?"

Marilyn dreamed she went out one night to saddle a horse. The barn was filled with them, all her horses, her pride and delight. She reached up to bridle one, a sorrel gelding, and suddenly felt—with disbelief that staved off the pain—powerful teeth bite down on her arm. She heard the bone crunch, saw the flesh tear, and then the blood . . .

She looked up in horror, into eyes which were reddened and strange.

A sudden blow threw her forward and she landed face-down in dust and straw. She could not breathe. Another horse, her gentle black mare, had kicked her in the back. She felt a wrenching, tearing pain in her leg. When finally she could move she turned her head and saw the great yellow teeth, stained with her blood, of both her horses as they fed upon her. And the other horses, all around her, were kicking at their stalls. The wood splintered and gave, and they all came to join in the feast.

The children came clattering in at lunchtime, tracking snow and mud across the red-brick floor. It had been snowing since morning, but the children were oblivious to it. They did not, as Marilyn had expected, rush out shrieking to play in the snow but went instead to the barn, as they did every weekend now. It was almost ready, they said.

Kelly slipped into her chair and powdered her soup with salt. "Wait till you see what we found," she said breathlessly.

"Animal, vegetable or mineral?" Derek asked.

"Animal *and* mineral."

"Where did you find it?" Marilyn asked.

The smallest child spilled soup in her lap and howled. When Marilyn got back to the table, everyone was talking about the discovery in the barn: Derek curious, the children mysterious.

"But what is it?" Marilyn asked.

"It's better to see it. Come with us after we eat."

The children had worked hard. The shrouded winter light spilled into the empty space of the barn through all the open half-doors of the stalls. The rotting straw and grain was all gone, and the dirt floor had been raked and swept clear of more than an inch of fine dust. The large design stood out clearly, white and clean against the hard earth.

It was not a horse. After examining it more closely, Marilyn wondered how she could have thought it was the depiction of a wild, rearing stallion. Horses have hooves, not three-pronged talons, and they don't have such a feline snake of a tail. The proportions of the body were wrong, too, once she looked more carefully.

Derek crouched and ran his fingers along the outline of the beast. It had been done in chalk, but it was much more than just a drawing. Lines must have been deeply scored in the earth, and the narrow trough then filled with some pounded white dust.

"Chalk, I think," Derek said. "I wonder how deep it goes?" He began scratching with a forefinger at the side of the thick white line.

Kelly bent and caught his arm. "Don't ruin it."

"I'm not, honey." He looked up at Marilyn, who was still standing apart, staring at the drawing.

"It must be the Indian curse," she said. She tried to smile, but she felt an unease which she knew could build into an open dread.

"Do you suppose this is what the spirit who haunts this land is supposed to look like?" Derek asked.

"What else?"

"Odd that it should be a horse, then, instead of some animal indigenous to the area. The legend must have arisen after the white man—"

"But it's not a horse," Marilyn said. "Look at it."

"It's not a horse exactly, no," he agreed, standing and dusting his hands. "But it's more a horse than it is anything else."

"It's so fierce," Marilyn murmured. She looked away into Kelly's eager face. "Well, now that you've cleaned up the barn, what are you going to do?"

"Now we're going to catch the horse."

"What horse?"

"The wild one, the one we hear at night."

"Oh, that. Well, it must be miles away by now. Someone else must have caught it."

Kelly shook her head. "I heard it last night. It was practically outside my window, but when I looked it was gone. I could see its hoof-prints in the snow."

"You're not going out again?"

The children turned blank eyes on her, ready to become hostile, or tearful, if she were going to be difficult.

"I mean," Marilyn said apologetically, "you've been out all morning, running around. And it's still snowing. Why don't you just let your food digest for a while—get out your colouring books, or a game or something, and play in here where it's warm."

"We can't stop now," Kelly said. "We might catch the horse this afternoon."

"And if you don't, do you intend to go out every day until you do?"

"Of course," Kelly said. The other children nodded.

Marilyn's shoulders slumped as she gave in. "Well, wrap up. And don't go *too* far from the house in case it starts snowing harder. And don't stay out too long, or you'll get frostbite." The children were already moving away from her as she spoke. They live in another world, Marilyn thought, despairing.

She wondered how long this would go on. The barn project had held within it a definite end, but Marilyn could not believe the children would ever catch the horse they sought. She was not even certain there was a horse out in that snow to be caught, even though she had been awakened more than once by the shrill, distant screaming that might have been a horse neighing.

Marilyn went to Derek's office and climbed again into the hidden window seat. The heavy curtains muffled the steady beat of Derek's typewriter, and the falling snow muffled the country beyond the window. She picked up another of the small green volumes and began to read.

"Within a month of his arrival, Martin Hoskins was known in Janeville for two things. One: he intended to bring industry, wealth and population to upstate New York, and to swell the tiny hamlet into a city. Second: a man without wife or children, Hoskins' pride, passion and delight was in his six beautiful horses.

"Martin had heard the legend that his land was cursed, but, as he wrote to a young woman in New York City, 'The Indians were driven out of these parts long ago, and their curses with them, I'll wager. For what is an Indian curse without an Indian knife or arrow to back it?'

"It was true that the great Indian tribes had been dispersed or destroyed, but a few Indians remained: tattered and homeless in the White Man's world. Martin Hoskins met one such young brave on the road to Janeville one morning.

" 'I must warn you, sir,' said the ragged but proud young savage. 'The land upon which you dwell is inhabited by a powerful spirit.'

" 'I've heard that tale before,' responded Hoskins, shortly but not unkindly. 'And I don't believe in your heathen gods; I'm not afraid of 'em.'

" 'This spirit is no god of ours, either. But my people have known of it, and respected it, for as many years as we have lived on this land. Think of this spirit not as a god, but as a force . . . something powerful in nature which cannot be reasoned with or fought—something like a storm.'

" 'And what do you propose I do?' asked Hoskins.

" 'Leave that place. Do not try to live there. The spirit cannot follow you if you leave, but it cannot be driven out, either. The spirit belongs to the land as much as the land belongs to it.'

"Martin Hoskins laughed harshly. 'You ask me to run from something I do not believe in! Well, I tell you this: I believe in storms, but I do not run from them. I'm strong; what can that spirit do to me?'

"The Indian shook his head sorrowfully. 'I cannot say what it may do. I only know that you will offend it by dwelling where it dwells, and the more you offend it, the more certainly will it destroy you. Do not try to farm there, nor keep animals. That land knows only one master and will not take to another. There is only one law, and one master on that land. You must serve it, or leave.'

" 'I serve no master but myself—and my God,' Martin said."

Marilyn closed the book, not wanting to read of Martin's inevitable, and terrible, end. He kept animals, she thought idly. What if he had been a farmer? How would the spirit of the land have destroyed him then?

She looked out the window and saw with relief that the children were playing. They've finally given up their hunt, she thought, and wondered what they were playing now. Were they playing follow-the-leader? Dancing like Indians? Or horses, she thought, suddenly, watching their prancing feet and tossing heads. They were playing horses.

Marilyn woke suddenly, listening. Her body strained forward, her heart pounding too loudly, her mouth dry. She heard it again: the wild, mad cry of a horse. She had heard it before in the night, but never so close, and never so human-sounding.

Marilyn got out of bed, shivering violently as her feet touched the cold, bare floor and the chilly air raised bumps on her naked arms. She went to the window, drew aside the curtains, and looked out.

The night was still and as clear as an engraving. The moon lacked only a sliver more for fullness and shone out of a cloudless, star-filled sky. A group of small figures danced upon the snowy ground, jerking and prancing and kicking up a spray of snow. Now and again one of them would let out a shrill cry: half a horse's neigh, half a human wail. Marilyn felt her hairs rise as she recognised the puppet-like dancers below: the children.

She was tempted to let the curtains fall back and return to bed—to say nothing, to do nothing, to act as if nothing unusual had happened. But these were *her* children now, and she wasn't allowed that sort of irresponsibility.

The window groaned as she forced it open, and at the faint sound the children stopped their dance. As one, they turned and looked up at Marilyn.

The breath stopped in her throat as she stared down at their upturned faces. Everything was very still, as if that moment had been frozen within a block of ice. Marilyn could not speak; she could not think of what to say.

She withdrew back into the room, letting the curtains fall back before the open window, and she ran to the bed.

"Derek," she said, catching hold of him. "Derek, wake up." She could not stop her trembling.

His eyes moved behind their lids.

"Derek," she said urgently.

Now they opened and, fogged with sleep, looked at her.

"What is it, love?" He must have seen the fear in her face, for he pushed himself up on his elbows. "Did you have a bad dream?"

"Not a dream, no. Derek, your Uncle Martin—he could have lived here if he hadn't been a master himself. If he hadn't kept horses. The horses turned on him because they had found another master."

"What are you talking about?"

"The spirit that lives in this land," she said. She was not trembling, now. Perspiration beaded her forehead. "It uses the . . . the servants, or whatever you want to call them . . . it can't abide anyone else ruling here. If we . . ."

"You've been dreaming, sweetheart." He tried to pull her down beside him, but she shook him off. She could hear them on the stairs.

"Is our door locked?" she suddenly demanded.

"Yes. I think so." Derek frowned. "Did you hear something? I thought . . ."

"Children are a bit like animals, don't you think? At least, people treat them as if they were—adults, I mean. I suppose children must . . ."

"I *do* hear something. I'd better go—"

"Derek—No—"

The doorknob rattled and there was a great pounding at the door.

"Who is that?" Derek said loudly.

"The children," Marilyn whispered.

The door splintered and gave way before Derek reached it, and the children burst through. There were so many of them, Marilyn thought, as she waited on the bed. And all she could seem to see was their strong, square teeth.

# R. Chetwynd-Hayes

# The Jumpity-Jim

RONALD CHETWYND-HAYES has been called the Dean of British Horror Writers. A full-time author since 1973, during the ensuing period he has written and published seven novels, eighteen collections of short stories, edited thirty-three anthologies, novelized two movies and had a couple of films made based on his work (*From Beyond the Grave* and *The Monster Club*).

In 1988 he was awarded both The Horror Writers of America and The British Fantasy special awards for his services to the field. His story "The Ninth Removal" was recently released by BBC Enterprises in their *Price of Fear* cassette series, featuring Vincent Price, and his latest novel *The Curse of the Snake God* is published by Piatkus Books.

The following story is one of Chetwynd-Hayes's most popular—it is also extremely *nasty*.

"KEEP YOURSELF neat and tidy at all times," Father said, "and learn your duties."

"Read a portion of Holy Scriptures every night before retiring," Mother instructed, and Father nodded his agreement.

Harriet waved to them from the coach window, more than a little frightened if the truth be told, for this was the first time she had been away from home and she was going into an unknown future. The coachman whipped up his horses, the guard blew a blast on his horn, and they were away, drawing clear of the village, leaving the happy years of childhood behind.

"You look distressed, my dear," a kindly looking matron on the opposite seat said. "You are leaving home for the first time?"

Harriet nodded while patting her eyes with a nice clean handkerchief, freshly laundered by Mother that morning.

"Never mind," the good lady consoled, "you'll soon get used to your new surroundings. It's good for youngsters to break away from the apron-strings. Going into service, I expect."

"Yes, Mam," Harriet nodded again. "Begging your pardon, but how did you know?"

The lady laughed. "Can always tell. Fresh young thing like you, all done up in your Sunday best. Service, I said to myself the minute you put foot inside this coach."

The four other passengers had been listening to this conversation with varying degrees of interest, and one young man who wore a beautiful waistcoat, smiled a rather supercilious smile.

"And what household is to be honoured by your service? Buckingham Palace?"

"Oh, no!" Harriet gasped. "But I am going to a nobleman's house. Lord Dunwilliam's."

"Are you, indeed!"

The young man produced a quizzing-glass and examined Harriet carefully for a few minutes, as though she were some rare specimen he had not encountered before. At length he dropped the glass, which dangled on the end of a gold chain, and pronounced his verdict.

"You should fit into Dunwilliam's establishment very nicely," he said. "Very nicely indeed."

Harriet stood in the courtyard of the Royal George and watched the departing mail-coach rumble its way up a slope and out on to the main highway. The last link with home had been broken and she was now alone, subject to the caprice of total strangers. She sat down on her black box, not daring to enter the inn, for Father had often stressed the evil which lurked in such places, and wondered what she should do. Father had said someone would be waiting to meet her, but so far none of the loungers that were clustered round the inn door advanced to claim her.

Presently, however, a tall, dark man, dressed in a cassock, entered the courtyard. His coming seemed to alarm everyone in sight, for they dispersed, scattering like corn husks before the wind. Harriet saw the priest had a long, harsh face—a visage she knew to be right and proper for a man of his calling—and she got quickly to her feet, performing a little bob, thus displaying a seemly respect for the cloth and a sense of righteous humility.

The reverend gentleman interrupted his journey towards the inn, which, if his expression was any criterion, boded ill for its occupants, and scowled down at the girl.

"And pray, child, what is a girl who displays all the outward signs of a proper upbringing doing in this place of iniquity? And unattended? Eh!"

He barked the "Eh" with such ferocity that Harriet trembled before bowing her knee into another bob, an action her mother had often stressed was most pleasing to the quality.

"If you please, sir, I am waiting to be picked up."

"What!"

The roar made Harriet realise she had not perhaps chosen her words well, and she hastened to explain.

"Begging your pardon, sir, but someone is to collect me. I am to be kitchen-maid, if it so please you, at Dunwilliam Grange . . ."

She stopped in mid-sentence, for the dark, awful eyes that glared down at her now held an expression that left no doubt she had again, inadvertently said the wrong thing.

"Repeat," the priest said, his jaw muscles quivering. "I say, if you have the brazen effrontery, repeat what you have just said."

"If you please, sir, I am to be kitchen-maid at . . ."

"Yes, go on. Where, child? Where?"

"Dunwilliam Grange, sir . . ."

One hand seized the front of her dress, the other tilted her chin, and the raucous voice rang out.

"The face is fair. Eh? I grant you the devil has grown cunning and now hides his evil under a pretty—nay—even an innocent mask. But I am not deceived. Eh? The form is shapely, well-calculated to inflame men's senses, but I warrant that somewhere the great beast has left his mark. Eh? Tell me, wench, where is it?"

"I don't know what you mean, sir."

Harriet dared not struggle, for she saw the reverend gentleman was sore afflicted; saliva was trickling down the corners of his mouth and his eyes were dreadfully bloodshot. She recalled that Gaffer Cheeseman had a similar appearance after he had drunk two gallons of cider on an empty stomach. The priest tightened his grip.

"Not know what I mean, eh? Going to Dunwilliam Grange and pleading the innocence of a lamb that has just seen the light of day? I would as lief believe the sun rose at midnight and the devil bathed in holy water. Now, I ask again, girl. Where is the mark? The secret tit from which the beast takes substance?"

"I have no mark, sir." Harriet was crying. "When you have slept, I am certain you will regret abusing me so. My father says cider breeds madness . . ."

The roar of rage was like that of Farmer Giles's bull when it spotted Mistress Jarvie crossing the field in a red cloak. The priest spun her round and, gripping her dress at the neck line, ripped it open to the waist. Harriet felt the cold air on her back, and she pulled away, only to have her hair grabbed. The now-spluttering voice shouted: "The flesh is white. Eh? So is the leper that is cast out from the haunts of men. But I will find the mark. Eh, I will find it."

"Enough!"

A sharp voice cut across the priest's tirade like the blade of a knife, and Harriet was suddenly released, to go sprawling face down on the cobble stones, where she lay sobbing for a few moments then, remembering her half-nude state, scrambled to her feet. A man was just dismounting from his horse, and tossing the reins to a nearby ostler. He sauntered over to the sobbing girl and glaring priest. Harriet, despite her distress, thought she had never seen such a beautiful gentleman before. He was tall, with a lean, bronzed face, and a pair of dark, penetrating eyes. His hair was jet-black, save for a single white streak which ran from the centre of his high forehead to the base of his skull. He was dressed all in black, relieved only by the silver trimmings on his cloak. He smiled, revealing even white teeth.

"I admire your taste, parson. But in public! Whatever would the dear bishop say?"

The clergyman crossed himself, then backed away a few paces.

"Avaunt, Satan."

The gentleman laughed. "I will be gone when the mood suits me. I will not ask why you molested this pretty creature, for you are as crazed as a cracked jug and I have not the time for the prattle of a madman. Where were you bound, girl?"

Harriet would have dropped a curtsey, but she suspected such an operation might cause her to release her torn dress, so she meekly bowed her head instead.

"To Dunwilliam Grange, if it so please you, sir."

"Another of your imported devil spawn?" the priest growled and the gentleman raised his hand in mock horror.

"You malign me. I rarely snatch from the cradle, but I grant you, she is a delicious morsel. What post are you to fill in my house, child?"

"You are—Lord Dunwilliam?" she gasped.

He sighed deeply. "I fear so."

"I am to be your kitchen-maid, my lord."

"Indeed? I was not aware that we needed one. It must be you that rogue Hackett was supposed to collect, but he ran the dog-cart into a ditch. Drunk as a priest at a bishop's convention."

He made an ironic bow in the parson's direction.

"Your pardon, Mr Dale, I forgot—you prefer stripping girls to opening a bottle."

"The day of reckoning is coming." The Reverend Dale shook his fist. "I know of the obscenities that take place in that proud house, but I tell you the time will come when its stones will be levelled to the ground."

"You'd best ride before me, girl." Lord Dunwilliam smiled down at Harriet. "'Twould not be wise to leave you here with that poor, mad fool, and heaven above knows when Hackett will be sober enough to drive a cart."

He beckoned to the ostler: "Take the girl's box into the inn. Someone will call for it later."

He mounted the great horse, then, leaning down, pulled Harriet up. She sat side-saddle, trying hard not to lean against him and very mindful of the strong arms that railed her in on either side when he took up the reins. They rode out of the courtyard and the Reverend Dale's voice followed them.

"God is not mocked. He will send forth his legions and they will crush the forces of evil. Cursed be ye that walk by night, for darkness will be your lot for all eternity . . ."

"The home of my fathers," said Dunwilliam in a low tone. "See girl, the nest in which I was hatched."

The grey-stoned house stood before a screen of trees; turreted, a face with many eyes, it was a structure of rare, if somewhat grim beauty. Harriet wondered if she dare enter such a grand place with a torn dress and a dirty face.

"It's very nice," she said.

Lord Dunwilliam chuckled.

"I doubt if there are many hereabouts who would agree with that description. How, in the name of sanity, did you ever become engaged as my kitchen-maid?"

"Mother, who was in service before she married, wrote to

an agency in London. For she knows her letters, and writes as good a hand as Parson himself. They sent someone down to see me, and I am to be on a month's trial."

"Um." His lordship grunted as they rode down one hill and then up another, finally to pass through the great iron gates of Dunwilliam Grange.

Mrs Browning was a woman of large proportions and such a grim aspect that Harriet almost wished herself back in the inn courtyard facing the Reverend Dale. The housekeeper allowed her cold gaze to travel slowly down from the girl's auburn head to the tips of her laced-up boots.

"How are you called, girl?"

"Harriet, mam."

"Most unsuitable. From now on you will be known as Jane." She called abruptly over one shoulder. "Mary, come here."

An extremely pretty girl left the kitchen table where she had been slicing potatoes and came quickly over to Mrs Browning, before whom she stood motionless, her head bowed.

"Yes, mam."

"Mary, you will take Jane upstairs and see that she returns suitably attired. She is to share your room."

"Yes, mam. Thank you, mam."

Harriet followed her guide up some very steep and winding stairs and presently came to a small room that overlooked the back garden. It was furnished with two narrow beds, a washstand and a large cupboard. Mary was brimful with curiosity and, scarcely had she closed the door, when questions came tripping off her tongue.

"How did your dress get all tore like that? And Jem the gardener says you come here on his lordship's horse. Did he tear your dress?"

"No." Harriet shook her auburn curls. "It was a horrible old parson."

"Ah, the Reverend Dale. He hates this place something cruel and says all of us who live here be limbs of Satan."

"Why?" Harriet had removed her tattered dress, which she was examining rather ruefully, and Mary opened the cupboard door and produced a black skirt and white blouse.

"Well, they do say all sort of weird goings-on took place in this house back in his lordship's father's time. There's a big room, right up under the roof, and people saw flashes of light and heard terrible cries. Then one morning his old lordship was found dead. 'Twas said he took poison or some such thing."

"How awful!" Harriet shuddered. "Aren't you frightened?"

Mary shook her head.

"No. I pay no heed to talk like that, only I wouldn't care to go wandering around the upper storey after nightfall. Besides, the pay's good, and although Mrs Browning is a tartar, the work ain't all that hard."

While they had been talking, Harriet had dressed, and now she wore a costume corresponding to Mary's; a long, black serge skirt and an off-the-shoulder blouse. She was not happy with this last item, Mother having on more than one occasion stated that the face and hands were the only parts of the body a respectable woman bared for the public gaze.

"It don't seem right," she began, but Mary laughed.

"You'll soon get used to it. 'Tis only the shoulders. Why, some ladies leave three parts of their boobs bare and aren't thought none the worse. It's a fad of her ladyship's. Indoors, we young 'uns have to wear this get-up. Don't do no harm. But it makes the parson howl."

She laid Harriet's torn dress out on the bed and sighed.

"Shame. But a needle and thread should soon put it to rights. Now, we best get down, or Mrs Browning will be raising old Cain and her tongue be sharp enough as it is."

Back in the kitchen Mrs Browning gave Harriet a quick glance, then said: "There's an overall hanging up behind the door. Put it on, then go into the scullery and start cleaning out the saucepans. We're all behind like a donkey's tail."

During the days that followed, Harriet began to realise to some degree why the Reverend Dale entertained such pronounced misgivings about the household at Dunwilliam

Grange. With the exception of Mrs Browning, all the female staff were young and extremely pretty. Another disquieting piece of imformation was that few completed their month's probation. The turnover in female staff was alarmingly high. Once, when washing-up in the scullery, she heard Jem the head gardener and Hackett, a bearded, morose individual, talking as they sat drinking beer at the kitchen table.

"The new 'un be shapely. 'Twould be a good tumble in the 'ay."

Harriet wondered what this remark might mean, but, realising that she was the "new 'un" under discussion, wiped her hands dry and stood listening.

"Won't last long," Hackett stated. "They never does. After a little chat with 'er ladyship, out they goes."

"That be a strange thing." Jem refilled his glass from an earthenware jug. "Why be that? Right as a trivet, until they 'as a little heart-to-heart with 'er ladyship. The number of boxes and blubbering wenches you've driven down to the Royal George . . . Don't they talk right or summat?"

"Maybe," Hackett murmured gruffly. "Maybe."

There was a full minute's silence and Harriet wondered if the conversation had come to an unsatisfactory conclusion. Then Hackett spoke again, but this in a low, though perfectly audible tone.

"Jem, if I tells you summat confidential like, will you promise to keep it under your 'at?"

"I'll be as silent as the grave," Jem promised. "I'm not one to blab, you knows that."

"Well," Hackett said and cleared his throat, "perhaps I shouldn't tell you, as his lordship gave me a gold piece to keep me mouth shut, but it's lain on me conscience and I'd like to unburden, if you knows what I mean."

"Aye, man. Get on with it."

"Well, about two year back, do you remember that red-headed piece, Clara? Only her real name was Jenny Binns. Well, she went upstairs for her little chat with 'er ladyship. Excited she was, thought maybe she'd get promotion to above stairs, and I didn't tell 'er no different. It must 'ave been about half-past six when 'is lordship comes over to the coach house; looked a bit down in the mouth 'e did. He sez: 'Hackett, Clara has been taken ill. I wants you to take 'er to the good Sister,' 'e sez. 'I'll ride over and see the Mother Superior.' Well, I thought that a bit funny, see? Any road, I went up to 'er ladyship's room, and there was the girl looking as if she's had a fit. Speechless she was, with 'er face all twisted up, and 'er eyes—strewth! You'd think she'd seen Old Nick 'imself."

"Do you think, maybe," Jem asked in a low, quivering voice, "she 'ad?"

"No, man. I don't 'old with that nonsense. But I tell you summat else. There were three ruddy great scratches down 'er back."

"No!" Jem gasped. "You're 'avin' me on."

"True as I sit 'ere. 'Er blouse was all tore, and scratches, like claw marks, down 'er back. Don't know what they thought of it up at the Convent. Mad dog, mayhap. Anyway, 'er ladyship was furious. Kept muttering about 'er almost being the one."

"What do you think she meant?" Jem asked.

"Gawd knows. But . . . Not a word mind. 'Ere comes old Ma Browning."

Harriet went back to her washing-up, trying to understand what the conversation had implied. Above all, what sort of person was Lady Dunwilliam?

"Mary, have you seen Lady Dunwilliam yet?"

"Once or twice."

Mary was bathing her feet in an earthenware bowl. "She walks in the small garden sometimes. Why?"

"I just wondered. You haven't been up to see her?"

"Oh, I see what you mean." Mary wiped her feet on a towel then, opening the window, emptied the contents of the bowl on to the garden below. "That'll make the cabbages grow. No. Mrs Browning said her ladyship would want a few words with me some time. But nothing's happened yet."

Mary climbed into bed and blew out the candle before snuggling deep down into the feather-mattress. She grunted with complete satisfaction.

"Never slept on a feather-mattress 'til I came here. Do you proud they do."

"What's she like?" Harriet asked.

"Who?"

"Lady Dunwilliam."

"Oh, I've never spoken to her. She's got a lovely face, but she's deformed."

"Deformed!"

"Yes." Mary turned over, making her bed creak. "She's got a hump. Terrible it is. A great bulge that comes up to her shoulders. I never seen anything like it."

"We had a hunchback in our village," Harriet said, "and the boys used to poke fun at him. He was a nasty man who beat his donkey."

"If you poked fun at Lady Dunwilliam, Mrs Browning would most likely beat you. Now go to sleep, do. We've got to be up early tomorrow."

The following morning Mrs Browning summoned Harriet from the scullery and handed her a stiff brush and dustpan.

"Nora is down with the flux. You must stand in for her. Get upstairs to the first landing and brush the carpet. Don't make a mess."

Harriet took the dustpan and brush and not without some trepidation, for she had never been in the upper part of the house before, made her way upstairs. Lord Dunwilliam had been kind when he had rescued her from the clutches of the Reverend Dale, but she instinctively knew it was the kindness he would have bestowed on a tormented dog, had the mood so moved him. Her parents had taught her to fear and respect people of quality, and fear was uppermost as she mounted the grand staircase.

The carpet was thick; her feet sank into the soft pile and she was trying hard to look in all directions at once. Massive gilt-framed pictures lined the walls; a magnificent chandelier was suspended from a high ceiling that dominated both staircase and hall. A footman, resplendent in a plum-coloured brocade livery and a powdered wig, minced his way across the first landing and stared at her with supercilious scorn.

"What are you doing up here, girl?"

"I am to clean the carpet." Harriet raised her head, not in the least impressed by brocade or wig, knowing the man's status to be little above her own.

"Then get on with it," he instructed, "and don't make any noise. Her ladyship is still asleep."

She poked her tongue out at his retreating figure, then sank to her knees and began to brush the carpet. In fact, it needed little attention and she found the work pleasant after a week of washing-up, scrubbing the kitchen floor and other menial tasks. She had reached the centre of the landing when a quiet voice asked: "Who are you?"

Harriet was afraid to look up. The voice was low and had that well-bred quality which told her it was one of authority. It spoke again.

"Stand up, girl, when I am speaking to you."

Harriet laid aside her dustpan and brush, then obeyed, to find herself facing the most beautiful woman she had ever seen.

"I am Lady Dunwilliam."

If she had said she was the Queen of England, Harriet would have felt no surprise, for the lovely fair-skinned face was regal, even arrogant. A mass of waving, ash-blonde hair tumbled down to her shoulders, a glorious cascade that Harriet wanted to touch. Her eyes were possibly the most outstanding feature, for they were dark-brown and contrasted dramatically with her dazzling fairness. But all this beauty was ruined by the grotesque hump that swelled out in a gradual curve from the small of her back to just above her shoulders. The weight, or perhaps the ungainly bulk of this awful deformity, made it impossible for Lady Dunwilliam to stand upright, and she stooped, reminding Harriet of the coalman preparing to empty his sack into Father's cellar. The dark, wonderful eyes were bitter, and lines of suffering were etched round the full mouth.

"It would seem you are deaf," Lady Dunwilliam said. "I asked who you were."

"Harriet—I mean Jane, my lady. The kitchen-maid, if it please you."

"It does not please me," the cold voice stated. "I am at a loss to know what the kitchen-maid is doing up on this landing. Surely you should be scouring pots, or something."

"Nora, the housemaid, is ill. And Mrs Browning said . . ."

"Never mind." A long-fingered hand waved aside the explanation as a spasm of pain passed over the lovely face.

"Leave off doing whatever you're supposed to be doing, and come with me."

She turned quickly and led the way into the bedroom. Harriet followed and found herself in a charming blue room that was in a state of chaos. Articles of clothing littered the floor, were draped over chairbacks and even the dressing-table. The bed was unmade; the sheets and blankets were twisted up and one pillow was ripped open: a great gaping wound from which feathers seeped like maggots from the belly of a dead horse.

"Clear this lot up," Lady Dunwilliam ordered, then sank down on to a dressing-stool, from where she watched the girl with sombre eyes. Harriet began to collect the clothes together, piling them on a chair.

"How long have you been here?" Lady Dunwilliam asked.

"A week, my lady."

"You can drop the ladyship business. Mam will suffice."

"Yes, my . . . Yes, mam."

An uncomfortable silence prevailed for some five minutes before Lady Dunwilliam spoke again.

"Do you like working in the kitchen?"

Harriet thought it good policy to express satisfaction with her mode of employment.

"Oh, yes mam."

"Then you must be either mad or stupid—and you appear to be neither." Her ladyship spoke sharply, and Harriet shivered. "Scouring saucepans, scrubbing floors. Being bullied by the excellent Mrs Browning. I am sure you must enjoy that."

Harriet did not answer, but turned her attention to the bed which she proceeded to strip before kneading the mattress. As she leant forward her eyes caught sight of a book. She quickly read the title. *"Unnatural enmities and their disposal* by Conrad Von Holstein." She must have gasped or betrayed some sign she was startled, for instantly Lady Dunwilliam asked: "What is it, child?"

"Nothing, mam."

"Don't lie. Was it that book? Can you read?"

"Yes, mam."

"An unusual accomplishment for a kitchen-maid. Who taught you?"

"My mother. She was in service at Sir William Sinclair's house and Lady Sinclair allowed her to study with the children."

Lady Dunwilliam pointed to a chair.

"Come and sit down and bring that book with you."

Harriet crept forward, clutching the book with moist hands, not at all sure she should obey. Mother had been most indignant when a milkmaid had once sat down in her presence. Besides, the invitation might be a test to see if she knew her place.

"Thank you, mam, but I'd rather . . ."

"Great balls of fire, girl, sit down."

Harriet perched on the very edge of the chair and waited.

"Open the book at page two hundred and seventy-two," her ladyship ordered.

Harriet found the book almost fell open at that page; the paper was well thumbed and had quite obviously been re-read many times.

"Let us see how well you can read," Lady Dunwilliam invited.

Harriet cleared her throat and began.

"'Chapter Eight. The Jumpity-Jim . . .

"'We are as blind men groping in eternal darkness, not knowing who or what is attendant upon us, or the pitfalls that are waiting for our stumbling feet. Many and diverse are the creatures that can be raised by those who have dipped a spoon in the unlimited sea of knowledge, but having once clothed them with a semblance of life, even the great Solomon would seek in vain for the power to control them.

"'Let it be known to all those who would follow the path of forbidden lore, that there is no creature more gruesome to behold, or more hell-binding in its relationship to the flesh, than the Primate Horrific, or, as it is known among the unlettered peasantry, the Jumpity-Jim.

"'The natural habitat of this creature is the third lower plane, and it can only be raised by a magician of the first order. But once brought into being, then I say woe unto him who has not protected himself with the tree circles of light, or cannot speak the words that are written in the blue book.

"'It is of foul aspect, having the face and form of an unborn monkey, yet is there a fearful parody of a human in its lineaments. It can leap to great heights and with mighty speed, and if he who has called it forth has protected himself, then will it find another . . .'"

"That is enough," Lady Dunwilliam's voice cut short the recital. "You read well, child, and are a credit to your mother's tuition."

Harriet gladly closed the book and looked at her employer with certain astonishment.

"'Tis most fearful reading, my lady, and, begging your pardon, I wonder why . . ."

"Why I interest myself in such things?" Lady Dunwilliam smiled. "Perhaps a crooked body breeds a crooked mind. 'Tis nonsense anyway. The poor fool who wrote it had but listened to tales babbled by peasants as they huddled round their fires on a dark night. None of them know the truth or can be expected to."

She rose and made her way towards the door, talking as she went.

"When you have finished here, come into my withdrawing-room. There is another service I require of you."

It took Harriet some twenty minutes to put the rooms to rights, then she went out on to the landing and, seeing an open door some little way along, went towards it. In the room that lay beyond she found Lady Dunwilliam seated behind a table, with a strange contraption made of polished walnut in front of her. It had a mass of wires and glass tubes rising up from its flat surface and curving down to disappear on either side. Two perpendicular, polished metal rods were fixed to left and right at the front, while a sheet of smoked glass, set in a metal frame, made a kind of screen at the rear.

"Come and sit beside me, girl," Lady Dunwilliam ordered, "but first remove that hideous overall, for I would see if you have the appearance for the kind of work I have in mind."

Harriet unbuttoned the offending garment and draped it carefully over a chair back; Lady Dunwilliam was watching her with a strangely intense look.

"Turn round."

Harriet did as she was told, turning her back to the lady, who appeared to be in a state of mounting excitement.

"Good, white shoulders," she muttered, "and a strong back." She raised her voice. "Come and sit beside me. Hurry."

As soon as Harriet was seated, Lady Dunwilliam pointed to the contraption and said: "This was invented by Lord Dunwilliam's father, and is meant to test a person's aptitude."

"Beg pardon, mam?"

"Great balls of fire!" Lady Dunwilliam appeared to grind her teeth, but hastily regained self-control. "Test your intelligence, girl. Never mind. This is what I want you to do. Grip those metal rods and stare straight at the glass screen. Now, do that."

Harriet, with some reluctance, gripped the metal rods as she had been bidden, and found they vibrated slightly. Lady Dunwilliam's voice was rather hoarse when she spoke again.

"Now, press them down. Gently . . . press down gently . . ."

Harriet felt the rods sink slowly downwards and as she pressed them, a reddish liquid began to bubble up through the glass tubes, while the machine gave out a faint humming sound.

"Good . . . good . . ." Lady Dunwilliam was whispering. "Now, listen carefully. Stare at the glass screen and empty your mind of all thoughts. I know it is not easy, but you must be a good girl and try. Empty your mind. There are no thoughts at all. Just emptiness."

Harriet found it very difficult indeed to think of nothing at all, but Mother had taught her always to obey her elders and betters, so she tried. And as she tried, the glass tubes filled with fast-moving red liquid, the machine hummed like a kettle just on the boil, and my lady was breathing heavily. The smoked-glass screen was getting bigger—or so it seemed—and its surface was most certainly becoming brighter, was developing a pulsating silver sheen that would have alarmed Harriet had she not been so enthralled. Suddenly, the screen cleared and became a three-dimensional picture, protraying a terrible, gloomy valley, illuminated by flickering flames that flared up from the peaks of flanking mountains. The valley and mountainsides were covered with dead trees; twisted shapes that reached out black, skeleton arms towards a red-tinted sky. Something moved on the topmost branch of the nearest tree: a small, long-legged, long-armed something, that dropped to the ground and went bounding down the valley in great, effortless jumps. It looked like a cross between a deformed monkey and a monstrous spider, but the swift, leaping jumps were its most horrible aspect.

Harriet screamed as she relaxed her grip on the metal rods, and instantly the picture disappeared to be replaced by the original smoked glass. The girl was in hysterics, screaming, then laughing, and Lady Dunwilliam was clawing at her arm, slapping her face, shaking her. "What did you see, girl? Stop it . . . stop it . . . tell me what you saw . . ."

". . . It was awful, mam," Harriet began, then lapsed into another fit of sobbing and my lady's patience snapped like an over-stretched cord.

"Talk, you stupid, hysterical slut . . . What did you see?"

"I saw a dark valley, and . . ."

"Yes . . . yes . . . go on," Lady Dunwilliam urged.

"There was something dreadful that went jumping . . ."

She was not allowed to continue, for Lady Dunwilliam

suddenly hugged her, kissed her on both cheeks, then sat back and watched her as though she were some long-sought-for treasure that had, against all expectations, come to hand.

"You have it." She giggled like a very young girl, and clapped her hands in an ecstasy of pure joy. "The true essence . . . you have it. You wonderful, wonderful child."

Harriet wiped her eyes, gradually coming to understand that she had recently displayed some unknown gift, or virtue, that might be to her advantage.

"Beg pardon, me lady, but what exactly have I . . . got?"

"Good heavens, child," Lady Dunwilliam was looking from side to side as though searching for a plausible explanation, "You have intelligence and imagination. The aptitude machine demonstrated that beyond all doubt. Who but an intelligent and imaginative girl could have created a dark valley and a funny little thing that jumped up and down on a piece of ordinary smoked-glass. I am very pleased with you, my dear."

"Thank you, mam." Harriet blushed with pleasure.

"I have been looking for a suitable companion with whom I can converse," Lady Dunwilliam went on, "for, as you can see, I lead a very lonely life, and really, I see no reason why you should not fill the post. What do you say to that?"

"Oh, my Lady . . ." Harriet began, but Lady Dunwilliam cut short her thanks with an imperious wave of her hand.

"That's settled then. There's a nice little room next to mine and you might as well move in right away."

"What will my duties be?" Harriet asked.

"Duties?" Lady Dunwilliam appeared to be at a loss for words for a short while, then, as though struck by a sudden thought, said: "Reading. You may read to me and keep my rooms tidy."

"I will endeavour to give satisfaction, mam," said Harriet.

For no apparent reason, Lady Dunwilliam suddenly began to laugh.

Youth is adaptable and Harriet soon got used to doing practically nothing at all. That is not to say her erstwhile companions of servitude either accepted the situation, or failed to show their shocked surprise. Whenever Lady Dunwilliam was out of sight and earshot, Harriet was winked at, sneered at, scowled upon, pinched, kicked and, on one occasion, punched in the ribs by Mary, who seemed to regard her as a deserter. She was also envied—and, by those who said they knew more than they were prepared to reveal, pitied. One morning, while dusting the china in Lady Dunwilliam's withdrawing-room, she looked up to find Mrs Browning staring at her with cold, expressionless eyes.

"Do you know why her ladyship has taken you to her bosom, girl?"

"She required a companion," Harriet stated boldly, for of late a feeling of self-confidence had moved in with the pretty dresses and her mistress's constant esteem.

"One of ten poor relations would have filled the post," Mrs Browning retorted with a sound that was as near a snort as was possible to a person of her demeanour. "'Tis no affair of mine, but pride goes before a fall, and I've not walked about with closed eyes and blocked ears these past ten years. Do you say your prayers at night?"

"Of course," Harriet expressed surprise at the question.

"Good," Mrs Browning nodded. "I would say them at twilight, just before the sun sets, for it's said the good Lord is most receptive then. Another thing." She paused in the doorway. "I wouldn't go roaming around on the top landing after nightfall. It was there, in the locked room, up under the roof, his late lordship—may his soul rest in peace—used to conduct his experiments, whatever they were. They still talk in the village about the horrible cries that could be heard a mile away. There's no servants left that was here then, and that's a fact a sensible girl would think about. So watch yourself, wear a crucifix, keep what I've said under your bonnet—and think about it."

Such revelations were as stones thrown into a placid pool; they caused unpleasant ripples of alarm, but then, warmed by Lady Dunwilliam's affability, well fed, comfortably bedded and with no arduous toil to mar her days, the feeling of well-being soon returned to Harriet. So pleasantly, in fact, did the days pass, she quite forgot there was such a person as Lord Dunwilliam, and therefore it came as a shock when she entered the withdrawing-room one morning, with her arms full of flowers, to find him seated in an armchair, his dusty boots propped up on a small table. He eyed Harriet with some surprise, then raised a slim eyebrow.

"The damsel in distress? You appear to have made yourself at home."

Harriet curtsied and almost dropped her flowers in the process.

"Her ladyship . . . she said I was to be her companion . . ."

Lord Dunwilliam seemed to uncoil like a handsome snake; he towered over her, his eyes suddenly alight with a gleam of dawning joy.

"She made you . . . her companion! Well, that is marvellous news."

Harriet had not thought his lordship would greet her elevation with anything but complete indifference, but here he was displaying all the emotion of a man who has been told he has just inherited a large fortune. He seized her roughly by the shoulder, kissed her soundly on both cheeks, then rushed from the room and tore upstairs.

For the first time she experienced a cold wave of apprehension. She remembered the story Hackett had related, Mrs Browning's sinister warning. Why should Lord Dunwilliam express undisguised joy when he learnt the kitchen-maid had been promoted to lady's companion? What should have been an unthinkable thought struck her. Was she to play Hagar to Lady Dunwilliam's Sarah? The very idea was extremely sinful and she decided not to think about it. Instead she went upstairs to her bedroom, where she sat by the window and looked out over the garden. Jem was pruning roses. A tall, ungainly figure who looked solid and matter-of-fact; a man of the soil, the kind of person Harriet had known all her life. She was about to go down and speak with him when she heard raised voices. They came from behind the closed door which led into Lady Dunwilliam's bedroom. The deep voice of Lord Dunwilliam was quite distinct, that of his wife a blurred murmur, but Harriet felt sure it was of the uttermost importance for her to hear as much of their conversation as possible. She bent down and applied her eye to the keyhole. His lordship was striding up and down, clearly much agitated; Lady Dunwilliam reclined in a chair and was tapping the palm of her hand with an ivory fan as though stressing her impatience.

"Are you absolutely certain?" Lord Dunwilliam was speaking. "You know what happened last time."

Harriet could not hear her ladyship's answer, then the man spoke again. "We must get her accustomed to the idea. God knows how. She seems simple and perhaps money and the promise of a life of ease might reconcile her. We can but try. There must be no talk. That mad fool, Dale, is already shouting "witchcraft" at the top of his voice—if he were to know the truth . . ."

The lady began to cry and Dunwilliam was about to put his arm around her shoulders, but, as though repulsed by the hideous hump, took one of her hands instead.

Harriet stood up, then walking over to the window, looked down at Jem, still peacefully pruning his roses.

"How long 'ave I been 'ere?" Jem sat on his wheelbarrow and lit an old clay pipe. "Well now, let me think. Must be nigh on eight year. Just after old Sir 'Ilary Sinclair died, I 'eard 'is lordship was in need of a 'ead gardener, and so 'ere I comes."

"Was Lord Dunwilliam married eight years ago?" Harriet asked, tapping her front teeth with a rose-stem.

"That 'e were," Jem nodded, "and 'ad been for two years. Poor lady, must be cruel 'ard for 'er, being afflicted the way she is. 'Specially with that pretty face."

"His lordship must be a very kind man," Harriet spoke with assumed artlessness. "I mean it's not every great gentleman who would marry a cripple."

"I guess 'e be kind enough," Jem agreed, "but they do say she weren't a hunchback when he married 'er. Sweet sixteen she were, and as straight as a larch. Some sickness took 'er after they'd been married nigh on a month, and when she was up and about she were as you see 'er now."

"No!" Harriet gasped. "Honestly?"

"So they say. Mind you, this was back in the old master's time and there be no servants 'ere now that there was then. But it sounds right. I can't see a up-and-bucko like his lordship marryin' a humpy. Must 'ave been a sickness affected 'er spine. Made it all crooked like."

Harriet agreed and wondered if the sickness were catching.

They dined together that evening. Lord Dunwilliam sat at one end of the table, his lady at the other and Harriet in the centre, while the pleasantly-shocked footman relayed news of this startling arrangement back to the kitchen.

"She looks very pretty, does she not, Charles?" said Lady Dunwilliam, and the gentleman nodded as he sipped his port wine.

"As a picture that has escaped from its frame."

"What white shoulders." Her ladyship laughed so joyfully, and looked so beautiful, one was inclined to forget the awful hump, and Lord Dunwilliam chuckled as though she had said something very witty.

"With a strong back to support them." He nodded gravely. "A veritable column of ivory."

This was too much for her ladyship, who shook with helpless merriment, so that the hump seemed to jump up and down, and her face was a mask with narrowed, gleaming eyes and a gaping mouth. Then, suddenly, the laughter was strangled by a gasp of pain, and the lady was bending forward, shaking her golden head, while making a series of animal-like cries. Lord Dunwilliam sat back in his chair and closed eyes that were bleak. His voice was scarcely above a whisper.

"Sit still, my darling. It will pass."

"What is wrong?" Harriet's pity was aroused, as also was her alarm, for her mistress seemed to be in mortal agony, what with the terrible groans that were being forced out from behind her clenched teeth, and the way her long fingers gripped the table edge. "Is there aught I can do?"

Lord Dunwilliam sat perfectly still, his eyes still closed, but the ghost of a smile creased his mouth.

"Nothing, child. 'Tis but a gripping pain."

The spasm passed as quickly as it had come and presently Lady Dunwilliam was smiling faintly, apologising for the alarm she had caused.

"Do not be frightened, my dear. I have these attacks if I get excited. I should never become excited."

"It must be soon," Lord Dunwilliam said, and his lady nodded.

"Aye, it must be soon. If I am to remain sane, it must be soon."

A day passed.

"You will wear this."

Lady Dunwilliam's eyes were bright and her hand shook as she tossed the dress on to the bed. Harriet said: "Yes, mam. Thank you, mam."

"And," Lady Dunwilliam added, "you will wear nothing underneath."

"But, my lady," Harriet gasped out her horror, "'twould not be decent."

"Great balls of fire!" An expression of anger passed over the beautiful face. "I am not concerned with your opinion of decency. I said, you are to wear nothing—nothing underneath."

"But, mam . . ." A tinge of colour tinted Harriet's pale cheeks, "I am a respectable girl . . ."

Lady Dunwilliam gripped the girl by both shoulders and shook her until her head rocked.

"Listen, girl. Listen. I have put up with your simpering face for nigh on four weeks. I have pampered you, listened to your childish prattle, and now you will do as I say, or by God's wounds I'll have his lordship strip you himself. Do you understand?"

Harriet was crying, sobbing, so that her body trembled like a wind-rocked tree, and so great was her fear she could only gasp: "Yes, my lady."

"Very well." Lady Dunwilliam went to the door. "We will come for you in ten minutes."

Left alone, Harriet reluctantly disrobed, then put on the dress, her horror growing when she viewed herself in the wardrobe mirror. The dress was black and completely backless. She turned round and looked back over one shoulder. Her back, save for a tape that held the dress in position, was bare from neck to waist.

She ran to the door, pulled it open and went racing down the stairs, determined to take refuge in the kitchen, trusting that Mrs Browning or some of the servants would protect her from the madness of Lady Dunwilliam.

The kitchen was empty. The fire was out, all the saucepans were piled neatly on their racks, the doors and windows were locked. She called Mrs Browning's name and, receiving no answer, went tearing up the stairs to the servants' quarters. She flung doors open, scampering like a trapped animal from room to room, but there was no one. Terror came racing down the empty corridors and she screamed, shriek after shriek that gave birth to an army of mocking echoes, like cries of the damned when the lid of hell has been raised. She fled back through the echoes, stumbled down one flight of stairs, fell down the next, picked herself up, then tore out into the main hall. The great front doors were locked and she pounded on the unresponsive wood, tugged at the gleaming handle, then sank down to the floor, sobbing like an abandoned child.

Footsteps came over the paved floor. A shadow moved over her and she looked up into the face of Lord Dunwilliam. Never had he appeared more beautiful; a wonderful gleam of compassion softened his sombre eyes, making him the lover-father, the dream-master who would love and chastise, order and protect. He reached down and pulled her up, then held her to him, murmuring softly.

"She should not have been so cruel. There now, don't cry so. She does not mean to hurt you, but it has been such a long time. Think of it—ten long years. She was younger than you when it happened and she was so sweet, soft and gentle, and so very, very beautiful."

"Please, my lord, let me go."

Harriet felt sure when she looked up into that beautiful, kindly face, her request would be granted, but he shook his head, while he smoothed back the tumbled hair from her forehead.

"I can't do that, child. You must surely understand that. I love her. Love demands so much. Honour, pity, the common decencies that enable a man to walk upright under the sun; all these must be sacrificed when the one we cherish cries out for help. You do see?"

"I am so frightened," Harriet said as he began to lead her across the hall and up the grand staircase. "Please, I'm frightened."

Lord Dunwilliam had an arm about her waist, and he held her left hand in his. The deep voice went on, carefully manufacturing words that had no meaning.

"One can learn to live with fear, so that after a while it is as natural as the air we breathe. Resignation and acceptance are the two words you must learn, then when you carry your burden through the darkest valley, there will always be a gleam of light ahead."

They went up two flights of stairs, then began to ascend a third and Harriet started to struggle, but the iron grip tightened around her waist and the deep voice gently protested.

"Do not struggle, my little bird. You will only break your wings against the bars, and you must not waste your strength. See, there's but a short way to go, and my love is waiting for you."

They came up on to the top landing, and there, like the mouth of a ravenous beast, was an open doorway. He led the now speechless girl into the room beyond, and, after seating her on a straight-backed chair, he went back and locked the door. The room was little more than a vast attic that possibly covered most of the rooms below. Above were cobweb-festooned rafters supporting the roof. Dormer windows lined the walls on either side. Glass vats, jumbled heaps of wire and glass tubes littered the floor, and there were signs of a long-ago fire, for some of the rafters and floorboards were charred. The only furniture Harriet could see was a large table and a few wooden chairs.

Lady Dunwilliam came slowly forward, her burning stare fixed on the girl's white face. She wore a loose, flower-patterned dressing-gown and her hair was piled up high on her head.

"No delay!" She spat out the words. "Let's get on with it."

"No!" Her husband's voice was like a whip-crack. "No. She must be prepared."

"Was *I*?" The woman glared at him, hammering her hips with clenched fists. "When your father trapped me, was I prepared? He but led me under that rafter . . ." She pointed to a charred beam. ". . . tore the dress from my back and . . ."

"Stop!" Lord Dunwilliam thundered. "She is young and untutored."

"What was I?" Lady Dunwilliam shrieked back. "A mature woman of the world? I was sixteen, fresh from the school-room, and happy to have suddenly acquired a kind father and a handsome husband. Father!" She laughed, a mad shriek that made Harriet whimper. "A devil incarnate. A monster."

"He but sought knowledge," Lord Dunwilliam murmured. "He followed the dark path and found it had no end."

Lady Dunwilliam sank down on to a chair and lowered her head.

"Tell her what you must," she said in a low tone, "but in the name of mercy, hurry."

Lord Dunwilliam took up a small black book from the table and handed it to Harriet. She recognised the title.

*Unnatural Enmities and their Disposal* by Conrad Von Holstein.

"My wife tells me you can read, Harriet."

She nodded.

"Now, I want you to turn to page two hundred and seventy-three and read from the top of the page. Will you do that?"

"Yes," she whispered.

"Very well. Begin when you are ready."

She turned over the yellow-edged pages and presently came to the place. The page stared up at her, the words mutely demanding a voice. She began to read.

"'The Primate Horrific or Jumpity-Jim hath little intelligence, being but a form of low existence that doth demand life essence and warm blood. Once it hath been raised it will leap about with much speed and agility, and, if that which it needs be not to hand, will depart with a mighty explosion.

"'But should there be within the radius of twenty feet, a virgin, who hath the right essence, and should the flesh of her back, that which lies between the neck and the upper portion of the loins, be bare, then will it leap thereon, and will become as part of the poor wretch, as doth the legs and other members that did God in his bountiful goodness provide.

"'Once the abomination has mounted the steed, it can in no wise be removed, unless a like-virgin, cursed with the same essence, can be induced, or forced, to accept the loathsome burden . . .'"

"That is enough, Harriet."

Lord Dunwilliam gently took the book from her limp hands and laid it on the table. She raised tear-filled eyes; never had he seemed so handsome, so kind.

"You have the right—essence, my dear. The instrument my father perfected told us that. You are also a virgin, or the glass screen would not have portrayed the dark valley. 'Twas our wedding eve when my father . . . But enough of that. You do understand what is expected of you?"

"No." She shook her head violently. "In God's name . . . No."

"There is no other way," his gentle voice insisted, "for we have searched for so long. One girl had a little power and it did move, causing my wife much pain and injuring the girl. But you are the one. For you the transportation will be easy and there will be a life of ease for you and your parents, for as long as any of you live."

Harriet could not speak. She was watching Lady Dunwilliam who was unfastening her robe, loosening the girdle, all the while smiling like one who has at last seen the gates of heaven through the smoke-clouds of purgatory. The robe fell to the floor and she was as Venus in her naked glory, a vision of white curves and moulded breasts. Then she turned round and Harriet tried to scream, but her vocal cords refused to function.

A hump? A promontory? A protuberance? Rather a curvature that arched up from the base of her spine, then terminated in a kind of craggy ridge which unnaturally deepened the thickness of the shoulders.

"Come," Lord Dunwilliam pulled Harriet to her feet. "You must stand side by side."

"No!" she screamed and his face grew grim. "No . . .!"

"Do not force me to tie you down."

The threat did much to command her obedience, for there was an added terror in the thought of being tied up, helpless, while—something—leapt upon her. She allowed him to lead her, unprotesting, to Lady Dunwilliam's side, flinched as a cold hand gripped hers, then she stood still and waited. Lord Dunwilliam took up a position in front of them and, after closing his eyes, began to chant a jumble of words. From far below there came the sound of splintering wood, but the three occupants of the room ignored it.

"Darkness, shadows that flow in a black stream, hear me. May that which feeds upon one, come forth and take nourishment from another. May that which has come from the nether-world and can never return, having taken on the flesh of the meat-eater, see the light of day and jump upon the waiting vessel."

"Aye, upon the waiting vessel," Lady Dunwilliam repeated.

"She is young and hath much strength," Lord Dunwilliam raised his voice to a higher pitch. "And she hath the right essence . . ."

Lady Dunwilliam began to writhe and moan; her grip tightened on Harriet's hand, so that the girl automatically turned as the sudden pain shot up her arm. The hump was moving. The skin was heaving, tremors were passing across the taut surface and on the crag-like ridge little eruptions were taking place. Small, ragged holes appeared, accompanied by little popping sounds. The voice of Lord Dunwilliam had a triumphant ring.

"The shoulders are white, aye, and the back is strong; the blood is thick and sweet and she is rich with essence . . ."

The skin split while Lady Dunwilliam screamed and a tiny, wizened head peeped out from its cocoon, like a chick about to emerge from its cracked egg. It was rather like a shrivelled, pink balloon and it jerked round to stare at Harriet with microscopic red eyes. The girl gave a hoarse cry and jerked her hand from Lady Dunwilliam's loosened grip, before tearing wildly across the room in an effort to escape. As she did so the woman was flung on to her face, while something went leaping up to the rafters, then down to the floor again: a black, pink-tinted something that moved so fast it was only a blur that streaked up and down across the room. With her back against the far wall, Harriet saw it zig-zagging towards her, coming forward with high leaps that carried it up to the rafters and down again; then there was a glimpse of that wizened, deflated face, the long pink body and four many-jointed legs, before she seized a nearby chair and hurled it straight at the approaching horror. Chair and thing collided and what appeared to be a pink ball went rolling over the floor to bounce against the nearest wall.

It lay there, a pulsating beach-ball, artistically striped with black where the legs were coiled tightly about its gleaming roundness and it began to rock slightly as though gathering momentum for another leap.

Lord Dunwilliam had laid his wife flat upon her back before dragging her under the table, where she lay moaning softly. He turned to Harriet and shouted his rage and fear.

"You must let it mount, otherwise it will go back to her. There is no door or wall that can hold it—"

His words were cut short by a sudden and violent interruption. The door first quivered, then splintered under a powerful blow; a second crash sent it hurling inwards and the Reverend Dale stood on the threshold, a thick beam of wood in one hand and a crucifix in the other. He was attired in a white surplice and a ferocious smile.

"Dunwilliam, the day of reckoning has come." He advanced into the room, the crucifix held high. "Ye have mocked and practised abominations, but hell is hungry for your soul and I have come to make an end. Aye . . ." He tilted his head to one side and glared down at Harriet. ". . . An end to you and the foulness that has assumed human form."

Dunwilliam faced him, a thoroughbred stallion squaring-up to a mad bull.

"Get out. This is not the place for a ranting, insane fool. You have not the slightest conception of what . . ."

"I have eyes." The priest pointed to the naked form of Lady Dunwilliam, then at Harriet. "They tell me all I wished to know. When you sent your servants packing for the day, where did you suppose they would go? Eh? To the village, where they prattled of the foulness you be practising with yon wench. You are cursed, Dunwilliam, you and your devil-bedded wife."

Dunwilliam struck the white face, then gripped the not-so-white surplice and punched the priest about the body. All the while shouting obscenities, bellowing out his mad rage. As the Reverend Dale struggled violently there came the sound of ripping cloth and he went hurtling backwards, the surplice split from neck to waist, baring his scrawny back. Dunwilliam retreated a few paces and looked down at his fallen adversary. A look of indescribable horror was dawning on the clergyman's face; a stupefied glare. His mouth fell open and a gurgling, retching sound emerged from his constricted throat. It slowly and painfully dissolved into words.

"What . . . foul . . . thing . . . is . . . on . . . my . . . back?"

He came up from the floor like a boxer at the count of nine; his questing hands went back and gently caressed that which crouched on his shoulders. He quickly withdrew them, then stared at his moist fingers with an uncomprehending glare. When he spoke again his voice was a low, hoarse whisper.

"I say again, Dunwilliam, what foul thing is on my back?"

Dunwilliam began to laugh. He roared, slapped his thighs, shook with uncontrollable merriment, while tears ran down his cheeks. Harriet could only watch the Jumpity-Jim. It was perfectly at home on the reverend's back; the head was nestling sideways, a little below Mr Dale's neck; the legs were folded neatly under the pink, narrow torso and a slimy excrescence, oozing out from every part of the body, was rapidly congealing into a chalk-white skin. Lord Dunwilliam at last gave utterance.

"Your 'holiness' has condemned you, Dale. A virgin! A virgin whose flesh is bare from neck to waist."

"What in God's name is it?" Dale was trying to shake his dreadful burden off. He twisted, jerked, then gasped when the creature tightened its hold.

"You must not get excited," Dunwilliam warned. "It's a Primate Horrific—a Jumpity-Jim." He grinned. "I should take it to a monastery. It will find many changes of abode there."

The Reverend Dale backed away towards the door, then, after vainly trying to speak, turned and went staggering out on to the landing. They heard him stumbling down the stairs. Five minutes passed before Harriet's strength returned and she too was able to creep from that room of horror. She left Lord Dunwilliam holding his wife and rocking her gently. They were both laughing softly.

Down on the lawn they were waiting. Terrified men with blazing torches and they shrank from the Reverend Mr Dale as though he were a leper. One man, braver than his fellows, approached the hump-backed figure and asked in a strangled whisper:

"What is it?"

The clergyman grinned, a terrible baring of teeth, and he beckoned the man nearer.

"Are you a virgin?" he whispered. "Eh? Are you a virgin? If so, take off your shirt and we'll dance a merry jig."

The man retreated, muttering, "Witchcraft . . . they have bewitched him and put the devil on his back."

"Witchcraft!" The word leapt from mouth to mouth as they moved with uplifted torches towards the house. Harriet they spat at, beat about the face and back, before she managed to escape from the garden and ran out on to the dusty road that led to the village. When she walked over the narrow bridge she did not look down into the dark waters of the river and did not therefore see the figure of Mr Dale floating, face downwards. She did, however, look back and see great scarlet tongues trying to lick the steel-blue sky. Dunwilliam Grange was burning.

She went on down the road, a pathetic, bowed figure, wandering the short but perilous path that separates the cradle from the grave. Her white back gleamed in the sunlight.

A little way back, something was zig-zagging across a meadow, leaping over hedges, swinging from the lower branches of an occasional tree. It came to a gate that barred the entrance to a dusty road. There it paused, the deflated, wizened head tilted to one side. Tired, hesitant footsteps came shuffling along the road, they passed the gate and went on behind a low hawthorn hedge.

The Jumpity-Jim jumped.

# Ramsey Campbell

# Out of Copyright

RAMSEY CAMPBELL has been described as perhaps the finest living exponent of the British weird fiction tradition. A multiple winner of both the British and World Fantasy Awards, over the past thirty years he has written fourteen novels and numerous short stories.

Recent publications include the novella *Needing Ghosts*, his latest novel *Midnight Sun*, and a collection entitled *Waking Nightmares*. He is also the co-editor of the *Best New Horror* series (Robinson/Carroll & Graf) and a recent issue of *Weird Tales* magazine is a Campbell special.

"Out of Copyright" is a blackly humorous tale of revenge from beyond the grave that should be especially chilling to all book collectors and anthology editors . . .

THE WIDOW GAZED WISTFULLY at the pile of books. "I thought they might be worth something."

"Oh, some are," Tharne said. "That one, for instance, will fetch a few pence. But I'm afraid your husband collected books indiscriminately. Much of this stuff isn't worth the paper it's printed on. Look, I'll tell you what I'll do—I'll take the whole lot off your hands and give you the best price I can."

When he'd counted out the notes, the wad over his heart was scarcely reduced. He carried the bulging cartons of books to his van, down three gloomy flights of stairs, along the stone path which hid beneath lolling grass, between gateposts whose stone globes grew continents of moss. By the third descent he was panting. Nevertheless he grinned as he kicked grass aside; the visit had been worthwhile, certainly.

He drove out of the cracked and overgrown streets, past rusty cars laid open for surgery, old men propped on front steps to wither in the sun, prams left outside houses as though in the hope that a thief might adopt the baby. Sunlight leaping from windows and broken glass lanced his eyes. Heat made the streets and his perceptions waver. Glimpsed in the mirror or sensed looming at his back, the cartons resembled someone crouching behind him. They smelled more dusty than the streets.

Soon he reached the crescent. The tall Georgian houses shone white. Beneath them the van looked cheap, a tin toy littering the street. Still, it wasn't advisable to seem too wealthy when buying books.

He dumped the cartons in his hall, beside the elegant curve of the staircase. His secretary came to the door of her office. "Any luck?"

"Yes indeed. Some first editions and a lot of rare material. The man knew what he was collecting."

"Your mail came," she said in a tone which might have announced the police. This annoyed him: he prided himself on his legal knowledge, he observed the law scrupulously. "Well, well," he demanded, "who's saying what?"

"It's that American agent again. He says you have a

moral obligation to pay Lewis's widow for those three stories. Otherwise, he says—let's see—'I shall have to seriously consider recommending my clients to boycott your anthologies'."

"He says that, does he? The bastard. They'd be better off boycotting him." Tharne's face grew hot and swollen; he could hardly control his grin. "He's better at splitting infinitives than he is at looking after his people's affairs. He never renewed the copyright on those stories. We don't owe anyone a penny. And by God, you show me an author who needs the money. Rolling in it, all of them. Living off their royalties." A final injustice struck him; he smote his forehead. "Anyway, what the devil's it got to do with the widow? She didn't write the stories."

To burn up some of his rage, he struggled down to the cellar with the cartons. His blood drummed wildly. As he unpacked the cartons, dust smoked up to the light-bulbs. The cellar, already dim with its crowd of bookshelves, grew dimmer.

He piled the books neatly, sometimes shifting a book from one pile to another, as though playing Patience. When he reached the ace, he stopped. *Tales Beyond Life*, by Damien Damon. It was practically a legend; the book had never been reprinted in its entirety. The find could hardly have been more opportune. The book contained *The Dunning of Diavolo*—exactly what he needed to complete the new Tharne anthology, *Justice From Beyond The Grave*. He knocked lumps of dust from the top of the book, and turned to the story.

> Even in death he would be recompensed. Might the resurrectionists have his corpse for a toy? Of a certainty—but only once those organs had been removed which his spirit would need, and the Rituals performed. This stipulation he had willed on his death-bed to his son. Unless his corpse was pacified, his curse would rise.
>
> Undeed, had the father's estate been more readily available to clear the son's debts, this

> might have been an edifying tale of filial piety. Still, on a night when the moon gleamed like a sepulture, the father was plucked tuberpallid from the earth.
>
> Rather than sow superstitious scruples in the resurrectionists, the son had told them naught. Even so, the burrowers felt that they had mined an uncommon seam. Voiceless it might be, but the corpse had its forms of protest. Only by seizing its wrists could the corpse-miners elude the cold touch of its hands. Could they have closed its stiff lids, they might have borne its grin. On the contrary, neither would touch the gelatinous pebbles which bulged from its face . . .

Tharne knew how the tale continued: Diavolo, the father, was dissected, but his limbs went snaking round the town in search of those who had betrayed him, and crawled down the throats of the victims to drag out the twins of those organs of which the corpse had been robbed. All good Gothic stuff—gory and satisfying, but not to be taken too seriously. They couldn't write like that nowadays; they'd lost the knack of proper Gothic writing. And yet they whined that they weren't paid enough!

Only one thing about the tale annoyed him: the misprint "undeed" for "indeed". Amusingly, it resembled "undead"—but that was no excuse for perpetrating it. The one reprint of the tale, in the 'twenties, had swarmed with literals. Well, this time the text would be perfect. Nothing appeared in a Tharne anthology until it satisfied him.

He checked the remaining text, then gave it to his secretary to retype. His timing was exact: a minute later the doorbell announced the book collector, who was as punctual as Tharne. They spent a mutually beneficial half-hour. "These I bought only this morning," Tharne said proudly. "They're yours for twenty pounds apiece."

The day seemed satisfactory until the phone rang. He heard the girl's startled squeak. She rang through to his office, sounding flustered. "Ronald Main wants to speak to you."

"Oh God. Tell him to write, if he still knows how. I've no time to waste in chatting, even if he has." But her cry had disturbed him; it sounded like a threat of inefficiency. Let Main see that someone round here wasn't to be shaken! "No, wait—put him on."

Main's orotund voice came rolling down the wire. "It has come to my notice that you have anthologized a story of mine without informing me."

Trust a writer to use as many words as he could! "There was no need to get in touch with you," Tharne said. "The story's out of copyright."

"That is hardly the issue. Aside from the matter of payment, which we shall certainly discuss, I want to take up with you the question of the text itself. Are you aware that whole sentences have been rewritten?"

"Yes, of course. That's part of my job. I am the editor, you know." Irritably Tharne restrained a sneeze; the smell of dust was very strong. "After all, it's an early story of yours. Objectively, don't you think I've improved it?" He oughtn't to sound as if he was weakening. "Anyway, I'm afraid that legally you've no rights."

Did that render Main speechless, or was he preparing a stronger attack? It scarcely mattered, for Tharne put down the phone. Then he strode down the hall to check his secretary's work. Was her typing as flustered as her voice had been?

Her office was hazy with floating dust. No wonder she was peering closely at the book—though she looked engrossed, almost entranced. As his shadow fell on the page she started; the typewriter carriage sprang to its limit, ringing. She demanded, "Was that you before?"

"What do you mean?"

"Oh, nothing. Don't let it bother you." She seemed nervously annoyed—whether with him or with herself he couldn't tell.

At least her typing was accurate, though he could see where letters had had to be retyped. He might as well write the introduction to the story. He went down to fetch *Who's*

*Who in Horror and Fantasy Fiction.* Dust teemed around the cellar lights and chafed his throat.

Here was Damien Damon, real name Sidney Drew: b. Chelsea, 30 April 1876; d. ? 1911? "His life was even more bizarre and outrageous than his fiction. Some critics say that that is the only reason for his fame . . ."

A small dry sound made Tharne glance up. Somewhere among the shelved books, a face peered at him through a gap. Of course it could be nothing of the sort, but it took him a while to locate a cover which had fallen open in a gap, and which must have resembled a face.

Upstairs he wrote the introduction. ". . . Without the help of an agent, and with no desire to make money from his writing, Damon became one of the most discussed in whispers writers of his day. Critics claim that it was scandals that he practised magic which gained him fame. But his posthumously published *Tales Beyond Life* shows that he was probably the last really first class writer in the tradition of Poe . . ." Glancing up, Tharne caught sight of himself, pen in hand, at the desk in the mirror. So much for any nonsense that he didn't understand writers' problems! Why, he was a writer himself!

Only when he'd finished writing did he notice how quiet the house had become. It had the strained unnatural silence of a library. As he padded down the hall to deliver the text to his secretary his sounds felt muffled, detached from him.

His secretary was poring over the typescript of Damon's tale. She looked less efficient than anxious—searching for something she would rather not find? Dust hung about her in the amber light, and made her resemble a waxwork or a faded painting. Her arms dangled, forgotten. Her gaze was fixed on the page.

Before he could speak, the phone rang. That startled her so badly that he thought his presence might dismay her more. He retreated into the hall, and a dark shape stepped back behind him—his shadow, of course. He entered her office once more, making sure he was audible.

"It's Mr Main again," she said, almost wailing.

"Tell him to put it in writing."

"Mr Tharne says would you please send him a letter." Her training allowed her to regain control, yet she seemed unable to put down the phone until instructed. Tharne enjoyed the abrupt cessation of the outraged squeaking. "Now I think you'd better go home and get some rest," he said.

When she'd left he sat at her desk and read the typescript. Yes, she had corrected the original; "undeed" was righted. The text seemed perfect, ready for the printer. Why then did he feel that something was wrong? Had she omitted a passage or otherwise changed the wording?

He'd compare the texts in his office, where he was more comfortable. As he rose, he noticed a few faint dusty marks on the carpet. They approached behind his secretary's chair, then veered away. He must have tracked dust from the cellar, which clearly needed sweeping. What did his housekeeper think she was paid for?

Again his footsteps sounded muted. Perhaps his ears were clogged with dust; there was certainly enough of it about. He had never noticed how strongly the house smelled of old books, nor how unpleasant the smell could be. His skin felt dry, itchy.

In his office he poured himself a large Scotch. It was late enough, he needn't feel guilty—indeed, twilight seemed unusually swift tonight, unless it was an effect of the swarms of dust. He didn't spend all day drinking, unlike some writers he could name.

He knocked clumps of dust from the book; it seemed almost to grow there, like grey fungus. Airborne dust whirled away from him and drifted back. He compared the texts, line by line. Surely they were identical, except for her single correction. Yet he felt there was some aspect of the typescript which he needed urgently to decipher. This frustration, and its irrationality, unnerved him.

He was still frowning at the pages, having refilled his glass to loosen up his thoughts, when the phone rang once. He grabbed it irritably, but the earpiece was as hushed as the house. Or was there, amid the electric hissing vague as a cascade of dust, a whisper? It was beyond the grasp of his hearing, except for a syllable or two which sounded like Latin—if it was there at all.

He jerked to his feet and hurried down the hall. Now that he thought about it, perhaps he'd heard his secretary's extension lifted as his phone had rung. Yes, her receiver was off the hook. It must have fallen off. As he replaced it, dust sifted out of the mouthpiece.

Was a piece of paper rustling in the hall? No, the hall was bare. Perhaps it was the typescript, stirred on his desk by a draught. He closed the door behind him, to exclude any draught—as well as the odour of something very old and dusty.

But the smell was stronger in his room. He sniffed gingerly at *Tales Beyond Life*. Why, there it was: the book reeked of dust. He shoved open the French windows, then he sat and stared at the typescript. He was beginning to regard it with positive dislike. He felt as though he had been given a code to crack; it was nerve-racking as an examination. Why was it only the typescript that bothered him, and not the original?

He flapped the typed pages, for they looked thinly coated with grey. Perhaps it was only the twilight, which seemed composed of dust. Even his Scotch tasted clogged. Just let him see what was wrong with this damned story, then he'd leave the room to its dust—and have a few well-chosen words for his housekeeper tomorrow.

There was only one difference between the texts: the capital I. Or had he missed another letter? Compulsively and irritably, refusing to glance at the grey lump which hovered at the edge of his vision, he checked the first few capitals. E, M, O, R, T . . . Suddenly he stopped, parched mouth open. Seizing his pen, he began to transcribe the capitals alone.

E mortuis revoco.
From the dead I summon thee.

Oh, it must be a joke, a mistake, a coincidence. But the next few capitals dashed his doubts. *From the dead I summon thee, from the dust I recreate thee*. . . The entire story concealed a Latin invocation. It had been Damien Damon's last story and also, apparently, his last attempt at magic.

And it was Tharne's discovery. He must rewrite his introduction. Publicized correctly, the secret of the tale could help the book's sales a great deal. Why then was he unwilling to look up? Why was he tense as a trapped animal, ears straining painfully? Because of the thick smell of dust, the stealthy dry noises that his choked ears were unable to locate, the grey mass that hovered in front of him?

When at last he managed to look up, the jerk of his head twinged his neck. But his gasp was of relief. The grey blotch was only a chunk of dust, clinging to the mirror. Admittedly it was unpleasant; it resembled a face masked with dust, which also spilled from the face's dismayingly numerous openings. Really, he could live without it, much as he resented having to do his housekeeper's job for her.

When he rose, it took him a moment to realize that his reflection had partly blotted out the grey mass. In the further moment before he understood, two more reflected grey lumps rose beside it, behind him. Were they hands, or wads of dust? Perhaps they were composed of both. It was impossible to tell, even when they closed over his face.

# Karl Edward Wagner

# The River of Night's Dreaming

KARL EDWARD WAGNER trained as a psychiatrist before becoming a full-time writer and editor with his heroic fantasy novel *Darkness Weaves With Many Shades* (1970). Since then he has continued the brutal exploits of his anti-hero Kane in *Death Angel's Shadow*, *Bloodstone*, *Dark Crusade*, *Night Winds* and *The Book of Kane*. A multiple winner of the British Fantasy Award and World Fantasy Award, his intelligent and provocative horror stories have been collected in such volumes as *In A Lonely Place*, *Why Not You and I?* and *Unthreatened By the Morning Light*. He has edited ten volumes of *The Year's Best Horror Stories*, and his most recent novel is a medical chiller, *The Fourth Seal*.

Fans of *The Rocky Horror Show* will recognize the title of Wagner's novella from his friend Richard O'Brien's lyrics. Based on a dream which came to the author as an almost complete narrative, this nightmarish tale owes much to Robert W. Chambers' masterpiece *The King in Yellow*, and was originally rejected by an editor for being too sexually explicit. You have been warned!

EVERYWHERE: GRAYNESS AND RAIN

The activities bus with its uniformed occupants. The wet pavement that crawled along the crest of the high bluff. The storm-fretted waters of the bay far below. The night itself, gauzy with gray mist and traceries of rain, feebly probed by the wan headlights of the bus.

Grayness and rain merged in a slither of skidding rubber and a protesting bawl of brakes and tearing metal.

For an instant the activities bus paused upon the broken guardrail, hung half-swallowed by the grayness and rain upon the edge of the precipice. Then, with thirty voices swelling a chorus to the screams of rubber and steel, the bus plunged over the edge.

Halfway down it struck glancingly against the limestone face, shearing off wheels amidst a shower of glass and bits of metal, its plunge unchecked. Another carom, and the bus began to break apart, tearing open before its final impact onto the wave-frothed jumble of boulders far below. Water and sound surged upward into the night, as metal crumpled and split open, scattering bits of humanity like seeds flung from a bursting melon.

Briefly, those trapped within the submerging bus made despairing noises—in the night they were no more than the cries of kittens, tied in a sack and thrown into the river. Then the waters closed over the tangle of wreckage, and grayness and rain silenced the torrent of sound.

She struggled to the surface and dragged air into her lungs in a shuddering spasm. Treading water, she stared about her—her actions still automatic, for the crushing impact into the dark waters had all but knocked her unconscious. Perhaps for a moment she *had* lost conciousness; she was too dazed to remember anything very clearly. Anything.

Fragments of memory returned. The rain and the night, the activities bus carrying them back to their prison. Then the plunge into darkness, the terror of her companions, metal bursting apart. Alone in another instant, flung helplessly into the night, and the stunning embrace of the waves.

Her thoughts were clearing now. She worked her feet out of her tennis shoes and tugged damp hair away from her face, trying to see where she was. The body of the bus had torn open, she vaguely realized, and she had been thrown out of the wreckage and into the bay. She could see the darker bulk of the cliff looming out of the grayness not far from her, and dimly came the moans and cries of other survivors. She could not see them, but she could imagine their presence, huddled upon the rocks between the water and the vertical bluff.

Soon the failure of the activities bus to return would cause alarm. The gap in the guardrail would be noticed. Rescuers would come, with lights and ropes and stretchers, to pluck them off the rocks and hurry them away in ambulances to the prison's medical ward.

She stopped herself. Without thought, she had begun to swim toward the other survivors. But why? She took stock of her situation. As well as she could judge, she had escaped injury. She could easily join the others where they clung to the rocks, await rescue—and once the doctors were satisfied she was whole and hearty, she would be back on her locked ward again. A prisoner, perhaps until the end of her days.

Far across the bay, she could barely make out the phantom glimmering of the lights of the city. The distance was great—in miles, two? three? more?—for the prison was a long drive beyond the outskirts of the city and around the sparsely settled shore of the bay. But she was athletically trim and a strong swimmer—she exercised regularly to help pass the long days. How many days, she could not remember. She only knew she would not let them take her back to that place.

The rescue workers would soon be here. Once they'd taken care of those who clung to the shoreline, they'd send divers to raise the bus—and when they didn't find her body among those in the wreckage, they'd assume she was drowned, her body washed away. There would surely be others who were missing, others whose bodies even now drifted beneath the bay. Divers and boatmen with drag hooks would search for them. Some they might never find.

*Her* they would never find.

She turned her back to the cliff and began to swim out into the bay. Slow, patient strokes—she must conserve her strength. This was a dangerous act, she knew, but then they would be all the slower to suspect when they discovered she was missing. The rashness of her decision only meant that the chances of escape were all the better. Certainly, they would search along the shoreline close by the wreck—perhaps use dogs to hunt down any who might have tried to escape along the desolate stretch of high cliffs. But they would not believe that one of their prisoners would attempt to swim across to the distant city—and once she reached the city, no bloodhounds could seek her out there.

The black rise of rock vanished into the gray behind her, and with it dwindled the sobbing wails of her fellow prisoners. No longer her fellows. She had turned her back on that existence. Beyond, where lights smeared the distant grayness, she would find a new existence for herself.

For a while she swam a breaststroke, switching to a backstroke whenever she began to tire. The rain fell heavily onto her upturned face; choppy waves spilled into her mouth, forcing her to abandon the backstroke each time before she was fully rested. Just take it slow, take your time, she told herself. Only the distant lights gave any direction to the grayness now. If she tried to turn back, she might swim aimlessly through the darkness, until . . .

Her dress, a drab prison smock, was weighing her down. She hesitated a moment—she would need clothing when she reached the shore, but so encumbered she would never reach the city. She could not waste strength in agonizing over her dilemma. There was no choice. She tugged at the buttons. A quick struggle, and she was able to wrench the wet dress over her head and pull it free. She flung the shapeless garment away from her, and it sank into the night. Another struggle, and her socks followed.

She struck out again for the faraway lights. Her bra and panties were no more drag than a swimsuit, and she moved through the water cleanly—berating herself for not having done this earlier. In the rain and the darkness it was impossible to judge how far she had swum. At least halfway, she fervently hoped. The adrenaline that had coursed through her earlier with its glib assurances of strength was beginning to fade, and she became increasingly aware of bruises and wrenched muscles suffered in the wreck.

The lights never appeared to come any closer, and by now she had lost track of time as well. She wondered whether the flow of the current might not be carrying her away from her destination whenever she rested, and that fear sent new power into her strokes. The brassiere straps chafed her shoulders, but this irritation was scarcely noticed against the gnawing ache of fatigue. She fought down her growing panic, concentrating her entire being upon the phantom lights in the distance.

The lights seemed no closer than the stars might have been—only the stars were already lost in the grayness and rain. At times the city lights vanished as well, blotted out as she labored through a swell. She was cut off from everything in those moments, cut off from space and from time and from reality. There was only the grayness and the rain, pressing her deeper against the dark water. Memories of her past faded—she had always heard that a drowning victim's life flashes before her, but she could scarcely remember any fragment of her life before they had shut her away. Perhaps that memory would return when at last her straining muscles failed, and the water closed over her face in an unrelinquished kiss.

But then the lights *were* closer—she was certain of it this time. True, the lights were fewer than she had remembered, but she knew it must be far into the night after her seemingly endless swim. Hope sped renewed energy into limbs that had moved like a mechanical toy, slowly winding down. There was a current here, she sensed, seeking to drive her away from the lights and back into the limitless expanse she had struggled to escape.

As she fought against the current, she found she could at last make out the shoreline before her. Now she felt a new rush of fear. Sheer walls of stone awaited her. The city had been built along a bluff. She might reach the shore, but she could never climb its rock face.

She had fought too hard to surrender to despair now. Grimly she attacked the current, working her way along the shoreline. It was all but impossible to see anything—only the looming wall of blackness that cruelly barred her from the city invisible upon its heights. Then, beyond her in the night, the blackness seemed to recede somewhat. Scarcely daring to hope, she swam toward this break in the wall. The current steadily increased. Her muscles stabbed with fatigue, but now she had to swim all the harder to keep from being swept away.

The bluff was indeed lower here, but as a defense against the floods, they had built a wall where the natural barrier fell away. She clutched at the mossy stones in desperation—her clawing fingers finding no purchase. The current dragged her back, denying her a moment's respite.

She sobbed a curse. The heavy rains had driven the water to highest levels, leaving no rim of shoreline beneath cliff or dike. But since there was no escape for her along the direction she had come, she forced her aching limbs to fight on against the current. The line of the dike seemed to be curving inward, and she thought surely she could see a break in the barrier of blackness not far ahead.

She made painful progress against the increasing current, and at length was able to understand where she was. The seawall rose above a river that flowed through the city and into the bay. The city's storm sewers swelling its stream, the river rushed in full flood against the manmade bulwark. Its force was almost more than she could swim against now. Again and again she clutched at the slippery face of the wall, striving to gain a hold. Each time the current dragged her back again.

Storm sewers, some of them submerged now, poured into the river from the wall—their cross currents creating whirling eddies that shielded her one moment, tore at her the next, but allowed her to make desperate headway against the river itself. Bits of debris, caught up by the flood, struck at her invisibly. Rats, swimming frenziedly from the flooded sewers, struggled past her, sought to crawl onto her shoulders and face. She hit out at them, heedless of their bites, too intent on fighting the current herself to feel new horror.

A sudden eddy spun her against a recess in the seawall, and in the next instant her legs bruised against a submerged ledge. She half-swam, half-crawled forward, her fingers clawing slime-carpeted steps. Her breath sobbing in relief, she dragged herself out of the water and onto a flight of stone steps set out from the face of the wall.

For a long while she was content to press herself against the wet stone, her aching limbs no longer straining to keep her afloat, her chest hammering in exhaustion. The flood washed against her feet, its level still rising, and a sodden rat clawed onto her leg—finding refuge as she had done. She crawled higher onto the steps, becoming aware of her surroundings once more.

So. She had made it. She smiled shakily and looked back toward the direction she had come. Rain and darkness and distance made an impenetrable barrier, but she imagined the rescue workers must be checking off the names of those they had found. There would be no checkmark beside her name.

She hugged her bare ribs. The night was chill, and she had no protection from the rain. She remembered now that she was almost naked. What would anyone think who saw her like this? Perhaps in the darkness her panties and bra would pass for a bikini—but what would a bather be doing out at this hour and in this place? She might explain that she had been sunbathing, had fallen asleep, taken refuge from the storm, and had then been forced to flee from the rising waters. But when news of the bus wreck spread, anyone who saw her would remember.

She must find shelter and clothing—somewhere. Her chance to escape had been born of the moment; she had not had time yet to think matters through. She only knew she could not let them recapture her now. Whatever the odds against her, she would face them.

She stood up, leaning against the face of the wall until she felt her legs would hold her upright. The flight of steps ran diagonally down from the top of the seawall. There was no railing on the outward face, and the stone was treacherous with slime and streaming water. Painfully she edged her way upward, trying not to think about the rushing waters below her. If she slipped, there was no way she could check her fall; she would tumble down into the black torrent, and this time there would be no escape.

The climb seemed as difficult as had her long swim, and her aching muscles seemed to rebel against the task of bearing her up the slippery steps, but at length she gained the upper landing and stumbled onto the storm-washed pavement atop the seawall. She blinked her eyes uncertainly, drawing a long breath. The rain pressed her black hair to her neck and shoulders, sluiced away the muck and filth from her skin.

There were no lights to be seen along here. A balustrade guarded the edge of the seawall, with a gap to give access to the stairs. A street, barren of any traffic at this hour, ran along the top of the wall, and, across the empty street, rows of brick buildings made a second barrier. Evidently she had come upon a district of warehouses and such—and, from all appearances, this section was considerably rundown. There were no streetlights here, but even in the darkness she could sense the disused aspect of the row of buildings with their boarded-over windows and filthy fronts, the brick street with its humped and broken paving.

She shivered. It was doubly fortunate that none were here to mark her sudden appearance. In a section like this, and dressed as she was, it was unlikely that anyone she might encounter would be of good Samaritan inclinations.

Clothing. She had to find clothing. Any sort of clothing. She darted across the uneven paving and into the deeper shadow of the building fronts. Her best bet would be to find a shop: perhaps some sordid second-hand place such as this street might well harbor, a place without elaborate burglar alarms, if possible. She could break in, or at worst find a window display and try her luck at smash and grab.

Just a simple raincoat would make her far less vulnerable. Eventually she would need money, shelter, and food, until she could leave the city for someplace faraway.

As she crept along the deserted street, she found herself wondering whether she could find anything at all here. Doorways were padlocked and boarded over; behind rusted gratings, windows showed rotting planks and dirty shards of glass. The waterfront street seemed to be completely abandoned—a deserted row of ancient buildings enclosing forgotten wares, cheaper to let rot than to haul away, even as it was cheaper to let these brick hulks stand than to pull them down. Even the expected winos and derelicts seemed to have deserted this section of the city. She began to wish she might encounter at least a passing car.

The street had not been deserted by the rats. Probably they had been driven into the night by the rising waters. Once she began to notice them, she realized there were more and more of them—creeping boldly along the street. Huge, knowing brutes; some of them large as cats. They didn't seem afraid of her, and at times she thought they might be gathering in a pack to follow her. She had heard of rats attacking children and invalids, but surely . . . She wished she were out of this district.

The street plunged on atop the riverside, and still there were no lights or signs of human activity. The rain continued to pour down from the drowned night skies. She began to think about crawling into one of the dark warehouses to wait for morning, then thought of being alone in a dark, abandoned building with a closing pack of rats. She walked faster.

Some of the empty buildings showed signs of former grandeur, and she hoped she was coming toward a better section of the riverfront. Elaborate entranceways of fluted columns and marble steps gave onto the street. Grotesque Victorian façades and misshapen statuary presented imposing fronts to buildings filled with the same musty decay as the brick warehouses. She must be reaching the old merchants' district of the city, although these structures as well appeared long abandoned, waiting only for the wrecking ball of urban renewal. She wished she could escape this street, for there seemed to be more rats in the darkness behind her than she could safely ignore.

Perhaps she might find an alleyway between buildings that would let her flee this waterfront section and enter some inhabited neighborhood—for it became increasingly evident that this street had long been derelict. She peered closely at each building, but never could she find a gap between them. Without a light, she dared not enter blindly and try to find her way through some ramshackle building.

She paused for a moment and listened. For some while she had heard a scramble of wet claws and fretful squealings from the darkness behind her. Now she heard only the rain. Were the rats silently closing about her?

She stood before a columned portico—a bank or church?—and gazed into the darker shadow, wondering whether she might seek shelter. A statue—she supposed it was of an angel or some symbolic figure—stood before one of the marble columns. She could discern little of its features, only that it must have been malformed—presumably by vandalism—for it was hunched over and appeared to be supported against the column by thick cables or ropes. She could not see its face.

Not liking the silence, she hurried on again. Once past the portico, she turned quickly and looked back—to see if the rats were creeping after her. She saw no rats. She could see the row of columns. The misshapen figure was no longer there.

She began to run then. Blindly, not thinking where her panic drove her.

To her right, there was only the balustrade, marking the edge of the wall, and the rushing waters below. To her left, the unbroken row of derelict buildings. Behind her, the night and the rain, and something whose presence had driven away the pursuing rats. And ahead of her—she was close enough to see it now—the street made a deadend against a rock wall.

Stumbling toward it, for she dared not turn back the way she had run, she saw that the wall was not unbroken—that a stairway climbed steeply to a terrace up above. Here the bluff rose high against the river once again, so that the seawall ended against the rising stone. There were buildings crowded against the height, fronted upon the terrace a level above. In one of the windows, a light shone through the rain.

Her breath shook in ragged gasps and her legs were rubbery, but she forced herself to half-run, half-clamber up the rain-slick steps to the terrace above. Here, again a level of brick paving and a balustrade to guard the edge. Boarded windows and desolate façades greeted her from a row of decrepit houses, shouldered together on the rise. The light had been to her right, out above the river.

She could see it clearly now. It beckoned from the last house on the terrace—a looming Victorian pile built over the bluff. A casement window, level with the far end of the terrace, opened out onto a neglected garden. She climbed over the low wall that separated the house from the terrace, and crouched outside the curtained window.

Inside, a comfortable-looking sitting room with old-fashioned appointments. An older woman was crocheting, while in a chair beside her a young woman, dressed in a maid's costume, was reading aloud from a book. Across the corner room, another casement window looked out over the black water far below.

Had her fear and exhaustion been less consuming, she might have taken a less reckless course, might have paused to consider what effect her appearance would make. But she remembered a certain shuffling sound she had heard as she scrambled up onto the terrace, and the way the darkness had seemed to gather upon the top of the stairway when she glanced back a moment gone. With no thought but to escape the night, she tapped her knuckles sharply against the casement window.

At the tapping at the window, the older woman looked up from her work, the maid let the yellow-bound volume drop onto her white apron. They stared at the casement, not so much frightened as if uncertain of what they had heard. The curtain inside veiled her presence from them.

*Please!* she prayed, without voice to cry out. She tapped more insistently, pressing herself against the glass. They would see that she was only a girl, see her distress.

They were standing now, the older woman speaking too quickly for her to catch the words. The maid darted to the window, fumbled with its latch. Another second, and the casement swung open, and she tumbled into the room.

She knelt in a huddle on the floor, too exhausted to move any farther. Her body shook and water dripped from her bare flesh. She felt like some half-drowned kitten, plucked from the storm to shelter. Vaguely she could hear their startled queries, the protective clash as the casement latch closed out the rain and the curtain swept across the night.

The maid had brought a coverlet and was furiously towelling her dry. Her attention reminded her that she must offer some sort of account of herself—before her benefactors summoned the police, whose investigation would put a quick end to her freedom.

"I'm all right now," she told them shakily. "Just let me get my breath back, get warm."

"What's your name, child?" the older woman inquired solicitously. "Camilla, bring some hot tea."

She groped for a name to tell them. "Cassilda." The maid's name had put this in mind, and it was suited to her surroundings. "Cassilda Archer." Dr Archer would indeed be interested in *that* appropriation.

"You poor child! How did you come here? Were you . . . attacked?"

Her thoughts worked quickly. Satisfy their curiosity, but don't make them suspicious. Justify your predicament, but don't alarm them.

"I was hitch-hiking." She spoke in uncertain bursts. "A man picked me up. He took me to a deserted section near the river. He made me take off my clothes. He was going to . . ." She didn't need to feign her shudder.

"Here's the tea, Mrs Castaigne. I've added a touch of brandy."

"Thank you, Camilla. Drink some of this, dear."

She used the interruption to collect her thoughts. The two women were alone here, or else any others would have been summoned.

"When he started to pull down his trousers . . . I hurt him. Then I jumped out and ran as hard as I could. I don't think he came after me, but then I was wandering lost in the rain. I couldn't find anyone to help me. I didn't have anything with me except my underwear. I think a tramp was following me. Then I saw your light and ran toward it.

"Please, don't call the police!" She forestalled their obvious next move. "I'm not hurt. I know I couldn't face the shame of a rape investigation. Besides, they'd never be able to catch that man by now."

"But surely you must want me to contact someone for you."

"There's no one who would care. I'm on my own. That man has my pack and the few bucks in my handbag. If you could please let me stay here for the rest of the night, lend me some clothes just for tomorrow, and in the morning I'll phone a friend who can wire me some money."

Mrs Castaigne hugged her protectively. "You poor child! What you've been through! Of course you'll stay with us for the night—and don't fret about having to relive your terrible ordeal for a lot of leering policemen! Tomorrow there'll be plenty of time for you to decide what you'd like to do.

"Camilla, draw a nice hot bath for Cassilda. She's to sleep in Constance's room, so see that there's a warm comforter, and lay out a gown for her. And you, Cassilda, must drink another cup of this tea. As badly chilled as you are, child, you'll be fortunate indeed to escape your death of pneumonia!"

Over the rim of her cup, the girl examined the room and its occupants more closely. The sitting room was distinctly old-fashioned—furnished like a parlor in an old photograph, or like a set from some movie that was supposed to be taking place at the turn of the century. Even the lights were either gas or kerosene. Probably this house hadn't changed much since years ago before the neighborhood had begun to decay. Anyone would have to be a little eccentric to keep staying on here, although probably this place was all Mrs Castaigne had, and Mr Castaigne wasn't in evidence. The house and property couldn't be worth much in this neighborhood, although the furnishings might fetch a little money as antiques—she was no judge of that, but everything looked to be carefully preserved.

Mrs Castaigne seemed well fitted to this room and its furnishings. Hers was a face that might belong to a woman of forty or of sixty—well featured but too stern for a younger woman, yet without the lines and age marks of an elderly lady. Her figure was still very good, and she wore a tight-waisted, ankle-length dress that seemed to belong to the period of the house. The hands that stroked her bare shoulders were strong and white and unblemished, and the hair she wore piled atop her head was as black as the girl's own.

It occurred to her that Mrs Castaigne must surely be too young for this house. Probably she was a daughter or more likely a granddaughter of its original owners—a widow who lived alone with her young maid. And who might Constance be, whose room she was to sleep in?

"Your bath is ready now, Miss Archer." Camilla reappeared. Wrapped in the coverlet, the girl followed her. Mrs Castaigne helped support her, for her legs had barely strength to stand, and she felt ready to pass out from fatigue.

The bathroom was spacious—steamy from the vast claw-footed tub and smelling of bath salts. Its plumbing and fixtures were no more modern than the rest of the house. Camilla entered with her and, to her surprise, helped her remove her scant clothing and assisted her into the tub. She was too tired to feel ill at ease at this unaccustomed show of attention, and when the maid began to rub her back with scented soap, she sighed at the luxury.

"Who else lives here?" she asked casually.

"Only Mrs Castaigne and myself, Miss Archer."

"Mrs Castaigne mentioned someone—Constance?—whose room I am to have."

"Miss Castaigne is no longer with us, Miss Archer."

"Please call me Cassilda. I don't like to be so formal."

"If that's what you wish to be called, of course . . . Cassilda."

Camilla couldn't be very far from her own age, she guessed. Despite the old-fashioned maid's outfit—black dress and stockings with frilled white apron and cap—the other girl was probably no more than in her early twenties. The maid wore her long blonde hair in an up-swept topknot like her mistress, and she supposed she only followed Mrs Castaigne's preferences. Camilla's figure was full—much more buxom than her own boyish slenderness—and her cinch-waisted costume accented this. Her eyes were a bright blue, shining above a straight nose and wide-mouthed face.

"You've hurt yourself." Camilla ran her fingers tenderly along the bruises that marred her ribs and legs.

"There was a struggle. And I fell in the darkness—I don't know how many times."

"And you've cut yourself." Camilla lifted the other girl's black hair away from her neck. "Here on your shoulders and throat. But I don't believe it's anything to worry about." Her fingers carefully touched the livid scrapes.

"Are you certain there isn't someone whom we should let know of your safe whereabouts?"

"There is no one who would care. I am alone."

"Poor Cassilda."

"All I want is to sleep," she murmured. The warm bath was easing the ache from her flesh, leaving her deliciously sleepy.

Camilla left her to return with large towels. The maid helped her from the tub, wrapping her in one towel as she dried her with another. She felt faint with drowsiness, allowed herself to relax against the blonde girl. Camilla was very strong, supporting her easily as she towelled her small breasts. Her fingers found the parting of her thighs, lingered, then returned again in a less than casual touch.

Her dark eyes were wide as she stared into Camilla's luminous blue gaze, but she felt too pleasurably relaxed to object when the maid's touch became more intimate. Her breath caught, and held.

"You're very warm, Cassilda."

"Hurry, Camilla." Mrs Castaigne spoke from the doorway. "The poor child is about to drop. Help her into her nightdress."

Past wondering, she lifted her arms to let Camilla drape the beribboned lawn nightdress over her head and to her ankles. In another moment she was being ushered into a bedroom, furnished in the fashion of the rest of the house, and to an ornate brass bed whose mattress swallowed her up like a wave of foam. She felt the quilts drawn over her, sensed their presence hovering over her, and then she slipped into a deep sleep of utter exhaustion.

"Is there no one?"

"Nothing at all."

"Of course. How else could she be here? She is ours."

Her dreams were troubled by formless fears—deeply disturbing as experienced, yet their substance was already forgotten when she awoke at length on the echo of her outcry. She stared about her anxiously, uncertain where she was. Her disorientation was the same as when she awakened after receiving shock, only this place wasn't a ward, and the woman who entered the room wasn't one of her wardens.

"Good morning, Cassilda." The maid drew back the curtains to let long shadows streak across the room. "I should say, good evening, as it's almost that time. You've slept throughout the day, poor dear."

Cassilda? Yes, that was she. Memory came tumbling back in a confused jumble. She raised herself from her pillows and looked about the bedchamber she had been too tired to examine before. It was distinctly a woman's room—a young woman's—and she remembered that it had been Mrs Castaigne's daughter's room. It scarcely seemed to have been unused for very long: the brass bed was brightly polished, the walnut of the wardrobe, the chests of drawers and the dressing table made a rich glow, and the gay pastels of the curtains and wallpaper offset the gravity of the high tinned ceiling and parquetry floor. Small oriental rugs and pillows upon the chairs and chaise longue made bright points of color. Again she thought of a movie set, for the room was altogether lacking in anything modern. She knew very little about antiques, but she guessed that the style of furnishings must go back before the First World War.

Camilla was arranging a single red rose in a crystal bud vase upon the dressing table. She caught her gaze in the mirror. "Did you sleep well, Cassilda? I thought I heard you cry out, just as I knocked."

"A bad dream, I suppose. But I slept well. I don't, usually." They had made her take pills to sleep.

"Are you awake, Cassilda? I thought I heard your voices." Mrs Castaigne smiled from the doorway and crossed to her bed. She was dressed much the same as the night before.

"I didn't mean to sleep so long," she apologized.

"Poor child! I shouldn't wonder that you slept so, after your dreadful ordeal. Do you feel strong enough to take a little soup?"

"I really must be going. I can't impose any further."

"I won't hear any more of that, my dear. Of course you'll stay with us until you're feeling stronger." Mrs Castaigne sat beside her on the bed, placed a cold hand against her brow. "Why, Cassilda, your face is simply aglow. I do hope you haven't taken a fever. Look, your hands are positively trembling!"

"I feel all right." In fact, she did not. She did feel as if she were running a fever, and her muscles were so sore that she wasn't sure she could walk. The trembling didn't concern her: the injections they gave her every two weeks made her shake, so they gave her little pills to stop the shaking. Now she didn't have those pills, but since it was time again for another shot, the injection and its side effects would soon wear off.

"I'm going to bring you some tonic, dear. And Camilla will bring you some good nourishing soup, which you must try to take. Poor Cassilda, if we don't nurse you carefully, I'm afraid you may fall dangerously ill."

"But I can't be such a nuisance to you," she protested as

a matter of form. "I really must be going."

"Where to, dear child?" Mrs Castaigne held her hands gravely. "Have you someplace else to go? Is there someone you wish us to inform of your safety?"

"No," she admitted, trying to make everything sound right. "I've no place to go; there's no one who matters. I was on my way down the coast, hoping to find a job during the resort season. I know one or two old girlfriends who could put me up until I get settled."

"See there. Then there's no earthly reason why you can't just stay here until you're feeling strong again. Why, perhaps I might find a position for you myself. But we shall discuss these things later when you're feeling well. For the moment, just settle back on your pillow and let us help you get well."

Mrs Castaigne bent over her, kissed her on the forehead. Her lips were cool. "How lovely you are, Cassilda," she smiled, patting her hand.

She smiled back, and returned the other woman's firm grip. She'd seen no sign of a TV or radio here, and an old eccentric like Mrs Castaigne probably didn't even read the papers. Even if Mrs Castaigne had heard about the bus wreck, she plainly was too overjoyed at having a visitor to break her lonely routine to concern herself with a possible escapee—assuming they hadn't just listed her as drowned. She couldn't have hoped for a better place to hide out until things cooled off.

The tonic had a bitter licorice taste and made her drowsy, so that she fell asleep not long after Camilla carried away her tray. Despite her long sleep throughout that day, fever and exhaustion drew her back down again—although her previous sleep robbed this one of restful oblivion. Again came troubled dreams, this time cutting more harshly into her consciousness.

She dreamed of Dr Archer—her stern face and mannish shoulders craning over her bed. Her wrists and ankles were fixed to each corner of the bed by padded leather cuffs. Dr Archer was speaking to her in a scolding tone, while her wardens were pulling up her skirt, dragging down her panties. A syringe gleamed in Dr Archer's hand, and there was a sharp stinging in her buttock.

She was struggling again, but to no avail. Dr Archer was shouting at her, and a stout nurse was tightening the last few buckles of the straitjacket that bound her arms to her chest in a loveless hug. The straps were so tight she could hardly draw breath, and while she could not understand what Dr Archer was saying, she recognized the spurting needle that Dr Archer thrust into her.

She was strapped tightly to the narrow bed, her eyes staring at the gray ceiling as they wheeled her through the corridors to Dr Archer's special room. Then they stopped; they were there, and Dr Archer was bending over her again. Then came the sting in her arm as they penetrated her veins, the helpless headlong rush of the drug—and Dr Archer smiles and turns to her machine, and the current blasts into her tightly strapped skull and her body arches and strains against the restraints and her scream strangles against the rubber gag clenched in her teeth.

But the face that looks into hers now is not Dr Archer's, and the hands that shake her are not cruel.

"Cassilda! Cassilda! Wake up! It's only a nightmare!"

Camilla's blonde and blue face finally focused into her awakening vision.

"Only a nightmare," Camilla reassured her. "Poor darling." The hands that held her shoulders lifted to smooth her black hair from her eyes, to cup her face. Camilla bent over her, kissed her gently on her dry lips.

"What is it?" Mrs Castaigne, wearing her nightdress and carrying a candle, came anxiously into the room.

"Poor Cassilda has had bad dreams," Camilla told her. "And her face feels ever so warm."

"Dear child!" Mrs Castaigne set down her candlestick. "She must take some more tonic at once. Perhaps you should sit with her, Camilla, to see that her sleep is untroubled."

"Certainly, madame. I'll just fetch the tonic."

"Please, don't bother . . ." But the room became a vertiginous blur as she tried to sit up. She slumped back and closed her eyes tightly for a moment. Her body *did* feel feverish, her mouth dry, and the trembling when she moved her hand to take the medicine glass was so obvious that Camilla shook her head and held the glass to her lips herself. She swallowed dutifully, wondering how much of this was a reaction to the Prolixin still in her flesh. The injection would soon be wearing off, she knew, for when she smiled back at her nurses, the sharp edges of color were beginning to show once again through the haze the medication drew over her perception.

"I'll be all right soon," she promised them.

"Then do try to sleep, darling." Mrs Castaigne patted her arm. "You must regain your strength. Camilla will be here to watch over you.

"Be certain that the curtains are drawn against any night vapors," she directed her maid. "Call me, if necessary."

"Of course, madame. I'll not leave her side."

She was dreaming again—or dreaming still.

Darkness surrounded her like a black leather mask, and her body shook with uncontrollable spasms. Her naked flesh was slick with chill sweat, although her mouth was burning dry. She moaned and tossed—striving to awaken order from out of the damp blackness, but the blackness only embraced her with smothering tenacity.

Cold lips were crushing her own, thrusting a cold tongue into her feverish mouth, bruising the skin of her throat. Fingers, slender and strong, caressed her breasts, held her nipples to hungry lips. Her hands thrashed about, touched smooth flesh. It came to her that her eyes were indeed wide open, that the darkness was so profound she could no more than sense the presence of other shapes close beside her.

Her own movements were languid, dreamlike. Through the spasms that racked her flesh, she became aware of a perverse thrill of ecstasy. Her fingers brushed somnolently against the cool flesh that crouched over her, with no more purpose or strength than the drifting limbs of a drowning victim.

A compelling lassitude bound her, even as the blackness blinded her. She seemed to be drifting away, apart from her body, apart from her dream, into deeper ever deeper darkness. The sensual arousal that lashed her lost reality against the lethargy and fever that held her physically, and rising out of the eroticism of her delirium shrilled whispers of underlying revulsion and terror.

One pair of lips imprisoned her mouth and throat now, sucking at her breath, while other lips crept down across her breasts, hovered upon her navel, then pounced upon the opening of her thighs. Her breath caught in a shudder, was sucked away by the lips that held her mouth, as the coldness began to creep into her burning flesh.

She felt herself smothering, unable to draw breath, so that her body arched in panic, her limbs thrashed aimlessly. Her efforts to break away were as ineffectual as was her struggle to awaken. The lips that stole her breath released her, but only for a moment. In the darkness she felt other flesh pinion her tossing body, move against her with cool strength. Chill fire tormented her loins, and as she opened her mouth to cry out, or to sigh, smooth thighs pressed down onto her cheeks and the coldness gripped her breath. Mutely, she obeyed the needs that commanded her, that overwhelmed her, and through the darkness blindly flowed her silent scream of ecstasy and of horror.

Cassilda awoke.

Sunlight spiked into her room—the colored panes creating a false prism effect. Camilla, who had been adjusting the curtains, turned and smiled at the sound of her movement.

"Good morning, Cassilda. Are you feeling better this morning?"

"A great deal better," Cassilda returned her smile. "I feel as if I'd slept for days." She frowned slightly, suddenly uncertain.

Camilla touched her forehead. "Your fever has left you; Mrs Castaigne will be delighted to learn that. You've slept away most of yesterday and all through last night. Shall I bring your breakfast tray now?"

"Please—I'm famished. But I really think I should be

getting up."

"After breakfast, if you wish. And now I'll inform madame that you're feeling much better."

Mrs Castaigne appeared as the maid was clearing away the breakfast things. "How very much better you look today, Cassilda. Camilla tells me you feel well enough to sit up."

"I really can't play the invalid and continue to impose upon your hospitality any longer. Would it be possible that you might lend me some clothing? My own garments . . ." Cassilda frowned, trying to remember why she had burst in upon her benefactress virtually naked.

"Certainly, my dear." Mrs Castaigne squeezed her shoulder. "You must see if some of my daughter's garments won't fit you. You cannot be very far from Constance, I'm certain. Camilla will assist you."

She was lightheaded when first she tried to stand, but Cassilda clung to the brass bedposts until her legs felt strong enough to hold her. The maid was busying herself at the chest of drawers, removing items of clothing from beneath neat coverings of tissue paper. A faint odor of dried rose petals drifted from a sachet beneath the folded garments.

"I do hope you'll overlook it if these are not of the latest mode," Mrs Castaigne was saying. "It has been some time since Constance was with us here."

"Your daughter is . . .?"

"Away."

Cassilda declined to intrude further. There was a dressing screen behind which she retired, while Mrs Castaigne waited upon the chaise longue. Trailing a scent of dried roses from the garments she carried, Camilla joined her behind the screen and helped her out of her nightdress.

There were undergarments of fine silk, airy lace, and gauzy pastels. Cassilda found herself puzzled, both from their unfamiliarity and at the same time their familiarity, and while her thoughts struggled with the mystery, her hands seemed to dress her body with practiced movements. First the chemise, knee-length and trimmed with light lace and ribbons. Seated upon a chair, she drew on pale stockings of patterned silk, held at mid-thigh by beribboned garters.

Then silk knickers, open front and back and tied at the waist, trimmed with lace and ruching where they flared below her stocking tops. A frilled petticoat fell almost to her ankles.

"I won't need that," Cassilda protested. Camilla had presented her with a boned corset of white and sky broché.

"Nonsense, my dear," Mrs Castaigne directed, coming around the dressing screen to oversee. "You may think of me as old-fashioned, but I insist that you not ruin your figure."

Cassilda submitted, suddenly wondering why she had thought anything out of the ordinary about it. She hooked the straight busk together in front, while Camilla gathered the laces at the back. The maid tugged sharply at the laces, squeezing out her breath. Cassilda bent forward and steadied herself against the back of the chair, as Camilla braced a knee against the small of her back, pulling the laces as tight as possible before tying them. Once her corset was secured, she drew over it a camisole of white cotton lace and trimmed with ribbon, matching her petticoat. Somewhat dizzy, Cassilda sat stiffly before the dressing table, while the maid brushed out her long black hair and gathered it in a loose knot atop her head, pinning it in place with tortoise-shell combs. Opening the wardrobe, Camilla found her a pair of shoes, with high heels that mushroomed outward at the bottom, which fit her easily.

"How lovely, Cassilda!" Mrs Castaigne approved. "One would scarcely recognize you as the poor drowned thing that came out of the night!"

Cassilda stood up and examined herself in the full-length dressing mirror. It was as if she looked upon a stranger, and yet she knew she looked upon herself. The corset constricted her waist and forced her slight figure into an "S" curve—hips back, bust forward—imparting an unexpected opulence, further enhanced by the gauzy profusion of lace and silk. Her face, dark-eyed and finely boned, returned her gaze watchfully from beneath a lustrous pile of black hair. She touched herself, almost in wonder, almost believing that the reflection in the mirror was a photograph of someone else.

Camilla selected for her a long-sleeved linen shirtwaist,

buttoned at the cuffs and all the way to her throat, then helped her into a skirt of some darker material that fell away from her cinched waist to her ankles. Cassilda studied herself in the mirror, while the maid fussed about her.

*I look like someone in an old illustration—a Gibson girl*, she thought, then puzzled at her thought.

Through the open window she could hear the vague noises of the city, and for the first time she realized that intermingled with these familiar sounds was the clatter of horses' hooves upon the brick pavement.

"You simply must not say anything more about leaving us, Cassilda," Mrs Castaigne insisted, laying a hand upon the girl's knee as she leaned toward her confidentially.

Beside her on the settee, Cassilda felt the pressure of her touch through the rustling layers of petticoat. It haunted her, this flowing whisper of sound that came with her every movement, for it seemed at once strange and again familiar—a shivery sigh of silk against silk, like the whisk of dry snow sliding across stone. She smiled, holding her teacup with automatic poise, and wondered that such little, common-place sensations should seem at all out of the ordinary to her. Even the rigid embrace of her corset seemed quite familiar to her now, so that she sat gracefully at ease, listening to her benefactress, while a part of her thoughts stirred in uneasy wonder.

"You have said yourself that you have no immediate prospects," Mrs Castaigne continued. "I shouldn't have to remind you of the dangers the city holds for unattached young women. You were extremely fortunate in your escape from those white slavers who had abducted you. Without family or friends to question your disappearance—well, I shan't suggest what horrible fate awaited you."

Cassilda shivered at the memory of her escape— a memory as formless and uncertain, beyond her *need* to escape, as that of her life prior to her abduction. She had made only vague replies to Mrs Castaigne's gentle questioning, nor was she at all certain which fragments of her story were half-truths or lies.

Of one thing she was certain beyond all doubt: the danger from which she had fled awaited her beyond the shelter of this house.

"It has been so lonely here since Constance went away," Mrs Castaigne was saying. "Camilla is a great comfort to me, but nonetheless she has her household duties to occupy her, and I have often considered engaging a companion. I should be only too happy if you would consent to remain with us in this position—at least for the present time."

"You're much too kind! Of course I'll stay."

"I promise you that your duties shall be no more onerous than to provide amusements for a rather old-fashioned lady of retiring disposition. I hope it won't prove too dull for you, my dear."

"It suits my own temperament perfectly," Cassilda assured her. "I am thoroughly content to follow quiet pursuits within doors."

"Wonderful!" Mrs Castaigne took her hands. "Then it's settled. I know Camilla will be delighted to have another young spirit about the place. And you may relieve her of some of her tasks."

"What shall I do?" Cassilda begged her, overjoyed at her good fortune.

"Would you read to me, please, my dear? I find it so relaxing to the body and so stimulating to the mind. I've taken up far too much of Camilla's time from her chores, having her read to me for hours on end."

"Of course." Cassilda returned Camilla's smile as she entered the sitting room to collect the tea things. From her delight, it was evident that the maid had been listening from the hallway. "What would you like for me to read to you?"

"That book over there beneath the lamp." Mrs Castaigne indicated a volume bound in yellow cloth. "It is a recent drama—and a most curious work, as you shall quickly see. Camilla was reading it to me on the night you came to us."

Taking up the book, Cassilda again experienced a strange sense of unaccountable *déjà vu*, and she wondered where she might previously have read *The King in Yellow*, if indeed she ever had.

"I believe we are ready to begin the second act," Mrs Castaigne told her.

Cassilda was reading in bed when Camilla knocked tentatively at her door. She set aside her book with an almost furtive movement. "*Entrez vous.*"

"I was afraid you might already be asleep," the maid explained, "but then I saw light beneath your door. I'd forgotten to bring you your tonic before retiring."

Camilla, *en déshabillé*, carried in the medicine glass on a silver tray. Her fluttering lace and pastels seemed a pretty contrast to the black maid's uniform she ordinarily wore.

"I wasn't able to go to sleep just yet," Cassilda confessed, sitting up in bed. "I was reading."

Camilla handed her the tonic. "Let me see. Ah, yes. What a thoroughly wicked book to be reading in bed!"

"Have you read *The King in Yellow?*"

"I have read it through aloud to madame, and more than once. It is a favorite of hers."

"It is sinful and more than sinful to imbue such decadence with so compelling a fascination. I cannot imagine that anyone could have allowed it to be published. The author must have been mad to pen such thoughts."

"And yet, you read it."

Cassilda made a place for her on the edge of the bed. "Its fascination is too great a temptation to resist. I wanted to read further after Mrs Castaigne bade me good night."

"It was Constance's book." Camilla huddled close beside her against the pillows. "Perhaps that is why madame cherishes it so."

Cassilda opened the yellow-bound volume to the page she had been reading. Camilla craned her blonde head over her shoulder to read with her. She had removed her corset, and her ample figure swelled against her beribboned chemise. Cassilda in her nightdress felt almost scrawny as she compared her own small bosom to the other girl's.

"Is it not strange?" she remarked. "Here in this decadent drama we read of Cassilda and Camilla."

"I wonder if we two are very much like them," Camilla laughed.

"They are such very dear friends."

"And so are we, are we not?"

"I do so want us to be."

"But you haven't read beyond the second act, dear Cassilda. How can you know what may their fate be?"

"Oh, Camilla!" Cassilda leaned her face back against Camilla's perfumed breasts. "Don't tease me so!"

The blonde girl hugged her fiercely, stroking her back. "Poor, lost Cassilda."

Cassilda nestled against her, listening to the heartbeat beneath her cheek. She was feeling warm and sleepy, for all that the book had disturbed her. The tonic always carried her to dreamy oblivion, and it was pleasant to drift to sleep in Camilla's soft embrace.

"Were you and Constance friends?" she wondered.

"We were the very dearest of friends."

"You must miss her very much."

"No longer."

Cassilda sat at the escritoire in her room, writing in the journal she had found there. Her petticoats crowded against the legs of the writing table as she leaned forward to reach the inkwell. From time to time she paused to stare pensively past the open curtains of her window, upon the deepening blue of the evening sky as it met the angled rooftops of the buildings along the waterfront below.

"I think I should feel content here," she wrote. "Mrs Castaigne is strict in her demands, but I am certain she takes a sincere interest in my own well-being, and that she has only the kindliest regard for me. My duties during the day are of the lightest nature and consist primarily of reading to Mrs Castaigne or of singing at the piano while she occupies herself with her needlework, and in all other ways making myself companionable to her in our simple amusements.

"I have offered to assist Camilla at her chores, but Mrs Castaigne will not have it that I perform other than the lightest household tasks. Camilla is a very dear friend to me, and her sweet attentions easily distract me from what might otherwise become a tedium of sitting about the house day to day. Nonetheless, I have no desire to leave my situation here, nor to adventure into the streets outside the house. We are not in an especially attractive section of the city here, being at some remove from the shops and in a district given over to waterfront warehouses and commercial establishments. We receive no visitors, other than the tradesmen who supply our needs, nor is Mrs Castaigne of a disposition to wish to seek out the society of others.

"Withal, my instincts suggest that Mrs Castaigne has sought the existence of a recluse out of some very great emotional distress which has robbed life of its interests for her. It is evident from the attention and instruction she has bestowed upon me that she sees in me a reflection of her daughter, and I am convinced that it is in the loss of Constance where lies the dark secret of her self-imposed withdrawal from the world. I am sensible of the pain Mrs Castaigne harbors within her breast, for the subject of her daughter's absence is never brought into our conversations, and for this reason I have felt loath to question her, although I am certain that this is the key to the mystery that holds us in this house."

Cassilda concluded her entry with the date: June 7th, 189—

She frowned in an instant's consternation. What *was* the date? How silly. She referred to a previous day's entry, then completed the date. For a moment she turned idly back through her journal, smiling faintly at the many pages of entries that filled the diary, each progressively dated, each penned in the same neat hand as the entry she had just completed.

Cassilda sat at her dressing table in her room. It was night, and she had removed her outer clothing preparatory to retiring. She gazed at her reflection—the gauzy paleness of her chemise, stockings, and knickers was framed against

Camilla's black maid's uniform, as the blonde girl stood behind her, brushing out her dark hair.

Upon the dressing table she had spread out the contents of a tin box she had found in one of the drawers, and she and Camilla had been looking over them as she prepared for bed. There were paper dolls, valentines, and greeting cards, illustrations clipped from magazines, a lovely cut-out of a swan. She also found a crystal ball that rested upon an ebony cradle. Within the crystal sphere was a tiny house, covered with snow, with trees and a frozen lake and a young girl playing. When Cassilda picked it up, the snow stirred faintly in the transparent fluid that filled the globe. She turned the crystal sphere upside down for a moment, then quickly righted it, and a snowstorm drifted down about the tiny house.

"How wonderful it would be to dwell forever in a crystal fairyland just like the people in this little house," Cassilda remarked, peering into the crystal ball.

Something else seemed to stir within the swirling snowflakes, she thought; but when the snow had settled once more, the tableau was unchanged. No: there was a small mound, there beside the child at play, that she was certain she had not seen before. Cassilda overturned the crystal globe once again, and peered more closely. There it was. Another tiny figure spinning amidst the snowflakes. A second girl. She must have broken loose from the tableau. The tiny figure drifted to rest upon the frozen lake, and the snowflakes once more covered her from view.

"Where is Constance Castaigne?" Cassilda asked.

"Constance . . . became quite ill," Camilla told her carefully. "She was always subject to nervous attacks. One night she suffered one of her fits, and she . . ."

"Camilla!" Mrs Castaigne's voice from the doorway was stern. "You know how I despise gossip—especially idle gossip concerning another's misfortunes."

The maid's face was downcast. "I'm very sorry, madame. I meant no mischief."

The older woman scowled as she crossed the room. Cassilda wondered if she meant to strike the maid. "Being sorry does not pardon the offense of a wagging tongue. Perhaps a lesson in behaviour will improve your manners in the future. Go at once to your room."

"Please, madame . . ."

"Your insolence begins to annoy me, Camilla."

"Please, don't be harsh with her!" Cassilda begged, as the maid hurried from the room. "She was only answering my question."

Standing behind the seated girl, Mrs Castaigne placed her hands upon her shoulders and smiled down at her. "An innocent question, my dear. However, the subject is extremely painful to me, and Camilla well knows the distress it causes me to hear it brought up. I shall tell you this now, and that shall end the matter. My daughter suffered a severe attack of brain fever. She is confined in a mental sanatorium."

Cassilda crossed her arms over her breasts to place her hands upon the older woman's wrists. "I'm terribly sorry."

"I'm certain you can appreciate how sorely this subject distresses me." Mrs Castaigne smiled, meeting her eyes in the mirror.

"I shan't mention it again."

"Of course not. And now, my dear, you must hurry and make yourself ready for bed. Too much exertion so soon after your illness will certainly bring about a relapse. Hurry along now, while I fetch your tonic."

"I'm sure I don't need any more medicine. Sometimes I think it must bring on evil dreams."

"Now don't argue, Cassilda dear." The fingers on her shoulders tightened their grip. "You must do as you're told. You can't very well perform your duties as companion if you lie about ill all day, now can you? And you *do* want to stay."

"Certainly!" Cassilda thought this last had not been voiced as a question. "I want to do whatever you ask."

"I know you do, Cassilda. And I only want to make you into a perfect young lady. Now let me help you into your night things."

Cassilda opened her eyes into complete darkness that swirled about her in an invisible current. She sat upright in her bed, fighting back the vertigo that she had decided must come from the tonic they gave her nightly. Something had wakened her. Another bad dream? She knew she often suffered them, even though the next morning she was unable to recall them. Was she about to be sick? She was certain that the tonic made her feel drugged.

Her wide eyes stared sleeplessly at the darkness. She knew sleep would not return easily, for she feared to lapse again into the wicked dreams that disturbed her rest and left her lethargic throughout the next day. She could not even be certain that this now might not be another of those dreams.

In the absolute silence of the house, she could hear her heart pulse, her breath stir anxiously.

There was another sound, more distant, and of almost the same monotonous regularity. She thought she heard a woman's muffled sobbing.

*Mrs Castaigne*, she thought. The talk of her daughter had upset her terribly. Underscoring the sobbing came a sharp, rhythmic crack, as if a rocker sounded against a loose board.

Cassilda felt upon the nightstand beside her bed. Her fingers found matches. Striking one, she lit the candle that was there—her actions entirely automatic. Stepping down out of her bed, she caught up the candlestick and moved cautiously out of her room.

In the hallway, she listened for the direction of the sound. Her candle forced a small nimbus of light against the enveloping darkness of the old house. Cassilda shivered and drew her nightdress closer about her throat; its gauzy lace and ribbons were no barrier to the cold darkness that swirled about her island of candlelight.

The sobbing seemed no louder as she crept down the hallway toward Mrs Castaigne's bedroom. There, the bedroom door was open, and within was only silent darkness.

"Mrs Castaigne?" Cassilda called softly, without answer.

The sound of muffled sobbing continued, and now seemed

to come from overhead. Cassilda followed its sound to the end of the hallway, where a flight of stairs led to the maid's quarters in the attic. Cassilda paused fearfully at the foot of the stairway, thrusting her candle without effect against the darkness above. She could still hear the sobbing, but the other sharp sound had ceased. Her head seemed to float in the darkness as she listened, but despite her dreamlike lethargy, she knew her thoughts raced too wildly now for sleep. Catching up the hem of her nightdress, Cassilda cautiously ascended the stairs.

Once she gained the landing above, she could see the blade of yellow light that shone beneath the door to Camilla's room, and from within came the sounds that had summoned her. Quickly Cassilda crossed to the maid's room and knocked softly upon the door.

"Camilla? It's Cassilda. Are you all right?"

Again no answer, although she sensed movement within. The muffled sobs continued.

Cassilda tried the doorknob, found it was not locked. She pushed the door open and stepped inside, dazzled a moment by the bright glare of the oil lamp.

Camilla, dressed only in her corset and undergarments, stood bent over the foot of her bed. Her ankles were lashed to the base of either post, her wrists tied together and stretched forward by a rope fixed to the headboard. Exposed by the open-style knickers, her buttocks were crisscrossed with red welts. She turned her head to look at Cassilda and the other girl saw that Camilla's cries were gagged by a complicated leather bridle strapped about her head.

"Come in, Cassilda, since you wish to join us," said Mrs Castaigne from behind her. Cassilda heard her close the door and lock it, before the girl had courage enough to turn around. Mrs Castaigne wore no more clothing than did Camilla, and she switched her riding crop anticipatorily. Looking from mistress to maid, Cassilda saw that both pairs of eyes glowed alike with the lusts of unholy pleasure.

For a long interval Cassilda resisted awakening, hovering in a languor of unformed dreaming despite the rising awareness that she still slept. When she opened her eyes at last, she stared at the candlestick on her nightstand, observing without comprehension that the candle had burned down to a misshapen nub of cold wax. Confused memories came to her, slipping away again as her mind sought to grasp them. She had dreamed . . .

Her mouth seemed bruised and sour with a chemical taste that was not the usual anisette aftertaste of the tonic, and her limbs ached as if sore from too strenuous exercise the day before. Cassilda hoped she was not going to have a relapse of the fever that had stricken her after she had fled the convent that stormy night so many weeks ago.

She struggled for a moment with that memory. The sisters in black robes and white aprons had intended to wall her up alive in her cell because she had yielded to the temptation of certain unspeakable desires . . . The memory clouded and eluded her, like a fragment of some incompletely remembered book.

There were too many elusive memories, memories that died unheard . . . Had she not read that? *The King in Yellow* lay open upon her nightstand. Had she been reading, then fallen asleep to such dreams of depravity? But dreams, like memories, faded mirage-like whenever she touched them, leaving only tempting images to beguile her.

Forcing her cramped muscles to obey her, Cassilda climbed from her bed. Camilla was late with her tray this morning, and she might as well get dressed to make herself forget the dreams. As she slipped out of her nightdress, she looked at her reflection in the full-length dressing mirror.

The marks were beginning to fade now, but the still painful welts made red streaks across the white flesh of her shoulders, back, and thighs. Fragments of repressed nightmare returned as she stared in growing fear. She reached out her hands, touching the reflection in wonder. There were bruises on her wrists, and unbidden came a memory of her weight straining against the cords that bound her wrists to a hook from an attic rafter.

Behind her, in the mirror, Mrs Castaigne ran the tip of her tongue along her smiling lips.

"Up and about already, Cassilda? I hope you've made up your mind to be a better young lady today. You were most unruly last night."

Her brain reeling under the onrush of memories, Cassilda stared mutely. Camilla, obsequious in her maid's costume, her smile a cynical sneer, entered carrying a complex leather harness of many straps and buckles.

"I think we must do something more to improve your posture, Cassilda," Mrs Castaigne purred. "You may think me a bit old-fashioned, but I insist that a young lady's figure must be properly trained if she is to look her best."

"What are you doing to me?" Cassilda wondered, feeling panic.

"Only giving you the instruction a young lady must have if she is to serve as my companion. And you *do* want to be a proper young lady, don't you, Cassilda."

"I'm leaving this house. Right now."

"We both know why you can't. Besides, you don't really want to go. You quite enjoy our cozy little *ménage à trois*."

"You're deranged."

"And you're one to talk, dear Cassilda." Mrs Castaigne's smile was far more menacing than any threatened blow. "I think, Camilla, the scold's bridle will teach this silly girl to mind that wicked tongue."

A crash of thunder broke her out of her stupor. Out of reflex, she tried to dislodge the hard rubber ball that filled her mouth, choked on saliva when she failed. Half-strangled by the gag strapped over her face, she strained in panic to sit up. Her wrists and ankles were held fast, and, as her eyes dilated in unreasoning fear, a flash of lightning beyond the window rippled down upon her spreadeagled body, held to the brass bedposts by padded leather cuffs.

Images, too chaotic and incomprehensible to form coherent memory, exploded in bright shards from her shattered mind.

She was being forced into a straitjacket, flung into a padded cell, and they were bricking up the door . . . no, it was some bizarre corset device, forcing her neck back, crushing her abdomen, arms laced painfully into a single glove at her back . . . Camilla was helping her into a gown of satin and velvet and lace, and then into a hood of padded leather that they buckled over her head as they led her to the gallows . . . and the nurses held her down while Dr Archer penetrated her with a grotesque syringe of vile poison, and Mrs Castaigne forced the yellow tonic down her throat as she pinned her face between her thighs . . . and Camilla's lips dripped blood as she rose from her kiss, and her fangs were hypodermic needles, injecting poison, sucking life . . . they were wheeling her into the torture chamber, where Dr Archer awaited her ("It's only a frontal lobotomy, just to relieve the pressure on these two diseased lobes.") and plunges the bloody scalpel deep between her thighs . . . and they were strapping her into the metal chair in the death cell, shoving the rubber gag between her teeth and blinding her with the leather hood, and Dr Archer grasps the thick black handle of the switch and pulls it down and sends the current ripping through her nerves . . . she stands naked in shackles before the black-masked judges, and Dr Archer gloatingly exposes the giant needle ("Just an injection of my elixir, and she's quite safe for two more weeks.") . . . and the nurses in rubber aprons hold her writhing upon the altar, while Dr Archer adjusts the hangman's mask and thrusts the electrodes into her breast . . . ("Just a shot of my Prolixin, and she's quite sane for two more weeks.") . . . then the judge in wig and mask and black robe smacks down the braided whip and screams, "She must be locked away forever!" . . . she tears away the mask and Dr Archer screams, "She must be locked inside forever!" . . . she tears away the mask and Mrs Castaigne screams, "She must be locked in here forever!" . . . she tears away the mask and her own face screams, "She must be locked in you forever!" . . . then Camilla and Mrs Castaigne lead her back into her cell, and they strap her to her bed and force the rubber gag between her teeth, and Mrs Castaigne adjusts her surgeon's mask while Camilla clamps the electrodes to her nipples, and the current rips into her and her brain screams and screams unheard . . . "I think she no longer needs to be drugged." Mrs Castaigne smiles and her lips are bright with blood. "She's one of us now. She always has been one of us" . . . and they leave her alone in darkness on the promise, "We'll begin again tomorrow," and the echo, "She'll be good for two more weeks."

She moaned and writhed upon the soiled sheets, struggling to escape the images that spurted like foetid purulence from her tortured brain. With the next explosive burst of lightning, her naked body lifted in a convulsive arc from the mattress, and her scream against the gag was like the first agonized outcry of the newborn.

The spasm passed. She dropped back limply onto the sodden mattress. Slippery with sweat and blood, her relaxed hand slid the rest of the way out of the padded cuff. Quietly in the darkness, she considered her free hand—suddenly calm, for she knew she had slipped wrist restraints any number of times before this.

Beneath the press of the storm, the huge house lay in darkness and silence. With her free hand she unbuckled the other wrist cuff, then the straps that held the gag in place, and the restraints that pinned her ankles. Her tread no louder than a phantom's, she glided from bed and crossed the room. A flicker of lightning revealed shabby furnishings and a disordered array of fetishist garments and paraphernalia, but she threw open the window and looked down upon the black waters of the lake and saw the cloud waves breaking upon the base of the cliff, and when she turned away from that vision her eyes knew what they beheld and her smile was that of a lamia.

Wraith-like she drifted through the dark house, passing along the silent rooms and hallways and stairs, and when she reached the kitchen she found what she knew was the key to unlock the dark mystery that bound her here. She closed her hand upon it, and her fingers remembered its feel.

Camilla's face was tight with sudden fear as she awakened at the clasp of fingers closed upon her lips, but she made no struggle as she stared at the carving knife that almost touched her eyes.

"What happened to Constance?" The fingers relaxed to let her whisper, but the knife did not waver.

"She had a secret lover. One night she crept through the sitting room window and ran away with him. Mrs Castaigne showed her no mercy."

"Sleep now," she told Camilla, and kissed her tenderly as she freed her with a swift motion that her hand remembered.

In the darkness of Mrs Castaigne's room she paused beside the motionless figure on the bed.

"Mother?"

"Yes, Constance?"

"I've come home."

"You're dead."

"I remembered the way back."

And she showed her the key and opened the way.

It only remained for her to go. She could no longer find shelter in this house. She must leave as she had entered.

She left the knife. That key had served its purpose. Through the hallways she returned, in the darkness her bare feet sometimes treading upon rich carpets, sometimes dust and fallen plaster. Her naked flesh tingled with the blood that had freed her soul.

She reached the sitting room and looked upon the storm that lashed the night beyond. For one gleam of lightning the room seemed festooned with torn wallpaper; empty wine bottles littered the floor and dingy furnishings. The flickering mirage passed, and she saw that the room was exactly as she remembered. She must leave by the window.

There was a tapping at the window.

She started, then recoiled in horror as another repressed memory escaped into consciousness.

The figure that had pursued her through the darkness on that night she had sought refuge here. It waited for her now at the window. Half-glimpsed before, she saw it now fully revealed in the glare of the lightning.

Moisture glistened darkly upon its rippling and exaggerated musculature. Its uncouth head and shoulders hunched forward bullishly; its face was distorted with insensate lust and drooling madness. A grotesque phallus swung between its misshapen legs—serpentine, possessed of its own life and volition. Like an obscene worm, it stretched blindly toward her, blood oozing from its toothless maw.

She raised her hands to ward it off, and the monstrosity pawed at the window, mocking her every terrified movement as it waited there on the other side of the rain-slick glass.

The horror was beyond enduring. There was another casement window to the corner sitting room, the one that overlooked the waters of the river. She spun about and lunged toward it—noticing from the corner of her eye that the creature outside also whirled about, sensing her intent, flung itself toward the far window to forestall her.

The glass of the casement shattered, even as its blubbery hands stretched out toward her. There was no pain in that release, only a dream-like vertigo as she plunged into the grayness and the rain. Then the water and the darkness received her falling body, and she set out again into the night, letting the current carry her, she knew not where.

"A few personal effects remain to be officially disposed of, Dr Archer—since there's no one to claim them. It's been long enough now since the bus accident, and we'd like to be able to close the files on this catastrophe."

"Let's have a look." The psychiatrist opened the box of personal belongings. There wasn't much; there never was in such cases, and had there been anything worth stealing, it was already unofficially disposed of.

"They still haven't found a body," the ward superintendent wondered, "do you suppose . . .?"

"Callous as it sounds, I rather hope not," Dr Archer confided. "This patient was a paranoid schizophrenic—and dangerous."

"Seemed quiet enough on the ward."

"Thanks to a lot of ECT—and to depot phenothiazines. Without regular therapy, the delusional system would quickly regain control, and the patient would become frankly murderous."

There were a few toiletry items and some articles of clothing, a brassiere and pantyhose. "I guess send this over to Social Services. These shouldn't be allowed on a locked ward," the psychiatrist pointed to the nylons, "nor these smut magazines."

"They always find some way to smuggle the stuff in," the ward superintendent sighed, "and I've been working here at Coastal State since back before the War. What about these other books?"

Dr Archer considered the stack of dog-eared gothic romance novels. "Just return these to the Patients' Library. What's this one?"

Beneath the paperbacks lay a small hardcover volume, bound in yellow cloth, somewhat soiled from age.

"Out of the Patients' Library too, I suppose. People have donated all sorts of books over the years, and if the patients don't tear them up, they just stay on the shelves forever."

"*The King in Yellow*," Dr Archer read from the spine, opening the book. On the flyleaf a name was penned in a graceful script: *Constance Castaigne*.

"Perhaps the name of a patient who left it here," the superintendent suggested. "Around the turn of the century this was a private sanatorium. Somehow, though, the name seems to ring a distant bell."

"Let's just be sure this isn't vintage porno."

"I can't be sure—maybe something the old-timers talked about when I first started here. I seem to remember there was some famous scandal involving one of the wealthy families in the city. A murderess, was it? And something about a suicide, or was it an escape? I can't recall . . ."

"Harmless nineteenth-century romantic nonsense," Dr Archer concluded. "Send it on back to the library."

The psychiatrist glanced at a last few lines before closing the book:

*Cassilda*. I tell you, I am lost! Utterly lost!

*Camilla* (terrified herself). You have seen the King . . .?

*Cassilda*. And he has taken from me the power to direct or to escape my dreams.

# Basil Copper

# Amber Print

FOR THIRTY YEARS, Basil Copper worked as a journalist and editor of a local newspaper before becoming a full-time writer in 1970. His first story in the horror field was "The Spider" in *The 5th Pan Book of Horror Stories* (1964) since when his novels of the macabre and gaslight gothic have included *The Great White Space*, *The Curse of the Fleers*, *Necropolis*, *The Black Death* and *House of the Wolf*. Copper's short fiction has been collected in *Not After Nightfall*, *From Evil's Pillow*, *When Footsteps Echo* and *And Afterward, the Dark* and he has written two non-fiction studies of the vampire and the werewolf.

Copper is also one of Britain's leading film collectors, with a private archive containing more than a thousand titles; with the following story, his expert knowledge is put to chilling effect in a movie buff's nightmare . . .

"IT REALLY IS A MOST REMARKABLE PRINT," said Mr Blenkinsop, leading the way into the large cluttered room behind the shop. His friend followed him in, his sallow cheeks flushing with pleasurable anticipation at Mr Blenkinsop's words.

"But where on earth did you get it?" Carter asked, for perhaps the thirteenth time that evening. "Decla went out in the twenties and U.F.A.'s Neubabelsberg Studios were gutted during the war, I understood . . ."

"Yes, yes, Henry, we know about that," said Mr Blenkinsop, impatience corroding the edges of his usually smooth, high voice. "All in good time. But first we must have a small drink by way of celebration."

Carter sat down in a deep leather armchair while his friend busied himself at a mahogany sideboard. It was a curious room which the overspill from Mr Blenkinsop's shop made even more bizarre. Deer's heads and antique weapons, rare glass and china, rosewood cabinets and ormolu clocks came and went in the gloom of the big sitting room, as Mr Blenkinsop took the items to be sold in the antique shop beyond. Mr Carter never knew what remarkable sight would meet his gaze when he next visited the private portions of his friend's premises.

The contrast was even more extraordinary when Mr Blenkinsop's *objets d'art* were carelessly set down among cans of movie film, projectors and other equipment of a much later age. Both men were bachelors and were thus able to indulge their tastes; in the case of Mr Blenkinsop the collection and sale of antiques and Victoriana. In that of Mr Carter there was no such duality. He followed the profession of accountant and apart from the purchase of rare books, his principal passion, like that of his friend, was the study of the history of the cinema and, above all, the collection, listing and showing of rare films collected from many sources and from many parts of the world.

Both men spent a great deal of time and money on this esoteric and expensive pursuit; both were among the principal collectors in the world, in a field which was followed perhaps by only 500 to 1,000 people on a global scale; both were authorities in their chosen sector; in Blenkinsop's case that of the German cinema of the twenties; in that of Carter, newsreels and actuality prints of the period 1895–1920. Above all, both men had enormous collections of films on many different gauges which, encased in cans, boxes and containers, spilled over from their intended racks and shelves and invaded every corner of their respective homes.

It was against this background that Carter had expressed only the polite interest due to his old friend, when the latter had enthused over the telephone about his latest acquisition. Mr Carter sat now, blinking amiably at Blenkinsop, as he fussed at the sideboard. He took the small cut-glass goblet filled with yellow liquid and sniffed at it appreciatively. Blenkinsop went back to the sideboard and returned with his own glass. The two old friends sat at the oval table for a few minutes, each lost in his own thoughts, sipping at the wine and glancing curiously at one another from time to time.

Carter was the first to break the silence, as Blenkinsop knew he would be.

"Well, are we going up, or aren't we?"

Mr Blenkinsop patted his knee with a soothing gesture, as though Mr Carter were a child who had somehow to be mollified. "Certainly, certainly," he said in his high, well-modulated voice. Then, glancing at his friend's expression, he smiled a quick smile and went on quickly, "We'll go now, then, if you really can't wait. Though I thought you said yet another print of Caligari wouldn't be of any real interest."

It was Carter's turn to smile. "Ah, but you were so damned mysterious on the telephone, George. And after all, a new print of a thing like that . . . and with scenes neither of us have got. Incredible, really. It's something I shall have to see."

Mr Blenkinsop smiled again with satisfaction. "That's why I asked you over, Henry. It's worth any collector's time. I'll refill your glass and then we'll make a start."

With both their glasses re-charged, the two men, outwardly quiet but each bubbling inwardly with suppressed thoughts—Carter with unformulated questions, Blenkinsop with unsolicited answers—began their long march which ended in the large attic beneath Mr Blenkinsop's roof. The night around them was heavy with noise; the creaking protests of old beams; the subtle shift of ancient timber floorings; the minute vibration as echoes raised by the passage of their feet died away along the corridors.

Mr Blenkinsop lived alone, except for a housekeeper who came in daily; he would allow no domestic interference above the level of the shop and the bedrooms on the first floor, so the two men's feet imprinted themselves as pallid indentations in the thick dust which coated the worn drugget of the passages. Mr Blenkinsop seemed to prefer the atmosphere of melancholy decay which pervaded the upper storeys of his old house; fortunately, it was quite detached from its neighbours in the street, as the noise in the early morning as Mr Blenkinsop projected an occasional sound film might have proved an intolerable intrusion on their privacy.

Mr Carter too, though he disliked dust and muddle—his training as an accountant ensured a clinical atmosphere and an immaculate marshalling of the cans and containers on the racks of his own collection—somehow had grown to tolerate the disorder of Mr Blenkinsop's menage; a disorder he could not have borne for one moment in his own establishment. It seemed all of a piece with the man himself and there was little or nothing Mr Carter would have changed in his old friend. Though he liked the atmosphere of the shop he preferred the great boarded room under the roof which Blenkinsop kept as his central archive; and beyond that the immaculate viewing theatre with its large modern screen, the half-dozen tip-up chairs salvaged from a bankrupt cinema; and the craftsman-built projection box with its plate glass windows and latest in sound equipment.

Here were the things Mr Carter most believed in and which were the substance of great argument between the two friends; the racks of reference books; the filing cabinets and index cards with their carefully documented scholarship; the looseleaf folders with the data on the films; the rewinders and viewers in three or four different gauges and, above all, the archive itself, the *raison d'etre* for all the paraphernalia that filled the two vast rooms.

On steel racks that stretched from floor to ceiling, was the accumulated treasure of more than seventy years of cinema history; from the Lumiere Programme of 1895, through Edwin S. Porter's *Great Train Robbery*, to the great films of the German silent period and beyond; from *Caligari*, *Vaudeville*, *The Last Laugh* and *The Joyless Street;* from the giant dragon of Fritz Lang's *Siegfried* to the massed legions of Abel Gance's *Napoleon.* From the cans the ghostly shades of great, long-dead artistes, picked out by the livid pencil of the projector's light, lived again for a brief while, before being temporarily banished to the gloom of the archive shelves.

Lya de Putti, Ivan Mosjoukine, Emil Jannings, Valentino, Conrad Veidt, Werner Krauss, Lars Hanson waited their turn to re-enact ancient dreams and desires that had been entrusted to celluloid thirty, forty, fifty years earlier. Blenkinsop was the instigator of a thousand adventures at the turn of a switch. And actors now past seventy were seen again—like Gosta Ekmann in *Faust*—in the full glory of youth, before time had taken its cruel toll of those once handsome limbs and unlined faces.

Though Carter did not share his friend's extreme passion for the silent drama, preferring to concentrate on the more arid but no less fascinating documentary field, he greatly enjoyed their evenings of magic under the great loft beams and appreciated the magnificent camerawork and the fine craftsmanship of the set designers and technicians of these pioneer works of the golden age of cinema. If he sometimes felt that Mr Blenkinsop's taste inclined towards the morbid—he had a large collection of early macabre films for instance—he was too polite to show it, though he really preferred the less frequent treat afforded by the work of the master comedians of which Blenkinsop also had a definitive collection.

But tonight was to see no contortions by Lloyd high above the street; no Langdon or Laurel; Chaplin or Linder; Keaton or Keystone; tonight the comics were banished and the leering nightmare of German expressionism was to dominate the screen. And yet, as Blenkinsop courteously held the door ajar for him, and Carter stepped through into the magical atmosphere of his old friend's loft, he once more wondered just what could be so special about this print of THE CABINET OF DOCTOR CALIGARI.

Blenkinsop followed him in, holding his glass of wine carefully as he negotiated the step; while Carter mused among the racks, Blenkinsop went on into the theatre, throwing switches as he went so that light progressively leaped up, banishing the gloom. Carter paused by a mountain of cans labelled COMING THROUGH THE RYE and wished for a moment that he could again see the Hepworth, instead of the over-familiar classic Blenkinsop was intent on showing him. Yet perhaps there might be something unusual about the evening; something really special, that would justify Blenkinsop's mysterious phone call and his air of suppressed tension, beneath the easy manner.

"Come in, come in," Blenkinsop called softly, re-appearing in the doorway of the projection room. As Carter lowered himself appreciatively into the comfortable padded seat his friend indicated with a wave of his slender hand, he sipped at his wine and asked mildly, "Don't I get to look at the print first?"

Mr Blenkinsop's eyes narrowed beneath his whitening hair. "So sorry, my dear fellow, the excitement of this coup has quite made me forget myself. The print is in here."

The two men squeezed through the doorway of the large projection box; it contained no less than five machines, but Carter had no time to spare for them. He had seen them many times before. He bent over the stand on which Blenkinsop's 35 mm. machines stood and gazed at the three metal cans before him. They bore Gothic German lettering; DAS KABINETT DES DOKTOR CALIGARI and numbers and technical details. He saw with surprise, as soon as he had the lid off, that the print was on 16 mm. and not 9.5 mm., as he had expected. Blenkinsop's dry chuckle sounded behind him.

"I thought that would puzzle you."

"An original print?" stammered Carter, starting to unwind the first spool. "From Decla? This is remarkable. Where did you . . ."

"Where did I buy it?" said Blenkinsop, interrupting the question he had been going to ask and answering it at the same time. "An old chap in Highgate Village. Or at least his widow. He had died some time before and she was selling up his collection. I think I got everything worth having. But this was quite the best thing there."

"I should think so," said Carter, gingerly unwinding the reel between thumb and forefinger and squinting up at the light. He saw that the film was tinted in various colours. There were so many main titles that he didn't have time to unreel them all. He handed the print back to his friend, who started to thread it on to his big Ampro sound machine.

"Just watch," said Blenkinsop, with an unusual smile, his eyes dark and impassive, as he inched the celluloid through the chrome-plated projector gate, "You've never seen anything like it."

Carter regained his seat and sipped reflectively at his wine as Blenkinsop extinguished the lights; there was a long pause and he suddenly felt nervous waiting alone in the dark. A thin crack of light came in from the archive room next door. The only sound was the hum of a distant car from the high road nearby and the occasional creak as the roofbeams settled. For the first time Carter became uneasily aware of all the illicit nitrate film Blenkinsop had stored on the premises; this was strictly against Home Office regulations, as nitrate film was notoriously unstable and highly inflammable. He refused to think what might happen if a fire should start up in this timbered portion of the house. Yet why should it, he told himself; it was curious that he should be thinking that way this evening. It was quite alien to his normal pattern of reasoning; he had been in Blenkinsop's loft hundreds of times and the nitrate films had been there at least twenty years, so why should he begin worrying about fire hazards now? He turned the crystal goblet between his fingers, his mind only half concentrating, when he became aware of the continued silence; there was a sudden crash which jangled his nerves and a loud exclamation from Mr Blenkinsop.

"All right?" Carter called out in a startled voice. Blenkinsop swore genteelly, which was a rarity for him.

"Sorry about that," he said cheerfully. "Knocked the tins down. Won't be a moment."

There was a click as he threw the switch, the projector whirred sweetly and a livid finger of blue light lanced out at the screen; crabbed handwriting grew before Mr Carter's eyes, blurred, then became distinct as Mr Blenkinsop focused up. DECLA-BIOSCOP PRESENTS said the screen. WERNER KRAUSS, CONRAD VEIDT, LIL DAGOVER. In THE CABINET OF DR CALIGARI the screen went on. Carter sat back as Blenkinsop eased himself into the next seat. The titles were written in sloping handwriting as the textbooks said the historic original prints of 1919 had been. The tinting was extraordinarily vivid, passing from amber to dark blue and then to greens and yellows and reds as the film progressed. Mr Blenkinsop squinted at the screen through his wineglass as the print clicked its way out of the projector gate and cast satisfied sidelong glances at his old friend. Director of Photography WILLY HAMEISTER the screen continued. DIRECTED BY ROBERT WIENE the screen shouted.

The picture went dark and Mr Carter almost exclaimed aloud when the first shots appeared; then followed the famous fairground sequence but as he had never seen it before. The picture glowed in its frame as though the long-dead characters could climb out and join the two men; the hues of the tinting joined and fused, dissolved and ran together again like living fire. It was diabolically clever photography and Mr Carter could now understand fully why the film had been such a sensation on its first release: it was truly an incredible print and he could well realise why Mr Blenkinsop should be so excited at its acquisition. But at the same time he felt vaguely uneasy as the surrealist sets glowed and wavered in the background of the scenes; it seemed to be hot in the little theatre too and a thin trickle of sweat ran down his collar. He nearly dropped his wineglass at the first appearance of Werner Krauss as Dr Caligari; that fine actor's soot-streaked features and carefully calculated gibbering and mowing had never affected him so powerfully.

As the story continued Mr Carter became more and more confused. As he well knew, Wiene's classic production concerned Dr Caligari, a charlatan who ran a fairground exhibition which featured Cesare, a weird somnambulist who could predict the future. But under cover of this the doctor sent Cesare out to commit murder after nightfall; at the end of Carl Mayer's celebrated screenplay, which caused a world sensation on its release, the nightmare sets, the stylised gesticulations of the actors, were seen to be nothing more than the distorted figments of a madman's imagination, the seemingly calm and sane narrator of the story.

Cesare, as played by Conrad Veidt in his first screen role, was a fine creation, still able to inspire terror and pity after the lapse of over 50 years, but this Cesare was something more. Perhaps it was the composition of the tinting or the edition Blenkinsop had got hold of was a special release print not generally seen, but Carter had never been so affected by the film; this Cesare was not only a distinguished actor portraying a criminal monster.

The malevolent stare of Cesare, seen in a series of smouldering close-ups, had something personal in it that brought unease to Mr Carter's soul and his discomfort was increased by a number of scenes which were completely new to him; a sequence of dwarfs re-enacting a tableau of mediaeval torture in Dr Sonnow's clinic; a long and complex passage where Cesare, in a wild landscape full of tottering verticals and wildly dancing shadows, began obscene preparations for the disembowelling of the heroine, Jane, who was strapped to an angled upright like a Giacometti sculpture; and a disgusting shot involving the slashing impact of a meat cleaver followed by a deluge of severed fingers on to the spectator.

The close-ups of Cesare continued and there was one climax, in the second part of the film, where it almost seemed as though he intended to climb out of the frame and come at the two men; the effect of this was so menacing that Mr Carter cracked his head against the projection box panelling behind him and cut a tooth in the process. As the writhing colours of the tinting wavered on and the sombre story mounted to the finale, Mr Carter became aware that Blenkinsop was completely and pleasurably absorbed in his new purchase; he might have been viewing a different film, so delighted did he seem. Carter began to wonder if he were ill; perspiration drenched his collar, his finger-nails dug into the padded arm of his chair, but he clenched his teeth and sat grimly on, his eyes hardly able to leave the fiery rectangle in front of him, on which such terrifying events were being depicted.

It ended at last, in the traditional manner, with Dr Sonnow expressing hope of his demented patient's recovery but as the screen went black Carter discovered that there was an epilogue, for the picture re-appeared and with a bubbling cry of horror which he could not repress, he saw the gaunt form of Cesare follow the doctor and hack again and again at his victim's body with a long knife he produced from the folds of his dark clothing. There was a final click from the projector and the picture faded; Carter became aware that he was lying back in his seat, looking at the ceiling. Blenkinsop hovered over him solicitously.

"Are you all right, old chap? That was quite a fit of coughing. I was extremely worried for a moment."

Carter sat up. Already he felt better and quite ashamed at having given way to his feelings. He looked at the trailing end of film still lashing around on its spool, as Blenkinsop moved to switch off the motor. Of course there was nothing wrong with the film but the amber print made such a difference to the performances. And he was sure some of the scenes were different from his copy.

But all he said to Blenkinsop was, "I must apologise for my outburst. I must have swallowed the wrong way."

Blenkinsop switched on the room lights and stood rubbing his hands, his face aglow with pleasure.

"You see what I mean. It was an unusual print, wasn't it?"

Carter felt that was pitching it in rather a low key, but he said cautiously, "Quite remarkable. There were a lot of passages in that which I hadn't seen before. It's different in many respects from the version in my collection."

"I thought you'd see that," said his friend, intent on rewinding the film back on to its spools. "Let's go down for another drink and then I'll tell you something. I never get tired of this film. I've already seen it seven times since I bought it."

Carter said nothing, but drained the few drops remaining in his wineglass and presently followed his friend downstairs, his mind full of conflicting thoughts.

As the two old friends sat at the oval table sipping their wine in the big room with its antiques and gilt furniture, some of the colour was returning to Carter's drained cheeks and he was already regretting the fuss he had made over the film. Neither seemed eager to broach the subject, however, and the ormolu clock had ticked on another twenty minutes before Carter felt it safe to steer the conversation back in that general direction.

"I felt it strange," he said diffidently, holding his glass up to the light of the chandelier. The rays striking through the glass made an amber pattern of his own face as he went on. "I mean, of course, it is a strange film, anyway. But this was something special. For instance, many of those shots were completely new. And I don't believe they've ever been mentioned in any reference book. That's something the Circle would like to know. Ted Walker would be interested . . ."

"Ah, but that's not all." Blenkinsop had leaned forward, his voice a hoarse quaver. "The scenes change all the time. I've never come across anything like this."

Mr Carter stopped examining the light through his glass and put it down slowly on the table. His head suddenly felt unsteady again.

"Eigh?" he said bewilderedly. "Keep changing? How do you mean?"

Mr Blenkinsop couldn't keep the excitement out of his voice. "That's exactly it. An optical illusion, of course. But every time I've seen the film it appears to me that it's never the same. There are always scenes that I haven't noticed before. Or the order changes. Though the basic plot and the progression of the key sequences remain. Or perhaps it's me."

There was a long silence between the friends.

"I'm not sure I understand," said Mr Carter slowly, weighing each word as though afraid of offending his friend. "How could the scenes change? You're sure you're not ill? Perhaps you had the sort of turn that affected me. That tinting might have a curious effect on the eyes. Strobing on the retina . . ."

But once again his reply was interrupted. Mr Blenkinsop was on his feet and pacing up and down the room in his agitation. "No, no, it's not that," he said, his eyes shining in a curious manner. "It's something else. Something that I have to find out for myself. There's a quality about this print that I haven't found in any other film. You're sure you wouldn't like to see it again?"

Mr Carter shook his head emphatically. He consulted his watch. It was already past ten. "Nothing would induce me to see it," he said firmly. "And I don't think you should either."

Mr Blenkinsop seemed rather startled at his manner. He tried a laugh which failed dismally. "Oh, surely," he said. "You can't be serious. You mean you wouldn't want to see it again—ever?"

Mr Carter looked at him quite steadily for a moment before replying.

"Never again, George," he said gently. "And you know the reason why. There's something unnatural about it. If it were my print I'd burn it, and you know what that means when a collector like myself speaks like that."

Mr Blenkinsop laughed again but there was little gaiety in the sound, which seemed to set the shadows starting in the dim room. "You'd never do it, Henry," he said briefly. "You'll feel better tomorrow."

The two old friends didn't return to the subject again. They spoke of other things, drank their wine and ten minutes later when Mr Carter said goodbye to Mr Blenkinsop all was quite normal between them. Except, as Mr Blenkinsop locked and bolted the glass-fronted door after his companion he felt, sadly, that something rare and precious had gone out of their friendship; and the cause, ridiculous as it might seem to either of them, was undoubtedly the amber print.

Mr Blenkinsop sat by himself in the room behind the shop for a few minutes more and poured himself another glass of wine. He glanced at the grandfather clock in the mahogany case in the corner and saw that it was still only ten-forty. There was plenty of time to see the amber print again before he sought his bed. He might not, it is true, see it all; it was perhaps overlong at 85 minutes for repeated viewing in one day and the subject was undeniably sombre. Yet it was such a beautiful copy and with so many unique features that it would repay endless study. Mr Blenkinsop did not regret time spent in such a manner; after all time was the one thing he had plenty of and it was difficult to imagine a more absorbing way of passing it.

He picked up his glass and walked with firm and purposeful steps up the staircase to the topmost floor. The old house was full of noises at this time of night; the timbers creaked reassuringly to themselves as though confirming their presence, one to the other. Mr Blenkinsop felt at ease as he let himself into his projection room and switched on the lights; the plush chairs welcomed him in the warm glow of the ceiling fittings. That was where he was most at home. The mundane problems of the shop and everyday dropped away and he was again in a world which he and Carter and a few other privileged souls alone really understood and appreciated. The world of art and scholarship; of amber prints and rarities; of notched titles and unique treasures that had to be pursued into remote suburbs after much advertising. Mr Blenkinsop's eyes gleamed and he rubbed his hands briskly as he stooped to the cans containing his precious print of CALIGARI. He laced up the machine.

The sweet sound of the projector's gears fell satisfyingly on his ears. He glanced once or twice at it to see that the loops were in order and that it was maintaining correct speed and then settled back in his seat. When he finally looked at the screen he was surprised to see that the titles had already disappeared; slightly annoyed, he groped around in the throbbing light that fell on the room and checked the cans. He thought for a moment he had put on the second reel in error but then saw that this was not so. The take-up spool certainly did not contain more than about thirty feet of film; surely not enough to have absorbed the long introductory credits.

Mr Blenkinsop then saw that an entirely different sequence was being enacted; Cesare and Dr Caligari were engaged in conversation with the heroine, Jane. While Caligari held the girl's attention the somnambulist was fingering the flowing white draperies of the girl's costume in a way Mr Blenkinsop didn't like at all. He frowned and found his vision suddenly blurring; he shook his head to clear his eyesight and the scene had changed once more. The sequence was the murder of the town clerk; the picture was bathed in amber light which pulsed and irradiated in a manner which filled Blenkinsop with alarm. As Cesare sidled nearer his unsuspecting victim, fondling a long butcher's knife, the very shadows painted on the walls of Reimann, Warm and Roehrig's sets seemed to pullulate like the corpuscles in a blood-cell. Mr Blenkinsop gulped and eased a shaking finger round his collar.

Mr Carter was right; there did appear to be something amiss with the film. Curious that he should not have noticed this before. Perhaps he was seeing it for the first time with his old friend's eyes. Mr Blenkinsop shook himself and concentrated on the screen again; this time all appeared normal and the spectator was once again at the fairground. Then the film seemed to judder in the gate, there was a vibration in the room and Mr Blenkinsop felt as though he were choking; his heart was like a great sponge squeezed by a giant hand.

He fought for breath as the picture went its inexorable way; he struggled towards the switch to turn off the machine. But something kept his eyes fixed with burning intensity on the screen. For the face of Francis, the hero's friend, had changed to that of his own. Mr Blenkinsop passed his free hand over his face as if to remind himself of its familiar contours. Perspiration was cascading down his cheeks in long rivulets; but still the Francis with the mirror-face that was himself enacted out the little drama of the fairground. And Mr Blenkinsop saw with mounting horror that it was indeed himself asking the fatal question.

HOW LONG HAVE I TO LIVE? said the screen title.

Cesare's face grimaced and gibbered with coruscating fire; the tinting ran from green to amber and then on to mauve in the frightful series of close-ups. The heavy-lidded eyes, thick with theatrical make-up, looked from the cabinet out at Mr Blenkinsop, who sat crucified in his padded chair. Cesare seemed about to invade the privacy of the room; the whole screen was running in sheets of pink fire which appeared to Mr Blenkinsop to be already lapping at the curtains which flanked the screen. The lips mouthed but no words came. But a hot breath licked at him from the front of the auditorium.

YOU WILL BE DEAD AT DAWN! the screen said.

Mr Blenkinsop must have shouted; how he managed it, he didn't know. He almost overturned the projector in his blundering panic. But somehow he managed to switch it off. The flickering and the frightful images died. To Blenkinsop's overheated imagination the figures of Caligari and Cesare seemed to run along the projector beam until they disappeared within the machine. He really must be ill; he operated the light switch like a man suffering from palsy and was shocked to find his palms running with the sweat of naked fear.

He downed the remaining wine in the glass which he had put on the projector stand and felt better; sitting on the edge of his chair he pressed his two hands together and waited for the shuddering of his nerves to recede. Then he forced himself to rewind the film and replace it in the can. He finally picked up the three cans and carried them out to the main archive, where he stacked them in their pre-ordained position in the Golden Age of German Cinema category.

He walked back down the long gallery, ostensibly to check on the title of a film at the other end, but in reality to prove something to himself. He had to master his nerves or he might never again be at ease in his own domain. He put his experience down to a combination of optical illusion, nerves and a possible fainting attack. Perhaps he had had a little too much to drink this evening; he had drunk several glasses of wine with Carter and possibly the extra on top? Yes, that was it.

He reached down a print of KOENIGSMARK and ran his hand over the label lovingly; as he went to replace it on the shelf he heard the sudden clatter of metal on metal at the other end of the gallery. He turned quickly, hearing the stealthy scraping which followed; curiously he felt no fear. The noise was that which might be made by someone who had difficulty in opening the lid of one of the film cans. A light rustling passed through the gallery. Mr Blenkinsop let the tin in his hand drop to the floor; the clatter as it hit the boards started hideous echoes from the ceiling rafters.

He trod quietly as he wormed his way into the next aisle. A long, attenuated shadow passed slowly across the white lozenge of light that spilled from the door of the projection room. Mr Blenkinsop had seen that shadow before and knew what it portended; the shadow grew and spread until it seemed to fill all the archive weighted with its hundreds of tins containing the enshrined performances of thousands of dead artistes. A brittle scratching fretted at his nerves in the silence which followed; Mr Blenkinsop rounded an angle in the gallery and found himself back in his original position.

His foot kicked against something; he looked down. The dim light fell on the label of a can. It said: DAS KABINETT DES DOKTOR CALIGARI. All three tins which contained the print were lying jumbled on the floor; all were, as Mr Blenkinsop had somehow expected, empty. He raised his eyes as the shadow grew before him until it filled the whole of the loft. Something fell with a soggy thump near him and an old, dusty top hat rolled forward into the light. Mr Blenkinsop understood everything as a soft hand closed on his arm; the fingers and sleeves were black as the night which surrounded him and the creeping shadow flowed onwards and took him to itself.

Mr Carter awoke with a choking cry at midnight, frightened beyond measure at a sinister dream which persisted into his waking life. He switched on the lights and looked at the clock; he had such an oppression of spirit which was completely outside his experience. So convinced was he that something was wrong that he had hastily dressed and was already starting his car before he fully realised what he intended to do.

Ten minutes later he had drawn up in front of Mr Blenkinsop's shop and was rapping timidly at the glass-panelled door. Lights shone from the upper storeys and there was a yellow radiance from the room behind the shop so that he knew Blenkinsop couldn't be abed. Nothing stirred. Mr Carter was in such an agitation of spirit that he surprised himself with his actions that night. When there was no reply to his repeated knockings, he went and fetched his car jack and unceremoniously smashed in the front door. He fumbled for the catch in the gloom, caring little whether he cut himself on the jagged glass or not. His ears were abnormally attuned to the sounds of the old house as he pounded up the stairs.

In the main gallery of the archive he found three large tins in the aisle; these seemed as though they had been burned and scorched. The label identified the contents as THE CABINET OF DOCTOR CALIGARI. Inside them was nothing but a putrescent mass of black liquid of the consistency of mud but with such a loathsome stench that Mr Carter was forced to clap his handkerchief over his nostrils. He noted scuffing marks in the dust of the floor. As the coroner afterwards remarked, it was with considerable courage that he went down the gallery to the crumpled remains of Mr Blenkinsop's body.

Some time later that evening, firebells were heard coming down the night wind and a haggard Mr Carter was banging on the door of a local police constable. Mr Blenkinsop's shop was detached and Mr Carter was perhaps justified in his actions, but nitrate film is impossible to stop once a fire is started and the authorities found hardly a bone left of Mr Blenkinsop to identify. Carter himself said he had no idea how the blaze began but a number of people had their own theories and it seemed odd, to say the least, that Mr Carter should have paid a second visit to his old friend's premises that night.

What cleared him of any culpability in Mr Blenkinsop's death was the testimony of several independent witnesses who stated that two tall and shadowy figures had been seen coming from Mr Blenkinsop's shop long after the fire had started and while Mr Carter was engaged in talking with the policemen. Astonishingly, the fire did not seem to harm them and those few people who tried to follow, soon lost them as they walked at an incredible pace and vanished in a maze of alleys adjoining the shop. The coroner had inquiries made, of course, but nothing fruitful ever arose from that line of investigation. An open verdict was returned.

Mr Carter now lives at Bexhill. Much aged, he is a changed man. He has sold his film collection and concentrates on stamps, mainly early Colonial issues. He sleeps badly and cannot bear to visit the cinema. He remembers only too well the shadows on the wall in the antique dealer's attic and the sight which prompted him to light the fire.

Not only the husk of Mr Blenkinsop's body, all liquefied as though the essence had been drawn out of it, or even the face, which had been erased as though some deadly hand had drawn a sponge across it. All these things, bad as they were, he could have borne. It was not those alone which prompted him to light the match. Just a piece of pasteboard clutched tightly between the stumps of what remained of the dead fingers. On the card was engraved in curlicue letters:

**Dr Caligari**

# Brian Lumley

# The House of the Temple

BRIAN LUMLEY fell under the spell of American horror writer H.P. Lovecraft while serving in the Army in Germany and Cyprus. He tried his own hand at writing similar tales, initially updating Lovecraft's famed Cthulhu Mythos, which resulted in two collections of short stories—*The Caller of the Black* and *The Horror at Oakdene*—and the novel *Beneath the Moors*.

He continued to adapt Lovecraft's themes in several series of books, but more recently has found his own voice with such bestselling novels as *Psychomech*, *Psychosphere*, *Psychamok*, *The House of Doors* and the five-volume *Necroscope* series. In 1989 he won the British Fantasy Award for his short story "Fruiting Bodies", which lends its title to his new collection.

In "The House of the Temple", the author returns to his literary roots; but despite using the trappings of Lovecraft's Mythos, the terror induced by this gripping novella is purely Lumley's own.

## 1. The Summons

I SUPPOSE UNDER THE CIRCUMSTANCES it is only natural that the police should require this belated written statement from me; and I further suppose it to be in recognition of my present highly nervous condition and my totally unwarranted confinement in this *place* that they are allowing me to draw the thing up without supervision. But while every kindness has been shown me, still I most strongly protest my continued detainment here. Knowing what I now know, I would voice the same protest in respect of detention in *any* prison or institute anywhere in Scotland . . . anywhere in the entire British Isles.

Before I begin, however, let me clearly make the point that, since no charges have been levelled against me, I make this statement of my own free will, fully knowing that in so doing I may well extend my stay in this detestable place. I can only hope that upon its reading, it will be seen that I had no alternative but to follow the action I describe.

You the reader must therefore judge. My actual sanity—if indeed I am still sane—my very *being*, may well depend upon your findings. . . .

I was in New York when the letter from my uncle's solicitors reached me. Sent from an address in the Royal Mile, that great road which reaches steep and cobbled to the esplanade of Edinburgh Castle itself, the large, sealed manila envelope had all the hallmarks of officialdom, so that even before I opened it I feared the worst.

Not that I had been close to my uncle in recent years (my mother had brought me out of Scotland as a small child, on the death of my father, and I had never been back) but certainly I remembered Uncle Gavin. If anything I remembered him better than I did my father; for where Andrew McGilchrist had always been dry and introverted, Uncle Gavin had been just the opposite. Warm, outgoing and generous to a fault, he had spoilt me mercilessly.

Now, according to the letter, he was dead and I was named his sole heir and beneficiary; and the envelope contained a voucher which guaranteed me a flight to Edinburgh from anywhere in the world. And then of course there was the letter itself, the contents of which further guaranteed my use of that voucher; for only a fool could possibly refuse my uncle's bequest, or fail to be interested in its attendant though at present unspecified conditions.

Quite simply, by presenting myself at the offices of Macdonald, Asquith and Lee in Edinburgh, I would already have fulfilled the first condition toward inheriting my uncle's considerable fortune, his estate of over three hundred acres and his great house where it stood in wild and splendid solitude at the foot of the Pentlands in Lothian. All of which seemed a very far cry from New York . . .

As to what I was doing in New York in the first place:

Three months earlier, in mid-March of 1976—when I was living alone in Philadelphia in the home where my mother had raised me—my fiancee of two years had given me back my ring, run off and married a banker from Baltimore. The novel I was writing had immediately metamorphosed from a light-hearted love story into a doom-laden tragedy, became meaningless somewhere in the transformation, and ended up in my waste-paper basket. That was that. I sold up and moved to New York, where an artist friend had been willing to share his apartment until I could find a decent place of my own.

I had left no forwarding address, however, which explained the delayed delivery of the letter from my uncle's solicitors; the letter itself was post-marked March 26th, and from the various marks, labels and redirections on the envelope, the U.S. Mail had obviously gone to considerable trouble to find me. And they found me at a time when the lives of both myself and my artist friend, Carl Earlman, were at a very low ebb. I was not writing and Carl was not drawing, and despite the arrival of summer our spirits were on a rapid decline.

Which is probably why I jumped at the opportunity the letter presented, though, as I have said, certainly I would have been a fool to ignore or refuse the thing . . . Or so I thought at the time.

I invited Carl along if he so desired, and he too grasped at the chance with both hands. His funds were low and getting lower; he would soon be obliged to quit his apartment for something less ostentatious; and since he, too, had decided that he needed a change of locale—to put some life back into his artwork—the matter was soon decided and we packed our bags and headed for Edinburgh.

It was not until our journey was over, however—when we were settled in our hotel rooms in Princes Street—that I remembered my mother's warning, delivered to me deliriously but persistently from her deathbed, that I should never return to Scotland, certainly not to the old house. And as I vainly attempted to adjust to jet-lag and the fact that it was late evening while all my instincts told me it should now be day, so my mind went back over what little I knew of my family roots, of the McGilchrist line itself, of that old and rambling house in the Pentlands where I had been born, and especially of the peculiar reticence of Messrs Macdonald, Asquith and Lee, the Scottish solicitors.

Reticence, yes, because I could almost feel the hesitancy in their letter. It seemed to me that they would have preferred *not* to find me; and yet, if I were asked what it was that gave me this impression, then I would be at a loss for an answer. Something in the way it was phrased, perhaps—in the dry, professional idiom of solicitors—which too often seems to me to put aside all matters of emotion or sensibility; so that I felt like a small boy offered a candy . . . and warned simultaneously that it would ruin my teeth. Yes, it seemed to me that Messrs. Mcdonald, Asquith and Lee might actually be *apprehensive* about my acceptance of their conditions—or rather, of my uncle's conditions—as if they were offering a cigar to an addict suffering from cancer of the lungs.

I fastened on that line of reasoning, seeing the conditions of the will as the root of the vague uneasiness which niggled at the back of my mind. The worst of it was that these conditions were not specified; other than to say that if I could not or would not meet them, still I would receive fifteen thousand pounds and my return ticket home, and that the residue of my uncle's fortune would then be used to carry out his will in respect of "the property known as Temple House."

Temple House, that rambling old seat of the McGilchrists where it stood locked in a steep re-entry; and the Pentland Hills a grey and green backdrop to its frowning, steep-gabled aspect; with something of the Gothic in its structure, something more of Renaissance Scotland, and an aura of antiquity all its own which, as a child, I could still remember loving dearly. But that had been almost twenty years ago and the place had been my home. A happy home, I had thought; at least until the death of my father, of which I could remember nothing at all.

But I did remember the pool—the deep, grey pool where it lapped at the raised, reinforced, east-facing garden wall—the pool and its ring of broken quartz pillars, the remains of the temple for which the house was named. Thinking back over the years to my infancy, I wondered if perhaps the pool had been the reason my mother had always hated the place. None of the McGilchrists had ever been swimmers, and yet water had always seemed to fascinate them. I would not have been the first of the line to be found floating face-down in that strange, pillar-encircled pool of deep and weedy water; and I had used to spend hours just sitting on the wall and staring across the breeze-rippled surface . . .

So my thoughts went as, tossing in my hotel bed late into the night, I turned matters over in my mind . . . And having retired late, so we rose late, Carl and I; and it was not until 2 p.m. that I presented myself at the office of Macdonald, Asquith and Lee on the Royal Mile.

## 2. The Will

SINCE CARL had climbed up to the esplanade to take in the view, I was alone when I reached my destination and entered MA and L's offices through a door of yellow-tinted bull's-eye panes, passing into the cool welcome of a dim and very *Olde Worlde* anteroom; and for all that this was the source of my enigmatic summons, still I found a reassuring air of charm and quiet sincerity about the place. A clerk led me into an inner chamber as much removed from my idea of a solicitor's office as is Edinburgh from New York, and having been introduced to the firm's Mr Asquith I was offered a seat.

Asquith was tall, slender, high-browed and balding, with a mass of freckles which seemed oddly in contrast with his late middle years, and his handshake was firm and dry. While he busied himself getting various documents, I was given a minute or two to look about this large and bewilderingly cluttered room of shelves, filing cabinets, cupboards and three small desks. But for all that the place seemed grossly disordered, still Mr Asquith quickly found what he was looking for and seated himself opposite me behind his desk. He was the only partner present and I the only client.

"Now, Mr McGilchrist," he began. "And so we managed to find you, did we? And doubtless you're wondering what it's all about, and you probably think there's something of a mystery here? Well, so there is, and for me and my partners no less than for yourself."

"I don't quite follow," I answered, searching his face for a clue.

"No, no of course you don't. Well now, perhaps this will explain it better. It's a copy of your uncle's will. As you'll see, he was rather short on words; hence the mystery. A more succinct document—which nevertheless hints at so much more—I've yet to see!"

"I Gavin McGilchrist," (the will began) "of Temple House in Lothian, hereby revoke all Wills, Codicils or Testamentary Dispositions heretofore made by me, and I appoint my Nephew, John Hamish McGilchrist of Philadelphia in the United States of America, to be the Executor of this my Last Will and direct that all my Debts, Testamentary and Funeral Expenses shall be paid as soon as conveniently may be after my death."

"I give and bequeath unto the aforementioned John Hamish McGilchrist everything I possess, my Land and the Property standing thereon, with the following Condition: namely that he alone shall open and read the Deposition which shall accompany this Will into the hands of the Solicitors; and that furthermore he, being the Owner, shall destroy Temple House to its last stone within a Threemonth of accepting this Condition. In the event that he shall refuse this undertaking, then shall my Solicitors, Macdonald, Asquith and Lee of Edinburgh, become sole Executors of my Estate, who shall follow to the letter the Instructions simultaneously deposited with them."

The will was dated and signed in my uncle's scratchy scrawl.

I read it through a second time and looked up to find Mr Asquith's gaze fixed intently upon me. "Well," he said, "and didn't I say it was a mystery? Almost as strange as his death . . ." He saw the immediate change in my expression, the frown and the question my lips were beginning to frame, and held up his hands in apology. "I'm sorry," he said, "so very sorry—for of course you know nothing of the circumstances of his death, do you? I had better explain:

"A year ago," Asquith continued, "your uncle was one of the most hale and hearty men you could wish to meet. He was a man of independent means, as you know, and for a good many years he had been collecting data for a book. Ah! I see you're surprised. Well, you shouldn't be. Your great-grandfather wrote *Notes of Nessie: the Secrets of Loch Ness*; and your grandmother, under a pseudonym, was a fairly successful romanticist around the turn of the century. You, too, I believe, have published several romances? Indeed," and he smiled and nodded, "it appears to be in the blood, you see?

"Like your great-grandfather, however, your Uncle Gavin McGilchrist had no romantic aspirations. He was a researcher, you see, and couldn't abide a mystery to remain unsolved. And there he was at Temple House, a bachelor and time on his hands, and a marvellous family tree to explore and a great mystery to unravel."

"Family tree?" I said. "He was researching the biography of a family? But which fam—" And I paused.

Asquith smiled. "You've guessed it, of course," he said. "Yes, he was planning a book on the McGilchrists, with special reference to the curse . . ." And his smile quickly vanished.

It was as if a cold draft, coming from nowhere, fanned my cheek. "The curse? My family had . . . a curse?"

He nodded. "Oh, yes. Not the classical sort of curse, by any means, but a curse nevertheless—or at least your uncle thought so. Perhaps he wasn't really serious about it at first, but towards the end—"

"I think I know what you mean," I said. "I remember now: the deaths by stroke, by drowning, by thrombosis. My mother mentioned them on her own deathbed. A curse on the McGilchrists, she said, on the old house."

Again Asquith nodded, and finally he continued. "Well, your uncle had been collecting material for many years, I suspect since the death of your father; from local archives, historical annals, various chronicles, church records, military museums, and so on. He had even enlisted our aid, on occasion, in finding this or that old document. Our firm was founded one hundred and sixty years ago, you see, and we've had many McGilchrists as clients.

"As I've said, up to a time roughly a year ago, he was as hale and hearty a man as you could wish to meet. Then he travelled abroad; Hungary, Romania, all the old countries of antique myth and legend. He brought back many books with him, and on his return he was a changed man. He had become, in a matter of weeks, the merest shadow of his former self. Finally, nine weeks ago on March 22nd, he left his will in our hands, an additional set of instructions for us to follow in the event you couldn't be found, and the sealed envelope which he mentions in his will. I shall give that to you in a moment. Two days later, when his gillie returned to Temple House from a short holiday—"

"He found my uncle dead," I finished it for him. "I see . . . And the strange circumstances?"

"For a man of his years to die of a heart attack . . ." Asquith shook his head. "He wasn't old. What?—an outdoors man, like him? And what of the shotgun, with both barrels discharged, and the spent cartridges lying at his feet just outside the porch? What had he fired at, eh, in the dead of night? And the look on his face—monstrous!"

"You saw him?"

"Oh, yes. That was part of our instructions; I was to see him. And not just myself but Mr Lee also. And the doctor, of course, who declared it could only have been a heart attack. But then there was the post-mortem. That was also part of your uncle's instructions . . . "

"And its findings?" I quietly asked.

"Why, that was the reason he wanted the autopsy, do you see? So that we should know he was in good health."

"No heart attack?"

"No," he shook his head, "not him. But dead, certainly. And that look on his face, Mr McGilchrist—that terrible, pleading look in his wide, wide eyes . . ."

## 3. The House

HALF AN HOUR later I left Mr Asquith in his office and saw myself out through the anteroom and into the hot, cobbled road that climbed to the great grey castle. In the interim I had opened the envelope left for me by my uncle and had given its contents a cursory scrutiny, but I intended to study them minutely at my earliest convenience.

I had also offered to let Asquith see the contents, only to have him wave my offer aside. It was a private thing, he said, for my eyes only. Then he had asked me what I intended to do now, and I had answered that I would go to Temple House and take up temporary residence there. He then produced the keys, assured me of the firm's interest in my business—its complete confidentiality and its readiness to provide assistance should I need it—and bade me good day.

I found Carl Earlman leaning on the esplanade wall and gazing out over the city. Directly below his position the castle rock fell away for hundreds of feet to a busy road that wound round and down and into the maze of streets and junctions forming the city center. He started when I took hold of his arm.

"What—? Oh, it's you, John! I was lost in thought. This fantastic view; I've already stored away a dozen sketches in my head. Great!" Then he saw my face and frowned. "Is anything wrong? You don't quite look yourself."

As we made our way down from that high place I told him of my meeting with Asquith and all that had passed between us, so that by the time we found a cab (a "taxi") and had ourselves driven to an automobile rental depot, I had managed to bring him fully up to date. Then it was simply a matter of hiring a car and driving out to Temple House . . .

We headed south-west out of Edinburgh with Carl driving our Range Rover at a leisurely pace, and within three-quarters of an hour turned right off the main road onto a narrow strip whose half-metalled surface climbed straight as an arrow toward the looming Pentlands. Bald and majestic, those grey domes rose from a scree of gorse-grown shale to cast their sooty, mid-afternoon shadows over lesser mounds, fields and streamlets alike. Over our vehicle, too, as it grew tiny in the frowning presence of the hills.

I was following a small-scale map of the area purchased from a filling station, (a "garage") for of course the district was completely strange to me. A lad of five on leaving Scotland—and protected by my mother's exaggerated fears at that, which hardly ever let me out of her sight—I had never been allowed to stray very far from Temple House.

Temple House . . . and again the name conjured strange phantoms, stirred vague memories I had thought long dead.

Now the road narrowed more yet, swinging sharply to the right before passing round a rocky spur. The ground rose up beyond the spur and formed a shallow ridge, and my map told me that the gully or reentry which guarded Temple House lay on the far side of this final rise. I knew that when we reached the crest the house would come into view, and I found myself holding my breath as the

Range Rover's wheels bit into the cinder surface of the track.

"There she is!" cried Carl as first the eaves of the place became visible, then its oak-beamed gables and greystone walls, and finally the entire frontage where it projected from behind the sheer rise of the gully's wall. And now, as we accelerated down the slight decline and turned right to follow a course running parallel to the stream, the whole house came into view where it stood half in shadow. That strange old house in the silent gully, where no birds ever flew and not even a rabbit had been seen to sport in the long wild grass.

"Hey!" Carl cried, his voice full of enthusiasm. "And your uncle wanted this place pulled down? What in hell for? It's beautiful—and it must be worth a fortune!"

"I shouldn't think so," I answered. "It might look all right from here, but wait till you get inside. Its foundations were waterlogged twenty years ago. There were always six inches of water in the cellar, and the panels of the lower rooms were mouldy even then. God only knows what it must be like now!"

"Does it look the way you remember it?" he asked.

"Not quite," I frowned. "Seen through the eyes of an adult, there are differences."

For one thing, the pool was different. The level of the water was lower, so that the wide, grass-grown wall of the dam seemed somehow taller. In fact, I had completely forgotten about the dam, without which the pool could not exist, or at best would be the merest pebble-bottomed pool and not the small lake which it now was. For the first time it dawned on me that the pool was artificial, not natural as I had always thought of it, and that Temple House had been built on top of the dam's curving mound where it extended to the steep shale cliff of the defile itself.

With a skidding of loose chippings, Carl took the Range Rover up the ramp that formed the drive to the house, and a moment later we drew to a halt before the high-arched porch. We dismounted and entered, and now Carl went clattering away—almost irreverently, I thought—into cool rooms, dark stairwells and huge cupboards, his voice echoing back to me where I stood with mixed emotions, savouring the atmosphere of the old place, just inside the doorway to the house proper.

"But this is *it*!" he cried from somewhere. "This is for me! My studio, and no question. Come and look, John—look at the windows letting in all this good light. You're right about the damp, I can feel it—but that aside it's perfect."

I found him in what had once been the main living-room, standing in golden clouds of dust he had stirred up, motes illumined by the sun's rays where they struck into the room through huge, leaded windows, "You'll need to give the place a good dusting and sweeping out," I told him.

"Oh, sure," he answered, "but there's a lot wants doing before that. Do you know where the master switch is?"

"Umm? Switch?"

"For the electric light," he frowned impatiently at me. "And surely there's an icebox in the kitchen?"

"A refrigerator?" I answered. "Oh, yes, I'm sure there is . . . Look, you run around and explore the place and do whatever makes you happy. Me, I'm just going to potter about and try to waken a few old dreams."

During the next hour or two—while I quite literally "pottered about" and familiarized myself once again with this old house so full of memories—Carl fixed himself up with a bed in his "studio," found the main switch and got the electricity flowing, examined the refrigerator and satisfied himself that it was in working order, then searched me out where I sat in the mahogany-panelled study upstairs to tell me that he was driving into Penicuik to stock up with food.

From my window I watched him go, until the cloud of dust thrown up by his wheel disappeared over the rise to the south, then stirred myself into positive action. There were things to be done—things I must do for myself, others for my uncle—and the sooner I started the better. Not that there was any lack of time; I had three whole months to carry out Gavin McGilchrist's instructions, or to fail to carry them out. And yet somehow . . . yes, there was this feeling of *urgency* in me.

And so I switched on the light against gathering shadows, took out the envelope left for me by my uncle—that envelope whose contents, a letter and a notebook, were for my eyes only—sat down at the great desk used by so many generations of McGilchrists, and began to read. . . .

## 4. The Curse

"MY DEAR, DEAR NEPHEW," the letter in my uncle's uneven script began, "—so much I would like to say to you, and so little time in which to say it. And all these years grown in between since last I saw you.

"When first you left Scotland with your mother I would have written to you through her, but she forbade it. In early 1970 I learned of her death, so that even my condolences would have been six months too late; well, you have them now. She was a wonderful woman, and of course she was quite right to take you away out of it all. If I'm right in what I now suspect, her woman's intuition will yet prove to have been nearer the mark than anyone ever could have guessed, and—

"But there I go, miles off the point and rambling as usual; and such a lot to say. Except—I'm damned if I know where to begin! I suppose the plain fact of the matter is quite simply stated—namely, that for you to be reading this is for me to be gone forever from the world of men. But gone . . . *where?* And how to explain?

The fact is, I cannot tell it all, not and make it believable. Not the way I have come to believe it. Instead you will have to be satisfied with the barest essentials. The rest you can discover for yourself. There are books in the old library that tell it all—if a man has the patience to look. And if he's capable of putting aside all matters of common knowledge, all laws of science and logic; capable of unlearning all that life has ever taught him of truth and beauty.

"Four hundred years ago we weren't such a race of damned sceptics. They were burning witches in these parts then, and if they had suspected of anyone what I have come to suspect of Temple House and its grounds. . . .

"Your mother may not have mentioned the curse—the curse of the McGilchrists. Oh, she believed in it, certainly, but it's possible she thought that to tell of it might be to invoke the thing. That is to say, by telling you she might bring the curse down on your head. Perhaps she was right, for unless my death is seen to be *entirely natural*, then certainly I shall have brought it down upon myself.

"And what of you, Nephew?

"You have three months. Longer than that I do not deem safe, and nothing is guaranteed. Even three months might be dangerously overlong, but I pray not. Of course you are at liberty, if you so desire, simply to get the thing over and done with. In my study, in the bottom right-hand drawer of my desk, you will find sufficient fuses and explosive materials to bring down the wall of the defile onto the house, and the house itself down into the pool, which should satisfactorily put an end to the thing.

"But . . . you had an inquiring mind as a child. If you look where I have looked and read what I have read, then you shall learn what I've learned and know that it is neither advanced senility nor madness but my own intelligence which leads me to the one, inescapable conclusion—that this House of the Temple, this Temple House of the McGilchrists, is accursed. Most terribly . . .

"I could flee the place, of course, but I doubt if that would save me. And if it did save me, still it would leave the final questions unanswered and the riddle unsolved. Also, I loved my brother, your father, and I saw his face when he was dead. If for nothing else, that look on your father's dead face has been sufficient reason for me to pursue the thing thus far. I thought to seek it out, to know it, destroy it—but now. . . .

"I have never been much of a religious man, Nephew, and so it comes doubly hard for me to say what I now say: that while your father is dead these twenty years and more, I now find myself wondering if he is truly at rest! And what will be the look on *my* face when the thing is over, one way or the other? Ask about that, Nephew, ask how *I* looked when they found me.

"Finally, as to your course of action from this point onward: do what you will, but in the last event be sure you bring about the utter dissolution of the seat of ancient evil known as Temple House. There are things hidden in the great deserts and mountains of the world, and others sunken under the deepest oceans, which never were meant to exist in any sane or ordered universe. Yes, and certain revenants of immemorial horror have even come among men. One such has anchored itself here in the Pentlands, and in a little while I may meet it face to face. If all goes well . . . But then you should not be reading this.

"And so the rest is up to you, John Hamish; and if indeed man has an immortal soul, I now place mine in your hands. Do what must be done and if you are a believer, then say a prayer for me . . .

Yr. Loving Uncle—
Gavin McGilchrist."

I read the letter through a second time, then a third, and the shadows lengthened beyond the reach of the study's electric lights. Finally, I turned to the notebook—a slim, ruled, board-covered book whose like might be purchased at any stationery store—and opened it to page upon page of scrawled and at first glance seemingly unconnected jottings, references, abbreviated notes and memoranda concerning . . . Concerning what? Black magic? Witchcraft? The "supernatural"? But what else would you call a curse if not supernatural?

Well, my uncle had mentioned a puzzle, a mystery, the McGilchrist curse, the thing he had tracked down almost to the finish. And here were all the pointers, the clues, the keys to his years of research. I stared at the great bookcases lining the walls, the leather spines of their contents dully agleam in the glow of the lights. Asquith had told me that my uncle brought many old books back with him from his wanderings abroad.

I stood up and felt momentarily dizzy, and was obliged to lean on the desk until the feeling passed. The mustiness of the deserted house, I supposed, the closeness of the room and the odour of old books. Books . . . yes, and I moved shakily across to the nearest bookcase and ran my fingers over titles rubbed and faded with age and wear. There were works here which seemed to stir faint memories—perhaps I had been allowed to play with these books as a child?—but others were almost tangibly strange to the place, whose titles alone would make aliens of them without ever a page being turned. These must be those volumes my uncle had discovered abroad. I frowned as I tried to make something of their less than commonplace names.

Here were such works as the German *Unter-Zee Kulten* and Feery's *Notes on the Necronomicon* in a French edition; and here Gaston le Fe's *Dwellers in the Depths* and a black-bound, iron-hasped copy of the *Cthäat Aquadingen*, its harsh title suggestive of both German and Latin roots. Here was Gantley's *Hydrophinnae*, and here the *Liber Miraculorem* of the Monk and Chaplain Herbert of Clairvaux. Gothic letters proclaimed of one volume that it was Prinn's *De Vermis Mysteriis*, while another purported to be the suppressed and hideously disquieting *Unaussprechlichen Kulten* of Von Junzt—titles which seemed to leap at me as my eyes moved from shelf to shelf in a sort of disbelieving stupefaction.

What possible connection could there be between these ancient, foreign volumes of elder madness and delirium and the solid, down-to-earth McGilchrist line of gentlemen, officers and scholars? There seemed only one way to find out. Choosing a book at random. I found it to be the *Cthäat Aquadingen* and returned with it to the desk. The light outside was failing now and the shadows of the hills were long and sooty. In less than an hour it would be dusk, and half an hour after that dark.

Then there would only be Carl and I and the night. And the old house. As if in answer to unspoken thoughts, settling timbers groaned somewhere overhead. Through the window, down below in the sharp shadows of the house, the dull green glint of water caught my eye.

Carl and I, the night and the old house—

And the deep, dark pool.

## 5. The Music

IT WAS ALMOST completely dark by the time Carl returned, but in between I had at least been able to discover my uncle's system of reference. It was quite elementary, really. In his notebook, references such as "CA 121/7" simply indicated an item of interest in the *Cthäat Aquadingen*, page 121, the seventh paragraph. And in the work itself he had carefully underscored all such paragraphs or items of interest. At least a dozen such references concerning the *Cthäat Aquadingen* occurred in his notebook, and as night had drawn on I had examined each in turn.

Most of them were meaningless to me and several were in a tongue or glyph completely beyond my comprehension, but others were in a form of old English which I could transcribe with comparative ease. One such, which seemed a chant of sorts, had a brief annotation scrawled in the margin in my uncle's hand. The passage I refer to, as nearly as I can remember, went like this:

"Rise, O Nameless Ones;
It is Thy Season
When Thine Own of Thy Choosing,
Through Thy Spells & Thy Magic,
Through Dreams & Enchantry,
May know Thou art come.
They rush to Thy Pleasure,
For the Love of Thy Masters—
—the Spawn of Cthulhu."

And the accompanying annotation queried: "Would they have used such as this to call the Thing forth, I wonder, or was it simply a blood lure? What causes it to come forth now? When will it next come?"

It was while I was comparing references and text in this fashion that I began to get a glimmer as to just what the book was, and on further considering its title I saw that I had probably guessed correctly. "Cthäat" frankly baffled me, unless it had some connection with the language or being of the pre-Nacaal Kthatans; but "Aquadingen" was far less alien in its sound and formation. It meant (I believed), "water-things," or "things of the waters"; and the—*Cthäat Aquadingen* was quite simply a compendium of myths and legends concerning water sprites, nymphs, demons, naiads and other supernatural creatures of lakes and oceans, and the spells or conjurations by which they might be evoked or called out of their watery haunts.

I had just arrived at this conclusion when Carl returned, the lights of his vehicle cutting a bright swath over the dark surface of the pool as he parked in front of the porch. Laden down, he entered the house and I went down to the spacious if somewhat old fashioned kitchen to find him filling shelves and cupboards and stocking the refrigerator with perishables. This done, bright and breezy in his enthusiasm, he inquired about the radio.

"Radio?" I answered. "I thought your prime concern was for peace and quiet? Why, you've made enough noise for ten since we got here!"

"No, no," he said. "It's not *my* noise I'm concerned about but yours. Or rather, the radio's. I mean, you've obviously found one for I heard the music."

Carl was big, blond and blue-eyed; a Viking if ever I saw one, and quite capable of displaying a Viking's temper. He had been laughing when he asked me where the radio was, but now he was frowning. "Are you playing games with me, John?"

"No, of course I'm not," I answered him. "Now what's all this about? What music have you been hearing?"

His face suddenly brightened and he snapped his fingers. "There's a radio in the Range Rover," he said. "There has to be. It must have gotten switched on, very low, and I've been getting Bucharest or something." He made as if to go back outside.

"Bucharest?" I repeated him.

"Hmm?" he paused in the kitchen doorway. "Oh, yes—gypsyish stuff. Tambourines and chanting—and fiddles. Dancing round campfires. Look, I'd better switch it off or the battery will run down."

"I didn't see a radio," I told him, following him out through the porch and onto the drive.

He leaned inside the front of the vehicle, switched on the interior light and searched methodically. Finally he put the light out with an emphatic click. He turned to me and his jaw had a stubborn set to it. I looked back at him and raised my eyebrows. "No radio?"

He shook his head. "But I heard the music."

"Lovers," I said.

"Eh?"

"Lovers, out walking. A transistor radio. Perhaps they were sitting in the grass. After all, it is a beautiful summer night."

Again he shook his head. "No, it was right there in the air. Sweet and clear. I heard it as I approached the house. It came from the house, I thought. And you heard nothing?"

"Nothing," I answered, shaking my head.

"Well then—damn it to hell!" he suddenly grinned. "I've started hearing things, that's all! Skip it . . . Come on, let's have supper . . ."

Carl stuck to his "studio" bedroom but I slept upstairs in a room adjacent to the study. Even with the windows thrown wide open, the night was very warm and the atmosphere sticky, so that sleep did not come easily. Carl must have found a similar problem for on two or three occasions I awakened from a restless half-sleep to sounds of his moving about downstairs. In the morning over breakfast both of us were a little bleary-eyed, but then he led me through into his room to display the reason for his nocturnal activity.

There on the makeshift easel, on one of a dozen old canvasses he had brought with him, Carl had started work on a picture . . . of sorts.

For the present he had done little more than lightly brush in the background, which was clearly the valley of the house, but the house itself was missing from the picture and I could see that the artist did not intend to include it. The pool was there, however, with its encircling ring of quartz columns complete and finished with lintels of a like material. The columns and lintels glowed luminously.

In between and around the columns vague figures writhed, at present insubstantial as smoke, and in the foreground the flames of a small fire were driven on a wind that blew from across the pool. Taken as a whole and for all its sketchiness, the scene gave a vivid impression of savagery and pagan excitement—strange indeed considering that as yet there seemed to be so little in it to excite any sort of emotion whatever.

"Well," said Carl, his voice a trifle edgy, "what do you think?"

"I'm no artist, Carl," I answered, which I suppose in the circumstances was saying too much.

"You don't like it?" he sounded disappointed.

"I didn't say that," I countered. "Will it be a night scene?"

He nodded.

"And the dancers there, those wraiths . . . I suppose they *are* dancers?"

"Yes," he answered, "and musicians. Tambourines, fiddles . . ."

"Ah!" I nodded. "Last night's music."

He looked at me curiously. "Probably . . . Anyway, I'm happy with it. At least I've started to work. What about you?"

"You do your thing," I told him, "and I'll do mine."

"But what are you going to do?"

I shrugged. "Before I do anything I'm going to soak up a lot of atmosphere. But I don't intend staying here very long. A month or so, and then—"

"And then you'll burn this beautiful old place to the ground." He had difficulty keeping the sour note out of his voice.

"It's what my uncle wanted," I said. "I'm not here to write a story. A story may come of it eventually, even a book, but that can wait. Anyway, I won't burn the house." I made a mushroom cloud with my hands. "She goes—up!"

Carl snorted. "You McGilchrists," he said. "You're all nuts!" But there was no malice in his statement.

There was a little in mine, however, when I answered: "Maybe—but I don't hear music where there isn't any!"

But that was before I knew everything . . .

## 6. The Familiar

DURING THE course of the next week Scotland began to feel the first effects of what is now being termed "a scourge on the British Isles," the beginning of an intense, ferocious and prolonged period of drought. Sheltered by the Pentlands, a veritable suntrap for a full eight to ten hours a day, Temple House was no exception. Carl and I took to lounging around in shorts and T-shirts, and with his blond hair and fair skin he was particularly vulnerable. If we had been swimmers, then certainly we should have used the pool; as it was we had to content ourselves by sitting at its edge with our feet in the cool mountain water.

By the end of that first week, however, the drought's effect upon the small stream which fed the pool could clearly be seen. Where before the water had rushed down from the heights of the defile, now it seeped, and the natural overflow from the sides of the dam was so reduced that the old course of the stream was now completely dry. As for our own needs: the large water tanks in the attic of the house were full and their source of supply seemed independent, possibly some reservoir higher in the hills.

In the cool of the late afternoon, when the house stood in its own and the Pentlands' shade, then we worked; Carl at his drawing or painting, I with my uncle's notebook and veritable library of esoteric books. We also did a little walking in the hills, but in the heat of this incredible summer that was far too exhausting and only served to accentuate a peculiar mood of depression which had taken both of us in its grip. We blamed the weather, of course, when at any other time we would have considered so much sunshine and fresh air a positive blessing.

By the middle of the second week I was beginning to make real sense of my uncle's fragmentary record of his research. That is to say, his trail was becoming easier to follow as I grew used to his system and started to detect a pattern.

There were in fact two trails, both historic, one dealing with the McGilchrist line itself, the other more concerned with the family seat, with the House of the Temple. Because I seemed close to a definite discovery, I worked harder and became more absorbed with the work. And as if my own industry was contagious, Carl too began to put in longer hours at his easel or drawing board.

It was a Wednesday evening, I remember, the shadows lengthening and the atmosphere heavy when I began to see just how my uncle's mind had been working. He had apparently decided that if there really was a curse on the McGilchrists, then that it had come about during the construction of Temple House. To discover why this was so, he had delved back into the years prior to its construction in this cleft in the hills, and his findings had been strange indeed.

It had seemed to start in England in 1594 with the advent of foreign refugees. These had been the members of a monkish order originating in the mountains of Romania, whose ranks had nevertheless been filled with many diverse creeds, colours and races. There were Chinamen amongst them, Hungarians, Arabs and Africans, but their leader had been a Romanian priest named Chorazos. As to why they had been hounded out of their own countries, that remained a mystery.

Chorazos and certain of his followers became regular visitors at the court of Queen Elizabeth I—who had ever held an interest in astrology, alchemy and all similar magics and mysteries—and with her help they founded a temple "somewhere sear Finchley." Soon, however, couriers from foreign parts began to bring in accounts of the previous doings of this darkling sect, and so the Queen took advice.

Of all persons, she consulted with Dr John Dee, that more than dubious character whose own dabbling with the occult had brought him so close to disaster in 1555 during the reign of Queen Mary. Dee, at first enamoured of Chorazos and his followers, now turned against them. They were pagans, he said; their women were whores and their ceremonies orgiastic. They had brought with them a "familiar," which would have "needs" of its own, and eventually the public would rise up against them and the "outrage" they must soon bring about in the country. The Queen should therefore sever all connections with the sect—and immediately!

Acting under Dee's guidance, she at once issued orders for the arrest, detention and investigation of Chorazos and his members . . . but too late, for they had already flown. Their "temple" in Finchley—a "columned pavilion about a central lake"—was destroyed and the pool filled in. That was in late 1595.

In 1596 they turned up in Scotland, this time under the guise of travelling faith-healers and herbalists working out of Edinburgh. As a reward for their work among the poorer folk in the district, they were given a land grant and took up an austere residence in the Pentlands. There, following a pattern established abroad and carried on in England, Chorazos and his followers built their temple; except that this time they had to dam a stream in order to create a pool. The work took them several years; their ground was private property; they kept for the main well out of the limelight, and all was well . . . for a while.

Then came rumours of orgiastic rites in the hills, of children wandering away from home under the influence of strange, hypnotic music, of a monstrous being conjured up from hell to preside over ceremonial murder and receive its grisly tribute, and at last the truth was out. However covertly Chorazos had organized his perversions, there now existed the gravest suspicions as to what he and the others of his sect were about. And this in the Scotland of James IV, who five years earlier had charged an Edinburgh jury with "an

Assize of Error" when they dismissed an action for witchcraft against one of the "notorious" North Berwick Witches.

In this present matter, however, any decision of the authorities was preempted by persons unknown—possibly the inhabitants of nearby Penicuik, from which town several children had disappeared—and Chorazos' order had been wiped out *en masse* one night and the temple reduced to ruins and shattered quartz stumps.

Quite obviously, the site of the temple had been here, and the place had been remembered by locals down the centuries, so that when the McGilchrist house was built in the mid-18th Century it automatically acquired the name of Temple House. The name had been retained . . . but what else had lingered over from those earlier times, and what *exactly* was the nature of the McGilchrist Curse?

I yawned and stretched. It was after eight and the sinking sun had turned the crests of the hills to bronze. A movement, seen in the corner of my eye through the window, attracted my attention. Carl was making his way to the rim of the pool. He paused with his hands on his hips to stand between two of the broken columns, staring out over the silent water. Then he laid back his head and breathed deeply. There was a tired but self-satisfied air about him that set me wondering.

I threw the window wide and leaned out, calling down through air which was still warm and cloying: "Hey, Carl—you look like the cat who got the cream!"

He turned and waved. "Maybe I am. It's that painting of mine. I think I've got it beat. Not finished yet . . . but coming along."

"Is it good?" I asked.

He shrugged, but it was a shrug of affirmation, not indifference. "Are you busy? Come down and see for yourself. I only came out to clear my head, so that I can view it in fresh perspective. Yours will be a second opinion."

I went downstairs to find him back in his studio. Since the light was poor now, he switched on all of the electric lights and led the way to his easel. I had last looked at the painting some three or four days previously, at a time when it had still been very insubstantial. Now—

Nothing insubstantial about it now. The grass was green, long and wild, rising to nighted hills of grey and purple, silvered a little by a gibbous moon. The temple was almost luminous, its columns shining with an eerie light. Gone the wraithlike dancers; they capered in cassocks now, solid, wild and weird with leering faces. I started as I stared at those faces—yellow, black and white faces, a half-dozen different races—but I started worse at the sight of the *thing* rising over the pool within the circle of glowing columns. Still vague, that horror—that leprous grey, tentacled, mushroom-domed monstrosity—and as yet mainly amorphous; but formed enough to show that it was nothing of this good, sane Earth.

"What the hell is it?" I half-gasped, half-whispered.

"Hmm?" Carl turned to me and smiled with pleased surprise at the look of shock on my blanched face. "I'm damned if I know—but I think it's pretty good! It will be when it's finished. I'm going to call it *The Familiar* . . ."

## 7. The Face

FOR A LONG WHILE I simply stood there taking in the contents of that hideous canvas and feeling the heat of the near-tropical night beating in through the open windows. It was all there: the foreign monks making their weird music, the temple glowing in the darkness, the dam, the pool and the hills as I had always known them, the *Thing* rising up in bloated loathsomeness from dark water, and a sense of realness I had never before and probably never again will see in any artist's work.

My first impulse when the shock wore off a little was to turn on Carl in anger. This was too monstrous a joke. But no, his face bore only a look of astonishment now—astonishment at my reaction, which must be quite obvious to him. "Christ!" he said, "is it that good?"

"That—*thing*—has nothing to do with Christ!" I finally managed to force the words out of a dry throat. And again I felt myself on the verge of demanding an explanation. Had he been reading my uncle's notes? Had he been secretly following my own line of research? But how could he, secretly or otherwise? The idea was preposterous.

"You really do *feel* it, don't you?" he said, excitedly taking my arm. "I can see it in your face."

"I . . . I feel it, yes," I answered. "It's a very . . . powerful piece of work." Then, to fill the gap, I added: "Where did you dream it up?"

"Right first time," he answered. "A dream—I think. Something left over from a nightmare. I haven't been sleeping too well. The heat, I guess."

"You're right," I agreed. "It's too damned hot. Will you be doing any more tonight?"

He shook his head, his eyes still on the painting. "Not in this light. I don't want to foul it up. No, I'm for bed. Besides, I have a headache."

"What?" I said, glad now that I had made no wild accusation. "You?—a strapping great Viking like you, with a headache?"

"Viking?" he frowned. "You've called me that before. My looks must be deceptive. No, my ancestors came out of Hungary—a place called Stregoicavar. And I can tell you they burned more witches there than you ever did in Scotland!"

There was little sleep for me that night, though toward morning I did finally drop off, slumped across the great desk, drowsing fitfully in the soft glow of my desk light. Prior to that, however, in the silence of the night—driven on by a feeling of impending . . . something—I had delved deeper into the old books and documents amassed by my uncle, slowly but surely fitting together that great jigsaw whose pieces he had spent so many years collecting.

The work was more difficult now, his notes less coherent, his writing barely legible; but at least the material was or should be more familiar to me. Namely, I was studying the long line of McGilchrists gone before me, whose seat had been Temple House since its construction two hundred and forty years ago. And as I worked so my eyes would return again and again, almost involuntarily, to the dark pool with its ring of broken columns. Those stumps were white in the silver moonlight—as white as the columns in Carl's picture—and so my thoughts returned to Carl.

By now he must be well asleep, but this new mystery filled my mind through the small hours. Carl Earlman . . . It certainly sounded Hungarian, German at any rate, and I wondered what the old family name had been. Ehrlichman, perhaps? Arlmann? And not Carl but Karl.

And his family hailed from Stregoicavar. That was a name I remembered from a glance into Von Junzt's *Unspeakable Cults*, I was sure. Stregoicavar: it had stayed in my mind because of its meaning, which is "witch-town." Certain of Chorazos' order of pagan priests had been Hungarian. Was it possible that some dim ancestral memory lingered over in Carl's mind, and that the pool with its quartz stumps had awakened that in his blood which harkened back to older times? And what of the gypsy music he had sworn to hearing on our first night in this old house? Young and strong he was, certainly, but beneath an often brash exterior he had all the sensitivity of the artist born.

According to my uncle's research my own great-grandfather, Robert Allan McGilchrist, had been just such a man. Sensitive, a dreamer, prone to hearing things in the dead of night which no one else could hear. Indeed, his wife had left him for his peculiar ways. She had taken her two sons with her; and so for many years the old man had lived here alone, writing and studying. He had been well known for his paper on the Lambton Worm legend of Northumberland: of a great worm or dragon that lived in a well and emerged at night to devour "bairns and beasties and foolhardy wanderers in the dark." He had also published a pamphlet on the naiads of the lochs of Inverness; and his limited edition book, *Notes on Nessie—the Secrets of Loch Ness* had caused a minor sensation when first it saw print.

It was Robert Allan McGilchrist, too, who restored the old floodgate in the dam, so that the water level in the pool could be controlled; but that had been his last work. A shepherd had found him one morning slumped across the gate, one hand still grasping the wheel which controlled its elevation, his upper body floating face-down in the water. He must have slipped and fallen, and his heart had given out. But the look on his face had been a fearful thing; and since the embalmers had been unable to do anything with him, they had buried him immediately.

And as I studied this or that old record or consulted this or that musty book, so my eyes would return to the dam, the pool with its fanged columns, the old floodgate—rusted now and fixed firmly in place—and the growing sensation of an onrushing doom gnawed inside me until it became a knot of fear in my chest. If only the heat would let up, just for one day, and if only I could finish my research and solve the riddle once and for all.

It was then, as the first flush of dawn showed above the eastern hills, that I determined what I must do. The fact of the matter was that Temple House frightened me, as I suspected it had frightened many people before me. Well, I had neither the stamina nor the dedication of my uncle. He had resolved to track the thing down to the end, and something—sheer hard work, the "curse," failing health, *something*—had killed him.

But his legacy to me had been a choice: continue his work or put an end to the puzzle for all time and blow Temple House to hell. So be it, that was what I would do. A day or two more—only a day or two, to let Carl finish his damnable painting—and then I would do what Gavin McGilchrist had ordered done. And with that resolution uppermost in my mind, relieved that at last I had made the decision, so I fell asleep where I sprawled at the desk.

The sound of splashing aroused me; that and my name called from below. The sun was just up and I felt dreadful, as if suffering from a hangover. For a long time I simply lay sprawled out. Then I stood up and eased my cramped limbs, and finally I turned to the open window. There was Carl, dressed only in his shorts, stretched out flat on a wide, thick plank, paddling out toward the middle of the pool!

"Carl!" I called down, my voice harsh with my own instinctive fear of the water. "Man, that's dangerous—you can't swim!"

He turned his head, craned his neck and grinned up at me. "Safe as houses," he called, "so long as I hang on to the plank. And it's cool, John, so wonderfully cool. This feels like the first time I've been cool in weeks!"

By now he had reached roughly the pool's center and there he stopped paddling and simply let his hands trail in green depths. The level of the water had gone down appreciably during the night and the streamlet which fed the pool was now quite dry. The plentiful weed of the pool, becoming concentrated as the water evaporated, seemed thicker than ever I remembered it. So void of life, that water, with never a fish or a frog to cause a ripple on the morass-green of its surface.

And suddenly that tight knot of fear was back in my chest, making my voice a croak as I tried to call out: "Carl, get out of there!"

"What?" he faintly called back, but he didn't turn his head. He was staring down into the water, staring intently at something he saw there. His hand brushed aside weed—

"Carl!" I found my voice. "For God's sake get out of it!"

He started then, his head and limbs jerking as if scalded, setting the plank to rocking so that he half slid off it. Then—a scrambling back to safety and a frantic splashing and paddling; and galvanized into activity I sprang from the window and raced breakneck downstairs. And Carl laughing shakily as I stumbled knee-deep in hated water to drag him physically from the plank, both of us trembling despite the burning rays of the new-risen sun and the furnace heat of the air.

"What happened?" I finally asked.

"I thought I saw something," he answered. "In the pool. A reflection, that's all, but it startled me."

"What did you see?" I demanded, my back damp with cold sweat.

"Why, what would I see?" he answered, but his voice trembled for all that he tried to grin. "A face, of course—my own face framed by the weeds. But it didn't look like me, that's all . . ."

## 8. The Dweller

Looking back now in the light of what I already knew—certainly of what I should have guessed at that time—it must seem that I was guilty of an almost suicidal negligence in spending the rest of that day upstairs on my bed, tossing in nightmares brought on by the nervous exhaustion which beset me immediately after the incident at the pool. On the other hand, I had had no sleep the night before and Carl's adventure had given me a terrific jolt; and so my failure to recognize the danger—how close it had drawn—may perhaps be forgiven.

In any event, I forced myself to wakefulness in the early evening, went downstairs and had coffee and a frugal meal of biscuits, and briefly visited Carl in his studio. He was busy—frantically busy, dripping with sweat and brushing away at his canvas—working on his loathsome painting, which he did not want me to see. That suited me perfectly for I had already seen more than enough of the thing. I did take time enough to tell him, though, that he should finish his work in the next two days; for on Friday or at the very latest Saturday morning I intended to blow the place sky high.

Then I went back upstairs, washed and shaved, and as the light began to fail so I returned to my uncle's notebook. There were only three or four pages left unread, the first dated only days before his demise, but they were such a hodge-podge of scrambled and near-illegible miscellanea that I had the greatest difficulty making anything of them. Only that feeling of a burgeoning terror drove me on, though by now I had almost completely lost faith in making anything whatever of the puzzle.

As for my uncle's notes: a basically orderly nature had kept me from leafing at random through his book, or perhaps I should have understood earlier. As it is, the notebook is lost forever, but as best I can I shall copy down what I remember of those last few pages. After that—and after I relate the remaining facts of the occurrences of that fateful hideous night—the reader must rely upon his own judgement. The notes then, or what little I remember of them:

"Levi's or Mirandola's invocation: '*Dasmass Jeschet Boene Doess Efar Duvema Enit Marous.*' If I could get the pronounciation right, perhaps . . . But what will the Thing be? And will it succumb to a double-barreled blast? That remains to be seen. But if what I suspect is firmly founded . . . Is It a tickthing, such as Von Junzt states inhabits the globular mantle of Yogg-Sothoth? (*Unaussprechlichen Kulten*, 78/16)—fearful hints—monstrous pantheon . . . And this merely a parasite to one of *Them!*

"The Cult of Cthulhu . . . immemorial horror spanning all the ages. The *Johansen Narrative* and the *Pnakotic Manuscript*. And the Innsmouth Raid of 1928; much was made of that, and yet nothing known for sure. Deep Ones, but . . . different again from this Thing.

"Entire myth-cycle . . . So many sources. Pure myth and legend? I think not. Too deep, interconnected, even plausible. According to Carter in SR, (AH '59) p. 250–51, *They* were driven into this part of the universe (or into this time-dimension) by 'Elder Gods' as punishment for a rebellion. Hastur the Unspeakable prisoned in Lake of Hali (again the lake or pool motif) in Carcosa; Great Cthulhu in R'lyeh, where he slumbers still in his death-sleep; Ithaqua sealed away behind icy Arctic barriers, and so on. But Yogg-Sothoth was sent *outside*, into a parallel place, conterminous with all space and time. Since YS is everywhere and when, if a man knew the gate he could call Him out . . .

"Did Chorazos and his acolytes, for some dark reason of their own, attempt thus to call Him out? And did they get this dweller in Him instead? And I believe I understand the reason for the pool. Grandfather knew. His interest in Nessie, the Lambton Worm, the Kraken of olden legend, naiads, Cthulhu . . . Wendy Smith's burrowers feared water; and the sheer *weight* of the mighty Pacific helps keep C. prisoned in his place in R'lyeh—thank God! Water subdues these things . . .

"But if water confines It, why does It *return* to the water? And how may It leave the pool if not deliberately called out? No McGilchrist ever called It out, I'm sure, not willingly; though some may have suspected that something was there. No swimmers in the family—not a one—and I think I know why. It is an instinctive, an ancestral fear of the pool! No, of the unknown *Thing* which lurks beneath the pool's surface . . ."

The thing which lurks beneath the pool's surface . . .

Clammy with the heat, and with a debilitating terror springing from these words on the written page—these scribbled thought-fragments which, I was now sure, were anything but demented ravings—I sat at the old desk and read on. And as the house grew dark and quiet, as on the previous night, again I found my eyes drawn to gaze down through the open window to the surface of the still pool.

*Except that the surface was no longer still!*

Ripples were spreading in concentric rings from the pool's dark centre, tiny mobile wavelets caused by—by what? Some disturbance beneath the surface? The water level was well down now and tendrils of mist drifted from the pool to lie soft, luminous and undulating in the moonlight, curling like the tentacles of some great plastic beast over the dam, across the drive to the foot of the house.

A sort of paralysis settled over me then, a dreadful lassitude, a mental and physical malaise brought on by excessive morbid study, culminating in this latest phenomenon of the old house and the aura of evil which now seemed to saturate its very stones. I should have done something—something to break the spell, anything rather than sit there and merely wait for what was happening to happen—and yet I was incapable of positive action.

Slowly I returned my eyes to the written page; and there I sat shivering and sweating, my skin crawling as I read on by the light of my desk lamp. But so deep my trancelike state that it was as much as I could do to force my eyes from one word to the next. I had no volition, no will of my own with which to fight that fatalistic spell; and the physical heat of the night was that of a furnace as sweat dripped from my forehead onto the pages of the notebook.

> ". . . I have checked my findings and can't believe my previous blindness! It should have been obvious. It happens when the water level falls below a certain point. It *has* happened every time there has been extremely hot weather—when the pool has started to *dry up!* Thing needn't be called out at all! As to why it returns to the pool after taking a victim: it must return before daylight. It is a fly-the-light. A haunter of the dark. A wampyre! . . . but not blood. Nowhere can I find mention of blood sacrifices. And no punctures or mutilations. What, then are Its 'needs?' Did Dee know? Kelly knew, I'm sure, but his writings are lost . . .
>
> "Eager now to try the invocation, but I wish that first I might know the true nature of the Thing. It takes the life of Its victim—but what else?"

> "I have it!—God, I know—and I wish I did not know! But that *look* on my poor brother's face . . . Andrew, Andrew . . . I know now why you looked that way. But if I can free you, you shall be freed. If I wondered at the nature of the Thing, then I wonder no longer. The answers were all there, in the *Cthaat A.* and *Hydrophinnae*, if only I had known exactly where to look. Yibb-Tstll is one such; Bugg-Shash, too. Yes, and the pool-thing

is another . . .

"There have been a number down the centuries —the horror that dwelled in the mirror of Nitocris; the sucking, hunting thing that Count Magnus kept; the red, hairy slime used by Julian Scortz—familiars of the Great Old Ones, parasites that lived on *Them* as lice live on men. Or rather, on their life-force! This one has survived the ages, at least until now. It does not take the blood but the very essence of Its victim. *It is a soul-eater!*

"I can wait no longer. Tonight, when the sun goes down and the hills are in darkness . . . But if I succeed, and if the Thing comes for me . . . We'll see how It faces up to my shotgun!"

My eyes were half-closed by the time I had finally scanned all that was written, of which the above is only a small part; and even having read it I had not fully taken it in. Rather, I had absorbed it automatically, without reading any immediate meaning into it. But as I re-read those last few lines, so I heard something which roused me up from my lassitude and snapped me alertly awake in an instant.

It was music: the faint but unmistakable strains of a whirling pagan tune that seemed to reach out to me from a time beyond time, from a hell beyond all known hells. . . .

## 9. The Horror

SHOCKED BACK to mental alertness, still my limbs were stiff as a result of several hours crouched over the desk. Thus, as I sprang or attempted to spring to my feet, a cramp attacked both of my calves and threw me down by the window. I grabbed at the sill . . . and whatever I had been about to do was at once forgotten.

I gazed out the open window on a scene straight out of madness or nightmare. The broken columns where they now stood up from bases draped with weed seemed to glow with an inner light; and to my straining eyes it appeared that this haze of light extended uniformly upwards, so that I saw a revenant of the temple as it had once been. Through the light-haze I could also see the centre of the pool, from which the ripples spread outward with a rapidly increasing agitation.

There was a shape there now, a dark oblong illuminated both by the clean moonlight and by that supernatural glow; and even as I gazed, so the water slopping above the oblong seemed pushed aside and the slab showed its stained marble surface to the air. The music grew louder then, soaring wildly, and it seemed to me in my shocked and frightened condition that dim figures reeled and writhed around the perimeter of the pool.

Then—horror of horrors!—in one mad moment the slab tilted to reveal a black hole going down under the pool, like the entrance to some sunken tomb. There came an outpouring of miasmal gases, visible in the eerie glow, and then—

Even before the thing emerged I knew what it would be, how it would look. It was that horror on Carl's canvas, the soft-tentacled, mushroom-domed terror he had painted under the ancient, evil influence of this damned, doomed place. It was the dweller, the familiar, the tick-thing, the star-born wampyre . . . it was the curse of the McGilchrists. Except I understood now that this was not merely a curse on the McGilchrists but on the entire world. Of course it had seemed to plague the McGilchrists as a personal curse—but only because they had chosen to build Temple House here on the edge of its pool. They had been victims by virtue of their *availability*, for I was sure that the pool-thing was not naturally discriminative.

Then, with an additional thrill of horror, I saw that the thing was on the move, drifting across the surface of the pool, its flaccid tentacles reaching avidly in the direction of the house. The lights downstairs were out, which meant that Carl must be asleep . . .

*Carl!*

The thing was across the drive now, entering the porch, the house itself. I forced cramped limbs to agonized activity, lurched across the room, out onto the dark landing and stumbled blindly down the stairs. I slipped, fell, found my feet again—and my voice, too.

"Carl!" I cried, arriving at the door of his studio. "Carl, *for God's sake!*"

The thing straddled him where he lay upon his bed. It glowed with an unearthly, a rotten luminescence which outlined his pale body in a sort of foxfire. Its tentacles writhed over his naked form and his limbs were filled with fitful motion. Then the dweller's mushroom head settled over his face, which disappeared in folds of the thing's gilled mantle.

"Carl!" I screamed yet again, and as I lurched forward in numb horror so my hand found the light switch on the wall. In another moment the room was bathed in sane and wholesome electric light. The thing bulged upward from Carl—rising like some monstrous amoeba, some sentient, poisonous jellyfish from an alien ocean—and turned toward me.

I saw a face, a face I knew across twenty years of time fled, *my uncle's face!* Carved in horror, those well remembered features besought, pleaded with me, that an end be put to this horror and peace restored to this lonely valley; that the souls of countless victims be freed to pass on from this world to their rightful destinations.

The thing left Carl's suddenly still form and moved forward, flowed toward me; and as it came so the face it wore melted and changed. Other faces were there, hidden in the thing, many with McGilchrist features and many without, dozens of them that came and went ceaselessly. There were children there, too, mere babies; but the last face of all, the one I shall remember above all others—*that was the face of Carl Earlman himself!* And it, too, wore that pleading, that imploring look—the look of a soul in hell, which prays only for release.

Then the light won its unseen, unsung battle. Almost upon me, suddenly the dweller seemed to wilt. It shrank from the light, turned and flowed out of the room, through the porch, back toward the pool. Weak with reaction I watched it go, saw it move out across the now still water, saw the slab tilt down upon its descending shape and heard the music fade into silence. Then I turned to Carl . . .

I do not think I need mention the look on Carl's lifeless face, or indeed say anything more about him. Except perhaps that it is my fervent prayer that he now rests in peace with the rest of the dweller's many victims, taken down the centuries. That is my prayer, but . . .

As for the rest of it:

I dragged Carl from the house to the Range Rover, drove him to the crest of the rise, left him there and returned to the house. I took my uncle's prepared charges from his study and set them in the base of the shale cliff where the house backed onto it. Then I lit the fuses, scrambled back into the Range Rover and drove to where Carl's body lay in the cool of night. I tried not to look at his face.

In a little while the charges detonated, going off almost simultaneously, and the night was shot with fire and smoke and a rising cloud of dust. When the air cleared the whole scene was changed forever. The cliff had come down on the house, sending it crashing into the pool. The pool itself had disappeared, swallowed up in shale and debris; and it was as if the House of the Temple, the temple itself and the demon-cursed pool had never existed.

All was silence and desolation, where only the moonlight played on jagged stumps of centuried columns, projecting still from the scree-and rubble-filled depression which had been the pool. And now the moon silvered the bed of the old stream, running with water from the ruined pool—

And at last I was able to drive on.

## **10.** The Unending Nightmare

THAT SHOULD HAVE been the end of it, but such has not been the case. Perhaps I alone am to blame. The police in

Penicuik listened to my story, locked me in a cell overnight and finally conveyed me to this place, where I have been now for more than a week. In a way I supposed that the actions of the police were understandable; for my wild appearance that night—not to mention the ghastly, naked corpse in the Range Rover and the incredible story I incoherently told—could hardly be expected to solicit their faith or understanding. But I do *not* understand the position of the alienists here at Oakdeene.

Surely they, too, can hear the damnable music?—that music which grows louder hour by hour, more definite and decisive every night—the music which in olden days summoned the pool-thing to its ritual sacrifice. Or is it simply that they disagree with my theory? I have mentioned it to them time and time again and repeat it now: that there are *other* pools in the Pentlands, watery havens to which the thing might have fled from the destruction of its weedy retreat beside the now fallen seat of the McGilchrists. Oh, yes, and I firmly believe that it did so flee. And the days are long and hot and a great drought is on the land . . .

And perhaps, too, over the years, a very real curse has loomed up large and monstrous over the McGilchrists. Do souls have a flavour, I wonder, a distinctive texture of their own? Is it possible that the pool-thing has developed an appetite, a *taste* for the souls of McGilchrists? If so, then it will surely seek me out; and yet here I am detained in this institute for the insane.

Or could it be that I am now in all truth mad? Perhaps the things I have experienced and know to be true have driven me mad, and the music I hear exists only in my mind. That is what the nurses tell me and dear God, I pray that it is so! But if not—if not . . .

For there is that other thing, which I have not mentioned until now. When I carried Carl from his studio after the pool-thing left him, I saw his finished painting. Not the whole painting but merely a part of it, for when it met my eyes they saw only one thing: the finished face which Carl had painted on the dweller.

This is the nightmare which haunts me worse than any other, the question I ask myself over and over in the dead of night, when the moonlight falls upon my high, barred window and the music floods into my padded cell:

If they should bring me my breakfast one morning and find me dead—*will my face really look like that?*

# Robert Bloch

# The Yougoslaves

ROBERT BLOCH will always be identified with his 1959 novel *Psycho* and Alfred Hitchcock's subsequent movie. However, the author began his career as a young devotee of the pulp magazine *Weird Tales* and began corresponding with author H.P. Lovecraft, who advised him to try his own hand at writing. He made his professional debut in 1935, quickly establishing his unique blend of psychological terror and grim graveyard humour. Winner of the science fiction field's Hugo Award in 1959 for "The Hell-Bound Train" and recipient of both the World Fantasy Award and Bram Stoker Award for Life Achievement, Bloch's work has been extensively adapted for radio, television and movies.

He has more than two dozen books and hundreds of short stories to his credit, and recent titles include *The Night of the Ripper*, *Lori*, the sequels *Psycho II* and *Psycho House* and, in collaboration with André Norton, *The Jekyll Legacy*.

The following short story proves that the Master has still not lost his touch, as he creates an unnerving twist on an old theme without resorting to gratuitous gore. It is based on a real-life experience the author had in Paris: "Part of it is fiction," he explains, adding "—but just *which* part will be up to the reader to decide."

I DIDN'T COME TO Paris for adventure.

Long experience has taught me there are no Phantoms in the Opera, no bearded artists hobbling through Montmartre on stunted legs, no straw-hatted *boulevardiers* singing the praises of a funny little honey of a Mimi.

The Paris of story and song, if it ever existed, is no more. Times have changed, and even the term "Gay Paree" now evokes what in theatrical parlance is called a bad laugh.

A visitor learns to change habits accordingly, and my hotel choice was a case in point. On previous trips I'd stayed at the Crillon or the Ritz; now, after a lengthy absence, I put up at the George V.

Let me repeat, I wasn't seeking adventure. That first evening I left the hotel for a short stroll merely to satisfy my curiosity about the city.

I had already discovered that some aspects of Paris remain immutable; the French still don't seem to understand how to communicate by telephone, and they can't make a good cup of coffee. But I had no need to use the phone and no craving for coffee, so these matters didn't concern me.

Nor was I greatly surprised to discover that April in Paris—*Paris in the spring, tra-la-la-la*—is apt to be cold and damp. Warmly-dressed for my little outing, I directed my footsteps to the archways of the Rue de Rivoli.

At first glance Paris by night upheld its traditions. All of the tourist attractions remained in place; the steel skeleton of the Eiffel Tower, the gaping maw of the Arch of Triumph, the spurting fountains achieving their miraculous transubstantiation of water into blood with the aid of crimson light.

But there were changes in the air—quite literally—the acrid odor of traffic fumes emanating from the exhausts of snarling sports cars and growling motor bikes racing along to the counter-point of police and ambulance sirens. Gershwin's tinny taxi-horns would be lost in such din; I doubt if he'd approve, and I most certainly did not.

My disapproval extended to the clothing of local pedestrians. Young Parisian males now mimicked the youths of other cities; bare-headed, leather-jacketed, and blue-jeaned, they would look equally at home in Times Square or on Hollywood Boulevard. As for their female companions, this seemed to be the year when every girl in France decided to don atrociously-wrinkled patent leather boots which turned shapely lower limbs into the legs of elephantiasis victims. The *chic* Parisienne had vanished, and above the traffic's tumult I fancied I could detect a sound of rumbling dismay as Napoleon turned over in his tomb.

I moved along under the arches, eyeing the lighted window displays of expensive jewelry mingled with cheap gimcracks. At least the Paris of tourism hadn't altered; there would still be sex shops in the Pigalle, and somewhere in the deep darkness of the Louvre the Mona Lisa smiled enigmatically at the antics of those who came to the city searching for adventure.

Again I say this was not my intention. Nonetheless, adventure sought me.

Adventure came on the run, darting out of a dark and deserted portion of the arcade just ahead, charging straight at me on a dozen legs.

It happened quickly. One moment I was alone; then suddenly and without warning, the children came. There were six of them, surrounding me like a small army—six dark-haired, swarthy-skinned urchins in dirty, disheveled garments, screeching and jabbering at me in a foreign tongue. Some of them clutched at my clothing, others jabbed me in the ribs. Encircling me they clamored for a beggar's bounty, and as I fumbled for loose change one of them thrust a folded newspaper against my chest, another grabbed and kissed my free hand, yet another grasped my shoulder and whirled me around. Deafened by the din, dazed by their instant attack, I broke free.

In seconds, they scattered swiftly and silently, scampering into the shadows. As they disappeared I stood alone again, stunned and shaken. Then, as my hand rose instinctively to press against my inner breast pocket, I realized that my wallet had disappeared too.

My first reaction was shock. To think that I, a grown

man, had been robbed on the public street by a band of little ragamuffins, less than ten years old!

It was an outrage, and now I met it with rage of my own. The sheer audacity of their attack provoked anger, and the thought of the consequences fueled my fury. Losing the money in the wallet wasn't important; he who steals my purse steals trash.

But there was something else I cherished; something secret and irreplaceable. I carried it in a billfold compartment for a purpose; after completing my sightseeing jaunt I'd intended to seek another destination and make use of the other item my wallet contained.

Now it was gone, and hope vanished with it.

But not entirely. The sound of distant sirens in the night served as a strident reminder that I still had a chance. There was, I remembered, a police station near the Place Vendome. The inconspicuous office was not easy to locate on the darkened street beyond an open courtyard, but I managed.

Once inside, I anticipated a conversation with an *Inspecteur*, a return to the scene of the affair in the company of sympathetic *gendarmes* who were knowledgeable concerning such offenses and alert in ferreting out the hiding place of my assailants.

The young lady seated behind the window in the dingy outer office listened to my story without comment or a change of expression. Inserting forms and carbons in her typewriter, she took down a few vital statistics—my name, date of birth, place of origin, hotel address, and a short inventory of the stolen wallet's contents.

For reasons of my own I neglected to mention the one item that really mattered to me. I could be excused for omitting it in my excited state, and hoped to avoid the necessity of doing so unless the *Inspecteur* questioned me more closely.

But there was no interview with an *Inspecteur*, and no uniformed officer appeared. Instead I was merely handed a carbon copy of the *Recepisse de Declaration*; if anything could be learned about the fate of my wallet I would be notified at my hotel.

Scarcely ten minutes after entering the station I found myself back on the street with nothing to show for my trouble but a buff-colored copy of the report. Down at the very bottom, on a line identified in print as *Mode Operatoire—Precisions Complementaires*, was a typed sentence reading "*Vol commis dans la Rue par de jeunes enfants yougoslaves*."

"Yougoslaves?"

Back at the hotel I addressed the question to an elderly nightclerk. Sleepy eyes blinking into nervousness, he nodded knowingly.

"Ah!" he said. "The gypsies!"

"Gypsies? But these were only children—"

He nodded again. "Exactly so." And then he told me the story.

Pickpockets and purse-snatchers had always been a common nuisance here, but within the past few years their presence had escalated.

They came out of Eastern Europe, their exact origin unknown, but "yougoslaves" or "gypsies" served as a convenient label.

Apparently they were smuggled in by skillful and enterprising adult criminals who specialized in educating children in the art of thievery, very much as Fagin trained his youngsters in the London of Dickens' *Oliver Twist*.

But Fagin was an amateur compared to today's professors of pilfering. Their pupils—orphans, products of broken homes, or no homes at all—were recruited in foreign city streets, or even purchased outright from greedy, uncaring parents. These little ones could be quite valuable; an innocent at the age of four or five became a seasoned veteran after a few years of experience, capable of bringing in as much as a hundred thousand American dollars over the course of a single year.

When I described the circumstances of my own encounter the clerk shrugged.

"Of course. That is how they work, my friend—in gangs." Gangs, expertly adept in spotting potential victims, artfully instructed how to operate. Their seemingly spontaneous outcries were actually the product of long and exacting rehearsal, their apparently impromptu movements perfected in advance. They danced around me because they had been choreographed to do so. It was a bandits' ballet in which each one played an assigned role—to nudge, to gesture, to jab and jabber and create confusion. Even the hand-kissing was part of a master plan, and when one ragged waif thrust his folded newspaper against my chest it concealed another who ducked below and lifted my wallet. The entire performance was programmed down to the last detail.

I listened and shook my head. "Why don't the police tell me these things? Surely they must know."

"*Oui, M'sieur.*" The clerk permitted himself a confidential wink. "But perhaps they do not care." He leaned across the desk, his voice sinking to a murmur. "Some say an arrangement has been made. The yougoslaves are skilled in identifying tourists by their dress and manner. They can recognize a foreign visitor merely by the kind of shoes he wears. One supposes a bargain has been struck because it is only the tourists who are attacked, while ordinary citizens are spared."

I frowned. "Surely others like myself must lodge complaints. One would think the police would be forced to take action."

The clerk's gesture was as eloquent as his words. "But what can they do? These yougoslaves strike quickly, without warning. They vanish before you realize what has happened, and no one knows where they go. And even if you managed to lay hands on one of them, what then? You bring this youngster to the police and tell your story, but the little ruffian has no wallet—you can be sure it was passed along immediately to another who ran off with the evidence. Also, your prisoner cannot speak or understand French, or at least pretends not to."

"So the gendarmes have nothing to go by but your words, and what can they do with the kid if they did have proof, when the law prohibits the arrest and jailing of children under thirteen?

"It's all part of the scheme. And if you permit me, it is a beautiful scheme, this one."

My frown told him I lacked appreciation of beauty, and he quickly leaned back to a position of safety behind the desk, his voice and manner sobering. "Missing credit cards can be reported in the morning, though I think it unlikely anyone would be foolish enough to attempt using them with a forged signature. It's the money they were after."

"I have other funds in your safe," I said.

"*Tres bien.* In that case I advise you to make the best of things. Now that you know what to expect, I doubt if you will be victimized again. Just keep away from the tourist traps and avoid using the Metro." He offered me the solace of a smile which all desk clerks reserve for complaints about stalled elevators, lost luggage, faulty electrical fixtures, or clogged plumbing.

Then, when my frown remained fixed, his smile vanished. "Please, my friend! I understand this has been a most distressing occurrence, but I trust you will chalk it up to experience. Believe me, there is no point in pursuing the matter further."

I shook my head. "If the police won't go after these children—"

"Children?" Again his voice descended to a murmur. "Perhaps I did not make myself clear. The yougoslaves are not ordinary kids. As I say, they have been trained by masters. The kind of man who is capable of buying or stealing a child and corrupting it for a life of crime is not likely to stop there. I have heard certain rumors, *M'sieur*, rumors which make a dreadful sort of sense. These kids, they are hooked on drugs. They know every manner of vice but nothing of morals, and many carry knives, even guns. Some have been taught to break and enter into homes, and if discovered, to kill. Their masters, of course, are even more dangerous when crossed. I implore you, for your own safety—forget what has happened tonight and go on your way."

"Thank you for your advice." I managed a smile and went on my way. But I did not forget.

I did not forget what had happened, nor did I forget I'd been robbed of what was most precious to me.

Retiring to my room, I placed the *Do Not Disturb* sign on the outer doorknob and after certain makeshift arrangements I sank eventually into fitful slumber.

By the following evening I was ready; ready and waiting. Paris by night is the City of Light, but it is also the city of shadows. And it was in the shadows that I waited, the shadows under the archways of the Rue de Rivoli. My dark clothing was deliberately donned to blend inconspicuously with the background; I would be unnoticed if the predators returned to seek fresh prey.

Somehow I felt convinced that they would do so. As I stood against a pillar, scanning the occasional passerby who wandered past, I challenged myself to see the hunted through the eyes of the hunters.

Who would be the next victim? That party of Japanese deserved no more than a glance of dismissal; it wasn't wise to confront a group. By the same token, those who traveled in pairs or couples would be spared. And even the lone pedestrians were safe if they were able-bodied or dressed in garments which identified them as local citizens.

What the hunters sought was someone like myself, someone wearing clothing of foreign cut, preferably elderly and obviously alone. Someone like the gray-headed old gentleman who was approaching now, shuffling past a cluster of shops already closed for the night. He was short, slight of build, and his uncertain gait hinted at either a physical impairment or mild intoxication. A lone traveler on an otherwise-deserted stretch of street—he was the perfect target for attack.

And the attack came.

Out of the deep dark doorway to an arcade the yougoslaves danced forth, squealing and gesticulating, to suddenly surround their startled victim.

They ringed him, hands outstretched, their cries confusing, their fingers darting forth to prod and pry in rhythm with the outbursts.

I saw the pattern now, recognized the roles they played.

Here was the hand-kisser, begging for bounty, here the duo tugging at each arm from the rear, here the biggest of the boys, brandishing the folded paper to thrust it against the oldster's chest while an accomplice burrowed into the gaping front of the jacket below. Just behind him the sixth and smallest of the band stood poised. The instant the wallet was snatched it would be passed to him, and while the others continued their distraction for a few moments more before scattering, he'd run off in safety.

The whole charade was brilliant in its sheer simplicity, cleverly contrived so that the poor old gentleman would never notice his loss until too late.

But I noticed—and I acted.

As the thieves closed in I stepped forward, quickly and quietly. Intent on their quarry, they were unaware of my approach. Moving up behind the youngster who waited to receive the wallet, I grasped his upraised arm in a tight grip, bending it back against his shoulderblade as I yanked him away into the shadows. He looked up and my free hand clamped across his oval mouth before he could cry out.

He tried to bite, but my fingers pressed his lips together. He tried to kick, but I twisted his bent arm and tugged him along offbalance, his feet dragging over the pavement as we moved past the shadowy archway to the curb beyond.

My rental car was waiting there. Opening the door, I hurled him down onto the seat face-forward. Before he could turn I pulled the handcuffs from my pocket and snapped them shut over his wrists.

Locking the passenger door, I hastened around to the other side of the car and entered, sliding behind the wheel. Seconds later we were moving out into the traffic.

Hands confined behind him, my captive threshed helplessly beside me. He could scream now, and he did.

"Stop that!" I commanded. "No one can hear you with the windows closed."

After a moment he obeyed. As we turned off onto a side street he glared up at me, panting.

"*Merde!*" he gasped.

I smiled. "So you speak French, do you?"

There was no reply. But when the car turned again, entering one of the narrow alleyways off the Rue St. Roch, his eyes grew wary.

"Where are we going?"

"That is a question for you to answer."

"What do you mean?"

"You will be good enough to direct me to the place where I can find your friends."

"Go to hell!"

"*Au contraire.*" I smiled again. "If you do not cooperate, and quickly, I'll knock you over the head and dump your body in the Seine."

"You old bastard—you can't scare me!"

Releasing my right hand from the steering wheel I gave him a clout across the mouth, knocking him back against the seat.

"That's a sample," I told him. "Next time I won't be so gentle." Clenching my fist, I raised my arm again, and he cringed.

"Tell me!" I said.

And he did.

The blow across the mouth seemed to have loosened his tongue, for he began to answer my questions as I reversed our course and crossed over a bridge which brought us to the Left Bank.

When he told me our destination and described it, I must confess I was surprised. The distance was much greater than I anticipated, and finding the place would not be easy, but I followed his directions on a mental map. Meanwhile I encouraged Bobo to speak.

That was his name—Bobo. If he had another he claimed he did not know it, and I believed him. He was nine years old but he'd been with the gang for three of them, ever since their leader spirited him off the streets of Dubrovnik and brought him here to Paris on a long and illegal route while hidden in the back of a truck.

"Dubrovnik?" I nodded. "Then you really are a yougoslave. What about the others?"

"I don't know. They come from everywhere. Where ever he finds them."

"Your leader? What's his name?"

"We call him Le Boss."

"He taught you how to steal like this?"

"He taught us many things," Bobo gave me a sidelong glance. "Listen to me, old man—if you find him there will be big trouble. Better to let me go."

"Not until I have my wallet."

"Wallet?" His eyes widened, then narrowed, and I realized that for the first time he'd recognized me as last night's victim. "If you think Le Boss will give you back your money, then you really are a fool."

"I'm not a fool. And I don't care about the money."

"Credit cards? Don't worry, Le Boss won't try to use them. Too risky."

"It's not the cards. There was something else. Didn't you see it?"

"I never touched your wallet. It was Pepe who took it to the van last night."

The van, I learned, was always parked just around the corner from the spot where the gang set up operations. And it was there that they fled after a robbery. Le Boss waited behind the wheel with the motor running; the stolen property was turned over to him immediately as they drove off to safer surroundings.

"So Le Boss has the wallet now," I said.

"Perhaps. Sometimes he takes the money out and throws the billfold away. But if there was more than money and cards inside as you say—" Bobo hesitated, peering up at me. "What is this thing you're looking for?"

"That is a matter I will discuss with Le Boss when I see him."

"Diamonds, maybe? You a smuggler?"

"No."

His eyes brightened and he nodded quickly. "Cocaine? Don't worry, I get some for you, no problem—good stuff, not the junk they cut for street trade. All you want, and cheap, too."

I shook my head. "Stop guessing. I talk only to Le Boss."

But Bobo continued to eye me as I guided the car out of the suburban residential and industrial areas, through a stretch of barren countryside, and into an unpaved side road bordering the empty lower reaches of the river. There were no lights here, no dwellings, no signs of life—only shadows, silence, and swaying trees.

Bobo was getting nervous, but now he forced a smile.

"Hey, old man—you like girls? Le Boss got one the other day."

"Not interested."

"I mean *little* girls. Fresh meat, only five, six maybe—"

I shook my head again and he sidled closer on the seat. "What about boys? I'm good, you'll see. Even Le Boss says so—"

He rubbed against me; his clothes were filthy and he smelled of sweat and garlic. "Never mind," I said quickly, pushing him away.

"Okay," he murmured. "I figured if we did a deal you'd give up trying to see Le Boss. It's just going to make things bad for you, and there's no sense getting yourself hurt."

"I appreciate your concern." I smiled. "But it's not me you're really worried about. You'll be the one who gets hurt for bringing me, is that not so?"

He stared at me without replying but I read the answer in his fear-filled eyes.

"What will he do to you?" I said.

The fear spilled over into his voice. "Please, *M'sieu*—don't tell him how you got here! I will do anything you want, anything—"

"You'll do exactly what I say," I told him.

He glanced ahead, and again I read his eyes.

"Are we here?" I asked. "Is this the place?"

"*Oui*. But—"

"Be silent." I shut off the motor and headlights, but not before the beam betrayed a glimpse of the river bank beyond the rutted side road. Through the tangle of trees and rampant underbrush I could see the parked van hidden from sight amidst the sheltering shadows ahead. Beyond it, spanning the river, was a crude and ancient wooden foot bridge, the narrow and rotting relic of a bygone era.

I slipped out of the car, circling to the other side, then opened the passenger door and collared my captive.

"Where are they?" I whispered.

"On the other side." Bobo's voice was faint but the apprehension it held was strong. "Please don't make me take you there!"

"Shut up and come with me." I jerked him forward toward the trees, then halted as I stared across the rickety old makeshift bridge. The purpose it served in the past was long forgotten, and so was the huge oval on the far bank which opened close to the water's edge.

But Le Boss had not forgotten. Once this great circular conduit was part of the earliest Paris sewer-system. Deep within its depths, dozens of connecting branches converged into a gigantic single outlet and spewed their waste into the water below. Now the interior channels had been sealed off, leaving the main tunnel dry but not deserted. For it was here, within a circle of metal perhaps twenty feet in diameter, that Le Boss found shelter from prying eyes, past the unused dirt road and the abandoned bridge.

The huge opening gaped like the mouth of Hell, and from within the fires of Hell blazed forth.

Actually the fires were merely the product of candle light flickering from tapers set in niches around the base of the tunnel. I sensed that their value was not only practical but precautionary, for they would be quickly extinguished in the event of an alarm.

Alarm?

I tugged at Bobo's soiled collar. "The lookout," I murmured. "Where is he?"

Reluctantly the boy stabbed a finger in the direction of a tall and tangled weed bordering the side of the bridge. In the shadows I made out a small shape huddled amid surrounding clumps of vegetation.

"Sandor." My captive nodded. "He's asleep."

I glanced up. "What about Le Boss and the others?"

"Inside the sewer. Farther back, where nobody can see them."

"Good. You will go in now."

"Alone?"

"Yes, alone." As I spoke I took out my key and unlocked the handcuffs, but my grip on Bobo's neck did not loosen.

He rubbed his chafed wrists. "What am I supposed to do?"

"Tell Le Boss that I grabbed you on the street, but you broke free and ran."

"How do I say I got here?"

"Perhaps you hitched a ride."

"And then—"

"You didn't know I was following you, not until I caught you here again. Tell him I'm waiting on this side of the river until you bring me my key. Once I get it I will go away—no questions asked, no harm done."

Bobo frowned. "Suppose he doesn't have the key?"

"He will," I said. "You see, it's just an old brass gate-key, but the handle is shaped into my family crest. Mounted in the crest is a large ruby."

Bobo's frown persisted. "What if he just pried it loose and threw the key away?"

"That's possible." I shrugged. "But you had better pray he didn't." My fingers dug into his neck. "I want that key, understand? And I want it now."

"He's not going to give it to you, not Le Boss! Why should he?"

For answer I dragged him toward the sleeping sentry in the weeds. Reaching into my jacket I produced a knife. As Bobo gaped in surprise, I aimed a kick at the slumbering lookout. He blinked and sat up quickly, then froze as I pressed the tip of the broad blade against his neck.

"Tell him that if you don't bring me back the key in five minutes I'll cut Sandor's throat."

Sandor believed me, I know, because he started to whimper. And Bobo believed me too, for when I released my grip on his collar he started running toward the bridge.

Now there was only one question. Would Le Boss believe me?

I sincerely hoped so. But for the moment all I could do was be patient. Yanking the sniveling Sandor to his feet, I tugged him along to position myself at the edge of the bridge, staring across it as Bobo reached the mouth of the sewer on the other side. The mouth swallowed him; I stood waiting.

Except for the rasp of Sandor's hoarse breathing, the night was still. No sound emanated from the great oval of the sewer across the river, and my vision could not penetrate the flashing of flame from within.

But the reflection of the light served me as I studied my prisoner. Like Bobo, he had the body of a child, but the face peering up at me was incongruously aged—not by wrinkles but by the the grim set of his cracked lips, the gaunt hollows beneath protruding cheekbones, and the sunken circles outlining the eyes above. The eyes were old, those deep dark eyes that had witnessed far more than any child should see. In them I read a present submissiveness, but that was merely surface reaction. Beyond it lay a cold cunning, a cruel craftiness governed not by intelligence but animal instinct, fully developed, ready for release. And he was an animal, I told myself; a predator, dwelling in a cave, issuing forth to satisfy ageless atavistic hungers.

He hadn't been born that way, of course. It was Le Boss who transformed the innocence of childhood into amoral impulse, who eradicated humanity and brought forth the beast beneath.

Le Boss. What was he doing now? Surely Bobo had reached him by this time, told his tale. What was happening? I held Sandor close at knife-point, my eyes searching the swirl of firelight and shadow deep in the tunnel's iron maw.

Then, suddenly and shockingly, the metal mouth screamed.

The high, piercing echo rose only for an instant before fading into silence, but I knew its source.

Tightening my grip on Sandor's ragged collar and pressing the knife blade close to his throat, I started toward the foot bridge.

"No!" he quavered. "Don't—"

I ignored his panting plea, his futile efforts to free himself. Thrusting him forward, I crossed the swaying structure, averting my gaze from the dank depths beneath and focusing vision and purpose on the opening ahead.

Passing between the flame-tipped teeth of the candles on either side, I dragged Sandor down into the sewer's yawning throat. I was conscious of the odor now, the odor of carrion corruption which welled from the dark inner recesses, conscious of the clang of our footsteps against the rounded metal surface, but my attention was directed elsewhere.

A dark bundle of rags lay across the curved base of the tunnel. Skirting it as we approached, I saw I'd been mistaken. The rags were merely a covering, outlining the twisted form beneath.

Bobo had made a mistake too, for it was his body that sprawled motionless there. The grotesque angle of his neck and the splinter of bone protruding from an outflung arm indicated that he had fallen from above. Fallen, or perhaps been hurled.

My eyes sought the rounded ceiling of the sewer. It was, as I'd estimated, easily twenty feet high, but I didn't have to scan the top to confirm my guess as to Bobo's fate.

Just ahead, at the left of the rounded iron wall, was a wooden ladder propped against the side of a long, broad shelf mounted on makeshift scaffolding which rose perhaps a dozen feet from the sewer's base. Here the candles were affixed to poles at regular intervals, illuminating a vast tumbled heap of handluggage, rucksacks, attache cases, boxes, packages, purses, and moldy, mildewed articles of clothing, piled into a thieves' mountain of stolen goods.

And here, before them on a soiled and aging mattress, amid a litter of emptied and discarded bottles, Le Boss squatted.

There was no doubt as to his identity; I recognized him by his mocking smile, the cool casualness with which he rose to confront me after I'd forced Sandor up the ladder and onto the platform.

The man who stood swaying before us was a monster. Forgive the term, but there is no other single word to describe him. Le Boss was well over six feet tall, and the legs enclosed in the dirt-smudged trousers of his soiled suit were bowed and bent by the sheer immensity of the burden they bore. He must have weighed over three hundred pounds,and the fat bulging from his bloated belly and torso was almost obscene in its abundance. His huge hands terminated in fingers as thick as sausages.

There was no shirt beneath the tightly-stretched suit jacket and from a cord around his thick neck a whistle dangled against the naked chest. His head was bullet-shaped and bald. Indeed, he was completely hairless—no hint of eyebrows surmounted the hyperthyroid pupils, no lashes guarded the red-rimmed sockets. The porcine cheeks and sagging jowls were beardless, their fleshy folds worm-white even in the candle light which glittered against the tiny, tawny eyes.

I needed no second glance to confirm my suspicions of what had occurred before my arrival here; the scene I pictured in my mind was perfectly clear. The coming of Bobo, the breathless, stammered story, his master's reaction of mingled disbelief and anger, the fit of drunken fury in which the terrified bringer of bad tidings had been flung over the side of the platform to smash like an empty bottle on the floor of the sewer below—I saw it all too vividly.

Le Boss grinned at me, his fleshy lips parted to reveal yellowed stumps of rotting teeth.

"Well, old man?" he spoke in French, but his voice was oddly accented; he could indeed be a yougoslave.

I forced myself to meet his gaze. "You know why I'm here," I said.

He nodded. "Something about a key, I take it."

"Your pack of thieves took it. But it's my property."

His grin broadened. "My property now." The deep voice rumbled with mocking relish. "Suppose I'm not inclined to return it?"

For answer I shoved Sandor before me and raised the knife, poising it against his neck. My captive trembled and made mewing sounds as the blade pressed closer.

Le Boss shrugged. "You'll have to do better than that, old man. A child's life isn't important to me."

I peered down at Bobo's body lying below. "So I see." Striving to conceal my reaction, I faced him again. "But where are the others?"

"Playing, I imagine."

"Playing?"

"You find that strange, old man? In spite of what you may think, I'm not without compassion. After all, they are only children. They work hard, and they deserve the reward of play."

Le Boss turned, gesturing down toward the far recesses of the sewer. My eyes followed his gaze through the shifting candle glow, and for the first time I became aware of movement in the dim depths. Faint noises echoed upward, identifiable now as the sound of childish laughter. Tiny shapes moved below and beyond, shapes which gleamed white amid the shadows.

The yougoslaves were naked, and at play. I counted four of them, scuffling and squatting in the far reaches of the tunnel.

But wait! There was a fifth figure, slightly smaller than the others who loomed over it and laughed as they pawed the squirming shape or tugged at the golden hair. Over their mirth rose the sound of sobbing, and over that, the echo of Bobo's voice.

*Hey, old man—you like girls? Fresh meat, only five, six maybe—*

Now I could see only too clearly. Two of the boys held their victim down, spread-eagled and helpless, while the other two—but I shall not describe what they were doing.

Glancing away, I again met Le Boss' smile. Somehow it seemed more hideous to me than the sight below.

He groped for a bottle propped against the pile of loot beside him and drank before speaking. "You are distressed, eh?"

I shook my head. "Not as much as you'll be unless you

give me back my key."

He smiled. "Empty threats will get you nothing but empty hands."

"My hands aren't empty." I jabbed the knife at Sandor's neck, grazing the flesh, and he squealed in terror.

Le Boss shrugged. "Go ahead. I told you it doesn't matter to me."

For a moment I stood irresolute. Then, with a sigh I drew the knife back from Sandor's throat and released my hold on his sweat-soaked collar. He turned and raced off to the ladder behind me, and I could hear his feet scraping against the rungs as he descended. Mercifully, the sound muffled the laughter from below.

Le Boss nodded. "That's better. Now we can discuss the situation like gentlemen."

I lifted the knife. "Not as long as I have this, and you have the key."

"More empty threats?"

"My knife speaks for me." I took a step forward as I spoke.

He chuckled. "I swear I don't know what to make of you, old man. Either you are very stupid or very brave."

"Both, perhaps." I raised the blade higher, but he halted my advance with a quick gesture.

"Enough," he wheezed. Turning, he stopped and thrust his pudgy hand into a tangle of scarves, kerchiefs, and handbags behind him. When he straightened again he was holding the key.

"Is this what you're after?"

"Yes. I knew you wouldn't discard it."

He stared at the red stone gleaming dully from the crested handle. "I never toss away valuables."

"Just human lives," I said.

"Don't preach to me, old man. I'm not interested in your philosophy."

"Nor I in yours." I stretched out my hand, palm upward. "All I want is my key."

His own hand drew back. "Not so fast. Suppose you tell me why."

"It's not the ruby," I answered. "Go ahead, pry it loose if you like."

Le Boss chuckled again. "A poor specimen—big enough, but flawed. It's the key itself that interests you, eh?"

"Naturally. As I told Bobo, it opens the gate to my estate."

"And just where is this estate of yours?"

"Near Bourg-la-Reine."

"That's not too far away." The little eyes narrowed. "The van could take us there within the hour."

"It would serve no purpose," I said. "Perhaps 'estate' is a misnomer. The place is small and holds nothing you'd be interested in. The furnishings are old, but hardly the quality of antiques. The house itself has been boarded up for years since my last visit. I have other properties elsewhere on the continent where I spend much of my time. But since I'll be here for several weeks on business, I prefer familiar surroundings."

"Other properties, eh?" Le Boss fingered the key. "You must be quite rich, old man."

"That's none of your affair."

"Perhaps not, but I was just thinking. If you have money, why not conduct your business in comfort from a hotel in Paris?"

I shrugged. "It's a matter of sentiment—"

"Really?" he eyed me sharply, and in the interval before speaking, I noted that the sounds below had ceased.

My voice broke the sudden silence. "I assure you—"

"*Au contraire*. You do not assure me in the least." Le Boss scowled. "If you do own an estate, then it's the key to the house that's important, not the one for the gate. Any locksmith could open it for you without the need of this particular key."

He squinted at the burnished brass, the dulled brilliance of the ruby imbedded in the ornate crest. "Unless, of course, it isn't a gate key after all. Looks to me more like the key to a strongbox, or even a room in the house holding hidden valuables."

"It's just a gate key." Again I held one hand out as the

other gripped the knife. "But I want it—now."

"Enough to kill?" he challenged.

"If necessary."

"I'll spare you that." Grinning, Le Boss reached down again into a bundle of discarded clothing. When he turned to face me again he held a revolver in his hand.

"Drop that toothpick," he said, raising the weapon to reinforce his command.

Sighing, I released my grip and the knife fell, clattering over the side of the open platform to the surface of the sewer below.

Impelled by blind impulse, I turned hastily. If I could get to the ladder—

"Stand where you are!"

It wasn't his words, but the sharp clicking sound that halted me. Slowly I pivoted to face the muzzle of his cocked revolver.

"That's better," he said.

"You wouldn't murder me—not in cold blood."

"Let's leave it up to the kids." As Le Boss spoke his free hand fumbled for the whistle looped around his neck. Enfolding it in blubbery lips, he blew.

The piercing blast echoed, reverberating from the rounded iron walls beside me and below. Then came the answering murmurs, the sudden thud of footsteps. Out of the corner of my eye I glanced down and saw the four naked figures—no, there were five now, including the fully clothed Sandor— moving toward the platform on which we stood.

Again I conjured up a vision of Hell, of demons dancing in the flames. But the flames were merely candle light and the bodies hurrying beneath were those of children. It was only their laughter which was demonic. Their laughter, and their gleefully contorted faces.

As they approached I caught a glimpse of what they held in their hands. Sandor had scooped up the knife from where it had fallen and the others held weapons of their own—a mallet, a wooden club, a length of steel pipe, the serrated stump of a broken wine bottle.

Le Boss chuckled once more. "Playtime," he said.

"Call them off!" I shouted. "I warn you—"

He shook his head. "No way, old man."

*Old man.* That, I swear, is what did it. Not the menace of the gun, not the sight of the loathsome little creatures below. It was just the phrase, the contempt with which it had been repeated over and over again.

I knew what he was thinking—an unarmed, helpless elderly victim had been trapped for torment. And for the most part he was right. I was weaponless, old, trapped.

But not helpless.

Closing my eyes, I concentrated. There are subsonic whistles which make no audible sound, and there are ways of summoning which require no whistles at all. And there's more than human vermin infesting abandoned sewers, lurking in the far recesses of tangled tunnels, but responsive to certain commands.

Almost instantly that response came.

It came in the form of a purposeful padding, of faint noises magnified by sheer numbers. It came in the sound of squeaks and chittering, first as distant echoes, then in closer cacophony as my summons were answered.

Now the yougoslaves had reached the ladder at the far side of the platform. I saw Sandor mount the lower rungs, knife held between clenched teeth—saw him halt as he too heard the sudden, telltale tumult. Behind Sandor his companions turned to seek its source.

They cried out then, first in surprise, then in alarm, as the gray wave surged toward them along the sewer's length; the gray wave, flecked with hundreds of red and glaring eyes, a thousand tiny teeth.

The wave raced forward, curling around the feet and ankles of the yougoslaves before the ladder, climbing and clinging to their legs and knees. Screaming, they lashed out with their weapons, trying to beat back the attack but the wave poured on, forward and upward. Furry forms leaped higher, claws digging into waists, teeth biting into bellies. Sandor pulled himself up the ladder with both hands, but below him the red eyes rose and the gray shapes launched up from behind to cover his unprotected back with a blanket of wriggling bodies.

Now the screams from below were drowned out by the volume of shrill screeching. The knife dropped from between Sandor's lips as he shrieked and toppled down into the writhing mass that had already engulfed his companions. Flailing helplessly, their faces sank from sight in the rising waves of the gray sea.

It happened so quickly that Le Boss, caught by surprise, could only stare in stunned silence at the shambles below.

It was I whose voice rose above the bedlam. "The key," I cried. "Give me the key."

For answer he raised his hand—not the one holding the key, but the one grasping the gun.

His fingers were trembling, and the muzzle wavered as I started toward him. Even so, at such close range I realized he couldn't miss. And he didn't.

As he squeezed the trigger the shots came in rapid succession. They were barely audible in the uproar from the tunnel, but I felt their impact as they struck my chest and torso.

I kept on, moving closer, hearing the final, futile click as he continued to press the trigger of his emptied revolver. Looking up, eyes red with rage, he hurled the weapon at my head. It whizzed past me, and now he had nothing left to clutch but the key. His hands started to shake.

My hand went out.

Snatching the key from his pudgy paw, I stared at his frantic face. Perhaps I should have told him he'd guessed correctly, the key was not meant to open a gate. I could have explained the ruby in the crest—the symbol of a lineage so ancient that it still adhered to the old custom of maintaining a tomb on the estate. The key gave me access to that tomb, not that it was really needed; my branch of the line had other resting places, and during my travels I always carried with me what was necessary to afford temporary rest of my own. But during my stay here the tomb was both practical and private. Calling a locksmith would be unwise and inconvenient, and I do not relish inconvenience.

All this I could have told him, and much more. Instead I pocketed the key bearing the great flawed ruby that was like a single drop of blood.

As I did so, I realized that the squeals and chittering below had faded into other sounds compounded of claws ripping through cloth, teeth grating against bone.

Unable to speak, unable to move, Le Boss awaited my approach. When I gripped his shoulders he must have fainted, for there was only a dead weight now to ease down onto the platform floor.

Below me my brothers sated their hunger, feasting on the bodies of the yougoslaves.

Bending forward to the fat neck beneath me, in my own way I feasted too.

What fools they were, these creatures who thought themselves so clever! Perhaps they could outwit others, but their little tricks could not prevail against me. After all, they were only yougoslaves.

And I am a Transylvanian.

# David Campton

# Firstborn

DAVID CAMPTON'S infrequent forays into short fiction have mostly been published in the *Whispers* anthologies, edited by Stuart David Schiff, and Karl Edward Wagner's *The Year's Best Horror Stories.*

Better known as a playwright, he has written more than seventy stage productions, ranging from romantic comedy to science fiction and horror (including an acclaimed adaptation of *Frankenstein*), as well as numerous scripts for television and radio. His one act black comedy *Smile* recently won first prize in a competition organised by The Drama Association of Wales.

"Firstborn" is a rare piece of fiction from Campton that is set firmly in the classic mad scientist tradition, but written with the author's distinctive wit and style. He is currently working on a story about a possessed parrot.

THERE WERE QUESTIONS to be answered.

As the gale hurled more snow at the window of Harry's cottage I asked myself what I was doing here. The pure malt I sipped was hardly the answer: the local product made a visit to this ice-raked wilderness bearable, but I wasn't here for the whisky. To be honest, I had hoped that, since coming into his late uncle's thousands, Harry might be good for another touch; otherwise, when he suggested the jaunt, I might not have so willingly traded civilisation for cold quarters in a converted barn. But what was a hot-house plant like Harry doing in the highest of the Highlands anyway?

Moreover Harry's elegant Elaine was here too in this croft north of Inverness. Why?—at this time of all times in a woman's life. Surely persons of substance expect their firstborn to be delivered with all the advantages of modern obstetrics. Instead of which Elaine, who at a pinch could always make do with the best, was holding her breath in the whitewashed bedroom next to us, while the local midwife did whatever local midwives do. The atmosphere was charged with unvoiced questions.

At a sharp cry from the next room Harry paused in mid-glass. The Scottish tones of the midwife's response, half-chiding, half-reassuring, were muffled by the closed door. Harry opened his mouth, but only managed a creak from the back of his throat. The expectant father's face shone in the light of the stoked-up fire. His eyes tried to focus on objects beyond the flicker of the leaping flames. He wanted to talk, and only needed enough Scotch in him to flush out the words. At last he plunged.

"Trust you, Gerry," he mumbled.

"Hope so." Detecting a certain lack of conviction in his tone, I hastened to reassure him. "After all, I owe so much to you." The literal truth—all those IOUs.

This comfort induced a wry smile. "That's why it has to be you. Here, I mean. In case . . . " He tossed another log onto the fire. "First you ought to know about . . . Not fair to face you with . . . Of course, it might not after all—in which case there's no harm . . . But if it should be necessary . . ." He kicked the log, sending a burst of sparks up the chimney.

Had I betrayed signs of uneasiness? He patted my shoulder, and paced from wall to wall of the tiny room—four steps each way. "That's why we're out here in the wilds, of course. Nobody else to . . . The midwife's a risk, but money's a great persuader, eh?"

I nodded agreement over the rim of my glass.

"How else did the old boy coax us down to Dorset?" he went on. "Money called. Elaine didn't even query the social life in Dorset, which meant that even she understood the situation. The wolves were gathering—you're familiar with the signs: bills in red with great threatening stamps all over them; 'phone dead; supplies cut off; friends suddenly out of town. At the clink of Uncle's money bags we packed the little we had to pack and accepted what he offered without leaving a forwarding address for our creditors.

"Uncle must have heard a whisper of our little local difficulties, but that didn't explain this uncharacteristic generosity. True, I was his surviving nearest and dearest, but until then he'd hardly acknowledged my existence. I didn't believe his guff about being lonely. He'd lived alone all his life and, being past the seventy mark, must have been used to his own company. For forty or more years he'd devoted himself to making money in the City with a ruthless singlemindedness that ruled out friends. He may have had an acquaintance or two at one time but almost certainly threw them to the sharks whenever profit was involved. Uncle loved Uncle and money, which didn't leave much affection over for anyone else. Not even my beautiful Elaine. He asked specially for Elaine. Obviously in some way or another we were expected to sing for our suppers; but a straw looks like a life-boat to a drowning man. Dorset was the Promised Land.

"Uncle had built the place there just over a year before. Between retirement and moving into this retreat he had lived abroad. He never mentioned those years to us: whatever we learned about them we gleaned from another source. The architect of the new building must have been utterly undistinguished, as not a single aspect of it was designed to catch the eye. The more remarkable features had been added to my uncle's own specifications, and we were only to learn about them in due course. His home was distant enough from civilisation to satisfy a demanding recluse. The taxi fare from the station took away my breath and all but a jingle of small change.

"I suppose it was typical of the very rich that Uncle never considered reimbursing our travelling expenses. So there we were on his doorstep like orphans at Barnardo's, dependent on his charitable whims.

"Oddly we felt neither downcast nor apprehensive. Sunshine helped—remember last May's early heatwave? Although the house was nothing to write home about, the garden was a delight. Bees were busily doing whatever bees are supposed to do, and the flowers were encouraging them. Their scent would have been worth a fortune in a bottle. Elaine seemed to think so too: she paused half-way up the garden path, nose twitching and an expression of silly bliss on her face. That slight indulgence gave Uncle time to establish himself on the front porch with welcoming gestures.

"He was an undersized monkey of a man whose grin stretched from ear to ear exposing an unconvincing set of teeth. His bright eyes twinkled like frost. Obviously we measured up to his expectations. Elaine particularly. He fondled her hand in both his shrivelled paws, and stood on tip-toe to kiss her cheek.

"His enthusing over how much he was going to enjoy having us with him had a ring of the double entendre. As Elaine's eyes met mine over his wrinkled head she raised a questioning brow. I replied with a reassuring smile—whatever lecherous impulses my superannuated relative may have harboured, he was surely past exercising them.

"After which we were introduced to the guest room, then given lunch. The appointments were new and luxurious. I suspected they had been ordered specially for us. The food was as good as deep-freeze and micro-wave could rise to.

The wine was excellent. I had a feeling that Elaine was going to be happy for a while. Between meals she was able to stretch out, suitably anointed, on the green velvet lawn exposing herself to the sun; her gleaming skin tanning to the caramel that blended so well with her butterscotch hair. I caught Uncle licking his lips like a small boy at a sweet-shop window. Well, age can have few compensations, and who was I to intrude on his naughty fantasies? I had daydreams of my own.

"I had plenty of time for them, too. The house, equipped with every modern labour saver, more or less ran itself while Uncle pottered among his plants. In spite of his initial pressing invitation the old boy paid far more attention to his seedlings than to his guests. He presided over meals and presumed that concluded his duties as host. His concentration on the paraphernalia of propagation almost amounted to mania. As an ancient is entitled to his eccentricities, I left him to them. By the third day, though, boredom had led me to the greenhouses.

"We hadn't been warned that they were out of bounds. When I tried one of the doors, and it wouldn't open, I assumed it was merely stuck. I was just heaving on the handle when Uncle bounded up, shrieking.

"I didn't exactly quail, because I'm not the quailing sort; but I must have looked somewhat blasted, because he suddenly cut his wrath short and apologised, giving me the monkey grin with nothing behind it but teeth. On my side I agreed that botanical experiments can be a sensitive area; and on his side he promised a guided tour of the potting sheds.

"While I'm fond enough of fruit and flowers on the table, I've never been one for prying into their private lives. However, I had nothing better to do, and as our comfort depended on keeping Uncle sweet, I trailed behind, playing up an interest I didn't exactly feel.

"The first greenhouse was all orchids. Some were pretty; some were bizarre. Uncle explained he had started with orchids. While still in the full vigour of his late fifties, piling thousands upon thousands, his medico had advised him to take up a hobby—'preparing for retirement,' he called it. Orchids were one of the suggestions. The doctor should have known that my uncle was incapable of doing anything by halves. Orchids became a consuming passion. Retiring years before he was expected to (actually shaking the F. T. Share Index), the relative devoted himself to his new pursuit. He embraced orchidomania as fervently as a religion. New horizons opened up. He had hoped one day to cultivate . . . Had I read Wells's 'Flowering of the Strange Orchid'? A pity that one had eluded him, because orchids now commanded less of his time. He reached beyond orchids . . .

"We left the orchid house. The orchid house was not locked. Making a detour through the kitchen, we picked up a basinful of mince, a slice or two of steak, and a couple of bones. There was a mortice lock on the door of the next hot-house.

"Thin brown fingers clutching the key, my uncle swore me to secrecy. I made some feeble joke, but pandered to his whims. Even then, before opening the door, he delivered a mini-lecture on his current obsession—the thin line between plant and animal life. The man-eating vine was a commonplace of horror stories—well, there *was* an area where fantasy fiction merged with fantastic fact.

"The plants nearest the door were almost commonplace—if giant fly-traps and sundews can be counted as commonplace. We fed these with pinches of mince. I was even allowed the treat of sprinkling meat onto waiting flowers. I admit I found their reaction grimly fascinating, with some blooms snapping shut on dinner, and others curling tendrils over their morsels of protein. Uncle enjoyed himself almost as much as the plants.

"The larger specimens were more impressive. They were approached with a certain reverence. You have to accord respect to any vegetation that can make a meal of half a pound of steak. I wasn't allowed to feed these. Nor did I wish to. I felt that, unless approached with care, one of them might snap off a finger as an hors d'oeuvre.

"Something crawled towards my neck, and I put a cautious hand up to it. It was no more than a trickle of sweat. The temperature and humidity in the glasshouse were uncomfortably high. Uncle grinned as he noticed the gesture, but he didn't comment. Instead he continued his exposition on South American discoveries, coupled with research into hybrids, grafting, cross-fertilisation, and so on, all mixed up with a poly-syllabic jargon that bemused me completely.

"Although I couldn't understand what he was talking about, I could see what he was doing. We ended by confronting an unhealthy-looking mass with blotched saucer-like leaves—or were they blooms? By this time most of the meat had been consumed, the other plants devoted to the process of digestion. Uncle had only bloody bones left in his tuck box. Were they for this mottled monster? Of course they were.

"I believe the thing was quivering with expectation. It practically grabbed at the hunks of skin and bone, my uncle musing meanwhile on whether the thing was capable of consuming a man. Not whole, he concluded, answering his own queries. A man would have to be chopped up first, and that hardly counted. However, his researches were continuing. He had entered an area of delicate and fascinating speculation. Was the question now one of cultivation or of breeding? Was conception the dividing line between animal and vegetable? Could that line be crossed?

"One of the saucers opened with a plop and a nauseating reek of gas. I'll swear it burped. Uncle suggested that I had seen enough for one day. I agreed with him—my shirt was sticking to my back, and my soggy condition had nothing to do with either the temperature or the humidity.

"Outside in the sunshine Elaine was tanning prettily. She purred contentedly as I rubbed oil between her shoulder blades. But Uncle's references to breeding had touched me on a sore spot. The fact is—Elaine and I had experienced some difficulty in that department. It seemed that I couldn't and she didn't want to. At least, not often. I don't know whether I couldn't because she didn't want to, or whether she didn't want to because I couldn't. As a sex-symbol,

Elaine was all symbol and no sex. None of which had escaped Uncle's beady eye.

"In fact at meal times—the only occasions on which the three of us seemed to come together—he would slip into the conversation occasional innuendos or half-jokes, meant to be funny because accompanied by a wrinkled grimace, but which I considered in rather poor taste. Naturally I didn't wince as I felt inclined, because a poor relation learns to laugh at the right time. Well, I suppose the old devil eventually did us a good turn.

"After a particularly good dinner—I can't recall what we ate, but the claret was remarkable—Uncle had been holding forth on his monomania. As a dutiful nephew I displayed some interest, and Elaine bestowed the occasional slow, sweet smile. Elaine has never been a great wit—being too involved with her private thoughts to follow much conversation—but her smile has warmed the cockles of many a monologuist's heart. She and I toyed relaxedly with our brandy snifters, content to let Uncle sparkle like the soda-water in his glass.

"On this occasion the bubbles must have gone to his head, because he prattled of his great experiment. At first I took this to mean the bone-crunching monster locked up in the hot-house but gradually came to realise that he was referring to some holy of holies. Apparently under the house lay unsuspected cellars, and he was offering to show us all. Elaine and I floated after him on an alcoholic cloud of euphoria.

"The cellar door was a cunningly devised panel in the kitchen. At the bottom of the stairs were doors to right and left. Behind the right-hand door lay the wine racks in an electronically controlled atmosphere at exactly the right temperature and humidity to keep their precious contents in condition.

"The same principle applied to the room behind the left-hand door, except that here conditions were equatorial. Within minutes of the door being shut behind us, our pores had opened like faucets, sweat running into our eyes. Even with vision somewhat blurred, though, we could not miss the vine that half-filled the cellar. The plant was supported by a frame of hausers, to which it clung with rope-like tendrils.

"As Uncle lectured on instinctive reactions in plants he held out a finger, and a green thread obligingly curled around it. A pretty demonstration. While we were admiring this performance I leaned unsteadily against the frame, whereupon something gripped me around the waist in a wrestler's hold, jerking me off my feet and among the dripping leaves.

"Uncle gently unwound the slippery bonds, clucking words like 'naughty, naughty'; though I could not be sure whether they applied to me, or to the vine.

"Cautiously standing back, we were invited to admire the buds that festooned the branches—green fingers varying in size, with the largest a handspan in length and over an inch in diameter. Streaks of red showed through a tracery of cracks near the top of one bud that was ready to open.

"Subdued excitement gripped Uncle. He knew what to expect. He stared at the bud, biting his lip and breathing heavily. On cue, while we watched, the bud burst open. Later I wondered if the fact that we were there may have had something to do with this prompt exhibition. After all the movement of the tendrils had shown that the plant reacted to our presence. Even if we had been obliged to wait, though, we would have been rewarded by the display. The flower was remarkable.

"A bright, shining red, it parodied my inefficient reproductive equipment—the main difference being its rampant vigour compared with my habitual ineptitude. No wonder it had been kept behind locked doors: its appearance in a shop window might have exposed a florist to prosecution under the Obscene Publications Act.

"Elaine has a delicate mind. Easily offended by schoolboy smut, she switches off completely at an off-colour remark. I glanced sideways, expecting blushes at one of Nature's jokes. In that heat a blush was difficult to detect, but her eyes had opened very wide and her mouth hung open. For the space of a few heartbeats nothing existed in her world but that flower. She looked so peculiarly vulnerable that something stirred deep inside me—a chemical reaction with pity and jealousy fizzing together. I wanted to take her in my arms and console her for what she had been missing—at the same time realising, almost with fury, that in her present mood she would be easy game for anyone offering as much.

"The show was not yet over. My uncle giggled as he tapped the stem of the flower. It bounced backwards and forwards suggestively; and before quivering to a stop, it exuded a few drops of viscous honey-dew with a heady perfume.

"I can't describe the scent, only its effect—more potent than any combination of claret and brandy. Elaine felt it too: the melting ice-maiden turned to me moist-lipped. Her hair was streaming. Perspiration and the atmosphere had drenched her clothes until they clung to every curve. She was making little animal noises.

"Dizzy with the perfume, I grabbed her and she clung to me. Murmuring incoherent excuses to my uncle we lunged from the cellar. I dimly remember him holding the cellar doors open for us, and his laughter cackling behind us. We left a trail of scattered garments all the way up the stairs to our bedroom. From then on we threshed about in an ecstatic frenzy until first light, when sheer exhaustion brought us down to earth and we crashed into sleep."

Harry fell silent, savouring his drink and perhaps the memory. We could hear the midwife purposefully busy. Harry gestured vaguely in her direction with his glass, as though emphasising the link between the drama in the next room and the bedroom farce some nine months past.

"Good for Uncle's potted plants," I murmured, quickly refilling my glass before the bottle was quite empty. Between the glow of the fire, the sighing of the wind, and Harry's reminiscent drawl, I was losing a battle against lethargy.

Another cry from Elaine. I sat up with an expletive, and with one stride Harry was over to the door. It opened as he reached it. The freckled midwife, firm of bosom and bicep, shook her head.

"Early yet," she hooted. "Back to your bottle and dinna' fash yourself. I promise ye'll be the first tae ken when the bairn appears."

She disappeared, shutting the bedroom door with the speed and efficiency of a cuckoo returning to its clock.

Harry ambled back to his chair, nursed his empty glass for a minute, then began to talk again. It passed the time.

"That wasn't the only occasion," he went on. "She'd come panting to bed, eager as a wild colt for a gallop, and I'd know it had been blossom-time again. Luckily some of that perfume seemed to cling to her. Her fingers would be covered with red pollen. One sniff, and I'd be bucking like a bronco. At first, after these bouts we'd go back to our old sterile ways, but gradually we began to grow towards each other. Nothing madly shattering, of course, but at least giving us a new interest in life. I'm more grateful to Uncle for that than for his thousands."

More silence from Harry.

"A sudden bereavement?" I hazarded.

He sighed, as Adam might have sighed, looking back on lost Paradise.

"It was the onion seller," he said simply.

I waited for what must follow.

"Uncle was undisturbable down in the cellar, and Elaine was soaking up the ultra-violet, when the onion seller appeared at the kitchen door. He was a slight man, kippered by wind and sun. Little black eyes had taken in every item of kitchen equipment between his question and my reply. In point of fact, he only seemed to know one word, which was 'onions'—an easy one, because it's almost the same in French as in English. I replied, 'Non'—showing off a bit—waving a hand at the deep-freeze, the micro-wave oven, and the washing-up machine, conveying the information that food in these parts was practically untouched by human hand. We just didn't need such items as old-fashioned onions. So off he trundled, bundles of onions swinging from his shoulders.

"He had a poor sense of direction because, instead of turning towards the front gate, he headed for the greenhouses. I had to swivel him round and point him in the direction he ought to go. He paused before going on to his next customer, and looked back at the house—not casually as one does at a gate, but intently as though searching for something which ought to have been there that he'd missed.

"I remember telling myself that the poor bastard wasn't going to do much business in this area, with at least two miles between us and the next house. Then I went on to consider he must have been pretty stupid, because even an unlettered clod must have seen there were no other houses down this lane, and no houses meant no sales. Finally I recalled that I hadn't seen an onion seller for years. He was an anachronism, like a muffin man ringing his bell around Earl's Court.

"By way of pleasantry I mentioned this to Uncle half-way through dinner that evening. He didn't find my joke very funny. In fact, it put him off his food. He set down his knife and fork very precisely, cogitated for a count of forty, then fired a stream of questions at me like an interrogating commissar.

"He wanted to be told exactly what the man had looked like, exactly what he had said, every detail of time, place, and scenario until he knew as much about the encounter as if he'd been there. When all that information had been gathered in, he pushed abruptly from the table, and whisked from the room without waiting for coffee, muttering something that sounded like 'Now, now, now.' He spent the rest of the night down in the cellar.

"He surfaced half-way through the following morning, just as I was massaging sun-tan oil into that awkward spot half-way up Elaine's spine. He wanted her assistance with a tricky process below-stairs. Knowing Elaine's limitations whenever anything practical is involved, I offered my services but was brushed aside. Uncle wanted Elaine and Elaine alone. I fastened her halter top and retired gracefully.

"My meditations were interrupted by the return of the onion seller; this time without the pretence of onions. In the twenty-four hours since our last encounter his vocabulary had improved remarkably. He still had a marked foreign accent but expressed himself forcefully. Making enquiries in the neighbourhood, he had been informed that an old gentleman lived alone on these premises. Encountering me yesterday, he had assumed he must have taken a wrong turn. However, a conversation last night with a taxi-driver convinced him that he had been right first time. He wanted my uncle. What's more, the expression on his face and the tone of his voice did not encourage me to call for the old man.

"Fortunately the cellar door was closed, and the stranger's darting glances failed to spot the vital panel. However, my formal reply that Uncle was not at home to callers was clearly not believed. The bright black eyes came to rest almost lovingly on a gleaming butcher's cleaver hanging with other equipment on the kitchen wall. I don't know why it was there: I'd never seen it in action. The foreigner, though, was obviously considering a use for it.

"Suddenly he changed his tactics. With a smile, intended to be warm and friendly, he promised m'sieur that if m'sieur knew everything m'sieur would understand everything, and if the worse came to worst, perhaps even forgive everything. It was a long story, but I did not interrupt because while the chap was talking; he was not molesting Uncle. My main fear was that Uncle himself might come popping out in the middle of the narrative. Luckily he didn't.

"It seemed that, in his own village, the onion seller once had a son—black hair, black eyes, and a lithe body brown as a nut. In the boy's thirteenth year an old man had come to live nearby. This old man was rich enough to indulge his hobby of raising peculiar plants. Some of these could only have been conceived by the Devil, but the boy was fascinated. As months passed, he began to spend all his spare time in the hellish garden created by the Englishman. He was occasionally paid for doing odd jobs—not overpaid, because the very rich understand the value of money, but money changed hands.

"Because of the money rumours started, but there was no truth in those stories. Truly those two were not interested in each other but only in the loathesome specimens. The boy was warned to stay away, but he defied authority, even enduring beatings.

"There came a time when the boy did not come home at all. His father went up to the house of the crazy plants, intent on a reckoning. The old man had suddenly decamped. The boy was there, though.

"The stranger's voice was flat and unemotional as he described how the young body had been found tangled with a vine. Quite dead, of course. What else could have been expected? After being impaled. Did m'sieur understand? A great shoot of the plant had been thrust up inside the victim. Tendrils of the vine had held him fast while he perished in agonies—that Thing inside him.

"The man could spin a yarn. I slumped back on the kitchen stool as he helped himself to the cleaver. After that I was quick to take evasive action, putting the length of a table between myself and that shining steelware. I fancy I babbled something about not being responsible for my relation's misdeeds. However, the cleaver was not required for immediate bloodletting. Only for breaking the windows of accursed greenhouses.

"I didn't try to stop him. After all, glass is replaceable—I am not. A minute or so later I heard a crashing and tinkling like a mad comedy act.

"My next inclination was to brief Uncle on these developments. It says something for the intruder's narrative powers that, until I opened the cellar door, all my attention had been focussed on the poor devil's sufferings. Only when I stood at the top of the stairs did I begin to put two and two together. I didn't like the total. Uncle was down there with Elaine—and the vine. I was soon down there too. Quicker than I had intended, because I missed my footing and bounced half the way. But I didn't even feel the bruises. Scrambling to my feet I crashed open the double door. Thank heavens, the old devil had been so sure of my behaving myself he hadn't troubled to lock it.

"The first thing to hit me was the perfume, now so concentrated it had passed beyond sweetness into a stink.

The vine, covered with red blooms, might have been dripping blood. Elaine was spread-eagled over it, tendril binding her body in a Saint Andrew's cross. Her head drooped. She was unconscious.

"I hurtled over to her and tried to pull her free. Uncle did his feeble best to stop me, but I sent him spinning with a well-aimed if unsporting kick to the groin. He needn't have bothered because, before I realised what was happening, the vine had got me too and I was struggling with a thick green coil around my middle.

"Uncle and I screamed obscenities at each other. I won that round on points, because in barbed phrases I described what was happening upstairs to the rest of his collection. He howled like a creature possessed and fled, leaving me to wrestle on.

"The plant had an unfair advantage. I had only two arms and two legs, whereas it seemed to produce fresh thongs at will. My resistance grew weaker as it bound me firmly to itself. Was all that an inbuilt natural reaction, or did it have a mind of its own?

"I lost count of time but eventually felt a cool draught on my face and realised that the heavy scent was drifting away. In his hurry Uncle had left both doors open. The grip of one of the tendrils relaxed and I was able to free a hand. Slowly I disengaged myself. I don't know whether the sudden drop in temperature was affecting the plant, or whether, having done what it was intended to do, it would have died anyway.

"Once I had disentangled myself, I released Elaine. As I lowered her to the cellar floor, her eyelids fluttered. At least she was still alive.

"Filled with hot fury against the monsters that had treated her with this indignity, I fell upon the vine, tearing great bunches of flowers from it. By now it was a defenceless object, visibly wilting, and eventually I realised that I would be better employed in rending my uncle limb from limb.

"It says something for the incoherence of my reasoning that I left Elaine lying there while I surfaced, calling down damnation on that gibbering little ape.

"I found parts of him in the ruins of the carnivores' hothouse. The onion seller had fed the rest to various plants. On seeing me, the boy's father smiled, bowed, and walked away. The police caught up with him on the outskirts of Poole. Indisputably insane, he was never brought to trial.

"None of the plants survived. A chap from the botanical gardens at Kew was quite cut up about that. Not as cut up as Uncle, of course. Fortunately there was enough left of him for identification and a respectable funeral . . . "

Silence again, except for the wind and the snow.

"Is that all?" I asked after a while.

"I don't know," replied Harry. "You see, when I'd calmed down somewhat, and had Elaine properly sedated and tucked up in bed, something was found."

"Something?" I prompted after another long silence.

"Where Elaine had been lying. A long, limp, dirty-brown object. Rather like a flabby bean pod, only it had never had beans in it."

"What was it?"

Harry took a deep breath and was about to answer when he stopped.

In the next room the midwife had started to scream.

# Manly Wade Wellman

# The Black Drama

MANLY WADE WELLMAN was born in the village of Kamundongo in Portuguese West Africa in 1903. Following childhood visits to London, he moved to the United States where he became a reporter before quitting his job in 1930 to become a professional writer. His long career spanned mainstream novels to works on the American Civil War, with a huge output of more than seventy-five books and two hundred short stories.

Much of that material was in the field of science fiction, fantasy and horror, and he became a prolific contributor to most of the pulp magazines of the '30s and '40s, including *Weird Tales*, *Wonder Stories* and *Astounding Stories*. He also wrote comic books, mystery novels, juveniles and county histories. Wellman twice won the World Fantasy Award before his death in 1986, and some of his finest supernatural fiction is collected in *Who Fears the Devil?*, *Worse Things Waiting* and *Lonely Vigils*.

The classic short novel that follows originally appeared under the pseudonym "Gans T. Field" over three issues of *Weird Tales* in 1938. It features his popular occult investigator, Judge Keith Hilary Pursuivant, in a mystery involving a lost play by Byron and a malevolent evil from the past. It is pulp fiction at its finest.

Powers, passions, all I see in other beings,
Have been to me as rain unto the sands
Since that all-nameless hour.

—Lord Byron: *Manfred*

## Foreword

UNLIKE MOST ACTORS, I do not consider my memoirs worth the attention of the public. Even if I did so consider them, I have no desire to carry my innermost dear secrets to market. Often and often I have flung aside the autobiography of some famous man or woman, crying aloud: "Surely this is the very nonpareil of bad taste!"

Yet my descendants—and, after certain despairful years, again I have hope of descendants—will want to know something about me. I write this record of utterly strange happenings while it is yet new and clear in my mind, and I shall seal it and leave it among my important possessions, to be found and dealt with at such time as I may die. It is not my wish that the paper be published or otherwise brought to the notice of any outside my immediate family and circle of close friends. Indeed, if I thought that such a thing would happen I might write less frankly.

Please believe me, you who will read; I know that part of the narrative will strain any credulity, yet I am ready with the now-threadbare retort of Lord Byron, of whose works more below: "Truth is stranger than fiction." I have, too, three witnesses who have agreed to vouch for the truth of what I have set down. Their only criticism is that I have spoken too kindly of them. If anything, I have not spoken kindly enough.

Like Peter Quince in *A Midsummer Night's*

*Dream*, I have rid my prolog like a rough colt. Perhaps, like Duke Theseus, you my readers will be assured thereby of my sincerity.

Signed,
Gilbert Connatt,
New York City
August 1, 1938

We, the undersigned, having read the appended statement of Gilbert Connatt, do hereby declare it to be true in substance.

Signed,
Sigrid Holgar
Keith Hilary Pursuivant
Jacob A. Switz

## 1. Drafted

The counterman in the little hamburger stand below Times Square gazed at me searchingly.

"Haven't I seen you somewhere?" he asked, and when I shook my head he made a gesture as of inspiration. "I got it, buddy. There was a guy in a movie like you—tall, thin—black mustache and eyes—"

"I'm not in pictures," I told him, quite truthfully as concerned the moment. "Make me a double hamburger."

"And coffee?"

"Yes." Then I remembered that I had but fifteen cents, and that double hamburgers cost a dime. I might want a second sandwich. "Make it a single instead."

"No, a double," piped somebody at my elbow, and a short, plump figure climbed upon the next stool. "Two doubles, for me and my friend here, and I'm paying. Gilbert Connatt, at half-past the eleventh hour I run onto you by the luck of the Switzes. I am glad to see you like an old father to see his wandering boy."

I had known that voice of old in Hollywood. Turning, I surveyed the fat, blob-nosed face, the crossed eyes behind shell-rimmed glasses, the thick, curly hair, the ingratiating smile. "Hello, Jake," I greeted him without enthusiasm.

Jake Switz waved at the counterman. "Two coffees with those hamburgers." His strange oblique gaze shifted back to me. "Gib, to me you are more welcome than wine at a wedding. In an uptown hotel who do you think is wondering about you with tears in her eyes as big as electric light bulbs?" He shrugged and extended his palms, as if pleased at being able to answer his own question. "Sigrid Holgar!"

I made no reply, but drew a frayed shirt-cuff back into the worn sleeve of my jacket. Jake Switz continued: "I've been wondering where to get hold of you, Gib. How would you like again to play leading man for Sigrid, huh?"

It is hard to look full into cross-eyes, but I managed it. "Go back to her," I bade him, "and tell her I'm not taking charity from somebody who threw me down."

Jake caught my arm and shook it earnestly. "But that ain't true, Gib. It's only that she's been so successful she makes you look like a loser. Gib, you know as well as you know your own name that it was you that threw her down—so hard she rang like a silver dollar."

"I won't argue," I said, "and I won't have charity."

I meant that. It hurt to think of Sigrid and myself as we had been five years ago—she an inspired but unsure newcomer from Europe, I the biggest star on the biggest lot in the motion picture industry. We made a film together, another, became filmdom's favorite lovers on and off screen. Then the quarrel; Jake was wrong, it was Sigrid's fault. Or was it? Anyway, she was at the head of the class now, and I had been kicked away from the foot.

The counterman set our sandwiches before us. I took a hungry bite and listened to Jake's pleadings.

"It would be you doing her and me a favor, Gib. Listen this one time—please, to give Jake Switz a break." His voice quavered earnestly. "You know that Sigrid is going to do a stage play."

"I've read about it in *Variety*," I nodded. "Horror stuff, isn't it? Like *Dracula*, I suppose, with women fainting and nurses dragging them out of the theater."

"Nurses!" repeated Jake Switz scornfully. "Huh, doctors we'll need. At our show Jack Dempsey himself would faint dead away on the floor, it's so horrible!" He subsided and began to beg once more. "But you know how Sigrid is. Quiet and restrained—a genius. She wouldn't warm up, no matter what leading man we suggested. Varduk, the producer, mentioned you. "Get Gilbert Connatt," he said to me. "She made a success with him once, maybe she will again." And right away Sigrid said yes."

I went on eating, then swallowed a mouthful of scalding coffee. Jake did the same but without relish. Finally he exploded into a last desperate argument.

"Gib, for my life I can't see how you can afford to pass it up. Here you are, living on hamburgers—"

I whirled upon him so fiercely that the rest of the speech died on his open lips. Rising, I tossed my fifteen cents on the counter and started for the door. But Jake yelled in protest, caught my shoulder and fairly wrestled me back.

"No, no," he was wailing. "Varduk would cut my heart out and feed it to the sparrows if I found you and lost you again. Gib, I didn't mean bad manners. I don't know nothing about manners, Gib, but have I ever treated you wrong?"

I had to smile. "No, Jake. You're a creature of instincts, and the instincts are rather better than the reasonings of most people. I think you're intrinsically loyal." I thought of the years he had slaved for Sigrid, as press agent, business representative, confidential adviser, contract maker and breaker, and faithful hound generally. "I'm sorry myself, Jake, to lose my temper. Let's forget it."

He insisted on buying me another double hamburger, and while I ate it with unblunted appetite he talked more about the play Sigrid was to present.

"Horror stuff is due for a comeback, Gib, and this will be the start. A lovely, Gib. High class. Only Sigrid could do it. Old-fashioned, I grant you, but not a grain of corny stuff in it. It was written by that English guy, Lord Barnum—no, Byron. That's it, Lord Byron."

"I thought," said I, "that there was some question about the real authorship."

"So the papers say, but they holler 'phony' at their own grandmothers. Varduk is pretty sure. He knows a thing or two, that Varduk. You know what he is going to do? He is getting a big expert to read the play and make a report." Jake, who was more press agent than any other one thing, licked his good-humored lips. "What a bust in the papers that will be!"

Varduk. . . . I had heard that name, that single name whereby a new, brilliant and mysteriously picturesque giant of the theatrical world was known. Nobody knew where he had come from. Yet, hadn't Belasco been a riddle? And Ziegfeld? Of course, they had never courted the shadows like Varduk, had never refused to see interviewers or admirers. I meditated that I probably would not like Varduk.

"Send me a pass when your show opens," I requested.

"But you'll be in it, Gib. Passes of your own you'll be putting out. Ha! Listen this once while I try to do you good in spite of yourself, my friend. You can't walk out after eating up the hamburgers I bought."

He had me there. I could not muster the price of that second sandwich, and somehow the shrewd little fellow had surmised as much. He chuckled in triumph as I shrugged in token of surrender.

"I knew you would, Gib. Now, here." He wrote on a card. "This is Varduk's hotel and room number. Be there at eight o'clock tonight, to read the play and talk terms. And here."

His second proffer was a wad of money.

"Get some clothes, Gib. With a new suit and tie you'll look like a million dollars come home to roost. No, no. Take the dough and don't worry. Ain't we friends? If you never pay me back, it will be plenty soon enough."

He beamed my thanks away. Leaving the hamburger stand, we went in opposite directions.

## 2. Byron's Lost Play

I DID NOT FOLLOW Jake's suggestion exactly. Instead of buying new garments throughout, I went to the pawnshop where I had of late raised money on the remnants of a once splendid wardrobe. Here I redeemed a blue suit that would become me best, and a pair of hand-made Oxfords. Across the street I bought a fresh shirt and necktie. These I donned in my coffin-sized room on the top floor of a cheap hotel. After washing, shaving and powdering, I did not look so bad; I might even have been recognized as the Gilbert Connatt who made history in the lavish film version of *Lavengro*, that classic of gipsydom in which a newcomer named Sigrid Holgar had also risen to fame. . . .

I like to be prompt, and it was eight o'clock on the stroke when I tapped at the door of Varduk's suite. There was a movement inside, and then a cheerful voice: "Who's there?"

"Gilbert Connatt," I replied.

The lock scraped and the door opened. I looked into the handsome, ruddy face of a heavy, towering man who was perhaps a year younger than I and in much better physical condition. His was the wide, good-humored mouth, the short, straight nose of the Norman Scot. His blond hair was beginning to grow thin and his blue eyes seemed anxious.

"Come in, Mr Connatt," he invited me, holding out his broad hand. "My name's Davidson—Elmo Davidson." And, as I entered, "This is Mr Varduk." He might have been calling my attention to a prince royal.

I had come into a parlor, somberly decorated and softly lighted. Opposite me, in a shadowed portion, gazed a pallid face. It seemed to hang, like a mask, upon the dark tapestry that draped the wall. I was aware first of a certain light-giving quality within or upon that face, as though it were bathed in phosphorescent oil. It would have been visible, plain even, in a room utterly dark. For the rest there were huge, deep eyes of a color hard to make sure of, a nose somewhat thick but finely shaped, a mouth that might have been soft once but now drew tight as if against pain, and a strong chin with a dimple.

"How do you do, Mr Connatt," said a soft, low voice, and the mask inclined politely. A moment later elbows came forward upon a desk, and I saw the rest of the man Varduk start out of his protective shadows. His dark, double-breasted jacket and the black scarf at his throat had blended into the gloom of the tapestry. So had his chestnut-brown curls. As I came toward him, Varduk rose—he was of middle height, but looked taller by reason of his slimness—and offered me a slender white hand that gripped like a smith's tongs.

"I am glad that you are joining us," he announced cordially, in the tone of a host welcoming a guest to dinner. "Miss Holgar needs old friends about her, for her new stage adventure is an important item in her splendid career. And this," he dropped his hand to a sheaf of papers on the desk, "is a most important play."

Another knock sounded at the door, and Elmo Davidson admitted a young woman, short and steady-eyed. She was Martha Vining, the character actress, who was also being considered for a rôle in the play.

"Only Miss Holgar to come," Davidson said to me, with a smile that seemed to ask for friendship. "We've only a small cast, you know; five."

"I am expecting one more after Miss Holgar," amended Varduk, and Davidson made haste to add: "That's right, an expert antiquary—Judge Keith Pursuivant. He's going to look at our manuscript and say definitely if it is genuine."

Not until then did Varduk invite me to sit down, waving me to a comfortable chair at one end of his desk. I groped in my pockets for a cigarette, but he pressed upon me a very long and very good cigar.

"I admire tobacco in its naked beauty," he observed with the wraith of a smile, and himself struck a match for me. Again I admired the whiteness of his hand, its pointed fingers and strong sensitivity of outline. Such hands generally betoken nervousness, but Varduk was serene. Even the fall of his fringed lids over those plumbless eyes seemed a deliberate motion, not an unthought wink.

Yet again a knock at the door, a brief colloquy and an ushering in by Elmo Davidson. This time it was Sigrid.

I got to my feet, as unsteady as a half-grown boy at his first school dance. Desperately I prayed not to look so moved as I felt. As for Sigrid, she paused and met my gaze frankly, with perhaps a shade's lightening of her gently tanned cheeks. She was a trifle thinner than when I had last seen her five years ago, and wore, as usual, a belted brown coat like an army officer's. Her hair, the blondest unbleached hair I have ever known, fell to her shoulders and curled at its ends like a full-bottomed wig in the portrait of some old cavalier. There was a green flash in it, as in a field of ripened grain. Framed in its two glistening cascades, her face was as I had known it, tapering from brow to chin over valiant cheekbones and set with eyes as large as Varduk's and bluer than Davidson's. She wore no make-up save a touch of rouge upon her short mouth—cleft above and full below, like a red heart. Even with low-heeled shoes, she was only two inches shorter than I.

"Am I late?" she asked Varduk, in that deep, shy voice of hers.

"Not a bit," he assured her. Then he saw my awkward expectation and added, with monumental tact for which I blessed him fervently, "I think you know Mr Gilbert Connatt."

Again she turned to me. "Of course," she replied. "Of course I know him. How do you do, Gib?"

I took the hand she extended and, greatly daring, bent to kiss it. Her fingers fluttered against mine, but did not draw away. I drew her forward and seated her in my chair, then found a backless settee beside her. She smiled at me once, sidewise, and took from my package the cigarette I had forsaken for Varduk's cigar.

A hearty clap on my shoulder and a cry of greeting told me for the first time that little Jake Switz had entered with her.

Varduk's brief but penetrating glance subdued the exuberant Jake. We turned toward the desk and waited.

"Ladies and gentlemen," began Varduk, seriously but not heavily, "a new-found piece of Lord Byron's work is bound to be a literary sensation. We hope also to make a theatrical sensation, for our new-found piece is a play.

"A study of Lord Byron evokes varied impressions and appeals. Carlyle thought him a mere dandy, lacking Mr Brummel's finesse and good humor, while Goethe insisted that he stood second only to Shakespeare among England's poets. His mistress, the Countess Guiccioli, held him literally to be an angel; on the other hand, both Lamartine and Southey called him Satan's incarnation. Even on minor matters—his skill at boxing and swimming, his depth of scholarship, his sincerity in early amours and final espousal of the Greek rebels—the great authorities differ. The only point of agreement is that he had color and individuality."

He paused and picked up some of the papers from his desk.

"We have here his lost play, *Ruthven*. Students know that Doctor John Polidori wrote a lurid novel of horror called *The Vampire*, and that he got his idea, or inspiration, or both, from Byron. Polidori's tale in turn inspired the plays of Nodier and Dumas in French, and of Planché and Boucicault in English. Gilbert and Sullivan joked with the story in *Ruddigore*, and Bram Stoker read it carefully before attempting *Dracula*. This manuscript," again he lifted it, "is Byron's original. It is, as I have said, a drama."

His expressive eyes, bending upon the page in the dimness, seemed to shed a light of their own. "I think that neither Mr Connatt nor Miss Vining has seen the play. Will you permit me to read?" He took our consent for granted, and began: "Scene, Malvina's garden. Time, late afternoon—Aubrey, sitting at Malvina's feet, tells his adventures."

Since *Ruthven* is yet unpublished, I take the liberty of outlining it as I then heard it for the first time. Varduk's voice was expressive, and his sense of drama good. We listened, intrigued and then fascinated, to the opening dialog in which young Aubrey tells his sweetheart of his recent adventures in wildest Greece. The blank verse struck me, at least, as being impressive and not too stiff, though better judges than I have called Byron unsure in that medium. Varduk changed voice and character for each rôle, with a skill almost ventriloquial, to create for us the illusion of an actual drama. I found quite moving Aubrey's story of how bandits were beaten off single-handed by his chance acquaintance, Lord Ruthven. At the point where Aubrey expresses the belief that Ruthven could not have survived the battle:

> "I fled, but he remained; how could one man,
> Even one so godly gallant, face so many?
> He followed not. I knew that he was slain—"

At that point, I say, the first surprise comes with the servant's announcement that Ruthven himself has followed his traveling companion from Greece and waits, whole and sound, for permission to present himself.

No stage directions or other visualization; but immediate dialog defines the title rôle as courtly and sinister, fascinating and forbidding. Left alone with the maid-servant, Bridget, he makes unashamed and highly successful advances. When he lifts the cap from her head and lets her hair fall down, it reminds one that Byron himself had thus ordered it among the maids on his own estate. Byron had made love to them, too; perhaps some of Ruthven's speeches in this passage, at least, came wholemeal from those youthful conquests.

Yet the seduction is not a gay one, and smacks of bird and snake. When Ruthven says to Bridget,

> "You move and live but at my will; dost hear?"

and she answers dully:

> "I hear and do submit,"

awareness rises of a darkling and menacing power. Again, as Aubrey mentions the fight with the bandits, Ruthven dismisses the subject with the careless,

"I faced them, and who seeks my face seeks death,"

one feels that he fears and spares an enemy no more than a fly. And, suddenly, he turns his attentions to Malvina:

> "Yes, I am evil, and my wickedness
> Draws to your glister and your purity.
> Now shall you light no darkness but mine own,
> An orient pearl swathed in a midnight pall—"

Oscar, husband of the betrayed Bridget, rushes in at this point to denounce Ruthven and draw away his bemused mistress. At a touch from the visitor's finger, Oscar falls dead. Aubrey, arming himself with a club of whitethorn—a sovereign weapon against demons—strikes Ruthven down. Dying, the enchanter persuades Aubrey and Malvina to drag him into the open and so leave him. As the moon rises upon his body, he moves and stands up:

> "Luna, my mother, fountain of my life,
> Once more thy rays restore me with their kiss.
> Grave, I reject thy shelter! Death, stand back! . . .

"Curtain," said Varduk suddenly, and smiled around at us.

"So ends our first act," he continued in his natural voice. "No date—nor yet are we obliged to date it. For purposes of our dramatic production, however, I intend to lay it early in the past century, in the time of Lord Byron himself. Act Two," and he picked up another section of the manuscript, "begins a century later. We shall set it in modern times. No blank verse now—Byron cleverly identifies his two epochs by offering his later dialog in natural prose. That was the newest of new tricks in his day."

Again he read to us. The setting was the same garden, with Mary Aubrey and her cousin Swithin, descendants of the Aubrey and Malvina of the first act, alternating between light words of love and attentions to the aged crone Bridget. This survivor of a century and more croaks out the fearsome tale of Ruthven's visit and what followed. Her grandson Oscar, Mary's brother, announces a caller.

The newcomer explains that he has inherited the estate of Ruthven, ancient foe of the Aubreys, and that he wishes to make peace. But Bridget, left alone with him, recognizes in him her old tempter, surviving ageless and pitiless. Oscar, too, hears the secret, and is told that this is his grandfather. Bit by bit, the significance of a dead man restless after a century grows in the play and upon the servants. They swear slavishly to help him. He seeks a double and sinister goal. Swithin, image of his great-grandfather Aubrey, must die for that ancestor's former triumph over Ruthven. Mary, the later incarnation of Malvina, excites Ruthven's passion as did her ancestress.

Then the climax. Mary, trapped by Ruthven, defies him, then offers herself as payment for Swithin's life. Swithin, refusing the sacrifice, thrusts Ruthven through with a sword, but to no avail. Oscar overpowers him, and the demoniac lord pronounces the beginning of a terrible curse; but Mary steps forward as if to accept her lover's punishment. Ruthven revokes his words, blesses her. As the Almighty's name issues from his lips, he falls dead and decaying.

"End of the play," said Varduk. "I daresay you have surmised what rôles I plan for you. Miss Holgar and Mr Connatt are my choices for Malvina and Aubrey in the first act, and Mary and Swithin in the second. Miss Vining will create the rôle of Bridget, and Davidson will undertake the two Oscars."

"And Ruthven?" I prompted, feeling unaccountably presumptuous in speaking uninvited.

Varduk smiled and lowered his fringed lids. "The part is not too difficult," he murmured. "Ruthven is off stage more than on, an influence rather than a flesh-and-blood character. I shall honor myself with this title rôle."

Switz, sitting near me, produced a watch. We had been listening to the play for full two hours and a half.

Again a knock sounded at the door. Davidson started to rise, but Varduk's slender hand waved him down.

"That will be Judge Pursuivant. I shall admit him myself. Keep your seats all."

He got up and crossed the floor, walking stiffly as though he wore tight boots. I observed with interest that in profile his nose seemed finer and sharper, and that his ears had no lobes.

"Come in, Judge Pursuivant," he said cordially at the door. "Come in, sir."

## 3. Enter Judge Pursuivant

KEITH HILARY PURSUIVANT, the occultist and antiquary, was as arresting as Varduk himself, though never were two men more different in appearance and manner. Our first impression was of a huge tweed-clad body, a pink face with a heavy tawny mustache, twinkling pale eyes and a shock of golden-brown hair. Under one arm he half crushed a wide black hat, while the other hand trailed a heavy stick of mottled Malacca, banded with silver. There was about him the same atmosphere of mature sturdiness as invests Edward Arnold and Victor McLaglen, and withal a friendly gayety. Without being elegant or dashing, he caught and held the regard. Men like someone like that, and so, I believe, do women who respect something beyond sleek hair and brash repartee.

Varduk introduced him all around. The judge bowed to Sigrid, smiled at Miss Vining, and shook hands with the rest of us. Then he took a seat at the desk beside Varduk.

"Pardon my trembling over a chance to see something that may have been written by Lord Byron to lie perdu for generations," he said pleasantly. "He and his works have long been enthusiasms of mine. I have just published a modest note on certain aspects of his—"

"Yes, I know," nodded Varduk, who was the only man I ever knew who could interrupt without seeming rude. "*A Defense of the Wickedest Poet*—understanding and sympathetic, and well worth the praise and popularity it is earning. May I also congratulate you on your two volumes of demonology, *Vampyricon* and *The Unknown that Terrifies*?"

"Thank you," responded Pursuivant, with a bow of his shaggy head. "And now, the manuscript of the play—"

"Is here." Varduk pushed it across the desk toward the expert.

Pursuivant bent for a close study. After a moment he drew a floor lamp close to cast a bright light, and donned a pair of pince-nez.

"The words 'by Lord Byron', set down here under the title, are either genuine or a very good forgery," he said at once. "I call your attention, Mr Varduk, to the open capital B, the unlooped down-stroke of the Y, and the careless scrambling of the O and N." He fumbled in an inside pocket and produced a handful of folded slips. "These are enlarged photostats of several notes by Lord Byron. With your permission, Mr Varduk, I shall use them for comparison."

He did so, holding the cards to the manuscript, moving them here and there as if to match words. Then he held a sheet of the play close to the light "Again I must say," he announced at last, "that this is either the true handwriting of Byron or else a very remarkable forgery. Yet—"

Varduk had opened a drawer of the desk and once more he interrupted. "Here is a magnifying glass, Judge Pursuivant. Small, but quite powerful." He handed it over. "Perhaps, with its help, you can decide with more accuracy."

"Thank you." Pursuivant bent for a closer and more painstaking scrutiny. For minutes he turned over page after page, squinting through the glass Varduk had lent him. Finally he looked up again.

"No forgery here. Every stroke of the pen is a clean one. A forger draws pictures, so to speak, of the handwriting he copies, and with a lens like this one can plainly see the jagged, deliberate sketchwork." He handed back the magnifying glass and doffed his spectacles, then let his thoughtful eyes travel from one of us to the others. "I'll stake my legal and scholastic reputation that Byron himself wrote these pages."

"Your stakes are entirely safe, sir," Varduk assured him with a smile. "Now that you have agreed—and I trust that you will allow us to inform the newspapers of your opinion—that *Ruthven* is Byron's work, I am prepared to tell how the play came into my possession. I was bequeathed it—by the author himself."

We all looked up at that, highly interested. Varduk smiled upon us as if pleased with the sensation he had created.

"The germ of *Ruthven* came into being one night at the home of the poet Shelley, on the shores of Lake Geneva. The company was being kept indoors by rain and wind, and had occupied itself with reading German ghost stories, and then tried their own skill at Gothic tales. One of those impromptu stories we know—Mary Godwin's masterpiece, *Frankenstein*. Lord Byron told the strange adventures of Ruthven, and Polidori appropriated them—that we also know; but later that night, alone in his room, Byron wrote the play we have here."

"In one sitting?" asked Martha Vining.

"In one sitting," replied Varduk. "He was a swift and brilliant worker. In his sixteen years of active creative writing, he produced nearly eighty thousand lines of published verse—John Drinkwater reckons an average of fourteen lines, or the equivalent of a complete sonnet, for every day. This prodigious volume of poetry he completed between times of making love, fighting scandal, traveling, quarreling, philosophizing, organizing the Greek revolution. An impressive record of work, both in size and in its proportion of excellence."

Sigrid leaned forward. "But you said that Lord Byron himself bequeathed the play to you."

Again Varduk's tight, brief smile. "It sounds fantastic, but it happened. Byron gave the manuscript to Claire Clairmont, his mistress and the mother of two of his children. He wanted it kept a secret—he had been called fiend incarnate too often. So he charged her that she and the children after her keep the play in trust, to be given the world a hundred years from the date of his death."

Pursuivant cleared his throat. "I was under the impression that Byron had only one child by Claire Clairmont, Mr Varduk. Allegra, who died so tragically at the age of six."

"He had two," was Varduk's decisive reply. "A son survived, and had issue."

"Wasn't Claire's son by Shelley?" asked Pursuivant.

Varduk shook his curly head. "No, by Lord Byron." He paused and drew a gentle breath, as if to give emphasis to what he was going to add. Then: "I am descended from that son, ladies and gentlemen. I am the great-grandson of Lord Byron."

He sank back into his shadows once more and let his luminous face seem again like a disembodied mask against the dark tapestry. He let us be dazzled by his announcement for some seconds. Then he spoke again.

"However, to return to our play. Summer is at hand, and the opening will take place at the Lake Jozgid Theater, in July, later to come to town with the autumn. All agreed? Ready to discuss contracts?" He looked around the circle, picking up our affirmative nods with his intensely understanding eyes. "Very good. Call again tomorrow. Mr Davidson, my assistant, will have the documents and all further information."

Jake Switz was first to leave, hurrying to telephone announcements to all the morning newspapers. Sigrid, rising, smiled at me with real warmth.

"So nice to see you again, Gib. Do not bother to leave with me—my suite is here in this hotel."

She bade Varduk good-night, nodded to the others and left quickly. I watched her departure with what must have been very apparent and foolish ruefulness on my face. It was the voice of Judge Pursuivant that recalled me to my surroundings.

"I've seen and admired your motion pictures, Mr Connatt," he said graciously. "Shall we go out together?

Perhaps I can persuade you to join me in another of my enthusiasms—late food and drink."

We made our adieux and departed. In the bar of the hotel we found a quiet table, where my companion scanned the liquor list narrowly and ordered samples of three Scotch whiskies. The waiter brought them. The judge sniffed each experimentally, and finally made his choice.

"Two of those, and soda—no ice," he directed. "Something to eat, Mr Connatt? No? Waiter, bring me some of the cold tongue with potato salad." Smiling, he turned back to me. "Good living is my greatest pursuit."

"Greater than scholarship?"

He nodded readily. "However, I don't mean that tonight's visit with Mr Varduk was not something to rouse any man's interest. It was full of good meat for any antiquary's appetite. By the way, were you surprised when he said that he was descended from Lord Byron?"

"Now that you mention it, I wasn't," I replied. "He's the most Byronic individual I have ever met."

"Right. Of course, the physical resemblances might be accidental, the manner a pose. But in any case, he's highly picturesque, and from what little I can learn about him, he's eminently capable as well. You feel lucky in being with him in this venture?"

I felt like confiding in this friendly, tawny man. "Judge Pursuivant," I said honestly, "any job is a godsend to me just now."

"Then let me congratulate you, and warn you."

"Warn me?"

"Here's your whisky," he said suddenly, and was silent while he himself mixed the spirit with the soda. Handing me a glass, he lifted the other in a silent toasting gesture. We drank, and then I repeated, "Warn me, you were saying, sir?"

"Yes." He tightened his wide, intelligent mouth under the feline mustache. "It's this play, *Ruthven*."

"What about it?"

His plate of tongue and salad was set before him at this juncture. He lifted a morsel on his fork and tasted it.

"This is very good, Mr Connatt. You should have tried some. Where were we? Oh, yes, about *Ruthven*. I was quite unreserved in my opinion, wasn't I?"

"So it seemed when you offered to stake your reputation on the manuscript being genuine."

"So I did," he agreed, cutting a slice of tongue into mouthfuls. "And I meant just that. What I saw of the play was Byronic in content, albeit creepy enough to touch even an occultist with a shiver. The handwriting, too, was undoubtedly Byron's. Yet I felt like staking my reputation on something else."

He paused and we each had a sip of whisky. His recourse to the liquor seemed to give him words for what he wished to say.

"It's a paradox, Mr Connatt, and I am by no means so fond of paradoxes as was my friend, the late Gilbert Chesterton; but, while Byron most certainly wrote *Ruthven*, he wrote it on paper that was watermarked less than ten years ago."

## 4. Into the Country

THE JUDGE WOULD not enlarge upon his perplexing statement, but he would and did play the most genial host I had ever known since the extravagant days of Hollywood. We had a number of drinks, and he complimented me on my steadiness of hand and head. When we parted I slept well in my little room that already seemed more cheerful.

Before noon the following day I returned to Varduk's hotel. Only Davidson was there, and he was far more crisp and to the point than he had been when his chief was present. I accepted the salary figure already set down on my contract form, signed my name, received a copy of the play and left.

After my frugal lunch—I was still living on the money Jake Switz had lent me—I walked to the library and searched out a copy of *Contemporary Americans*. Varduk's name I did not find, and wondered at that until the thought occurred that he, a descendant of Byron, was undoubtedly a British subject. Before giving up the volume I turned to the P's. This time my search bore fruit:

*PURSUIVANT, Keith Hilary; b. 1891, Richmond, Va., only son of Hilary Pursuivant (b. 1840, Pursuivant Landing, Ky.; Col. and Maj.-Gen., Va. Volunteer Infantry, 1861–65; attorney and journalist; d. 1891) and Anne Elizabeth (Keith) Pursuivant (b. 1864, Edinburgh; d. 1891).*

*Educ. Richmond pub. sch., Lawrenceville and Yale. A. B., male, 1908. Phi Beta Kappa, Skulls and Bones, football, forensics. LL. B., Columbia, 1911. Ph.D., Oxford, 1922. Admitted to Virginia bar, 1912. Elected 1914, Judge district court, Richmond. Resigned, 1917, to enter army. Major, Intelligence Div., U.S.A., 1917–19. D.S.C., Cong. Medal of Honor,* Legion d'Honneur *(Fr.). Ret. legal practice, 1919.*

*Author:* The Unknown That Terrifies, Cannibalism in America, Vampyricon, An Indictment of Logic, *etc.*

*Clubs: Lambs, Inkhorn, Gastronomics, Saber.*

*Hobbies: Food, antiquaries, demonology, fencing.*

*Protestant. Independent. Unmarried.*

*Address: Low Haven, RFD No. 1, Bucklin, W.Va.*

Thus the clean-picked skeleton of a life history; yet it was no hard task to restore some of its tissues, even coax it to life. Son of a Southern aristocrat who was a soldier while young and a lawyer and writer when mature, orphaned of his Scotch mother in the first year of his existence—had she died in giving him life?—Keith Pursuivant was born, it seemed, to distinction. To graduate from Yale in 1908 he must have been one of the youngest men in his class, if not the youngest; yet, at seventeen, he was an honor student, an athlete, member of an exclusive senior society and an orator. After that, law school, practise and election to the bench of his native community at the unheard-of age of twenty-three.

Then the World War, that sunderer of career-chains and remolder of men. The elder Pursuivant had been a colonel at twenty-one, a major-general before twenty-five; Keith, his son, deserting his brilliant legal career, was a major at twenty-six, but in the corps of brain-soldiers that matched wits with an empire. That he came off well in the contest was witnessed by his decorations, earnest of valor and resource.

"Ret. legal practise, 1919." So he did not remain in his early profession, even though it promised so well. What then? Turn back for the answer. "Ph.D., Oxford, 1922." His new love was scholarship. He became an author and philosopher. His interests included the trencher—I had seen him eat and drink with hearty pleasure—the study hall, the steel blade.

What else? "Protestant"—religion was his, but not narrowly so, or he would have been specific about a single sect. "Independent"—his political adventures had not bound him to any party. "Unmarried"—he had lived too busily for love? Or had he known it, and lost? I, too, was unmarried, and I was well past thirty. "Address: Low Haven"—a country home, apparently pretentious enough to bear a name like a manor house. Probably comfortable, withdrawn, full of sturdy furniture and good books, with a well-stocked pantry and cellar.

I felt that I had learned something about the man, and I was desirous of learning more.

On the evening mail I received a envelope addressed in Jake Switz's jagged handwriting. Inside were half a dozen five-dollar bills and a railway ticket, on the back of which was scribbled in pencil: "Take the 9 a.m. train at Grand Central. I'll meet you at the Dillard Falls Junction with a car. J. Switz."

I blessed the friendly heart of Sigrid's little serf, and went home to pack. The room clerk seemed surprised and relieved when I checked out in the morning, paying him in full. I reached the station early and got on the train, securing a good seat in the smoking-car. Many were boarding the car, but none looked at me, not even the big fellow who seated himself into position at my side. Six years before I had been mobbed as I stepped off the Twentieth Century Limited in this very station—a hundred women had rent away my coat and shirt in rags for souvenirs—

"Would you let me have a match, Mr Connatt?" asked a voice I had heard before. My companion's pale blue eyes were turned upon me, and he was tucking a trusty-looking pipe beneath his blond mustache.

"Judge Pursuivant!" I cried, with a pleasure I did not try to disguise. "You here—it's like one of those Grand Hotel plays."

"Not so much coincidence as that," he smiled, taking the match I had found. "You see, I am still intrigued by the paradox we discussed the other night; I mean, the riddle of how and when *Ruthven* was set down. It so happens that an old friend of mine has a cabin near the Lake Jozgid Theater, and I need a vacation." He drew a cloud of comforting smoke. "Judiciously I accepted his invitation to stay there. You and I shall be neighbors."

"Good ones, I hope," was my warm rejoinder, as I lighted a cigarette from the match he still held.

By the time our train clanked out of the subterranean caverns of Grand Central Station, we were deep in pleasant talk. At my earnest plea, the judge discussed Lord Byron.

"A point in favor of the genuineness of the document," he began, "is that Byron was exactly the sort of man who would conceive and write a play like *Ruthven*."

"With the semi-vampire plot?" I asked "I always thought that England of his time had just about forgotten about vampires."

"Yes, but Byron fetched them back into the national mind. Remember, he traveled in Greece as a young man, and the belief was strong in that part of the world. In a footnote to *The Giaour*—you'll find his footnotes in any standard edition of his works—he discusses vampires."

"Varduk spoke of those who fancied Byron to be the devil," I remembered.

"They may have had more than fancy to father the thought. Not that I do not admire Byron, for his talents and his achievements; but something of a diabolic curse hangs over him. Why," and Pursuivant warmed instantly to the discussion, "his very family history reads like a Gothic novel. His father was 'Mad Jack' Byron, the most sinful man of his generation; his grandfather was Admiral 'Foulweather Jack' Byron, about whose ill luck at sea is more than a suggestion of divine displeasure. The title descended to Byron from his great-uncle, the 'Wicked Lord,' who was a murderer, a libertine, a believer in evil spirits, and perhaps a practising diabolist. The family seat, Newstead Abbey, had been the retreat of medieval monks, and when those monks were driven from it they may have cursed their dispossessors. In any case, it had ghosts and a 'Devil's Wood.'"

"Byron was just the man for that heritage," I observed.

"He certainly was. As a child he carried pistols in his pockets and longed to kill someone. As a youth he chained a bear and a wolf at his door, drank wine from a human skull, and mocked religion by wearing a monk's habit to orgies. His unearthly beauty, his mocking tongue, fitted in with his wickedness and his limp to make him seem an incarnation of the hoofed Satan. As for his sins—" The judge broke off in contemplation of them.

"Nobody knows them all," I reminded.

"Perhaps he repented," mused my companion. "At least he seems to have forgotten his light loves and dark pleasures, turned to good works and the effort to liberate the Greeks from their Turkish oppressors. If he began life like an imp, he finished like a hero. I hope that he was sincere in that change, and not too late."

I expressed the desire to study Byron's life and writings, and Pursuivant opened his suitcase on the spot to lend me Drinkwater's and Maurois' biographies, a copy of the collected poems, and his own work, *A Defense of the Wickedest Poet.*

We ate lunch together in the dining-car, Pursuivant pondering his choice from the menu as once he must have pondered his decision in a case at court. When he made his selection, he devoured it with the same gusto I had observed before. "Food may be a necessity," quoth he between bites, "but the enjoyment of it is a blessing."

"You have other enjoyments," I reminded him. "Study, fencing—"

That brought on a discussion of the sword as weapon and symbol. My own swordsmanship is no better or worse than that of most actors, and Pursuivant was frank in condemning most stage fencers.

"I dislike to see a clumsy lout posturing through the duel scenes of *Cyrano de Bergerac* or *Hamlet*," he growled. "No offense, Mr Connatt. I confess that you, in your motion-picture interpretation of the rôle of Don Caesar de Bazan, achieved some very convincing cut-and-thrust. From what I saw, you have an understanding of the sport. Perhaps you and I can have a bout or so between your rehearsals."

I said that I would be honored, and then we had to collect our luggage and change trains. An hour or more passed on the new road before we reached our junction.

Jake Switz was there as he had promised to be, at the wheel of a sturdy repainted car. He greeted us with a triumphant story of his astuteness in helping Elmo Davidson to bargain for the vehicle, broke off to invite Pursuivant to ride with us to his cabin, and then launched into a hymn of praise for Sigrid's early rehearsals of her rôle.

"Nobody in America seems to think she ever made anything but movies," he pointed out. "At home in Sweden, though, she did deep stuff—Ibsen and them guys—and her only a kid then. You wait, Gib she'll knock from the theater public their eyes out with her class."

The road from the junction was deepset between hills, and darkly hedged with high trees. "This makes the theater hard to get at," Jake pointed out as he drove. "People will have to make a regular pilgrimage to see Holgar play in *Ruthven*, and they'll like it twice as well because of all the trouble they took."

Pursuivant left us at the head of a little path, with a small structure of logs showing through the trees beyond. We waved good-bye to him, and Jake trod on his starter once more. As we rolled away, he glanced sidewise at me. His crossed eyes behind their thick lenses had grown suddenly serious.

"Only one night Sigrid and I been here, Gib," he said,

somewhat darkly, "and I don't like it."

"Don't tell me you're haunted," I rallied him, laughing. "That's good press-agentry for a horror play, but I'm one of the actors. I won't be buying tickets."

He did not laugh in return.

"I won't say haunted, Gib. That means ordinary ghosts, and whatever is here at the theater is worse than ghosts. Listen what happened."

## 5. Jake's Story

SIGRID, with Jake in attendance as usual, had left New York on the morning after Varduk's reading of *Ruthven*. They had driven in the car Jake had helped Davidson to buy, and thus they avoided the usual throngs of Sigrid's souvenir-demanding public, which would have complicated their departure by train. At Dillard Falls Junction, Varduk himself awaited them, having come up on a night train. Jake took time to mail me a ticket and money, then they drove the long, shadowy way to the theater.

Lake Jozgid, as most rural New Yorkers know, is set rather low among wooded hills and bluffs. The unevenness of the country and the poverty of the soil have discouraged cultivation, so that farms and villages are few. As the party drove, Varduk suggested an advantage in this remoteness, which suggestion Jake later passed on to Judge Pursuivant and me; where a less brilliant or more accessible star might be ignored in such far quarters, Sigrid would find Lake Jozgid to her advantage. The world would beat a path to her box office, and treasure a glimpse of her the more because that glimpse had been difficult of attainment.

The theater building itself had been a great two-story lodge, made of heavy logs and hand-hewn planks. Some sporting-club, now defunct, had owned it, then abandoned it when fish grew scarce in the lake. Varduk had leased it cheaply, knocked out all partitions on the ground floor, and set up a stage, a lobby and pew-like benches. The upper rooms would serve as lodgings for himself and his associate

Davidson, while small outbuildings had been fitted up to accommodate the rest of us.

Around this group of structures clung a thick mass of timber. Sigrid, who had spent her girlhood among Sweden's forests, pointed out that it was mostly virgin and inquired why a lumber company had never cut logs here. Varduk replied that the property had been private for many years, then changed the subject by the welcome suggestion that they have dinner. They had brought a supply of provisions, and Jake, who is something of a cook in addition to his many other professions, prepared a meal. Both Sigrid and Jake ate heartily, but Varduk seemed only to take occasional morsels for politeness' sake.

In the evening, a full moon began to rise across the lake. Sitting together in Varduk's upstairs parlor, the three saw the great soaring disk of pale light, and Sigrid cried out joyfully that she wanted to go out and see better.

"Take a lantern if you go out at night," counseled Varduk over his cigar.

"A lantern?" Sigrid repeated. "But that would spoil the effect of the moonlight."

Her new director blew a smooth ring of smoke and stared into its center, as though a message lay there. Then he turned his brilliant eyes to her. "If you are wise, you will do as I say," he made answer.

Men like Varduk are masterful and used to being obeyed. Sometimes they lose sight of the fact that women like Sigrid are not used to being given arbitrary commands without explanation. She fell silent and a little frigid for half an hour—often I had seen her just as Jake was describing her. Then she rose and excused herself, saying that she was tired from the morning's long drive and would go to bed early. Varduk rose and courteously bowed her to the stairs. Since her sleeping-quarters, a cleverly rebuilt woodshed, were hardly a dozen steps from the rear of the lodge building itself, neither man thought it necessary to accompany her.

Left alone, Varduk and Jake carried on an idle conversation, mostly about publicity plans. Jake, who in the show business had done successfully almost everything but acting, found in his companion a rather penetrating and accurate commentator on this particular aspect of production. Indeed, Varduk debated him into a new attitude—one of restraint and dignity instead of novel and insistent extravagance.

"You're right," Jake announced at length. "I'm going to get the releases that go out in tomorrow's mail. I'll cut out every 'stupendous' and 'colossal' I wrote into them. Good night, Mr Varduk."

He, too, trotted downstairs and left the main building for his own sleeping-room, which was the loft of an old boat-house. As he turned toward the water, he saw a figure walking slowly and dreamily along its edge—Sigrid, her hands tucked into the pockets of the light belted coat she had donned against possible night chills, her head flung back as though she sought all of the moonlight upon her rapt face.

Although she had wandered out to the brink of the sandy beach and so stood in the open brightness, clumps of bushes and young trees grew out almost to the lake. One tufty belt of scrub willow extended from the denser timber to a point within a dozen feet of Sigrid. It made a screen of gloom between Jake's viewpoint and the moon's spray of silver. Yet, he could see, light was apparently soaking through its close-set leaves, a streak of soft radiance that was so filtered as to look murky, greenish, like the glow from rotting salmon.

Even as Jake noticed this flecky glimmer, it seemed to open up like a fan or a parasol. Instead of a streak, it was a blot. This extended further, lazily but noticeably. Jake scowled. And this moved lakeward, without leaving any of itself at the starting-point.

With its greatening came somewhat of a brightening, which revealed that the phenomenon had some sort of shape—or perhaps the shape was defining itself as it moved. The blot's edges grew unevenly, receding in places to swell in others. Jake saw that these swellings sprouted into pseudopodal extensions (to quote him, they "jellied out"), that stirred as though groping or reaching. And at the top was a squat roundness, like an undeveloped cranium. The lower rays of light became limbs, striking at the ground as though to walk. The thing counterfeited life, motion—and attention. It was moving toward the water, and toward Sigrid.

Jake did not know what it was, and he says that he was suddenly and extremely frightened. Yet he does not seem to have acted like one who is stricken with fear. What he did, and did at once, was to bawl out a warning to Sigrid, then charge at the mystery.

It had stolen into the moonlight, and Jake encountered it there. As he charged, he tried to make out the details; but what little it had had of details in the darkness now went misty, as its glow was conquered in the brighter flood of moonglow. Yet it was there, and moving toward Sigrid. She had turned from looking across the water, and now shrank back with a tremulous cry, stumbling and recovering herself ankle-deep in the shallows.

Jake, meanwhile, had flung himself between her and what was coming out of the thicket. He did not wait or even set himself for conflict, but changed direction to face and spring upon the threatening presence. Though past his first youth, he fancied himself as in fairly tough condition, and more than once he had won such impromptu fist-fights as spring up among the too-temperamental folk of the theater. He attacked as he would against a human adversary, sinking his head between his shoulders and flinging his fists in quick succession.

He got home solidly, against something tangible but sickeningly loose beneath its smooth skin or rind. It was like buffeting a sack half full of meal. Though the substance sank in beneath his knuckles, there was no reeling or retreat. A squashy return slap almost enveloped his face, and his spectacles came away as though by suction. At the same time he felt a cable-like embrace, such as he had imagined a python might exert. He smelled putrescence, was close to being sick, and heard, just behind him, the louder screaming of Sigrid.

The fresh knowledge of her danger and terror made him strong again. One arm was free, and he battered gamely with his fist. He found his mark, twice and maybe three times. Then his sickness became faintness when he realized that his knuckles had become slimy wet.

A new force dragged at him behind. Another enemy . . . then a terrible voice of command, the voice of Varduk:

"Let go at once!"

The grasp and the filthy bulk fell away from Jake. He felt his knees waver like shreds of paper. His eyes, blurred without their thick spectacles, could barely discern, not one, but several lumpy forms drawing back. And near him stood Varduk, his facial phosphorescence out-gleaming the rotten light of the creatures, his form drawn up sternly in a posture of command.

"Get out!" cried Varduk again. "By what power do you come for your victim now?"

The uncouth shapes shrank out of sight. Jake could not be sure whether they found shelter behind bushes and trees or not; perhaps they actually faded into invisibility. Sigrid had come close, stepping gingerly in her wet shoes, and stooped to retrieve Jake's fallen glasses.

"We owe you our lives," she said to Varduk. "What were those—"

"Never mind," he cut her off. "They will threaten you no more tonight. Go to your beds, and be more careful in the future."

This was the story that Jake told me as we drove the final miles to the Lake Jozgid Theater.

He admitted that it had all been a desperate and indistinct scramble to him, and that explanation he had offered next morning when Varduk laughed and accused him of dreaming.

"But maybe it wasn't a dream," Jake said as he finished. "Even if it was, I don't want any more dreams like it."

## **6.** The Theater in the Forest

JAKE'S NARRATIVE did not give me cheerful expectations of the Lake Jozgid Theater. It was just as well, for my first glimpse of the place convinced me that it was the exact setting for a play of morbid unreality.

The road beyond Pursuivant's cabin was narrow but not too bad. Jake, driving nimbly over its sanded surface, told me that we might thank the public works program for its good condition. In one or two places, as I think I have said already, the way was cut deeply between knolls or bluffs, and here it was gloomy and almost sunless. Too, the woods thickened to right and left, with taller and taller ranks of trees at the roadside. Springtime's leafage made the trees seem vigorous, but not exactly cheerful; I fancied that they were endowed with intelligence and the power of motion, and that they awaited only our passing before they moved out to block the open way behind us.

From this sand-surfaced road there branched eventually a second, and even narrower and darker, that dipped down a thickly timbered slope. We took a rather difficult curve at the bottom and came out almost upon the shore of the lake, with the old lodge and its outbuildings in plain view.

These structures were in the best of repair, but appeared intensely dark and weathered, as though the afternoon sky shed a brownish light upon them. The lodge that was now the theater stood clear in the center of the sizable cleared space, although lush-looking clumps and belts of evergreen scrub grew almost against the sheds and the boathouse. I was enough of an observer to be aware that the deep roofs were of stout ax-cut shingles, and that the heavy timbers of the walls were undoubtedly seasoned for an age. The windows were large but deep-set in their sturdy frames. Those who call windows the eyes of a house would have thought that these eyes were large enough, but well able to conceal the secrets and feelings within.

As we emerged from the car, I felt rather than saw an onlooker. Varduk stood in the wide front door of the lodge building. Neither Jake nor I could agree later whether he had opened the door himself and appeared, whether he had stepped into view with the door already open, or whether he had been standing there all the time. His slender, elegant figure was dressed in dark jacket and trousers, with a black silk scarf draped Ascot fashion at his throat, just as he had worn at his hotel in New York. When he saw that we were aware of him, he lifted a white hand in greeting and descended two steps to meet us coming toward him. I offered him my hand, and he gave it a quick, sharp pressure, as though he were investigating the texture of my flesh and bone.

"I am glad to see you here so soon, Mr Connatt," he said cordially. "Now we need wait only for Miss Vining, who should arrive before dark. Miss Holgar came yesterday, and Davidson this morning."

"There will be only the six of us, then?" I asked.

He nodded his chestnut curls. "A caretaker will come here each day, to prepare lunch and dinner and to clean. He lives several miles up the road, and will spend his nights at home. But we of the play itself will be in residence, and we alone—a condition fully in character, I feel, with the attitude of mystery and reserve we have assumed toward our interesting production. For breakfasts, Davidson will be able to look after us."

"Huh!" grunted Jake. "That Davidson can act, manage, stage-hand, cook—he does everything."

"Almost everything," said Varduk dryly, and his eyes turned long and expressionlessly upon my friend, who immediately subsided. In the daylight I saw that Varduk's eyes were hazel; on the night I had met him at his hotel they had seemed thunder-dark.

"You, too, are considered useful at many things around the theater, Switz," Varduk continued. "I took that into consideration when Miss Holgar, though she left her maid behind, insisted on including you in the company. I daresay, we can depend on you to help Davidson with the staging and so on."

"Oh, yes, sure," Jake made reply. "Certainly. Miss Holgar, she wants me to do that."

"Very good." Varduk turned on the heel of his well-polished boot. "Suppose," he added over his shoulder, "that you take Mr Connatt up to the loft of the boathouse. Mr Connatt, do you mind putting up with Switz?"

"Not in the least," I assured him readily, and took up two of my bags. Jake had already lifted the third and heaviest.

We nodded to Varduk and skirted the side of the lodge, walked down to the water, then entered the boathouse. It was a simple affair of well-chinked logs. Two leaky-looking canoes still occupied the lower part of it, but we picked our way past them and ascended a sturdy staircase to a loft under the peaked roof. This had been finished with wall-board and boasted a window at each end. Two cots, a rug, a wash-stand, a table and several chairs made it an acceptable sleeping-apartment.

"This theater is half-way to the never-never land," I commented as I began to unpack.

"I should live so—I never saw the like of it," Jake said earnestly. "How are people going to find their way here? Yesterday I began to talk about signs by the side of the road. Right off at once, Varduk said no. I begged like a poor relation left out of his uncle's will. Finally he said yes—but the signs must be small and dignified, and put up only a day before the show begins."

I wanted to ask a question about his adventure of the previous night, but Jake shook his head in refusal to discuss it. "Not here," he said. "Gib, who knows who may be listening?" He dropped his voice. "Or even *what* might be listening?"

I lapsed into silence and got out old canvas sneakers, flannel slacks and a Norfolk jacket, and changed into them. Dressed in this easy manner, I left the boathouse and stood beside the lake. At once a voice hailed me. Sigrid was walking along the water's edge, smiling in apparent delight.

We came face to face; I bent to kiss her hand. As once before, it fluttered under my lips, but when I straightened again I saw nothing of distaste or unsteadiness in her expression.

"Gib, how nice that you're here!" she cried. "Do you like the place?"

"I haven't seen very much of it yet," I told her. "I want to see the inside of the theater."

She took her hand away from me and thrust it into the pocket of the old white sweater she wore. "I think that I love it here," she said, with an air of gay confession. "Not all of the hermit stories about me are lies. I could grow truly fat—God save the mark!—on quiet and serenity."

"Varduk pleases you, too?" I suggested.

"He has more understanding than any other theatrical executive in my experience," she responded emphatically. "He fills me with the wish to work. I'm like a starry-eyed beginner again. What would you say if I told you that I was sweeping my own room and making my own bed?"

"I would say that you were the most charming housemaid in the world."

Her laughter was full of delight. "You sound as if you mean it, Gib. It is nice to know you as a friend again."

It seemed to me that she emphasized the word "friend" a trifle, as though to warn me that our relationship would nevermore become closer than that. Changing the subject, I asked her if she had swum in the lake; she had, and found it cold. How about seeing the theater? Together we walked toward the lodge and entered at a side door.

The auditorium was as Jake had described it to me, and I saw that Varduk liked a dark tone. He had stained the paneling, the benches, and the beams a dark brown. Brown, too, was the heavy curtain that hid the stage.

"We'll be there tonight," said Sigrid, nodding stageward. "Varduk has called the first rehearsal for immediately after dinner. We eat together, of course, in a big room upstairs."

"May I sit next to you when we eat?" I asked, and she laughed yet again. She was being as cheerful as I had ever known her to be.

"You sound like the student-hero in a light opera, Gib. I don't know about the seating-arrangement. At lunch I was at the head of the table, and Varduk at the foot. Jake and Mr Davidson were at either side of me."

"I shall certainly arrive before one or the other of them," I vowed solemnly.

Varduk had drifted in as we talked, and he chuckled at my announcement.

"A gallant note, Mr Connatt, and one that I hope you can capture as pleasantly for the romantic passages of our *Ruthven*. By the bye, our first rehearsal will take place this evening."

"So Miss Holgar has told me," I nodded. "I have studied the play rather prayerfully since Davidson gave me a copy. I hope I'm not a disappointment in it."

"I am sure that you will not be," he said kindly. "I did not choose disappointing people for my cast."

Davidson entered from the front, to say that Martha Vining had arrived. Varduk moved away, stiff in his walk as I had observed before. Sigrid and I went through the side door and back into the open.

That evening I kept my promise to find a place by Sigrid at the table. Davidson, entering just behind me, looked a trifle chagrined but sat at my other side, with Martha Vining opposite. The dinner was good, with roast mutton, salad and apple tart. I thought of Judge Pursuivant's healthy appetite as I ate.

After the coffee, Varduk nodded to the old man who served as caretaker, cook and waiter, as in dismissal. Then the producer's hazel eyes turned to Sigrid, who took her cue and rose. We did likewise.

"Shall we go down to the stage?" Varduk said to us. "It's time for our first effort with *Ruthven*."

## 7. Rehearsal

WE WENT DOWN a back stairway that brought us to the empty stage. A light was already burning, and I remember well that my first impression was of the stage's narrowness and considerable depth. Its back was of plaster over the outer timbers, but at either side partitions of paneling had been erected to enclose the cell-like dressing-rooms. One of the doors bore a star of white paint, evidently for Sigrid. Against the back wall leaned several open frames of wood, with rolls of canvas lying ready to be tacked on and painted into scenery.

Varduk had led the way down the stairs, and at the foot he paused to call upward to Davidson, who remained at the rear of the procession. "Fetch some chairs," he ordered, and the tall subordinate paused to gather them. He carried down six at once, his long strong arms threaded through their open backs. Varduk showed him with silent gestures where to arrange them, and himself led Sigrid to the midmost of them, upstage center.

"Sit down, all," he said to the rest of us. "Curtain, Davidson." He waited while the heavy pall rolled ponderously upward against the top of the arch. "Have you got your scripts, ladies and gentlemen?"

We all had, but his hands were empty. I started to offer him my copy, but he waved it away with thanks. "I know the thing by heart," he informed me, though with no air of boasting. Remaining still upon his feet, he looked around our seated array, capturing every eye and attention.

"The first part of *Ruthven* is, as we know already, in iambic pentameter—the 'heroic verse' that was customary and even expected in dramas of Byron's day. However, he employs here his usual trick of breaking the earlier lines up into short, situation-building speeches. No long and involved declamations, as in so many creaky tragedies of his fellows. He wrote the same sort of opening scenes for his plays the world has already seen performed—*Werner*, *The Two Foscari*, *Marino Faliero* and *The Deformed Transformed*."

Martha Vining cleared her throat. "Doesn't *Manfred* begin with a long, measured soliloquy by the central character?"

"It does," nodded Varduk. "I am gratified, Miss Vining, to observe that you have been studying something of Byron's work." He paused, and she bridled in satisfaction. "However," he continued, somewhat maliciously, "you would be well advised to study farther, and learn that Byron stated definitely that *Manfred* was not written for the theater. But, returning to *Ruthven*, with which work we are primarily concerned, the short, lively exchanges at the beginning are Aubrey's and Malvina's." He quoted from memory,

"'Scene, Malvina's garden. Time, late afternoon—Aubrey, sitting at Malvina's feet, tells his adventures.' Very good, Mr Connatt, take your place at Miss Holgar's feet."

I did so, and she smiled in comradely fashion while waiting for the others to drag their chairs away. Glancing at our scripts, we began:

"I'm no Othello, darling."
"Yet I am
Your Desdemona. Tell me of your travels."
"Of Anthropophagi?"
"'And men whose heads do grow beneath—'"
"I saw no such,
Not in all wildest Greece and Macedon."
"Saw you no spirits?"
"None, Malvina—none."
"Not even the vampire, he who quaffs the blood
Of life, that he may live in death?"
"Not I.
How do you know that tale?"
"I've read
In old romances—"

"Capital, capital," interrupted Varduk pleasantly. "I know that the play is written in a specific meter, yet you need not speak as though it were. If anything, make the lines less rhythmic and more matter-of-fact. Remember, you are young lovers, half bantering as you woo. Let your audience relax with you. Let it feel the verse form without actually hearing."

We continued, to the line where Aubrey tells of his travel-acquaintance Ruthven. Here the speech became definite verse:

"He is a friend who charms, but does not cheer,
One who commands, but comforts not, the world.
I do not doubt but women find him handsome,
Yet hearts must be uneasy at his glance."

Malvina asks:

"His glance? Is it so piercing when it strikes?"

And Aubrey:

"It does not pierce—indeed, it rather weighs,
Like lead, upon the face where it is fixed."

Followed the story, which I have outlined elsewhere, of the encounter with bandits and Ruthven's apparent sacrifice of himself to cover Aubrey's retreat. Then Martha Vining, as the maid Bridget, spoke to announce Ruthven's coming, and upon the heels of her speech Varduk moved stiffly toward us.

"Aubrey!" he cried, in a rich, ringing tone such as fills theaters, and not at all like his ordinary gentle voice. I made my due response:

"Have you lived, Ruthven? But the horde
Of outlaw warriors compassed you and struck—"

In the rôle of Ruthven, Varduk's interruption was as natural and decisive as when, in ordinary conversation, he neatly cut another's speech in two with a remark of his own. I have already quoted this reply of Ruthven's:

"I faced them, and who seeks my face seeks death."

He was speaking the line, of course, without script, and his eyes held mine. Despite myself, I almost staggered under the weight of his glance. It was like that which Aubrey actually credits to Ruthven—lead-heavy instead of piercing, difficult to support.

The rehearsal went on, with Ruthven's seduction of Bridget and his court to the nervous but fascinated Malvina. In the end, as I have synopsized earlier, came his secret and miraculous revival from seeming death. Varduk delivered the final rather terrifying speech magnificently, and then abruptly doffed his Ruthven manner to smile congratulations all around.

"It's more than a month to our opening date in July," he said, "and yet I would be willing to present this play as a finished play, no later than this day week. Miss Holgar, may I voice my special appreciation? Mr Connatt, your confessed fear of your own inadequacy is proven groundless. Bravo, Miss Vining—and you, Davidson." His final tag of praise to his subordinate seemed almost grudging. "Now for the second act of the thing. No verse this time, my friends. Finish the rehearsal as well as you have begun."

"Wait," I said. "How about properties? I simulated the club-stroke in the first act, but this time I need a sword. For the sake of feeling the action better—"

"Yes, of course," granted Varduk. "There's one in the corner dressing-room." He pointed. "Go fetch it, Davidson."

Davidson complied. The sword was a cross-hilt affair, old but keen and bright.

"This isn't a prop at all," I half objected. "It's the real thing. Won't it be dangerous?"

"Oh, I think we can risk it," Varduk replied carelessly. "Let's get on with the rehearsal. A hundred years later, in the same garden, Swithin and Mary, descendants of Aubrey and Malvina, on stage."

We continued. The opening, again with Sigrid and myself a-wooing, was lively and even brilliant. Martha Vining, in her rôle of the centenarian Bridget, skilfully cracked her voice and infused a witch-like quality into her telling of the Aubrey-Ruthven tale. Again the entrance of Ruthven, his suavity and apparent friendliness, his manner changing as he is revealed as the resurrected fiend of another age; finally the clash with me, as Swithin.

I spoke my line—"My ancestor killed you once, Ruthven. I can do the same today." Then I poked at him with the sword.

Varduk smiled and interjected, "Rather a languid thrust, that, Mr Connatt. Do you think it will seem serious from the viewpoint of our audience?"

"I'm sorry," I said. "I was afraid I might hurt you."

"Fear nothing, Mr Connatt. Take the speech and the swordplay again."

I did so, but he laughed almost in scorn. "You still put no life into the thrust." He spread his hands, as if to offer himself as a target. "Once more. Don't be an old woman."

Losing a bit of my temper, I made a genuine lunge. My right foot glided forward and my weight shifted to follow my point. But in mid-motion I knew myself for a danger-dealing fool, tried to recover, failed, and slipped.

I almost fell at full length—would have fallen had Varduk not been standing in my way. My sword-point, completely out of control, drove at the center of his breast—I felt it tear through cloth, through flesh—

A moment later his slender hands had caught my floundering body and pushed it back upon its feet. My sword, wedged in something, snatched its hilt from my hand. Sick and horrified, I saw it protruding from the midst of Varduk's body. Behind me I heard the choked squeal of Martha Vining, and an oath from Jake Switz. I swayed, my vision seemed to swim in smoky liquid, and I suppose I was well on the way to an unmasculine swoon. But a light chuckle, in Varduk's familiar manner, saved me from collapsing.

"That is exactly the way to do it, Mr Connatt," he said in a tone of well-bred applause.

He drew the steel free—I think that he had to wrench rather hard—and then stepped forward to extend the hilt.

"There's blood on it," I mumbled sickly.

"Oh, that?" he glanced down at the blade. "Just a deceit for the sake of realism. You arranged the false-blood device splendidly, Davidson." He pushed the hilt into my slack grasp. "Look, the imitation gore is already evaporating."

So it was, like dew on a hot stone. Already the blade shone bright and clean.

"Very good," said Varduk. "Climax now. Miss Holgar, I think it is your line."

She, too, had been horrified by the seeming catastrophe, but she came gamely up to the bit where Mary pleads for Swithin's life, offering herself as the price. Half a dozen exchanges between Ruthven and Mary, thus:

"You give yourself up, then?"

"I do."

"You renounce your former manners, hopes and wishes?"

"I do."

"You will swear so, upon the book yonder?" (Here Ruthven points to a Bible, open on the garden-seat.)

"I do." (Mary touches the Bible.)

"You submit to the powers I represent?"

"I know only the power to which I pray. 'Our Father, which wert in heaven—'"

Sigrid, as I say, had done well up to now, but here she broke off. "It isn't correct there," she pointed out. "The prayer should read, 'art in heaven'. Perhaps the script was copied wrongly."

"No," said Martha Vining, "It's 'wert in heaven' on mine."

"And on mine," I added.

Varduk had frowned a moment, as if perplexed, but he spoke decisively. "As a matter of fact, it's in the original. Byron undoubtedly meant it to be so, to show Mary's agitation."

Sigrid had been reading ahead. "Farther down in the same prayer, it says almost the same thing—'Thy will be done on earth as it was in heaven.' It should be, 'is in heaven.'"

I had found the same deviation in my own copy. "Byron hardly meant Mary's agitation to extend so far," I argued.

"Since when, Mr Connatt," inquired Varduk silkily, "did you become an authority on what Byron meant, here or elsewhere in his writings? You're being, not only a critic, but a clairvoyant."

I felt my cheeks glowing, and I met his heavy, mocking gaze as levelly as I could. "I don't like sacrilegious mistakes," I said, "and I don't like being snubbed, sir."

Davidson stepped to Varduk's side. "You can't talk to him like that, Connatt," he warned me.

Davidson was a good four inches taller than I, and more muscular, but at the moment I welcomed the idea of fighting him. I moved a step forward.

"Mr Davidson," I said to him, "I don't welcome dictation from you, not on anything I choose to do or say."

Sigrid cried out in protest, and Varduk lifted up a hand. He smiled, too, in a dazzling manner.

"I think," he said in sudden good humor, "that we are all tired and shaken. Perhaps it's due to the unintentional realism of that incident with the sword—I saw several faces grow pale. Suppose we say that the rehearsals won't include so dangerous-looking an attack hereafter; we'll save the trick for the public performance itself. And we'll stop work now; in any case, it's supposed to be unlucky to speak the last line of a play in rehearsal. Shall we all go and get some rest?"

He turned to Sigrid and offered his arm. She took it, and they walked side by side out of the stage door and away. Martha Vining followed at their heels, while Davidson lingered to turn out the lights. Jake and I left together for our own boathouse loft. The moon was up, and I jumped when leaves shimmered in its light—I remembered Jake's story about the amorphous lurkers in the thickets.

But nothing challenged us, and we went silently to bed, though I, at least, lay wakeful for hours.

## 8. Pursuivant Again

WHEN FINALLY I SLEPT, it was to dream in strange, unrelated flashes. The clearest impression of all was that Sigrid and Judge Pursuivant came to lead me deep into the dark woods beyond the lodge. They seemed to know their way through pathless thickets, and finally beckoned me to follow into a deep, shadowed cleft between banks of earth. We descended for miles, I judged in my dream, until we came to a bare, hard floor at the bottom. Here was a wide, round hatchway of metal, like a very large sewer lid. Bidding me watch, Sigrid and the judge bent and tugged the lid up and away. Gazing down the exposed shaft, it was as if I saw the heavens beneath my feet—the fathomlessness of the night sky, like velvet all sprinkled with crumbs of star-fire. I did not know whether to be joyful or to fear; then I had awakened, and it was bright morning.

The air was warmer than it had been the day before, and I donned bathing-trunks and went downstairs, treading softly to let Jake snore blissfully on. Almost at the door of the boathouse I came face to face with Davidson, who smiled disarmingly and held out his hand. He urged me to forget the brief hostility that had come over us at rehearsal; he was quite unforced and cheerful about it, yet I surmised that Varduk had bade him make peace with me. However, I agree that we had both been tired and upset, and we shook hands cordially.

Then I turned toward the water, and saw Sigrid lazily crawling out into the deep stretches with long, smooth strokes. I called her name, ran in waist-deep, and swam as swiftly as I could, soon catching up. She smiled in welcome and turned on her side to say good-morning. In her brief bathing-suit she did not look so gaunt and fragile. Her body was no more than healthily slim, and quite firm and strong-looking.

As we swam easily, I was impelled to speak of my dream, and she smiled again.

"I think that was rather beautiful, I mean about the heavens below your feet," she said. "Symbolism might have something to say about it. In a way the vision was prophetic—Judge Pursuivant has sent word that he will call on us."

"Perhaps the rest was prophetic, too," I ventured boldly. "You and I together, Sigrid—and heaven at our feet—"

"I've been in long enough," she announced suddenly, "and breakfast must be ready. Come on, Gib, race me back to shore."

She was off like a trout, and I churned after her. We finished neck and neck, separated and went away to dress. At breakfast, which Davidson prepared simply but well of porridge, toast and eggs, I did not get to sit next to Sigrid; Davidson and Jake had found places at her left and right hands. I paid what attentions I could devise to Martha Vining, but if Sigrid was piqued by my courtliness in another direction, she gave no sign.

The meal over, I returned to my room, secured my copy of *Ruthven* and carried it outdoors to study. I chose a sun-drenched spot near the lodge, set my back to a tree, and leafed through the play, underlining difficult passages here and there. I remembered Varduk's announcement that we would never speak the play's last line in rehearsal, lest bad luck fall. He was superstitious, for all his apparent wisdom and culture; yet, according to the books Judge Pursuivant had lent me, so was Lord Byron, from whom Varduk claimed descent. What was the ill-omened last line, by the way?

I turned to the last page of the script.

The final line, as typewritten by Davidson, contained only a few words. My eyes found it:

"RUTHVEN (placing his hand on Mary's head):"

And no more than that. There was place for a speech after the stage direction, apparently the monster's involuntary cry for blessing upon the brave girl, but Davidson had not set down such a speech.

Amazed and in some unaccountable way uneasy, I walked around the corner of the lodge to where Martha Vining, seated on the door-step, also studied her lines. Before I had finished my first question, she nodded violently.

"It's the same way on my script," she informed me. "You mean, the last speech missing. I noticed last night, and mentioned it before breakfast to Miss Holgar. She has no last line, either."

A soft chuckle drifted down upon us. Varduk had come to the open door.

"Davidson must have made a careless omission," he said. "Of course, there is only one typescript of the play, with carbon copies. Well, if the last line is missing, isn't it a definite sign that we should not speak it in rehearsal?"

He rested his heavy gaze upon me, then upon Martha Vining, smiled to conclude the discussion, and drew back into the hallway and beyond our sight.

Perhaps I may be excused for not feeling completely at rest on the subject.

Judge Pursuivant arrived for lunch, dressed comfortably in flannels and a tweed jacket, and his performance at table was in healthy contrast to Varduk, who, as usual, ate hardly anything. In the early afternoon I induced the judge to come for a stroll up the slope and along the main road. As soon as we were well away from the lodge, I told him of Jake's adventure, the outcome of the sword-accident at rehearsal, and the air of mystery that deepened around the omitted final speech of the play.

"Perhaps I'm being nervous and illusion-ridden," I began to apologize in conclusion, but he shook his great head.

"You're being nothing of the sort, Connatt. Apparently my semi-psychic intuition was good as gold. I did perfectly right in following this drama and its company out here into the wilderness."

"You came deliberately?" I asked, and he nodded.

"My friend's cabin in the neighborhood was a stroke of good luck, and I more than half courted the invitation to occupy it. I'll be frank, Connatt, and say that from the outset I have felt a definite and occult challenge from Varduk and his activities."

He chopped at a weed with his big malacca stick, pondered a moment, then continued.

"Your Mr Varduk is a mysterious fellow. I need not enlarge on that, though I might remind you of the excellent reason for his strange character and behavior."

"Byron's blood?"

"Exactly. And Byron's curse."

I stopped in mid-stride and turned to face the judge. He smiled somewhat apologetically.

"I know, Connatt," he said, "that modern men and women think such things impossible. They think it equally impossible that anyone of good education and normal mind should take occultism seriously. But I disprove the latter impossibility, at least—I hold degrees from three world-famous universities, and my behavior, at least, shows that I am neither morbid nor shallow."

"Certainly not," I assented, thinking of his hearty appetite, his record of achievement in many fields, his manifest kindness and sincerity.

"Then consent to hear my evidence out." He resumed his

walk, and I fell into step with him. "It's only circumstantial evidence, I fear, and as such must not be entirely conclusive. Yet here it is:

"Byron was the ideal target for a curse, not only personally but racially. His forebears occupied themselves with revolution, dueling, sacrilege and lesser sins—they were the sort who attract and merit disaster. As for his immediate parents, it would be difficult to choose a more depraved father than Captain 'Mad Jack' Byron, or a more unnatural mother than Catherine Gordon of Gight. Brimstone was bred into the child's very soul by those two. Follow his career, and what is there? Pride, violence, orgy, disgrace. Over his married life hangs a shocking cloud, an unmentionable accusation—rightly or not we cannot say. As for his associates, they withered at his touch. His children, lawful and natural, died untimely and unhappy. His friends found ruin or death. Even Doctor Polidori, plagiarist of the *Ruthven* story, committed suicide. Byron himself, when barely past his first youth, perished alone and far from home and friends. Today his bright fame is blurred and tarnished by a wealth of legend that can be called nothing less than diabolic."

"Yet he wasn't all unlucky," I sought to remind my companion. "His beauty and brilliance, his success as a poet—"

"All part of the curse. When could he be thankful for a face that drew the love of Lady Caroline Lamb and precipitated one of London's most fearful scandals? As for his poetry, did it not mark him for envy, spite and, eventually, a concerted attack? I daresay Byron would have been happier as a plain-faced mechanic or grocer."

I felt inclined to agree, and said as much. "If a curse exists," I added, "would it affect Varduk as a descendant of Byron?"

"I think that it would, and that his recent actions prove at once the existence of a curse and the truth of his claim to descent. A shadow lies on that man, Connatt."

"The rest of the similarity holds," I responded. "The charm and the genius. I have wondered why Miss Holgar agrees to this play. It is archaic, in some degree melodramatic, and her part is by no means dominant. Yet she seems delighted with the rôle and the production in general."

"I have considered the same apparent lapse of her judgment," said Pursuivant, "and came to the conclusion that you are about to suggest—that Varduk has gained some sort of influence over Miss Holgar."

"Perhaps, then, you feel that such an influence would be dangerous to her and to others?"

"Exactly."

"What to do, then?"

"Do nothing, gentlemen," said someone directly behind us.

We both whirled in sudden surprise. It was Elmo Davidson.

## **9.** Davidson Gives a Warning

I SCOWLED AT Davidson in surprised protest at his intrusion. Judge Pursuivant did not scowl, but I saw him lift his walking-stick with his left hand, place his right upon the curved handle, and gave it a little twist and jerk, as though preparing to draw a cork from a bottle. Davidson grinned placatingly.

"Please, gentlemen! I didn't mean to eavesdrop, or to do anything else sneaking. It was only that I went for a walk, too, saw the pair of you ahead, and hurried to catch up. I couldn't help but hear the final words you were saying, and I couldn't help but warn you."

We relaxed, but Judge Pursuivant repeated "Warn?" in a tone deeply frigid.

"May I amplify? First of all, Varduk certainly does not intend to harm either of you. Second, he isn't the sort of man to be crossed in anything."

"I suppose not," I rejoined, trying to be casual. "You must be pretty sure, Davidson, of his capabilities and character."

He nodded. "We've been together since college."

Pursuivant leaned on his stick and produced his well-seasoned briar pipe. "It's comforting to hear you say that. I mean, that Mr Varduk was once a college boy. I was beginning to wonder if he wasn't thousands of years old."

Davidson shook his head slowly. "See here, why don't we sit down on the bank and talk? Maybe I'll tell you a story."

"Very good," agreed Pursuivant, and sat down. I did likewise, and we both gazed expectantly at Davidson. He remained standing, with hands in pockets, until Pursuivant had kindled his pipe and I my cigarette. Then:

"I'm not trying to frighten you, and I won't give away any real secrets about my employer. It's just that you may understand better after you learn how I met him.

"It was more than ten years ago. Varduk came to Revere College as a fresh-man when I was a junior. He was much the same then as he is now—slender, quiet, self-contained, enigmatic. I got to know him better than anyone in school, and I can't say truly that I know him, not even now.

"Revere, in case you never heard of the place, is a small school with a big reputation for grounding its students hock-deep in the classics."

Pursuivant nodded and emitted a cloud of smoke. "I knew your Professor Dahlberg of Revere," he interjected. "He's one of the great minds of the age on Greek literature and history."

Davidson continued: "The buildings at Revere are old and, you might say, swaddled in the ivy planted by a hundred graduating classes. The traditions are consistently mellow, and none of the faculty members come in for much respect until they are past seventy. Yet the students are very much like any others, when class is over. In my day, at least, we gave more of a hoot for one touch-down than for seven thousand odes of Horace."

He smiled a little, as though in mild relish of memories he had evoked within himself.

"The football team wasn't very good, but it wasn't very bad, either. It meant something to be on the first team, and I turned out to be a fairish tackle. At the start of my junior year, the year I'm talking about, a man by the name of Schaefer was captain—a good fullback though not brilliant, and the recognized leader of the campus.

"Varduk didn't go in for athletics, or for anything else except a good stiff course of study, mostly in the humanities. He took a room at the end of the hall on the third floor of the men's dormitory, and kept to himself. You know how a college dorm loves that, you men. Six days after the term started, the Yellow Dogs had him on their list."

"Who were the Yellow Dogs?" I asked.

"Oh, there's a bunch like it in every school. Spiritual descendants of the Mohocks that flourished in Queen Anne's reign; rough and rowdy undergraduates, out for Halloween pranks every night. And any student, particularly any frosh, that stood on his dignity—" He paused and let our imagination finish the potentialities of such a situation.

"So, one noon after lunch at the training-table, Schaefer winked at me and a couple of other choice spirits. We went to our rooms and got out our favorite paddles, carved from barrel-staves and lettered over with fraternity emblems and wise-cracks. Then we tramped up to the third floor and knocked loudly at Varduk's door.

"He didn't answer. We tried the knob. The lock was on, so Schaefer dug his big shoulder into the panel and smashed his way in."

Davidson stopped and drew a long breath, as if with it he could win a better ability to describe the things he was telling.

"Varduk lifted those big, deep eyes of his as we appeared among the ruins of his door. No fear, not even surprise. Just a long look, traveling from one of us to another. When he brought his gaze to me, I felt as if somebody was pointing two guns at me, two guns loaded to their muzzles."

I, listening, felt like saying I knew how he had felt, but I did not interrupt.

"He was sitting comfortably in an armchair," went on Davidson, rocking on his feet as though nervous with the memory, "and in his slender hands he held a big dark book. His forefinger marked a place between the leaves.

"'Get up, frosh,' Schaefer said, 'and salute your superiors.'

"Varduk did not move or speak. He looked, and Schaefer bellowed louder, against a sudden and considerable uneasiness.

"'What are you reading there?' he demanded of Varduk in his toughest voice.

"'A very interesting work,' Varduk replied gently. 'It teaches how to rule people.'

"'Uh-huh?' Schaefer sneered at him. 'Let's have a look at it.'

"'I doubt if you would like it,' Varduk said, but Schaefer made a grab. The book came open in his hands. He bent, as if to study it.

"Then he took a blind, lumbering step backward. He smacked into the rest of us all bunched behind him, and without us I think he might have fallen down. I couldn't see his face, but the back of his big bull-neck had turned as white as plaster. He made two efforts to speak before he managed it. Then all he could splutter out was 'Wh-what—'"

Davidson achieved rather well the manner of a strong, simple man gone suddenly shaky with fright.

"'I told you that you probably wouldn't like it,' Varduk said, like an adult reminding a child. Then he got up out of his armchair and took the book from Schaefer's hands. He began to talk again. 'Schaefer, I want to see you here in this room after you finish your football practise this afternoon.'

"Schaefer didn't make any answer. All of us edged backward and got out of there."

Davidson paused, so long that Pursuivant asked, "Is that all?"

"No, it isn't. In a way, it's just the beginning. Schaefer made an awful fool of himself five or six times on the field that day. He dropped every one of his passes from center when we ran signals, and five or six times he muffed the ball at drop-kick practise. The coach told him in front of everybody that he acted like a high school yokel. When we finished and took our showers, he hung back until I came out, so as to walk to the dormitory with me. He tagged along like a frightened kid brother, and when we got to the front door he started upstairs like an old man. He wanted to turn toward his own room on the second floor; but Varduk's voice spoke his name, and we both looked up, startled. On the stairs to the third flight stood Varduk, holding that black book open against his chest.

"He spoke to Schaefer. 'I told you that I wanted to see you.'

"Schaefer tried to swear at him. After all, here was a frail, pale little frosh, who didn't seem to have an ounce of muscle on his bones, giving orders to a big football husky who weighed more than two hundred pounds. But the swear words sort of strangled in his throat. Varduk laughed. Neither of you have ever heard a sound so soft or merciless.

"'Perhaps you'd like me to come to your room after you,' Varduk suggested.

"Schaefer turned and came slowly to the stairs and up them. When he got level with Varduk, I didn't feel much like watching the rest. As I moved away toward my room, I saw Varduk slip his slender arm through Schaefer's big, thick one and fall into step with him, just as if they were going to have the nicest schoolboy chat you can imagine."

Davidson shuddered violently, and so, despite the warm June air, did I. Pursuivant seemed a shade less pink.

"Here, I've talked too much," Davidson said, with an air of embarrassment. "Probably it's because I've wanted to tell this story—over a space of years. No point in holding back the end, but I'd greatly appreciate your promise—both your promises—that you'll not pass the tale on."

We both gave our words, and urged him to continue. He did so.

"I had barely got to my own digs when there was a frightful row outside, shouts and scamperings and screamings; yes, screamings, of young men scared out of their wits. I jumped up and hurried downstairs and out. There lay Schaefer on the pavement in front of the dormitory. He was dead, with the brightest red blood all over him. About twenty witnesses, more or less, had seen him as he jumped out of Varduk's window.

"The faculty and the police came, and Varduk spent hours with them, being questioned. But he told them something satisfactory, for he was let go and never charged with any responsibility.

"Late that night, as I sat alone at my desk trying to drive from my mind's eye the bright, bright red of Schaefer's blood, a gentle knock sounded at my door. I got up and opened. There stood Varduk, and he held in his hands that black volume. I saw the dark red edging on its pages, the color of blood three hours old.

"'I wondered,' he said in his soft voice, 'if you'd like to see the thing in my book that made your friend Schaefer so anxious to leave my room.'

"I assured him that I did not. He smiled and came in, all uninvited.

"Then he spoke, briefly but very clearly, about certain things he hoped to do, and about how he needed a helper. He said that I might be that helper. I made no reply, but he knew that I would not refuse.

"He ordered me to kneel, and I did. Then he showed me how to put my hands together and set them between his palms. The oath I took was the medieval oath of vassalage. And I have kept my oath from that day to this."

Davidson abruptly strode back along the way to the lodge. He stopped at half a dozen paces' distance.

"Maybe I'd better get along," he suggested. "You two may want to think and talk about what I have said, and my advice not to get in Varduk's way."

With that he resumed his departure, and went out of sight without once looking back again.

## **10.** That Evening

JUDGE PURSUIVANT and I remained sitting on the roadside bank until Davidson had completely vanished around a tree-clustered bend of the way. Then my companion lifted a heavy walking-boot and tapped the dottle from his pipe against the thick sole.

"How did that cheerful little story impress you?" he inquired.

I shook my head dubiously. My mustache prickled on my upper lip, like the mane of a nervous dog. "If it was true," I said slowly, "how did Davidson dare tell it?"

"Probably because he was ordered to."

I must have stared foolishly. "You think that—"

Pursuivant nodded. "My knowledge of underworld argot is rather limited, but I believe that the correct phrase is 'lay off'. We're being told to do that, and in a highly interesting manner. As to whether or not the story is true, I'm greatly inclined to believe that it is."

I drew another cigarette from my package, and my hand trembled despite itself. "Then the man is dangerous—Varduk, I mean. What is he trying to do to Sigrid?"

"That is what perplexes me. Once, according to your little friend Jake Switz, he defended her from some mysterious but dangerous beings. His behavior argues that he isn't the only power to consider."

The judge held a match for my cigarette. His hand was steady, and its steadiness comforted me.

"Now then," I said, "to prevent—whatever is being done."

"That's what we'd better talk about." Pursuivant took his stick and rose to his feet. "Let's get on with our walk, and make sure this time that nobody overhears us."

We began to saunter, while he continued, slowly and soberly:

"You feel that it is Miss Holgar who is threatened. That's no more than guesswork on your part, supplemented by the natural anxiety of a devoted admirer—if you'll pardon my mentioning that—but you are probably right. Varduk seems to have exerted all his ingenuity and charm to induce her to take a part in this play, and at this place. The rest of you he had gathered more carelessly. It is reasonably safe to say that whatever happens will happen to Miss Holgar."

"But what will happen?" I urged, feeling very depressed.

"That we do not know as yet." I began to speak again, but he lifted a hand. "Please let me finish. Perhaps you think that we should do what we can to call off the play, get Miss Holgar out of here. But I reply, having given the matter deep thought, that such a thing is not desirable."

"Not desirable?" I echoed, my voice rising in startled surprise. "You mean, she must stay here? In heaven's name, why?"

"Because evil is bound to occur. To spirit her away will be only a retreat. The situation must be allowed to develop—then we can achieve victory. Why, Connatt," he went on warmly, "can you not see that the whole atmosphere is charged with active and supernormal perils? Don't you know that such a chance, for meeting and defeating the power of wickedness, seldom arises? What can you think of when you want to run away?"

"I'm not thinking of myself, sir," I told him. "It's Sigrid. Miss Holgar."

"Handsomely put. All right, then; when you go back to the lodge, tell her what we've said and suggest that she leave."

I shook my head, more hopelessly than before. "You know that she wouldn't take me seriously."

"Just so. Nobody will take seriously the things we are beginning to understand, you and I. We have to fight alone—but we'll win." He began to speak more brightly. "When is the play supposed to have its first performance?"

"Sometime after the middle of July. I've heard Varduk say as much several times, though he did not give the exact date."

Pursuivant grew actually cheerful. "That means that we have three weeks or so. Something will happen around that time—presumably on opening night. If time was not an element, he would not have defended her on her first night here."

I felt somewhat reassured, and we returned from our stroll in fairly good spirits.

Varduk again spoke cordially to Pursuivant, and invited him to stay to dinner. "I must ask that you leave shortly afterward," he concluded the invitation. "Our rehearsals have something of secrecy about them. You won't be offended if—"

"Of course not," Pursuivant assured him readily, but later the judge found a moment to speak with me. "Keep your eyes open," he said earnestly. "He feels that I, in some degree familiar with occult matters, might suspect or even discover something wrong about the play. We'll talk later about the things you see."

The evening meal was the more pleasant for Judge Pursuivant's high-humored presence. He was gallant to the ladies, deferential to Varduk, and witty to all of us. Even the pale, haunted face of our producer relaxed in a smile once or twice, and when the meal was over and Pursuivant was ready to go, Varduk accompanied him to the door, speaking graciously the while.

"You will pardon me if I see you safely to the road. It is no more than evening, yet I have a feeling—"

"And I have the same feeling," said Pursuivant, not at all heavily. "I appreciate your offer of protection."

Varduk evidently suspected a note of mockery. He paused. "There are things, Judge Pursuivant," he said, "against which ordinary protection would not suffice. You have borne arms, I believe, yet you know that they will not always avail."

They had come to the head of the front stairs, leading down to the lobby of the theater. The others at table were chattering over a second cup of coffee, but I was straining my ears to hear what the judge and Varduk were saying.

"Arms? Yes, I've borne them," Pursuivant admitted. "Oddly enough, I'm armed now. Should you care to see?"

He lifted his malacca walking-stick in both hands, grasping its shank and the handle. A twist and a jerk, and it came apart, revealing a few inches of metal. Pursuivant drew forth, as from a sheath, a thin, gleaming blade.

"Sword cane!" exclaimed Varduk admiringly. He bent for a closer look.

"And a singularly interesting one," elaborated Pursuivant. "Quite old, as you can see for yourself."

"Ah, so it is," agreed Varduk. "I fancy you had it put into the cane?"

"I did. Look at the inscription."

Varduk peered. "Yes, I can make it out, though it seems worn." He pursed his lips, then read aloud, very slowly: "*Sic pereant omnes inimici tui, Domine.* It sounds like Scripture."

"That's what it is, Mr Varduk," Pursuivant was saying blandly. "The King James Version has it: 'So let all thine enemies perish, O Lord.' It's from Deborah's song—fifth chapter of *Judges*."

Varduk was plainly intrigued. "A warlike text, I must say. What knight of the church chose it for his battle cry?"

"Many have chosen it," responded the judge. "Shall we go on?"

They walked down the stairs side by side, and so out of my sight and hearing.

When Varduk returned he called us at once to rehearsal. He was as alert as he had been the night before, but much harder to please. Indeed, he criticized speeches and bits of stage business that had won his high praise at the earlier rehearsal, and several times he called for repetitions and new interpretations. He also announced that at the third rehearsal, due the next day, he would take away our scripts.

"You are all accomplished actors," he amplified. "You need nothing to refresh good memories."

"I'd like to keep my book," begged Martha Vining, but Varduk smiled and shook his head.

"You'll be better without," he said definitely.

When we approached the climactic scene, with Swithin's attempt to kill Ruthven and Mary's attempted sacrifice, Varduk did not insist on stage business; in fact, he asked us flatly to speak our lines without so much as moving from our places. If this was to calm us after the frightening events of the night before, it did not succeed. Everyone there remembered the accidental sword-thrust, and Varduk's seeming invulnerability; it was as though their thoughts were doleful spoken words.

Rehearsal over—again without the final line by Ruthven—Varduk bade us a courteous good-night and, as before, walked out first with Sigrid and Martha Vining. I followed with Jake, but at the threshold I touched his arm.

"Come with me," I muttered, and turned toward the front of the lodge.

Varduk and the two women had gone out of sight around the rear of the building. Nobody challenged us as we walked silently in the direction of the road, but I had a sensation as of horrors all around me, inadequately bound back with strands that might snap at any moment.

"What's it about, Gib?" asked Jake once, but at that moment I saw what I had somehow expected and feared to see.

A silent figure lay at the foot of the upward-sloping driveway to the road. We both ran forward, coming up on either side of that figure.

The moon showed through broken clouds. By its light we recognized Judge Pursuivant, limp and apparently lifeless. Beside him lay the empty shank of his walking-stick. His right fist still clenched around the handle, and the slender blade set therein was driven deeply into the loam.

I did not know what to do, but Jake did. He knelt, scooped the judge's head up and set it against his knee, then slapped the flaccid cheeks with his open palm. Pursuivant's eyelids and mustache fluttered.

Jake snorted approvingly and lifted his own crossed eyes to mine. "I guess he's all right, Gib. Just passed out is all. Maybe better you go to Varduk and ask for some brand—"

He broke off suddenly. He was staring at something behind me.

I turned, my heart quivering inside my chest.

Shapes—monstrous, pallid, unclean shapes—were closing in upon us.

## 11. Battle and Retreat

I DOUBT if any writer, however accomplished, has ever done full justice to the emotion of terror.

To mention the icy chill at the backbone, the sudden sinewless trembling of the knees, the withering dryness of throat and tongue, is to be commonplace; and terror is not commonplace. Perhaps to remember terror is to know again the helplessness and faintness it brings.

Therefore it must suffice to say that, as I turned and saw the closing in of those pale-glowing blots of menace, I wanted to scream, and could not; to run, and could not; to take my gaze away, and could not.

If I do not describe the oncoming creatures—if creatures indeed they were—it is because they defied clear vision then and defy clear recollection now. Something quasi-human must have hung about them, something suggestive of man's outline and manner, as in a rough image molded by children of snow; but they were not solid like snow. They shifted and swirled, like wreaths of thick mist, without dispersing in air. They gave a dim, rotten light of their own, and they moved absolutely without sound.

"It's them," gulped Jake Switz beside me. He, too, was frightened, but not as frightened as I. He could speak, and move, too—he had dropped Pursuivant's head and was rising to his feet. I could hear him suck in a lungful of air, as though to brace himself for action.

His remembered presence, perhaps the mere fact of his companionship before the unreasoned awfulness of the glow-shadowy pack that advanced to hem us in, gave me back my own power of thought and motion. It gave me, too, the impulse to arm myself. I stooped to earth, groped swiftly, found and drew forth from its bed the sword-cane of Judge Pursuivant.

The non-shapes—that paradoxical idea is the best I can give of them—drifted around me, free and weightless in the night air like luminous sea-things in still, dark water. I made a thrust at the biggest and nearest of them.

I missed. Or did I? The target was, on a sudden, there

no longer. Perhaps I had pierced it, and it had burst like a flimsy bladder. Thus I argued within my desperate inner mind, even as I faced about and made a stab at another. In the same instant it had gone, too—but the throng did not seem diminished. I made a sweeping slash with my point from side to side, and the things shrank back before it, as though they dared not pass the line I drew.

"Give 'em the works, Gib!" Jake was gritting out. "They can be hurt, all right!"

I laughed, like an impudent child. I felt inadequate and disappointed, as when in dreams a terrible adversary wilts before a blow I am ashamed of.

"Come on," I challenged the undefinable enemy, in a feeble attempt at swagger. "Let me have a real poke at—"

"Hold hard," said a new voice. Judge Pursuivant, apparently wakened by this commotion all around him, was struggling erect. "Here, Connatt, give me my sword." He fairly wrung it from my hand, and drove back the misty horde with great fanwise sweeps. "Drop back, now. Not toward the lodge—up the driveway to the road."

We made the retreat somehow, and were not followed. My clothing was drenched with sweat, as though I had swum in some filthy pool. Jake, whom I remember as helping me up the slope when I might have fallen, talked incessantly without finishing a single sentence. The nearest he came to rationality was, "What did . . . what if . . . can they—"

Pursuivant, however, seemed well recovered. He kicked together some bits of kindling at the roadside. Then he asked me for a match—perhaps to make me rally my sagging senses as I explored my pockets—and a moment later he had kindled a comforting fire.

"Now," he said, "we're probably safe from any more attention of that bunch. And our fire can't be seen from the lodge. Sit down and talk it over."

Jake was mopping a face as white as tallow. His spectacles mirrored the fire-light in nervous shimmers.

"I guess I didn't dream the other night, after all," he jabbered. "Wait till I tell Mister Varduk about this."

"Please tell him nothing," counseled Judge Pursuivant at once.

"Eh?" I mumbled, astonished. "When the non-shapes—"

"Varduk probably knows all about these things—more than we shall ever know," replied the judge. "I rather think he cut short his walk across the front yards so that they would attack me. At any rate, they seemed to ooze out of the timber the moment he and I separated."

He told us, briefly, of how the non-shapes (he liked and adopted my paradox) were upon him before he knew. Like Jake two nights before, he felt an overwhelming disgust and faintness when they touched him, began to faint. His last voluntary act was to draw the blade in his cane and drive it into the ground, as an anchor against being dragged away.

"They would never touch that point," he said confidently. "You found that out, Connatt."

"And I'm still amazed, more about that fact than anything else. How would such things fear, even the finest steel?"

"It isn't steel." Squatting close to the fire, Pursuivant again cleared the bright, sharp bodkin. "Look at it, gentlemen—silver."

It was two feet long, or more, round instead of flat, rather like a large needle. Though the metal was bright and worn with much polishing, the inscription over which Pursuivant and Varduk had pored was plainly decipherable by the firelight. *Sic pereant omnes inimici tui, Domine* . . . I murmured it aloud, as though it were a protective charm.

"As you may know," elaborated Judge Pursuivant, "silver is a specific against all evil creatures."

"That's so," interjected Jake. "I heard my grandfather tell a yarn about the old country, how somebody killed a witch with a silver bullet."

"And this is an extraordinary object, even among silver swords," Pursuivant went on. "A priest gave it to me, with his blessing, when I did a certain thing to help him and his parish against an enemy not recognized by the common law of today. He assured me that the blade was fashioned by Saint Dunstan himself."

"A saint make a silver weapon!" I ejaculated incredulously.

Pursuivant smiled, exactly as though we had not lately feared and fought for our lives and souls. His manner was that of a kindly teacher with a dull but willing pupil.

"Saint Dunstan is not as legendary or as feeble as his name sounds. As a matter of fact, he flourished heartily in the Tenth Century—not long before the very real Norman Conquest. He was the stout son of a Saxon noble, studied magic and metal-working, and was a political power in England as well as a spiritual one."

"Didn't he tweak Satan's nose?" I inquired.

"So the old poem tells, and so the famous painting illustrates," agreed Pursuivant, his smile growing broader. "Dunstan was, in short, exactly the kind of holy man who would make a sword to serve against demons. Do you blame me for being confident in his work?"

"Look here, Judge," said Jake, "what were those things that jumped us up?"

"That takes answering." Pursuivant had fished a handkerchief from a side pocket and was carefully wiping the silver skewer. "In the first place, they are extraterrestrial—supernatural—and in the second, they are noisomely evil. We need no more evidence on those points. As for the rest, I have a theory of a sort, based on wide studies."

"What is it, sir?" I seconded Jake. Once again the solid assurance of the judge was comforting me tremendously.

He pursed his lips. "I've given the subject plenty of thought ever since you, Connatt, told me the experience of your friend here. There are several accounts and considerations of similar phenomena. Among ancient occultists was talk of elementary spirits—things super-normal and sometimes invisible, of sub-human intelligence and personality and not to be confused with spirits of the dead. A more modern word is "elemental", used by several cults. The things are supposed to exert influences of various kinds, upon various localities and people.

"Again, we have the poltergeist, a phenomenon that is coming in for lively investigation by various psychical scholars of today. I can refer you to the definitions of Carrington, Podmore and Lewis Spence—their books are in nearly every large library—but you'll find that the definitions and possible explanations vary. The most familiar manifestation of this strange but undeniable power is in the seeming mischief that it performs in various houses—the knocking over of furniture, the smashing of mirrors, the setting of mysterious fires—"

"I know about that thing," said Jake excitedly. "There was a house over in Brooklyn that had mysterious fires and stuff."

"And I've read Charles Fort's books—*Wild Talents* and the rest," I supplemented. "He tells about such happenings. But see here, isn't the thing generally traced to some child who was playing tricks?"

Pursuivant, still furbishing his silver blade, shook his head. "Mr Hereward Carrington, the head of the American Psychical Institute, has made a list of more than three hundred notable cases. Only twenty or so were proven fraudulent, and another twenty doubtful. That leaves approximately seven-eighths unexplained—unless you consider super-normal agency an explanation. It is true that children are often in the vicinity of the phenomena, and some investigators explain this by saying that the poltergeist is attracted or set in motion by some spiritual current from the growing personality of the child."

"Where's the child around here?" demanded Jake. "He must be a mighty bad boy. Better someone should take a stick to him."

"There is no child," answered the judge. "The summoning power is neither immature nor unconscious, but old, wicked and deliberate. Have you ever heard of witches' familiars?"

"I have," I said. "Black cats and toads, with demon spirits."

"Yes. Also grotesque or amorphous shapes—similar, perhaps, to what we encountered tonight—or disembodied voices and hands. Now we are getting down to our own case. The non-shapes—thanks again, Connatt, for the expression—are here as part of a great evil. Perhaps they came of themselves, spiritual vultures or jackals, waiting to share in the prey. Or they may be recognized servants of a vast and dreadful activity for wrong. In any case they are here, definite and dangerous."

Again I felt my nerve deserting me. "Judge Pursuivant," I pleaded, "we must get Miss Holgar out of here."

"No. You and I talked that out this afternoon. The problem cannot be solved except at its climax."

He rose to his feet. The fire was dying.

"I suggest that you go to your quarters. Apparently you're safe indoors, and just now the moon's out from behind the clouds. Keep your eyes open, and stay in the clear. The things won't venture into the moonlight unless they feel sure of you. Anyway, I think they're waiting for something else."

"How about you?" I asked.

"Oh, I'll do splendidly." He held up the sword of Saint Dunstan. "I'll carry this naked in my hand as I go."

We said good-night all around, rather casually, like late sitters leaving their club. Pursuivant turned and walked along the road. Jake and I descended gingerly to the yard of the lodge, hurried across it, and gained our boathouse safely.

## 12. Return Engagement

ONE OF THE MOST extraordinary features of the entire happening was that it had so little immediate consequence.

Judge Pursuivant reached his cabin safely, and came to visit us again and again, but never remained after dark. If Varduk knew of the attack by the non-shapes, and if he felt surprise or chagrin that Pursuivant had escaped, he did not betray it. By silent and common consent, Jake and I forbore to discuss the matter between ourselves, even when we knew that we were alone.

Meanwhile, the moon waned and waxed again while we rehearsed our play and between rehearsals swam, tramped and bathed in the sun. Not one of us but seemed to profit by the exercise and fresh air. Sigrid's step grew freer, her face browner and her green-gold hair paler by contrast. I acquired some weight, but in the proper places, and felt as strong and healthy as I had been when first I went from the Broadway stage to Hollywood, eight years before. Even Jake Switz, whose natural habitat lay among theatrical offices and stage doors, became something of a hill-climber, canoeist and fisherman. Only Varduk did not tan, though he spent much time out of doors, strolling with Davidson or by himself. Despite his apparent fragility and his stiffness of gait, he was a tireless walker.

One thing Jake and I did for our protection; that was to buy, on one of our infrequent trips to the junction, an electric flashlight apiece as well as one for Sigrid. These we carried, lighted, when walking about at night, and not once in the month that followed our first encounter with the non-shapes did we have any misadventure.

The middle of July brought the full moon again, and with it the approach of our opening night.

The theatrical sections of the papers—Varduk had them delivered daily—gave us whole square yards of publicity. Jake had fabricated most of this, on his typewriter in our boathouse loft, though his most glamorous inventions included nothing of the grisly wonders we had actually experienced. Several publishers added to the general interest in the matter by sending to Varduk attractive offers for the manuscript of *Ruthven*, and receiving blunt refusals. One feature writer, something of a scholar of early Nineteenth Century English literature, cast a doubt upon the authenticity of the piece. In reply to this, Judge Pursuivant sent an elaboration of his earlier statement that *Ruthven* was undoubtedly genuine. The newspaper kindly gave this rejoinder considerable notice, illustrating it with photographs of the judge, Varduk and Sigrid.

On July 20, two days before opening, Jake went out to nail signs along the main road to guide motor parties to our theater. He was cheerfully busy most of the morning, and Sigrid deigned to let me walk with her. We did not seek the road, but turned our steps along the brink of the water.

An ancient but discernible trail, made perhaps by deer, ran there.

"Happy, Sigrid?" I asked her.

"I couldn't be otherwise," she cried at once. "Our play is to startle the world—first here, then on Broadway—"

"Sigrid," I said, "what is there about this play that has such a charm for you? I know that it's a notable literary discovery, and that it's pretty powerful stuff in spots, but in the final analysis it's only melodrama with a clever supernatural twist. You're not the melodramatic type."

"Indeed?" she flung back. "Am I a type, then?"

I saw that I had been impolitic and made haste to offer apology, but she waved it aside.

"What you said might well be asked by many people. The pictures have put me into a certain narrow field, with poor Jake Switz wearing out the thesaurus to find synonyms for 'glamorous.' Yet, as a beginner in Sweden, I did *Hedda Gabler* and *The Wild Duck*—yes, and Bernard Shaw, too; I was the slum girl in *Pygmalion*. After that, a German picture, *Cyrano de Bergerac*, with me as Roxane. It was luck, perhaps, and a momentary wish by producers for a new young foreign face, that got me into American movies. But, have I done so poorly?"

"Sigrid, nobody ever did so nobly."

"And at the first, did I do always the same thing? What was my first chance? The French war bride in that farce comedy. Then what? Something by Somerset Maugham, where I wore a black wig and played a savage girl of the tropics. Then what? A starring rôle, or rather a co-starring rôle—opposite you." She gave me a smile, as though the memory were pleasant.

"Opposite me," I repeated, and a thrill crept through me. "*Lavengro*, the costume piece. Our costumes, incidentally, were rather like what we will wear in the first part of *Ruthven*."

"I was thinking the same thing. And speaking of melodrama, what about *Lavengro*? You, with romantic curly sideburns, stripped to the waist and fighting like mad with Noah Beery. Firelight gleaming on your wet skin, and me mopping your face with a sponge and telling you to use your right hand instead of your left—"

"By heaven, there have been lots of worse shows!" I cried, and we both laughed. My spirits had risen as we had strolled away from the lodge grounds, and I had quite forgotten my half-formed resolve to speak a warning.

We came to a stretch of sand, with a great half-rotted pine trunk lying across it. Here we sat, side by side, smoking and scrawling in the fine sand with twigs.

"There's another reason why I have been happy during this month of rehearsal," said Sigrid shyly.

"Yes?" I prompted her, and my heart began suddenly to beat swiftly.

"It's been so nice to be near you and with you."

I felt at once strong and shivery, rather like the adolescent hero of an old-fashioned novel. What I said, somewhat ruefully, was, "If you think so, why have you been so hard to see? This is the first time we have walked or been alone together."

She smiled, and in her own individual way that made her cheeks crease and her eyes turn aslant. "We saw a lot of each other once, Gib. I finished up by being sorry. I don't want to be sorry again. That's why I've gone slowly."

"See here, Sigrid," I blurted suddenly. "I'm not going to beat around the bush, or try to lead up diplomatically or dramatically, but—oh, hang it!" Savagely I broke a twig in my hands. "I loved you once, and in spite of the fact that we quarreled and separated, I've never stopped. I love you right this instant—"

She caught me in strong, fierce arms, and kissed me so soundly that our teeth rang together between lips crushed open. Thus for a second of white-hot surprise; then she let go with equal suddenness. Her face had gone pale under its tan—no acting there—and her eyes were full of panicky wonder.

"I didn't do that," she protested slowly. She, too, was plainly stunned. "I didn't. But—well, I did, didn't I?"

"You certainly did. I don't know why, and if you say so I won't ask; but you did, and it'll be hard to retire from the position again."

After that, we had a lot more to say to each other. I admitted, very humbly, that I had been responsible for our estrangement five years before, and that the reason was the very unmanly one that I, losing popularity, was jealous of her rise. For her part, she confessed that not once had she forgotten me, nor given up the hope of reconciliation.

"I'm not worth it," I assured her. "I'm a sorry failure, and we both know it."

"Whenever I see you," she replied irrelevantly, "bells begin to ring in my ears—loud alarm bells, as if fires had broken out all around me."

"We're triple idiots to think of love," I went on. "You're the top, and I'm the muck under the bottom."

"You'll be the sensation of your life when *Ruthven* comes to Broadway," rejoined Sigrid confidently. "And the movie magnates will fight duels over the chance to ask for your name on a contract."

"To hell with the show business! Let's run away tonight and live on a farm," I suggested.

In her genuine delight at the thought she clutched my shoulders, digging in her long, muscular fingers. "Let's!" she almost whooped, like a little girl promised a treat. "We'll have a garden and keep pigs—no, there's a show."

"And the show," I summed up, "must go on."

On that doleful commonplace we rose from the tree-trunk and walked back. Climbing to the road, we sought out Jake, who with a hammer and a mouthful of nails was fastening his last sign to a tree. We swore him to secrecy with terrible oaths, then told him that we intended to marry as soon as we returned to New York. He half swallowed a nail, choked dangerously, and had to be thumped on the back by both of us.

"I should live so—I knew this would happen," he managed to gurgle at last. "Among all the men you know, Sigrid Holgar, you got to pick this *schlemiel*!"

We both threatened to pummel him, and he apologized profusely, mourning the while that his vow kept him from announcing our decision in all the New York papers.

"With that romance breaking now, we would have every able-bodied man, woman and child east of the Mississippi trying to get into our show," he said earnestly. "With a club we'd have to beat them away from the ticket window. Standing-room would sell for a dollar an inch."

"It's a success as it is," I comforted him. "*Ruthven*, I mean. The house is a sell-out, Davidson says."

That night at dinner, Sigrid sat, not at the head of the table, but on one side next to me. Once or twice we squeezed hands and Jake, noticing this, was shocked and burned his mouth with hot coffee. Varduk, too, gazed at us as though he knew our secret, and finally was impelled to quote something from Byron—a satiric couplet on love and its shortness of life. But we were too happy to take offense or even to recognize that the quotation was leveled at us.

## **13.** The Black Book

OUR FINAL REHEARSAL, on the night of the twenty-first of July, was fairly accurate as regards the speeches and attention to cues, but it lacked fire and assurance. Varduk, however, was not disappointed.

"It has often been said, and often proven as well, that a bad last rehearsal means a splendid first performance," he reminded us. "To bed all of you, and try to get at least nine hours of sleep." Then he seemed to remember something. "Miss Holgar."

"Yes?" said Sigrid.

"Come here, with me." He led her to the exact center of the stage. "At this spot, you know, you are to stand when the final incident of the play, and our dialog together, unfolds."

"I know," she agreed.

"Yet—are you sure? Had we not better be sure?" Varduk turned toward the auditorium, as though to gage their position from the point of view of the audience. "Perhaps I am being too exact, yet—"

He snapped his fingers in the direction of Davidson, who seemed to have expected some sort of request signal. The big assistant reached into the pocket of his jacket and brought out a piece of white chalk.

"Thank you, Davidson." Varduk accepted the proffered fragment. "Stand a little closer center, Miss Holgar. Yes, like that." Kneeling, he drew with a quick sweep of his arm a small white circle around her feet.

"That," he informed her, standing up again, "is the spot where I want you to stand, at the moment when you and I have our final conflict of words, the swearing on the Bible, and my involuntary blessing upon your head."

Sigrid took a step backward, out of the circle. I, standing behind her, could see that she had drawn herself up in outraged protest. Varduk saw, too, and half smiled as if to disarm her. "Forgive me if I seem foolish," he pleaded gently.

"I must say," she pronounced in a slow, measured manner, as though she had difficulty in controlling her voice, "that I do not feel that this little diagram will help me in the least."

Varduk let his smile grow warmer, softer. "Oh, probably it will not, Miss Holgar; but I am sure it will help me. Won't you do as I ask?"

She could not refuse, and by the time she had returned across the stage to me she had relaxed into cheerfulness again. I escorted her to the door of her cabin, and her good-night smile warmed me all the way to my own quarters.

Judge Pursuivant appeared at noon the next day, and Varduk, hailing him cordially, invited him to lunch.

"I wonder," ventured Varduk as we all sat down together, "if you, Judge Pursuivant, would not speak a few words in our favor before the curtain tonight."

"I?" The judge stared, then laughed. "But I'm not part of the management."

"The management—which means myself—will be busy getting into costume for the first act. You are a scholar, a man whose recent book on Byron has attracted notice. It is fitting that you do what you can to help our opening."

"Oh," said Pursuivant, "if you put it like that—but what shall I tell the audience?"

"Make it as short as you like, but impressive. You might announce that all present are subpoenaed as witnesses to a classic moment."

Pursuivant smiled. "That's rather good, Mr Varduk, and quite true as well. Very good, count on me."

But after lunch he drew me almost forcibly away from the others, talking affably about the merits of various wines until we were well out of earshot. Then his tone changed abruptly.

"I think we know now that the thing—whatever it is—will happen at the play, and we also know why."

"Why, then?" I asked at once.

"I am to tell the audience that they are 'subpoenaed as witnesses.' In other words, their attention is directed, they must be part of a certain ceremony. I, too, am needed. Varduk is making me the clerk, so to speak, of his court—or his cult. That shows that he will preside."

"It begins to mean something," I admitted. "Yet I am still at a loss."

Pursuivant's own pale lips were full of perplexity. "I wish that we could know more before the actual beginning. Yet I, who once prepared and judged legal cases, may be able to sum up in part:

"Something is to happen to Miss Holgar. The entire fabric of theatrical activity—this play, the successful effort to interest her in it, the remote theater, her particular rôle, everything—is to perform upon her a certain effect. That effect, we may be sure, is devastating. We may believe that a part, at least, of the success depends on the last line of the play, a mystery as yet to all of us."

"Except to Varduk," I reminded.

"Except to Varduk."

But a new thought struck me, and for a moment I found it comforting.

"Wait. The ceremony, as you call it, can't be all evil," I said. "After all, he asks her to swear on a Bible."

"So he does," Pursuivant nodded. "What kind of a Bible?"

I tried to remember. "To tell the truth, I don't know. We haven't used props of any kind in rehearsals—not even the sword, after that first time."

"No? Look here, that's apt to be significant. We'll have to look at the properties."

We explored the auditorium and the stage with a fine show of casual interest. Davidson and Switz were putting final touches on the scenery—a dark blue backdrop for evening sky, a wall painted to resemble vine-hung granite, benches and an arbor—but no properties lay on the table backstage.

"You know this is a Friday, Gib?" demanded Jake, looking up from where he was mending the cable of a floodlight. "Bad luck, opening our play on a Friday."

"Not a bit," laughed Pursuivant. "What's begun on a Friday never comes to an end. Therefore—"

"Oi!" crowed Jake. "That means we'll have a record-breaking run, huh?" He jumped up and shook my hand violently. "You'll be working in this show till you step on your beard."

We wandered out again, and Sigrid joined us. She was in high spirits.

"I feel," she said excitedly, "just as I felt on the eve of my first professional appearance. As though the world would end tonight!"

"God forbid," I said at once, and "God forbid," echoed Judge Pursuivant. Sigrid laughed merrily at our sudden expressions of concern.

"Oh, it won't end that way," she made haste to add, in the tone one reserves for children who need comfort. "I mean, the world will begin tonight, with success and happiness."

She put out a hand, and I squeezed it tenderly. After a moment she departed to inspect her costume.

"I haven't a maid or a dresser," she called over her shoulder. "Everything has to be in perfect order, and I myself must see to it."

We watched her as she hurried away, both of us sober.

"I think I know why you fret so about her safety," Pursuivant said to me. "You felt, too, that the thing she said might be a bad omen."

"Then may her second word be a good omen," I returned.

"Amen to that," he said heartily.

Dinnertime came, and Pursuivant and I made a quick meal of it. We excused ourselves before the others—Sigrid looked up in mild astonishment that I should want to leave her side—and went quickly downstairs to the stage.

On the property table lay the cudgel I was to use in the first act, the sword I was to strike with in the second, the feather duster to be wielded by Martha Vining as Bridget, a tray with a wine service to be borne by Davidson as Oscar. There was also a great book, bound in red cloth, with red edging.

"That is the Bible," said Pursuivant at once. "I must have a look at it."

"I still can't see," I muttered, half to myself, "how this sword—a good piece of steel and as sharp as a razor—failed to kill Varduk when I—"

"Never mind that sword," interrupted Judge Pursuivant. "Look at this book, this 'Bible' which they've refused to produce up to now. I'm not surprised to find out that—well, have a look for yourself."

On the ancient black cloth I saw rather spidery capitals, filled with red coloring matter: *Grand Albert.*

"I wouldn't look inside if I were you," warned the judge. "This is in all probability the book that Varduk owned when Davidson met him at Revere College. Remember what happened to one normal young man, ungrounded in occultism, who peeped into it."

"What can it be?" I asked.

"A notorious gospel for witches," Pursuivant informed me. "I've heard of it—Descrepe, the French occultist, edited it in 1885. Most editions are modified and harmless, but this, at first glance, appears to be the complete and infamous Eighteenth Century version." He opened it.

The first phase of his description had stuck in my mind. "A gospel for witches; and that is the book on which Sigrid must swear an oath of renunciation at the end of the play!"

Pursuivant was scowling at the fly-leaf. He groped for his pince-nez, put them on. "Look here, Connatt," he said.

I crowded close to his elbow, and together we read what had been written long ago, in ink now faded to a dirty brown:

*Geo Gordon (Biron) his book*

*At 1 hr. befor midnt, on 22 July, 1788 givn him. He was brot to coeven by Todlin he the saide Geo. G. to be bond to us for 150 yers. and serve for our glory he to gain his title & hav all he desirs. at end of 150 yrs. to give acctg. & not be releasd save by delivring anothr as worthie our coeven.*

*(Signed)*

*For coeven* — *For Geo. Gordon (Biron)*

*Terragon* — *Todlin*

"And look at this, too," commanded Judge Pursuivant. He laid his great forefinger at the bottom of the page. There, written in fresh blue ink, and in a hand somehow familiar:

*This 22nd of July, 1938, I tender this book and quit this service unto Sigrid Holgar.*

*George Gordon, Lord Byron.*

## **14.** Zero Hour

PURSUIVANT closed the book with a loud snap, laid it down on the table, and caught me by the arm.

"Come away from here," he said in a tense voice. "Outside, where nobody will hear." He almost dragged me out through the stage door. "Come along—down by the water—it's fairly open, we'll be alone."

When we reached the edge of the lake we faced each other. The sun was almost set. Back of us, in front of the lodge, we could hear the noise of early arrivals for the theater—perhaps the men who would have charge of automobile parking, the ushers, the cashier.

"How much of what you read was intelligible to you?" asked Pursuivant.

"I had a sense that it was rotten," I said. "Beyond that, I'm completely at sea."

"I'm not." His teeth came strongly together behind the words. "There, on the flyleaf of a book sacred to witches and utterly abhorrent to honest folk, was written an instrument pledging the body and soul of a baby to a 'coeven'—that is, a congregation of evil sorcerers—for one hundred and fifty years. George Gordon, the Lord Byron that was to be, had just completed his sixth month of life."

"How could a baby be pledged like that?" I asked.

"By some sponsor—the one signing the name 'Todlin.' That was undoubtedly a coven name, such as we know all witches took. Terragon was another such cognomen. All we can say of 'Todlin' is that the signature is apparently a woman's. Perhaps that of the child's eccentric nurse, Mistress Gray—"

"This is beastly," I interposed, my voice beginning to tremble. "Can't we do something besides talk?"

Pursuivant clapped me strongly on the back. "Steady," he said. "Let's talk it out while that writing is fresh in our minds. We know, then, that the infant was pledged to an unnaturally long life of evil. Promises made were kept—he became the heir to the estates and title of his grand-uncle, 'Wicked Byron,' after his cousins died strangely. And surely he had devil-given talents and attractions."

"Wait," I cut in suddenly. "I've been thinking about that final line or so of writing, signed with Byron's name. Surely I've seen the hand before."

"You have. The same hand wrote *Ruthven*, and you've seen the manuscript." Pursuivant drew a long breath. "Now we know how *Ruthven* could be written on paper only ten years old. Byron lives and signs his name today."

I felt almost sick, and heartily helpless inside. "But Byron died in Greece," I said, as though reciting a lesson. "His body was brought to England and buried at Hucknall Torkard, close to his ancestral home."

"Exactly. It all fits in." Pursuivant's manifest apprehension was becoming modified by something of grim triumph. "Must he not have repented, tried to expiate his curse and his sins by an unselfish sacrifice for Grecian liberty? You and I have been over this ground before; we know how he suffered and labored, almost like a saint. Death would seem welcome—his bondage would end in thirty-six years instead of a hundred and fifty. What about his wish to be burned?"

"Burning would destroy his body," I said. "No chance for it to come alive again."

"But the body was not burned, and it has come alive again. Connatt, do you know who the living-dead Byron is?"

"Of course I do. And I also know that he intends to pass something into the hands of Sigrid."

"He does. She is the new prospect for bondage, the 'other as worthie.' She is not a free agent in the matter, but neither was Byron at the age of six months."

The sun's lower rim had touched the lake. Pursuivant's pink face was growing dusky, and he leaned on the walking-stick that housed a silver blade.

"Byron's hundred and fifty years will end at eleven o'clock tonight," he said, gazing shrewdly around for possible eavesdroppers. "Now, let me draw some parallels.

"Varduk—we know who Varduk truly is—will, in the character of Ruthven, ask Miss Holgar, who plays Mary, a number of questions. Those questions, and her answers as set down for her to repeat, make up a pattern. Think of them, not as lines in a play, but an actual interchange between an adept of evil and a neophyte."

"It's true," I agreed. "He asks her if she will 'give herself up,' 'renounce former manners,' and to swear so upon—the book we saw. She does so."

"Then the prayer, which perplexes you by its form. The 'wert in heaven' bit becomes obvious now, eh? How about the angel that fell from grace and attempted to build up his own power to oppose?"

"Satan!" I almost shouted. "A prayer to the force of evil!"

"Not so loud, Connatt. And then, while Miss Holgar stands inside a circle—that, also, is part of the witch ceremony—he touches her head, and speaks words we do not know. But we can guess."

He struck his stick hard against the sandy earth.

"What then?" I urged him on.

"It's in an old Scottish trial of witches," said Pursuivant. "Modern works—J. W. Wickwar's book, and I think

Margaret Alice Murray's—quote it. The master of the coven touched the head of the neophyte and said that all beneath his hand now belonged to the powers of darkness."

"No! No!" I cried, in a voice that wanted to break.

"No hysterics, please!" snapped Pursuivant. "Connatt, let me give you one stark thought—it will cool you, strengthen you for what you must help me achieve. Think what will follow if we let Miss Holgar take this oath, accept this initiation, however unwittingly. At once she will assume the curse that Varduk—Byron—lays down. Life after death, perhaps; the faculty of wreaking devastation at a word or touch; gifts beyond human will or comprehension, all of them a burden to her; and who can know the end?"

"There shall not be a beginning," I vowed huskily. "I will kill Varduk—"

"Softly, softly. You know that weapons—ordinary weapons—do not even scratch him."

The twilight was deepening into dusk. Pursuivant turned back toward the lodge, where windows had begun to glow warmly, and muffled motor-noises bespoke the parking of automobiles. There were other flecks of light, too. For myself, I felt beaten and weary, as though I had fought to the verge of losing against a stronger, wiser enemy.

"Look around you, Connatt. At the clumps of bush, the thickets. What do they hide?"

I knew what he meant. I felt, though I saw only dimly, the presence of an evil host in ambuscade all around us.

"They're waiting to claim her, Connatt. There's only one thing to do."

"Then let's do it, at once."

"Not yet. The moment must be *his* moment, one hour before midnight. Escape, as I once said, will not be enough. We must conquer."

I waited for him to instruct me.

"As you know, Connatt, I will make a speech before the curtain. After that, I'll come backstage and stay in your dressing-room. What you must do is get the sword that you use in the second act. Bring it there and keep it there."

'I've told you and told you that the sword meant nothing against him."

"Bring it anyway," he insisted.

I heard Sigrid's clear voice, calling me to the stage door. Pursuivant and I shook hands quickly and warmly, like teammates just before a hard game, and we went together to the lodge.

Entering, I made my way at once to the property table. The sword still lay there, and I put out my hand for it.

"What do you want?" asked Elmo Davidson behind me.

"I thought I'd take the sword into my dressing-room."

"It's a prop, Connatt. Leave it right where it is."

I turned and looked at him. "I'd rather have it with me," I said doggedly.

"You're being foolish," he told me sharply, and there is hardly any doubt but that I sounded so to him. "What if I told Varduk about this?"

"Go and tell him, if you like. Tell him also that I won't go on tonight if you're going to order me around." I said this as if I meant it, and he relaxed his commanding pose.

"Oh, go ahead. And for heaven's sake calm your nerves."

I took the weapon and bore it away. In my room I found my costume for the first act already laid out on two chairs—either Davidson or Jake had done that for me. Quickly I rubbed color into my cheeks, lined my brows and eyelids, affixed fluffy side-whiskers to my jaws. The mirror showed me a set, pale face, and I put on rather more make-up than I generally use. My hands trembled as I donned gleaming slippers of patent leather, fawn-colored trousers that strapped under the insteps, a frilled shirt and flowing necktie, a flowered waistcoat and a bottle-green frock coat with velvet facings and silver buttons. My hair was long enough to be combed into a wavy sweep back from my brow.

"Places, everybody," the voice of Davidson was calling outside.

I emerged. Jake Switz was at my door, and he grinned his good wishes. I went quickly on-stage, where Sigrid already waited. She looked ravishing in her simple yet striking gown of soft, light blue, with billows of skirt, little puffs of sleeves, a tight, low bodice. Her gleaming hair was caught back into a Grecian-looking coiffure, with a ribbon and a white flower at the side. The normal tan of her skin lay hidden beneath the pallor of her make-up.

At sight of me she smiled and put out a hand. I kissed it lightly, taking care that the red paint on my lips did not smear. She took her seat on the bench against the artificial bushes, and I, as gracefully as possible, dropped at her feet.

Applause sounded beyond the curtain, then died away. The voice of Judge Pursuivant became audible:

"Ladies and gentlemen, I have been asked by the management to speak briefly. You are seeing, for the first time before any audience, the lost play of Lord Byron, *Ruthven*. My presence here is not as a figure of the theater, but as a modest scholar of some persistence, whose privilege it has been to examine the manuscript and perceive its genuineness.

"Consider yourselves all subpoenaed as witnesses to a classic moment." His voice rang as he pronounced the phrase required by Varduk. "I wonder if this night will not make spectacular history for the genius who did not die in Greece a century and more ago. I say, he did not die—for when does genius die? We are here to assist at, and to share in, a performance that will bring him his proper deserts.

"Ladies and gentlemen, I feel, and perhaps you feel as well, the presence of the great poet with us in this remote hall. I wish you joy of what you shall observe. And now, have I your leave to withdraw and let the play begin?"

Another burst of applause, in the midst of which sounded three raps. Then up went the curtain, and all fell silent. I, as Aubrey, spoke the first line of the play:

"I'm no Othello, darling. . . ."

## **15.** "Whither? I Dread to Think—"

SIGRID and I struck on the instant the proper note of affectionate gayety, and I could feel in the air that peculiar audience-rhythm by which an actor knows that his effort to capture a mood is successful. For the moment it was the best of all possible worlds, to be exchanging thus the happy and brilliant lines with the woman I adored, while an intelligent and sympathetic houseful of spectators shared our happy mood.

But, if I had forgotten Varduk, he was the more imposing when he entered. His luminous pallor needed no heightening to seize the attention; his face was set off, like some gleaming white gem, by the dark coat, stock, cape, boots, pantaloons. He spoke his entrance line as a king might speak in accepting the crown and homage of a nation. On the other side of the footlights the audience grew tense with heightened interest.

He overpowered us both, as I might have known he would, with his personality and his address. We might have been awkward amateurs, wilting into nothingness when a master took the stage. I was eclipsed completely, exactly as Aubrey should be at the entrance of Ruthven, and I greatly doubt if a single pair of eyes followed me at my first exit; for at the center of the stage, Varduk had begun to make love to Sigrid.

I returned to my dressing-room. Pursuivant sat astride a chair, his sturdy forearms crossed upon its back.

"How does it go?" he asked.

"Like a producer's dream," I replied, seizing a powder puff with which to freshen my make-up. "Except for the things we know about, I would pray for no better show."

"I gave you a message in my speech before the curtain. Did you hear what I said? I meant, honestly, to praise Byron and at the same time to defy him. You and I, with God's help, will give *Ruthven* an ending he does not expect."

It was nearly time for me to make a new entrance, and I left the dressing-room, mystified but comforted by Pursuivant's manner. The play went on, gathering speed and impressiveness. We were all acting inspiredly, maugre the bizarre nature of the rehearsals and other preparations, the dark atmosphere that had surrounded the piece from its first introduction to us.

The end of the act approached, and with it my exit. Sigrid and I dragged the limp Varduk to the center of the stage and retired, leaving him alone to perform the sinister resurrection scene with which the first act closes. I loitered in the wings to watch, but Jake Switz tugged at my sleeve.

"Come," he whispered. "I want to show you something."

We went to the stage door. Jake opened it an inch.

The space behind the lodge was full of uncertain, half-formed lights that moved and lived. For a moment we peered. Then the soft, larval radiances flowed toward us. Jake slammed the door.

"They're waiting," he said.

From the direction of the stage came Varduk's final line:

"Grave, I reject thy shelter! Death, stand back!"

Then Davidson dragged down the curtain, while the house shook with applause. I turned again. Varduk, back-stage, was speaking softly but clearly, urging us to hurry with our costume changes. Into my dressing-room I hastened, my feet numb and my eyes blurred.

"I'll help you dress," came Pursuivant's calm voice. "Did Jake show you what waits outside?"

I nodded and licked my parched, painted lips.

"Don't fear. Their eagerness is premature."

He pulled off my coat and shirt. Grown calm again before his assurance, I got into my clothes for Act Two—a modern dinner suit. With alcohol I removed the clinging side-whiskers, repaired my make-up and brushed my hair into modern fashion once more. Within seconds, it seemed, Davidson was calling us to our places.

The curtain rose on Sigrid and me, as Mary and Swithin, hearing the ancestral tale of horror from Old Bridget. As before, the audience listened raptly, and as before it rose to the dramatic entrance of Varduk. He wore his first-act costume, and his manner was even more compelling. Again I felt myself thrust into the background of the drama; as for Sigrid, great actress though she is, she prospered only at his sufferance.

Off stage, on again, off once more—the play was Varduk's, and Sigrid's personality was being eclipsed. Yet she betrayed no anger or dislike of the situation. It was as though Varduk mastered her, even while his character of Ruthven overpowered her character of Mary. I felt utterly helpless.

In the wings I saw the climax approach. Varduk, flanked by Davidson as the obedient Oscar, was declaring Ruthven's intention to gain revenge and love.

"Get your sword," muttered Jake, who had taken Davidson's place at the curtain ropes. "You're on again in a moment."

I ran to my dressing-room. Pursuivant opened the door, thrust something into my hand.

"It's the silver sword," he told me quickly. "The one from my cane. Trust in it, Connatt. Almost eleven o'clock—go, and God stiffen your arm."

It seemed a mile from the door to the wings. I reached it just in time for my entrance cue—Sigrid's cry of "Swithin will not allow this."

"Let him try to prevent it," grumbled Davidson, fierce and grizzled as the devil-converted Oscar.

"I'm here for that purpose," I said clearly, and strode into view. The sword from Pursuivant's cane I carried low, hoping that Varduk would not notice at once. He stood with folded arms, a mocking smile just touching his white face.

"So brave?" he chuckled. "So foolish?"

"My ancestor killed you once, Ruthven," I said, with more meaning than I had ever employed before. "I can do so again."

I leaped forward, past Sigrid and at him.

The smile vanished. His mouth fell open.

"Wait! That sword—"

He hurled himself, as though to snatch it from my hand. But I lifted the point and lunged, extending myself almost to the boards of the stage. As once before, I felt the flesh tear before my blade. The slender spike of metal went in, in, until the hilt thudded against his breast-bone.

No sound from audience or actors, no motion. We made a tableau, myself stretched out at lunge, Varduk transfixed, the other two gazing in sudden aghast wonder.

For one long breath's space my victim stood like a figure of black stone, with only his white face betraying anything of life and feeling. His deep eyes, gone dark as a winter night, dug themselves into mine. I felt once again the intolerable weight of his stare—yet it was not threatening, not angry even. The surprise ebbed from it, and the eyes and the sad mouth softened into a smile. Was he forgiving me? Thanking me? . . .

Sigrid found her voice again, and screamed tremulously. I released the cane-hilt and stepped backward, automatically. Varduk fell limply upon his face. The silver blade, standing out between his shoulders, gleamed red with blood. Next moment the red had turned dull black, as though the gore was a millennium old. Varduk's body sagged. It shrank within its rich, gloomy garments. It crumbled.

The curtain had fallen. I had not heard its rumble of descent, nor had Sigrid, nor the stupefied Davidson. From beyond the folds came only choking silence. Then Pursuivant's ready voice.

"Ladies and gentlemen, a sad accident has ended the play unexpectedly—tragically. Through the fault of nobody, one of the players has been fatally—"

I heard no more. Holding Sigrid in my arms I told her, briefly and brokenly, the true story of *Ruthven* and its author. She, weeping, gazed fearfully at the motionless black heap.

"The poor soul!" she sobbed. "The poor, poor soul!"

Jake, leaving his post by the curtain-ropes, had walked on and was leading away the stunned, stumbling Davidson.

I still held Sigrid close. To my lips, as if at the bidding of another mind and memory, came the final lines of *Manfred*:

"He's gone—his soul hath ta'en its earthless flight—
Whither? I dread to think—but he is gone."

# Charles L. Grant

# Crystal

CHARLES L. GRANT is a prolific editor, short story writer and novelist. He has won the Nebula Award, the British Fantasy Award and the World Fantasy Award and published more than 100 short stories. His first story, "The House of Evil", appeared in 1968, and after publishing several science fiction novels, he began to develop his unique brand of "quiet" horror in more than thirty novels, including *The Hour of the Oxrun Dead*, *The Nestling*, *The Pet*, *For Fear of the Night*, *Dialing the Wind* and *In a Dark Dream*.

His stories have been collected in *Tales from the Nightside*, *A Glow of Candles* and *Nightmare Seasons*, and he is the editor of the successful *Shadows*, *Midnight* and *Greystone Bay* anthology series.

"Crystal" is a deeply disturbing tale of possession and death set in a tourist's-eye view of London.

THE SHOP WASN'T A VERY SMART ONE as shops in the district went, but Brian had weeks ago learned that it catered mostly to tourists and the occasional country family in town for a holiday, and so needed only a bit of flash, a few items with the royal family on them, and a dozen different street maps from which to choose the best way of getting lost.

Now, Brian, he thought then in a silent scold, that's not the way to think, is it? This is London, boy, and you're practically a native. You're not going to get lost, you're not going to be shortchanged, you're not going to be taken for a foreigner at all. Until, that is, you open your fat Yank mouth.

His reflection in the shop window smiled wryly at him, and he nodded to it just as a young man and his girl wandered by, saw him, and gave him a puzzled look, the boy lifting an eyebrow and the girl shoving a laugh into her palm. Startled, he watched them until, if he wanted to watch them further, he'd have to look directly at their backs; so he stuffed his hands into his pockets and returned to his contemplation of the display.

Seeing nothing.

Hearing nothing of the homewardbound traffic grumbling past him on High Holborn.

Until a face in the window caught his attention. A young woman, striking in a dark-haired, pallid sort of way, and he smiled again, hopes rising, until he realized with a derisive snort it was a picture he was looking at. And not a very good one, at that. Oval, in fading color, framed in cheap silver.

He leaned closer.

No. Not cheap at all. In fact, the frame only appeared to be simple, but there around the edges were etchings of long-stemmed roses, so delicately done the sunlight blotted them out until he moved his shadow over their stems. He cocked his head and leaned closer still; he felt his left hand bunching around the roll of money he kept in his trousers; and when a horn blared behind him, he jumped and moved instantly and casually into the store.

The shopkeeper was a rotund man and thickly mustached. He remained behind the rear counter when Brian asked about the picture, saying that if he were interested, he was more than welcome to take it out of the window and bring it into the light. Brian shrugged. He didn't want to appear too stupid, nor too interested. Nevertheless, he made his way slowly back along the narrow aisle, angling sideways between a group of women chattering in Texas-Southern accents about how *darling* everything was and wouldn't Cousin Annie just *love* a picture of that *adorable* Prince Andrew. Carefully, he reached around a newspaper display and picked up the frame.

It was heavy, much heavier than it had a right to be.

He turned it around and looked at the portrait.

Narrow face; narrow chin; wide, dark eyes that matched the dark hair curling under her jaw. The hint of a lace-trimmed velvet bodice. Bare shoulders. Nothing more.

Attractive, he decided, but with an odd distance in her gaze.

He hefted it. Tilted it to the light when he felt the shopkeeper watching. Frowned as if in concentration and debate, shrugged as if in reluctant decision, and carried it back, waiting patiently as the women fussed with the unfamiliar coinage, finally giving up and handing the man some bills, their faces sharp in daring him not to give them their due.

Brian grinned, and the man grinned back over a blue-tinted head. One of the ladies turned around and glared, obviously taking him for a local and extending the dare to him.

But he only nodded politely and handed over the picture as soon as the women moved on, chattering again, exclaiming, and wondering aloud why the English, with all their experience, didn't have money like the Americans, it would make things so much easier all around, don't you think?

"You must get tired of it, Mr Isling," Brian said sympathetically as he pulled out his roll and coins and gave him the correct amount.

"Not so much anymore, Mr Victor," was the smiling answer. "At least I don't have to put my feet up in a hotel, do I, when the day is over."

"Oh, they're not that bad." But his expression put the lie to it, and the man laughed, put the purchase in a paper bag, and thanked him for the sale.

Halfway up the aisle, Brian turned. "Do you know who she is?" he asked.

"Who?"

He held up the bag.

"No. Not really, that is. There's a name on the back. Crystal. I reckon that's either her or the artist."

"Do you get many of them?"

Isling hesitated, then shook his head. "Only one of that lot, far as I know. We get them now and then, the odd piece. Sometimes they last until I junk them; sometimes they go as soon as I put them out."

"And this one?"

"Put it out this morning."

"It must have known I was coming."

The shopkeeper's laughter followed him to the street, where he turned left, elbows in to protect his ribs from his dubious prize, trying to decide if he should go back to his room now, or find someplace to eat and examine his folly there. Wherever it was, it would have to be someplace quiet, someplace that would allow him peace, to figure out why the hell he'd spent so much on a whim.

He slid the frame just far enough out of the bag to take a puzzled look, heard someone scream a warning, and looked up in time to see a black, square-framed taxi jump the curb and head straight for him. He shouted and leapt to one side, lost his balance and fell over the curbing into the street. The taxi plowed on, scattering pedestrians and postcard displays until it slammed through the window of the shop he'd just left. There was a man's yell, a faint whump, a whiff of gas, and suddenly the pavement was alive with smoke and fire.

Brian immediately crossed his arms protectively over his head, half expecting that any moment some fiery shard of metal would soon crash down on him, that glass lances would shred him. And he stayed on his side until he heard someone asking him if he was all right. Cautiously, he lowered his arms. Sirens were already blaring, and through the thick smoke he could see figures rushing about the shop with fire extinguishers hissing.

"Do you need help?"

He didn't object when hands cupped under his arms and pulled gently, until he gathered his feet beneath him and stood. He swayed a bit, and coughed. Someone brushed grime from his denim jacket, a piece of something from his hair, then led him away from the scene, talking all the while about the danger of living in the city these days, and if it wasn't the damned IRA or the damned Arabs, it was the damned taxis going wrong and he'd be damned if he didn't think the damned Apocalypse was coming.

Brian's eyes stopped their watering, but his right leg still hurt where he'd cracked it on the street, and his right shoulder felt as if it had been yanked from its socket. He groaned and gripped his arm, tensing with the anticipation of feeling the flow of blood.

"You need a doctor?"

After a moment he shook his head, closed his eyes tightly, and willed the pain to go away, come back later when he wasn't shaking so much. When he opened them again, his benefactor was gone and the police were already cordoning off the area. He walked off, still a bit wobbly but able to convince those who saw him that he wasn't drunk or crazy.

And it wasn't until he'd cut through Russell Square several minutes later and was heading toward his place near the university that he realized the bag was still clamped under his sore arm. A sign, he decided, and leaned against the nearest lamppost, took the picture out, and smiled at the woman.

"Crystal," he said, "why do I get the feeling you've just saved my life?"

"Don't flatter yourself, boy. It was a mistake."

Brian nearly dropped the package at the voice, then whirled and scowled. "Melody," he said, "you could have taken ten years off me, sneaking up like that."

Melody Tyce only laughed, parts and sections of her rippling in accompaniment as she tried to get a closer look at what he was holding in his hand. "You talking to pictures now, Brian?"

Quickly, he tucked Crystal back into her bag and tucked it back under his arm. "None of your business."

She laughed again and pushed coquettishly at the mass of blond hair that ill-framed her pudgy face. She was much too large for so much atop her head, and, he thought, for the snug clothes she wore. It made her seem as if she were trying too hard, which he knew wasn't the case where he was concerned. She was a good-natured woman who had taken him under her wing, sending him to the restaurants where meals were good and just as good with their prices, to the shops where his clothes wouldn't look as if they'd fallen off the rack, and to the clubs where he might, were he more aggressive, even meet a young lady.

"Oh, come on," she persisted. "What do you have? Not one of *those* things, is it?"

"No," he said with a grin. "Something I picked up in a shop, that's all."

"Ah. A souvenir."

"Yes. Sort of."

She nodded. "Better. You're forgiven, then, for talking to yourself."

"I wasn't talking—" He made to ease her away, to give him some room, and the package slipped to the pavement. Instantly she pounced on it, and since the picture had slipped out of its covering, she was able to take a good look as she handed it back.

"Well, I'll be damned," she said.

"What?" He moved to her side and peered at the woman's face over her shoulder. "You know her?"

"I should." Her thumb ran along the frame, tracing the roses, while she sighed. "Where'd you get it, Brian?"

He told her.

She sighed again.

"Hey, what?" he said as she pushed it back into his hands and walked off. "C'mon, Mel, what gives?"

Midway down the block she stopped, shaking her head and looking up at the clean white facade of what had once been a Georgian townhouse, was now only one of several bed-and-breakfast hotels that lined the narrow street.

"Mel, what do you mean, you should know her?" Then he followed her gaze into the top-floor window, over the narrow entrance. "No," he said. "No, you're kidding."

"Clear as day, it's her."

They took the steps together, and he held the door, frowning but not wanting to push her with more questions. What she was claiming was clearly absurd—that the picture was of her mother, who lived in a large room two floors above the entrance and seldom showed herself to any of the guests. It couldn't be. She was, by his estimation after the one time he had seen her, well over eighty and almost as large as Melody herself.

At the back of the square foyer now used as a lobby was a large desk. Melody hurried behind it and dropped into a wing-back chair, slapped her hands on the blotter, stared at him without expression. "I gave that to Ben two weeks ago," she said. "Told him to take it to a friend that has a shop in Salisbury. He promised me he would."

"But why, if it's true?"

"Oh, it's true, Brian. And the why of it? Because she don't like seeing herself like that anymore. It makes her—"

"Oh," he said. "Oh. I see." And he supposed that seeing his own photograph, taken now, thirty years in the future would probably drop him into an unstoppable depression. "Oh, hell."

"It's all right," she assured him. "I should have known it wouldn't be that easy. Bad pennies, if you know what I mean."

He said nothing more, just gave her a sympathetic look and started up the winding staircase toward his own room on the middle floor. And once inside, he flopped into his armchair and puffed his cheeks, blew out a breath, and set the picture on the table beside him.

"So," he said as he unlaced his shoes and kicked them under the bed. "So that's what you looked like, you old bat. Not bad. Mind telling me what happened?"

He laughed shortly, hoisted himself back up, and stripped to his underwear. There was a basin in one corner, and a mirror over it in which he saw the spreadings of a pair of marvelous bruises—one on his shoulder, another reaching up over his hip. Suddenly he began to tremble, and a chill of perspiration slipped over his chest and back. He coughed, he choked, and he barely made it to the toilet at the end of the hall before he lost his breakfast, and the bit of lunch he'd taken during his walk.

Ten minutes later he lay on the bed, staring at the ceiling.

Delayed reaction, he thought, and almost immediately fell asleep.

Dreamless.

Long.

Waking shortly after sunset when a screech of brakes made him sit up, his breath short and his hands clenched into white-knuckled fists.

"Jesus," he said, reached up and switched on the tiny light affixed to the wall. The floor-to-ceiling windows were open, the curtains drifting with the breeze; the armchair a dark blotch in front of a fireplace bricked over, its shadow on the wall slightly wavering, as if under water.

He rubbed his eyes until they burned, then forced his fingers to relax, groaning when the aches, dull and throbbing, erupted along the side. He wondered if he ought not to see a doctor, and by the time he had decided it wasn't worth it, he was sleeping again.

Dreaming, this time, of phantom taxis and phantom drivers and old Ben Isling crushed to death behind his counter.

He spent most of the following day in the hotel, watching television, eating sandwiches, fussed over by Melody, who told him more than once that if he wanted to get rid of the picture, she could take it out to her friend in Salisbury herself. The other guests wandered in and out of the cozy front room, clucking, shaking their heads, giving him all the sympathy he required, until Melody finally laughed and told him he ought to charge admission.

But Bess didn't come. Bess Orbache, a young American like himself, using the city as a way to bury her past. Or so he thought each time she refused him a history, or even a hint. He hoped she was all right; he knew, however, she was more than all right, she was competent and confident and didn't need him for a squire.

On the third day, he walked to get the stiffness from his leg, had dinner and too much to drink at a pub he haunted, and finally, when there was no place to go, went to his bed.

And dreamed of taxis and explosions and something crawling black and wet through his window.

He woke with a start, blinking sleep away without sitting up. A few deep breaths to calm him, and he turned his head to the left, and saw the door to his room several inches ajar.

God, he thought, and felt himself grow cold, not once moving his gaze from the bit of hallway he could see. There was no one out there, not anymore, but he held his breath anyway, against the odd chance.

This is silly, you know, he told himself when he felt his shoulders trembling; you're just the victim of a beautiful woman who wanted to see your body before asking you to her suite at the Savoy for a night of—

Someone screamed.

"Jesus," he said, and leapt to his feet, wincing at the ache in his bruised leg as he stumbled back into his clothes. By the time he was dressed, the hallway was filling with those guests still at home, most of them crowding to the center stairwell. As best he could tell from the babble and the whispers, someone on the floor below had been discovered in his room; murder, it was said, a throat cut and enough blood to paint most of one wall.

A young woman, shorter than he, her long brown hair touched prematurely with strands of gray, swayed a bit as the descriptions grew more graphic, and he put a hand on her back to prevent her from falling.

"I'm all right!" she snapped, then looked over her shoulder. "Oh, sorry, Brian. I thought it was Mr White."

He smiled, tapped her once with a finger, and they backed away to a free corner. "Mr White? Thanks a lot, Bess. It's just what I needed."

Her answering smile was more forced than easy, the faint spray of her freckles nearly vanishing in the attempt, and he leaned back against the wall, a hand in a hip pocket. Thurmond White was a lone traveler—fresh from Virginia, though he had no identifiable accent—with one eye out for bargains and the other out for lonely women. Bess, it seemed, was one of his prime candidates for either category, and twice Brian had to rescue her in the lobby by pretending they had a date. White hadn't been gracious, and hadn't given up the fight.

Bess, for her part, allowed him to take her to dinner both times, once more to the theater, once again to a film. Their good-nights were so chaste he wanted to scream.

They said nothing as they watched the dozen or so guests shift around for better views; they tensed when they heard the sirens stop outside, heard footsteps on the carpeted stairs, heard voices raised in authority.

"I don't think I want to talk to the cops," he said at last, and with a nod for her to join him, slipped back into his room.

She took the chair at once; he sat cross-legged on the bed.

"I heard you nearly caught it the other day," she said, staring around the room as if it were light-years different from her own down the hall. "Are you all right?"

He explained what had happened, didn't bother to exaggerate the injuries he'd received. She wasn't that impressed, though she didn't seem to mind that he couldn't stop looking at the T-shirt she wore—a thin one, and of a solid black that accentuated the tan of her bare arms and the curve of her chest. With a few variations, it was what she had worn since the first day he had met her; he assumed she had several of them and knew what they did.

Then he told her about waking up and finding the door open.

"Oh, my God," she said, sitting suddenly forward. "Brian, do you realize you could have been a victim? My God!" She scanned the room again, this time checking the shadows for a lurking killer. "My God!" And she was grinning.

A flare of light when the wind parted the curtains, and she looked to the side table and saw the picture of Crystal.

"Melody's mother," he said to her unasked question.

"You're kidding. That old bat?"

"So she says."

Bess reached for the frame, changed her mind with a frown, and suggested that he make sure he kept his door locked. When he told her he did, she reminded him it had been open.

"Or opened," she amended with a sly, menacing smile.

"Right," he said. "Now look, I don't know about you, but living dangerously makes me hungry."

"I already ate."

"Eat again."

She looked at him, considered, and nodded, then took his arm, stroked it once, and led him into the hall, where they were stopped by a constable who asked them if they'd mind looking in at the downstairs lounge, just a few questions, no problems, the inspector would take only a moment of their time.

Melody Tyce met them on the landing and looked at him strangely.

The inspector took exactly ten minutes, thanked them, and took their names.

"I'll be damned," Bess said as they walked out to the street.

"I'm not surprised," he said. "Sooner or later one of his women was bound to catch on."

"You knew him well?" she asked dubiously.

"No. But White was the kind of guy . . . I don't know. The kind of guy who just travels around, seeing what he can get from where he is before going somewhere else. I don't know. Old before his time, you know what I mean?"

"Sure," she said, skipping a step. "Decadent."

He thought about it, and shook his head. "No. Just lost, I think."

"Ah," she said. "Very profound."

Maybe, he thought, and wondered if she knew how much the description seemed to fit him. If she did, she said nothing, and once their meal was over, they walked home in silence, not holding hands, not brushing arms, and when she skipped up the steps to her room he stood in the foyer shaking his head.

Was it something I said? he thought with a grin.

And thought about it again the next morning when Melody acted as if he had just contracted the plague. Her manner was stiff, her eyes blank when she looked at him, and as he headed out for a day trip to the Tower, he looked back and saw her standing in the doorway, arms folded under her breasts.

From Traitor's Gate, then, to the armor museum, he walked through the tour and thought of nothing but Bess. She was getting to him. She was taunting him. The idea she was toying with him got him so mad that he returned to the hotel before he was ready and sat on the steps, waiting for her, ready to demand an explanation of her disinterest.

The sun set.

He went up to his room only once, to change clothes, and turned Crystal's face away when her eyes seemed to follow.

Back outside he sat again, hands on knees, seeing a patrol car pass and remembering Mr White and Ben. I am, he thought then, pretty damn lucky after all.

A light switched on in a room overhead, and he looked up and back, and saw a shadow behind curtains. Melody's mother, and he rolled his shoulders in a shudder.

Bess showed up just after nine, smiled broadly when she realized he'd been waiting just for her, and nodded when all the dialogues he'd imagined came out as an invitation to a late dinner up the street.

They ate at the nearest Garfunkel's, neither of them wanting to walk very far, neither in the mood for anything fancy. She took a place on the wall-length booth, he the aisle chair. The only adventurous thing they attempted was switching plates when he was unable to face the bland meat he'd been served. And neither of them spoke of more than the cool weather, the bright skies, the tourists who seemed to be crowding into everything and not giving the true Anglophiles a chance to indulge, until Bess looked peculiarly at the veal she'd been nibbling.

"Something wrong?"

"The cheese," she said, her face abruptly pale, the freckles suddenly too dark.

He reached over with a fork and took a bit on a tine, tasted it with his tongue, and shrugged. "Seems all right to me."

She gagged and covered her mouth with her napkin, looking apologetic and near frightened at the same time. When she reached for and failed to grab her glass of water, he half rose and began to search for a waitress, looked back in time to see her slump to one side in the false leather booth. With a cry for help, he kicked back his chair and attempted to stretch her out along the seat. She moaned. He muttered encouragement and chafed her wrists, reached around and grabbed a napkin to dip into water when he saw the perspiration breaking over her brow.

A doctor pushed him aside.

Two minutes later she was dead.

Five minutes after the place was closed down, and within the hour he was standing in front of the hotel, looking up at the lighted window where Melody's mother lived. Questioned and released from the scene, the urge to wander had been suppressed in favor of a sudden macabre curiosity. He supposed, if he were inclined to believe in such things, that the portrait was some sort of good-luck charm; and right now it was difficult not to believe. The taxi, White's murder, the rat poison-tainted food; add them up and they tallied deaths that should have been his. Add them another way, however, and they tallied a run of good fortune that had nothing to do with anyone's likeness. Melody had said it herself, in fact—that she had gotten rid of it because her mother didn't like it. She called it a bad penny, which, to Brian's mind, had nothing at all to do with good luck.

The questions shifted as a shadow approached them.

He stepped back toward the curb, not bothering to look away.

The curtains parted just enough for him to see a slant of face, a slash of vivid blue, before they closed again and the shadow backed away.

He almost went in. He almost ran up the steps and slammed open the door. But a sudden image of Bess' stricken face loomed over the stoop, and he turned away and began walking—past buildings that even in the dark seemed a century out of place, past short-skirted girls who giggled softly in the shadows, past theatergoers in fine clothes, and belligerent shills who told him he'd better not wait, mate, if he didn't want to miss the city's greatest show.

He saw none of the neon, none of the headlamps, none of the faces that turned toward him and away.

Good luck, he thought sourly; what the hell kind of good luck was it for Bess, and Mr White, and old Ben at the shop?

Coincidence.

Poisoned meat.

He was angry at himself for not feeling more sorrow at young Bess's dying, but he had hardly known her except as someone he couldn't have; he felt nothing at all for Thurmond White, in spite of the man's brashness and his ill-mannered ways; and Ben just happened to be standing where he was, at his post in the shop as the taxi crashed through.

Coincidence.

Good luck.

Bad pennies; and he whirled, nearly knocking over an old woman, and broke into a run that soon covered him with sweat, had his shift clinging to his chest, filled his shoes with slimy damp. The dark streets were quiet save for the slap of his soles; the last of the leaves hissed as he passed. Twice he had to dodge cars as he crossed in a street's center; once he had to outrun a dog he'd surprised rooting in garbage.

He ran back to the hotel and stood on the pavement, and when Melody came to the door he only glared and nodded.

She had a sweater cloaked over her wide shoulders, and she fussed with the top button as she came down the steps.

"It's her," he said tightly, pointing at the window.

"I admit, it's unusual."

He could barely see her face, but he could sense her hesitant smile. "Unusual? Christ, Mel, it's impossible!"

She took his hand and tugged. When he resisted, she tugged again. "Won't hurt, Brian. It won't hurt to look."

He shook off her grip, but followed her just the same, into the lobby, up the stairs, through the fire door and around to the front. She knocked and tilted her head, gave him a smile and walked in, and he rode with her on her shadow.

A single bed, a single chair, a dresser on the far wall.

A crystal chandelier that blinded him until he squinted.

Melody stood beside him.

The other woman stood with her back to the curtains.

She wore a red velvet nightdress trimmed in faint gold, a complement to the ebony that spilled over her shoulders. Her face told him she was sixty, perhaps even thirty; her hands told him she was thirty, perhaps even twenty; and she was as far from fat as he was from content.

She was the woman in his picture, framed by the silvered drapes.

"She tries very hard, my granddaughter does," said the woman named Crystal, in a soft, whipping voice. "Her mother was no better."

He heard Melody sobbing; he didn't look around.

"I suspect she took a fancy to you, a little before I did." The smile was brief and cold. "For different reasons, of course. She fancies she loves you."

He did look then, and looked away from the tears; then reached behind him for the doorknob. "You're crazy," he said.

"You're alive," she told him.

He snorted, courage returned when he wasn't looking in her eyes. "Look, lady—"

"You're here," she said quietly, "because you've noplace else to go, isn't that so? No home. No family. You live in the past, and England is perfect for ambitions like that. And so do I, Brian. So do I." The rustle of velvet. "My past, not yours."

He yanked the door open and stepped into the hall; and once out of the wash of white light, he took a deep breath, and shuddered, and headed for the stairs. It was time, he thought, to move on. Another city, perhaps the Continent. Maybe even go back to the States. It didn't matter as long as he didn't stay here.

Melody hurried up behind him.

"Tote the tab," he said as he climbed toward his room. "I'll be down in a few minutes."

"You don't get it yet, do you?" she said.

"Get it?" he look down. "C'mon, Mel, you know me."

She wiped her nose with a sleeve. "Do you know who had that picture before you?"

"You did. You told me."

"No. Not me. Mr White."

He blinked, and grinned. "Mel, this isn't the time. I—"

"I killed him."

He fumbled for the banister and lowered himself to the step. "You didn't."

"She was tired of him. With a few exceptions, he was growing to like older women."

"So?"

"Older women, Brian, don't have much time left."

He stood angrily. "Jesus, Mel, what the hell are you pulling here, huh?" His eyes closed, and opened. "Oh, I get it. Your grandmother has the power to take what life is left from a person, right? She then gives that portrait to someone, and it brings them good luck—like not dying when they should." He spread his hands. "No problem, Mel. If it'll make you feel better, I'll leave it behind. O.K.? Are you happy?"

He started up again (*my past*) and reached the landing, then turned around (*not yours*) because he saw the cab, and the blood, and young Bess on a stretcher.

"Let me get this straight," he said to Melody, who was still waiting. "You arranged, somehow, for me to get the picture because Mr White didn't pick the girls, he picked older women?"

"You were the type," she said. "She always knows the type."

"And . . . " He put a finger to his chin. "And no matter where I go, because of me people are going to die just to keep her where she is."

Melody lifted a helpless hand.

"You," he said, "are insane. So is that imposter in there, or was the old woman the fake?"

He pulled open the fire door—

"Brian, how did you feel when poor Bess was dead?"

—and stepped into the hall, snatched his key from his pocket, and slammed into his room.

He didn't turn on the lights.

He didn't look at Crystal's picture.

He stood at the window and stared down at the street through the gauze of the curtains.

What a stupid thing to say, he thought, spinning the key in one hand; I felt lousy, I felt rotten, I felt . . .

And he knew then what Crystal wanted.

Not the dead, not the dying, but the fact that good old Brian, like Thurmond White, would never really care.

A polite knock on the door.

"What!" he said as a tour coach drifted by.

"The bill," Melody said. "Do you still want it?"

A pair of young women in jeans and down jackets huddled on the opposite pavement, knapsacks at their feet, and they were studying a map.

"Brian?"

"No," he said loudly, and parted the curtain.

One of them looked up and saw him, poked her companion, and they smiled.

He heard Melody shift the picture so it faced his bed.

"Brian, she's waiting."

Girls, he thought; they're not much older than girls.

He watched them without expression, watched their flirting and their intent, and when he nodded at the last, the light in the room above switched off, and he waited.

Listening to the girls hurry over to the door.

Listening as Melody left to let them in.

Waiting, and sighing, because he didn't feel a thing.

# F. Paul Wilson

# Buckets

F. PAUL WILSON is another of those horror writers who is also a doctor. His short fiction was first published in 1971, while he was still studying as a medical student, and since then he has appeared in all the major science fiction and fantasy magazines. Over two million copies of his books are in print in America and he is the author of ten novels, including *The Keep* (filmed in 1983), *The Tomb*, *The Touch*, *Black Wind*, *Dydeetown World*, *The Tery* and *Reborn*, while his short fiction has been collected in *Soft & Others*.

The following story was originally written for a never-published anthology about "Doctors and Halloween", and the author admits that he knew it would be "extremely unpopular with a fair number, perhaps even a majority of readers.

"As you will see, 'Buckets' leaves no room for a neutral stance," says Wilson. "But given the premise, how else could it be written? And despite the fact that it was written in 1985, it seems to get more timely with each passing year."

Prepare to make up your own mind . . .

"MY, AREN'T YOU AN EARLY BIRD!"

Dr. Edward Cantrell looked down at the doe-eyed child in the five-and-dime Princess Leia costume on his front doorstep and tried to guess her age. A beautiful child of about seven or eight, with flaxen hair and scrawny little shoulders drawn up as if she were afraid of him, as if he might bite her. It occurred to him that today was Wednesday and it was not yet noon. Why wasn't she in school? Never mind. It was Halloween and it was none of his business why she was getting a jump on the rest of the kids in the trick-or-treat routine.

"Are you looking for a treat?" he asked her.

She nodded slowly, shyly.

"Okay! You got it!" He went to the bowl behind him on the hall table and picked out a big Snickers. Then he added a dime to the package. It had become a Halloween tradition over the years that Dr. Cantrell's place was where you got dimes when you trick-or-treated.

He thrust his hand through the open space where the screen used to be. He liked to remove the storm door screen on Halloween; it saved him the inconvenience of repeatedly opening the door against the kids pressing against it for their treats; and besides, he worried about one of the little ones being pushed backward off the front steps. A lawsuit could easily follow something like that.

The little girl lifted her silver bucket.

He took a closer look. No, not silver—shiny stainless steel, reflecting the dull gray overcast sky. It reminded him of something, but he couldn't place it at the moment. Strange sort of thing to be collecting Halloween treats in. Probably some new fad. Whatever became of the old pillowcase or the shopping bag, or even the plastic jack-o'-lantern?

He poised his hand over the bucket, then let the candy bar and dime drop. They landed with a soft *squish*.

Not exactly the sound he had expected. He leaned forward to see what else was in the bucket but the child had swung around and was making her way down the steps.

Out on the sidewalk, some hundred feet away along the maple-lined driveway, two older children waited for her. A stainless-steel bucket dangled from each of their hands.

Cantrell shivered as he closed the front door. There was a new chill in the air. Maybe he should put on a sweater. But what color? He checked himself over in the hall mirror. Not bad for a guy looking fifty-two in the eye. That was Erica's doing. Trading in the old wife for a new model twenty years younger had had a rejuvenating effect on him. Also, it made him work at staying young-looking—like three trips a week to the Short Hills Nautilus Club and watching his diet. He decided to forgo the sweater for now.

He almost made it back to his recliner and the unfinished New York *Times* when the front bell rang again. Sighing resignedly, he turned and went back to the front door. He didn't mind tending to the trick-or-treaters, but he wished Erica were here to share door duty. Why did she have to pick today for her monthly spending spree in Manhattan? He knew she loved Bloomingdale's—in fact, she had once told him that after she died she wanted her ashes placed in an urn in the lingerie department there—but she could have waited until tomorrow.

It was two boys this time, both about eleven, both made up like punkers with orange and green spiked hair, ripped clothes, and crude tattoos, obviously done with a Bic instead of a real tattooer's pen. They stood restlessly in the chill breeze, shifting from one foot to the other, looking up and down the block, stainless-steel buckets in hand.

He threw up his hands. "Whoa! Tough guys, eh? I'd better not mess around with the likes of—!"

One of the boys glanced at him briefly, and in his eyes Cantrell caught a flash of such rage and hatred—not just for him, but for the whole world—that his voice dried away to a whisper. And then the look was gone as if it had never been and the boy was just another kid again. He hastily grabbed a pair of Three Musketeers and two dimes, leaned through the opening in the door, and dropped one of each into their buckets.

The one on the right went *squish* and the one on the left went *plop*.

He managed to catch just a glimpse of the bottom of the bucket on the right as the kid turned. He couldn't tell what was in there, but it was red.

He was glad to see them go. *Surly pair*, he thought. Not a word out of either of them. And what was in the bottom of that bucket? Didn't look like any candy he knew, and he considered himself an expert on candy. He patted the belly that he had been trying to flatten for months. More than an expert—an *aficionado* of candy.

Further speculation was forestalled by a call from Monroe Community Hospital. One of his postpartum patients needed a laxative. He okayed a couple of ounces of milk of mag. Then the nurse double-checked his pre-op orders on the hysterectomy tomorrow.

He managed to suffer through it all with dignity. It was Wednesday and he always took Wednesdays off. Jeff Sewell was supposed to be taking his calls today, but all the floors at the hospital had the Cantrell home phone number and they habitually tried here first before they went hunting for whoever was covering him.

He was used to it. He had learned ages ago that there was no such thing as a day off in Ob-Gyn.

The bell rang again, and for half a second Cantrell found himself hesitant to answer it. He shrugged off the reluctance and pulled open the door.

Two mothers and two children. He sucked in his gut when he recognized the mothers as longtime patients.

*This is more like it!*

"Hi, Dr. Cantrell!" the red-haired woman said with a big smile. She put a hand atop the red-haired child's head. "You remember Shana, don't you? You delivered her five years ago next month."

"I remember *you*, Gloria," he said, noting her flash of pleasure at having her first name remembered. He never forgot a face. "But Shana here looks a little bit different from when I last saw her."

As both women laughed, he scanned his mind for the other's name. Then it came to him:

"Yours looks a little bigger, too, Diane."

"She sure does. What do you say to Dr. Cantrell, Susan?"

The child mumbled something that sounded like "Ricky Meat" and held up an orange plastic jack-o'-lantern with a black plastic strap.

"That's what I like to see!" he said. "A real Halloween treat holder. Better than those stainless-steel buckets the other kids have been carrying!"

Gloria and Diane looked at each other. "Stainless-steel buckets?"

"Can you believe it?" he said as he got the two little girls each a Milky Way and a dime. "My first three Halloween customers this morning carried steel buckets for their treats. Never seen anything like it."

"Neither have we," Diane said.

"You haven't? You should have passed a couple of boys out on the street."

"No. We're the only ones around."

Strange. But maybe they had cut back to the street through the trees as this group entered the driveway.

He dropped identical candy and coins into the identical jack-o'-lanterns and heard them strike the other treats with a reassuring rustle.

He watched the retreating forms of the two young mothers and their two happy kids until they were out of sight. *This is the way Halloween should be*, he thought. Much better than strange hostile kids with metal buckets.

And just as he completed the thought, he saw three small white-sheeted forms of indeterminate age and sex round the hedge and head up the driveway. Each had a shiny metal bucket in hand.

He wished Erica were here.

He got the candy bars and coins and waited at the door for them. He had decided that before he parted with the goodies he was going to find out who these kids were and what they had in their little buckets. Fair was fair.

The trio climbed to the top step of the stoop and stood there waiting, silently watching him through the eye holes of their sheets.

Their silence got under his skin.

*Doesn't anybody say "Trick or treat?" anymore?*

"Well, what have we here?" he said with all the joviality he could muster. "Three little ghosts! The Ghostly Trio!"

One of them—he couldn't tell which—said, "Yes."

"Good! I like ghosts on Halloween! You want a treat?"

They nodded as one.

"Okay! But first you're gonna have to earn it! Show me what you've got in those buckets and I'll give you each a dime and a box of Milk Duds! How's that for a deal?"

The kids looked at each other. Some wordless communication seemed to pass between them, then they turned and started back down the steps.

"Hey, kids! Hey, wait!" he said quickly, forcing a laugh. "I was only kidding! You don't have to show me anything. Here! Just take the candy."

They paused on the second step, obviously confused.

Ever so gently, he coaxed them back. "C'mon, kids. I'm just curious about those buckets, is all. I've been seeing them all day and I've been wondering where they came from. But if I frightened you, well, hey, I'll ask somebody else later on." He held up the candy and the coins and extended his hand through the door. "Here you go."

One little ghost stepped forward but raised an open hand—a little girl's hand—instead of a bucket.

He could not bear to be denied any longer. He pushed open the storm door and stepped out, looming over the child, craning his neck to see into that damn little bucket. The child squealed in fright and turned away, crouching over the bucket as if to protect it from him.

*What are they trying to hide? What's the matter with them? And what's the matter with me?*

Really. Who *cared* what was in those buckets?

*He* cared. It was becoming an obsession with him. He'd go crazy if he didn't find out.

Hoping nobody was watching—nobody who'd think he was a child molester—he grabbed the little ghost by the shoulders and twisted her toward him. She couldn't hide the bucket from him now. In the clear light of day he got a good look into it.

Blood.

Blood with some floating bits of tissue and membrane lay maybe an inch and a half deep in the bottom.

Startled and sickened, he could only stand there and stare at the red, swirling liquid. As the child tried to pull the bucket away from him, it tipped, spilling its contents over the front of her white sheet. She screamed—more in dismay than terror.

"Let her go!" said a little boy's voice from beside him. Cantrell turned to see one of the other ghosts hurling the contents of its bucket at him. As if in slow motion, he saw the sheet of red liquid and debris float toward him through the air, spreading as it neared. The warm spray splattered him up and down and he reeled back in revulsion.

By the time he had wiped his eyes clear, the kids were halfway down the driveway. He wanted to chase after them, but he had to get out of these bloody clothes first. He'd be taken for a homicidal maniac if someone saw him running after three little kids looking like this.

Arms akimbo, he hurried to the utility room and threw his shirt into the sink. *Why*? his mind cried as he tried to remember whether hot or cold water set a stain. He tried cold and began rubbing at the blood in the blue oxford cloth.

He scrubbed hard and fast to offset the shaking of his hands. What a horrible thing for anyone to do, but especially *children!* Questions tumbled over each other in confusion: What could be going through their sick little minds? And where had they gotten the blood?

But most of all, *Why me*?

Slowly the red color began to thin and run, but the bits of tissue clung. He looked at them more closely. *Damn if that doesn't look like . . .*

Recognition triggered an epiphany. He suddenly understood everything.

He now knew who those children were—or at least who had put them up to it—and he understood why. He sighed with relief as anger flooded through him like a cleansing flame. He much preferred being angry to being afraid.

He dried his arms with a paper towel and went to call the cops.

"Right-to-lifers, Joe! Has to be them!"

Sergeant Joe Morelli scratched his head. "You sure, Doc?"

Cantrell had known the Morelli family since Joe's days as a security guard at the Mall, waiting for a spot to open up on the Monroe police force. He had delivered all three of Joe's kids.

"Who else could it be? Those little stainless-steel buckets they carry—the ones I told you about—they're the same kind we use in D and C's, and get this: We used to use them in abortions. The scrapings from the uterus slide down through a weighted speculum into one of those buckets."

And it was those bloody scrapings that had been splattered all over him.

"But why you, Doc? I know you do abortions now and then—all you guys do—but you're not an abortionist per se, if you know what I'm saying."

Cantrell nodded, not mentioning Sandy. He knew the subject of Joe's youngest daughter's pregnancy two years ago was still a touchy subject. She had only been fifteen but he had taken care of everything for Joe with the utmost discretion. He now had a devoted friend on the police force.

A thought suddenly flashed through Cantrell's mind: *They must know about the women's center! But how could they?*

It was due to open tomorrow, the first of the month. He had been so careful to avoid any overt connection with it, situating it downtown and going so far as to set it up through a corporate front. Abortions might be legal, but it still didn't sit well with a lot of people to know that their neighbor ran an abortion mill.

Maybe that was it. Maybe a bunch of sicko right-to-lifers had connected him with the new center.

"What gets me," Joe was saying, "is that if this is real abortion material like you say, where'd they get it?"

"I wish I knew." The question had plagued him since he had called the police.

"Well, don't you worry, Doc," Joe said, slipping his hat over his thinning hair. "Whatever's going on, it's gonna stop. I'll cruise the neighborhood. If I see any kids, or even adults with any of these buckets, I'll ID them and find out what's up."

"Thanks, Joe," he said, meaning it. It was comforting to know a cop was looking out for him. "I appreciate that. I'd especially like to get this ugly business cleared up before the wife and I get home from dinner tonight."

"I don't blame you," he said, shaking his head. "I know I wouldn't want Marie to see any buckets of blood."

The trick-or-treaters swelled in numbers as the afternoon progressed. They flowed to the door in motley hordes of all shapes, sizes, and colors. A steady stream of Spocks, Skywalkers, Vaders, Indiana Joneses, Madonnas, Mötley Crües, Twisted Sisters, and even a few ghosts, goblins, and witches.

And always among them were one or two kids with steel buckets.

Cantrell bit his lip and repressed his anger when he saw them. He said nothing, did not try to look into their buckets, gave no sign that their presence meant anything to him, pretended they were no different from the other kids as he dropped candies and coins into the steel buckets among the paper sacks and pillowcases and jack-o'-lanterns, all the while praying that Morelli would catch one of the little bastards crossing the street and find out who was behind this bullshit.

He saw the patrol car pull into the drive around 4:00. Morelli finally must have nailed one of them! *About time*! He had to leave for the women's center soon and wanted this thing settled and done with.

"No luck, Doc," Joe said, rolling down his window. "You must have scared them off."

"Are you crazy?" His anger exploded as he trotted down the walk to the driveway. "They've been through here all afternoon!"

"Hey, take it easy, Doc. If they're around, they must be

hiding those buckets when they're on the street, because I've been by here about fifty times and I haven't seen one steel bucket."

Cantrell reined in his anger. It would do no good to alienate Joe. He wanted the police force on his side.

"Sorry. It's just that this is very upsetting."

"I can imagine. Look Doc. Why don't I do this: Why don't I just park the car right out at the curb and watch the kids as they come in. Maybe I'll catch one in the act. At the very least, it might keep them away."

"I appreciate that, Joe, but it won't be necessary. I'm going out in a few minutes and won't be back until much later tonight. However, I do wish you'd keep an eye on the place—vandals, you know."

"Sure thing, Doc. No problem."

Cantrell watched the police car pull out of the driveway, then he set the house alarm and hurried to the garage to make his getaway before the doorbell rang again.

## The Midtown Women's Medical Center

Cantrell savored the effect of the westering sun glinting off the thick brass letters over the entrance as he walked by. Red letters on a white placard proclaimed "Grand Opening Tomorrow" from the front door. He stepped around the side of the building into the alley, unlocked the private entrance, and stepped inside.

Dark, quiet, deserted. *Damn!* He had hoped to catch the contractor for one last check of the trim. He wanted everything perfect for the opening.

He flipped on the lights and checked his watch. Erica would be meeting him here in about an hour, then they would pick up the Klines and have drinks and dinner at the club. He had just enough time for a quick inspection tour.

*So clean*, he thought as he walked through the waiting room—the floors shiny and unscuffed, the carpet pile unmatted, the wall surfaces unmarred by chips or finger smudges. Even the air smelled new.

This center—*his* center—had been in the planning stages for three years. Countless hours of meetings with lawyers, bankers, planning boards, architects, and contractors had gone into it. But at last it was ready to go. He planned to work here himself in the beginning, just to keep overheads down, but once the operation got rolling, he'd hire other doctors and have them do the work while he ran the show from a distance.

He stepped into Procedure Room One and looked over the equipment. Dominating the room was the Rappaport 206, a state-of-the-art procedure table with thigh and calf supports on the stirrups, three breakaway sections, and fully motorized tilts in all planes—Trendelenburg, reverse Trendelenburg, left and right lateral.

Close by, the Zarick suction extractor—the most efficient abortion device on the market—hung gleaming on its chrome stand. He pressed the "on" button to check the power but nothing happened.

"It won't work tonight," said a child's voice behind him, making him almost scream with fright.

He spun around. Fifteen or twenty kids stood there staring at him. Most were costumed, and they all carried those goddamn steel buckets.

"All right!" he said. "This does it! I've had just about enough! I'm getting the police!"

He turned to reach for the phone but stopped after one step. More kids were coming in from the hall. They streamed in slowly and silently, their eyes fixed on him, piercing him. They filled the room, occupying every square foot except for the small circle of space they left around him and the equipment. And behind them he could see more, filling the hall and the waiting room beyond. A sea of faces, all staring at him.

He was frightened now. They were just kids, but there were so damn many of them! A few looked fifteen or so, and one looked to be in her early twenties, but by far most of them appeared to be twelve and under. Some were even toddlers! What sort of sick mind would involve such tiny children in this?

And how did they get in? All the doors were locked.

"Get out of here," he said, forcing his voice into calm, measured tones.

They said nothing, merely continued to stare back at him.

"All right, then. If you won't leave, *I* will! And when I return—" He tried to push by a five-year-old girl in a gypsy costume. Without warning she jabbed her open hand into his abdomen with stunning force, driving him back against the table.

"Who are you?" This time his voice was less calm, his tones less measured.

"You mean you don't recognize us?" a mocking voice said from the crowd.

"I've never seen any of you before today."

"Not true," said another voice. "After our fathers, you're the second most important man in our lives."

This was insane! "I don't know *any* of you!"

"You should." Another voice—were they trying to confuse him by talking from different spots in the room?

"*Why?*"

"Because you killed us."

The absurdity of the statement made him laugh. He straightened from the table and stepped forward. "Okay. That's it. This isn't the least bit funny."

A little boy shoved him back, roughly, violently. His strength was hideous.

"M-my wife will be here s-soon." He was ashamed of the stammer in his voice, but he couldn't help it. "She'll call the police."

"Sergeant Morelli, perhaps?" This voice was more mature than the others—more womanly. He found her and looked her in the eye. She was the tall one in her early twenties, dressed in a sweater and skirt. He had a sudden crazy thought that maybe she was a young teacher and these were her students on a class trip. But these kids looked like they spanned all grades from pre-school to junior high.

"Who are you?"

"I don't have a name," she said, facing him squarely. "Very few of us do. But this one does." She indicated a little girl at her side, a toddler made up like a hobo in raggedy clothes with burnt cork rubbed on her face for a beard. An Emmett Kelly dwarf. "Here, Laura," she said to the child as she urged her forward. "Show Dr. Cantrell what you looked like last time he saw you."

Laura stepped up to him. Behind the makeup he could see that she was a beautiful child with short dark hair, a pudgy face, and big brown eyes. She held her bucket out to him.

"She was eleven weeks old," the woman said, "three inches long, and weighed fourteen grams when you ripped her from her mother's uterus. She was no match for you and your suction tube."

Blood and tissue swirled in the bottom of her bucket.

"You don't expect me to buy this, do you?"

"I don't care what you buy, Doctor. But this is Sandra Morelli's child—or at least what her child would look like now if she'd been allowed to be born. But she wasn't born. Her mother had names all picked out—Adam for a boy, Laura for a girl—but her grandfather bullied her mother into an abortion and you were oh-so-willing to see that there were no problems along the way."

"This is absurd!" he said.

"Really?" the woman said. "Then go ahead and call Sergeant Morelli. Maybe he'd like to drive down and meet his granddaughter. The one you killed."

"I killed no one!" he shouted. "*No one*! Abortion has been legal since 1974! Absolutely legal! And besides—she wasn't really alive!"

*What's the matter with me*? he asked himself. *I'm talking to them as if I believe them*!

"Oh, yes," the woman said. "I forgot. Some political appointees decided that we weren't people and that was that. Pretty much like what happened to East European Jews back in World War II. We're not even afforded the grace of being called embryos or fetuses. We're known as 'products of conception.' What a neat, dehumanizing little phrase. So much easier to scrape the 'products of conception' into a bucket than a person."

"I've had just about enough of this!" he said.

"So?" a young belligerent voice said. "What're y'gonna do?"

He knew he was going to do nothing. He didn't want to have another primary-grade kid shove him back against the table again. No kid that size should be that strong. It wasn't natural.

"You can't hold me responsible!" he said. "They came to me, asking for help. They were pregnant and they didn't want to be. My God! *I* didn't make them pregnant!"

Another voice: "No, but you sure gave them a convenient solution!"

"So blame your mothers! *They're* the ones who spread their legs and didn't want to take responsibility for it! How about *them*?"

"They are not absolved," the woman said. "They shirked their responsibilities to us, but the vast majority of them are each responsible for only one of us. You, Dr. Cantrell, are responsible for *all* of us. Most of them were scared teenagers, like Laura's mother, who were bullied and badgered into 'terminating' us. Others were too afraid of what their parents would say so they snuck off to women's medical centers like this and lied about their age and put us out of their misery."

"Not all of them, sweetheart!" he said. He was beginning to feel he was on firmer ground now. "Many a time I've done three or four on the same woman! Don't tell me *they* were poor, scared teenagers. Abortion was their idea of birth control!"

"We know," a number of voices chorused, and something in their tone made him shiver. "We'll see them later."

"The point is," the woman said, "that you were always there, always ready with a gentle smile, a helpful hand, an easy solution, a simple way to get them off the hook by getting rid of us. And a bill, of course."

"If it hadn't been me, it would have been someone else!"

"You can't dilute your own blame. Or your own responsibility," said a voice from behind his chair. "Plenty of doctors refuse to do abortions."

"If you were one of those," said another from his left, "we wouldn't be here tonight."

"The *law* lets me do it. The Supreme Court. So don't blame me. Blame those Supreme Court justices."

"That's politics. We don't care about politics."

"But I believe in a woman's right to control her own life, to make decisions about her own body!"

"We don't care *what* you believe. Do you think the beliefs of a terrorist matter to the victims of his bombs? Don't you understand? This is *personal*!"

A little girl's voice said, "I could have been adopted, you know. I would've made someone a good kid. But I never had the chance!"

They all began shouting at once, about never getting Christmas gifts or birthday presents or hugs or tucked in at night or playing with matches or playing catch or playing house or even playing doctor—

It seemed to go on endlessly. Finally the woman held up her bucket. "All their possibilities ended in here."

"Wait a goddamn minute!" he said. He had just discovered a significant flaw in their little show. "Only a few of them ended up in buckets! If you were up on your facts, you'd know that no one uses those old D and C buckets for abortions anymore." He pointed to the glass trap on the Zarick suction extractor. "This is where the products of conception wind up."

The woman stepped forward with her bucket. "They carry this in honor of me. I have the dubious distinction of being your first victim."

"You're not *my* victims!" he shouted. "The law—"

She spat in his face. Shocked and humiliated, Cantrell wiped away the saliva with his shirt sleeve and pressed himself back against the table. The rage in her face was utterly terrifying.

"The *law*?" she hissed. "Don't speak of legalities to me! Look at me! I'd be twenty-two now and this is how I'd look if you hadn't murdered me. Do a little subtraction, Doctor: 1974 was a lot less than twenty-two years ago. I'm Ellen Benedict's daughter—or at least I would have been if you hadn't agreed to do that D and C on her when she couldn't find a way to explain her pregnancy to her impotent husband!"

*Ellen Benedict!* God! How did they know about Ellen Benedict?

Even *he* had forgotten about her!

The woman stepped forward and grabbed his wrist. He was helpless against her strength as she pressed his hand over her left breast. He might have found the softness beneath her sweater exciting under different circumstances, but now it elicited only dread.

"Feel my heart beating? It was beating when your curette ripped me to pieces. I was only four weeks old. And I'm not the only one here you killed before 1974—I was just your first. So you can't get off the hook by naming the Supreme Court as an accomplice. And even if we allowed you that cop-out, other things you've done since '74 are utterly abominable!" She looked around and pointed into the crowd. "There's one! Come here, honey, and show your bucket to the doctor."

A five- or six-year-old boy came forward. He had blond bangs and the biggest, saddest blue eyes the doctor had ever seen. The boy held out his bucket.

Cantrell covered his face with his hands. "I don't want to see!"

Suddenly he felt his hands yanked downward with numbing force and found the woman's face scant inches from his own.

"*Look*, damn you! You've seen it before!"

He looked into the upheld bucket. A fully formed male fetus lay curled in the blood, its blue eyes open, its head turned at an unnatural angle.

"This is Rachel Walraven's baby as you last saw him."

*The Walraven baby! Oh, God, not that one! How could they know?*

"What you see is how he'd look now if you hadn't broken his neck after the abortifacient you gave his mother made her uterus dump him out."

"He couldn't have survived!" he shouted. He could hear the hysteria edging into his voice. "He was pre-viable! Too immature to survive! The best neonatal ICU in the world couldn't have saved him!"

"Then why'd you break my neck?" the little boy asked.

Cantrell could only sob—a single harsh sound that seemed to rip itself from the tissues inside his chest and burst free into the air. What could he say? How could he tell them that he had miscalculated the length of gestation and that no one had been more shocked than he at the size of the infant that had dropped into his gloved hands. And then it had opened its eyes and stared at him and my God it seemed to be trying to breathe! He'd done late terminations before where the fetus had squirmed around awhile in the bucket before finally dying, but this one—!

*Christ*! he remembered thinking, *what if the damn thing lets out a cry*? He'd get sued by the patient and be the laughing stock of the staff. Poor Ed Cantrell—can't tell the difference between an abortion and a delivery! He'd look like a jerk!

So he did the only thing he could do. He gave its neck a sharp twist as he lowered it into the bucket. The neck didn't even crack when he broke it.

"Why have you come to me?" he said.

"Answer us first," a child's voice said. "Why do you do it? You don't need the money. Why do you kill us?"

"I told you! I believe in every woman's right to—"

They began to boo him, drowning him out. Then the boos changed to a chant: "*Why? Why? Why? Why*?"

"Stop that! Listen to me! I told you why!"

But still they chanted, sounding like a crowd at a football game: "*Why? Why? Why? Why*?"

Finally he could stand no more. He raised his fists and screamed. "All right! Because I can! Is that what you want to hear? I do it because I *can*!"

The room was suddenly dead silent.

The answer startled him. He had never asked himself *why* before. "Because I can," he said softly.

"Yes," the woman said with equal softness. "The ultimate power."

He suddenly felt very old, very tired. "What do you want of me?"

No one answered.

"Why have you come?"

They all spoke as one: "Because today, this Halloween, this night . . . *we* can."

"And we don't want this place to open," the woman said.

So that was it. They wanted to kill the women's center before it got started—*abort* it, so to speak. He almost smiled at the pun. He looked at their faces, their staring eyes. *They mean business*, he thought. And he knew they wouldn't take no for an answer.

Well, this was no time to stand on principle. Promise them anything, then get the hell out of here to safety.

"Okay," he said, in what he hoped was a meek voice. "You've convinced me. I'll turn this into a general medical center. No abortions. Just family practice for the community."

They watched him silently. Finally a voice said, "He's lying."

The woman nodded. "I know." She turned to the children. "Do it," she said.

Pure chaos erupted as the children went wild. They were like a berserk mob, surging in all directions. But silent. So silent.

Cantrell felt himself shoved aside as the children tore into the procedure table and the Zarick extractor. The table was ripped from the floor and all its upholstery shredded. Its sections were torn free and hurled against the walls with such force that they punctured through the plasterboard.

The rage in the children's eyes seemed to leak out into the room, filling it, thickening the air like an onrushing storm, making his skin ripple with fear at its ferocity.

As he saw the Zarick start to topple, he forced himself forward to try to save it but was casually slammed against the wall with stunning force. In a semi-daze, he watched the Zarick raised into the air; he ducked flying glass as it was slammed onto the floor, not just once, but over and over until it was nothing more than a twisted wreck of wire, plastic hose, and ruptured circuitry.

And from down the hall he could hear similar carnage in the other procedure rooms. Finally the noise stopped and the room was packed with children again.

He began to weep. He hated himself for it, but he couldn't help it. He just broke down and cried in front of them. He was frightened. And all the money, all the plans . . . destroyed.

He pulled himself together and stood up straight. He would rebuild. All this destruction was covered by insurance. He would blame it on vandalism, collect his money, and have the place brand-new inside of a month. These vicious little bastards weren't going to stop him.

But he couldn't let them know that.

"Get out, all of you," he said softly. "You've had your fun. You've ruined me. Now leave me alone."

"We'll leave you alone," said the woman who would have been Ellen Benedict's child. "But not yet."

Suddenly they began to empty their buckets on him, hurling the contents at him in a continuous wave, turning the air red with flying blood and tissue, engulfing him from all sides, choking him, clogging his mouth and nostrils.

And then they reached for him . . .

Erica knocked on the front door of the center for the third time and still got no answer.

*Now where can he be?* she thought as she walked around to the private entrance. She tried the door and found it unlocked. She pushed in but stopped on the threshold.

The waiting room was lit and looked normal enough.

"Ed?" she called, but he didn't answer. Odd. His car was out front. She was supposed to meet him here at five. She had taken a cab from the house—after all, she didn't want Ginger dropping her off here; there would be too many questions.

This was beginning to make her uneasy.

She glanced down the hallway. It was dark and quiet.

*Almost* quiet.

She heard tiny little scraping noises, tiny movements, so soft that she would have missed them if there had been any other sound in the building. The sounds seemed to come from the first procedure room. She stepped up to the door and listened to the dark. Yes, they were definitely coming from in there.

She flipped on the light . . . and felt her knees buckle.

The room was red—the walls, the ceiling, the remnants of the shattered fixtures, all dripping with red. The clots and the coppery odor that saturated the air left no doubt in Erica's reeling mind that she was looking at blood. But on the floor—the blood-puddled linoleum was littered with countless shiny, silvery buckets. The little rustling sounds were coming from them. She saw something that looked like hair in a nearby bucket and took a staggering step over to see what was inside.

It was Edward's head, floating in a pool of blood, his eyes wide and mad, looking at her. She wanted to scream but the air clogged in her throat as she saw Ed's lips begin to move. They were forming words but there was no sound, for there were no lungs to push air through his larynx. Yet still his lips kept moving in what seemed to be silent pleas. But pleas for what?

And then he opened his mouth wide and screamed—silently.

# David A. Riley

# The Satyr's Head

DAVID RILEY's short fiction has been published over the years in a variety of books and magazines including *The Pan Book of Horror Stories*, *The Year's Best Horror Stories*, *New Writings in Horror & the Supernatural*, *Death*, *First World Fantasy Awards*, *World of Horror*, *Whispers*, *Fantasy Tales* and *Fear*.

The following novella originally gave its title to David Sutton's anthology *The Satyr's Head and Other Tales of Terror* (1975), and the author has now expanded this nightmarish story of dark possession to novel-length. He has recently completed another novel, *Cursed Be the Ground*, and is currently working on a third, *Goblin Mire*.

# 1.

As Henry Lamson looked from the gate of his brother's farm on the outskirts of Pire he noticed that someone was walking along the lane in his direction. Although it did nothing to disconcert him at the time, he did wonder, as he bid farewell to the silhouetted figures in the doorway, before setting off for his bus stop, why someone should have been coming back from the moors at this time of the night, especially when it had been pouring down with rain all day.

Shrugging his shoulders, Lamson pulled his raincoat collar up high about his neck against the drizzle and picked his way as carefully as he could between the puddles in the deeply rutted lane. He wished now, as his feet sank in the half hidden mud, that he had thought to bring a torch with him when he came on his visit, since the moon, though full, only faintly showed through the clouds and the lane was for the most part in shadow.

Engrossed as he was in finding a reasonably dry route along the lane, he did not notice until a few minutes later, when the lights of his brother's farm had disappeared beyond the hedgerow, that the figure he had seen was nearing him quickly. Already he could hear his scrambling footsteps along the lane.

Petulantly pausing to disentangle a snapped thorn branch that had caught onto his trouser leg, he turned to watch the hunched figure hobbling towards him. A threadbare overcoat of an undeterminable colour swayed from about his body. In one hand he grasped a worn flat cap, whilst the other was thrust in his overcoat pocket for warmth.

When he finally succeeded in freeing himself of the twig, Lamson made to continue on his way. The man was obviously nothing more than a tramp, and an old one at that. As he started off, though, he heard him call out in a cracked bellow that rose and died in one breath.

"'Arf a mo' there!"

Irritated already at the drizzle that was soaking inexorably through his overcoat, Lamson sighed impatiently.

As the tramp hurried towards him through the gloom he slowly made out his bristly, coarse and wrinkled face, its dirt-grained contours glossy with rain.

The old man stumbled to a halt and raucously coughed a volley of phlegm on the ground. The pale grey slime merged in with the mud. Lamson watched him wipe his dribbling mouth with the top of his cap. Disgusted at the spectacle, Lamson asked coldly what the matter was. "Are you feeling ill?" He hoped that he wasn't. The last thing he wanted was to be burdened with someone like this.

"Ill?" The old man laughed smugly. "Ne'er 'ad a day's illness in my life. Ne'er!" He coughed and spat more phlegm upon the ground. Lamson looked away from it. Perhaps mistaking the reason for this action, the tramp said: "But I don't want to 'old you up. I'll walk alon' with you if you don't mind me doin'. That's all I called you for. It's a lonely place to be by yoursel'. Too lonely, eh?"

Lamson was uncertain as to whether this was a question or not. Relieved, however, that his unwanted companion was at least not adverse to continuing down the lane, he nodded curtly and set off again, the old man beside him.

"A raw night, to be sure," the old man said, with a throaty chuckle. Lamson felt a wave of revulsion sweep over him as he glanced at the old man's face in the glimmering light of one of the few lamp posts down the lane. He had never before seen anyone whose flesh gave off such an unnatural look of roughness. Batrachian in some indefinable way, with thick and flaccid lips, a squat nose and deeply sunken eyes, he had the appearance of almost complete depravity. Lamson stared at the seemingly scaly knuckles of his one bare hand.

"Have you come far?" Lamson asked.

"Far?" The man considered the word reflectively. "Not really *far*, I s'ppose," he conceded, with a further humourless chuckle. "And you," he asked in return, "are you goin' far, or just into Pire?"

Lamson laughed. "Not walking, I'm not. Just onto the bus stop at the end of the lane where I should just about catch the seven fifty-five for the centre." He looked across at a distant farm amidst the hills about Pire. Its minuscular windows stood out in the blackness like feeble fire flies through the intervening miles of rain. He glanced at his watch. In another eight minutes his bus would be due. As he looked up, Lamson was relieved to see the hedgerow end, giving way at a junction to the tarmac road that ran up along the edge of the moors from Fenley. The bus shelter stood beside a dry-stone wall, cemented by Nature with tangled patches of grass. Downhill, between the walls and lines of trees, were the pin-pointed lines of street lights etched across the valley floor. It was an unfailingly awe-inspiring sight, and Lamson felt as if he had passed through the sullen voids of Perdition and regained Life once more.

On reaching the bus shelter he stepped beneath its corrugated roof out of the rain. Turning round, as he nudged a half empty carton of chips to one side, he saw that the man was still beside him.

"Are you going into Pire as well?" Lamson asked. He tried, not too successfully, to keep his real feelings out of his voice. Not only did he find the tramp's company in itself distasteful, but there was a fetid smell around him that was reminiscent in some way of sweat and of sea weed rotting on a stagnant beach. It was disturbing in that it brought thoughts or half thoughts of an unpleasant type to his mind.

Apparently oblivious of the effect he was having on Lamson, the tramp was preoccupied in staring back at the moors. Willows and shrubs were thrown back and forth in the gusts, intensifying the loneliness of the place. Finally replying to Lamson's enquiry, he said: "There's no where else a body can go, is there? I've got to sleep. An' I can't sleep out in this." His flat, bristly, toad-like head turned round. There was a dim yellow light in his eyes. "I'll fin' a doss somewhere."

Lamson looked back to see if the bus was as yet in sight, though there were another four minutes to go before it was due. The empty expanse of wet tarmac seemed peculiarly lonely in the jaundiced light of the sodium lamps along the road.

Fidgeting nervously beside him, the old man seemed to have lost what equanimity had possessed him before. Every movement he made seemed to cry out of the desire to be on his way once more. It was as if he was morbidly afraid of something on the moors behind him. Lamson was bewildered. What could there be on the moors to worry him? Yet, whether there was really something there for him to worry about or not, there was no mistaking the relief which he showed when they at last heard the whining roar of the double decker from Fenley turning the last bend in the slope uphill, its headlights silhouetting the bristling shrubs along the road and glistening the droplets of rain. A moment later it drew up before them, comfortingly bright against the ice-grey hills and sky. Climbing on board, Lamson sat down beside one of the windows, rubbing a circle in the misted glass to look outside. He was dismayed when the tramp slumped down beside him. In the smoke-staled air the smell around the old man became even more noticeable than before, whilst his cold, damp body seemed to cut him off from the warmth he had welcomed on entering the bus.

Apparently unconcerned by such matters, the tramp grinned sagaciously, saying that it was good to be moving once more. His spirits were blatantly rising and he ceased looking back at the moors after a couple of minutes, seemingly satisfied.

In an effort to ignore the fetor exuded by the man, Lamson concentrated on looking out of the window, watching the trees and meadows pass by as they progressed into Pire, till they were supplanted by the gardened houses of the suburbs.

"'Ave you a light?" The frayed stub of a cigarette was stuck between the tramp's horny fingers.

His lips drawn tight in annoyance, Lamson turned round to face him as he searched through his pockets. Was there to be no end to his intolerable bother? he wondered. His eyes strayed unwillingly about the scaly knuckles of the man's hand, to the grimily web-like flaps of skin stretched at their joints. It was a disgustingly malformed object and Lamson was certain that he had never before seen anyone whose every aspect excited nothing so much as sheer nausea.

Producing a box of matches he struck one for him, then waited while he slowly sucked life into his cigarette.

When he settled back a moment later, the tramp brought the hand he had kept thrust deep in his overcoat pocket out and held it clenched before Lamson.

"Ever seen anythin' like this afore?" he asked cryptically. Like the withered petals of a grotesque orchid, his fingers uncurled from the palm of his hand. Prepared as he was for some forgotten medal of the Great War, tarnished and grimy, with a caterpillar segment of wrinkled ribbon attached, Lamson was surprised when he saw instead a small but well-carved head of dull black stone which looked as though it might have been broken from a statue about eighteen inches in height.

He met the intentive eyes of the tramp as the bus trundled to a momentary stop and two boisterous couples on a night out climbed on board, laughing and giggling at some murmured remark. Oblivious of them, Lamson let the tramp place the object in his hand. Though he was attracted by it he was simultaneously and inexplicably repelled. There was a certain hungry look to the man's face on the broken head which seemed to go further than that of mere hunger for food. Though from the deep pits in it and the numerous stains marking it, he could tell that it was of considerable age and antiquity, the head's features were singularly difficult for him to identify with any specific race. It had the fine features of the Aryan, subjugated with an almost disgustingly mongrel bestiality. The lips, unlike the other features, were particularly non-Aryan, and reminded Lamson unpleasantly in their loose obesity of the tramp's. If he had been of a less sceptical turn of mind or more inclined to the mystic he might have struck for the type of origin a Madame Blavatsky would have labelled it with, of Atlantis or Mu or some such crypto-mythological land. The leprous evil that seemed to have eaten at the head's initial nobility like a cancerous disease was far from at variance to the necromantic legends of such dark cultures as these.

Lamson turned the head about in his fingers, savouring the pleasant, soap-like surface of the stone.

"A strange thing to find out there, you'd think, wouldn't you?" the old man said, pointing his thick black stub of a thumb back at the moors.

"So you found it out there?" Somehow there was just enough self-control in Lamson's voice for him to rob it of its disbelief. Though he would have wanted nothing more a few minutes earlier than to be rid of the man, he felt a yearning now to own the head for himself that dettered him from insulting the tramp. After all, there was surely no other reason for the man showing him it except to sell it. And although he had never before felt any intense fascination in archeology there was something about the head which made Lamson desire it now. He was curious about it as a small boy is curious about a toy he has seen in a shop window.

Intent on adding whatever gloss of credibility to his tale that he could, the old tramp went on, saying: "It were in a brook. I found i' by chance as I were gettin' some water for a brew. It'd make a nice paperweight, I thought. I thought so as soon as I saw it there. It'd make a nice paperweight, I thought." He laughed self-indulgently, wiping his mouth with the sleeve of his coat. "'Cept that I've got no paper to put it on."

Lamson looked down at the carving and smiled.

When the bus drew up at the terminus Lamson was surprised, though not dismayed, when the tramp hurriedly climbed off and merged with the passing crowds outside. His bow-legged gait and crookedly unkempt figure were too suggestive of sickness and deformity for Lamson's tastes, and he felt more eager than ever for a salutary drink of beer in a pub before going on home to his flat.

Pressing his way through the queues outside the Cinerama on Market Street, he made for the White Bull, whose opaque doors swung open steamily before him with an outblowing bubble of warm, beery air. One drink later and another in hand, he stepped across to a vacant table up in a corner of the lounge, placing his glass beside a screwed up bag of crisps. A group of men were arguing amongst themselves nearby, one telling another, as of someone giving profound advice: "A standing prick has no conscience." There was a nodding of heads and another affirmed: "That's true enough."

Disregarding them as they sorted out what they were having for their next round of drinks, Lamson reached in his pocket and brought out the head. A voice from the television fixed above the bar said: "You can be a Scottish nationalist or a Welsh nationalist and no one says anything about it, but as soon as you say you're a British nationalist someone starts calling out 'Fascist!'" Two of the men nodded to each other in agreement.

Holding the head in the palm of his hand Lamson realised for the first time just how heavy it was. If not for the broken neck, which showed clearly enough that it was made out of stone, he would have thought it to have been moulded from lead. As he peered at it he noticed that there were two small ridges on its brows that looked as though they had once been horns. As he studied them he felt that if they had remained in their entirety the head would have looked almost satyric, despite the bloated lips. In fact, the slightly raised eyebrows and long straight nose—or what remained of them—were still reminiscent of Pan.

He heard a glass being placed on the table beside him. When he looked up he saw that it was Alan Sutcliffe. "I didn't see you in here before. Have you only just got in?"

Sutcliffe wiped his rain-spotted glasses on a handkerchief as he sat down, nodding his head. He replaced his glasses, then thirstily drank down a third of his pint before unbuttoning his raincoat and loosening the scarf about his neck. His face was flushed as if he had been running. "I didn't think I'd get here in time to have a drink. I have to be off again soon to go onto the Film Society. What've you got there?" he asked abruptly. "Been digging out your garden or something?"

Almost instinctively Lamson cupped his hands about the head. "It'd be a strange garden in a second floor flat, wouldn't it?" he replied acidly. Drawing his hands inwards towards his body, he covered what little still showed of the head with the ends of his scarf. Somehow he felt ashamed of the thing, almost as if it was obscene and repulsive and peculiarly shameful. "Where did you say you were off to?" he asked, intending to change the subject. "The Film Society? What are they presenting tonight?"

"*Nosferatu*. Why? Do you fancy coming along to see it as well? It's something of a classic, I believe. Should be good."

Lamson shook his head. "Sorry, but I don't really feel like it tonight. I only stopped in for a pint or two before going on home and getting an early night. I've had a long day already helping my brother, Peter, redecorating the inside of his farm. I'm about done in."

Glancing significantly at the clock above the bar Sutcliffe drained his glass, saying as he placed it back on the table afterwards: "I'll have to be off now. It starts in another ten minutes."

"I'll see you tomorrow, then, as we planned," Lamson said. "At twelve, if that's still okay?"

Sutcliffe nodded as he stood up to go. "We'll meet at the Wimpy, then I can get a bite to eat before we set off for the match."

"Right then."

As Sutcliffe left, Lamson opened his sweat-softened hands and looked at the head concealed in the cramped shadows inbetween. Now that his friend had gone he felt puzzled at his reaction with the thing. What was it about it that should affect him like this? he wondered fruitlessly. Then, placing it back in his pocket, he decided that he had had enough of the pub and strode outside, buttoning his coat against the rain.

## 2.

SUNLIGHT WAS POURING with a cold liquidity through his bedroom window when Lamson awoke. It shone across the cellophane covering the spines of the books shelved opposite his bed, obscuring their titles. It seemed glossy and bright and clean, with the freshness of newly fallen snow.

Yawning contentedly he stretched, then drew his dressing gown onto his shoulders as he gazed out of the window. Visible beyond the roof opposite was the radiantly blue and cloudless sky. He felt the last dull dregs of sleep sloughing from him as he rubbed the fine granules that had collected in his eyes away. Somewhere he could hear a radio playing a light pop tune, though it was almost too faint to make out.

Halfway through washing he remembered the dreams. They had completely passed from his mind on wakening and it was with an unpleasant shudder that they returned to him now. The veneer of his cheerfulness was dulled by the recollection, and he paused in his ablutions to look back at his bed. They were dreams he was not normally troubled with and he was loathe to think of them now

"To Hell with them!" he muttered self-consciously as he returned to scrubbing the threads of dirt from underneath his nails.

The measured chimes of the clock on the neo-Gothic tower, facing him across the neat churchyard of St. James, were tolling midday when Lamson walked past the Municipal Library. Sutcliffe, who worked at a nearby firm of accountants as an articled clerk, would be arriving at the Wimpy a little further along the street any time now. Going inside, Lamson ordered himself a coffee and took a seat by the window. He absent-mindedly scratched his hand, wondering nonchalantly, when he noticed what he was doing, if he had accidently brushed it against some of the nettles that grew up against the churchyard wall. A few minutes later Sutcliffe arrived and the irritation passed from his mind, forgotten.

"You're looking a bit bleary-eyed today," Sutcliffe remarked cheerfully. "An early night indeed! Too much bed and not enough sleep, that's your trouble."

"I slept well enough last night," Lamson replied. "Too well, perhaps."

"Come again?"

"Some dreams—" he started to explain, before he was interrupted by Sutcliffe as the waitress arrived, saying: "A wimpy and chips and coffee, please." When she'd gone Sutcliffe said: "I'm sorry. What was that you were saying?" But the inclination to tell him had gone and Lamson merely shrugged the topic's dismissal, broaching instead the Rovers' chances that afternoon in their match against Rochdale. As they spoke, though, his mind was not on what they were talking about. He was troubled, though he did not properly know why, by the dreams he had been about to relate to his friend, but which on reconsideration he had decided to keep to himself. He was glad that he had a full day ahead of him, what with the football match this afternoon and a date with Joan at the Tavern tonight. Sutcliffe was taking his fiancee there with them and it promised to be an enjoyable evening for them all. He only wished that his relationship with Joan was less peculiarly platonic. A lack of passion, she'd complained to him once not long ago, that was his trouble. Whether this was his fault or hers, he did not know. A bit of both, he supposed when he thought about it. Yet, if things did not improve very soon, he knew that their friendship, whatever his own inner feelings might be, would start to cool. Was this the cause of the dreams? he wondered to himself as he tried to concentrate on what Sutcliffe was saying. There did not seem to be any other reason for them that he could think of at the moment, and decided that this must be it.

As Lamson walked home through the vaporous gloom beneath the old street lamps along Beechwood Avenue, after having left Joan at her parents' home, his mind was deep in thought. It had been, as he had expected, an enjoyable evening, but only because of the new folk group they had been able to listen to at the Tavern. Joan had been no different than before: friendly and feminine in every way that he could wish, talkative—but not too much so—intelligent, amusing, and yet . . . and yet what was missing? Or was it him? What was it, he wondered, that made him feel so *fatherly* towards her, instead of the way in which at all other times he wished, even yearned, to be?

If not for the unexpected sound of someone slipping on the pavement some distance behind him, he would not have been brought out of his revery until reaching Station Road and the last, short stretch to his flat. As it was he half intentionally, half instinctively turned round to see if someone had fallen. But all he glimpsed on the otherwise deserted avenue was the vague impression of someone merging hurriedly with the shadowy privet bushes midway between the feeble light of two lamp posts further back. So fleeting was the impression, in fact, that he would have taken it for the blurred motion of a cat that had raced across the avenue but for the distinct recollection of something *slipping* on the footpath.

For a moment or two he waited and watched in vain, certain that whoever or whatever hid in the gloom of the privets had not moved since he turned and was only waiting for him to turn round again to emerge. It was disturbing, and he tried to play down his nervousness with the thought that it must be some kids playing an idiotic game of hide and seek in the dark. Unconvinced though he was by this explanation, he found it substantial enough as an excuse to turn round with at least the pretence of indifference and continue on his way home. Yet it was with a definite feeling of relief, however, when he reached Station Road, where the bright shop windows, neon signs and passing cars brought him back into reality. With more speed than he usually employed he strode along to the door leading into his flat and raced up the two flights of stairs to his rooms.

As he closed the door behind him he noticed the small black head he had bought from the tramp perched where he had left it on the dresser, its outline gleaming in the reflection of the street lights outside. It was looking towards him, crooked at an obtuse angle on its broken neck. Somehow it looked larger in the gloom, as if it had somehow mysteriously grown since he bought it. Dismissing the ridiculous thought with a snigger of contempt, he threw his overcoat onto the bed and stepped to the window to draw the curtains together, before switching on the light. He felt at the radiator opposite his bed by the bookcase. It was just lukewarm. As he stared morosely about the room he wondered what had made him buy the head. What perverse attraction had drawn him to it before had gone, and all he could see in it now was ugliness and decay. He picked it up. It wasn't as if he could legitimately claim that he'd bought it out of some kind of archeological interest. It was years since he'd half heartedly pottered in that subject while he'd still been at school, and what enthusiasm he may have once had for it had been lost to him long ago. For a moment he rubbed the small lumps on its brows, but he felt too tired suddenly to study it tonight. There was a nagging ache in the small of his back and his arms felt stiff, while the rash-like irritation had returned to tingle on the backs of his hands.

Lamson dropped the stone head back on the dresser and began to get changed into his pyjamas. He felt too tired now to think or even place his clothes, as he invariably did, folded up neatly on the table by his bed. For a moment he struggled to keep awake, but he could not resist. He did not want to resist. All he wanted to do was to surrender himself, his body and soul, to the dull black nothingness of sleep.

Sleep quickly overcame him as he lay on his bed and closed his eyes.

And in his sleep he dreamed.

There was a wood in his dream, a great, deep, darkly mysterious wood, that filled him with unease as he listened to its decrepit oaks groaning in the wind.

He stood alone before it. But he did not feel alone. He could sense something watching him malevolently from the gloomy depths of the wood.

The twilight passed into the darkness of night. Shadows glided silently about the trees, gathering as if to stare out at him with small, round, rubicund eyes. Or was it his own eyes, playing tricks with the dark?

Then he saw something emerge out of the waist-high ferns, crawling on all fours across the ground. It was almost black, its naked flesh dry and coarse, strung tight about its jutting bones. Its legs, though hairless, were as the legs of a goat, whilst shrunken breasts, some twelve in number, hung limply from its chest. They swayed as it moved, its jaundiced eyes gleaming from the deep black depths of their sockets with a foul anticipation. There was a convulsive twitching in its long, thin, bony hands.

Unable to move, Lamson watched it crawl towards him. Its penis was hard with lust, the dark nipples of its breasts enlarged and tight. Its lips were wet with overflowing saliva as it drew towards him. Though partially human it was hideously inhuman, a foul, unearthly, cacodemoniacal Pan. Stiff black horns curved upwards from its brows. A scaled and rat-like tail flicked from its spine. He could see the mounting tension of its poised phallus. He tried to scream. With all his strength he tried to scream, to cry out and tear himself away from the hideous creature creeping towards him, but there was nothing he could do. He was paralysed and defenceless.

A murmured chanting sibilantly issued from the encircling trees, flitting with the winds.

"*Ma dheantar aon scriosadh, athru, gearradh, lot no milleadh ar an ordu feadfar diultu d'e a ioc.*"

The rhythmic chanting began to mimic the frenzied beating of a heart, faster and deeper, as the satyr, swaying its lean torso to the rhythms of the chants, came upon Lamson. Its left hand grasped him about the thigh, pulling him down till he knelt on the ground. Its fetid breath blew hot into his face like the searing gusts of a newly opened furnace. He could see the wrinkles in its clammy flesh and the sores suppurating on its lips. With renewed urgency he wrenched himself free and tried to roll out of its way across the grass. But before he even saw it move he felt its hands grasping him once more. He kicked out at it, whimpering. Its talons tore a deep gash in his pyjama trousers. Its palm slid searchingly down his leg. Once more he kicked.

With a slow deliberation it reached out for the cord of his pyjamas and ripped it free. It was crouched over him, its softly repulsive underbelly almost touching his legs. In the feeble light its body seemed huge.

With a sudden exertion Lamson managed at last to emit a scream. As its hands reached for him between his legs darkness sprang up about him like a monstrous whirlpool. He felt dizzy and sick, shuddering with horror as he awoke, his body drenched with perspiration in the tangled blankets of his bed. At the same instant he felt the final climax of an orgasm clasp hold of him. He lay back and gasped, weak with the intensity of his ejaculation. He felt fouled suddenly, as if dragged through the sordid cesspools of some hideous sin.

Nauseated, he looked across from his bed at the carving. Its coarse features seemed even more awful to him now than before, and he did not doubt but that in some repulsively Freudian way its lecherous features—mirrored, as he now realised, on the demon creature of his nightmare—had influenced his sleeping mind. As he looked at it he found it difficult to understand how he had failed to notice the unclean lust rampant about its face before, like some infernal incubus roused by the harlots of Hell.

As he washed himself clean a few minutes later he wondered if it would not be better to get rid of the head, to throw it away and forget it, and in doing so hopefully rid himself of the dreams. Only once while he dressed did a discordant thought make him wonder if, perhaps, the dreams were not connected in some way with his unsatisfactory relationship with Joan. But the two were at such polarised extremes in his mind that he could not connect them with anything other than shame. As he looked at the stone this shame transferred itself to this object, intensifying into a firm resolution to get rid of the thing. How could he possibly make any kind of headway with Joan, he told himself, with such a foul obscenity as that thing troubling him?

When Lamson left his flat a short time later, carrying the head in his raincoat pocket, it was with steps so unsteady that he wondered if he was becoming ill. The irritation on his hands had, if anything, become even worse, while aches and pains announced their presence from all over his body while he walked. He wondered if he had overstrained himself when he was helping his brother redecorate the farm, though he'd felt fit enough the day before.

The Sunday morning streets were agreeably deserted as he walked along them. The only cars in sight were parked by the kerb. In a way he was glad that the dream had woken him as early as it had. Just past eight thirty now, it would be a while yet, he knew, before the city would start to stir into life today.

"*Dirty o-old ma-an, dirty o-old ma-an!*"

He looked across to where the sing-song voices came from. Two small boys of about ten or eleven years in age—perhaps less—were stood at the corner of the street in Burton's doorway. Cheeky little brats, Lamson thought as he noticed the shuffling figure their jeers were directed at, a stooped old man slowly making his way down the street leading off from the main road. Although Lamson could not see his face he could tell that the old man knew that they were calling out at him. Slow though his pace was, it was also unmistakeably hurried, as if he was trying to get out of their way as quickly as he could on his decrepit legs.

"Clear off!" Lamson shouted angrily, feeling sorry for the old man. The kids yelped and ran off down an alley, laughing. If he had not felt so weary himself he would have run after them. How could they act so callously? He watched the old man as he continued on his way. There was something about the painful stoop of his back and the way his legs bent that struck a cord of remembrance somewhere. He could almost have been the tramp he met on the moors, except that he hadn't been anything like as decrepit as this man obviously was, not unless his health had failed disastrously over the last couple of days.

Lamson crossed the road and headed up past St. James church, putting the old man out of his mind. The pleasant singing of the birds in the elms in the churchyard helped to ease his spirits, and he breathed in the scent of the grass with a genuine feeling of pleasure. He only wished that his legs didn't feel so tired and stiff. He wondered again if he was coming down with a bug of some kind.

He paused suddenly by the wall and felt in his pocket, his fingers moving speculatively about the stone head that bulged heavily inside it. Though he did not know properly why, he decided that the churchyard was too near his flat for him to get rid of the stone here. It would be better if he made his way to the canal where he could lose it without trace properly.

As he turned round to leave he noticed a slight movement out of the corner of his eye. With a feeling of trepidation he paused, turned round and anxiously scanned the solemn rows of lichened headstones. Nothing moved, except for a light film of drizzle that began to filter down through the overhanging boughs of the trees. Yet, even though he could not see anything to account for what he seemed to glimpse—like a blurred shadow moving on the edge of his sight—he was sure that he was not mistaken. He stepped up the street to where a narrow gate led into the churchyard. He looked across it once again and wished that he could make himself leave this suddenly disturbing, if prosaic place, but he could not. With slow, but far from resolute steps he walked down the asphalt path between the headstones, his senses attuned to the least disturbance about him: the cold moisture of the drizzle on his hands and face, the hissing of the leaves as the rain passed through them, the singing of the birds that echoed and re-echoed about him, and the distant murmur of a car along Station Road as the clock tolled a quarter to nine. The air seemed strangely still. Or was it his own overwrought imagination, keyed up by the horrendous nightmare, scenes from which still flickered uncomfortably across his mind? He felt a fluttering sensation in his stomach as he looked along the rough-hewn stones of the church with its incised windows of stained glass.

Quickening his pace as the drizzle began to fall with more weight he passed round the church. As he walked by the trees on the far side of the building, where they screened it off from the bleak back walls of a derelict mill, he began to notice something move. Was it a dog? he wondered, though it seemed a little large. He whistled, though there was no response other than a thin, frail echo.

He strode between a row of ornate monuments of polished marble. Was that someone there, crouched down in the bushes? "Excuse me!" he called enquiringly. Then stopped. Calling out to a dog, indeed! he thought as he glimpsed what he took to be a large black hound—perhaps an Irish wolf hound—scuttering off out of sight between the trees.

As he walked back to the street he decided that it was about time he got on his way to the canal before the rain got any worse.

The rain did worsen. By the time he reached the towpath of the canal he began to regret ever having come out on a morning like this on such a pointless exercise. The rain covered the fields on either side of the canal in a dull grey veil. What colours there were had been reduced to such a washed-out monochrome that the scene reminded him of that in an old and faded photograph. Facing him across the dingy waters of the canal were rows of little sheds and barbed wire fences. Crates of neglected rubbish had been abandoned in the sparsely grassed fields, together with the tyreless carcasses of deserted cars. The fields rose up to the back of a grim row of tenements whose haphazard rooftops formed a jagged black line against the sky. Only the mouldering wood of the derelict mills and their soot-grimed bricks on his side of the canal stood out with any clarity. A dead cat floated in a ring of scum in the stagnant water at his feet, its jellied eyes sightlessly staring at the sky with a dank luminescence.

As he took the stone head from his pocket he heard someone move behind him. Having thought that he was safely alone he spun round in surprise. Crouched deep in the dark shadows between the walls of the mill, where a gate had once stood, was a man. A long, unbuttoned overcoat hung about his hunched body. It was a coat that Lamson recognised instantly.

"So it was you those kids were shouting at," Lamson accused, as the tramp tottered out into the light. "Have you been following me?" he asked. But there was no response other than a slight twitching of the old man's blistered lips into what he took to be a smile, though one that was distinctively malignant and sly. "You were following me last night, weren't you?" he went on. "I heard you when you slipped, so there's no point in denying it. *And* I saw you this morning when those kids spotted you. I thought they were being cruel when they shouted out at you, but I don't know now. Perhaps they were right. Perhaps you are a dirty old man, a dirty, insidious and evil old man." Even now there was no more response from the tramp than that same repugnant smile. "Haven't you got a tongue?" Lamson snapped. "Grinning there like a gargoyle. It's a pity you're not made out of stone. Well? You were talkative enough when we met on the moors. Have you taken vows of silence since then? Come on! Speak up, damn you!" He clenched his fists, fighting back the impulse to hit him in the face, though it was almost too strong to resist. What an ugly old creature he was, what with his pock-marked face all rubbery and grey and wet, and those bloated, repulsive lips. Was he some kind of half-breed? he wondered, though of what mixture he could not imagine. A thin, grey trickle of saliva hung down from a corner of his mouth. There was a streak of blood in it. As he stared at him he realised that he looked far worse, far, far worse than before, as if whatever disease had already swollen and eroded his features had suddenly accelerated its effect.

The tramp stared down at the stone, clenched tight in Lamson's hands. "Were you after gettin' rid o' it? Is that why you've come to this place?" he asked finally.

"Since it's mine I have every right to, if that's what I want to do," Lamson said, taken aback at the accusation.

"An' why should you choose to do such a thing, I wonder. You liked it well enough when I first showed it to you on the bus. Couldn't 'ardly wait to buy it off o' me, could you? 'Ere's the money, give me the stone, quick as a flash! Couldn't 'ardly wait. An' yet 'ere you are, all 'et up an' nervous, can't 'ardly wait to get rid o' the thing. What's the poor sod been a doin' to you? Givin' you nightmares, 'as it?"

"What do you mean?"

"What should I mean? Just a joke. That's all. Can't you tell? Ha, ha, ha!" He spat a string of phlegm onto the ground. "Only a joke," he went on, wiping his mouth in between with his sleeve.

"Only a joke, was it?" Lamson asked, his anger inflamed with indignation at the old man's ill-concealed contempt for him. "And I suppose it was only a joke when you followed me here as well? Or did you have some other purpose in mind? Did you?"

"P'raps I was only tryin' to make sure that you came to no 'arm. Wouldn't want no 'arm to come to you now, would I? After all, you bought the 'ead off o' me fair an' square, didn't you? Though it does seem an awful shame to toss it into the canal there to me. Awful shame it'd be. Where'd you get another one like it, I ask you? Where'd you get another bit o' stone like that? It's unique, you know, that's what it is right enough: unique. Wouldn't want to throw it into no canal, would you? Where's the sense in it? Or the use? Could understand it if there was somethin' unpleasant about it. Somethin' bad an' nasty. But what's bad an' nasty about that? Don't give you no nightmares, does it? Nothin' like that? Course not! Little bit o' stone like that? An' yet, 'ere you are, gettin' ready to toss it away, an' no reason to it. I can't understand it at all, I can't, I swear it." He shook his head reproachfully, though there was a cunning grin about his misshapen mouth, as if laughing at a secret joke. "Throwin' it away," he went on in the same infuriatingly mocking voice. "Ne'er would 'a' thought o' doin' such a thin'. Old bit o' stone like that. You know 'ow much it might be worth? Can you even guess? Course not! An' yet you get it for next to nothin' off o' me, only keep it for a day or two, then the next thin' I knows 'ere you are all ready to toss it like an empty can into the canal. An' that's what you've come 'ere for, isn't it?"

"And if it is, why are you here?" Lamson asked angrily. The old man knew too much—far, far too much. It wasn't natural. "What are you?" he asked. "And why have you been spying on me? Come on, give me an answer."

"An answer, is it? Well, p'raps I will. It's too late now, I can tell, for me to do any 'arm in lettin' you know. 'E's 'ad 'Is 'ands on you by now, no doubt, eh?"

Lamson felt a stirring in his loins as he remembered the dream he had woken from barely two hours ago. But he couldn't mean that. It was impossible for him to know about it, utterly, completely, irrefutably impossible! Lamson tried to make himself leave, but he couldn't, not until he had heard what the old man had to say, even though he knew that he didn't want to listen. He had no choice. He couldn't. "Are you going to answer my questions?" he asked, his voice sounding far more firm than he felt.

The tramp leered disgustedly. "'Aven't 'ad enough, 'ave you? Want to 'ear about it as well?"

"As well as what?"

The tramp laughed. "You know. Though you pretend that you don't, you know all right. You know." He wiped one watering, red-rimmed eye. "I 'xpect you'll please 'Im a might bit more 'an me. For a while, at least. *I* wasn't much for 'Im, even at the first. Too old. Too sick. Even then I was too sick. Though I'm sicker now. A lot sicker now. But that's 'ow it is. That's 'ow it's got to be, I s'ppose. 'E wears you out. That's what 'E does. Wears you out. But you, now, you, you're as young as 'E could ask for. An' fit. Should last for a while. A long, long while, I think, before 'E wears *you* out. *Careful!* Wouldn't wanna drop 'Im, now, would you?"

It seemed as if something cold and clammy had clenched itself like a tumourous hand deep inside him. With a shudder of revulsion Lamson looked down at the stone in his hands. Was he mistaken or was that a look of satisfaction on its damnable face? He stared at it hard, feeling himself give way to a nauseating fear that drained his limbs of their strength.

"I thought you were o' the right sort for 'Im when I saw you on that lane," the tramp said. "I'm ne'er wrong 'bout such things."

As if from a great distance Lamson heard himself ask what he meant. "Right sort? What the fucking Hell do you mean: *the right sort?*"

"Should 'a' thought you'd know," he replied, touching him on the hand with his withered fingers. Lamson jerked his hand away. "You dirty old sod!" he snapped, fear and disgust adding tension to his voice. "You . . . you . . ." He did not want to face the things hinted at. He didn't! They were lies, all lies, nothing but lies! With a sudden cry of half-hearted annoyance, both at the tramp and at himself for his weakness, he pushed past and ran back along the towpath. He ran as the rain began to fall with more force and the sky darkened overhead. He ran as the city began to come to life and church bells tolled their beckoning chimes for the first services of the day.

## 3.

"I CAN'T UNDERSTAND YOU," Sutcliffe said as he collected a couple of pints from the bar and brought them back to their table by the snug. "Excuse me," he added, as he pushed his chair between a pair of outstretched legs from the next table. "Another inch. Right. Thanks." Loosening his scarf, he sat down with a shake of his tousled head. "Like the Black Hole of Calcutta in here," he said. He took a sip of his pint, watching Lamson as he did so. His friend's face looked so pale and lifeless these days, its unhealthiness emphasised by the dark sores that had erupted about his mouth.

"In what way can't you understand me?" Lamson asked. There was a dispirited tiredness to his voice which Sutcliffe could tell didn't come from boredom or disinterest.

Folding his arms, Sutcliffe leant over the table towards him. "It's two weeks now since you last went out with Joan. And that was the night we all went to the Tavern. Since then nothing. No word or anything. *From you.* But Joan has called round to your flat four times this week, though you weren't apparently in. Unless you've found someone else, you'd better know that she won't keep on waiting for you to see her. She has her pride. And she can tell when she is being snubbed. Don't get me wrong, Henry. I wouldn't like you to think that I'm interfering, but it was Joan herself who asked me to mention this to you if I bumped into you. So, if you have some reason for avoiding her, I'd be glad if you'd let me know." He shrugged. "If you'd prefer to tell me to mind my own business I'd understand, of course. But, even if only for Joan's sake, I'd rather you'd say something."

Suppressing a cough, Lamson wiped his mouth with a handkerchief held ready in his hand. He wished that he could tell Sutcliffe the reason why he was avoiding Joan, for a deliberate avoidance it was. "I haven't been feeling too good recently," he replied evasively.

"Is it anything serious?"

Lamson shook his head. "No, it's nothing serious. I'll be better in a while. A bad dose of flu, I think. But it's been lingering on, that's all."

Sutcliffe frowned. He did not like the way in which his friend was acting these days, so unlike the open and friendly manner in which he had always behaved before, at least with him. Even allowing for flu, that neither explained the change in his character nor the peculiar swellings about his mouth. If it was flu, it was of a type far more serious than any he had ever known himself. And how, for Christ's sake, could this explain the way in which his skin seemed to have become coarse and dry, especially about the knuckles on his hands?

"Have you been eating the right kinds of foods?" Sutcliffe asked. "I know what it can be like living in a flat. Tried it once for a while myself. Never again. Give me a boarding house anytime. Too much like hard work for me to cook my own meals, I can tell you. I dare say that you find it much like that yourself."

"A little," Lamson admitted, staring at his beer without interest or appetite as three men wearing election roseettes pressed by towards the bar. One of them said: "I wouldn't be at all surprised if it wasn't something all these Asians have been bringing into the country. There's been an increase in

T.B. already, and that was almost unheard of a few years ago."

"It's certainly like nothing I've ever heard of, that's for sure."

As the men waited for their drinks one of them turned round, smiling in recognition when he saw Lamson. "Hello there. I didn't notice you were here when we came in."

"Still working hard, I see," Lamson said, nodding at the red, white and blue rosette pinned to the man's lapel.

"No rest for the wicked. Someone's got to do the Devil's work," he joked as the two men with him smiled in appreciation. He was short and fat and looked as if he meant what he said, despite the humourous twinkle in his eyes. "It's the local elections soon," he added.

Collecting their drinks the men sat down at the table beside Lamson and Sutcliffe.

"I overheard you talking about T.B. Has there been a sudden outbreak or something?" Lamson asked.

"Not T.B.," the man said. "We've just been talking to an old woman who told us that a tramp was found dead in her back alleyway earlier this week. From what we were able to gather from her even the ambulancemen who were called to take him away were shaken by what they saw."

"What was it?" Sutcliffe asked. "A mugging?"

"No," the man said. "Apparently he died from some kind of disease. They're obviously trying to keep news about it down, though we're going to try and find out what we can about it. So far there's been no mention in the press, though that's hardly surprising in our local rag. They wouldn't know what real news was if it jumped up and bit 'em. So, just what it is that the old fellow died of we don't know, though it must have been serious. Sickening, is how the old woman described him, though how she got a look at him is anybody's guess. But you know what some of these old woman are like. Somehow or other she got a bloody good look—too good a look, I think, for her own peace of mind in the end. According to what she said there were swellings and sores and odd looking bruises all over his body. And blood dripping out of his mouth, almost as if his insides had been eaten away."

Lamson shuddered.

"What's the matter?" Sutcliffe asked as he lit a cigarette.

Lamson smiled weakly. "Just someone walking over my grave, that's all," he said, taking a long drink of his beer. The three men drained theirs. Putting his glass down, empty, Eddie, the man who'd been speaking, stood up. "We'd better be off back to our canvassing or someone will be doing a clog dance on our graves. And we'll be in them!"

As they left, Lamson said that he could do with a whisky.

"Just because of hearing about some poor old sod of a tramp?" Sutcliffe asked.

"It's not him," Lamson replied. "God rest his miserable soul. He was probably better off dead anyway." Though what he said was meant to sound off-hand his voice lacked the lightness of tone to carry it off successfully. Realising this, he pushed his glass away. "I'm sorry, Alan. I must seem poor company tonight. I think it would perhaps be better if I set off home. Perhaps we'll meet up again tomorrow night. Yes?"

"If you say so," Sutcliffe replied amicably. "You do look a bit under the weather tonight." A Hell of a lot under the weather, he added silently to himself. "Anyhow, now that you mention it, it's about time I was on my way home as well. I'll walk along with you to my bus stop. It's on your way."

As they stepped out of the pub Sutcliffe asked if he had been sleeping well recently.

"What makes you ask?"

"Your eyes," Sutcliffe said as the wind pushed against them, a torn newspaper scuttering along the gutter. "Red rimmed and bleary. You ought to get yourself a few early nights. Or see if your doctor can prescribe you some sleeping pills. It's what you need."

Lamson stared down the road as they walked along it. How cold and lonely it looked, even with the cars hissing by through the puddles of rain and the people walking hurriedly along the pavement. There was the smell of fish and chips and the pungent aroma of curry as they passed a take-away, but even this failed to make him feel at home on the street. He felt foreign and lost, alienated to the things and places which had previously seemed so familiar to him. Even with Sutcliffe he felt almost alone, sealed within himself.

As they parted a few minutes later at Sutcliffe's stop outside the Cinerama on Market Street, his friend said: "I'll be expecting you tomorrow. You've been keeping far too much to yourself recently. If you don't watch out you'll end up a hermit, and that's no kind of fate for a friend of mine. So mind that you're ready when I call round. Will seven o'clock be all right with you?"

Lamson said that it was. There was no point in trying to evade him. Sutcliffe was far too persistent for that. Nor did he really want to evade him, not deep down. He pulled his collar up about his neck and started off purposefully for his flat.

There was a gloom to his bedroom which came from more than just an absence of light, since even during the day it was here. It was a gloom which seemed to permeate everything within it like a spreading stain. As soon as Lamson stepped inside he was aware of the gloom, in which even the newest of his possessions seemed faded and cheap. He looked at the stone. It drew his attention almost compulsively. Of everything it was the only object in the room that had not been affected by this strange malaise. Was it gloating? he wondered. Gloating at the way in which it had triumphed over everything else in the flat, including (or especially) the framed photo of Joan, with her blond hair curled so characteristically about her face. You're trapped with me, it seemed to say like some grotesque spider that had caught him on its Stygian web, smirking and sneering with its repulsively hybrid, goat-like features, swollen over the past two weeks till it rested on the dresser almost as large as a full sized human skull.

Lamson rubbed his hands together vigorously, trying to push the thoughts out of his mind. I *must* get rid of the thing, he told himself (as he had continually done, though without result, for the past two weeks). He glanced at his unmade bed with distaste and a feeling of shame. "Oh, God," he whispered self-consciously, "if only I could get rid of the obsession. Because that's all it is. No more. Only an obsession which I *can* and *must* somehow forget." Or was it? There was no way in which he could get away from the doubt. After all, he thought, how could he satisfactorally explain the way in which the tramp had seemed able to read his thoughts and know just what it was that he'd dreamt? Or was he only a part of this same, single-minded and delusionary obsession? he wondered, somewhat hopefully, as his mind grew dull with tiredness. He glanced at his watch. How much longer, he wondered, could he fight against falling asleep? One hour? Two? Eventually, though, he would have to give in. It was one fight, as he so well knew by now, which no one could win, no matter how much they might want to or with how much will.

In an effort to concentrate his thoughts he picked out a book from the shelf randomly. It was *Over the Bridge* by Richard Church. He had quite enjoyed reading it once, several months before, but the words did not seem to have any substance in his brain any more. Letters, like melting figures of ice, lost form and swam and merged as if the ink was still wet and was slowly soaking through the pages as he watched.

When, as was inevitable, he finally lost consciousness and slept, he became aware of a change in the atmosphere. There was a warmth which seemed womb-like and wrong in the open air. It disturbed him as he looked up at the stars prickling the sky, the deep, black, canopied darkness of the sky.

On every side trees rose from the gloom, their boughs bent over like thousands upon thousands of enormous fingers, black in their damp decay. Their leaves were like limpets, pearly and wet as they shivered in the rising winds. Before him a glade led down beneath the trees. Undecided as to which way he should go, Lamson looked about himself uncertainly, hoping for a sign, for some indication—however faint or elusive—as to which path was the one he should take. There seemed to be so many of them, leading like partially erased pencil lines across a grimy sheet of paper through the over-luxuriant grass. Somewhere there was a sound, though it was so dimmed and distorted by the distance seperating him from its source. Sibilantly, vaguely, the rhythmic words wound their ways between the trees.

Finding himself miming them, he turned his back to the sounds and started for the glade. Even as he moved he knew that he had made a mistake. But he knew also, and with a sudden, wild wrenching of his heart, that there was no escape. Not now. It was something which he knew had either happened before or was pre-ordained, that no matter what he did there was no way in which he could escape from what was going to happen next. He felt damned—by God, the Devil, and himself.

Crestfallen, as the awfulness of what he knew was about to happen next came over him, he felt a sudden impulse to scream. Something large and heavy rustled awkwardly through the ferns. Fear, like lust, swelled within him. He felt a loathing and a horror and, inexplicably, a sense of expectation as well, as if some small part of him yearned for what it knew was about to take place. He began to sob. How could he escape from this thing—how could he even *hope* to escape from this thing—if some perverse element within him did not want to be free?

He turned round to retrace his steps up the glade, but there was something dark stretched across his path, barring his way, some yards ahead of him. It turned towards him and rose. Starlight, filtering through the trees, glittered darkly across its teeth as it smiled.

Lamson turned round and tried to run back down the glade, but the creature was ready, bounding after him like a great black goat. He felt its claws sink into his shoulders as it forced him suddenly forwards, knocking him face down onto the ground. He tried to scream but his cries were gagged on dried leaves and soil, as his mouth was brutally pushed into them and the creature's furiously powerful fingers tore at his clothes, strewing them about him. The winds blew cool against his hot, naked flesh as sweat from the lunging, piston-like body ran down the hollow of his spine.

There was a crash somewhere and the dream ripped open. The next instant he seemed to blink his eyes to find the comforting sight of his bedroom in front of him. The book he had been reading when sleep overcame him earlier lay against his feet on the floor.

He breathed out a sigh of relief as he glanced at his watch. It was now three thirty-five in the morning. He shivered. His body was covered in sweat and felt awful, aching in every joint. He put on his dressing gown and crossed to the window, opening the curtains to look down at the twilit street below. It was empty and quiet, peaceful as it very rarely was during the day. But it was also, undeniably, lonely. Cold and lonely and lifeless. The sight of its bleak grey lines could not make him forget the dream for long, nor keep away from him the wretched feeling of despair that remembering it brought along with it, a despair made all the more unbearable at the realisation that its cause, deep down, must lie rooted in his character. There was no way in which he could deny to himself the perverted aspects it presented to him. But was he perverted as well? Or had the old tramp been lying? After all, why should he be any more perceptive of that kind of thing than anyone else? It was his suggestion, that was all, his *vile* suggestion that was making his mind work in that direction now. He knew it. Just like some kind of post-hypnotic suggestion. And if this was it and it was the tramp's horrible insinuations that had caused this neurotic and evil obsession, then it was up to him to vent these desires in the most normal way that he could. Otherwise, he knew, they would only worsen, just as they were worsening already.

Decided on this course he rested quietly for the rest of the night drinking coffee and listening to the radio. When the sky began to lighten at last he welcomed the new day with a fervour he had not felt for many weeks. At last, it seemed to him, there was finally a chance of ridding himself of this nightmare. At last . . .

## 4.

IT WAS NOT TILL MIDDAY that Henry Lamson dressed and stepped outside. In realising that he had to prove to himself that he was normal, and thereby rid himself of the perverse obsession that was gradually driving him off the rails, he had decided that the easiest way open to him was to call on Clara Sadwick, a local prostitute who rented rooms on Park Road above a newsagent's shop. As he walked towards it down the sodden street the place had a dingy and slightly obscene look to it, with its unpainted window frames and faded curtains, pulled together tight behind their grimy, fly-specked windows. As he stepped inside and began to climb the bare staircase to the first floor landing he gazed bleakly at the mildewed paper on the walls. A naked light bulb hung from a cord at the head of the stairs. He wondered what he had let himself in for at a place like this. Fortifying himself, though, with the thought that in going through with what was to follow he might end the dreams that had been tormenting him for the past three weeks, he pressed on the buzzer by the door facing him at the top. One-fifteen she had said on the phone when he rang her up an hour before from a call box down the road. It was just a minute off that time now. He ran his fingers nervously through his uncombed hair.

After a short pause the door opened before him.

"Believe in punctuality, don't you," Clara said with an off-hand familiarity which made him feel more relaxed as she stepped back and looked at the slim gold watch on her wrist. She was dressed in a denim skirt, fluffy red slippers and a purple, turtle-neck sweater, which clung about her ample breasts. She smiled as she showed him in. "Make yourself at home," she said breezily.

"Thank you," Lamson said as he hung his coat on a hook on the wall and looked about the room. In the far corner, partially hidden behind a faded Japanese screen, was a bed. In front of the old gas fire stood a coffee table crammed with dirty dishes and plates. He wondered if she had been having a party or whether, as seemed dismayingly more likely, she merely washed them up when there were no more clean ones left. He hoped, fleetingly, that she was a little more conscientious about cleaning herself.

Clara ground the cigarette she'd been smoking into a saucer, then said: "It'll be fifteen quid. Cash first, if you don't mind. It's not that I don't trust you, but I can hardly take you to court if you refuse to pay up afterwards."

Lamson smiled to cover his embarrassement and said that he understood. "You can't be too careful, can you?" he added sententiously as he sorted out the notes from his wallet. "Fifteen pounds, you said?" he went on, placing the money in her waiting hand.

"Many thanks," she replied, taking it to a drawer and locking it inside.

She looked back at him, coyly. "Well, I suppose we had better begin," she said, folding back the screen from the bed. Without any further word she kicked off her slippers and began to unbutton her skirt. Within a few minutes she was dressed only in her tights and bra. She looked up then as if only just remembering his presence, and told him to hurry. "I haven't all day to wait for you getting undressed. Unless, of course, you prefer having it with your clothes still on." She shook her head, laughing almost like a young girl, though she was in her late thirties, unfastening her bra and letting it fall forward from her breasts. Lamson swallowed as he stared at the limpid mounds of pale white flesh they uncovered, their puckered orbs matching the gooseflesh that was starting to rise on her cosily rounded arms. She shivered, complaining to him again at his slowness. "Do you want me to help you?" she asked sarcastically.

Lamson shook his head as he loosened his trousers and let them fall, unaided, to the floor. Stepping out of them onto the lukewarm oilcloth he looked at her again. "Come on, luv," she said, reaching out for him as she rolled back on the rumpled, quilt-covered bed. "Off with the rest of them and we can begin." Although Lamson felt embarrassed at his nakedness as he slipped out of the last of his clothes, and could feel the blood burning in his cheeks, he was surprised, and not just a little alarmed, to find that there was no other reaction, that he seemed, in fact, to be incapable of carrying out what he had paid her for. Seemingly unaware of this, though—or, if she was, taking no apparent notice of it—she smiled as he approached her. Lightly, questingly, her hands felt about his body as he pushed his face into her breasts.

He smelt the faint aroma of sweat and eau de cologne, his mind whirling with haphazard and conflicting sensations. She pressed his mouth against her hardening nipples as he moved further up her body. Yet still he could not find the desire to possess her. "Come on, dearie, come on," he heard her whisper between gasps. He raised himself onto his elbows and looked down into her face. In the same instant her hands grasped him between his legs. He gasped as her fingers lengthened and tightened gently about his penis, guiding him towards her. It was as if his loins were being instilled with a surcharge of life. He looked down at her eyes. Joan's face seemed to merge with her's, hiding the cheapness and vulgarity that had been there a moment before. It was almost angelic. Never before had he looked upon a face such as this, upon which all his pent up emotions of warmth, affection and even love could be gladly poured. His eyes passed lingeringly about her warm, soft cheeks, where the blood made a pleasant suffusion of pink. She smiled encouragingly, and yet with an apparent innocence which drove him into an almost unbearable desire to possess her. He felt her thighs rise on either side of his legs, pressing him to her. He could feel himself grow stiff, entering her, slowly, cautiously passing into the warmth within her summoning body. He could have cried out at the exquisite pangs that were racing through him, obliterating conscious thought.

Even through the pleasure that was overwhelming his mind Lamson became suddenly aware that the room was darkening. Then something sharp and dry scraped painfully across his back. He cried out in alarm as it stuck, like a vicious hook, embedded in his skin and dragging him away from her. The pain crescendoed suddenly as he was tugged from the bed and sent hurtling to the floorboards. Contorted in agony he looked up and glimpsed something dark stride over him. There was a scream. It seemed to cut deep down into his ears like slivers of broken glass, and he desperately tried to crawl back onto his knees. Then the screaming stopped just as suddenly as it started. Instead there was a ripping sound, like something being torn apart.

"No! God, no!" he sobbed, dizzy with nausea, his sight seeming to blur. Whatever stood over him still moved, its weight shifting from one leg to the other in sickening rhythm to the rips and tears from the bed. Feebly Lamson tried to reach out across the sheets to stop whatever was happening when something soft and warm touched his fingers. Something wet. It clung to him as he recoiled from it, screaming hysterically as darkness rose up about him and he fell into a faint.

It could have been hours, or even just minutes afterwards, when he opened his eyes once more. However long it was, the tawdry bedchamber had gone. Instead he was stretched out on the floor of his flat, facing the window. A blow-fly buzzed aggressively, though without result, against the window pane. Besides this there was silence.

As he slowly climbed to his feet his first reaction was one of intense relief. He could have laughed out loud in that one brief instant in joy at the fact that it had never happened, that it was all just a horrible dream, that he had never even left his room. Then he noticed the spots of blood on his shirt. There were scabs of it clotted about his hands and fingers. His stomach heaved with revulsion as he stared down at the ugly stains covering him like the deadly marks of a plague. "Oh my God!" he muttered, rushing convulsively to the sink to wash them from him. His hands still dripping, he grabbed hold of his shirt and tugged it from him, grinding his teeth against the pain in his back as the scabs swathed across it were torn open. His shirt had been glued to him by them. When the pain had subsided sufficiently he gingerly felt across his back, his fingers trembling cautiously along the blood-clogged grooves that had been gouged into him. Crestfallen with horror, he stared at his haggard face in the mirror above the sink. Did it happen? Was it not a dream after all, but some vile distortion of reality?

He stepped back into his bedroom and looked at the head, perched where he had left it. The thing stared at him with its coal-black, swollen eyes. *You* know, he thought suddenly, you know what happened, you black swine of a devil! But no, this was madness. How could he believe that the thing had some sort of connection with what had happened? It must have been something else. But what, though? he wondered. What else but something equally bizarre, equally preposterous could account for it? What? *What?*

Outside he heard the two tone siren of a police car as it sped down the road. After it had gone there was another. Lamson strode to the window and looked down as an ambulance hurtled by, its blue light blinking with a furious beat.

He leant against the windowsill. Resignedly, he knew that it did happen, it really did happen. By now they must have found her blood-soaked body—or what was left of it. He gazed down at the red stains still sticking to his fingers and wondered what he could do. Like a Brand of Cain threads of blood clung to the hardened scales about his knuckles. If only he had thrown that stone away when he had intended to originally. If he had he was sure that none of this would have ever happened.

He grabbed hold of the stone, clenching it tightly in both hands as if he would crush it into dust. Something black seemed to move on the edge of his sight. He turned round in surprise, but there was nothing there. Steady, now, steady, he told himself. Don't lose your grip altogether.

He placed the head back on the drawers and took a deep breath to compose himself. He wondered if he had left it too late to get rid of the head. Or was there time yet? After all, there was no saying what the thing might make him do next. Reluctantly he looked again at the head. How he wished that he could convince himself that it was nothing more than just an inanimate lump of stone. Once more he picked it up, his fingers experiencing the same kind of revulsion he would have felt on touching a diseased piece of flesh. "Damn you!" he whispered tensely, suddenly flexing his arms. There was a movement by his side, furtive and vague. He whipped round. "Where are you hiding?" he asked shakily, searching round the empty room. There seemed to be a sound somewhere like the clattering of hooves. Or was there? It echoed metallically, almost unreal. "Come on, now, where are you hiding?" Something touched his arm. It was hard and dry. He caught a glimpse of blackness shaped like an arm. He cried out inarticulately in revulsion. "Go away!" he choked, retreating to the window. He turned round to look outside, raising his hands and glancing at the huge black head that was clasped in his fingers. He coughed harshly, feeling the phlegm rising in his throat. It involuntarily dribbled from his lips, spilling on the floor. Looking down he saw that there was a string of blood in it. He closed his eyes tightly. He knew what it meant, though he wished fervently that he could believe that it didn't. He wished that he could have known earlier what he now knew and done then what he was about to do, when it wasn't already too late. "God help me!" he cried as he tugged his arms free of the fingers that plucked at him, and flung the stone through the window. There was a crash as the glass was shattered and he fell to the floor. Something rose up above him, seeming monstrously large in the gloom of his faltering sight.

"Are you going up to see Mr. Lamson?" the elderly woman asked, detaining Alan Sutcliffe with a nervously insistent hand.

"I am," he replied. "Why? Is there something wrong?" He did not try to hide his impatience. He was nearly half an hour late already.

"I don't know," she said, glancing up the stairs apprehensively. "It was late this afternoon when it happened. I was cleaning the dishes after having my tea when I heard something crash outside. When I looked I found that there was broken glass all over the flagstones. It had come from up there," she pointed up the stairs, "from the window of Mr. Lamson's flat. I could see that his window had been broken."

His impatience mellowing into concern, Sutcliffe asked if anyone had been up to see Lamson since then. "Do you know if he's been hurt? He hasn't been too well recently and he might be sick."

"I went up to his rooms, naturally," the woman said. "But he wouldn't answer his door. On no account would he, even when I called out to him, though he was in there right enough. I could hear him, you see, bumping around inside. Tearing something up, I think he was, like books. But he wouldn't open the door to me. He wouldn't even answer my calls. Not one word. There was nothing more I could do, was there?" she apologised. "I didn't know he was ill."

"That's all right," Sutcliffe said, thanking her for warning him. "I'll be able to see how he is when I call up. I'm sure he'll answer his door to me when I call to him. By the way," he went on to ask, turning round suddenly on the first step up the stairs, "do you know what it was that broke the window?"

"Indeed I do," the woman said. She felt in the pocket of her apron. "I found this on the pavement when I went out to clear up the glass. It's been cracked in two, as you can see. I couldn't find the body." She handed him the stone. "Ugly looking thing, isn't it?"

"It certainly is." Sutcliffe felt at the worn features on its face. It was pleasantly soap-like and warm. He wondered why Lamson should have thrown something like this through his window. "Do you mind if I hold onto it for a while?" he asked.

"You can keep it for good for all I care. I don't want it, I'm certain of that, Lord knows! It'd give me the jitters if I kept an evil-looking thing like that in my rooms."

Thanking her again, Sutcliffe bounded up the stairs. He wondered worriedly if Lamson had thrown it through the window as a cry for help. Just let me be in time if it was, he thought, knocking at the door to his flat. "Henry! Are you in there? It's me, Alan. Come on, open up!" There was no sound. Again he knocked, louder this time. "Henry! Open up, will you?" Apprehensively he waited an instant more, then took hold of the door handle, turning it. "Henry, I'm coming in. Keep back away from the door." Heavily he lunged against the door with his shoulder. The thin wood started to give way almost at once. Again he lunged against it, then again, then the door swung open, propelling Sutcliffe in with it.

"Where are you, Henr—" he began to call out as he steadied himself, before he saw what lay curled up against the windowsill. Shuddering with nausea Sutcliffe clasped a hand to his mouth and turned away. Naked and almost flayed to the bone, with tears along his doubled back, Lamson was crouched like a grotesque foetus amongst the blood-soaked tatters of his clothes. His head was twisted round and it was obvious that his neck had been broken. But it was none of this, neither the mutilations nor the gore nor the look of horror and pain on Lamson's rigidly contorted face, that were to haunt him in the weeks and months to come, but an expression that lay across his friend's dead face which he knew should have never been there—a look of joyful ecstasy. And there was a hunger there, too, but a hunger that went further than that of mere hunger for food.

# Stephen Laws

# Junk

STEPHEN LAWS is one of the rising young stars of horror fiction. He began writing when he was eight, and by his late twenties he was scripting television plays, while his short stories of the supernatural were published locally and broadcast on radio. After winning a fiction competition in 1981, Laws decided to try his hand at a novel. The result was *Ghost Train*, which received enthusiastic reviews on both sides of the Atlantic and led to him being described as "England's answer to Stephen King". This success has continued with his three subsequent novels, *Spectre*, *The Wyrm* and *The Frighteners*.

The following tale of techno-terror will leave you reeling as you meet a mysterious stranger with a very unusual hobby . . .

THE NIGHTMARE BEGAN on a warm, sultry August afternoon. McLaren had been standing outside his ramshackle "office," leaning against the rusting hulk of a Ford Cortina, his belly full of beer after a boozing session at the pub around the corner. For half an hour he had stood there, smoking one of the cheap cigars his brother-in-law brought him back from Spain regularly. The cheap aroma seemed to radiate from him continuously: in his clothes, his hair, his breath.

From his vantage point, he had a clear view of the entire junkyard from which he made his living. He watched as Tony Bastable manoeuvred the jib of the crane, bringing the huge mechanical claw down heavily onto a battered Austin Allegro, crushing the roof like tissue paper. It gave McLaren a curious sense of satisfaction to see the car crushed like that. Only the week before, some fat cat had been sitting behind the wheel of that car, probably on his way to some big business meeting. Looking forward to champagne and caviar; not realising that the articulated truck just ahead of him was about to jack-knife on a patch of oil on the motorway and that his nice new Allegro was going to slam, bang right into the back of it, leaving lots of little pieces of fat cat all over the road.

The Allegro was hoisted into the air and swung across the yard to The Crusher. In a few minutes, all that would remain would be a solid cube of metal.

McLaren took the cigar from between his teeth and crumpled it in his hand in much the same way that the mechanical claw had just crushed the Allegro.

"You are, no doubt, the proprietor of this establishment?"

The voice which sounded from behind McLaren made him jump forward a couple of feet, shoulders hunched up into his bull neck as if expecting an attack. But it was not a loud voice. Silky soft and with a thick accent.

"What the hell do you want to creep up on me like that for?" boomed McLaren, taking in the tall, angular figure which appeared to have materialised from nowhere. The stranger was tall, impeccably dressed and wore a homburg hat.

"My apologies. I assume that you were engrossed in your thoughts," said The Stranger. His pale face had an expression of vulpine amusement. When he smiled, McLaren could see two rows of perfectly even teeth that would have put the Osmond brothers to shame. Striking eyes sparkled with amusement beneath dark, heavy brows.

"Never mind. What do you want?" McLaren thought: *Only Jews wear homburgs. But he doesn't look Jewish. That accent sounds . . . I dunno . . . Hungarian or something.* The Stranger had his hands clasped at chest level, as if he were about to pray. Big white pulpy fingers writhed like a handful of worms.

"I am looking for certain . . . bits and pieces."

"Well, bits and pieces are what you see scattered all over the yard, mister. What you looking for in particular?"

"May I browse for a while?"

"This isn't a bloody library, mister. Now, what do you want?"

"Ah, a businessman," said The Stranger, in a way that McLaren didn't like one bit. Like he was being humoured or something. "You have it in mind to make an immediate transaction. Very well. I require a transmission from a 1963 Ford Cortina."

McLaren opened his fingers and let the crumpled cigar fall to the ground before dusting off his hands. "Pretty specific. But we don't have one in working order."

The Stranger smiled again as if to humour him. The afternoon sun seemed to be playing tricks with his eyes and teeth, which seemed to capture and reflect the light. McLaren noted in particular the curious effect the sun played on his eyes. It was like the photograph that he'd taken at his nephew's wedding last spring. The flash cube had turned everyone's irises a deep reflective red. And now The Stranger stood before him, like some forgotten and uninvited intruder at that wedding, grinning into the camera.

"The transmission need not be in working order."

From the other side of the yard, McLaren heard The Crusher begin to growl, followed by the squealing shriek of metal as the Allegro began its first crushing compression.

"Indeed, the condition of the transmission is not, within limits, of outstanding importance."

Again, the silky voice. The eyes with their stolen embers of sun. The scream of tortured metal.

"However, I do require that the equipment in question be taken from a 1963 Ford Cortina . . . *any* 1963 Ford Cortina . . . But the automobile must have ended its days as the result of a crash. And at least one passenger in the car must have been killed instantaneously."

"Get out of my junkyard, mister. Before I set my dog on you. I've got a business to run. I suggest that you save however much you were going to pay me and use it on a shrink. Now, get out." McLaren turned away from The Stranger to lean on the wreck behind him. "Atlas!" he shouted. On the other side of the yard was a shed which Jackie Shannon, the night watchman, laughingly called the "office." The shed was surrounded by a mesh fence, and McLaren's Alsatian dog prowled restlessly back and forth like a caged wild animal . . . which, in effect, it was. On hearing its name called, the dog leapt up against the mesh with a sharp, ringing clatter. McLaren smiled and turned back to The Stranger to see if he had taken the point.

The Stranger now stood less than three feet away from him. Silently, he appeared to have glided uncomfortably close to McLaren while his back was turned. The Stranger's grin was wider but there was no trace of humour on the face. The eyes burned with amber fire now, which came not from the sun, but from within. McLaren involuntarily pressed himself back against the wreck.

The Stranger's thumbs began to intertwine back and forth, back and forth in the white nest of his fingers. The squealing of metal against metal seemed to be reaching a new crescendo as The Stranger spoke again, his soft, satin voice still silken clear over the cacophony.

"At least one fatality, Mr. McLaren."

*How does he know my name?* thought McLaren with something like panic beginning to take hold. *Because your name's on the sign over the gate, that's why, you idiot!* But the answer failed to stem the fear which crept over him. His uneasiness in

The Stranger's company had now turned to an unreasoning terror. Sweat trickled between his shoulderblades and moulded his shirt to his back. It ran down his face and dripped from the tip of his bulbous nose.

"Age or sex is immaterial. But I expect you to provide me with my requirements by tomorrow evening at the same time. Do I make myself clear?"

McLaren could not find his voice. It lay shrivelled and fearful in the pit of his stomach.

"Do I make myself clear?" said the vulpine face again as it began to move terribly and hypnotically closer.

"Yes!" McLaren's fear had found the mislaid response. The face halted inches from his own and McLaren could see now without any question that the flames of hell burned hungrily in The Stranger's eyes. A white hand like the dried, shrivelled husk of a dead spider moved to McLaren's chest and he felt something being pushed into his top jerkin pocket.

"Tomorrow, Mr. McLaren."

McLaren wanted to look away from that horrible face but was afraid that if he did, those frighteningly sharp teeth would dart quickly forward for his throat.

And then The Stranger was gone, turning sharply on his heels and striding purposefully towards the junkyard gates. The screeching sound had dwindled to a dull churning and crunching. Atlas gave vent to a long, low, pitiful howl. McLaren turned to see the dog slinking back from the mesh fence towards the shed. When he looked back to watch the departing figure, there was no one in sight. But that was crazy! It was a good three-minute walk to the gates.

But The Stranger was gone.

*Tomorrow.*

McLaren wiped the sweat from his face. His hand was trembling violently. Now able to move at last, he pushed himself away from the wreck and began to pick his way nervously amidst the junk towards the shed, casting anxious glances back over his shoulder.

Tony was still concentrating on The Crusher. "Hi, Frank!" he called as McLaren stumbled quickly to the mesh gate and let himself in without once looking his way. "Up yours then, you bastard!" he growled under his breath as a four-foot metal cube of Austin Allegro trundled past on a conveyor belt.

McLaren moved quickly to the shed. Atlas rounded the corner, glanced sheepishly at his master and then, as if sensing the fear which still lingered around McLaren like an invisible cloud of his rancid cigar smoke, slunk away out of sight again. McLaren clattered across the shed to a small safe, twisted the dials to the right combination and pulled out a bottle of MacInlays and a glass. Sitting at a cluttered table in the centre of the room, McLaren poured a glassful and downed it in one, staring out through the grease-stained window which overlooked the spot where he had encountered The Stranger. He drank another and then remembered the something that The Stranger had stuffed into his top pocket. Fingers still trembling, he pulled out twenty ten-pound notes.

*Two hundred quid!* For a lousy transmission that doesn't have to work.

*A 1963 Ford Cortina which has been involved in an accident*, a voice seemed to echo somewhere. *And at least one person must have been killed instantaneously in the wreck.*

McLaren drank again and watched as Tony climbed into the crane, swung the jib over The Crusher, plucked up the metal cube from the conveyor belt and swung it across the yard, late afternoon sun glinting on the wrinkled metal.

McLaren spent four of the crisp brand-new ten-pound notes on booze in the Crane and Lever that night. And as the alcohol seeped into his corpulent bulk, the unreasoning fear which had overcome him in the presence of The Stranger began gradually to dissolve. By closing time in the pub, he had rationalised the situation completely. The man was an eccentric, a queer, a pervert. He got his kicks from weird mementoes. Hadn't he once read somewhere that pieces from the car wreck which had killed James Dean in the fifties were treasured souvenirs? So what if this fella was sick? He had paid two hundred smackers, cash in advance, and the stuff he wanted didn't even have to be in working order. And, anyway, he knew for a fact that there was a battered Cortina just behind the compound with its transmission intact. It was useless, of course; strictly junk value. Two kids on a bender had been cut out of the car on the Coast Road. One of them had been dead on arrival at the County Hospital. McLaren had always been interested in how his cars came to the junkyard. Now it looked as if his interest was going to pay off.

On the following day, when the effects of the alcohol had worn off, McLaren's reasoning did not seem as watertight as it had previously. He suffered from butterflies in the stomach from the moment he climbed out of bed and they stayed with him as he supervised the extraction of the transmission from the Cortina. His nervousness also angered him so that when Tony asked him why the hell he was bothering with this piece of junk, McLaren had told him to get the hell on with it and earn his living.

As the afternoon crept on towards the appointed time, McLaren's apprehension and temper grew. By 4:00 P.M. the bottle of whisky in his safe was empty. Atlas had sensed his master's discomfort and was keeping well out of the way under the table in the "office." At 4:31 P.M. the dog looked up, sniffed the air, snarled and then slunk quickly out of the office.

McLaren knew before looking out of the window that The Stranger would be standing in the same place as yesterday, hands held clasped in front of him, staring at the office.

McLaren made his way over to the silent figure, trying to avoid looking at the face with the ivory glint of teeth and the twin orbs of copper-fire. There was a twelve-foot gap between them when McLaren stopped. The transmission rested against the twisted hulk of machinery which McLaren now leant against, waiting for The Stranger to break the silence.

"This is the transmission I requested?"

"Yeah . . ."

"Capital, capital. I think that this will suit my purpose admirably."

*Bloody creep.*

"I trust that you can store this equipment for me in a secure place here in your yard?" The silky smooth voice purred like a contented cat gloating over a recently slaughtered mouse.

"Well . . ."

"For a suitable fee, of course." The Stranger's thumbs were intertwining again as he surveyed the battered transmission.

"How long do you want me to keep it for you?" ventured McLaren, wiping the sweat from his brow and averting his gaze from The Stranger to scan the junkyard behind him unnecessarily.

"Not for long. I have numerous other requirements which I trust you will be able to provide."

*Look, mister. Why don't you take your junk and just clear off? Leave me alone. Take your eyes and your teeth to someone else.*

"Like what?"

"A rear axle from a 1971 Morris Marina. Undamaged. And the driver must have suffered leg injuries in the crash. Fatal or otherwise, but the leg injuries are the important factor."

*Jesus!*

Thirty seconds and thirty pounds later, McLaren was walking back to the office, feeling his hands shaking again and not wanting to turn around in case he really did see The Stranger suddenly vanish in a puff of smoke. Tomorrow. Same time, same place. That evening, there were two new whisky bottles in the safe and another on the office table.

And so the days began to blur into each other.

McLaren fought his fear with the whisky bottle and decided, at the height of his drunkenness, on various means of dealing with The Stranger: How about the threat of physical violence? Setting the dog on him and telling him never to come back? (If, that is, Atlas could be persuaded to stop crawling on his belly.) Hiring a couple of heavies from the Crane and Lever to lean on him? Calling the police to complain about the nuisance?

But every evening at the allotted time, McLaren found

himself standing trembling beside the twisted hulk with The Stranger as he showed him the latest acquisition. McLaren was becoming a very rich man. But for the first time in his life, the money meant nothing to him. He hoped fervently that each latest piece of junk would be the last. But it never was.

> The rear seat from an Anglia: the back-seat passenger must have been killed, preferably decapitated.
>
> The front wheels from a Volkswagen: condition irrelevant. But two bystanders must have been injured in the crash. At least one fatality required. Leg injuries essential.
>
> An unruptured petrol tank from a Datsun Cherry: one child fatality required.

And for reasons McLaren could not explain, he found himself obeying The Stranger's strictly specific requirements to the letter even though they were becoming more and more bizarre, more and more difficult to find. Panic often threatened to overtake him on his quest, which now took him to other junkyard owners: men who had once called him friend but now only took his money, noted his whisky-tainted breath and, shaking their heads sadly, directed him to the required junk. Somehow, McLaren succeeded in meeting The Stranger's requirements every time.

Until, that is, The Stranger made his request for the *unmarked windscreen from a hit-and-run car. No particular model of car necessary. But the victim must have suffered damage to the eyes.*

McLaren knew immediately that, this time, he would never be able to meet The Stranger's requirements. It was impossible. How the hell could he provide something like that?

On The Stranger's next visit, he said so.

And then wished that he hadn't as The Stranger turned his doll-like visage on him and the ember-filled eyes sparkled displeasure. When The Stranger smiled, it was with the face of something that had been dead for a long time. McLaren burbled that he would have the windscreen ready for him at the same time tomorrow night.

When The Stranger had gone, McLaren stood looking miserably at the pile of junk which lay cluttered in the middle of his junkyard. The recently acquired two hundred and fifty pounds fluttered loosely in one dangling hand. The pile made no sense at all. He could make no reason of this ill-assorted heap of scrap metal. It was useless. Rubbish. Junk. When McLaren moved towards the office at last, he failed to notice that two of The Stranger's ten-pound notes had fallen from his loose grasp and now lay fluttering on the muddy ground.

The following day passed agonisingly slowly for McLaren in a whisky-sodden haze. He had tried everywhere for the windscreen knowing that the request was impossible. How the hell would anyone know if any of his own cars or any of the wrecks in the other junkyards he visited were hit-and-run? Only the police were apt to have that kind of information. And in one of the junkyards he visited that day, the owner had threatened to give him a good working over after he had made his sick request.

At three o'clock that afternoon, McLaren sat in his office trying to drown the fear in his guts once more with alcohol. After a while, it seemed to be working. But McLaren knew that he must keep himself sufficiently "topped-up" to carry out the plan which he had finally prepared. He was faced with no other alternative. And if his fear of The Stranger was allowed to surface, he would never be able to do it.

First of all, he made a none-too-steady tour of the junkyard and found an intact windscreen from a Citroën. Then he called Tony over and instructed him to take it out carefully . . . *very carefully* . . . ignoring the look of disgust on his employee's face. What the hell? He was drunk and he knew it, and only by staying drunk was he going to solve his problem.

By the time that Tony had propped the windscreen up against the pile of junk which had been accumulated by The Stranger, the sun was beginning to sink in the late afternoon sky.

"Mind if I ask a question?" said Tony, lighting a cigarette

as he cast a glance over the peculiar debris.

McLaren grunted. It could have meant yes or no.

"What the hell's all this stuff for?"

"You get paid to do a job, Tony. And that's all. Just do it and don't stick your nose in." McLaren finished his statement with a rattling belch.

"You always were a pig, McLaren." Tony blew a stream of smoke in his direction. "And until now, I've just put up with it because I needed the work. Now I don't. So you can stuff your job as of now."

McLaren stepped forward.

"Try it and I'll lay you out," said Tony easily. McLaren stopped, swaying slightly. "But before I do go I think I should give you a piece of advice. See a shrink. You're acting pretty weird, McLaren. I think that whisky bottle has addled your brains."

Casting a last, derisory glance at The Stranger's junk, Tony walked past McLaren towards the gates.

*Oh, yeah?* thought McLaren. *Big man! If you'd been through what I've been through, you wouldn't be so loudmouthed. If you'd had to look into those bloody eyes, just what state would your nerves be in?* He wanted to say all of those things to Tony. But only one word would come out.

"Bastard!"

Tony ignored him. Funnily enough, McLaren's parting remark was entirely factual.

Back in the office, McLaren replenished himself, cooing gratefully to the bottle, caressing its neck like some strange glass pet. Underneath the table, Atlas began to make low, grumbling sounds in his throat. It was time.

The Stranger stood in the usual spot, his own angular shadow joining with the sharp, ragged shadows of the surrounding junk as the sun finally began to creep past the horizon. McLaren's hands were no longer trembling as he stood up purposefully, the chair clattering backward to the floor. The dog whined and began to crawl across the floor on its stomach until it had reached the far corner.

Walking stiff-legged, eyes staring, McLaren moved to the bench, found what he was looking for and tucked it tightly into his belt behind him, feeling its hard coolness in the small of his back. The walk across the junkyard to The Stranger seemed to take place in a dream-like slow motion. He seemed to be walking on a moving treadmill and never actually getting any closer.

The Stranger was smiling or grimacing . . . McLaren couldn't decide which . . . but he hoped above everything else that he could not read his mind and see his intention. The Stranger's mouth opened, lips writhing back from glistening teeth, as McLaren arrived.

"You have obtained the necessary?"

"Yes . . . it's over there behind you." *All this whisky and I'm still so goddamned frightened. Can he hear it? Can he hear how frightened I am?*

"Good. Let me see it."

McLaren gestured for him to move forward and The Stranger turned to look at his pile of junk. The windscreen was propped against the transmission. It dimly reflected The Stranger's angular shape as he leaned down to touch it. McLaren had moved up behind him as The Stranger crouched down and stroked the glass.

And then McLaren heard the sharp intake of breath that sounded more like the warning of a rattlesnake about to strike. The Stranger was turning from his crouched position, mouth twisting in a cruel grimace. One eye was swivelling back to look at him like some hideous chameleon.

"This is *not* . . . " began The Stranger as McLaren stepped swiftly forward, fumbling at the small of his back. In the next instant, the spanner had cracked open The Stranger's skull like a ripe melon. The mouth grinned, eyes rolled up to white and The Stranger jerked over backward with the spanner still embedded in his brain, arms and legs writhing in a dance of death. Then he was still.

McLaren stood frozen in position, one arm held out before him in the act of the fatal blow. Stunned, he stared at The Stranger. It had been so easy. So damned easy. One blow. And he was dead.

Lurching away, McLaren vomited a stream of pure alcohol onto the ground, his stomach heaving and straining until there was nothing left to come.

The Stranger lay twisted and angular like some hideous praying mantis, the whites of his dead eyes still reflecting the dying light as McLaren finally moved towards him again. He purposefully avoided those eyes as he leaned behind the twisted car wreck against which The Stranger's junk was propped, trembling fingers finding the oil-smeared tarpaulin he had placed there earlier. McLaren felt so terribly cold, so bloodless, as he threw the tarpaulin on the ground beside the corpse. Wiping one trembling hand across his mouth, he kicked the body over onto the tarpaulin, unable to bring himself to touch The Stranger with his hands. The body rustled easily over onto the sheet. The spanner squelched from its resting place.

Controlling his stomach, McLaren drew the canvas up around the body and rolled it over; once, twice, three times . . . until The Stranger's corpse was firmly wrapped in a cocoon of tarpaulin. McLaren threw an anxious glance back at the office. Jackie Shannon, the night watchman, would be arriving at any time. There wasn't much time. McLaren grabbed the tarpaulin around The Stranger's feet and began to drag his package across the junkyard. The sun had finally slipped past the horizon as McLaren reached the rusted hulk of the Ford Cortina, the jagged piled silhouettes of rusted cars and twisted metal painted with the blue-black of night. It was like some bizarre elephant's graveyard.

Hinges screeched as he pulled open the driver's door and McLaren heard Atlas give vent to a long, solitary howl from the office. Now McLaren would have to use his hands and felt disgust as he roughly bundled the corpse across the driver's seat, still glancing fearfully behind him for any sign of Shannon. Finally, the bundle was stuffed into the car and McLaren slammed the door shut with unnecessary force, feeling the cold sweat on his face, the dull ache in his gut.

Within seconds, he was in the driving cab of the crane. As he had so rightly guessed, Tony had left the keys in the dash. The engine roared into life and the grab swung across the yard to hover like some mythical roc's claw above the wreck and its grisly occupant. The engine gasped and the claw suddenly descended under its own weight, crumpling the roof of the car. The claw tightened, punching in the windows, splintering and cracking the bodywork. In silhouette, it seemed as if some stalking *Tyrannosaurus rex* had caught its prey and was in the process of taking the corpse to its lair.

The black, rectangular maw of The Crusher yawned wide to receive the car as the crane gently lowered the wreck. For five agonisingly long seconds the prey refused to be parted from the hunter, before finally crashing down into the machine. Five minutes later, McLaren stood at The Crusher's control, still furtively looking over his shoulder, eyes darting, fingers twitching, beads of sweat marbling his face.

He set The Crusher in motion.

The squealing and rending of metal was almost too much for him. He turned his back on The Crusher, hands clasped to his ears to deafen the insane cacophony of tortured metal. McLaren tried to shut out the recurring mental image of what must be happening to the tarpaulin-wrapped body in the car. It would all be over soon. But now, as the car began to reach the first stage of its compression before the hydraulic ram could start on the inexorable forward movement which would finally reduce the car to a solid cube of metal, the squealing had taken on a new and decidedly more horrific tone.

It seemed to sound like someone screaming.

*No, that can't be!* thought McLaren, squeezing his hands tightly over his ears. *He was dead. I know he was dead. I crushed his skull . . .*

The squealing and crunching abruptly subsided to a lower, rumbling noise under the unstoppable grumbling of The Crusher. The conveyor belt began to move.

McLaren moved away from The Crusher controls and around to one side, straining nervously forward to catch sight of the car's remains.

A cube of compressed metal, four feet square, trundled out of The Crusher's maw.

McLaren walked around it. There was no blood. No telltale shoe poking out of the side. No hideous, clutching hands. He turned back to the crane and climbed into the cabin.

The claw descended. The cube was hoisted across the junkyard. McLaren swung the cube up high over the inpenetrable tangle of steel and iron in the middle of his yard, until it dangled over the most inaccessible depths of his junk pile. The claw opened.

The cube plunged into the junk pile with a screeching crash and the pile seemed to shift uncomfortably, adjusting its bulk to take account of this unwelcome intruder. It groaned, murmured, protested. And then, with a final squeal of protest, the cube began to slip. Slowly at first, and then faster and faster the cube slid into the widening, yawning fissure of a junk earthquake.

*Perfect!* thought McLaren, licking dry lips. *Bloody perfect!*

The cube vanished from sight under an avalanche of metal, a twisted wreath of wiring and steel frame crashing down and effectively burying it from sight for good. The junk heap rumbled once and was still.

*Perfect!*

"Working late, Mr. McLaren?"

The voice just outside the cab door sent a bolt of electric blue lightning racing through McLaren's heart, bottlenecking in his throat with a convulsive heave. Shannon had climbed up to the cab and watched as McLaren had manoeuvred the cube into the junk heap.

"Just . . . it was . . . " McLaren heard himself say. "Bloody stuff was no good! Just in the way all the time." And then, hastily and defensively: "Wouldn't have had to do it myself if it hadn't been for Bastable. I had to sack the bastard this afternoon!"

"Tony? Really?" Shannon began to climb back down as McLaren switched off and began to follow him, legs like jelly. "Ah, well. I could see it coming. His heart was never in it."

Back at the office, McLaren could hear that Atlas was barking fit to burst again. But this time, it seemed to him that his dog's barking seemed healthier, less fearful. McLaren began to feel a great pressure lifting from him.

"Fancy a glass of whisky?" he asked Shannon.

Shannon's jaw dropped. This kind of offer from McLaren was unknown. "Don't mind if I do," he replied after he had regained his composure, adding mentally: *Sacking people must agree with you. I'd better watch my step.*

McLaren smiled heartily and clapped Shannon's back so heavily that the old man's dentures nearly popped out.

"Celebrating, Mr. McLaren?"

"Just let's say I've got a pressing problem off my mind."

The nightmare began again a week later.

McLaren had found himself unable to go anywhere near the pile of junk which he had accumulated for The Stranger. Every time he passed it, he promised himself that he would have it gathered up and slung out later. Later. Always later. And then, a week to the day that he had rid himself of that *thing*, he noticed that the junk was gone.

His first reaction was one of relief. He had given no order to any of his men to get rid of the stuff and normally he would have flown into a vindictive rage because of that fact. But not this time. He asked his workmen in as casual and appreciative a manner as possible, who had done it . . . George, Ray and Barney Hill. Even Jackie Shannon. And something like unease began to creep over McLaren as each worker in turn denied having touched any of the stuff. He fought it down. *Somebody* must have moved the bloody stuff. But whatever that person's reason for keeping quiet about it, McLaren decided to be thankful for this not-so-small mercy and ask no more questions. The junk was gone. That was the important thing.

On Thursday morning, McLaren let himself in through the main compound gate for another working day and as he approached the office could see immediately that something was wrong. Shannon was standing in the doorway hopping from foot to foot, obviously waiting anxiously for him. Atlas was pacing back and forward behind the mesh.

"What's up, Jackie?"

"Prowlers, Mr. McLaren. Early this morning; about three o'clock."

"Catch anybody?" asked McLaren, pushing past him

into the office and making straight for the freshly boiled kettle.

"Never saw a soul. Heard them, though. I reckon Atlas put the wind up them."

"Where?"

"Over on the other side of the compound. They couldn't have been professionals, Mr. McLaren. They made one hell of a racket. Crashing and banging, pulling the bloody junk about. I let Atlas go and then followed him. I reckon when they heard him barking, they scarpered. They must have been fast, though . . . I didn't see a soul. Not even with those arc lights blazing away."

"Probably kids," said McLaren. *Then why the hell do I feel scared all of a sudden? What the hell's the matter with me?*

"Did you check the fence?"

"No breaks. They must have come over the top. Must have been keen if they wanted to risk losing a bollock on that barbed wire. Shall I report it?"

"Naw," said McLaren, gulping hot, strong tea. "Not worth it. Just keep your eyes open tonight." *Tomorrow night. In the junkyard. In the dark. And I'll be home, drinking whisky. Far away from this place. Far away and safe.*

Why did the junkyard at night suddenly seem such an unpleasant prospect?

McLaren gulped his tea and started a long, unsuccessful day of trying to rid himself of a bloody awful creepy feeling that he thought had vanished with the passing of The Stranger.

It had been a long, arduous day. McLaren, still feeling clammy, had spent two hours in the Crane and Lever that evening until the whisky had numbed him to it. Returning home, he had finished off a six-pack from the fridge and fallen asleep in front of the television. His dreams were vague and troubled. The images were confused and disturbing. The junkyard at night. The crane. The Crusher. A tall, angular shadow standing up against the compound fence, fingers hooked through the mesh, face obscured apart from two hideously shining red eyes looking straight at him with hungry intent. The sound of The Crusher. The squealing and shrieking of rending metal. The shrieking of steel turning to the shrieking of a human voice. Closer and louder. Closer . . . louder . . . *Close . . . closer . . . here . . . Now!*

McLaren woke with a scream clenched tightly in his teeth; his heart was hammering, and he half expected to find himself standing alone in the junkyard listening to the sounds of shambling footsteps behind him. The familiarity of his living room made him slump backward with a deep sigh. The television buzzed angrily at him, the speckled snowstorm on the screen the sole light in the room.

But why could he still hear the shrieking?

He panicked again. But no, it wasn't The Crusher, or the car, or The Stranger. It was the telephone.

Groaning again, McLaren struggled to his feet, accidentally kicking over an empty beer can with a reverberating clank. He wiped his face, yawned and then answered the telephone.

It was Shannon.

"I'm sorry to bother you so late, Mr. McLaren. But I think you'd better come down here straightaway."

McLaren looked at his watch. It was one-thirty. "What the hell's wrong?"

"It's Atlas. He's been hurt pretty bad."

"How? No . . . wait! I'll be right down!"

As always, the junkyard was brilliantly floodlit, but the harsh black shadows that filled the ragged gaps and crevices of the junk pile brought the crawling taste of fear back to McLaren. The booze had worn off. He felt dry and hollow; and the hollowness was filling up rapidly with that creepy sick feeling again. The gates were open . . . Shannon had obviously seen to that . . . and McLaren's car roared through, kicking up dust. The car screeched to a halt and McLaren flung himself out past the night watchman and into the office, unaware of Shannon's agitated burblings, and realising for the first time (*truly* for the first time) how much he loved that dog and didn't want to lose it. He knew that it was going to be bad.

But not as bad as this.

Atlas lay on a blanket beside the table, making low, hopeless gurgling sounds in the back of his throat. It whimpered when it saw him. McLaren moved forward and saw the blood. The dog's body was covered in deep lacerations, its foreleg almost severed at the knee. Shannon had tied a makeshift tourniquet above the knee with masking tape.

". . . Oh God, Atlas . . . " was all that McLaren could say as he knelt beside his dying dog, knowing that it had lost too much blood to be saved. It licked his hand. McLaren choked back tears.

"*What the hell happened here?*"

"That's what I've been trying to tell you, Mr. McLaren. There's something weird going on. I don't think I want to work here no more . . ."

"*What have you done to my dog?*"

"We've been hearing noises all night, Mr. McLaren." Shannon's voice struggled to retain control. "Somebody's out there in the junk, moving stuff around. And every time we got near to where we thought the noise was coming from, it stopped and then started again somewhere else. Atlas was sniffing around at the foot of that big pile of junk in the middle of the yard . . . just like he'd found something in there. Then he started squealing. When I got to him I saw that he'd got his leg caught in some wiring. I couldn't get him loose, Mr. McLaren! He just kept getting more tangled in the junk. He bit me while I was trying to help him. Look!"

Shannon showed him the crescent-shaped mark on his forearm but McLaren was looking beyond him, through the open door and into the junkyard. "Show me, Jackie. Show me where it happened." McLaren's voice was quavering. Instinctively, he knew where it had happened. But he still had to see. "Show me."

"The dog . . .?"

"He's as good as dead. Show me."

McLaren followed Shannon outside.

"I'm sorry, Mr. McLaren. Really I am. But we just couldn't find whatever was making the noise. It stopped after Atlas was hurt . . ."

"Show me."

They walked through the starkly lit, deeply shadowed automobile graveyard, passing ruined metal carcasses heaped one upon the other. The crane stood its silent dinosaur vigil, dagger-toothed head stooped and waiting. As McLaren had guessed, Shannon headed straight for the centre pile where The Stranger's remains lay buried in a four-foot-cube coffin. McLaren became aware of a buzzing in his head and tried to shake it off, finally realising at last that the sound was coming from one of the arc lights overhead. The first of their multiple shadows reached the pile before them. Shannon pointed at the foot of the pile.

"There. That's where it happened." A pool of Atlas' blood glistened darkly like machine oil.

*What am I going to do?* thought McLaren desperately.

"Maybe we should get the police . . . " began Shannon.

"No!" snapped McLaren. "No police!" *God knows what they might find if they start snooping around.*

And then the lights started to go out.

During their walk the buzzing sound had grown steadily louder before ending abruptly. At that moment, one of the arc lights beside the office had suddenly gone out. Both men turned to look as another light went out on the far side of the compound. They turned again. Another light went out. And then another. Section by section, the junkyard was being plunged into utter darkness.

"What the . . .?"

Only one arc light now remained in operation: the light which towered above the centre pile at which they were standing. McLaren and Shannon stood vulnerably in the droning spotlight.

"Power failure?" said Shannon in hopeless dismay.

The last light went out.

McLaren almost allowed his first instinctive reaction to take hold. He had plunged headfirst into his own most recent nightmare and he wanted to run screaming from the junkyard. Fighting to control himself, knowing that he was not going to wake up this time in the safety of his own armchair, McLaren fumbled through the dark to touch Shannon's arm. Shannon jerked in shock at the touch.

"Use the flashlight."

Shannon unfastened the torch from his belt and switched it on, the beam sweeping over the twisted wreckage of the junk pile.

"We'll walk back to the office slowly. No point in breaking our necks on a piece of junk."

Something shifted in the junk pile behind them.

Shannon swung around and the torch beam danced over the pile again.

"Keep walking!" said McLaren, pulling Shannon's arm.

"There's something in there," said Shannon tightly. "I can see . . . sparks . . . or something."

"Come on!"

"No, wait, look there." Shannon switched off the torch. The darkness swamped them again. McLaren could feel his heart racing. Despite himself, he turned to look.

Deep inside the junk pile, obscured by tangled machinery and wiring, McLaren could see a brief spluttering of light. Sparks danced and hissed somewhere in the very heart of the junk pile as if someone was at work in there with an oxyacetylene torch.

"*We've got to get out, Jackie!*"

The junk shifted again. The sparks crackled and jumped.

"No . . . wait a minute, Mr. McLaren . . . I can see something . . . I can see . . . " Shannon had moved forward, pulling away from McLaren's grip.

"Jackie, I'm going for the police. Come on. It's kids or something." McLaren kept backing away as Shannon put one hand on the pile of junk and strained forward to peer inside. He raised the torch and pointed it through a ragged gap.

"Come on, Jackie!"

"No . . . wait a minute, Mr. McLaren . . . I can see something . . . I can see . . . " Shannon switched on the torch, pushing forward headfirst into a gap in the junk pile.

At first, McLaren thought that he was back on that terrible day again and that he had just switched on The Crusher. The horrifying screech of metal had turned into the screaming of a human voice. The screaming had started again—loud, desperate and horrifying. A screeching and crunching noise that froze McLaren in his tracks. But of course, it was not The Crusher. It was Shannon.

And McLaren could only stand and watch in horror as something unseen began to drag Shannon into the junk pile by his head. The torch clattered down into the pile, providing an angled cross-lit framework of the tangled junk as Shannon thrashed, screamed and kicked. The junk shifted. Shannon slipped further inside, his shrieking now hoarse and mortally desperate. His legs kicked spasmodically, the junk shifted again and Shannon disappeared quivering and silent into the pile. The hissing and spluttering sparks danced again.

At last, McLaren screamed. He turned and ran blindly into the dark, away from the junk pile. Too late, he became aware of something directly before him. Something slammed into his forehead, sparks danced in his brain and he was aware now that he was lying on his back. He groaned, wiped his hand across his head and felt blood. He looked up. A length of girder was protruding from the open window of a ruined Ford Estate car. McLaren had run straight into it. And he knew that the girder had not been there before.

Frantically, he clambered to his feet and began moaning in terror as the pile began to slither and crash behind him like a living thing. McLaren blundered away again, trying to orientate himself and find the direction which would lead him to the office.

But as he ran, he felt like a stranger in someone else's junkyard. The terrain was unknown to him. The landscapes of piled junk, the jagged peaks and valleys of wrecked cars and ruined machinery were completely alien.

*It's as if something's been moving the junk around so that I would get lost!* McLaren heard himself thinking, blind terror now taking hold. He continued to run, screaming and scrabbling through the junk like an animal as the centre pile crashed and heaved in the darkness. *Something's breaking out! That's what it is . . . he's breaking out!* Jagged steel edges lacerated his hands and shredded his sleeves as he plunged blindly ahead. Something screeched rustily in the darkness behind him.

*Please, God, let me get out! I'll be a good boy . . . I promise . . . Just let me out!*

McLaren's foot tangled in a broken radio set and he crashed heavily to the ground again, knocking the breath out of his lungs. Sobbing painfully, he scrabbled into the shadows of a rusted car hulk, squeezing himself partially beneath it.

The noises from the centre pile ceased.

McLaren struggled to control his wheezing, now the only sound in the darkness. The centre pile was obscured by other mazed mounds of twisted junk. There was no sound; no movement of any kind. McLaren tried to assess his exact whereabouts in the junkyard, scanning the darkness and the black silhouettes of metal carcasses. None of the junk was familiar. He closed his eyes, hands clasped to heaving chest, and concentrated. He thought quickly back to his first approach towards the centre pile with Shannon, gauged how far his desperate flight had taken him, and then looked around again. If he headed *over there . . .*

And then McLaren heard the first sound off to his right. A hollow, shivering clank from somewhere in the darkness. It didn't come from the centre pile, of that much he was certain. Perhaps, he thought, with rising hope, it was Ray, or George, or . . .

Something moved across the open patch of ground on McLaren's right. Something that was long, twisted and indistinct. It seemed to hop, skip and then turn end over end as it moved quickly across the ragged ground, rattling and clanking. McLaren refused to believe that it was a car exhaust, moving of its own volition and headed in the direction of the centre pile. He also refused to believe it when a car battery began to roll end over end across the yard from the other direction, again on its way to the centre pile. Junk did not move by itself. Tyres did not suddenly squeeze themselves out of the junk and roll sedately away into the darkness. Headlights, axles and car seats did not emerge from the night, scuttling and bouncing on to their unknown destination. Even when a rearview mirror whistled past his face, clipping his ear and drawing blood, McLaren did not believe. Things like that only happened in nightmares. And if this was a nightmare, he would be waking up soon. A wild, living tangle of valves and wiring whispered past his arm, like some insane man-made tumbleweed.

The screeching, hammering and grinding from the centre pile began again. McLaren squeezed further under the car wreck, face smeared with blood and rust. This had to be a dream.

For two hours, McLaren lay in that position, listening to the crashing and rending of metal, the hiss and sputtering of something that made sparks. And for two hours, he firmly believed that he would awake at any second in his armchair at home. When he did, he would make straight for the fridge and break open another six-pack. After a while, the procession of ambulatory junk had stopped. Now there was only the noise.

When the noise stopped, McLaren screwed his eyes shut, willing himself to wake up. *It's time to wake up now! This is it! The nightmare's finished. Come on . . .*

Something large and decidedly ferocious coughed once in the darkness and then began to roar throatily. The sound was filled with threat and rage. It was hungry. It wanted somebody. It wanted him.

It began to move in his direction.

McLaren scrabbled out from under the car, sobbing desperately. The roaring sound filled the night air, reverberating and echoing from the mounds of junk. He raced in the direction he had identified earlier.

*I want to get out!*

McLaren rounded a corner, tottering on one foot, trying to find the office. It was useless. Everything looked so bloody different. Behind him, something large and monstrous ploughed through a mound of junk with explosive force.

He ran. And ran. And ran.

The junkyard was a maze. McLaren was lost. And behind him, getting ever closer as it followed his scent, came a bellowing, fearful Minotaur. McLaren leapt over an old tractor engine with an agility born out of mortal terror and slipped into another unfamiliar alley. The bellowing behind him changed tone to a gasping, hydraulic hiss. It was as if some great animal was angrily drawing in breath and scanning the junk for any sign of its quarry. McLaren pressed tightly and silently into the darkness, holding his breath. The gasping noise began to move away. McLaren listened until the noise had receded into the distance and when it had vanished, he exhaled desperately, heaving air into his lungs. When he had recovered sufficiently, he began to creep forward through the junk, scanning the twisted wreckage for movement, searching desperately for the office. On his left, the dim outline of an arc light reared up against the night sky. Using it as a guide, he searched for the others. One, two, three . . . and *there* was the light with the broken girder.

*That means the office is over there!*

Quietly, fearfully, McLaren picked his way through the junk to the arc light, slipping between rusted car wrecks, squeezing through gaps and crevices. The night swamped everything. Fighting down claustrophobia, McLaren pushed through yet another tangle of metal. As he pushed at a ruined lawn mower, the junk shifted with a grinding clatter. McLaren froze, expecting the bellowing, hissing unseen thing in the dark to round a corner and roar down upon him. But there was no noise.

McLaren eased through the junk, hope and relief flooding his soul as he saw the dim outline of his office and the compound fence. His car was parked and waiting. Beyond it, the gates were wide open. In one minute flat, he would be roaring away from the nightmare forever.

He ran quickly forward, crouching low and darting anxious glances in the darkness as he made for his car. Something metallic snared his shin in the pitch-blackness. He cursed under his breath at the pain. Finally, he reached the dim outline of his car, knowing that the keys were still in the dash. The doors were not locked. He would be gone in seconds.

Quicker than thought, he wrenched open the door and dived into the driving seat. He slammed the door and reached for the keys. They were gone. He fumbled in the darkness for them. They had not fallen on the floor, as far as he could see. Muttering a short prayer, McLaren reached up for the light switch above the windscreen, which did not seem to be where it should be. His fingers found an unfamiliar switch. He pressed it and a blue light came on overhead.

Now he knew that he was not in his car.

McLaren was sitting in a nightmare tangle of wiring and twisted metal; a bizarre creation of freshly welded junk. Rusted piping throbbed with hideous life. A twisted radiator grille, soldered to the exhaust which McLaren remembered procuring for The Stranger, hissed angry steam. With mounting terror, McLaren recognised the other items of The Stranger's junk, all hideously welded into some nightmarish, contorted and utterly alien design.

He was sitting inside some monstrous machine that only barely resembled a car. He knew now what had chased him in the junkyard.

Something pulsed in the darkness beneath the dashboard. McLaren didn't want to look, but did.

Shannon's severed head gazed up at McLaren, the eye sockets pierced by living wires. But it wasn't the head that made McLaren scream. It was the object on which Shannon's head rested and into which the wiring from his eye sockets had been soldered.

It was the hideous cube of metal which McLaren had buried in the junk pile. The cube which contained the mangled remains of The Stranger.

The eye socket wiring sputtered, Shannon's jaw twitched and McLaren saw the machine's headlights flare on beyond the rusted frame of the shattered windscreen. Now it could see. McLaren scrabbled at the door but could not find a handle.

"*Let me out! For God's sake let me . . .!*"

A band of corrugated steel flashed from the darkness around his waist, pinning McLaren to the seat like some insane seatbelt. Frantically clawing at the unyielding metal,

McLaren failed to see the dashboard slowly open before him. Steam hissed angrily. The interior blue light flickered as the monstrous engine coughed into rumbling life.

"*No no no No! No! No! . . .* "

A rusted pipe, slick with oil, stabbed outward from the dashboard. McLaren watched it plunge into his chest in a crimson implosion with a look of mild surprise on his face. The pipe tore into his heart, sucking greedily. Beneath McLaren's spasming legs, the tangled cube of metal began to vibrate.

Now refueled, the Doomsday Machine roared out of the yard, scattering junk.

The noise of its coughing, roaring engine was soon swallowed by the beckoning night.

# Graham Masterton

# Pig's Dinner

ONE-TIME EDITOR OF *Mayfair* and *Penthouse*, Graham Masterton's first published book was titled *Your Erotic Fantasies*. He went on to write more how-to sex manuals, such as the phenomenally successful *How to Drive Your Man Wild in Bed* before turning his talents to horror with *The Manitou* (filmed in 1978 with Tony Curtis as the hero). Since then he has produced a string of best-selling horror novels such as *Charnel House*, *Tengu*, *Mirror*, *Feast*, *Night Warriors*, *Death Dreams* and *Walkers*. He also writes historical sagas and in 1989 edited *Scare Care*, an anthology of supernatural tales to benefit abused and needy children.

The story that follows was written especially for this anthology, and is perhaps the most stomach-churning tale in the book. The author describes it as "a story to put you off bacon sandwiches for life"—and I can't argue with that . .

DAVID CLIMBED TIREDLY out of the Land Rover, slammed the ill-fitting door, and trudged across the yard with his hands deep in the pockets of his donkey-jacket. It had stopped raining at last, but a coarse cold wind was blowing diagonally across the yard, and above his head the clouds rushed like a muddy-pelted pack of mongrel dogs.

Today had been what he and his brother Malcolm always sardonically called "a pig of a day."

He had left the piggery at half-past five that morning, driven all the way to Chester in the teeming rain with a litter of seven Landrace piglets suffering from suspected swine erysipelas. He had waited two-and-a-half hours for a dithering young health inspector who had missed his rail connection from Coventry. Then he had lunched on steak-and-kidney pudding with a deputy bank manager whose damp suit had reeked like a spaniel, and who had felt himself unable to grant David the loan that he and Malcolm desperately needed in order to repair the roof of the old back barn.

He was wet, exhausted and demoralized. For the first time since they had taken over the piggery from their uncle four-and-a-half years ago, he could see no future for Bryce Prime Pork, even if they sold half of their livestock and most of their acreage, and re-mortgaged their huge Edwardian house.

He had almost reached the stone steps when he noticed that the lights in the feed plant had been left burning. Damn it, he thought. Malcolm was always so careless. It was Malcolm's over-ambitious investment in new machinery and Malcolm's insistence on setting up their own slaughtering and deep-freezing facilities that had stretched their finances to breaking-point. Bryce Prime Pork had been caught between falling demand and rising costs, and David's dream of becoming a prosperous gentleman farmer had gradually unraveled all around him.

He crossed the sloping yard toward the feed plant. Bryce Prime Pork was one of the cleanest piggeries in Derbyshire, but there was still a strong smell of ammonia on the evening wind, and the soles of David's shoes slapped against the thin black slime that seemed to cover everything in wet weather.

He opened the door to the feed plant and stepped inside. All the lights were on; but there was no sign of Malcolm. Nothing but sacks of fish meal, maize, potatoes, decorticated ground-nut meal, and grey plastic dustbins filled with boiled swill. They mixed their own pig-food, rather than buying proprietary brands—not only because it cost them three or four percent less, but because Malcolm had developed a mix of swill, cereal and concentrate which not only fattened the pigs more quickly, but gave them award-winning bacon.

David walked up and down the length of the feed plant. He could see his reflection in the night-blackened windows: squatter, more hunched than he imagined himself to be. As he passed the stainless-steel sides of the huge feed grinder, he thought that he looked like a Golem, or a troll, dark and disappointed. Maybe defeat did something to a man's appearance, squashed him out of shape, so that he couldn't recognize himself any longer.

He crossed to the switches by the door, and clicked them off, one after another, and all along the feed plant the fluorescent lights blinked out. Just before he clicked the last switch, however, he noticed that the main switch which isolated the feed-grinder was set to "off."

He hesitated, his hand an inch away from the light-switch. Neither Malcolm nor Dougal White, their foreman, had mentioned that there was anything wrong with the machinery. It was all German, made in Dusseldorf by Müller-Koch, and after some initial teething troubles with the grinder blades, it had for more than two years run with seamless efficiency.

David lifted the main switch to "on"—and to his surprise, with a smooth metallic scissoring sound, like a carving-knife being sharpened against a steel, the feed-grinder started up immediately.

But in the very next instant, he heard a hideously distorted shriek—a gibbering monkeylike yammering of pain and terror that shocked him into stunned paralysis—unable to understand what the shriek could be, or what he could do to stop it.

He fumbled for the "off" switch, while all the time the

screaming went on and on, growing higher and higher-pitched, racketing from one side of the building to the other, until David felt as if he had suddenly gone mad.

The feed-grinder gradually minced to a halt, and David crossed stiff-legged as a scarecrow to the huge conical stainless-steel vat. He clambered up the access ladder at the side, and while he did so the screaming died down, and gave way to a complicated mixture of gurgles and groans.

He climbed up to the lip of the feed vat, and saw to his horror that the entire shining surface was rusty-coloured with fresh blood—and that, down at the bottom of the vat, Malcolm was standing, staring up at him wild-eyed, his hands braced tightly against the sloping sides.

He *appeared* to be standing, but as David looked more closely, he began to realize that Malcolm had been churned into the cutting-blades of the feed-grinder almost up to his waist. He was encircled by a dark glutinous pool of blood and thickly-minced bone, its surface still punctuated by occasional bubbles. His brown plaid shirt was soaked in blood, and his face was spattered like a map.

David stared at Malcolm and Malcolm stared back at David. The silent agony which both joined and fatally seperated them at that instant was far more eloquent than any scream could have been.

"Oh, Christ," said David. "I didn't know."

Malcolm opened and closed his mouth, and a huge pink bubble of blood formed and burst.

David clung tightly to the lip of the feed-grinding vat and held out his hand as far as he could.

"Come on, Malcolm. I'll pull you up. Come on, you'll be all right."

But Malcolm remained as he was, staring, his arms tensed against the sides of the vat, and shook his head. Blood poured in a thick ceaseless ribbon down his chin.

"Malcolm, come on, I can pull you out! Then I'll get an ambulance!"

But again Malcolm shook his head: this time with a kind of dogged fury. It was then that David understood that there was hardly anything left of Malcolm to pull out—that it wasn't just a question of his legs being tangled in the machinery. The grinder blades had consumed him up to the hip—reducing his legs and the lower part of his body to a thick smooth paste of bone and muscle, an emulsion of human flesh that would already be dripping down into the collecting churn underneath.

"Oh God, Malcolm, I'll get somebody. Hold on, I'll call for an ambulance. Just hold on!"

"No," Malcolm told him, his voice muffled with shock.

"Just hold on, for Christ's sake!" David screamed at him.

But Malcolm repeated, "No. I want it this way."

"What?" David demanded. "What the hell do you mean?"

Malcolm's fingers squeaked against the bloody sides of the vat. David couldn't begin to imagine what he must be suffering. Yet Malcolm looked up at him now with a smile—a smile that was almost beatific. Or maybe more sly than beatific.

"It's wonderful, David. It's wonderful. I never knew that pain could feel like this. It's better than anything that ever happened. Please, switch it back on. Please."

"Switch it *back on*?"

Malcolm began to shudder. "You must. I want it so much. Life, love—they don't count for anything. Not compared with this."

"No," said David. "I can't."

"David," Malcolm urged him, "I'm going to die anyway. But if you don't give me this . . . believe me, I'm never going to let you sleep for the rest of your life."

David remained at the top of the ladder for ten long indecisive seconds.

"Believe me," Malcolm nodded, in that voice that sounded as if it came straight from hell, "it's pure pleasure. Pure pleasure. Beyond pain, David, out of the other side. You can't experience it without dying. But David, David, what a way to go!"

David stayed motionless for one more moment. Then, without a word, he climbed unsteadily back down the ladder. He tried not to think of anything at all as he grasped the feed-grinder's main power switch, and clicked it to "on."

From the feed-grinder came a cry that was partly naked agony and partly exultation. It was a cry that made David rigid with horror, and his ill-digested lunch rose in the back of his throat in a sour thick, tide.

He was gripped by a sudden terrible compulsion that he needed to *see*. He scrambled back up the access ladder, gripped the rim of the vat, and stared down at Malcolm with a feeling that was almost like being electrocuted.

The grinding-blades scissored and chopped, and the entire vat surged with blood. Malcolm was still bracing himself at the very bottom, his torso tensed as the grinder blades turned his pelvis and his lower abdomen into a churning mixture of blood, muscle and shredded cloth.

His face was a mask of concentration and tortured ecstasy. He was enjoying it, reveling in it, relishing every second of it. The very extinction of his own life; the very destruction of his own body.

*Beyond pain*, he had told David. *Out of the other side*.

Malcolm held his upper body above the whirling blades as long as he could, but gradually his strength faded and his hands began to skid inch by inch down the bloody metal sides. His screams of pleasure turned into a cry like nothing that David had ever heard before—piercing, high-pitched, an ullulation of unearthly triumph.

His white stomach was sliced up; skin, fat, intestines; and he began a quivering, jerking last descent into the maw of the feed-grinder.

"David!" he screamed. "David! It's won—!"

The blades hacked into his ribs. He was whirled around with his arms lifted as if he were furiously dancing. Then there was nothing but his head, spinning madly in a froth of pink blood. Finally, with a noise like a sink-disposal unit chopping up chicken-bones, his head was gone, too, and the grinder spun faster and faster, without any more grist for its relentless mill.

Shaking, David climbed down the ladder and switched the grinder off. There was a long, dying whine, and then silence, except for the persistent worrying of the wind.

What the hell was he going to do now? There didn't seem to be any point in calling for an ambulance. Not only was it pointless—how was he going to explain that he had switched the feed-grinder back on again, with Malcolm still inside it?

The police would quickly realize that the grinder didn't have the capacity to chop up Malcolm's entire body before David had had the opportunity to switch it off. And he doubted very much if they would understand that Malcolm had been beyond saving—or that even if Malcolm *hadn't* begged David to kill him—even if he hadn't said how ecstatic it was—finishing him off was probably the most humane thing that David could have done.

He stood alone in the shed shivering with shock and indecision. He and Malcolm had been arguing a lot lately—everybody knew that. Only two weeks ago, they had openly shouted at each other at a livestock auction in Chester. It would only take one suggestion that he might have killed Malcolm deliberately, and he would face arrest, trial, and jail. Even if he managed to show that he was innocent, a police investigation would certainly ruin the business. Who would want to buy Bryce Prime Pork products if they thought that the pigs had been fed from the same grinder in which one of the Bryce brothers had been ground up?

Unless, of course, nobody found out that he *had* been ground up.

Unless nobody found him at all.

David seemed to remember a story that he had read, years ago, about a chicken-farmer who had murdered his wife and fed her to the chickens, and then fed the chickens to other chickens, until no possible trace of his wife remained.

He heard a glutinous dripping noise from the feed-grinder. It wouldn't be long before Malcolm's blood would coagulate, and become almost impossible for him to wash thoroughly away. He hesitated for just one more moment; then he switched on the lights again, and went across to the sacks of bran, middlings and soya-bean meal.

Tired and fraught and grief-stricken as he was, tonight he was going to make a pig's dinner.

*

He slept badly, and woke early. He lay in bed for a long time, staring at the ceiling. He found it difficult to believe now that what had happened yesterday evening had been real. He felt almost as if it had all been a roughly-photographed, luridly-coloured film. But he felt a cold change inside his soul that told him it had actually happened. A change in himself that would affect him for the rest of his life—what he thought, what he said, what people he could love, what risks he was prepared to take.

Just after dawn, he saw the lights in the pig-houses flicker on, and he knew that Dougal and Charlie had arrived. He dressed, and went downstairs to the kitchen, where he drank half a pint of freezing-cold milk straight out of the bottle. He brought some of the milk directly back up again, and had to spit it into the sink. He wiped his mouth on a damp tea-towel and went outside.

Dougal was tethering a Landrace gilt and fixing up a heater for her piglets in a "creep", a boxlike structure hanging alongside her. Piglets under four weeks needed more heat than their mother could provide. Charlie was busy in a pen further along, feeding Old Jeffries, their enormous one-eyed Large Black boar. They bred very few Large Blacks these days: the Danish Landraces were much more docile and prolific, and gave excellent bacon. But Malcolm had insisted on keeping Old Jeffries for sentimental reasons. Old Jeffries had been given to them by their uncle when they took over the business, and had won them their first rosette. "Old Jeffries and I are going to be buried in the same grave," he always used to say.

"Morning, Mr David," said Dougal. He was a sandy-haired Wiltshireman with a pudgy face and protuberant eyes.

"Morning, Dougal."

"Mr Malcolm not about yet?"

David shook his head. "No . . . he said something about going to Chester."

"Well . . . that's queer. We were going to divide up the weaner pool today."

"That's all right. I can help you do that."

"Mr Malcolm didn't say when he'd be back?"

"No," said David. "He didn't say a word."

He walked along the rows of pens until he came to Old Jeffries' stall. Charlie had emptied a bucketful of fresh feed into Old Jeffries' trough, and the huge black boar was greedily snuffling his snout into it; although his one yellow eye remained fixed on David as he ate.

"He really likes his breakfast today," Charlie remarked. Charlie was a young curly-haired teenager from the village. He was training to be a veterinarian, but he kept himself in petrol and weekly Chinese takeaways by helping out at Bryce Prime Pork during the holidays.

"Yes . . ." said David. He stared in awful fascination as Old Jeffries snorted and guzzled at the dark red mixture of roughage, concentrate and meat meal that (in two horrific hours of near-madness) he had mixed last night out of Malcolm's soupy remains. "It's a new formula we've been trying."

"Mr Malcolm sorted out that bearing on the feed-grinder, then?" asked Charlie.

"Oh—oh, yes," David replied. But he didn't take his eyes off Old Jeffries, grunting into his trough; and Old Jeffries didn't for one moment take his one yellow eye off David.

"What did the health inspector say?" asked Charlie.

"Nothing much. It isn't erysipelas, thank God. Just a touch of zinc deficiency. Too much dry food."

Charlie nodded. "I thought it might be that. But this new feed looks topnotch. In fact, it smells so good, I tasted a little bit myself."

For the first time, David looked away from Old Jeffries. "You did what?"

Charlie laughed. "You shouldn't worry. You know what Malcolm says, he wouldn't feed anything to the pigs that he wouldn't eat himself. I've never come across anybody who loves his livestock as much as your brother. I mean, he really puts himself into these pigs, doesn't he? Body and soul."

Old Jeffries had finished his trough, and was enthusiastically cleaning it with his long inky tongue. David couldn't help watching him in fascination as he licked the last fragments of meat meal from his whiskery cheeks.

"I'm just going to brew up some tea," he said, clapping Charlie on the back.

He left the piggery; but when he reached the door, he could still see Old Jeffries staring at him one-eyed from the confines of his pen, and for some inexplicable reason it made him shudder.

You're tired, shocked, he told himself. But as he closed the piggery door he heard Old Jeffries grunt and whuffle as if he had been dangerously roused.

The telephone rang for Malcolm all day; and an irritated man in a badly-muddied Montego arrived at the piggery, expecting to talk to Malcolm about insurance. David fended everybody off, saying that Malcolm had gone to Chester on business and no, he didn't know when he was coming back. Am I my brother's keeper?

That night, after Dougal had left, he made his final round of the piggery, making sure that the gilts and the sows were all tethered tight, so that they didn't accidentally crush their young; checking the "creeps" and the ventilators; switching off lights.

His last visit was to Old Jeffries. The Large Black stood staring at him as he approached; and made a noise in his throat like no noise that David had ever heard a boar utter before.

"Well, old man," he said, leaning on the rail of the pen. "It looks as if Malcolm knew what he was talking about. You and he are going to be buried in the same grave."

Old Jeffries curled back his lip and grunted.

"I didn't know what else to do," David told him. "He was dying, right in front of my eyes. God, he couldn't have lived more than five minutes more."

Old Jeffries grunted again. David said, "Thanks, O.J. You're a wonderful conversationalist." He reached over to pat the Large Black's bristly head.

Without any warning at all, Old Jeffries snatched at David's hand, and clamped it between his jaws. David felt his fingers being crushed, and teeth digging right through the palm of his hand. He shouted in pain, and tried to pull himself away, but Old Jeffries twisted his powerful sloped-back neck and heaved David bodily over the railings and into his ammonia-pungent straw.

David's arm was wrenched around behind him, and he felt his elbow crack. He screamed, and tried to turn himself around, but Old Jeffries' four-toed trotter dug into his ribcage, cracking his breastbone and puncturing his left lung. Old Jeffries weighed over 300 kilograms, and even though he twisted and struggled, there was nothing he could do to force the boar off him.

"Dougal!" he screamed, even though he knew that Dougal had left over twenty minutes ago. "Oh God, help me! Somebody!"

Grunting furiously, Old Jeffries trampled David and worried his bloody hand between his teeth. To his horror, David saw two of his fingers drop from Old Jeffries' jaw, and fall into the straw. The boar's bristly sides kept scorching his face: taut and coarse and pungent with the smell of pig.

He dragged himself backwards, out from under the boar's belly, and grabbed hold of the animal's back with his free hand, trying to pull himself upright. For a moment, he thought he had managed it, but then Old Jeffries let out a shrill squeal of rage, and burrowed his snout furiously and aggressively between David's thighs.

"No!" David screamed. "No! Not that! Not that!"

But he felt sharp teeth tearing through corduroy, and then half of his inside thigh being torn away from the bone, with a bloody crackle of fat and tissue. And then Old Jeffries ripped him between the legs. He felt the boar's teeth puncture his groin, he felt cords and tubes and fats being wrenched away. He threw back his head and he let out a cry of anguish, and wanted to die then, right then, with no more pain, nothing but blackness.

But Old Jeffries retreated, trotting a little way away from him with his gory prize hanging from his mouth. He stared at David with his one yellow eye as if he were daring him to take it back.

David sicked up bile. Then, letting out a long whimpering sound, he climbed up on to his feet, and cautiously limped to the side of the pen. He could feel that he was losing pints of blood. It pumped warm and urgent down his trouser-leg. He knew that he was going to die. But he wasn't going to let this pig have him. He was going to go the way that Malcolm had gone. Beyond pain, out on the other side. He was going to go in ecstasy.

He opened the pen, and hobbled along the piggery, leaving a wide wet trail of blood behind him. Old Jeffries hesitated for a few moments, and then followed him, his trotters clicking on the concrete floor.

David crossed the yard to the feed buildings. He felt cold, cold, cold—colder than he had ever felt before. The wind banged a distant door over and over again, like a flat-toned funeral drum. Old Jeffries followed him, twenty or thirty yards behind, his one eye shining yellow in the darkness.

*To market, to market, to buy a fat pig*
*Home again, home again, jiggety-jig.*

Coughing, David opened the door of the feed building. He switched on the lights, leaning against the wall for support. Old Jeffries stepped into the doorway and watched him, huge and black, but didn't approach any closer. David switched the feed-grinder to "on", and heard the hum of machinery and the scissoring of precision-ground blades.

It seemed to take him an age to climb the access ladder to the rim of the vat. When he reached the top, he looked down into the circular grinder, and he could see the blades flashing as they spun around.

*Ecstasy*, that's what Malcolm had told him. *Pleasure beyond pain.*

He swung his bloodied legs over the rim of the vat. He closed his eyes for a moment, and said a short prayer. Dear God, forgive me. Dear mother, please forgive me.

Then he released his grip, and tumble-skidded down the stainless steel sides, his feet plunging straight into the grinder blades.

He screamed in terror; and then he screamed in agony. The blades sliced relentless into his feet, his ankles, his shins, his knees. He watched his legs ground up in front of his eyes in a bloody chaos of bone and muscle, and the pain was so intense that he pounded at the sides of the vat with his fists. This wasn't ecstasy. This was sheer nerve-tearing pain—made even more intense by the hideous knowledge that he was already mutilated beyond any hope of survival—that he was as good as dead already.

The blades cut into his thighs. He thought he had fainted but he hadn't fainted, *couldn't* faint, because the pain was so fierce that it penetrated his subconscious, penetrated every part of his mind and body.

He felt his pelvis shattered, crushed, chopped into paste. He felt his insides drop out of him. Then he was caught and tangled in the same way that Malcolm had been caught and tangled, and for a split-second he felt himself whirled around, a wild Dervish dance of sheer agony. Malcolm had lied. Malcolm had lied. Beyond pain there was nothing but more pain. On the other side of pain was a blinding sensation that made pain feel like a caress.

The blades bit into his jaw. His face was obliterated. There was a brief whirl of blood and brains and then he was gone.

The feed-grinder whirred and whirred for over an hour. Then—with no feed to slow down its blades—it overheated and whined to a halt.

Blood dripped; slower and slower.

Old Jeffries remained where he was, standing in the open doorway, one-eyed, the cold night wind ruffling his bristles.

Old Jeffries knew nothing about retribution. Old Jeffries knew nothing about guilt.

But perhaps something that Old Jeffries didn't understand had penetrated the black primitive knots of his cortex—a need for revenge so powerful that it had been passed from a dead soul to a bestial brain. Or perhaps he had simply acquired a taste for a new kind of feed.

Old Jeffries trotted back to his pen and waited patiently for morning, and for Charlie to arrive, to fill up his trough with yet another pig's dinner.

STEPHEN JONES is the winner of the World Fantasy Award, the Horror Writers of America Bram Stoker Award and eight-time recipient of The British Fantasy Award. A full-time columnist, film-reviewer, illustrator, television producer/director and horror movie publicist (*Hellraiser*, *Hellbound*, *Nightbreed* etc.), he is the co-editor of *Horror: 100 Best Books*, *Best New Horror*, *Gaslight & Ghosts*, *Now We Are Sick*, and the *Fantasy Tales* and *Dark Voices* series, and compiler of *Clive Barker's The Nightbreed Chronicles*, *Clive Barker's Shadows in Eden* and *James Herbert: By Horror Haunted*.